PULP FICTION

PULP FICTION
THE CRIMEFIGHTERS

Edited by
OTTO PENZLER

Introduction by
HARLAN COBEN

Quercus

Printed in Great Britain by Clays Ltd, St Ives plc

For Sally Owen
my irreplaceable colleague –
with affection and gratitude

CONTENTS

FOREWORD

Dear Reader:

Oh man, do I envy you.

Welcome to the world of pulp fiction. If you have been here before, well, skip this introduction and dive in. You already have some idea of the delights that await. For the rest of you, I will keep this brief.

I know some writers who claim that they have never read pulp fiction. I put them in two classes. The larger group I call, for a lack of a better term, liars. Of course they have read pulp fiction. They may not know it. They may, because of the various connotations derived from the word 'pulp', not want to admit it. But come on now.

Reading pulp fiction is a bit like, uh, something else. Ninety percent of the writers out there admit they do it. Ten percent lie about it.

The second group, the writers who really have never read pulp fiction (yes, I know this contradicts the last paragraph where I basically said one hundred percent read it, but go with me here) – these are writers the rest of us do not associate with. They have poor self-esteem. They had a troubled home life. They are not fun at parties.

Discovering pulp fiction now, right now, is a bit like finding a lost treasure. You are unearthing something that will entertain, enlighten, amuse, horrify, mangle, jangle, keep you riveted. Decades after they were written, these stories still manage to have an edge.

Edge. That might be the key for me. These stories still cut, still tear, still even shock a bit. These guys experimented. They wrote on the move. They wrote, like Shakespeare and Oscar Wilde, for money. They went places maybe they shouldn't have and we love them for it.

I like edge. I like it a lot. I think you will too.

Otto Penzler has carefully selected the greatest of the great from the history of pulp fiction. Legendary writers you've already heard of like Dashiell Hammett, Erle Stanley Gardner, Cornell Woolrich and Raymond Chandler are here. Legendary writers that you should have heard of like Frederick Nebel, Paul Cain, Carroll John Daly, George Harmon Coxe, Charles Booth, Leslie White, William Rollins, Norbert Davis, Horace McCoy and Thomas Walsh are also where they should be – with the greats.

In short: you got the goods here.

Finally, you have a great tour guide for this treasure hunt. Otto Penzler knows more about pulp fiction than pretty much anyone else I know. He also has self-esteem, a fine home life, and man, is he fun at parties.

Okay, put a bullet in this. I'm done. Turn the page, dammit. Start reading.

Harlan Coben
January 2006

INTRODUCTION

Like jazz, the hard-boiled private detective is entirely an American invention, and it was given life in the pages of pulp magazines. Pulp now is a nearly generic term, frequently misused to indicate hack work of inferior literary achievement. While that often may be accurate, pulp was not intended to describe literary excellence or lack thereof, but was derived from the word pulpwood, which is the very cheap paper that was used to produce popular magazines after World War I. These, in turn, were the offspring of 'Dime Novels,' mainly magazine-sized mystery, Western and adventure novels produced for young or unsophisticated readers.

At their peak of popularity, there were hundreds of pulp magazines published every month, covering every type of fiction. While there were magazines devoted to stories of railroads, aviation, jungle adventure, 'spicy' stories, Westerns, romance, science fiction, horror and any other subject that enterprising publishers thought would attract a readership, the most successful pulps were those featuring such super-heroes as The Shadow, The Spider, Doc Savage, The Phantom Detective and anyone else who had a mask and a cape, and those devoted mainly to detective fiction (with the notable exception of *Weird Tales*, the long-lived pulp devoted to fantasy and science fiction).

There is more than one way to judge the success of a pulp magazine, including longevity, circulation and profitability, but the undisputed champion in the area of having developed the greatest writers and having had the most long-lasting literary influence was *Black Mask*, and most of the stories in this collection were originally published in its pages.

Had it done no more than publish Carroll John Daly's first story, *Black Mask* would have achieved immortality. On May 15, 1923, with the publication of 'Three Gun Terry,' the hard-boiled private eye made his first appearance, quickly followed by Daly's creation of Race Williams, the first series character in hard-boiled fiction.

While Daly was truly a hack writer devoid of literary pretension, aspiration and ability, he laid the foundation for the form that continues to flourish to this day in the work of such writers as Robert B. Parker, Joe Gores, James Crumley, Bill Pronzini, Michael Connelly and James Lee Burke (although the latter two employ series characters who are cops, they function in the same individualistic way that private investigators do, and frequently use the smart-aleck speech patterns as their kindred free-lancers do).

Dashiell Hammett produced his first Continental Op story for *Black Mask* later in the same year, and the future of the genre was secure, as the editors and the reading public quickly recognized that this was serious literature in the guise of popular fiction. Every significant writer of the pulp era worked for *Black Mask*, including Paul Cain, Horace McCoy, Frederick Nebel, Raoul Whitfield, Erle Stanley Gardner, Charles G. Booth, Roger Torrey, Norbert Davis, George Harmon Coxe and, of course, the greatest of them all, Raymond Chandler.

It was the era between the two world wars in which the pulps flourished, their garish covers enticing readers, and their cheap prices providing mass entertainment through the years of the Great Depression. It has been widely stated that the advent of television tolled the death knell for the pulps, but it is not true. They were replaced by the creation and widespread popularity of paperback books, virtually unkown as a mass market commodity before WWII.

There is quotable prose in these pages, and characters that you will remember, and fascinating evocations of another time and place, but the writers mainly had the goal of entertaining readers when these stories were produced. No reasonable reader will ever complain that the stories are slow moving, that they lack action and conflict – in short, that they are dull. Many of the contributors to this book went on to successful writing careers in other arenas, including Hollywood, but here is the real stuff: stories written at breakneck speed and designed to be read the same way.

Crimefighters in the pulps were seldom the sensitive type who understood that a difficult childhood or an unloving grandmother were responsible for the violence of the criminals with whom he came into contact. No, his role was to battle bad guys, and he did it without fear, without pity, and without remorse. It was a black-and-white world in the pulps, a simple conflict between the forces of goodness and virtue and those who sought to plunder, harm and kill the innocent. In the pages of the pulps, and between the covers of this book, Good is triumphant over Evil. Perhaps that is the key to the enormous popularity they enjoyed for so many years.

Otto Penzler
New York, January 2006

ONE, TWO, THREE
PAUL CAIN

One of the true mystery men of pulp fiction, Paul Cain was discovered to be the pseudonym of the successful screenwriter Peter Ruric. Then, not so many years ago, it was further learned that even that name was a disguise for the author's actual name, George Carrol Sims (1902–1966).

His fame as a writer of crime fiction rests with a single novel, *Fast One* (1933), which Raymond Chandler called 'some kind of high point in the ultra hard-boiled manner.'

The novel had its genesis in a series of short stories published in *Black Mask*, beginning with 'Fast One' in the March 1932 issue, followed by four other adventures of Gerry Kells and his alcoholic girlfriend, S. Granquist. Cain had been writing pulp stories in New York but moved to Los Angeles when Cary Grant began filming *Gambling Ship*, which was loosely based on these stories. The sale of the film to Hollywood inspired him to pull the stories together as a novel, which was both savaged by the review media at the time while praised by others. It sold few copies and he never wrote another.

He did write films, however, most famously *The Black Cat* (1934), about a Satanic cult that starred Boris Karloff, with whom he became friends, as well as *Affairs of a Gentlemen* (1934), *Grand Central Murders* (1942) and *Mademoiselle Fifi* (1944).

'One, Two, Three' was first published in *Black Mask* in May, 1933, and collected in his short story collection, *Seven Slayers* (1946).

ONE, TWO, THREE

PAUL CAIN

I'd been in Los Angeles waiting for this Healey to show for nearly a week. According to my steer, he'd taken a railroad company in Quebec for somewhere in the neighborhood of a hundred and fifty grand on a swarm of juggled options or something. That's a nice neighborhood.

My information said further that he was headed west and that he dearly loved to play cards. I do, too.

I'll take three off the top, please.

I missed him by about two hours in Chicago and spent the day going around to all the ticket-officers, getting chummy with agents, finally found out Healey had bought a ticket to LA, so I fanned on out there and cooled.

Pass.

Sunday afternoon I ran into an op for Eastern Investigators, Inc., named Gard, in the lobby of the Roosevelt. We had a couple drinks and talked about this and that. He was on the Coast looking for a gent named Healey. He was cagey about who the client was, but Eastern handles mostly missing persons, divorces, stuff like that.

Monday morning Gard called me and said the Salt Lake branch of his outfit had located Healey in Caliente, Nevada. He said he thought I might like to know. I told him I wasn't interested and thanked him and then I rented a car in a U Drive place and drove up to Caliente.

I got there about four in the afternoon and spotted Healey in the second joint I went into. He was sitting in a stud game with five of the home boys and if they were a fair sample of local talent I figured I had plenty of time.

Healey was a big man with a round cheery face, smooth pink skin. His mouth was loose and wet and his eyes were light blue. I think his eyes were the smallest I've ever seen. They were set very wide apart.

He won and lost pretty evenly, but the game wasn't worth a nickel. The home boys were old-timers and played close to their vests and Healey's luck was the only thing that kept him even. He finally scared two of them out of a seventy or eighty-dollar pot and that made him feel so good that he got up and came over to the the bar and ordered drinks for the boys at the table. He ordered lemonade for himself.

I said: 'Excuse me, but haven't I seen you around Lonnie Thompson's

3

in Detroit?' Lonnie makes a book and I had most of my dope on Healey from him.

He smiled and said: 'Maybe,' and asked me what I drank.

I ordered whiskey.

He asked me if I'd been in town long and I said I'd just driven up from LA to look things over and that things didn't look so hot and that I would probably drive back to LA that night or the next morning.

I bought him another lemonade and had another whiskey and we talked about Detroit. In a little while he went back to the table and sat down.

That was enough for a beginning. I had registered myself with him as one of the boys. I went out and drove a couple of blocks to the Pine Hotel and took a room. The Pine was practically the only hotel in town, but I flipped the register back a day or so and found Healey's name to make sure. Then I went up and washed and lay down to smoke a cigarette and figure out the details.

According to Lonnie Thompson, Healey was a cash boy – carried his dough in paper and traveler's cheques. I couldn't be sure of that but it was enough. The point was to get him to LA and in to one of two or three places where I could work on him.

I guess I must have slept almost an hour because it was dark when I woke up. Somebody was knocking at the door and I got up and stumbled over and switched on the light and opened the door. I was too sleepy to take Healey big – I mumbled something about coming in and sitting down, and went over to the basin and put some cold water on my face.

When I turned around he was sitting on the bed looking scared. I offered him a cigarette and he took it and his hand was shaking.

He said: 'Sorry I woke you up like that.'

I said: 'That's all right,' and then he leaned forward and spoke in a very low voice:

'I've got to get out of here right away. I want to know how much it's worth to you to take me down to Los Angeles.'

I almost fell off the chair. My first impulse was to yell, 'Sure,' and drag him down to the car; but he was scared of something and when a man's scared is a swell time to find out what it's all about.

I stalled. I said: 'Oh, that's all right,' sort of hesitantly.

He said: 'Listen. . . . I got here Saturday morning. I was going to stay here long enough to establish residence and then apply for one of those quick divorces, under the Nevada law.

'My wife has been on my tail six weeks with a blackmail gag,' he went on. 'She's here. When I got back to the hotel a little while ago she came into my room and put on an act.'

I thought then I knew who Gard's client was.

'She came in this afternoon. She's got the room next to mine.'

He was silent so long that I laughed a little and said: 'So what?'

'I've got to duck, quick,' he went on. 'She's a bad actor. She came into my room and put on an act. She's got a guy with her that's supposed to be her brother and he's a bad actor, too. You said you were going to drive back to LA. I saw your name on the register when I came in and I thought you might take me along. I can't rent a car here and there isn't a train till midnight.'

He pulled the biggest roll I ever saw out of his pocket and skimmed off a couple notes. 'If it's a question of money . . .'

I shook my head with what I hoped was a suggestion of dignity. I said: 'I'd decided to go back myself tonight. It will be a pleasure to take you, Mister Healey,' and I got up and put on my coat. 'How about your stuff?'

He looked blank until I said: 'Luggage,' and then he said: 'That's all right – I'll leave it.' He smiled again. 'I travel light.'

At the top of the stairs he whispered: 'This is sure a big lift.' Then he remembered that he had to sneak up to his room to get something and said he'd meet me at the car. I told him where it was. He said he'd paid his hotel bill.

I went on downstairs and checked out.

My car was wedged in between a Ford truck and a light-blue Chrysler roadster. There was plenty of room ahead of the roadster, so I went up and snapped off the hand-brake and pushed it ahead about eight feet. Then I got into my car and leaned back and waited.

The whole layout looked pretty bad, what with him scared to death of a deal he admitted was blackmail and all. He said he didn't want his luggage and then right on top of it, he had to go up to his room to get something. That would be taking a chance on running into the wife again. I wondered if she was his wife.

I couldn't figure out how a wife could blackmail a husband while she was jumping from state to state with a man who was 'supposed' to be her brother; but then almost anything is possible in Nevada.

After about five minutes I began to get nervous. I opened the door of the car and stepped out on the side-walk, and as I closed the door there were five shots close together some place upstairs in the hotel.

I can take trouble or leave it alone; only I always take it. Like a sap, I went into the hotel.

The clerk was a big blond kid with glasses. He came out from behind the counter as I went in the door; we went upstairs together, two or three at a time.

There was a man in long woolly underwear standing in the corridor on the third floor and he pointed to a door and we went in. Healey was lying flat on his face in the middle of the room, and beyond him, close to the wall, was the body of a woman, also face downward.

The clerk turned a beautiful shade of green; he stood there staring at Healey. I went over and rolled the woman over on her back. She couldn't have been much over twenty-two or three; little, gray-eyed blonde. There was a knife in her side, under the arm. There was a .38 automatic near her outstretched hand. She was very dead.

The man in the woolly underwear peeked in and then hurried across the hall and into another room. I could hear him yelling the news to somebody there.

I went over and tapped the clerk on the shoulder and pointed at the girl. The clerk swallowed a couple of times, said: 'Miss Mackay,' and looked back at Healey. He was hypnotized by the way Healey's back looked. Hamburger.

Then about two dozen people came into the room all at once.

The sheriff had been in a pool-hall across the street. He rolled Healey over and said: 'This is Mister Healey,' as if he'd made a great discovery.

I said: 'Uh-huh. He's been shot.'

I guess the sheriff didn't like the way I said it very well. He glanced at the clerk and then asked me who I was. I told him my name and the clerk nodded and the sheriff scratched his head and went over and looked at the girl. I wanted to say that she'd been knifed, but I restrained myself.

Shaggy underwear was back with his pants on. He said he hadn't heard anything except somebody swearing and then, suddenly, the shots.

I asked him how long after the shots it had been when he came into the corridor and he said he wasn't sure, but it was somewhere around half a minute.

The first interesting thing that turned up was that it wasn't Healey's room – it was Miss Mackay's room. His was next door. That probably meant that Healey had deliberately gone into her room; that she hadn't surprised him in his room while he was getting something he'd forgotten.

Number two was that the knife was Healey's. Half a dozen people had seen him with it. It was an oversize jack-knife with a seven-inch blade – one of the kind that snaps open when you press a spring. Somebody said Healey had a habit of playing mumbletypeg with it when he was trying to out-sit a raise or scare somebody into splitting a pot.

Number three was the topper. The dough was gone. The sheriff and a couple of deputies searched Healey and went through both rooms with a fine-tooth comb. They weren't looking for big money because they didn't know about it; they were looking for evidence.

All they found on Healey were four hundred-dollar bills tucked into his watch pocket, and the usual keys, cigarettes, whatnot. There were no letters or papers of any kind. There was one big suitcase in his room and it was full of dirty clothes. The roll he'd flashed on me was gone.

In the next half-hour I found out a lot of things. The girl had come to the hotel alone. No one else had checked in that day, except myself. The door to the girl's room was about twenty feet from the top of the back stairs and there was a side-door to the hotel that they didn't lock until ten o'clock.

It looked like a cinch for the man Healey had told me about, the one who was supposed to be Miss Mackay's brother.

Healey had probably gone upstairs to take care of the girl. I knew that his being scared of her was on the level because I know bona-fide fear when I see it. She evidently had plenty on him. He'd arranged his getaway with me and then gone up to carve the girl, shut her up forever.

The alleged brother had come in the side-door and had walked in on the knife act and opened up Healey's back with the automatic at about six feet.

Then he'd grabbed the roll and whatever else Healey had in his pocket that was of any value – maybe a book of traveler's cheques – had tossed the gun on the floor and screwed back down the back stairway and out the side-door. Something like that. It wasn't entirely plausible, but it was all I could figure right then.

By the time I'd figured that much out the sheriff had it all settled that Healey had knifed the girl and then she'd plugged him five times, in a ten-inch square in his back. With about three inches of steel in her heart.

That was what the sheriff said so I let it go. They didn't know about the brother and I didn't want to complicate their case for them. And I did want a chance to look for that roll without interference.

When I got out to the car the blue Chrysler was gone. That wasn't important except that I wondered who had been going away from the hotel when it looked like everybody in town was there or on the way there.

I didn't get much information at the station. The agent said he'd just come on duty; the telegraph operator had been there all afternoon but he was out to supper. I found him in a lunchroom across the street and he said there'd been a half-dozen or so people get off the afternoon train from Salt Lake; but the girl had been alone and he wasn't sure who the other people had been except three or four hometowners. That was no good.

I tried to find somebody else who had been in the station when the train came in but didn't have any luck. They couldn't remember.

I went back to the car and that made me think about the blue Chrysler again. It was just possible that the Mackay girl had come down from Salt Lake by rail, and the boyfriend or brother or whatever he was had driven down. It didn't look particularly sensible but it was an idea. Maybe they didn't want to appear to be traveling together or something.

I stopped at all the garages and gas-stations I could find but I couldn't get a line on the Chrysler. I went back to the hotel and looked at the register and found out that Miss Mackay had put down Chicago as her home, and I finagled around for a half hour and talked to the sheriff and the clerk and everybody who looked like they wanted to talk but I didn't get any more angles.

The sheriff said he'd wired Chicago because it looked like Healey and

Miss Mackay were both from Chicago, and that he'd found a letter in one of Healey's old coats from a Chicago attorney. The letter was about a divorce, and the sheriff had a hunch that Miss Mackay was Mrs. Healey.

I had a sandwich and a piece of pie in the hotel restaurant and bundled up and went out and got in the car and started for LA.

I didn't get up till around eleven o'clock Tuesday morning. I had breakfast in my room and wired a connection in Chi to send me all he could get on Miss Mackay and her brother. I called the desk and got the number of Gard's room and on the way down stopped in to see him.

He was sitting in his nightshirt by the window, reading the morning papers. I sat down and asked him how he was enjoying his vacation and he said swell, and then he said: 'I see by the papers that our friend Healey had an accident.'

I nodded.

Gard clucked: 'Tch, tch, tch. His wife will sure be cut up.'

I smiled a little and said, 'Uh-huh,' and Gard looked up and said: 'What the hell are you grinning about and what do you mean: Uh-huh?'

I told him that according to my paper Mrs. Healey was the lady who had rubbed Healey – the lady who was on her way back East in a box.

Gard shook his head intelligently and said: 'Wrong. That one was an extra. Mrs. Healey is alive and kicking and one of the sweetest dishes God ever made.'

I could see that he was going to get romantic so I waited and he told me that Mrs. Healey had been the agency's client in the East and that she'd come in from Chicago Monday morning by plane and that he'd met her in the agency office, and then he went on for five or ten minutes about the color of her eyes and the way she wore her hair, and everything.

Gard was pretty much of a ladies' man. He told it with gestures.

Along with the poetry he worked in the information that Mrs. Healey, as he figured it, had had some trouble with Healey and that they'd split up and that she wanted to straighten it all out. That was the reason she'd wired the Salt Lake office of his agency to locate Healey. And almost as soon as they'd found Healey he'd shoved off for LA and the agency had wired her in Chicago to that effect. She'd arrived the morning Healey had been spotted in Caliente and had decided to wait in LA for him.

Gard said he had helped her find an apartment. He supposed the agency had called her up and told her that bad news about Healey. He acted like he was thinking a little while and then asked me if I didn't think he ought to go over and see if he could help her in any way. 'Comfort her in her bereavement,' was the way he put it.

I said: 'Sure – we'll both go.'

Gard didn't go for that very big, but I told him that my having been such a pal of Healey's made it all right.

We went.

Mrs. Healey turned out a great deal better than I had expected from Gard's glowing description. As a matter of fact she was swell. She was very dark, with dark blue eyes and blue-black hair; her clothes were very well done and her voice was cultivated, deep. When she acknowledged Gard's half-stammered introduction, inclined her head towards me and asked us to sit down, I saw that she had been crying.

Gard had done pretty well in the way of helping her find an apartment. It was a big luxurious duplex in the Garden Court on Kenmore.

I said we wanted her to know how sorry we were about it all and that I had known Healey in Detroit, and if there was anything we could do – that sort of thing.

There wasn't much else to say. There wasn't much else said.

She asked Gard to forgive her for bothering him so much the previous evening with her calls, but that she'd been nervous and worried and kept thinking that maybe Healey had arrived in LA after the agency was closed and that she hadn't been notified. They'd been watching the trains of course.

Gard said that was all right and got red and stammered some more. He was stunned by the lady. So was I. She was a pip.

She said she thought she'd stay in California and she told us delicately that she'd made arrangements for Healey's body to be shipped to his folks in Detroit.

Finally I said we'd better go and Gard nodded and we got up. She thanked us again for coming and a maid helped us with our coats and we left.

Gard said he had to go downtown so I took a cab and went back to the hotel. There was a wire from Chicago: JEWEL MACKAY TWO CONVICTIONS EXTORTION STOP WORKS WITH HUSBAND ARTHUR RAINES ALIAS J L MAXWELL STOP LEFT CHICAGO WEDNESDAY FOR LOS ANGELES WITH RAINES STOP DESCRIPTION MACKAY FOUR ELEVEN ONE HUNDRED TWO BLONDE GRAY EYES RAINES FIVE SIX ONE HUNDRED TWENTY-FIVE RED BROWN EYES STOP MAY LOCATE THROUGH BROTHER WILLIAM RAINES REAL ESTATE SOUTH LABREA REGARDS

ED.

I got the number of Raines' real estate office from the telephone book and took a cab and went down and looked it over. I didn't go in. Then I told the driver to take me to the Selwyn Apartments on Beverly Boulevard. That was the place the telephone book had listed as Raines' residence.

It took a half-hour of jabbering about spark plugs with the Bohunk in the Selwyn garage to find out that Mister Raines had gone out about ten o'clock with another gentleman, and what Mister Raines looked like and what kind of a car he drove. The gentleman who had been with him was tall – or maybe he was short. Or maybe it had been a lady. The Bohunk wasn't sure.

I jockeyed the cab around to a good spot in the cross street and went into the drug-store on the opposite corner and drank Coca-Colas. Along about the fifth Coca-Cola the car I was looking for pulled up in front of the Selwyn. A medium-sized middle-aged man who I figured to be the brother got out of the driver's seat and went into the apartment house. The other man in the car moved over into the driver's seat and started west on Beverly. By that time I was back in the cab and after him.

Of course I couldn't be sure it was Raines. It looked like a little man. I had to take that chance.

We followed the car out Beverly to Western, up Western. I wondered what had become of the blue Chrysler. Then we drew up close behind Raines' car at an intersection and I nearly fell out the window. The man in the car ahead turned around and looked back; we looked smack at one another for five seconds.

I'd seen him before! I'd seen him the night before in Miss Mackay's room at the Pine Hotel in Caliente! He'd been one of the raft of people who'd busted in with the sheriff and stood around ah-ing and oh-ing. The man had guts. He'd come in while Healey and the girl were still warm to see what a neat job he'd done.

The traffic bell rang and I knew he'd recognized me, too. He went across that intersection like a bat out of hell, up Western to Fountain.

He lost us on Fountain. I talked to my driver like a father. I got down on my knees and begged him to keep that car in sight. I called him all the Portuguese pet-names I could think of and made up a few new ones, but Raines ran away from us on Fountain.

On the way back to the hotel I stopped at the Hollywood Branch of the Automobile Club and had a friend of mine look up the license number of the car. Of course it was the brother's car, in the brother's name. That didn't get me anywhere. I was pretty sure Raines wouldn't go back to his brother's place now that he knew I'd spotted him; and it was a cinch he wouldn't use that car very long.

He didn't know what I wanted. He might figure me for a dick and scram out of LA – out of the country. I sat in my room at the hotel and thought soft thoughts about what a chump I'd been not to go to him directly when he'd stopped with his brother in front of the Selwyn, and the speed of taxi-cabs as compared to automobiles – things like that. It looked like the Healey case was all washed up as far as I was concerned.

I went out about five o'clock and walked. I walked down one side of Hollywood Boulevard to Bronson and back up the other side to Vine and went into the U Drive joint and rented the car again. I was nervous and jumpy and disgusted, and the best way for me to get over feeling that way is to drive it off.

I drove out through Cahuenga Pass a ways and then I had an idea and drove back to the Selwyn Apartments. The idea wasn't any good. William Raines told the clerk to send me up and he asked me what he could do for me and smiled and offered me a drink.

I said I wanted to get in touch with his brother on a deal that would do us both a lot of good. He said his brother was in Chicago and that he hadn't seen him for two years. I didn't tell him he was a liar. It wouldn't have done any good. I thanked him and went back down to the car.

I drove down to LA and had dinner in a Chinese place. Then I went back by the Santa Fe and found out about trains – I figured on going back to New York the next day.

On the way back to Hollywood I drove by the Garden Court. Not for any particular reason – I thought about Mrs. Healey and it wasn't much out of the way.

The blue Chrysler was sitting squarely across the street from the entrance.

I parked up the street a little way and got out and went back to be sure. I lit a match and looked at the card on the steering column; the car was registered to another U Drive place, downtown, on South Hope.

I went across the street and walked by the desk with my nose in the air. The Spick elevator boy didn't even look at the folded bill I slipped him, he grinned self-consciously and said that a little red-haired man had gone up to four just a couple minutes ago. Mrs. Healey was on four and there were only three apartments on a floor.

I listened at the door but could only hear a confused buzz that sounded like fast conversation. I turned the knob very slowly and put a little weight against the door. It was locked. I went down to the end of the hall and went out as quietly as possible through a double door to a fire-escape platform. By standing outside the railing and holding on with one hand and leaning far out I could see into the dining-room of Mrs. Healey's apartment, could see a couple inches of the door that led, as well as I could remember, into the drawing-room. It was closed.

There is nothing that makes you feel quite so simple as hanging on a fire-escape, trying to look into a window. Particularly when you can't see anything through the window. After a few minutes I gave it up and climbed back over the railing.

I half sat on the railing and tried to figure things out. What business would the guy who shot Healey have with Mrs. Healey? Did the blackmail angle that Raines and Mackay had held over Healey cover Mrs. Healey, too? Was Raines milking his lowdown for all it was worth? It was too deep for me.

I went back into the hall and listened at the door again. They were a little louder but not loud enough to do me any good. I went around a bend in the hall to what I figured to be the kitchen-door and gave it the slow

11

turn and it opened. I mentally kicked myself for wasting time on the fire-escape, tip-toed into the dark kitchen and closed the door.

It suddenly occurred to me that I was in a quaint spot if somebody should come in. What the hell business did I have there! I fixed that, to myself, with some kind of vague slant about protecting Mrs. Healey and edged over to the door, through to the room I'd been looking into from the fire-escape.

The door into the drawing-room was one of those pasteboard arrangements that might just as well not be there. The first thing I heard was a small, suppressed scream like somebody had smacked a hand over somebody else's mouth, and then something like a piece of furniture being tipped over. It was a cinch someone was fighting in there, quietly – or as quietly as possible.

There wasn't much time to think about whether I was doing the right thing or not. If I'd thought about it I'd probably have been wrong, anyway. I turned the knob, swung the door open.

Mrs. Healey was standing against the far wall. She was standing flat against the wall with one hand up to her mouth. Her eyes were very wide.

There were two men locked together on the floor near the central table and as I came in they rolled over a turn or so and one broke away and scrambled to his feet. It was Raines. He dived after a nickel-plated revolver that was lying on the floor on the far side of the table, and the other man, who had risen to his knees, dived after it, too. The other man was Gard.

He beat Raines by a hair but Raines was on his feet; he kicked the gun out of Gard's hand, halfway across the room. Gard grabbed his leg and pulled him down and they went round and round again. They fought very quietly; all you could hear was the sound of heavy breathing and an occasional bump.

I went over and picked up the gun and stooped over the mess of arms and legs and picked out Raines' red head and took hold of the barrel of the gun. I took dead aim and let Raines have it back of the ear. He relaxed.

Gard got up slowly. He ran his fingers through his hair and jiggled his shoulders around to straighten his coat and grinned foolishly.

I said: 'Fancy, meeting you here.'

I turned around and looked at Mrs. Healey. She was still standing against the wall with her hand across her mouth. Then the ceiling fell down on top of my head and everything got dark very suddenly.

Darkness was around me when I opened my eyes, but I could see the outlines of a window and I could hear someone breathing somewhere near me. I don't know how long I was out. I sat up and my head felt like it was going to explode; I lay down again and closed my eyes.

After a while I tried it again and it was a little better. I crawled towards what I figured to be a door and ran into the wall and I got up on my feet and felt along the wall until I found the light switch.

Raines was lying in the same place I'd smacked him, but his hands and feet were tied with a length of clothes-line and there was a red, white and blue silk handkerchief jammed into his mouth. His eyes were open and he looked at me with an expression that I can only describe as bitter amusement.

Gard was lying belly-down on the floor near the door into the dining-room. He was the hard breather I'd heard in the darkness. He was still out.

I ungagged Raines and sat down. I kept having the feeling that my head was going to blow up. It was a very unpleasant feeling.

In a little while Raines got his jaws limbered up and started talking. The first thing he said was: 'What a bright boy *you* turned out to be!' I was too sick to know very much about what that meant – or care.

He went on like that for some time, talking in a high, squeaky voice, and the idea gradually filtered through the large balloon-shaped ache that my head had turned into.

It seems that Raines and the Mackay gal had juggled Healey into a swell spot. One of their angles was that Healey, in an expansive moment, had entirely forgotten about Mrs. Healey and married Miss Mackay. They had a lot of material besides; everything from the Mann Act to mayhem. When he'd made the hundred and fifty grand lick in Quebec they'd jumped him in Chicago.

Healey had ducked out of Chi and they'd trailed him, first to Salt Lake, then to Caliente. Monday night, Raines had helped Mackay put on the act in the hotel that Healey had told me about.

Raines hadn't got off the train with her or checked into the hotel with her because they didn't want to be seen together in case anything went wrong, but he ducked up that handy back stairway and they'd given Healey the act, showing him exactly the color and size of the spot they had him on.

Then, when Healey came down to my room, Raines had gone down and planted across the street in case Healey tried to powder.

Raines hadn't been there five minutes before Mrs. Healey and a man rolled up in the blue Chrysler. Raines recognized Mrs. Healey because she'd spotted Healey with Miss Mackay and Raines in a cabaret in Chicago once and crowned Miss Mackay with a beer bottle. It seems Mrs. Healey was a nice quiet girl.

They parked in front of the hotel and the man went in a minute, probably to buy a cigar and get a peek at the register. Then he came out and talked to Mrs. Healey a little while and went back in the little alleyway that led to the side door. He was only there a minute; he probably found out that it was practical to go into the hotel that way and came back and told her.

Along about that time in Raines' yarn I woke up to the fact that he was

13

referring to the man who was with Mrs. Healey as 'this guy.' I opened my
eyes and looked at him and he was looking at Gard.

Gard had stayed in the car while Mrs. Healey went back through the
alleyway and into the hotel. After a couple minutes he got nervous and got
out and walked up the street a little ways, and Raines went across the street
and went upstairs to find out what it was all about. That must have been
about the time I was checking out.

Gard must have been coming back down the other side of the street and
he saw me come out and finagle with his car and get into mine, and he
stayed away until hell started popping upstairs and I went into the hotel.

Raines stopped a minute. I got up and went over and rolled Gard over
on his back. He groaned and opened his eyes and blinked up at me and
then he sat up slowly and leaned against the wall.

Raines said Mrs. Healey must have tried Healey's door and then waited
till Healey came up the front stairway after he left me, and she ducked
around a corner and watched Healey go into Mackay's room. By that time
Raines was at the top of the back stairway and he watched Mrs. Healey
take a gun out of her bag and go down and listen at Miss Mackay's door.
When Healey opened the door after whittling Mackay, she backed him into
the room and closed the door. Raines said she probably told him a few
pertinent truths about himself and relieved him of what was left of the
hundred and fifty and then opened him up with the .38.

It was a swell spot for her, with the Mackay gal there with a knife in her
heart. Raines said he figured she'd intended to rub Healey from the start,
before he could divorce her – Healey had said she'd sworn to kill him,
before he left Chicago. A nice quiet girl – Mrs. Healey. A lady.

She'd dodged Raines on the stairs and he'd chased her down to the car,
but by that time Gard was back in the car with the engine running and
they'd shoved off fast. Then Raines had come back up with the sheriff and
his gang to look things over. That's where I'd seen him.

He'd taken the midnight train for LA and it had taken him all day
Tuesday to locate Mrs. Healey. He'd been putting the screws on her and
Gard for a split of the important money and Gard had gone into a
wrestling number with him just before I arrived.

By the time Raines had got all that out of his system Gard was sitting up
straight with his mouth open and his hands moving around fast and that
dumb, thoughtful look on his face as if he wanted to say something. When
Raines stopped to breathe. Gard said that the lady had talked him into
driving her up to Caliente because she said she was too nervous to wait for
Healey in LA – she said she had to see Healey and try to make their scrap
up right away, or she'd have a nervous breakdown or something, and Gard
– the big chump – fell for it.

He said he was the most surprised man in the world when the shooting
started, and that when she came galloping down and they scrammed for

LA she'd told him that she'd walked in on Mackay ventilating Healey, just like the sheriff said, and that Mackay had shot at her as she ran away. Gard had fallen for that, too. She had the poor sap hypnotized.

Gard knew I'd been up at Caliente, of course – he'd seen me; so when I walked into his place in the morning he'd figured I had some kind of slant on what it was all about and he'd taken me over to her place so they could put on their 'comfort her in her bereavement' turn for my benefit.

Then, Tuesday night, when I'd walked in on the shakedown and knocked Raines out, Gard, who had had a load of what Raines had to say to Mrs. Healey and who half believed it, calculated that his best play was to take the air with her. He was too much mixed up in it to beat an accessory rap anyway, so he'd sapped me with a bookend and they'd tied Raines, who was coming to, and he'd helped her pack her things. They were going to light out for New Zealand or some quiet place like that; only she'd sneaked up behind him and smacked him down at the last minute. A lovely lady.

We all stopped talking about that time – Raines and Gard and me – and looked at one another.

Gard laughed. He squinted at me and said: 'You looked silly when I clipped you with the bookend!'

Raines said: 'You didn't look particularly intelligent when our girl-friend let *you* have it.'

Gard snickered on the wrong side of his face and got up and went out into the kitchen for a drink of water. He found a bottle out there – almost a full fifth of White Horse. He brought it in, I untied Raines and we all had a snort.

I was thinking about what suckers we'd been, I'd popped Raines and Gard had popped me and Mrs. Healey had popped Gard – all of us. One, two, three. Tinker to Evers to Chance – only more so.

I think we were all pretty washed up with La Belle Healey. It was a cinch Gard wouldn't want any more of her. I don't know about Raines. But I know I didn't.

We finished the bottle and Raines snooped around and found a full one and we did a little business with that.

I didn't find out I had a concussion till next morning. I was a week and two days in the hospital at twenty dollars a day, and the doctor nicked me two-fifty. He'll get the rest of it when he catches me.

The whole Healey play, what with one thing and another, cost somewhere in the neighborhood of a grand. I got a lame skull and about two-bits' worth of fun out of it.

I pass.

THE CREEPING SIAMESE

DASHIELL HAMMETT

The argument could be made that the most influential writer of the 20th century was Dashiell Hammett. As writers turned from the orotund style of Henry James and his Victorian predecessors to lean and swift prose, later scholars have pointed to the undeniably profound force of Ernest Hemingway. But who influenced Hemingway? Hammett did.

Publishing dates are hard facts, not esoteric theories. Hammett's first Continental Op story appeared in *Black Mask* on October 1, 1923. The quintessential hard-boiled private eye appeared frequently in the ensuing years. Hemingway's first book, *In our Time*, was published in Paris in a limited edition in 1924, and published in a tiny edition of 1,335 copies in the United States in October, 1925, by which time Hammett was already well established and a highly popular regular contributor to the most important pulp magazine of its time.

In addition to the nameless operative of the Continental Detective Agency, Hammett (1894–1961) created Sam Spade, the hero of the most famous American Detective novel ever written or filmed, *The Maltese Falcon*, which had been serialized in *Black Mask*, as were all of his novels excepting the last, *The Thin Man*.

Written at the height of his success and powers, 'The Creeping Siamese' was published in *Black Mask* in March, 1926, the year before he began to serialize his first novel, *Red Harvest*.

THE CREEPING SIAMESE
DASHIELL HAMMETT

Standing beside the cashier's desk in the front office of the Continental Detective Agency's San Francisco branch, I was watching Porter check up my expense account when the man came in. He was a tall man, raw-boned, hard-faced. Grey clothes bagged loosely from his wide shoulders. In the late afternoon sunlight that came through partially drawn blinds, his skin showed the color of new tan shoes.

He opened the door briskly, and then hesitated, standing in the doorway, holding the door open, turning the knob back and forth with one bony hand. There was no indecision in his face. It was ugly and grim, and its expression was the expression of a man who is remembering something disagreeable.

Tommy Howd, our freckled and snub-nosed office boy, got up from his desk and went to the rail that divided the office.

'Do you—?' Tommy began, and jumped back.

The man had let go the doorknob. He crossed his long arms over his chest, each hand gripping a shoulder. His mouth stretched wide in a yawn that had nothing to do with relaxation. His mouth clicked shut. His lips snarled back from clenched yellow teeth.

'Hell!' he grunted, full of disgust, and pitched down on the floor.

I heaved myself over the rail, stepped across his body, and went out into the corridor.

Four doors away, Agnes Braden, a plump woman of thirty-something who runs a public stenographic establishment, was going into her office.

'Miss Braden!' I called, and she turned, waiting for me to come up. 'Did you see the man who just came in our office?'

'Yes.' Curiosity put lights in her green eyes. 'A tall man who came up in the elevator with me. Why?'

'Was he alone?'

'Yes. That is, he and I were the only ones who got off at this floor. Why?'

'Did you see anybody close to him?'

'No, though I didn't notice him in the elevator. Why?'

'Did he act funny?'

'Not that I noticed. Why?'

'Thanks. I'll drop in and tell you about it later.'

I made a circuit of the corridors on our floor, finding nothing. The raw-boned man was still on the floor when I returned to the office, but he had been turned over on his back. He was as dead as I had thought. The Old Man, who had been examining him, straightened up as I came in. Porter was at the telephone, trying to get the police. Tommy Howd's eyes were blue half-dollars in a white face.

'Nothing in the corridors,' I told the Old Man. 'He came up in the elevator with Agnes Braden. She says he was alone, and she saw nobody close to him.'

'Quite so.' The Old Man's voice and smile were as pleasantly polite as if the corpse at his feet had been a part of the pattern in the carpet. Fifty years of sleuthing have left him with no more emotion than a pawnbroker. 'He seems to have been stabbed in the left breast, a rather large wound that was staunched with this piece of silk' – one of his feet poked at a rumpled ball of red cloth on the floor – 'which seems to be a sarong.'

Today is never Tuesday to the Old Man: it *seems* to be Tuesday.

'On his person,' he went on, 'I have found some nine hundred dollars in bills of various denominations, and some silver; a gold watch and a pocket knife of English manufacture; a Japanese silver coin, 50 *sen*; tobacco, pipe and matches; a Southern Pacific timetable; two handkerchiefs without laundry marks; a pencil and several sheets of blank paper; four two-cent stamps; and a key labeled *Hotel Montgomery, Room 540.*

'His clothes seem to be new. No doubt we shall learn something from them when we make a more thorough examination, which I do not care to make until the police come. Meanwhile, you had better go to the Montgomery and see what you can learn there.'

In the Hotel Montgomery's lobby the first man I ran into was the one I wanted: Pederson, the house copper, a blond-mustached ex-bartender who doesn't know any more about gum-shoeing than I do about saxophones, but who does know people and how to handle them, which is what his job calls for.

'Hullo!' he greeted me. 'What's the score?'

'Six to one, Seattle, end of the fourth. Who's in 540, Pete?'

'They're not playing in Seattle, you chump! Portland! A man that hasn't got enough civic spirit to know where his team—'

'Stop it, Pete! I've got no time to be fooling with your childish pastimes. A man just dropped dead in our joint with one of your room-keys in his pocket – 540.'

Civic spirit went blooey in Pederson's face.

'540?' He stared at the ceiling. 'That would be that fellow Rounds. Dropped dead, you say?'

'Dead. Tumbled down in the middle of the floor with a knife-cut in him. Who is this Rounds?'

'I couldn't tell you much off-hand. A big bony man with leathery skin. I wouldn't have noticed him excepting he was such a sour looking body.'

'That's the bird. Let's look him up.'

At the desk we learned that the man had arrived the day before, registering as H. R. Rounds, New York, and telling the clerk he expects to leave within three days. There was no record of mail or telephone calls for him. Nobody knew when he had gone out, since he had not left his key at the desk. Neither elevator boys nor bell-hops could tell us anything.

His room didn't add much to our knowledge. His baggage consisted of one pigskin bag, battered and scarred, and covered with the marks of labels that had been scraped off. It was locked, but traveling bags locks don't amount to much. This one held us up about five minutes.

Rounds' clothes – some in the bag, some in the closet – were neither many nor expensive, but they were all new. The washable stuff was without laundry marks. Everything was of popular makes, widely advertised brands that could be bought in any city in the country. There wasn't a piece of paper with anything written on it. There wasn't an identifying tag. There wasn't anything in the room to tell where Rounds had come from or why.

Pederson was peevish about it.

'I guess if he hadn't got killed he'd of beat us out of a week's bill! These guys that don't carry anything to identify 'em, and that don't leave their keys at the desk when they go out, ain't to be trusted too much!'

We had just finished our search when a bell-hop brought Detective Sergeant O'Gar, of the police department Homicide Detail, into the room.

'Been down to the Agency?' I asked him.

'Yeah, just came from there.'

'What's new?'

O'Gar pushed back his wide-brimmed black village-constable's hat and scratched his bullet head.

'Not a heap. The doc says he was opened with a blade at least six inches long by a couple wide, and that he couldn't of lived two hours after he got the blade – most likely not more'n one. We didn't find any news on him. What've you got here?'

'His name is Rounds. He registered here yesterday from New York. His stuff is new, and there's nothing on any of it to tell us anything except that he didn't want to leave a trail. No letters, no memoranda, nothing. No blood, no signs of a row, in the room.'

O'Gar turned to Pederson.

'Any brown men been around the hotel? Hindus or the like?'

'Not that I saw,' the house copper said. 'I'll find out for you.'

'Then the red silk was a sarong?' I asked.

21

'And an expensive one,' the detective sergeant said. 'I saw a lot of 'em the four years I was soldiering on the islands, but I never saw as good a one as that.'

'Who wears them?'

'Men and women in the Philippines, Borneo, Java, Sumatra, Malay Peninsula, parts of India.'

'Is it your idea that whoever did the carving advertised himself by running around in the streets in a red petticoat?'

'Don't try to be funny!' he growled at me. 'They're often enough twisted or folded up into sashes or girdles. And how do I know he was knifed in the street? For that matter, how do I know he wasn't cut down in your joint?'

'We always bury our victims without saying anything about 'em. Let's go down and give Pete a hand in the search for your brown men.'

That angle was empty. Any brown men who had snooped around the hotel had been too good at it to be caught.

I telephoned the Old Man, telling him what I had learned – which didn't cost me much breath – and O'Gar and I spent the rest of the evening sharp-shooting around without ever getting on the target once. We questioned taxicab drivers, questioned the three Roundses listed in the telephone book, and our ignorance was as complete when we were through as when we started.

The morning papers, on the streets at a little after eight o'clock that evening, had the story as we knew it.

At eleven o'clock O'Gar and I called it a night, separating in the direction of our respective beds.

We didn't stay apart long.

II

I opened my eyes sitting on the side of my bed in the dim light of a moon that was just coming up, with the ringing telephone in my hand.

O'Gar's voice: '1856 Broadway! On the hump!'

'1856 Broadway,' I repeated, and he hung up.

I finished waking up while I phoned for a taxicab, and then wrestled my clothes on. My watch told me it was 12:55 A.M. as I went downstairs. I hadn't been fifteen minutes in bed.

1856 Broadway was a three-story house set behind a pocket-size lawn in a row of like houses behind like lawns. The others were dark. 1856 shed light from every window, and from the open front door. A policeman stood in the vestibule.

'Hello, Mac! O'Gar here?'

'Just went in.'

22

I walked into a brown and buff reception hall, and saw the detective sergeant going up the wide stairs.

'What's up?' I asked as I joined him.

'Don't know.'

On the second floor we turned to the left, going into a library or sitting room that stretched across the front of the house.

A man in pajamas and bathrobe sat on a davenport there, with one bared leg stretched out on a chair in front of him. I recognized him when he nodded to me: Austin Richter, owner of a Market Street moving picture theater. He was a round-faced man of forty-five or so, partly bald, for whom the Agency had done some work a year or so before in connection with a ticket-seller who had departed without turning in the day's receipts.

In front of Richter a thin white-haired man with doctor written all over him stood looking at Richter's leg, which was wrapped in a bandage just below the knee. Beside the doctor, a tall woman in a fur-trimmed dressing-gown stood, a roll of gauze and a pair of scissors in her hands. A husky police corporal was writing in a notebook at a long narrow table, a thick hickory walking stick laying on the bright blue table cover at his elbow.

All of them looked around at us as we came into the room. The corporal got up and came over to us.

'I knew you were handling the Rounds job, sergeant, so I thought I'd best get word to you as soon as I heard they was brown men mixed up in this.'

'Good work, Flynn,' O'Gar said. 'What happened here?'

'Burglary, or maybe only attempted burglary. They was four of them – crashed the kitchen door.'

Richter was sitting up very straight, and his blue eyes were suddenly excited, as were the brown eyes of the woman.

'I beg your pardon,' he said, 'but is there – you mentioned brown men in connection with another affair – is there another?'

O'Gar looked at me.

'You haven't seen the morning papers?' I asked the theatre owner.

'No.'

'Well, a man came into the Continental office late this afternoon, with a stab in his chest, and died there. Pressed against the wound, as if to stop the bleeding, was a sarong, which is where we got the brown men idea.'

'His name?'

'Rounds, H. R. Rounds.'

The name brought no recognition into Richter's eyes.

'A tall man, thin, with dark skin?' he asked. 'In a grey suit?'

'All of that.'

Richter twisted around to look at the woman.

'Molloy!' he exclaimed.

'Molloy!' she exclaimed.

'So you know him?'

Their faces came back toward me.

'Yes. He was here this afternoon. He left—'

Richter stopped, to turn to the woman again, questioningly.

'Yes, Austin,' she said, putting gauze and scissors on the table, and sitting down beside him on the davenport. 'Tell them.'

He patted her hand and looked up at me again with the expression of a man who has seen a nice spot on which to lay down a heavy load.

'Sit down. It isn't a long story, but sit down.'

We found ourselves chairs.

'Molloy – Sam Molloy – that is his name, or the name I have always known him by. He came here this afternoon. He'd either called up the theater or gone there, and they had told him I was home. I hadn't seen him for three years. We could see – both my wife and I – that there was something the matter with him when he came in.

'When I asked him, he said he'd been stabbed, by a Siamese, on his way here. He didn't seem to think the wound amounted to much, or pretended he didn't. He wouldn't let us fix it for him, or look at it. He said he'd go to a doctor after he left, after he'd got rid of the thing. That was what he had come to me for. He wanted me to hide it, to take care of it until he came for it again.

'He didn't talk much. He was in a hurry, and suffering. I didn't ask him any questions. I couldn't refuse him anything. I couldn't question him even though he as good as told us that it was illegal as well as dangerous. He saved our lives once – more than my wife's life – down in Mexico, where we first knew him. That was in 1916. We were caught down there during the Villa troubles. Molloy was running guns over the border, and he had enough influence with the bandits to have us released when it looked as if we were done for.

'So this time, when he wanted me to do something for him, I couldn't ask him about it. I said, "Yes," and he gave me the package. It wasn't a large package: about the size of – well – a loaf of bread, perhaps, but quite heavy for its size. It was wrapped in brown paper. We unwrapped it after he had gone, that is, we took the paper off. But the inner wrapping was of canvas, tied with silk cord, and sealed, so we didn't open that. We put it upstairs in the pack room, under a pile of old magazines.

'Then, at about a quarter to twelve tonight – I had only been in bed a few minutes, and hadn't gone to sleep yet – I heard a noise in here. I don't own a gun, and there's nothing you could properly call a weapon in the house, but that walking stick' – indicating the hickory stick on the table – 'was in a closet in our bedroom. So I got that and came in here to see what the noise was.

'Right outside the bedroom door I ran into a man. I could see him better, than he could see me, because this door was open and he showed against the window. He was between me and it, and the moonlight showed him fairly clear. I hit him with the stick, but didn't knock him down. He turned and ran in here. Foolishly, not thinking that he might not be alone, I ran after him. Another man shot me in the leg just as I came through the door.

'I fell, of course. While I was getting up, two of them came in with my wife between them. There were four of them. They were medium-sized men, brown-skinned, but not so dark. I took it for granted that they were Siamese, because Molloy had spoken of Siamese. They turned on the lights here, and one of them, who seemed to be the leader, asked me:

'"Where is it?"

'His accent was pretty bad, but you could understand his words good enough. Of course I knew they were after what Molloy had left, but I pretended I didn't. They told me, or rather the leader did, that he knew it had been left here, but they called Molloy by another name – Dawson. I said I didn't know any Dawson, and nothing had been left here, and I tried to get them to tell me what they expected to find. They wouldn't though – they just called it "*it*".

'They talked among themselves, but of course I couldn't make out a word of what they were saying, and then three of them went out, leaving one here to guard us. He had a Luger pistol. We could hear the others moving around the house. The search must have lasted an hour. Then the one I took for the leader came in, and said something to our guard. Both of them looked quite elated.

'"It is not wise if you will leave this room for many minutes," the leader said to me, and they left us – both of them – closing the door behind them.

'I knew they were going, but I couldn't walk on this leg. From what the doctor says, I'll be lucky if I walk on it inside of a couple of months. I didn't want my wife to go out, and perhaps run into one of them before they'd got away, but she insisted on going. She found they'd gone, and she phoned the police, and then ran up to the pack room and found Molloy's package was gone.'

'And this Molloy didn't give you any hint at all as to what was in the package?' O'Gar asked when Richter had finished.

'Not a word, except that it was something the Siamese were after.'

'Did he know the Siamese who stabbed him?' I asked.

'I think so,' Richter said slowly, 'though I am not sure he said he did.'

'Do you remember his words?'

'Not exactly, I'm afraid.'

'I think I remember them,' Mrs. Richter said. 'My husband, Mr. Richter, asked him, "What's the matter, Molloy? Are you hurt, or sick?"'

'Molloy gave a little laugh, putting a hand on his chest, and said, "Nothing much. I run into a Siamese who was looking for me on my way here, and got careless and let him scratch me. But I kept my little bundle!" And he laughed again, and patted the package.'

'Did he say anything else about the Siamese?'

'Not directly,' she replied, 'though he did tell us to watch out for any Asiatics we saw around the neighborhood. He said he wouldn't leave the package if he thought it would make trouble for us, but that there was always a chance that something would go wrong, and we'd better be careful. And he told my husband' – nodding at Richter – 'that the Siamese had been dogging him for months, but now that he had a safe place for the package he was going to "take them for a walk and forget to bring them back." That was the way he put it.'

'How much do you know about Molloy?'

'Not a great deal, I'm afraid,' Richter took up the answering again. 'He liked to talk about the places he had been and the things he had seen, but you couldn't get a word out of him about his own affairs. We met him first in Mexico, as I have told you, in 1916. After he saved us down there and got us away, we didn't see him again for nearly four years. He rang the bell one night, and came in for an hour or two. He was on his way to China, he said, and had a lot of business to attend to before he left the next day.

'Some months later I had a letter from him, from the Queen's Hotel in Kandy, asking me to send him a list of the importers and exporters in San Francisco. He wrote me a letter thanking me for the list, and I didn't hear from him again until he came to San Francisco for a week, about a year later. That was in 1921, I think.

'He was here for another week about a year after that, telling us that he had been in Brazil, but, as usual, not saying what he had been doing there. Some months later I had a letter from him, from Chicago, saying he would be here the following week. However, he didn't come. Instead, some time later, he wrote from Vladivostok, saying he hadn't been able to make it. Today was the first we'd heard of him since then.'

'Where's his home? His people?'

'He always says he has neither. I've an idea he was born in England, though I don't know that he ever said so, or what made me think so.'

'Got any more questions?' I asked O'Gar.

'No. Let's give the place the eye, and see if the Siamese left any leads behind 'em.'

The eye we gave the house was thorough. We didn't split the territory between us, but went over everything together – everything from roof to cellar – every nook, drawer, corner.

The cellar did most for us: it was there, in the cold furnace, that we found the handful of black buttons and the fire-darkened garter clasps. But the upper floors hadn't been altogether worthless: in one room we had found the crumpled sales slip of an Oakland store, marked *1 table cover*, and in another room we had found no garters.

'Of course it's none of my business,' I told Richter when O'Gar and I joined the others again, 'but I think maybe if you plead self-defense you might get away with it.'

He tried to jump up from the davenport, but his shot leg failed him. The woman got up slowly.

'And maybe that would leave an out for you,' O'Gar told her. 'Why don't you try to persuade him?'

'Or maybe it would be better if you plead the self-defense,' I suggested to her. 'You could say that Richter ran to your help when your husband grabbed you, that your husband shot him and was turning his gun on you when you stabbed him. That would sound smooth enough.'

'My husband?'

'Uh-huh, Mrs. Rounds-Molloy-Dawson. Your late husband, anyway.'

Richter got his mouth far enough closed to get words out of it.

'What is the meaning of this damned nonsense?' he demanded.

'Them's harsh words to come from a fellow like you,' O'Gar growled at him. 'If this is nonsense, what do you make of that yarn you told us about creeping Siamese and mysterious bundles, and God knows what all?'

'Don't be too hard on him,' I told O'Gar. 'Being around movies all the time has poisoned his idea of what sounds plausible. If it hadn't, he'd have known better than to see a Siamese in the moonlight at 11:45, when the moon was just coming up at somewhere around 12:45, when you phoned me.'

Richter stood up on his one good leg.

The husky police corporal stepped close to him.

'Hadn't I better frisk him, sergeant?'

O'Gar shook his bullet head.

'Waste of time. He's got nothing on him. They cleaned the place of weapons. The chances are the lady dropped them in the bay when she rode over to Oakland to get a table cover to take the place of the sarong her husband carried away with him.'

That shook the pair of them. Richter pretended he hadn't gulped, and the woman had a fight of it before she could make her eyes stay still on mine.

O'Gar struck while the iron was hot by bringing the buttons and garters clasps we had salvaged out of his pocket, and letting them trickle from one hand to another. That used up the last bit of the facts we had.

I threw a lie at them.

'Never me to knock the press, but you don't want to put too much confidence in what the papers say. For instance, a fellow might say a few pregnant words before he died, and the papers might say he didn't. A thing like that would confuse things.'

The woman reared up her head and looked at O'Gar.

'May I speak to Austin alone?' she asked. 'I don't mean out of your sight.'

27

The detective sergeant scratched his head and looked at me. This letting your victims go into conference is always a ticklish business: they may decide to come clean, and then again, they may frame up a new out. On the other hand, if you don't let them, the chances are they get stubborn on you, and you can't get anything out of them. One way was as risky as another. I grinned at O'Gar and refused to make a suggestion. He could decide for himself, and, if he was wrong, I'd have him to dump the blame on. He scowled at me, and then nodded to the woman.

'You can go over into that corner and whisper together for a couple of minutes,' he said, 'but no foolishness.'

She gave Richter the hickory stick, took his other arm, helped him hobble to a far corner, pulled a chair over there for him. He sat with his back to us. She stood behind him, leaning over his shoulder, so that both their faces were hidden from us.

O'Gar came closer to me.

'What do you think?' he muttered.

'I think they'll come through.'

'That shot of yours about being Molloy's wife hit center. I missed that one. How'd you make it?'

'When she was telling us what Molloy had said about the Siamese she took pains both times she said "my husband" to show that she meant Richter.'

'So? Well—'

The whispering in the far corner had been getting louder, so that the s's had become sharp hisses. Now a clear emphatic sentence came from Richter's mouth.

'I'll be damned if I will!'

Both of them looked furtively over their shoulders, and they lowered their voices again, but not for long. The woman was apparently trying to persuade him to do something. He kept shaking his head. He put a hand on her arm. She pushed it away, and kept on whispering.

He said aloud, deliberately:

'Go ahead, if you want to be a fool. It's your neck. I didn't put the knife in him.'

She jumped away from him, her eyes black blazes in a white face. O'Gar and I moved softly toward them.

'You rat!' she spat at Richter, and spun to face us.

'I killed him!' she cried. 'This thing in the chair tried to and—'

Richter swung the hickory stick.

I jumped for it – missed – crashed into the back of his chair. Hickory stick, Richter, chair, and I sprawled together on the floor. The corporal helped me up. He and I picked Richter up and put him on the davenport again.

The woman's story poured out of her angry mouth:

28

'His name wasn't Molloy. It was Lange, Sam Lange. I married him in Providence in 1913 and went to China with him – to Canton, where he had a position with a steamship line. We didn't stay there long, because he got into some trouble through being mixed up in the revolution that year. After that we drifted around, mostly around Asia.

'We met this thing' – she pointed at the now sullenly quiet Richter – 'in Singapore, in 1919, I think – right after the World War was over. His name is Holley, and Scotland Yard can tell you something about him. He had a proposition. He knew of a gem-bed in upper Burma, one of many that were hidden from the British when they took the country. He knew the natives who were working it, knew where they were hiding their gems.

'My husband went in with him, with two other men that were killed. They looted the natives' cache, and got away with a whole sackful of sapphires, topazes and even a few rubies. The two other men were killed by the natives and my husband was badly wounded.

'We didn't think he could live. We were hiding in a hut near the Yunnan border. Holley persuaded me to take the gems and run away with them. It looked as if Sam was done for, and if we stayed there long we'd be caught. I can't say that I was crazy about Sam anyway; he wasn't the kind you would be, after living with him for a while.

'So Holley and I took it and lit out. We had to use a lot of the stones to buy our way through Yunnan and Kwangsi and Kwangtung, but we made it. We got to San Francisco with enough to buy this house and the movie theater, and we've been here since. We've been honest since we came here, but I don't suppose that means anything. We had enough money to keep us comfortable.

'Today Sam showed up. We hadn't heard of him since we left him on his back in Burma. He said he'd been caught and jailed for three years. Then he'd got away, and had spent the other three hunting for us. He was that kind. He didn't want me back, but he did want money. He wanted everything we had. Holley lost his nerve. Instead of bargaining with Sam, he lost his head and tried to shoot him.

'Sam took his gun away from him and shot him in the leg. In the scuffle Sam had dropped a knife – a kris, I think. I picked it up, but he grabbed me just as I got it. I don't know how it happened. All I saw was Sam staggering back, holding his chest with both hands – and the kris shining red in my hand.

'Sam had dropped his gun. Holley got it and was all for shooting Sam, but I wouldn't let him. It happened in this room. I don't remember whether I gave Sam the sarong we used for a cover on the table or not. Anyway, he tried to stop the blood with it. He went away then, while I kept Holley from shooting him.

'I knew Sam wouldn't go to the police, but I didn't know what he'd do. And I knew he was hurt bad. If he dropped dead somewhere, the chances are he'd be traced here. I watched from a window as he went down the street, and nobody seemed to pay any attention to him, but he looked so conspicuously wounded to me that I thought everybody would be sure to remember him if it got into the papers that he had been found dead somewhere.

'Holley was even more scared than I. We couldn't run away, because he had a shot leg. So we made up that Siamese story, and I went over to Oakland, and bought the table cover to take the place of the sarong. We had some guns and even a few oriental knives and swords here. I wrapped them up in paper, breaking the swords, and dropped them off the ferry when I went to Oakland.

'When the morning papers came out we read what had happened, and then we went ahead with what we had planned. We burned the suit Holley had worn when he was shot, and his garters – because the pants had a bullet-hole in them, and the bullet had cut one garter. We fixed a hole in his pajama-leg, unbandaged his leg, – I had fixed it as well as I could, – and washed away the clotted blood until it began to bleed again. Then I gave the alarm.'

She raised both hands in a gesture of finality and made a clucking sound with her tongue.

'And there you are,' she said.

'You got anything to say?' I asked Holley, who was staring at his bandaged leg.

'To my lawyer,' he said without looking up.

O'Gar spoke to the corporal.

'The wagon, Flynn.'

Ten minutes later we were in the street, helping Holley and the woman into a police car.

Around the corner on the other side of the street came three brown-skinned men, apparently Malay sailors. The one in the middle seemed to be drunk, and the other two were supporting him. One of them had a package that could have held a bottle under his arm.

O'Gar looked from them to me and laughed.

'We wouldn't be doing a thing to those babies right now if we had fallen for that yarn, would we?' he whispered.

'Shut up, you, you big heap!' I growled back, nodding at Holley, who was in the car by now. 'If that bird sees them he'll identify 'em as his Siamese, and God knows what a jury would make of it!'

We made the puzzled driver twist the car six blocks out of his way to be sure we'd miss the brown men. It was worth it, because nothing interfered with the twenty years apiece that Holley and Mrs. Lange drew.

HONEST MONEY

ERLE STANLEY GARDNER

It is the numbers that are so impressive when thinking about Erle Stanley Gardner. He created the most famous criminal defense attorney in literature, Perry Mason, when he published *The Case of the Velvet Claws* on March 1, 1933. He went on to produce 80 Mason novels which, in all editions, sold more than 300,000,000 copies.

The novels were the ultimate in formulaic genre fiction, with the lawyer taking on the role of detective to prove his client innocent at trial, turning to point a finger at the real culprit, who generally broke down and confessed. The television series based on the character, starring Raymond Burr, was enormously successful for nine years, running from September 21, 1957 to May 22, 1966, and showing in reruns pretty much ever since.

Before Perry Mason, however, there was Ken Corning, an equally hard-hitting, fearless and incorruptible defense attorney who made his debut in *Black Mask* magazine in November 1932. Had he been named Perry Mason, and his secretary named Della Street instead of Helen Vail, it would be impossible to tell the difference between the two. 'Honest Money' is the first story in the series.

Gardner (1889–1970) began his lengthy writing career in the pulps in *Breezy Stories* in 1921, eventually producing hundreds of short stories, countless articles, more than a hundred novels, and numerous non-fiction books on the law and, as a noted outdoorsman, on travel and environmental issues. At the time of his death, he was the best-selling writer in history.

HONEST MONEY

ERLE STANLEY GARDNER

The clock on the city hall was booming the hour of nine in the morning when Ken Corning pushed his way through the office door. On the frosted glass of that door appeared the words: '*Kenneth D. Corning, Attorney at Law – Enter.*'

Ken Corning let his eye drift over the sign. It was gold leaf and untarnished. It was precisely thirty days since the sign painter had collected for the job, and the sign painter had collected as soon as his brush had finished the last letter of the last word of that sign.

The credit of young attorneys in York City wasn't of the best. This was particularly true of young lawyers who didn't seem to have an 'in' with the administration.

Helen Vail was dusting her desk. She grinned at Ken.

He reached a hand to his inside pocket.

'Pay day,' he said.

Her eyes glinted with a softness that held a touch of the maternal.

'Listen, Ken, let it go until you get started. I can hang on a while longer. . . .'

He took out a wallet, started spreading out ten–dollar bills. When he had counted out five of them, he pushed the pile over to her. There were two bills left in the wallet.

'Honest, Ken. . . .'

He pushed his way to the inside office. 'Forget it,' he said. 'I told you we'd make it go. We haven't started to fight yet.'

She followed him in, the money in her hand. Standing in the doorway, very erect, chin up, she waited for him to turn to meet her gaze.

The outer door of the entrance office made a noise.

She turned. Looking over her shoulder, Ken could see the big man who stood on the threshold. He looked as though his clothes had been filled with apply jelly. He quivered and jiggled like a jellyfish on a board. Fat encased him in layers, an unsubstantial, soft fat that seemed to be hanging to his bones with a grip that was but temporary.

His voice was thin and falsetto.

'I want to see the lawyer,' he shrilled.

Helen turned on her heel, called over her shoulder: 'All right, Mr. Corning. I'll enter up this retainer.' To the man she said: 'You'll have to wait. Mr. Corning's preparing an important brief. He'll see you in a minute or two.'

The pneumatic door check swung the door to.

Ken Corning turned in his swivel-chair and sent swift hands to his tie. From the outer office sounded the furious clack of a typewriter. Three minutes passed. The roller of the machine made sounds as the paper was ripped from it. The door of the private office banged open. Helen Vail pushed her way in, in an ecstasy of haste, crinkling a legal paper in her hands.

'All ready for your signature,' she said.

The pneumatic door check was swinging the door closed as Ken reached for the paper. On it had been written with the monotony of mechanical repetition, over and over: 'Now is the time for all good men to come to the aid of the party.'

The door completed its closing. The latch clicked.

'Get his name?' asked Ken.

'Sam Parks. He's nervous. It's a criminal case. I'd have kept him waiting longer, but he won't stand for it. He's looking at his watch – twice in the last sixty seconds.'

Ken patted her hand.

'Okey. Good girl. Shoot him in.'

Helen walked to the door, opened it, smiled sweetly. 'You may come in now, Mr. Parks.'

She held the door open. Ken could see the big man heaving his bulk free of the chair. He saw him blot out the light in the doorway as the girl stepped aside. He was signing a paper as the big man entered the office and paused. Ken kept his eyes on the paper until the door catch clicked. Then he looked up with a smile.

'Mr. Parks, is it?' he asked.

The big man grunted, waddled over to the chair which was placed so close to the new desk as to invite easy intimacy. He sat down, then, apparently feeling that the chair was too far away, started hitching it closer and closer to the desk. His voice was almost a shrill whisper.

'My wife,' he said, 'has been arrested.'

Ken laid down the pen, looked professional.

'What,' he asked, 'is the charge?'

The big man's shrill voice rattled off a string of swift words: 'Well, you see it was this way. We had a place, a little restaurant, and the officers came busting in without a warrant . . . tell me, can they come into a place without a warrant, that way?'

Ken replied crisply: 'They did, didn't they?'

'Yes.'

'Okey, then they can. They're not supposed to, but they did, they do and they can. What happened?'

'Well, that was about all. They claimed we were selling booze.'

Ken's voice was sharp.

'Find any?'

'A little.'

'How much?'

'Ten or fifteen gallons.'

'Then they arrested you both?'

The fat man blinked glassy eyes.

'Just her. They didn't take me.'

'Why?'

He fidgeted, and the layers of fat jiggled about.

'Well, we sort of outslicked 'em. There had been a guy eating at one of the tables. He got wise as soon as the first man walked in on the raiding party. He ducked out the back. I sat down at his table and finished up his food. The wife pretended she didn't know me, and asked the officers if she could collect my bill before they took her. They said she could. I paid her fifty cents for the food and gave her a ten-cent tip. Then they closed up the place, took the booze away with 'em, and put me out. The wife said she ran the place alone.'

Ken Corning twisted a pencil in his fingers.

'I'll want a retainer of a hundred and fifty dollars,' he said, 'and then I'll see what I can do and report.'

The glassy eyes squinted.

'You ain't in with the gang here?'

'I'm a newcomer.'

The man opened his coat, disclosed a wrinkled vest and shirt, soggy with perspiration. He pulled a leather wallet from an inside pocket and pulled out a hundred dollar bill and a fifty. The wallet was crammed with money. He tossed the money carelessly on the desk.

'The first thing to do,' he said, 'is to see the wife. Tell her you're going to represent her, see? Let her know I'm on the job, and tell her to keep a stiff upper lip, and to keep quiet, see? Tell her to keep quiet, see?'

Ken Corning folded the money, got to his feet, stood there, signifying that the interview was over.

'Come back when I send for you. Leave your name and address and your wife's name with the girl in the outer office so I can get my records straight. Leave a telephone number where you can be reached.'

The man turned on the threshold.

'You ain't in with the ring?' he asked, and there was a note of anxiety in his voice.

Ken Corning reached for a law book, shook his head.

The pneumatic door clicked shut.

Ken set down the law book and fingered the money. He turned it over and over in his fingers. He cocked his head on one side, listening. After a moment he heard the click of the outer door catch. Then Helen Vail was standing on the threshold of the inner office. Her eyes were starry.

Ken Corning waved the money.

'Start an account for that bird, and credit it with a hundred and fifty.'

She was smiling at him when the door opened. Broad shoulders pushed their way across the outer office. From his desk, Ken could see the man as he crossed the outer office. Helen Vail barred the inner office door.

'Whom do you wish?' she asked.

The man laughed, pushed past her, walked directly to Ken Corning's desk. He flipped back a corner of his coat with a casual hand.

'Who,' he asked, 'was the guy that just left here, and what'd he want?'

Ken Corning pushed back the swivel-chair as he got to his feet.

'This,' he said, 'is my private office.'

The broad shouldered man laughed. His face was coarse skinned, but the gray eyes had little lights in them that might have meant humor, or might have meant a love of conflict.

'Keep your shirt on, keep your shirt on,' he said. 'I'm Perkins from the booze detail. There was a speak knocked over last night. The woman who was running it tried to slip a bribe, and she's booked on a felony. That big guy was sitting in there, eating chow. He claimed he was a customer. I happened to see him come in here. He looked phoney, so I tagged along. I want to know what he wanted.'

Ken Corning's voice was hard.

'This,' he said, 'is a law office, not an information bureau.'

The gray eyes became brittle hard. The jaw jutted forward. Perkins crowded to the desk.

'Listen, guy,' he said, 'you're new here. Whether you're going to get along or not depends on whether you play ball or not. I asked you who that guy was. I asked because I wanted to know. . . .'

Corning moved free of the swivel-chair.

'You getting out?' he asked.

The lips of the broad shouldered man twisted in a sneer.

'So that's your line of chatter?'

'That's my line of chatter.'

The man turned on his heel, strode towards the door. He turned with his hand on the knob.

'Try and get some favors out of the liquor detail!' he said.

Ken's tone was rasping. He stood with his feet planted wide apart, eyes glinting.

'I don't want favors,' he said, 'from anybody!'

The broad shouldered man walked from the office, heels pounding the floor. Slowly the automatic door check swung the door shut.

*

Ken was ready to leave his office, seeking an interview with his client at the jail, when the door of his private office framed the white features of Helen Vail.

'It's Mr. Dwight,' she said.

'What is?'

'The man who just came in. Carl Dwight. He's outside. He wants to see you.'

Ken whistled. 'Show him in,' he said.

She motioned towards the desk.

'Shall I get you some papers?'

'Not with him. He's a wise bird. He knows. Shoot him in.'

Helen stood to one side of the door and beckoned. Carl Dwight came in. He walked with a slight limp. His lips were smiling. He had pale eyes that seemed covered with a thin white film, like boiled milk. Those eyes didn't smile. His skin was swarthy and oily. There was a cut on his forehead, a slight bruise on his left cheek bone.

He wasn't large, and yet he radiated a suggestion of ominous power. He said, crisply: 'I'm busy. You're busy. You know of me. I know of you. I've had my eye on you for the last week or two. You're a likely looking young man. I want to give you a retainer. Here's five hundred dollars. That'll be for this month. There'll be five hundred dollars more coming next month, and the month after that.'

His gloved hand laid an envelope on the desk.

Ken picked up the envelope. It was unsealed. There were five one hundred–dollar bills in it.

'What,' asked Ken cautiously, 'am I supposed to do?'

The gloved hand waved in an airy gesture.

'Just use your head,' said Dwight. 'I've got rather extensive interests here. You've probably heard of me, know who I am.'

Ken Corning chose his words carefully.

'You,' he said, 'are reputed to be the head of the political machine in this county. You are reputed to be the man who tells the mayor what to do.'

The filmed eyes blinked. The swarthy skinned man made clucking noises in his throat.

'That, of course, is an exaggeration, Mr. Corning. But I have interests in the county, interests which are rather extensive. Now you can sort of look out for those interests. And, by the way, there's a criminal case, the matter of a woman who was running rather a disreputable joint, gambling, hooch and all that. Parks was the name, I believe.

'Do you know, I think it might be rather a good thing to have that case disposed of rather rapidly. A plea of guilty, let us say. I'm certain you'll agree that it's a dead open and shut case. She tried to bribe an officer. There were witnesses. She gave him fifty dollars. Having such things aired in front of a jury don't do any good.'

He got to his feet. The swarthy skin crinkled in a smile, a sallow, bilious smile. The filmed eyes regarded Ken Corning with the wisdom of a serpent.

'So now,' he smirked, 'we understand each other perfectly. I think you'll like it in York City, Corning.'

Ken slowly got to his feet.

'Yes,' he said, 'I understand you perfectly. But you don't understand me, not by a long ways. Take back this damned money before I slap your face with it!'

Dwight teetered back and forth on his feet, made little clucking noises with his mouth.

'Like that, eh?' he said.

'Like that,' agreed Corning.

Dwight sneered.

'You won't last long. You can't . . .'

He didn't finish. Ken Corning reached out with the envelope which he held by a corner, and slapped it across Dwight's mouth. The filmed eyes blazed into light. The mouth twisted in a snarl. Dwight snatched at the envelope, crammed it in his pocket, whirled and started to the door. He paused on the threshold.

'Wait,' he said, significantly.

And Ken Corning, standing by his desk, feet braced wide apart, jaw thrust forward, said: 'You're damned tooting I'll wait. I'll be waiting long after you think you're finished with me!'

The attorneys' room in the county jail was a dull, cheerless place. There was a long desk which ran down the center of the room. Above this desk was a heavy wire screen. The prisoner could sit on one side of the desk, the attorney on the other.

Esther Parks came into the room through the doorway which led to the cell corridor. Ken Corning watched her with interest. Her face was heavy, her walk plodding. She was a big woman, broad-hipped and big-shouldered. Her eyes were like oysters on a white plate.

She plowed her way forward.

The attendant who had charge of the room stood at the doorway, beyond earshot, but where he could see everything that went on in the room.

The woman sat down on the stool opposite Ken Corning. Her face was within three feet of his. Her big hands were folded upon the scarred wood of the long desk. The heavy screen separated them.

'Hello,' she said.

Ken Corning kept his voice low pitched.

'Hello. I'm the attorney that your husband engaged to represent you. He thought you were just charged with unlawful possession of liquor. You're not. They've got you on the charge of offering a bribe to an officer. That's a felony.'

He paused expectantly.

The woman said: 'Uh-huh.'

Ken stared into the oyster eyes.

'Well,' he said, 'I'm to do the best I can for you. Can we go to trial and beat the charge?'

The eyes didn't change expression. The heavy face rippled into dull speech.

'I was running a speak, me and Sam. We went in mostly for cheap food with drinks to sell to the right parties. I don't see why they had to pick on us. Everybody's doing it, that is, everybody anywhere round our neighborhood.'

Ken frowned and shook his head.

'I'm telling you it isn't the liquor charge they've got you on. I could square that with a fine. It's the bribery charge. Can we beat that?'

The woman's voice was blurred in its accent, indifferent and stolid in tone.

'I don't know. I gave him the money. They all take the money. Twice before I've had men call on me and say they was the law. I've given 'em money. I gave this man money. Then he collared me. They didn't spot Sam. He sat down at a table and ate some grub.'

Ken Corning made little drumming noises with the tips of his fingers. He regarded the woman through the wire mesh of the screen.

'Have they asked you for a statement?' he wanted to know.

A flicker of intelligence appeared in the pale, watery eyes.

'I ain't so dumb. I told 'em to wait until my lawyer showed up, then they could talk with him.'

'Who was it?' asked Corning, 'the one who wanted the statement?'

She moved her head in a gesture of slow negation.

'I dunno. Somebody from the Sheriff's office, or the District Attorney's office. He was a young fellow and he had a man with him that took down what I said in shorthand.'

'What did you say?'

'Nothin'.'

Corning squinted his eyes thoughtfully.

'How did it happen that they didn't spot Sam as your husband? Usually when they make these raids they've had a stoolie go in and make a purchase or two. They have all the dope on where the stuff is kept and who runs the place.'

The woman's head turned again, slowly, from side to side.

'I dunno. They just didn't spot Sam, that was all. I was behind the counter at the cash register. They came walkin' in. I think I heard somebody say "There she is," or "That's her, now," or somethin' like that.

I didn't pay so much attention. They made the pinch, and I tried to hand 'em the dough.

'It was their fault I slipped 'em the money, too. One of the men held up the jug that had the hooch in it, and said: "Well, sister, what are you goin' to do about this?" I seen he had me, dead to rights, so I opened the cash register, an' asked him if he'd listen to reason. He said he would. I slipped him the cash, an' then they said something to each other and told me to come along with them.

'Sam had got wise to what was goin' on, an' he'd gone over to the table an' was boltin' down food. I asked the law if I could close up the joint, take the cash an' collect from the gent at the table. They said I could, an' I did, an' that's all I know about it. They took me here.'

Ken Corning clamped his mouth into a thin line.

'Then we've got to plead guilty,' he said.

She shrugged her shoulders.

'That's your job. I dunno. I'm tellin' you what happened. I figured Sam would get a mouthpiece an' spring me.'

Corning continued to drum with his fingers.

'Look here,' he said, 'there's something funny about this case. I'm going to keep a close mouth for a while, and see if I can find out what's back of it. You seem to be on the outs with the ring that's running the town. Do you know why?'

The big head shook slowly.

'Well,' said Corning, 'sit tight for a while. Don't talk to anyone. If anyone asks you any questions, no matter who it is, tell them to see your lawyer, Mr. Corning. Can you remember to do that?'

'Uh-huh.'

'I'll have you arraigned and get bail set. Can you raise bail?'

'How much?'

'Maybe three thousand dollars?'

'No.'

'Two thousand?'

'Maybe.'

'Any property you could put up as security with a bail bond company for the purpose of getting them to issue a bail bond?'

'No. Just cash. We had a lease on the joint. It paid fair money. Lately it ain't been payin'.'

Ken Corning got to his feet.

'All right,' he said. 'Sit tight. Remember what I told you. Don't talk. I'm going to see what I can do.'

The attendant moved forward.

'This way,' he said to the woman, in a voice that was a mechanical monotone.

*

Don Graves, the Deputy District Attorney in charge of the case of the People vs. Esther Parks, was almost totally bald, despite the fact that he was in his early thirties. His face ran to nose. The eyes on either side were round and lidless. He had a peculiar peering appearance like that of a startled anteater.

He turned the nose directly towards Ken Corning, so that the twin eyes bored unblinkingly into those of the attorney, and said: 'We won't reduce the charge. She bribed an officer. That's a serious offense.'

Ken kept his temper.

'That's a hard charge to prove, and you know as well as I do that the officer kept angling to get her to give him money. You get a jury of twelve people together, and some of 'em are going to think it's a hell of a note to send a woman to the pen because she had some hooch and an officer kept sticking his palm out at her. It's only natural to slip a man something when he makes a stall like that. That isn't being criminal. That's just human nature.'

The deputy licked his lips with the tip of a pale tongue that seemed, somehow, to be utterly cold.

'The penal code don't say so, brother.'

Ken Corning frowned.

'The penal code says lots of things – so does the Constitution.'

Don Graves said: 'Yeah,' and made as though he'd turn away.

Corning raised his voice.

'Well, listen, about bail. If you'll suggest to the magistrate that bail be reduced to a thousand dollars cash, I think she can raise it.'

Graves turned back to Corning, stared lidlessly at him.

'You heard what the magistrate said: ten thousand bucks cash, or twenty thousand bond.'

Corning's rage flared up.

'A hell of a bail that is. You'd think the woman was guilty of a murder or something. If you don't know that these cheap dicks are sticking their palms out right and left and shaking down the people that run the little speaks, you're just plain crazy! You keep riding me around, and I'll take this jane before a jury and see what twelve men in a box have to say about the way you're getting so damned virtuous in York City all of a sudden.'

The lidless eyes remained hard and peering.

'Go ahead,' said Graves.

'I will!' snapped Corning.

Graves spoke as Ken Corning was halfway to the door.

'Tell you what I *will* do, Corning.'

Corning paused, turned.

'Take her into court right away, plead her guilty as charged, and I'll ask to have a minimum sentence imposed.'

Corning asked: 'Fine or imprisonment?'

41

'Imprisonment,' said Graves. 'To hell with a fine.'

Corning's retort was emphatic. 'To hell with *you!*' he said, and slammed the door.

Helen Vail had the afternoon papers for him when he walked into his office.

'News?' she asked.

He grinned at her, took the papers, touched her fingertips as he took them, and suddenly patted her hand.

'Good girl,' he said.

'Why?'

'Oh, I don't know. You just are.'

'How about the case?'

'I don't know. There's something funny. You'd think the woman had done a murder or something. And Graves, that billiard ball guy with the snake eyes, told me he'd let me cop a minimum sentence if I'd rush her through the mill and make a plea.'

Helen Vail's eyes were sympathetic.

'You mean send the woman to the pen because she slipped one of these dicks a little dough?'

'Exactly.'

'What'd you tell him?'

Corning grinned.

'That, precious, is something your little shell-like ears shouldn't hear.'

And he walked into the inner office, taking the papers with him. He sat in his swivel-chair, put his feet on the desk, turned to the sporting page, browsed through the headlines, turned back to the front page.

The telephone rang.

He called out to Miss Vail: 'I've got it, Helen,' and scooped the receiver to his ear, holding the newspaper in one hand, the telephone in the other.

The shrill, piping voice of Sam Parks came over the wire.

'Listen, is this Corning, the lawyer?'

'Yes.'

'Okey. This is Parks. I was in to see you this morning about my wife. Listen, I know why they're trying to give her the works. I can't tell you over the telephone. I'm coming over. You be there?'

'Come right away,' said Corning.

'Yeah!' shrilled Parks excitedly, and banged the receiver into place. Ken Corning hung up, turned to the paper. There was a frown creasing his forehead. He looked at his watch. It was five minutes to four. Street noises came up through the open window. The afternoon was warm, the air laden with the scents of late summer.

Ken's eyes drifted unseeingly to the front page of the newspaper. Why should so much stir be made over the matter of a commonplace woman in a third-grade speakeasy giving some money to an officer who held out his hand for it? Why should a raid be made on a place where the officers hadn't collected enough information to know who was running the place, and had let the husband slip through their fingers?

He stared at the newspaper, let his forehead crinkle in thought, and tried to fit the ends of the puzzle together.

Minutes passed.

The clock on the city hall boomed the hour of four, and the big gilt hands crept around until the minute hand marked the quarter hour.

There was the sound of a truck backfiring in the street,

Something came trebling up through the window, the scream of a child, or of a very frightened woman. Then there was the sound of rubber tires, skidding into a turn on pavement, the shout of a man.

There was a second silence, and then the noise made by many voices, the sound of feet running on cement. A siren wailed in the distance.

Ken Corning, lost in contemplation, did not interpret the significance of those sounds until the siren had become a scream, until the clanging bell of the ambulance sounded almost directly beneath his office window, and until the door of his private office opened and Helen Vail stared at him.

'There seems to have been a man hurt,' she said.

Ken Corning put down the paper and went to the window. Helen put her hand on his shoulder as they leaned out. Corning was conscious of the touch of her hair against his cheek, the pressure of her hand on his shoulder. He slid his right arm out, around her waist.

They looked down upon the street.

There was no traffic. Such vehicles as were on the street were stalled. Men swarmed about like busy ants, moving in seething disorder. An ambulance was backing towards the curb. A uniformed officer was clearing a path for it. Stalled cars, their motors running, belched forth thin smoke films which made the air a light blue color.

A black circle of men were not moving. They were grouped about something which lay on the sidewalk. From that form there was a dark stain which had welled along the cement until it trickled in a thin, sluggish stream into the gutter.

The man was big and fat. He was lying on his back.

'Good heavens!' said the voice of Helen Vail, 'it's the man who was in the office.'

Ken Corning swung from the window. He reached the doorway of the private office in three strides, and gained the stairs. He went down them two at a time. He reached the sidewalk as the men were loading the stretcher. He pushed his way through the crowd. Men muttered comments, turned and stared at him, growled warnings to watch what he was doing. Corning paid no attention to them.

He reached the inner circle, saw the stretcher bearers heaving against the weight of the bulk that they strove to place in the ambulance.

Parks had been shot twice. To all appearances he was dead. The bullet holes welled a red trail which dripped from the stretcher. The eyes were half open and waxy. The skin was like discolored dough. The hands trailed limply at the ends of dangling arms.

One of the stretcher bearers spoke sharply.

'Give us a hand here, some of you guys!'

Ken Corning pushed through the circle as two of the spectators swirled forward. A uniformed officer also bent to give a lift. Corning asked a question: 'Who saw it? How did it happen?'

Men stared at him with blank curiosity. He was hatless, wandering about asking how it had happened, and men regarded him as a part of the incident which had broken into the routine of their daily life. They watched him with that expression of impersonal curiosity with which fish in an aquarium stare at spectators who press against the glass tank.

On the fifth repetition of the question, a man gave an answer.

'I saw it. He drove up in an automobile and parked the car. He started walking along the street. The guy that shot him was in a roadster. He pulled right in to the curb, and he didn't drive away until he was sure the guy was dead. The first shot smacked him over. He shot again when the guy was on the cement. I seen him twitch when the second bullet struck!'

Corning led the man to one side.

'Drove up in a car, eh? Which car?'

He indicated the line of parked machines.

The witness shrugged his shoulders. 'I ain't sure. I think it was the flivver over there. I remember that it was a car that had a smashed fender. You know, there wasn't no reason why I should notice him until . . .'

'Yes,' said Corning, 'I know. Now you want some advice?'

The man looked at him with curious eyes.

'Huh?' he asked.

'Get away from here and don't tell your story to a soul. Go to headquarters, get the homicide squad's office and ask for Sergeant Home. He's on the square. Tell your story to him, and ask that your name be withheld. Otherwise, if you got a good look at the man that did the shooting, you might find yourself parked on a marble slab. Killers don't like witnesses.'

The man's face paled. 'Gee,' he said; then, after an interval: 'Gee whiz!'

He spun on his heel, started walking rapidly away. From time to time he glanced over his shoulder.

His tip gave Ken Corning the chance to be the first man to examine the light car with the bent fender.

He looked at the registration certificate which was strapped about the steering post of the car. That showed the machine was registered in the name of Esther Parks, and the address which was given was the same address as that of the place which had been raided when the woman was arrested.

Ken felt of the seat. It was still warm.

He noticed an afternoon newspaper lying on the floorboards. He picked it up. There was nothing else on the inside of the car to give any inkling as to who had driven or owned it. Ken felt in the flap pocket of the right-hand door. His groping fingers encountered a lady's handkerchief, a pair of pliers, the cap from an inner tube, and a bit of pasteboard. He pulled out the pasteboard.

It was red, bearing the insignia of the police department. It was, he found when he deciphered the scrawled lines which were placed in the printed blanks, a ticket for parking within fifteen feet of a fire hydrant on Seventh Street, between Madison and Harkley. The time was checked at three-forty-five, of that day.

Ken pocketed the ticket and walked around to the front of the car, inspecting the dent in the fender. There was but little paint left upon the nondescript car which Parks had been driving. That little paint had been cracked and chipped where the fender had crumpled. And, on the tip of that crumpled fender, was a spot of bright red enamel, evidently taken from the car with which the flivver had collided.

Ken examined the front of the springs, the radiator, found further evidences of a collision, further bits of red paint. The accident had evidently been very recent.

Aside from those things, there was nothing to indicate anything whatever about the occupant of the car, or the errand upon which it had been driven.

Ken walked to the curb, looked at the crowd which was commencing to move along under orders of the uniformed police. The traffic was moving now, crawling past at a snail's pace, horns blaring. An officer, accompanied by a woman, moved along the parked lane of cars, inspecting them.

Corning felt that this woman had seen the fat man emerge from a machine, but couldn't identify the machine. Ken let himself drift away with the scattering spectators. He walked around the block, and back to his office. He climbed the stairs, smiled at Helen Vail's white face.

'Was it . . . ?'

He nodded, passed into the inner office. She came and stood in the doorway. Ken smoothed out the newspaper he had taken from the car Parks had driven. He spread it out.

A knife had cut away a section of the front page.

'Was it because he came here?' asked Helen, mustering her courage.

Ken Corning reached for the other afternoon newspaper he had been reading when the sound of the shots had interrupted him. He nodded absently as he spread the two front pages out on the desk, one over the other.

The paper from the death car showed the page of the other paper through the opening where the knife had cut. That which had been cut out was a picture with a small paragraph or two below it.

Ken looked at the picture.

It showed a man with a square-cut chin, shell glasses, a firm, thin mouth, high cheek bones and a high forehead. Below it appeared the words *Mayor Appoints Harry B. Dike as New Head of Water Department.*

Corning read the few paragraphs appearing below the headlines of the accompanying news article. Those paragraphs recited the enviable record Harry B. Dike had enjoyed in connection with his own business enterprises and such civic activities as had claimed his time. It also mentioned that Dike was firmly opposed to the granting of contracts and concessions to those who enjoyed political pull, and that, in the future, the water department would be conducted upon a basis of efficiency with all work thrown open to the lowest responsible bidders, although the department would reserve the right to let private contracts.

The article sounded very promising. It gave the location of Dike's office in the Monadnock Building. The Monadnock Building was on Seventh Street, between Madison and Harkley.

Helen Vail watched Corning as he clamped his hat down on his forehead.

'Ken,' she said, 'you're going out . . . on this thing, into danger?'

Her face was a dead white. The eyes were starry and tender.

He laughed at her, saw the pale lips stiffen, quiver and tremble into the first sign of a sob, then lift into a half smile. He patted her shoulder, grinned at her.

'Listen, kid, I'm a newcomer here. I'm here to stay. Some of these chaps don't recognize that fact yet, that's all. It's time they did. I'm just going out and let a few of them know that when I hung out my shingle in this town I did it with my eyes open. I planted my feet here, and I'm staying here.'

And he strode across the office, went through the outer door, made time to the street, caught a taxi. 'Monadnock Building,' he said, as he settled back against the cushions, 'and make it snappy.'

The cab lurched into motion.

'Man shot here a while back,' said the communicative driver. 'Raised hell with traffic.'

Corning said: 'Yeah,' without interest and the conversaion languished. The cab swung in to the curb at Seventh Street, Corning paid the meter, consulted the directory of the Monadnock Building, found that Dike's office was on the seventh floor, and took the elevator up.

There was no one in the reception office except a typist who was tapping frantically at the keys of a noiseless typewriter, and a rather stern-faced but pretty secretary who sat stiffly behind a desk in the corner of the room, three telephones in front of her.

Corning walked to her, smiled.

'I'm anxious to get in touch with a man who was to have met me here earlier this afternoon, but I had a puncture and was delayed. He's a great big man, fat, about forty-eight, wearing a gray suit that's in need of pressing . . .'

Her voice was crisply efficient.

'You mean Mr. Parks. He's been here and gone.'

Corning made a gesture of disappointment, but his mouth clamped shut to keep from showing his elation.

'Mr. Dike's in?'

'Yes. He's busy. You haven't an appointment?'

'No. Can you answer the question? What kind of a car does he drive?'

'A Cadillac. It's a sedan. Then he had a roadster, a Buick.'

'Thanks. I think I'm interested in the Cadillac. It's a bright red, isn't it?'

'It's red, yes.'

'I'm afraid I've got to disturb Mr. Dike. Tell him it's Mr. Corning, and that I'm in a hurry.'

She shook her head.

'He's not to be disturbed. You haven't an appointment, and . . .'

Corning gained the door to the inner office in a swift stride, without waiting for her to finish the sentence.

'And I'm in a hurry,' he said, and opened the door.

Harry B. Dike was even more dignified in his frosty appearance than the newspaper photograph would have indicated to a casual observer. The light glinted from the bald reaches of his high forehead. His eyes were steel gray and bored steadily out from behind his shell spectacles. He looked up from a desk which contained a sheaf of papers, stared at Corning and said: 'Get out! I'm busy.'

His eyes went down to the papers.

Corning walked across the room.

Dike didn't look up again. He was moving the point of a pencil along the typewritten lines of a document. 'Get out,' he said, 'or I'll call a cop and have you thrown in for disturbing the peace. I've canceled my appointments. I don't want any life insurance, any books or a new automobile.'

Corning sat down.

Dike scowled at him, banged the pencil down on his desk and reached for the telephone.

'I'm Kenneth D. Corning, attorney for Sam Parks, the man who called on you a little while earlier this afternoon,' he said.

Dike dropped the telephone. His eyes widened, darkened, then became fixedly steady in gaze and expression. He said coldly: 'What's that to me?'

'It has to do with your acceptance of the position of Superintendent of the Water Department,' said Corning. 'I think it would be far better for you to refuse the appointment – particularly in view of the fact that Parks was murdered about twenty minutes ago.'

The face did not change by so much as a line.

'You mean that you think I had something to do with the murder?' asked Dike coldly.

Corning's tone was equally cold.

'Yes,' he said.

The two men stared at each other.

'Corning,' said Dike, as though trying to place the name. 'A newcomer here, eh? I presume you're crazy. But if you've got anything to say, I'll listen.'

Corning spoke, his tone dispassionate.

'He made the mistake of coming to you first. I presume he wanted a shakedown. When things didn't go to suit him here he called me. It was Dwight's men who put him on the spot. You probably weren't directly connected with it. You notified Dwight, that's all. You weren't entirely surprised to hear of the murder, but you hadn't exactly expected it.'

Dike got to his feet.

'All right. You've had your say. Now get out.'

Corning held his ground.

'You accept that position of Superintendent of the Water Department,' he said, slowly and forcefully, 'and I'll have you before the grand jury for murder.'

Dike laughed scornfully.

'A man calls at my office. Later on he's found murdered. I have been sitting here all the time. Simply because he came here you think that I should give up my career, eh?'

Corning played his bluff.

'Forget it,' he said. 'I know what I'm doing. Parks talked before he died. It was on the road to the hospital. I rode with him in the ambulance.'

That statement shook Dike's self-control. The eyes wavered. The mouth twitched. Then he gripped himself and was as granite once more.

'I presume he said I ran alongside his flivver and stabbed him!' he snorted.

Corning grinned.

'So you know it was a flivver, eh? Well, I'll tell you what he said. He said that he and his wife were out driving and that they had an automobile accident. The car that they ran into was your car. You were in it, and there was another man in it, Carl Dwight, the head of the machine that's milking the city of millions in graft money. The people had been demanding a change in the water department because of that very graft. The mayor made them a gesture by putting you in charge. You were supposed to put an end to the graft on water contracts. Yet you were out riding with Dwight, the man you were supposed to fight.

'You didn't get the man's name. But you found out about the woman. She was driving the car. You learned she was running a speakeasy. You thought it'd be a good plan to get her where her testimony wouldn't count. So Dwight raided her place and framed a felony rap on her. She didn't know the full significance of what she'd seen. You thought it'd be a good plan to forestall developments. The testimony of a convicted felon wouldn't go very far in a court of law.'

Corning ceased talking. His fists were clenched, his eyes cold and steady.

Dike's gaze was equally steady.

'Corning,' he said, 'you are a very vigorous and impulsive young man. You are also either drunk or crazy. Get out and stay out.'

Corning turned towards the door.

'I thought,' he said, 'that I would have the satisfaction of telling you what I know, and showing you that you can't gain anything by railroading this woman. Also you'll either resign your post, or you'll be mixed up in murder.'

Dike scooped up the telephone.

'When you go out,' he said, 'tell my secretary to put the spring catch on the door. I don't want any more crazy guys busting in here.'

Corning grinned at him.

'I'll put the catch on the door myself,' he said, and pushed the thumb snap down, walked out and closed the door behind him. The typist paused in her pounding of the keys to watch him. The secretary stared with wide eyes. Corning walked to the corridor and took the elevator.

He stepped into a drug store on the corner and called police headquarters. He asked for the homicide squad, and got Sergeant Home on the line.

'This,' he said, 'is a tip.'

'What is?' gruffed the sergeant.

'What you're hearing. A man named Parks was killed this afternoon. He'd been driving a flivver that had collided with a red car. Harry B. Dike owns a red car that's been in a collision. Parks had been to call on Dike just before he got killed. Carl Dwight has been in some sort of a smash. There's a cut on his forehead, and he walks with a limp. Sam Parks has a wife, Esther. You've got her in jail right now on a felony charge.'

Sergeant Home's voice betrayed his excitement.

'Tell me, who is this speaking? Where do you get that dope?'

Ken snapped his answer into the transmitter.

'Have a man you can trust at the *Columbino* at eight tonight. Have him wear a white carnation and sit near the front door. Look up the information I've given you in the meantime.'

And Corning slammed the receiver back on the hook, waited a moment for a free line, and then called Harry Dike's office on the telephone. The line was busy. He called three times with the same result. The fourth time he got Dike on the line, after some argument with the secretary.

'Corning,' he snapped crisply. 'I'm giving you one last chance to get out of the tangle Dwight's got you in. I'll be at the *Columbino* tonight at eight. If you want to make a written statement and get out of the mess I won't put the screws down.'

Dike's voice was smoothly suave.

'Kind of you, I'm sure, but I don't think I care to see you there. However . . . where are you now?'

Corning laughed into the transmitter.

'Wouldn't you like to know!' he said, and hung up.

He waited in front of the drug-store, keeping in the background, yet being where he could watch the entrance to Dike's office building.

Carl Dwight didn't show up. But a speeding automobile, slamming into the curb at the fire hydrant, disgorged Perkins, the detective. Half a dozen minutes later a taxicab paused to let out Fred Granger, who was Dwight's right-hand man.

Perkins came out, almost on the run, within fifteen minutes. Granger didn't come out for half an hour. Dike followed him. Ten minutes after that, a police car bearing a detective stopped in front of the office building.

Ken Corning terminated his vigil, stepped into a barber shop, had a shave, hot towels, massage, haircut and shampoo. He was careful not to go near any of his regular haunts, or leave a trail which could be picked up.

The *Columbino* ran fairly wide open. Anyone could get in there who had the price. It went in somewhat for music, atmosphere and an aura of respectability. The liquor was very good.

It was early when Ken Corning walked into the place, exactly eight o'clock, and there were but few patrons, most of them eating. The dance floor would fill up later on, and by midnight the place would be going full blast.

A man in evening clothes, with a conspicuous white carnation in his buttonhole, had a table in the front of the place. Ken heaved a sigh as he saw that Home had investigated his tip, found out enough to go ahead on the lead.

Ken Corning ordered a full dinner with a cocktail at the start, a bottle of wine with the meal, a cordial afterwards. Momentarily he expected action, and the action did not come.

It was nine-fifteen when he reluctantly called for the waiter and paid the check. The man with the white carnation continued to sit by the door.

Evidently the powers that ruled the city had decided to ignore Ken Corning, and Ken was disquieted at the thought. Things were not turning out as he had anticipated.

The waiter was gone some little time. Ken waited for the change. The man in the dinner coat with white carnation looked at his watch, pursed his lips. Ken got the idea that this man had a definite time limit fixed. At nine-thirty, probably, he would leave.

The waiter returned.

'I beg your pardon,' he said, 'but the manager wants to see you in his office. There's a bit of trouble, sir.'

Ken got to his feet, followed the waiter. He was walking lightly, his hands slightly away from his sides, his head carried alertly, eyes watchful.

The manager stared coldly from behind the desk.

The waiter turned to go. Ken thought that something brushed against his coat. He couldn't be sure. He glanced at the waiter's retreating back.

The manager said: 'I'm sure it's a mistake, but it's something I'll have to investigate.'

'What is?' asked Corning.

'This,' said the manager, and placed on the desk in front of him the bill which Ken Corning had given the waiter. 'It's counterfeit.'

Ken laughed.

'Well,' he said, 'it happens that I can give a complete history of that bill. It was paid me this morning by way of retainer in a legal matter, in the presence of my secretary. What's more, I don't think it's counterfeit.'

A door opened. A man stepped purposefully into the room.

The manager waved his hand.

'I'll let you discuss that with McGovern, of the Secret Service. You probably don't know it, but we've been flooded with clever counterfeits here the last week. McGovern has been waiting on call.'

Ken turned to meet the man's eyes.

McGovern smiled, and the smile was frank.

'If you can tell me where you got it, that's all I need to know,' he said. 'One look at you's enough to convince me *you're* no counterfeiter.'

Ken smiled in return, then let the smile fade.

'Look here,' he said, 'this bill came from a client. I have an idea certain interests would like to frame something else on that client and his wife. The man is dead. The wife isn't – yet. I don't want to play into any frame-up. . . .'

The other smiled, waved his hand.

'Just a formality, but you'll have to tell me. You're dealing with the Federal Secret Service now. You won't find any political frame-ups with us. As a matter of form, would you mind letting me see the rest of your money?'

Ken laughed, reached in his coat, took out his wallet.

That wallet felt strangely bulky. He stared at it. It wasn't his wallet. It was crammed with currency. He made a move as though to put it back in his pocket. The Federal man whipped down a swift arm.

'Here,' he said, 'none of that. Acting funny ain't going to help you.'

He grabbed the wallet, opened it, whistled.

There was a moment of silence.

'That,' said Ken, 'is not my wallet. I demand that the waiter who brought me in here be called. I want to have him searched. He slipped this wallet into my pocket and took mine out. He's a professional dip, and this is a plant.'

The lip of the Federal man curled.

'Yeah,' he said. 'How often I've heard that one! You've got to come along. Want to go quietly, or would you rather make a fuss?'

Ken stared at the wallet.

'I'll go quietly if you'll pick up the waiter and take him along, too,' said Ken.

The Federal turned to the manager.

'Who was it?' he asked.

'Frank,' said the manager.

'Get him,' said the Federal. 'In the meantime I'll take this guy along in a cab. Come on. You can tell your story where it'll be appreciated. They don't pay me to listen, only to do things.'

Ken went out through the cabaret.

The man in the dinner coat, who wore the white carnation, was looking at his watch with an air of finality. Ken walked rapidly so that he was a step or two ahead of McGovern. There were couples standing on the floor. Many of the tables were vacant. The music stopped when Ken was some twenty feet from the table occupied by the man in the dinner coat who wore the white carnation. There was a perfunctory spatter of applause and then couples stood, waiting, staring at the orchestra expectantly.

Ken Corning raised his voice and called over his shoulder to McGovern: 'This is just a frame-up, because I've got some evidence in that Parks murder case.'

McGovern spoke in an even, ominous tone. 'Shut up!' he said.

Ken flashed a glance to the man who wore the white carnation. He was signaling a waiter for his check. There was nothing on his face to indicate that he had heard what Ken had said; or hearing, was in anywise concerned with it. The orchestra struck up an encore. As the couples started to twine and twist to the strains of the dance, Ken flashed a glance at McGovern, then at the man who wore the white carnation. The man was handing the waiter a bill. The waiter was pushing an oblong of pink pasteboard at him from which had been figured the items of the check. The man pushed away the pasteboard, made a sweeping gesture with his hand as though to indicate that the waiter should keep the change. Staring at his face, it was impossible for Ken to tell whether the man had hurried his exit because Ken was leaving, or whether he had simply grown tired of waiting, and decided to knock off for the day.

Behind him, McGovern said: 'Get your hat and coat and don't try any funny business.'

Ken moved up to the checking stand. A girl with a beautiful face flashed him a smile that was meant to be dazzling, but was only mechanical, took the square of pasteboard which he handed her and pushed Ken's hat out over the counter.

The man who wore the white carnation in his dinner coat had evidently found some people he knew. He was chatting with them, a young man of about thirty, and a red-haired woman who could not have been over twenty-three. As he chatted, he reached up and plucked the white carnation from the dinner jacket, dropped it to the floor and stepped on it.

Ken said to McGovern: 'Can I talk with you? Will you listen to reason?'

McGovern said: 'Sure, I'll listen to any guy who wants to talk; only remember that anything you say will be used against you.'

Ken lured him over to the far corner of the checking counter and said: 'All right now, listen. I told you that this thing was a frame-up because I was a witness in the Parks case. You don't seem to be interested.'

McGovern said: 'Why should I be interested? That's a state case, I'm a Federal. You tell me where you got this counterfeit money from and where the plates are and I'll sit here and listen to you until daylight. But if you've got anything to say on the Parks case you can tell it to the state authorities – I'm not interested.'

Ken fixed his eyes on McGovern and said: 'Listen, suppose that I could show you that this man Parks had something on the administration and was going to keep Dike from accepting the position of Superintendent of the Water Department? Suppose I could show you that Carl Dwight is mixed up with Dike; that, in place of being enemies, those two fellows are working hand in glove regardless of all this newspaper talk about Dike wanting to clean up the graft. . . .'

McGovern took his arm above the elbow and gave him a push.

'Listen, guy, I told you I wasn't interested in all that stuff. Are you going to tell me where you got the plates or where you've got the rest of this queer cached?'

Ken Corning's eyes narrowed.

'Okey,' he said, 'I tried to give you the breaks and you wouldn't listen. Now I'll take a look at *your* credentials before I leave this place.

McGovern grinned easily and dropped his right hand to the side pocket.

'Gee,' he said, 'you sure are full of alibis and stalls. Come on and let's get going. This is all in the day's work with me and I want to get home and get my beauty sleep. You can stall all night, but you can't keep me from taking you to jail and booking you on a charge of possession of counterfeit money. If you want my authority, here it is.'

Ken felt something hard prodding against his ribs. He glanced down to where the right hand of McGovern was holding the gun concealed by the right-hand side pocket of his coat. He said: 'Oh, it's like that, is it?'

McGovern said: 'Yes, guy, it's like that. You're going to take it and like it. Get started out of here. You've got counterfeit money in your possession and there are witnesses that you tried to pass it. You can either go quietly or you can get your insides blown out right here. Which is it going to be?'

Ken grinned and said: 'Under the circumstances, I guess I'll go quietly.'

McGovern said: 'Now you're talking sense. You can't gain anything by talking any other way. I'm on the square and I'm going to take you in, but I ain't going to stand here all night and listen to a lot of hooey and I ain't going to have you pull any smart aleck stuff on me. Get started!'

Corning moved towards the door. He noticed that the man who had worn the white carnation was moving towards the door also and that the man who had been with the red-haired girl was walking with him. The red-haired girl moved off towards the left and went into the women's dressing room. The man who had worn the white carnation lit a cigarette. He seemed in no hurry. Ken Corning went out of the door painfully conscious of the pressure of the gun which was held against his ribs. The doorman looked at them and said: 'Taxicab?'

McGovern shook his head and said: 'No, I've got a car.'

The big limousine which had been parked near the curb with motor running slid smoothly up to the front of the cabaret and stopped. The doorman started to open the door and McGovern spoke sharply: 'That's all right,' he said, 'I'm a Federal dick and this man is a prisoner. He's desperate and may try to start something. Keep back, I'll handle this!'

He reached out and opened the door. His gun prodded Ken in the ribs. 'Get in,' he said.

Ken put his right foot on the running-board of the limousine. He could see two men seated in the back seat. They were grinning. Ken swung his body in a pivot, grabbing with his left hand at the gun which McGovern was holding against his ribs and pushing down with all his strength.

McGovern fired twice before Ken's fist connected with his jaw. Neither shot hit. Somebody shot from the interior of the limousine but the bullet hit the plate-glass window, shattered it into a thousand fragments and deflected. McGovern went down like a sack of cement. Ken swung himself on him and reached for the gun. Over his shoulder he could see the swirl of motion from the interior of the limousine. A man jumped to the running-board while Ken was still struggling for the possession of the gun. Ken heard him say: 'All right, guy, take a load of this!'

Two shots roared out as though they had been one explosion. The man who had stood on the running-board of the limousine pitched forward and struck on his face. Ken jerked the gun from the pocket of McGovern and saw that the man in the dinner jacket was standing on the steps of the cabaret, an automatic in his hand. The man who had been with the red-haired girl was standing on the sidewalk a little bit to one side with a double-action revolver spouting fire. The doorman was running heavily, his gold-braided coat flapping grotesquely behind him. The limousine had lurched into motion. Somebody was rolling down the back window, which had not been shattered. Guns blazed over Ken's head. A bullet whistled past his cheek. The two men standing in the front of the cabaret answered the fire.

Ken got McGovern's gun in his hand and took a couple of shots at the limousine. He heard the bullets give forth a clinking sound as they struck against the metal of the body. The limousine swung far over to one side as it rounded the corner to the accompaniment of screaming tires.

The man in the dinner coat ran towards Ken as McGovern, recovering from the daze of Ken's blow, started to struggle to his feet.

Ken said: 'Those men were trying to take me for a ride. This guy posed as a Federal agent . . .'

McGovern spoke up and said: 'I am a Federal agent. This crook's been shoving the queer. He's got a wallet of phoney stuff on him right now.'

The man in the dinner coat laughed and said: 'Federal, hell! I know you, you're Jim Harper, and you've done time!'

A uniformed policeman, on beat, ran up. The man in the dinner coat spoke to him sharply: 'All right, Bell. Get the crowd back. I'll handle what's left of this.'

A curious crowd was commencing to form a ring around the men, and the uniformed policeman started to herd them back.

The man in the dinner coat said: 'That's all right, buddy, I know this guy, he's a crook. You're a witness in the Parks case, huh?'

Ken Corning stared at him with round eyes and shook his head.

'No,' he said, 'I'm not a witness, I'm attorney for Mrs. Parks and I came here to meet a witness but he didn't show up.'

The man in the dinner jacket stared at Ken Corning for a long five seconds. Then his right eyelid slowly closed in a solemn wink: 'So,' he said, '*that's* your story, eh?'

Ken Corning kept his face perfectly straight and his eyes perfectly steady. 'That,' he said, 'is my story and I'm sticking to it. I'm not a witness, I'm a lawyer. I was to meet a witness here. These guys tried to keep me from meeting him, that's all.'

The man in the dinner coat said: 'Who were they? Would you recognize any of them if you saw them again?'

Ken Corning shook his head.

'No,' he said, 'the light wasn't good enough. I couldn't see them.'

The man in the dinner coat turned to the fake Federal agent. Ken Corning slipped away. No one tried to stop him. There was the sound of a police siren, approaching fast, as he turned the corner.

Ken Corning walked into his office.

The morning sun streamed in at the east window. Helen Vail stared at him with eyes that were dark with emotion, warm with pride.

'Got your name in the papers, didn't you?'

He grinned at her.

'How about our client?' she asked.

He spread his hands, palm up, made a sweeping gesture.

'Gone. Case is closed, dismissed.'

'And all we get then is the hundred and fifty dollar retainer?'

Ken nodded.

'That's all. The woman was driving the car. Her husband wasn't with her. I figured that he must have been, but he wasn't. Dike and Dwight had been having a secret meeting. They'd been out in the country at a road-house where they were safe. Coming back they were riding in the same car. Dike was driving and he was a little bit 'lickered.' The woman was driving the flivver and they had a smash. She was a little bit belligerent and insisted on taking down the license number of the automobile. They paid her for her damage but she acted a little suspicious so Dwight got the license number of her automobile and found out who she was. They knew that she was running a speak, and figured that she was too dumb to know what it was all about, but they wanted her out of the way, just the same. With the deal Dike was planning to pull, it would have been fatal if somebody had uncovered this woman as a witness, so Dwight decided that he'd get her convicted of a felony. That would have discredited her testimony if she'd ever been called as a witness.

'She probably was suspicious, because she told her husband about it. Nobody knows just how much she told him or how much he knew, but it's a cinch that he knew enough to put two and two together when he saw Dike's picture in the paper with the blurb about his taking over the Water Department and eliminating graft.'

Helen Vail watched him with wide eyes.

'Can we prove any of that?' she asked.

Ken Corning shook his head. 'We can't prove anything,' he said. 'Wouldn't do us any good if we could. They've dismissed the case against the woman, released her from custody and she's gone. They probably made a deal with her, gave her some money and started her traveling.'

'Why would they do that?' asked Helen Vail. 'Her testimony is just as damaging now as it ever was.'

Ken Corning smiled and motioned towards the morning paper.

'Read the news,' he said, 'and you'll notice that Dike has declined the appointment. He said that his private business was taking up too much of his time for him to make the sacrifice of accepting a public position.'

Helen Vail blinked her eyes thoughtfully and said: 'How about the people in the automobile – don't you know any of them?'

Ken Corning said: 'You mean the ones who were trying to take me for a ride?'

She nodded her head.

Ken laughed and said: 'Sure I do. Perkins was one of them. He was the detective who barged into the office here. He's a cheap heel who does dirty work for the Dwight machine.'

'But,' she said, 'you told the officers that you couldn't recognize any of them.'

Ken Corning laughed mirthlessly and said: 'Of course I did. I'd never get anywhere trying to pin anything on Perkins. He'd produce an alibi and get acquitted. Then they'd turn around and prosecute me for perjury. I'm bucking a machine in this town, and the machine is well entrenched with a lot of money back of it. I'm not a fool!'

'How about the man who pretended to be a Federal officer?' she asked.

'He's got to take the rap. They've got the goods on him. They might have managed to make some sort of stall there, only I knew it was coming. I had worked the wallet that the waiter had planted on me out of my pocket. When they opened the door of the limousine I tossed the wallet in with my left hand before I grabbed at this guy's gun and socked him with my right.'

She shuddered and said: 'Oh, Ken, I don't like it.'

He stood with his feet planted far apart, his jaw thrust forward, hands thrust into the pocket of his coat.

'I like it,' he said, 'and I'm going to make them like it. I'm going to bust this town wide open. They're going to stop me if they can. They'll try to frame me, try to take me for a ride, try to freeze me out. I'm going to stay! I'm going to be here after they're gone.'

'But, Ken,' she objected, 'you've done all this work and risked your life and we only get a hundred and fifty dollars out of it.'

Ken Corning nodded and laughed.

'A hundred and fifty dollars,' he said, 'and it's honest money.'

Then he walked into his private office and the door clicked shut.

Helen Vail could hear him moving around in the inner office. He was whistling cheerfully as though he didn't have a care in the world.

She opened the drawer of her desk, took out a ledger which was innocent of entry, took a pen and wrote in a hand which trembled slightly: 'People versus Parks – cash retainer $150.00.'

FROST RIDES ALONE

HORACE McCOY

A somewhat prolific author of pulp stories, primarily for *Black Mask*, Horace McCoy (1897–1955) is mainly remembered for his dark, tragic and occasionally violent novels, several of which have been made into notable films.

A memorable work of noir fiction and a classic film is *They Shoot Horses, Don't They?* (1935), filmed in 1969 with Sydney Pollack as the director, which achieved its aim of illustrating the pain and hopelessness of the Great Depression, using a marathon dance contest as a metaphor, with the exhausting and pointless expenditure of energy for participants being analogous to the plight of the majority of Americans.

The film *The Turning Point* (1952), directed by William Dieterle, became the novel *Corruption City* in 1959; *Kiss Tomorrow Goodbye* (1948) starred James Cagney and was directed by Gordon Douglas when it was filmed in 1950; *No Pockets In a Shroud* (1937) was filmed in France in 1975; and *Scalpel* (1952) was filmed the following year as *Bad for Each Other*, the screenplay co-written by McCoy and directed by Irving Rapper. The only one of McCoy's novels to have no film version is *I Should Have Stayed Home* (1938), and McCoy's screenplay was published in 1978.

Captain Jerry Frost of the Texas (Air) Rangers made his debut in 'Dirty Work' in *Black Mask* in September 1929; 'Frost Rides Alone' was published in the March 1930 issue.

FROST RIDES ALONE

HORACE McCOY

F rost felt that he and the woman were being followed, had been followed since they crossed the Border. As they emerged from the Plaza Madero and turned down the crooked street towards the Café Estrellita he became acutely aware that footsteps were proceeding in the same direction as himself and that the owner was trying to attract as little attention as possible.

To satisfy himself that he was not the victim of his own imagination, so often the case when he invaded old Mexico after nightfall, he halted briefly before a shop window, wherein baubles were exhibited, and whispered a caution to his companion. The moment they stopped the footfalls ceased. No one passed. Quite evidently someone was following.

Fully alive now, his nerves on edge, Frost spoke to his companion, and they walked on. In the distance he could see the lights of the Café Estrellita and outside the shadowy forms of customers at the sidewalk tables. Frost walked slowly, his ears strained, but did not look around. He was still being followed. Moreover, the number of steps behind him had increased. There were now two or three men. The street was narrow and the footsteps loud: overhead the stars blinked and from a hidden patio nearby there floated the dim tinkle of a guitar.

As the woman passed the dark, dank interiors she gave way to a swift rush of apprehension and took Frost's arm nervously. He leaned over and whispered: 'Don't get excited, but I'd like to know if you can use a gun.'

She moved her head closer. 'I'm sort of jumpy,' she apologized lamely, 'but really, I can use a gun. Fact is—' her confidence returned '—I've got one.' She patted her voluminous handbag. She went on lightly. 'I haven't been a newspaper woman ten years without learning a few things.'

Frost said, 'Oh!' rather contritely, and steered her into the café without looking back at his pursuers.

La Estrellita was a little square room overcrowded with tables at which, outside and inside, sat perhaps half a hundred persons. The ceiling was almost obscured by cigarette smoke, and there was all the variety of noises commonly associated with Border joints. It was the hour when Algadon blazed with the specific intent of luring tourists, although the patronage here was now, as far as Frost determined in a hurried glance, mostly native.

At one end of the room was a bar at which two Mexicans were mixing drinks; behind them was the traditional frosted mirror and long rows of bottles. A square-shouldered, semi-bald man was busy plying a rag with what amounted to violence and one look at him left no doubt concerning his origin. He was one of those old-time American bartenders driven into Mexico by prohibition.

Glasses and spoons littered one end of the bar and near this end, on a raised platform, sat a quintet of native musicians languidly strumming their guitars. They simulated indifference, ennui, hoping to chisel a round of drinks from a sympathetic tourist. The house was bare of sympathy.

Frost led his companion inside and half way to the table he had mentally selected he recognized the unmistakable form of Ranger Captain George Stuart. Frost slowly passed Stuart's table and said under his breath:

'Don't look up, George. Just get set. Hell's fixing to pop.'

The only indiction Stuart heard was an almost imperceptible movement of his fingers as he knocked the ashes off his cigarette. Twenty years on the Border had given him perfect control of all his faculties, had deadened his emotions.

Frost went to a table near the end of the bar and helped his companion into a chair. Then he sat down, facing the room and glanced at George Stuart.

There passed a look of understanding. Stuart crossed his legs and as he did so slid his six-gun inside his thigh by means of his elbow. At that moment three men came through the doorway, looked hurriedly about the room and walked to a table near Frost. As they sat down their chairs scraped and the sounds were audible above the maudlin talk and the soporific music.

The three of them were young, Mexican in cast of countenance, with sharp faces and narrow eyes – of a general type with which the Border, from end to end, teems: shrewd, crafty wastrels who will turn any sort of a trick for any sort of a price.

Frost ordered two bottles of beer from a waiter, and looked at his companion.

'I'm afraid,' he said, striving to be unconcerned, 'I've got you into a mess – and the only way out is straight ahead.'

'You think,' she asked, inclining her head slightly, 'those men—'

'I don't know,' Frost said. 'But I've got a sweet hunch you're liable to get a good story before this party ends. There's a window directly behind you. If – if anything happens, get out and keep going.'

'You talk,' she said, 'as if you regretted bringing me.'

Frost eyed her. 'I never have regrets,' he said, 'they're cowardly. Just the same it didn't look this foggy when we started. If we tried to get out now we'd never live to reach the street.'

'As bad as that?' She was smiling and the smile annoyed Frost. He didn't answer. He thought her question was stupid. Hell, of course it was bad. She had no business here. But that was the way with the newspaper tribe – all of them. Especially women. They thought that their profession was protection. Helen Stevens, however, seemed more officious than any other Frost had known. Probably, he presumed, because she was to author a series about Hell's Stepsons for an indubitably important organization, the Manhattan Syndicate, Inc. But, even then, Frost told himself again, this time bitterly, she had no business here.

Few spots on the Border are safe for a woman after dark; Algadon was no spot for a woman at any time. But Helen Stevens had insisted and as the final persuasive force she had even brought a letter from the Adjutant-General. And here she was.

It looked bad.

The waiter returned with the bottles and two glasses. He poured the drinks, placed the bottles on a tray, and started away.

'*Psst!*' said Frost. '*Deja los botella.*'

The waiter turned, surprised. '*Como?*'

'*Deja los botella!*' Frost repeated, more sharply.

The waiter lifted his eyes as if invoking divine compassion on the fool before him; and put the empty bottles back on the table. He moved away, slightly puzzled; but no more so than the newspaper woman.

'How odd!' she observed.

'Not at all,' Frost said. 'I've got a lot of funny little habits like that.' He didn't feel it necessary to tell her experience had taught him there was nothing comparable to the efficiency of a beer bottle at close quarters; or that he had a deep-seated hunch it would be at close quarters soon.

He took a sip from his glass and looked at his companion. Her face was unworried, lovely. He thought of that moment on route to La Estrellita when she had, momentarily frightened, touched his arm. Her face betrayed no fear now – nor anything that remotely approached fear. From the tranquillity of her demeanor she might have been sitting in the refinement of an opera loge instead of a Mexican dive where the air was charged with expectancy. Frost felt, irreverently, that if he, accustomed to tension, was slightly ill at ease, she, unaccustomed to anything of the sort, should at least have shared a portion of that discomfort. It mildly annoyed him that she didn't.

She reached for the glass with her long fingers and as she lifted it she drummed her fingers lightly against the stem. Out of the corner of his eye Frost saw one of the three men who had followed him lean over and whisper to his comrades. He also saw George Stuart move forward in his chair, ready to get into action in a split second.

Helen Stevens was speaking in a dulcet voice. 'Is this,' she was saying, 'typical of Border towns?'

'Is it possible,' Frost countered, 'that you are a stranger to Border towns?'

She laughed and her eyes beamed spiritedly. 'Of course.'

'In that case it's typical. Just the same,' Frost went on, 'I wish we hadn't come.'

'Why?' she demanded. She seemed positively to be enjoying it. 'I'm glad,' she went on, rippling, 'that I can see you against your proper background.' She inclined her head. 'Captain, I'm afraid you dramatize yourself fearfully.'

For the second time in the past few minutes Frost was the victim of mixed emotions. She alternately stirred him and irritated him. Now he was in no mood for tea-room repartee.

'Please,' he said, 'let's not get personal.' He contemplated that remark and decided it wasn't exactly what he wanted to say. It sounded flat. So he hurried on, 'Miss Stevens, you mustn't get me wrong. Our men have been having a tough time along this river with an important gang. We are constantly expecting things to happen – anything. To you that may seem dramatic. But I am only cautious—' he lifted his eyes '—and thinking of you.'

'You needn't,' she said suddenly. 'I'm all right.'

Somehow he didn't quite think so. He was alarmed – rather definitely alarmed. Notwithstanding his attitude of indifference he felt that something was going to happen before they got out of La Estrellita. He knew the signs. It was the sort of a prelude that always traveled along in the same slot. Never any change. Had he been alone he could have forced the issue. But he was not alone. There was a woman with him – a personal charge. That sort of cramped his style. Jerry Frost had been in the habit of meeting trouble half-way.

Three men had followed him. Why? Footpads intent on robbing a tourist? He dismissed that thought. They knew very well who he was – should have known – and even if they didn't, George Stuart was there. Every man, woman and child in Algadon knew the rock-ribbed Stuart. He was part and parcel of the Border country. Men who stalk American game along the Rio with a Ranger within the same walls are bent on a mission more sinister than robbery.

Did they think Frost had on his person the valuable black book he got from Flash Singleton in the little episode at Jamestown – the little black book the gangster had carried, giving names and information? He didn't know. But there was a voice within him – a small, still voice that roused him to the alert. It bred expectancy. Helen Stevens had thought, and said so, that this was theatricality. Frost smiled reflectively. She could think what she damn well pleased. He had no fault to find with his intuition. It had saved him too often.

'Do you think,' she whispered, 'any of the gang is here now?'

'*No se*,' he shrugged. 'They're everywhere.'

'But I thought I'd read that Hell's Stepsons had broken it up.'

He cast her what was intended to be a rueful grimace, but it hardly was that. 'No,' he admitted, 'we've made only a small dent in it. We've caught only the little fish.'

She moved again, this time her body. She placed her hand on Frost's wrist and swayed her head a little. 'I hope,' she said suddenly and, he thought, softly, 'you get the big ones!'

Frost felt she was animated by deep sincerity, and as quickly as his suspicions had mounted they disappeared. They might have been dissipated by the touch of her hand, by the proximity of her lovely face, by the faint smile on her lips; but dissipated they most assuredly were. Helen Stevens was a good-looking woman of the type which has been vaguely classified as a man's woman. It had been a long time since such a creature had been as close to him. He became poignantly and swiftly aware that he had been missing something.

He patted her hand gratefully, sighed like a silly schoolboy and said: 'I hope so, too.'

There was a scuffling sound from the front of the house and a man got up unsteadily. After an hour he had become aware that the orchestra was not functioning well.

'*Una cancion!*' he cried. '*Canta!*'

'*Si, si*,' came the chorus.

The musicians on the platform be-stirred themselves and stroked the strings with a little more life than they had previously evidenced. They played a few bars as a vamp and then lifted their voices in a plaintive rendering of *La Cucaracha*, camp song of that immortal renegade – Villa.

They finished and were rewarded with loud applause. It was to be expected. *La Cucaracha* is a sort of provincial national air. It brought back flashing memories of the Chihuahua stable cleaner who later flung his defy in the teeth of the government: '*Que chico se me hace el mar para hacer un buche de agua* . . . I'll use the ocean to gargle!'

The lethargy in La Estrellita was falling away.

Frost looked at the table where the three men were sitting. They were, to him, plainly agitated. Their heads bobbed excitedly, and one of them exchanged wise looks with the bartender. After that the bartender moved slowly down the rail with affected nonchalance. Frost pretended to be thoroughly immersed in his drink and his companion. But he was not too immersed in either.

Something was about to occur.

'Remember,' he said aside to the woman, 'the window is directly behind you. It looks like trouble is coming. Understand?'

'Perfectly,' she said quietly. She reached for her bag, and opened it in

65

her lap. Her hand slipped inside and closed about the butt of a gun. 'Don't worry.'

'I won't,' he said. He meant it. The calmness and sureness of her decision relieved him. Again he admired her, found himself wondering what sort of a companion she would be in more agreeable surroundings.

One of the three Mexicans got up. The impression he meant to convey was drunkenness. Frost got no such impression.

He caught the eye of George Stuart and nodded. Stuart nodded likewise.

The Mexican started off between the tables, ostensibly intent on reaching the bar. He never got that far. He purposely stepped out of the way to trip against Frost's foot, almost falling to the floor. He righted himself and poured out a volume of Spanish; swept the glasses from the table.

Here it was. The big blow-off. Here it was. Frost had been waiting, taut as a bow-string.

He leaped from his chair and put all his power into a short uppercut that landed flush on the Mexican's chin and sent him reeling ten feet away against a table.

'Beat it!' he said to the woman.

His right hand went to his hip after his gun and his left hand groped for the empty bottle. But he had lost a precious few seconds. He turned to find himself looking down the blue barrels of two pistols held in the hands of the remaining pursuers. It was too late to draw his own weapon.

The career of Jerry Frost might have ended on the spot had it not been for George Stuart. He had come from behind softly, but fast, and brought the butt of his gun down upon the head of one of the Mexicans. It was a terrific blow. The man groaned and fell to the floor. Stuart quickly threw his arms about the other's shoulders.

Frost availed himself of the lull to take a step backward and look for Helen Stevens. She was missing; and he had no tme to speculate on where she was or how she got away. Through the door came five men, as tough looking as any Frost had ever seen. They were rushing forward recklessly, intent on but one purpose. Everybody in the room had risen by now, offering the quintet slight impediment.

Frost swung the beer bottle with all the force he could muster, and it crashed against the head of the man with whom Stuart was wrestling. The Mexican's cheek bone ripped through the skin as if by magic, and blood poured down his face. He instantly grew limp; and Stuart let him slide to the floor.

An unseen hand pressed the switch and La Estrellita was swept into darkness.

A pistol cracked, light blue and scarlet, and the bullet whistled by Frost's head. Pandemonium arose. Frost stepped to one side; not a moment too soon. The pistol barked again. From the flash Frost deduced he had been in direct line of fire. If—

There was a stampede towards the door. Frost lashed out in the dark, heard a grunt, and lashed out again. A third time he swung the beer bottle; this time it shattered. Spanish blasphemy ascended. La Estrellita was an inferno. Tables and chairs rattled, glasses crashed, and a loud voice shouted:

'*Luz! Luz!*'

Someone was calling for lights and it struck Frost that the sensible thing to do now was retreat before the lights went up. So he shouted for Stuart to follow him, ducked quickly, and moved towards the window. His escape was made difficult by the cursing, wedging mob. Everybody was fighting to get outside. Frost lunged with his fists, and a blow banged against his jaw. He reeled, almost fell but came up swinging. Outside he could hear the shrill whistles of the police. The Mexican constabulary was calling, like no other police in the world, for order.

Frost set his teeth and flailed his arms. And every time they went out they struck something. He dived forward and some of the mob went down before the force of his body. He got up and climbed over, carrying others in his mad march to the exit.

He wanted to shout at Stuart again to let him know where he was, but even in that chaos of mind and flesh, Frost realized to cry out now would be to betray himself by his voice. So he fought his way slowly to the window.

He could see it as a rectangle of outside light a few feet ahead and he pushed and struggled and continued to swing. He thrilled to the power in his long arms and his fists . . . a form loomed in front of him in clear silhouette and he started a blow from the floor. His fist crashed against the blurred vision that was a head; there was a smothered exclamation, and the man went down.

Frost shifted his arms and got his pistol, and as he came near the window he swung again and again; then of a sudden he became aware that his legs were not moving. They were imprisoned in a human vise.

He fell forward.

But he did not hit the floor. He fell on top of several squirming bodies; and realized he had been pulled down in the confusion. Fearful lest he be trampled, he yanked himself up again by means of somebody's coat and was thankful he still had his pistol. He came to his knees, then full up, and, finding he had sufficient space to move his legs, kicked lustily at the form on the floor. There was an oath.

He reached for the window, anchored his hand and pulled. He finally made it. He climbed up and literally fell into the night. With the first intake of air he thought of the woman and Stuart.

Where were they? Safe? There had been, he reflected, but two pistol shots. So far as he could determine neither had found a mark. Mexican marksmanship is, notoriously, bad; their first love is the blade. And the blade is, generally, silent. Had? . . . The thought sent Frost into a rage. Still, Stuart was a veteran. He had been in hundreds of brawls . . . and yet. . . .

Regardless of everything now, Frost lifted his voice:

'George! George!'

As if in answer to his reckless cry, George Stuart tumbled through the window.

'Thank God!' Frost panted. 'Hurt?'

'Nope!' Laconically. Then: 'You?'

'Bruised.' Then: 'George, I've got to find the woman!'

They moved quickly across the street. The mêlée in the café continued. The police were puffing at their whistles and occasionally shouting in an official voice that did no good; there was general discord.

'In the meantime,' George said, 'we're in a fine shape to stop a slug or two. Let's step on it.'

They walked rapidly towards the international bridge.

Stuart said, 'Who the hell was that dame?'

'A newspaper woman the Old Man sent down – but I'd rather not talk about it.'

'I don't blame you,' Stuart said. 'You had a swell idea – bringing her to this town. She damn near got us messed up.'

'I know that now. But it could have been worse.' He went on quietly, 'You saved my life, George.'

George Stuart rubbed his chin reflectively and pretended he didn't hear.

'Where do you suppose she went?' he asked.

'I tried to tell her what was coming,' Frost said. 'If she was smart she went across.'

They had gone so far now the sounds in La Estrellita were but murmurs. Overhead the stars blinked on; once in a while the Rangers caught the music of guitars as an indolent part of Algadon, impervious to the excitement, sang on.

'Know those yeggs who started the fight?' Stuart asked, matching the strides of the long-legged flyer.

'Never saw 'em before,' Frost said. 'I guess they were hired by the gang. I wonder,' he mused, 'where it'll all end?'

Stuart had no answer for that one. They walked along silently.

'I hope,' Frost went on, as if to himself, 'she got back okey. I sort of had the idea she could look out for herself.'

'Well,' put in Stuart truculently, 'she had a swell opportunity of doing that little thing tonight.'

'And she wasn't bad looking,' Frost went on in the same tone.

'Yeh – I saw that, too.'

At the international boundary they exchanged pleasantries they did not feel with the customs officials. Frost asked for the woman. The officers said they were sorry, but no woman had passed into the States. Frost stoutly insisted they must be mistaken; they insisted just as stoutly they could not be.

George Stuart was familiar with their technique. He said, 'Well?' to Frost in such a tone his meaning was clear.

'A mess,' Frost exploded – 'a first-class mess. God,' he breathed, 'if anything's happened . . . Well,' resolutely, 'I can't go back without her. That much is a cinch.'

Stuart lighted a cigarette and said, 'Anything you say, Jerry. Wanna take a look at La Estrellita?' thus leaving the plan of action to the flyer.

'It's not a question of wanting to, George. But the Old Man sent her—'

'Sure.' Stuart turned to the officials and requested, with a trace of belligerence, that if the woman who had crossed with Frost returned she be detained. He then divested himself of certain pertinent remarks. 'Jerry – you're the biggest damn fool I ever saw. You know how you stand around here,' and, having unburdened himself, he again became the fighting man with a terse, 'Hell, let's go!'

And with no more than that they swung back to La Estrellita, whence they had so recently and so narrowly escaped with their lives.

The café had quieted somewhat when they returned. Stuart and Frost made their way inside. A few patrons had come back (a great many had never left), but many of the tables were over-turned and everywhere there were unmistakable signs of the fight, notwithstanding the expeditious work of the café's ubiquitous emergency corps. The five-man Mexican orchestra was back on the platform playing in the same listless fashion which forever characterizes their music. This was a bland lot of musicians. A brawl, a pistol fight, a knife duel – nothing to them. Every night was just another night.

Their hands on their hips, the Rangers stood inside the door of the café and returned glare for glare. There were low murmurs of recognition as they entered.

They summoned the proprietor.

'I know this guy Rasaplo,' Stuart said. 'Lemme do all the talking.'

Rasaplo waddled up solicitously, portly after the vogue of Mexican café owners, with long mustachios and sagging jowls that could be either fierce or cherubic. At this moment he chose for them to be cherubic. He rubbed his hands as if Frost and Stuart were patron saints who had stepped from their *nichos*, and smiled broadly.

'*Señors*,' he said, 'I am sorry – vair sorry.' He looked from one face to the other, seeking some indication of official forgiveness. There was none. The Rangers stared at him and through him. Rasaplo quailed somewhat.

'Now lissen,' Stuart said, his voice steely. 'The *capitan* here brought a woman with him – *la mujer Americana. Ella desvaneca* – disappeared. *Sabe what that means?*'

Rasaplo's eyes widened in surprise. His whole person registered consternation. Great actors, those fellows. Rasaplo lifted his hands in horror.

'*Imposible!*' he managed. 'Never in La Estrellita. Never! La Estrellita ees—'

'Yeh,' Stuart cut in; 'I know that speech backwards! La Estrellita is a little nursery where mommas leave their children.' He clucked heatedly. 'Nix on that patriotism stuff, Rasaplo! Your dump ain't no different from any of the others along this creek. Now get this – the woman disappeared in here tonight – and she's got to be found. Tell me something before I—'

'But,' Rasaplo wheezed, 'I am in the back room when a gun go boom! and the place get dark. I know no more.'

Stuart looked at Frost and nodded. 'Well, in that case,' he began, his meaning clear, 'I guess we'll—'

Rasaplo said quickly, 'Mebbe Pete know. Pete always know.' He went briskly to the bar and engaged a bartender in conversation. He was the one Frost had seen moving down the rail before the lights went out. From the way the patrons eyed the scene the Rangers could tell they still were annoyed at having their evening interrupted. They were content, however, merely to stare.

But the bartender was mystified, too. There was no misinterpreting his gestures. He didn't know how the fight started, and he didn't remember any woman. All he knew was that after the lights went on again several natives were carried out, semi-conscious.

Rasaplo darted a swift look around, leaned over the bar a little farther, and something changed hands. Stuart and Frost both saw it at the same time. They went forward.

'Gimme that!' Stuart commanded.

Rasaplo grinned abashed, and handed over a letter. 'They give it to the boy to mail,' he said. 'I do not know anything.'

The letter was addressed to Captain Jerry Frost, Gentry, Texas, and there was a two-cent U.S. stamp in the corner. Frost ripped it open. A note on the back of a menu. It said:

'*Thanks, Captain, for the woman.*'

It was written in that peculiar, flamboyant foreign style. Frost fingered it blankly and held it up for Stuart to see. Stuart said to Rasaplo: 'Where's the waiter who got this?'

Rasaplo summoned a sleek servitor, who eyed Stuart and Frost with an expression that can only be called baleful.

'Who gave you this?' Frost held up the letter.

The waiter shrugged his shoulders to say he couldn't remember all the patrons; but made no answer.

'Who gave you this?' Frost repeated.

'I no remember,' he said. 'A man—' as if that would help.

Rasaplo inserted his broad bulk into the scene to give his employee whatever protection he could muster. 'He know nothing,' he said. 'He get the letter and boom! the place go dark. Mebbe we get *miedo* – and no mail letter. But—' His voice, colorless, trailed off.

Stuart gestured disgustedly to Frost. For the time being they knew they were against a blank wall. Trying to elicit criminal information from some Mexicans can be – in some instances, is – nothing short of impossible. Indeed, some of them are so clumsy in trying to remain innocent they incriminate themselves.

The Rangers knew they could do no more; and, too, they were chancing further trouble by remaining in La Estrellita.

'Come on, let's go see the cops.' On the way out Stuart went on: 'But don't expect too much of the law here. It's quite probably the rottenest force in the world. Maybe, though—'

They went around the corner to the police station, and Frost soon learned that Stuart had properly classified the Algadon police. They said they hadn't the faintest idea what happened to the woman; moreover, they gave the impression, and it was true, that they weren't in the least interested. They were without the slightest degree of enthusiasm, and raised their brows superciliously to convey the thought that if the Rangers couldn't look out for their own women they shouldn't expect anyone else to.

Stuart said to Frost: 'I'd like to sock this gang in the jaw.'

Frost nodded abstractedly. He wasn't particularly concerned with that. It was the woman. His last hope, for the present, had fled. She had been his responsibility, his personal charge, and to return to Gentry without her likely would cause complications. She could be one of a thousand places. He rephrased Stuart's words: he had been a damn fool.

And the Old Man. He'd raise hell. Well, what the hell? He'd just have to raise it, that was all. There wasn't anything they could do about it now. Anyway, it was partly his fault. He'd never brought her over if the Old Man hadn't written that letter. 'Let her have a look at Algadon by night,' he had said. The exact words. Let her have a look by night. . . . Well, she'd had one.

Frost damned his thoughts and turned to Stuart. 'Should I have kept her there and taken a chance?' he asked. 'Didn't I do the right thing when I told her to get out?'

'Sure,' said Stuart broadly, consolingly. Under his breath he rasped: 'I'd like to sock this gang in the nose!'

Back at the boundary the Customs officers said no woman had passed since Frost and Stuart were last there, and the Rangers swore roundly and stamped across the bridge. There were headed for the police department in Gentry.

Fifteen minutes later the telegraph wires of the Border country were humming a message, soon to be broadcast over the nation:

Kidnaped in Algadon, Mexico, on the night of February Eleventh: Woman answering to name of Helen Stevens, representative of Manhattan Newspaper Syndicate of New York City. About five feet five inches, hundred ten pounds, light brown hair, blue eyes, teeth unmarked, wearing brown coat and skirt, flat-heeled two-tone shoes. Notify Texas Air Rangers, Captain Jerry Frost Gentry, Texas.

Stuart and Frost then went to the barracks of Hell's Stepsons and dived into bed. George Stuart, again exhibiting remarkable mental control, went immediately to sleep.

Not so Frost. He rolled, pitched, tossed and fretted at his impotence.

Within seventy-two hours the Manhattan Syndicate, Inc., of New York City, had taken official cognizance of the disappearance of one of its representatives by bringing the matter to the attention of the ranking officer of the sovereign State of Texas. Powerfully allied, as are all important syndicates, it lost no time in applying all the pressure at its command.

Messages were exchanged and the austere Mexican government moved, as a gesture of courtesy, a detachment of *rurales* into Algadon. Nobody, of course, expected them to achieve results.

Helen Stevens had disappeared as completely as if the earth had swallowed her.

Yet the law, tank-like in its motion, rumbled on.

The spotlight was fixed on Hell's Stepsons, and its glare was not favorable. The spectacular work done in the past was forgotten.

On the fourth day after her disappearance there was a conference within the great, gilt-domed state capitol at Austin, in the inner office of the governor's suite. There were three men there: the Great Man himself, the Adjutant-General and Captain Frost.

'It is unfortunate,' the Governor was saying; 'most unfortunate.' He was tapping his glasses against his chin: a dignified patriarch, product of the expansive state he represented – rugged, sincere and honest.

'Yes,' the Adjutant-General agreed. He was commander of that crack constabulary, the Texas Rangers, the personification of the ideals of that brigade. Big and gaunt he was; you knew at a glance, the sort of an official who would, if needs be, climb into the saddle himself and take the trail.

'The woman,' the Governor went on, 'is well connected. We cannot, in any event, let up in the search.'

'But, sir,' mildly demurred the Adjutant-General, 'we *are* trying. I feel,' he went on, 'somewhat responsible in a personal sense. I insisted Captain Frost take her across.'

'No,' Frost said quickly; 'the fault was mine.'

'Well,' the Governor declared, 'whose fault it was is beside the point. We have got to do something at once.'

'They're a tough lot,' Frost mused. He spread his hands on the desk. He was, for obvious reasons, highly uncomfortable. 'Gentlemen,' he said, 'I agree that we are being made to look bad. But what else can we do?'

'It has been my experience,' said the Adjutant-General, 'that this gang never strikes blindly. There always is a motive back of every crime. What was it in this case? Why did they kidnap Helen Stevens? Revenge? Hardly. Ransom?' He shook his head. 'No – something else. Some reason we don't know yet.'

Frost nodded. 'If I had the slightest idea where she was,' he said, 'I'd go get her – no matter where that happened to be.'

Silence.

Then the Governor said, 'Perhaps we ought to ask for a bigger appropriation for the Ranger force. Increase them. Move some of them south.' He looked sagacious. 'The only bad feature about movement like that is the publicity. Our opponents always construe that as inefficiency. It gives them something to talk about. I dislike having this case noised around.'

'Well,' Frost said bluntly, 'the only way to keep it in the family is to let me have a crack at it alone.'

Then the unbelievable happened. The immense, carved door swung open noiselessly, and the Governor's secretary entered.

'I'm sorry, sir,' he addressed the Great Man, 'but I've a message for Captain Frost.'

'For me?' Frost asked.

'Yes, sir – forwarded from Gentry.'

The Governor said: 'Come in, Leavell, come in.'

The secretary walked to Captain Frost and handed him the message. Frost made no move to open it until the secretary had departed.

'May I—'

'Certainly,' said the Governor.

A deep silence fell. Frost read the message without even a blink of the eye and passed it over the desk to the Governor.

He put on his glasses and read aloud:

Coast Guard Cutter Forty-Nine sighted Rum-Runner Catherine B longitude ninety-seven east latitude twenty-seven near Brownsville with woman aboard answering description Stevens stop cutter outdistanced stop rum boat one of former Al Thomas fleet.

O'Neill.

The Governor removed his glasses and tapped them against his chin again. The Adjutant-General looked at Frost. Frost looked out the window.

'I sort of thought so,' he soliloquized.

'Al Thomas,' mused the Governor. 'Who is that?'

'A gunman killed in a plane smash a couple of months ago after a dogfight with Hell's Stepsons,' Frost replied. 'His men seem to be carrying on.'

'"Cutter outdistanced,"' the Governor went on. 'I wonder how—'

'Please, sir,' Frost put in. He was on his feet now. Hours of inactivity, of recrimination, of criticism, rushed to a climax which crystallized his attitude. 'Please, sir – I'd like to play this alone. Single-handed. It started mine and—' his voice was grim – 'I'd like it to finish the same way. I don't want any help.'

'But, Captain—' he began.

'Of course, Jerry,' said the Adjutant-General in a placating voice. 'You can't go streaking off like this!'

Frost raised his hand. His face was in a cast of resolve. 'Please,' he said again, firmly. He looked at the Adjutant-General and the Adjutant-General understood. 'I've got to go it alone.'

The Governor nodded; Frost saluted and went out.

As the door closed the Adjutant-General smiled and offered an observation to his chief. 'I'd hate like hell to have him after me.'

Coast Guard Cutter Forty-Nine's base was at Corpus Christi, and it was towards there that Frost turned when he hopped off from Austin. He was at Cuero in fifty minutes, stopping only long enough to wire Jimmy O'Neill that he was on his way and to notify Hans Traub he again was temporarily in command of the Air Rangers.

'I'm riding alone on the Stevens case,' he telegraphed.

Two hours and fifty minutes after he had circled the dome of the state capitol, he dipped into the airport at Corpus Christi and taxied his battle plane into a hangar. He got O'Neill on the phone at the government docks.

'Coming right over, Jimmy.'

'Great,' said O'Neill. 'Ox Clay is here. You'll like him.'

Frost did like Ox Clay. That name ought to awaken memories of sporting page devotees because Ox Clay was pretty well known back in '21 and '22 when he was ripping football lines to shreds for the Middies: little, square-jawed, built like a bullet, and innumerable laugh wrinkles around his eyes. 'Hello, Jerry,' he greeted the flyer. 'I've heard so damn much about you I feel as if we're old friends.'

'You're no stranger yourself.' Frost returned. He said to O'Neill: 'Well, Jimmy, I've just left one of those high and mighty conferences. Believe you me, Missus Frost's young son has got to do something and do it pronto. 'What's it all about?'

'Ox can tell you more than I can, Jerry. He was riding Forty-Nine himself.'

'I'll say I was,' Clay retorted with a grimace. 'And the way that baby slipped away from Forty-Nine was nobody's business. We took a couple of shots – it wasn't good target practice. We only scared her faster.'

'What about the woman?'

'I was getting to that. It's that Stevens skirt – no two ways about it. They let us get pretty close – and then kidded us by pulling away. But nobody can tell me I didn't see her during those first few minutes – brown suit, brown hair—'

'Right!' said Frost. 'Sounds like my little playmate. What about the boat?'

'Well, she used to belong to the Singleton outfit. Name's the *Catherine B*. Lately taken over by Thomas, and then his gang got it when you fellows rubbed him out. She's the prize of the Gulf, can store about three thousand cases and make close to forty knots. We've never got her because she's fast and then there are hundreds of little coves along the coast she ducks in when trouble appears. When we saw her she was heading to sea.'

'We've got plenty of dope on that outfit,' O'Neill said. 'But so far it hasn't done us any good. We know they load on the stuff at Tampico, Vera Cruz and God knows where else – and about a hundred miles out they transfer it to the launches.'

'I see,' Frost said. 'The launches don't dare get out farther than that?'

'Exactly,' Clay put in. 'They work close to the Mexican side. There must be five hundred coves between here and the Laguna de la Madre.'

'If we could grab the *Catherine B*,' O'Neill said; 'we'd stop a lot of the smuggling. What's your idea about this, Jerry?'

'Well, I'm going to have a look for her,' Frost said quietly.

They thought he was kidding.

'Bring your bathing suit?' Clay asked.

'I'm serious,' Frost said.

'Really?' Incredulously.

'Hell, yes. Why not? I'll get pontoons and try to take her. She can't outrun my boat.'

'It'd be suicide,' said Clay, shaking his head.

Frost laughed. 'Lissen, Ox – I admit it may seem funny to you, but it doesn't to me. Besides, I've *got* to do it. How am I going to know when I see her?'

'Easy,' said Clay. 'Brass taffrails. She's ebony black all over but for her taffrails. You can see 'em rain or shine. She carries one funnel, looks perfect alow and aloft, has a heavy stern and her cutwater and bow lines are as pretty as I ever saw.'

Frost laughed. 'I don't get that conservation,' he said. 'But I did understand about the brass. I don't guess I can miss her.'

'You can't,' O'Neill said.

'Definitely made up your mind to go it alone?' asked Clay.

'Yep. Would it be possible for me to requisition silencers?'

Ox Clay swung open a drawer and took out two pistols fitted with longish muzzles. 'Presto!' he said. He handed them to Frost. 'I'll let you use mine.'

Frost stared at them curiously. 'This,' he said, 'is the first time I ever saw a silencer. Are they apt to jam?'

Clay grinned. 'The first shots will be all right. After that you gamble. Hope they'll do you, Jerry. They're my contribution to your success.'

Frost took an automatic out of his hip-holster and one from under his chamois jacket. He said: 'I'll trade for the time being. Now one thing more and I'll blow a bugle over your grave. Will you phone Roland at the field that I'm on my way and be sure and be in.'

'I'll phone, but don't think that gang on the *Catherine B* will be a pushover. It's a tough mob.'

'I know.' Frost shook hands with each of them. 'Well,' he said; 'so long.'

'So long. Good luck.'

'Thanks.'

He sheathed his pistols and walked out. Ox Clay looked at Jimmy O'Neill.

'Lotsa guts,' he observed.

'You said it!'

Major Oliver Roland, commander of the flying field at Corpus Christi was a stout admirer of Jerry Frost personally and professionally, being a veteran airman himself, but he thought Frost's plan to take the air in an effort to locate the kidnaped woman was a wild idea.

'It's all wet,' as he put it.

Frost said no.

'Ridiculous – and dangerous.'

'Neither,' Frost retorted crisply. 'I can't afford to think of either one.'

'You ought to.' Sternly: 'Just because you've had a lot of success along the Border you think you're invulnerable That makes you cocky and breeds overconfidence. You mustn't get that way.'

Roland's tone was firm, but inoffensive, and Frost grinned. 'I'm not overconfident. I've got good reasons not to be.' He was thinking of that time not so long ago when he escaped in an enemy plane, to think he had the world by the tail on a down-hill pull, and was promptly shot down by his companions. 'I'm not overconfident,' he repeated. 'But I am curious – curious as hell. It's up to me to get that woman – and with your help I intend to!'

Oliver Roland knew flyers. He looked into Frost's eyes – clear. He looked at his mouth – tight. He looked at his chin – square under pressure of the jaws. He decided the young man knew what he was doing.

'Very well,' he surrendered. 'Want a flying boat?'

'Nope, pontoons. Just pontoons. Will you fit me?'

Roland nodded. 'On the condition that you forget where you got 'em.'

'My memory's awful,' Frost smiled.

It required little more than two hours to fit the pontoons and service the ship; and then the silver-winged bird cascaded through the Gulf of Mexico, left the water in a stream of fume, and turned its eager wings southward.

That bird was a fighting ship of the Texas Rangers, carried two thousand rounds of ammunition, a veteran pilot who had a brace of silencer-equipped pistols, and, what was infinitely more important, a stout heart.

Jerry Frost was riding alone. He climbed to fifteen thousand feet better to deaden the roar of his motor, and swung down the jagged coast line. The Gulf lay beneath, a somber expanse as far as his eyes could see, its surface rippling with whitecaps: long, thin, broken lines like the foreground of an etching. Far down the lanes he could see the funnels of a boat which seemed to hang on the edge of the world, so slowly did it move.

The coast line was dotted with innumerable coves and the waves rolled against them to be broken into effervescence. Frost reflected that Ox Clay had been entirely correct. There were so many of these serrated sanctuaries which afforded natural shelter for the lawless they could well defy the maps. No cartographer possibly could have marked them all.

Frost rocketed down the coast line for a hundred miles and then veered over the Gulf in a wider flight. Already he had come to realize that finding the *Catherine B* out here was no sinecure for a young man who wanted action. There was, however, one consoling thought: he, at least, was in the air with a definite objective.

The *Catherine B* had been seen in Longitude 97 east and Latitude 27. He consulted the map on his board. That would be, as near as he could roughly estimate, fifty miles out of the Laguna de la Madre in a line with Rockport and Vera Cruz. Of course, she wouldn't be there now. But she had started – and there was a reason why. It was not, manifestly, chance. She was on her way to keep a rendezvous.

Frost kept cudgeling his brain seeking a motive for the kidnaping of Helen Stevens. It probably was the least remunerative thing the gang could have done. What could they hope to gain? Didn't they know they would only attract official attention? And that the less attention they attracted the more success would attend their missions?

It seemed, to Frost, inconsistent, imbecilic. But – they had her. He couldn't very well get away from that – they had her. And it was up to him.

It seemed simple. 'Two and two,' he said to his instrument board; 'make four.'

A long way out from the Mexican coast his eyes were caught by a tiny boat that was slipping through the water, leaving a long wake, and he deduced she must be running all of thirty knots. Even from his height he knew the speed was unusual. His heart jumped. He came as close as he dared and maneuvered to get the sun on her. He looked closely. No brass reflection. A rum-runner, but, now, inconsequential. Frost was not interested.

He rolled back closer to the coast and maintained his vigil for thirty more minutes. Then he looked down and was surprised to see another boat. Bang, like that. He had been looking away for only a moment and when he gazed below the boat was there.

He thought probably the lowering sun was playing tricks on him, so he stared intently. No mistake. A boat. Speeding southwest; occasionally outlined against wide swells. If the first launch he saw was speeding there was no adjective for this one. She was, comparatively, doing more than that. And she looked capacious and businesslike now that he could see well. Worth investigating.

He turned the nose of his ship up and climbed. Over to the left was a perfect cirro–cumulus formation which invited him with its natural protection, and he went for it. As he took a gap in the fleece his eyes caught a reflection.

Brass!

The *Catherine B!*

He offered a silent prayer for the cloud bank and took a hurried compass reading. The course the boat was holding was in a straight line with Galveston. The big traffic route! But it could dare. It could show its stern to ninety-nine out of a hundred. . . .

Frost knew it would be fatal to attempt a landing now. Too much light yet. Something might happen. He thought about that rather sharply. An unknown grave in the Gulf was not appealing. That was the way Nungesser and Coli went. And Pedlar. And Erwin. Poor old Bill. There was a tug at Frost's throat. He had gone through many a dogfight with the Dallas ace. . . .

No, Frost knew, he couldn't go down now. Must wait. Hang back and wait for the dark. A big gamble then. A big gamble. Now it would be death.

He guessed the dusk was less than an hour away, but it was a bad guess. It was eighty minutes away and they were the longest eighty minutes Frost ever spent. Occasionally he stole through a rift in the bank to check his quarry to make sure it was within range. The *Catherine B* had now reduced its speed and was drifting idly: quite plainly at its trysting place.

Frost was forcibly struck by the profundity of the situation. Below was a rum boat a hundred miles at sea; above was a formation of clouds which concealed an eagle of justice. Soon that mass of clouds would part to disgorge a winged courier of the law. Why did those clouds happen – just happen to be there? Providence? Frost went off into an endless speculation about the omnipotence of the Creator.

And he found time to breathe a cautious prayer. Cautious because he had never done so openly. It struck him as cowardly. So he prayed quietly and cautiously.

He had decided to go down now in a few minutes.

The sun reached the end of the world, slid off the rim, and reached with long, tenuous fingers for a final hold, missed and fell into the lap of night. Frost was constantly amazed at the swiftness of the sunset; had always been amazed. Yet it is a source of indefinable joy to airmen to see the sun sink from the sky, for at fifteen thousand feet you seem pretty close to the heart of things. Frost probably always would be stirred by such manifestations, no matter how exigent the conditions under which he viewed them. They mildly disquieted him; made him wish he had been an artist.

'Hell,' he said to his instrument board, 'you're only a lousy airman. Get your head back into this cockpit!'

Night slipped up and five minutes later it was dark. Frost dropped out of the cloud bank among, it seemed, the fledgling stars which were timidly trying their wings, and looked for the *Catherine B*. The Gulf had lost the blackness so apparent in the sunlight and now had become opaque to a faint luminosity. A wayward light flickered below on deck. The light revealed the boat Frost had come to take – and he had determined to take it. Bellerophon felt the same way about the Chimaera.

Frost took off his gauntlet and slipped the silencer-equipped .38 into the seat beside him. Its touch comforted him, reassured him. Of a sudden he picked it up and pulled the trigger. No other sound broke above the throttled humming of the motor.

'Hot stuff!' he said to the sky. To the instrument board he said: 'Well, here we go!'

He fell into a glide and kicked his switch off. It was his farewell to the air. Dropping fifteen thousand feet his motor would get cold, too cold to start again in an emergency. But, he told himself, there must be no emergency.

A quarter of a mile back he nosed up into a sort of drift, timing the distance with that weird sense all good flyers possess. And his landing was a tribute to long years of feeling his air. The premium he collected was munificent – his life. To have failed meant death.

The *Catherine B*, on the spot of its meeting, drooled in a wide circle, and as the little battle plane slowly moved by the stern, Frost could plainly read her markings:

CATHERINE B
Galveston

Frost kicked his rudder bar around and turned in towards the boat. He flattened out against its sides when he saw a spurt of flame and heard the crash of the report. The man shot from the rail amidships. Frost leveled his gun and fired. Then he quickly threw his anchor rope over the rail. There had been no far-carrying report from his gun, but the man dropped. He was out on the wing in a moment, over the rail in another, and had tied his ship off with a loop knot.

Attracted by the explosion, a husky fellow shoved half his bulk through the wheelhouse door and Frost saw him level his gun. The Ranger shot from the hip; the man collapsed in the door and rolled on deck. He never knew what had hit him. Frost ran forward.

There was a scuffling sound aft and a man's head and shoulders appeared. He seemed to rise out of nowhere. But he was cautious, had come to investigate what he thought was a shot.

Frost tensed his muscles and gripped his pistol. He pressed himself close to the skylights as the man stepped out gingerly and came towards the wheel-house. He was roughly dressed. He had nearly reached Frost's side, when he stopped suddenly and sucked in his breath in a swift intake. He had seen the plane.

In a flash Frost was beside him. He rammed the gun into his ribs.

'One crack and off goes your head! Get down flat!'

Silently, the man obeyed. He stretched out an arm's length from the second man who had been shot.

Frost said tensely: 'That guy is dead. You didn't hear my gun go off because it's got a silencer, see? Now answer my questions and answer 'em quick!'

'All right,' the man grunted.

'How many on this tub?'

'Six.'

'One of them a woman?'

'Two women.'

'Two!'

Frost thought that over.

'What's this boat doing out here?'

'Meeting the *Mermaid* at midnight.'

'Liquor?'

'Yep.'

'Well, I'll have to give you the works to get you out of the way,' Frost said grimly. He meant it. The man knew he meant it. The game had gone too far to take chances.

'I'm a Texas Ranger.'

'I know,' was the answer. 'We been expecting you. But not like this. You're Frost.'

'Expecting me?' Frost thought probably he hadn't heard aright.

'Sure. Catherine said you'd come.'

'Who's Catherine?'

Flash's girl.'

Frost rolled his tongue against his cheek. 'Singleton?'

'Yep.'

'I didn't know he had a girl.'

'I'll say he had.'

Frost hesitated, his mind in a turmoil. The man misconstrued the silence.

'You ain't gonna kill me?' he pleaded. 'I'll do anything—'

'Okey,' Frost said offhand. 'Go over there and call the crew up here. And remember that I've killed two of this crew – and you'll be number three if you make a false move. I'll slug you right through the back of your head. Get up!'

The man walked to the poop ladder, Frost a step behind.

'Hey – Hans!' he yelled through his cupped hands.

Shortly there was a mumble from below.

'Come above and bring Marcelle with you. Hurry!'

Two men climbed out on deck and stood beside the ladder. They hardly were up before Frost stepped out from behind the man and leveled his gun. 'Get up in a hurry!' he barked.

They slowly complied.

'Now,' Frost went on tensely, 'unless you do exactly as I say I'll kill you!'

He looked at the man called Hans. 'Throw your gun away!'

The light was feeble, but Frost could see the man scowl. He made no move to comply; he merely grunted.

'Get that gun overboard!'

Still the man said nothing. One of those hard-boiled seamen.

Put-t!

The flame leaped from Frost's gun; there was a muttered oath and the man grabbed his shoulder and moaned, 'I'm hit! I'm hit!'

'Get that gun overboard! The next time you stop it with your head!'

There was no mistaking the command now. Frost disliked to shoot the man, but this was no time to quibble. They must be impressed with his determination.

81

The man groaned and threw his gun overboard with the arm that was still serviceable.

'Get that hand back in the air! And you – throw that gun over! Now yours!'

The men discarded their pistols. Frost lined them up and backed them towards the hatch. 'Unbatten it!' he commanded.

They did.

'Pile in!'

'What?'

'Pile in!'

'But, we'll—'

'*In there!*'

The wounded man called Hans was the last one down. The others aided him. They disappeared below the top, and Frost wrestled the hatch and battened it down as if heading for the open sea. Then he retrieved his pistol and moved to the wheelhouse. The man who lay on deck had been shot through the mouth, and evidently was a first officer. Frost noticed the wheel was chained, so he dragged the body against the skylights and went to the foredeck where he had glimpsed the first sailor.

He had pitched forward on his face, his gun at his feet. Before Frost stooped to inspect him, he kicked the gun across the deck into the water. Then he tugged the man over, saw he, too, was dead, and came back to the after companion. The night now had come on full. The stars were gleaming and a pale moon glowed off the starboard.

Frost went down the steps slowly. He walked along the passage and heard sounds of music, struggling to free itself of the confinement and get into the air. He could sense the struggle. He paused at the cabin door and listened. An electric gramaphone. Someone evidently was unworried. He rapped on the door.

It opened and he thrust his foot inside. He pried it open with his leg and entered, his gun drawn.

He faced a woman – and gasped.

'You!'

'You!'

His companion of La Estrellita!

Here – in full panoply, arrayed like a queen; against a background of luxury. For a moment he was nonplussed. A lot had happened. This was the crowning blow. He gradually recovered, and thought about the awkward picture he presented there with his pistol drawn.

'Miss Stevens,' he coughed, embarrassed. 'Er—'

'How do you do, Captain?' she said. 'Sit down.' Frost did so. 'Do you find it helps the effect when you visit a young lady with drawn revolver?'

Frost grinned. 'Well, I hardly expected to find you like this. I thought—'

'Yes,' she beamed; 'they are good to me, aren't they?'

She nonchalantly moved across the cabin to a wall telephone. He thought that rather an odd thing for a prisoner to do – telephone. That simple act brought the pieces of the puzzle together with a click. Frost had just been told there were two women on board. One he expected to find a prisoner – Helen Stevens. But this woman was no prisoner—

Catherine!

With pent-up fury he leaped from his chair and was beside her before she could get an answer. He snatched the telephone out of her hand and replaced it. He faced her, flushing with anger.

'Get away!' he said. 'And I hope it won't be necessary for me to kill you!'

She lifted her face in a half sneer. 'Well,' she said, moving in a swagger, 'how long do you think you can get away with this high-handed stuff?'

'Don't make me laugh,' Frost said.

There was the sound of a knock on a door in another wall than that by which he had entered.

'Who's in there?' he demanded.

'Find out for yourself,' she snapped.

'I will,' he said. He observed her with something not unlike admiration. 'So you're Catherine, eh?' He was a little taken aback. Disappointed. Once he had had an adventure with her. Men do not easily forget such things. Now it all came back in a rush . . . her indifference to the danger in La Estrellita . . . the tapping of her fingers on the glass was a signal. . . .

He glared: 'You tried to trap me, didn't you? Tried to get me killed?'

She laughed. 'Why not? You bumped off the only man I ever loved, and for that I'm going to *get* you, Frost. What a pity those saps didn't kill you that night in Algadon!'

'Yes,' he mused; 'what a pity! You know – you're a damned attractive woman to be mixed up with a rotten gang like this.'

'I'm going to stay mixed. You can't bluff me, Frost. I don't scare worth a damn.'

'Maybe you don't. Oh, by the way; I neglected to tell you I locked three of your thugs in the hold. Also,' this casually, 'I had to bump off a couple of 'em. Now who's the woman in the other room?'

'Nobody. That is—'

'Get that door open, or I'll tear it down!'

She got up sullenly and unlocked the narrow door. Through it another woman stumbled, her hair disheveled, her clothes wrinkled, her face worried. She saw Frost and stopped short.

'It's all right,' Frost said reassuringly, 'I'm a policeman. Who are you?'

'I'm—'

'Don't you talk!' came the swift interruption. 'This bum means no good.' She tried to reach the woman's side, but Frost intervened.

'Never mind her,' he said. 'I'm Frost of the Rangers.'

'Oh! Frost!' she murmured the words. 'I'm Helen Stevens. I've been a prisoner for a week.'

'Huh! Are you a newspaper woman?'

'Yes.'

Frost grinned broadly, spread his legs and said: 'Well, sit down, ladies, and get comfortable. This ought to be good.'

Then it was that Frost observed both women were about the same height and build, and that the genuine Helen Stevens wore a brown ensemble similar to the one worn by his companion that night in La Estrellita. He began to see the light.

'A week ago,' said Helen Stevens, 'I was kidnaped in Jamestown, drugged and brought here. I don't know why. I never had an enemy in my life.'

'There's no puzzle there,' Frost said. 'This jane here is the ex-sweetheart of an ex-racketeer who was allied with the Black Ship gang and bumped off by Hell's Stepsons. She wanted revenge on me; the way to get that was remove you and assume your identity.' He smiled appreciatively. 'That right, Mrs. Singleton?'

'You go to hell!'

'So,' mused Helen Stevens, slightly more at ease, 'you're Captain Frost. I was on my way to see you – had a letter from the Adjutant-General. It was stolen with my luggage!'

'I got it,' Frost grinned. 'You'll learn after a while that this is a high-powered gang you're dealing with.'

Helen Stevens was surveying the broad figure of Jerry Frost, remembering tales of his prowes in the skies of France and in the jungles of Latin America – *El Beneficio* they called him then – surveying him in frank admiration.

'I think,' Frost said, 'it would be wise to get going. This boat has got a date I'd rather not keep. First, I'm afraid we'll have to tie up the hellcat.'

The hellcat got to her feet, her eyes burning with passionate hatred, and leaped at Frost. She landed in his lap and they both went over backwards with the chair. His pistol rattled on the hardwood floor.

'Get that gun!' he yelled, a moment before she clawed at his face. She interposed a few choice oaths, and hammered Frost about the ears with her fists. They squirmed on the floor inelegantly until he managed to get a hammer-lock on her arm. She swore and cried out in pain.

'Pipe down and I'll let you go!' Frost said. 'Otherwise I'll break it off.' His eyes fell on the silk cord knotted around port hole draperies and he said to Helen Stevens, 'Get that cord.'

She untied it and brought it to him. Frost slipped it around the woman's wrists and tied her hands behind her. Then he took off his belt and strapped it tightly around her ankles. To complete the job he took out his handkerchief and crammed it in her mouth.

'Now,' he said; 'I need a bandage.'

Helen Stevens did not hesitate. She lifted her dress, revealed a sheeny knee and a silk petticoat. She ripped it, jerked off a strip and handed it to Frost.

'Great stuff!' he said. 'I'm beginning to think you'll do!'

'You're damned right I'll do!' she admitted.

Frost tied the gag and then stepped back to inspect his craftmanship. Apart from the woman's squirming, and nobody has ever invented a way to stop that, he had to confess it was very good.

'Not bad for a beginner,' he observed.

The woman grunted and her eyes flashed. Frost picked her up and deposited her, none too carefully, on a lounge. He whispered in her ear: 'Now we're going up to take the wheel.' She grunted again, and in a fit of temper wriggled to the floor with a bang.

Frost looked at her loftily. 'All right, baby – suit yourself.'

Helen Stevens handed him his pistol and said: 'Don't you think it would be wise to use the radio and let somebody know where we are?'

Frost slanted his head from side to side as if he had known her a century; decided she, too, was a fluffy bit of femininity. His light mood was sharpened by his success. 'Another great idea,' he said. 'Let's have a look.'

They came on deck together, he holding her hand. It was, like the night, warm and soft – he remembered snatches of books and stories he'd read about women . . . regal poise . . . generations of aristocrats to produce one like this . . . long lashes . . . and full red lips. . . . He even tried to recall some poetry.

He looked at her suddenly as if he knew she had read his thoughts. He was blushing. . . . She laughed. He laughed too – not knowing what else to do.

They entered the wheelhouse of the *Catherine B* as she rose on a long swell, poised herself, and settled into the valley of the Gulf. It was dark and quiet, only a light glowed from the compass box; Frost found the switch and pulled it. A light sprang into life at the top of the pilothouse.

On one side was the wireless and without further ado Frost seated himself and cut on the switch. The motor hummed, tiny sparks glowed, and he adjusted the head set. He tapped out a message hurriedly. Presently there was a light cracking sound in the headphone and he bent over his task. He finished and sat up.

'They're on their way,' he said.

He took a look at the binnacle and moved to the chart table. 'Now to figure out which way to go,' he remarked. 'I'd hate to wind up in Cuba.' He studied the chart for a few silent minutes. Then he moved the wheel and unchained it. 'Look,' he said, 'think you can hold this wheel on one-eighteen when I get her on that course?'

'Sure,' she said, still the adventuress.

'I'll have a look around,' Frost said. He went to the side of the box and yanked at the control. From somewhere in the boat's depth a bell tinkled. It slowly gained speed. Frost spun the wheel and held her circling until she was on the course he had determined upon as most likely to intercept the cutter he had summoned. Frost reached into his shoulder-holster and took out his other pistol. He laid it on the table beside her. 'That's a .38,' he said; 'fitted with a silencer. And it's ready to blast.' She nodded and he went out.

Frost noted that the *Catherine B* was holding steadily at about half speed. He went to the rail and unloosed the rope that anchored his plane, snubbed it along the rail and finally tied it off the stern. Then he walked for'ard and went below through the fo'csle.

Helen Stevens, left alone on as weird an adventure as any newspaper woman ever had, gripped the wheel, her teeth clenched, and stared into that disk of white light that held the magic number, 118, wavering across a red line.

Some time later Frost emerged from the shadows of the deck-house and came forward into the wheelhouse wearing a wide smile.

'We're all alone but for the engineer,' he said. 'Now I'll take charge of that.' He took the wheel, and she stood beside him and shivered.

'You might as well get comfortable,' he said.

'I'm all right,' she said. 'I think this is a good time to begin that belated interview. Born?'

'Yes?'

She laughed. 'Where?'

'I'd rather talk about you,' Frost said. 'How long are you going to be around Texas?'

'That depends.'

'On what?'

'How long it takes to get this story.'

'In that case—' he smiled.

And she smiled.

They probably would have been talking yet had not a siren sounded off the port side some two hours later. Frost rang the signal for power off and went out of the wheelhouse.

'Ahoy, there!'

'Who's there?'

'U.S. Coast Guard!'

'Okey! This is Frost – Texas Rangers!'

The cutter pulled up alongside, its fenders bumped and they lashed on.

Half a dozen huskies vaulted the rails. The leader shifted his pistol to his right hand and came forward fast. Frost could see in the half-light he was some sort of an officer.

'Frost?'

'Right!'

'I'm Al Bennett.' They shook hands. 'We picked up your message. I radioed Clay in Corpus that I'd located you.'

Thanks,' said Frost. 'Can you send a man over to take the wheel? I've got somebody in there who's just about washed up.'

'Sure,' said Bennett. 'Bucko – on the wheel!'

The man saluted smartly and preceded Frost and Bennett into the wheelhouse.

'Miss Stevens this is Mr. Bennett, of the Coast Guard.' Bennett nodded his head. 'So you're the little girl who's been leading us such a merry chase?'

'I'm afraid so,' she said. She took Frost's arm.

'Bennett, there's three of the crew in the hold – one winged. For'ard there's a man dead and beside the sky-light there's another one in the same fix. There is a woman below I had to tie up.'

Bennett looked at him, his eyes wide.

'Say,' he said, 'is it possible you took this baby all alone?'

'It was a cinch.' Lightly.

'Yeh? Well. I don't mind telling you the whole Coast Guard has been trying to land this bark for weeks.'

'Will you,' asked Frost, disregarding the praise, 'see that we get into port okey?'

'You bet.' He went to the door and spoke to the crew who had come over in the recent boarding. 'Pass the word along for the cutter to shove off. You men stay aboard with me. We're going to Corpus.' He came back to the wheel.

'We'll go below,' Frost said. 'Er—'

'Sure,' said Bennett, grinning.

'Business,' Frost went on. 'She's getting—'

'Sure—'

But Frost, self-conscious, refused to let Bennett be diplomatic. Helen Stevens finally had to rush to the rescue. 'I'm interviewing him,' she explained.

Bennett laughed, full. 'That's okey with me, Miss,' he said. 'But you'd better shove off. Ox Clay and Jimmy O'Neill are on their way out here.'

Frost and the woman walked out – close together.

The moment they disappeared Bennett turned to the man at the wheel and said: 'Ever hear of anything like it?'

'Beats me.'

Bennett looked aft at the shadowy form that rose and fell behind like a phantom. It was Frost's battle plane.

'I guess,' said Bennett, soberly, 'a guy has got to be a little goofy to try something like this. It wouldn't work once in a hundred times. They must be right about that guy, Frost. I've read of those one-man cyclones, but I never saw one before.'

'You said it,' contributed the man at the wheel.

The *Catherine B*, in the firm hands of the Coast Guard, slipped on towards Corpus Christi with a grim greyhound of the Gulf for a convoy, and another on the way.

In four hours they would be in port.

STAG PARTY

CHARLES G. BOOTH

Once an enormously successful novelist and writer of pulp stories, Charles G. Booth (1896–1949) is a name largely forgotten today, his fiction generally unread, while the films with which he was involved have taken on cult status and more.

He won an Academy Award for writing the best original story of the spy thriller, *The House on 92nd Street* (1945), an early work of documentary realism. His novel *Mr. Angel Comes Aboard* was filmed as *Johnny Angel* in 1945, a year after publication, and he wrote the novel *The General Died at Dawn*, which was filmed with Gary Cooper in 1936.

Born in Manchester, England, he emigrated to Canada before moving to Los Angeles in 1922, eventually becoming a contract writer for 20th Century Fox.

As with much of his fiction, 'Stag Party' has a strong sense of place and evokes its time wonderfully. The hero, preparing for a showdown with gangsters in an underworld-run nightclub, dresses in his dinner jacket so that he'll look his best for the confrontation.

Originally published in the November 1933, issue of *Black Mask*, 'Stag Party' is the first and longest of three novellas featuring McFee of the Blue Shield Detective Agency to be collected in one of the rarest private eye volumes of the 1940s, *Murder Strikes Thrice* (1946), published by the short-lived paperback publisher Bond.

STAG PARTY

CHARLES G. BOOTH

Stirring his coffee McFee – Blue Shield Detective Agency – thought he had seen the girl somewhere. She had dull red hair. She had a subtle red mouth and experienced eyes with green lights in them. That was plenty. But over her provocative beauty, lay a hard sophistication as brightly polished as new nickel.

McFee said, 'You ought to be in pictures.'

'I've been in pictures.' Her voice was husky. 'That's where you've seen me.'

'No, it isn't,' McFee said. 'Sit down. Coffee?'

'Black.'

The girl let herself drop into the chair on the other side of the table. Her wrap fell back. She wore an evening gown of jade green velvet and a necklace of square-cut emeralds. Her eyes were guarded but urgent; desperate, perhaps.

Abruptly, she asked, 'Do I look like a fool?'

'I dunno what a fool looks like.' McFee finished his apple pie, sugared his coffee. His movements, the flow of his words, the level staring of his V-thatched, somber eyes were as precisely balanced as the timing of a clock. The girl was restlessly tapping the table pedestal with a green satin pump when McFee asked: Some'dy tell you I was here?'

'Jules – at the door. He's been with Cato's ever since I can remember.'

A waiter came, drew the booth curtains, went away. McFee gave the girl a cigarette. A flame came into each of her eyes and she began to pelt him with little hard bullets of words.

'I am Irene Mayo. Rance Damon and I were dining here one night Rance pointed you out. He said, "That's McFee, the Blue Shield operative." Jules told us you often dropped in for coffee around midnight—'

McFee muttered, 'Coffee and Cato's apple pie.'

'Yes. That's what Jules told us. And Rance said, "Irene, if you ever run into a jam get McFee." So I knew if you were here—'

'What sort of jam you in?'

'I don't know.' The girl stared at the ruddy vitality of McFee, shivered.

'Rance and I left my apartment – the St. Regis – around eleven. We were going to the Cockatoo for supper and some dancing, but we didn't get there.'

'Pretty close,' McFee said.

She nodded. 'Rance had just turned into Carter, from Second, when he saw Sam Melrose—'

'That's funny,' McFee said. He tapped a newspaper beside his coffee cup. 'The Trib says Melrose is aboard Larry Knudson's yacht. Has been all week.'

Irene Mayo flared out, 'That's what Rance said. That's why he went after him. Melrose has been evading the Grand Jury ever since they opened up that Shelldon scandal. Rance said they couldn't serve him.'

'I dunno that indicting him'll do any good,' McFee muttered, frowning. 'Sam took the town over when Gaylord rubbed out, and he's got his hooks in deep. Damon saw Melrose and went after him, you said—'

'Into the Gaiety Theatre. Rance parked on Second. The house was dark – after eleven—'

McFee cut in, 'Melrose owns the Gaiety now.'

'Rance told me. He said he'd be back in fifteen minutes – less, maybe. But he had to see Melrose.' The girl's green eyes dilated a little. 'I waited an hour and fifteen minutes. He didn't come back. I couldn't stand it any longer. I went to the lobby doors. They were locked. The box office was locked. I could see into the theatre. It was dark.'

McFee said, 'You tried the alley fire exits?'

'I didn't think of those. But why would Rance—'

The girl stared at McFee with terrified eyes. 'Nothing can have happened – I mean, Melrose wouldn't dare—'

'I dunno, Sam Melrose—'

McFee saw the girl's red mouth lose its subtlety in the sharp twitching of the lip muscles. He stood up. 'Put that coffee under your belt and stay here till I come back.'

2

McFee crossed Third and went down Carter. A late street car rumbled somewhere along Brant, but the town was quiet. He walked fast for half a block.

Cato's had been at Third and Carter when the town was young and the Gaiety Theatre had billed Martin Thomas in Othello and William Gillette in Sherlock Holmes. That had been before business moved west and the corner had gone pawn shop and fire sale, and buttoned itself on to Chinatown. Second and Carter's had been McFee's nursery. Cato's hadn't moved because Signor Cato and Papa Dubois had known the value of tradition to the restaurant business, and because M. Papoulas, the present proprietor, also knew it. But Cato's had kept its head up. The Gaiety had gone burleyque.

McFee tried the lobby doors. They were tight. The interior of the theatre was black. Light from the street seeped into the lobby. On the walls were life-sized tinted photographs of the girls. A legend under one of them said Mabel Leclair. She Knocked 'Em Cold on Broadway.

An alley separated the Gaiety Building from the Palace Hotel at Second. The Gaiety had two exit doors in the north side of the alley. On the south side the Palace had a service entrance. Instead of turning into the alley, McFee went to where Maggie O'Day had her ten-by-four hole-in-the-wall in the hotel building. She was putting her stock away. McFee bought a pack of cigarettes.

He said, 'Seen Sam Melrose lately, Maggie?'

She was a little dark witch of a woman with rouged cheek bones and tragic purple-brown eyes. Like McFee and the Gaiety girls, she belonged to the picture. Always had. In the Gaiety's Olga Nethersole-melodrama days, she had played minor parts. That had been about the time the late Senator Gaylord was coming into power. Things had happened, and she had gone to singing in Sullivan's saloon on Second, until a street car accident had crippled her hip. Now she leaned on a crutch in her hole-in-the-wall and shook dice with the dicks and the Gaiety girls. Midnight or later she rolled herself home in a wheel chair she kept in the Gaiety alley.

'Sam's getting up in the world,' the old woman answered.

'See him go into the Gaiety a while back?'

'Sam go into the Gaiety—' The old woman's voice thinned into silence. She stared at McFee. 'It wasn't Sam I saw . . . It wasn't Sam—' And then, vehemently, 'I can't be seeing everybody. . . .'

McFee said gently, 'You better go home, Maggie.'

He turned into the Gaiety alley, barked his shin against Maggie O'Day's wheel chair. He tried the nearer exit door. It was unbolted. The door creaked as McFee pulled on it. He slipped inside.

The darkness fell all around McFee. It had a hot, smothering touch. It plucked at his eyeballs. He chewed a cigarette, listened. Vague murmurings were audible. The sort of noises that haunt old theatres. Dead voices. . . . Sara Kendleton, Martin Thomas, Mrs. Fiske, Edwin South. But that sort of thing didn't touch McFee. He knew the Gaiety for the rattletrap barn it was and waited, his hat on the back of his head and his ears wide open.

Suddenly he was on his toes.

The sound coming towards him was a human sound. It came down the side aisle from the stage end. It was a rustling sound, like dead leaves in a wind; then it identified itself as the slow slurring of a body dragging exhaustedly over a flat surface. Against a wall. Over a floor. It stopped. The taut quietness that followed throttled McFee. A groan flowed through the darkness, a low strangling cough. The slurring sound was resumed. It was closer now, but there was a bitter-end exhaustion in it.

McFee, chewing his cigarette, felt at the gun and the flashlight in his pocket. He took three steps forward, his arms spread wide.

The man pitched forward and fell against his chest.

McFee slid him down to the floor of the aisle. The man's chest was wet. He felt a warm stickiness on his hands. He made light, spread it over the man's face. It was Rance Damon. His eyes were wide open, fixed in horror; his lips were bloodless. McFee felt at the heart.

Damon was dead.

McFee muttered, 'He's been a while dying.'

The hole was in the chest. A good deal of blood had flowed.

Damon was around thirty, a dark, debonair lad with straight hair as black as Maggie O'Day's had once been. His bright eloquence, the bold ardor of his restless eyes, had stepped him along. The late Senator Gaylord (Senator by courtesy) had placed him in the District Attorney's office. Damon had become a key man. You had to figure on him. But his mouth was lax.

'The boys'll have to plant a new in-man,' McFee said. He sniffed the odor of gin. 'Party, I guess.' And then, 'Well, well! Rubbed out doing his little stunt!'

McFee had lifted Damon's left arm. The fingers clutched a tangle of five-century notes. Ten of them.

A trail of blood spots on the aisle floor led backstage. The wall was smeared where Damon had fought his way agonizingly along it. McFee followed the sign, back of the boxes, up a short stair, through a door into the backstage. A dingy curtain shut him off from the house. He stood under the drops, among a bedroom set, and waved his light. Damon had crawled across the stage into the wing, where a final resurgence of life lifted him up.

Entering the dressing room from which Damon had come, McFee saw high, fly-blown walls that pictured the evolution of the burleyque girl. He had appreciated it on previous occasions. A quart bottle of gin, two-thirds empty, stood on a rickety dressing table, two glasses beside it. He did not touch them. A table lamp lay on the floor, broken. Dancing costumes lay about. A rug was turned up.

Make-up material had been swept off the dressing table – powder, crimson grease paint, lipstick, eyebrow buffer. The tube of grease paint had been stepped on by someone, burst open. The stuff smeared the floor. It looked like coagulated blood.

Near the door lay a .32 automatic pistol. One shell had been ejected.

McFee went back to the aisle.

Irene Mayo was kneeling beside the body.

McFee said, 'I'm sorry, sister.'

The cold beam of his torch made her eyes look enormous in her white, drawn face. Her mouth quivered. She pressed her hand against it, stifled a sob. But after a moment she said dully, 'He would have been governor some day.'

McFee answered moodily, 'Damon had the makings.' He stared down into the girl's uplifted eyes, at the purple shadows beneath them. The emeralds at her throat blazed coldly. He added, 'If it's in a man's blood you can't stop him.'

'Unless you kill him.' The girl spoke passionately. 'It's in me, too, but there's more than that in me. If it's the last thing I do—'

McFee cut in, 'You saw Melrose?'

'No—' The girl hesitated, her eyes hardening. 'But Rance saw him. Rance said—' Her eyes fell apprehensively. 'I don't understand about that money—'

'Were you in love with Damon?'

'I don't know.' She spoke slowly. 'I liked him. He took me around a lot. He was a dear – yes, I did love him!' She rocked distractedly, said in a frenzy, 'I'll spend every dollar I have to get Melrose.'

'Good kid.'

'Are you with me, McFee?'

Instead of replying, McFee put out his flash, said softly, 'There's someone in the house.'

The girl stood up, moved close to him, her wrap drawn tightly around her body. Her breath fanned McFee's cheeks. Neither of them moved. McFee pushed the girl flat against the wall.

'Stay here,' he whispered.

'McFee—'

'Easy, sister.'

McFee took off his shoes. He felt for his gun, went up the sloping aisle on the balls of his feet. A rustling sound became audible, quieted. He reached the top of the aisle, turned, felt his way towards the foyer. McFee sniffed. Perfume. Thick, too. He grinned, put away his gun. A door was on his right – the manager's office. He turned into the room.

McFee stopped. Someone was breathing heavily. He heard a sob – suppressed. A floor board creaked. McFee thought he located the woman. He took three steps forward, his arms wide apart, as when he had gone to meet Rance Damon. Caught the glitter of a necklace. As he flung one arm around the woman's neck, he slammed the other against her mouth and shut off her scream. She fought, but McFee held her.

He said softly, 'One yip and I'll blow you in two.'

The woman became quiet. McFee removed his hand.

'Lemme go, McFee,' she said huskily.

'Leclair – swell! Anyb'dy else on the party?'

'Rance Damon—' The woman leaned on McFee's arm. 'Oh, my God!' she wept. 'Damon – that's all—'

Mabel Leclair's blond beauty was unconfined and too abundant. The petulant immaturity of her features ran at odds with the hardness in her round blue eyes. She presented a scanty negligee effect.

McFee asked, 'That kind of a party?'

The woman's hands and negligee were bloody. She looked down at them and went sick. McFee directed the light into her eyes. 'Sit down,' he said. She fell moaning into a chair.

McFee snapped a desk lamp switch. The room contained a shabby desk, chairs, a safe, a water cooler and a couch. The dingy walls were a photograph album burleyque theme.

From the door Irene Mayo cried out, 'She killed him—'

'I did not!' the Leclair woman screamed, and jumped up. 'What you doing here? What'd I kill him for? We were having a party – oh—' The blood on her hands sickened her again. She wiped them on her negligee. She thrust her hands behind her back, shut her eyes, rocked her head. 'Get me a drink,' she whimpered, and fell into the chair.

'You had plenty, sister. What kind of party?'

'Just a party, McFee.' She tried to smile wisely. 'Rance dropped in to see me—'

Irene Mayo cut in, 'That's a lie!'

'You think so?' The Leclair woman spoke wickedly. 'Kid, I never seen the buttercup I couldn't pick. And I've picked 'em from Broadway west.'

McFee said harshly, 'Got anything to say before I call the cops?'

'Wait a minute, Handsome.' The woman's eyes took fright again, but she seemed to be listening, too. 'Lemme tell you. Rance was drinking some. Not much. I hadn't touched it. Honest, McFee – well, mebbe I had a coupla quick ones, but I wasn't lit. I'm telling you, McFee. I was standing in front of the dressing table. Rance was standing beside me, next to the couch. He heard some'dy on the stage. The door was open – the backstage was dark. Rance turned around. And that's when he got it. Right in the chest. I saw the flash – that's all. McFee, I'm telling you! He spun round – kind of. I caught him—' The woman shuddered, shut her eyes.

'Yes?' said McFee.

'He was bleeding—' She wrung her hands. 'He slid out of my arms – slow. I thought he'd never drop. The look in his eyes knocked me cuckoo. I fainted. When I came to—' She covered her face.

'When you came to—'

'It was dark. We'd bust the lamp, falling. McFee, he wasn't dead. He was groaning somewhere. I lit a match. He'd dragged himself out backstage. He wouldn't quit crawling. I was scared to switch on the lights—' McFee's cold eyes alarmed the woman. She reiterated desperately. 'I'm giving you the straight of it. Rance and me—'

'What you here for?'

'To phone the cops.'

'Did you phone 'em?'

'No. You came in. I was scared stiff. I thought it might be Rance's murderer coming back—'

'Phone anyb'dy?'

'No.' The woman stared at McFee, the listening look in her eyes. 'I didn't phone anybody.'

McFee said, 'You're a liar.' He picked up the desk telephone. The receiver was moist. Leclair stared at McFee. 'Who'd you call?'

'Go roll your hoop.'

Irene Mayo leaned against the wall, a little to the left of the door. Her eyes were tragic and scornful. McFee was about to unhook the telephone when she gestured warningly.

In the foyer a man said, 'Put that telephone down, McFee.'

Mabel Leclair laughed.

4

The man moved into the lane of light that flowed out of the office. It was Joe Metz, who ran the Spanish Shawl Club, a Melrose enterprise. McFee threw a glance at the red-headed girl. She seemed to understand what was in his mind.

McFee flung the telephone at the desk lamp. Glass shattered. The room went dark. Leclair screamed. McFee dropped behind the desk.

Joe Metz called, 'You birds cover those exits. Smoke him, if you have to . . . McFee!'

The latter, feeling around for the telephone, said, 'Speaking.'

'I've got three of the boys with me. Nice boys. Boys you've played ball with—' Metz was inside the room now. 'They don't wanna hurt you—'

McFee answered, 'You'll have me crying pretty soon.' Prone on his stomach, he found the instrument, put the receiver to his ear, his lips to the mouthpiece. 'Tell me some more, Joe.'

Central did not respond.

Mabel Leclair ejaculated, 'He's got the telephone, Joe!'

'That's all right,' Metz drawled. 'I've cut the wire. How about sitting in a little game, McFee?'

'Speak your piece,' McFee said, and then: 'I got a gun on the door.'

'Handsome, it's this way,' Metz said. 'Sam Melrose has named the next district attorney – Claude Dietrich. Now the Gaiety's a Melrose house and Sam don't want a deputy district attorney dying in it two months before election. So we gotta get Damon away. But that's not the half of it.' Metz spoke with a careful spacing of his words. 'Damon was in a position to get Sam something he hadda have, election coming on. So Sam turned Blondy loose on the boy – Sam has more swell ideas than a tabloid editor. Damon was a nut for the frills. He fell for Leclair like a bucket of bricks. Blondy makes a deal with Damon. The boy's taken money before. Taking five grand from Blondy is duck soup—'

McFee said, 'Five grand for what?'

'Oh, some photographs, an affidavit, a letter Melrose wrote, a coupla cancelled checks, some testimony from a lad that died – the usual junk.'

'Grand Jury file on the Shelldon blow-off?' McFee asked.

'That's right – you're a good guy, McFee. The Grand Jury turned it over to the D.A. Melrose thought it ought to disappear.'

'Lemme see,' McFee said. 'There's a murder tied up with the indictment, isn't there?'

'Sam'll beat that. But you know how it is, election coming on.'

'Well, I haven't got it.'

'Now, look here, McFee, you aren't in any shape to stand off me and the boys. Melrose wants that Grand Jury indictment.'

McFee had begun to creep noiselessly towards Metz and the door. 'Who give you the notion that I got it?'

Metz said coldly, 'You gotta have it – or know where it is. Damon had the money and the Shelldon file in his hands when that .32 bumped him. He flopped into Blondy's arms. She threw a faint—' Metz interrupted himself to say, 'There's places where women is swell, but a jam like that ain't one of 'em.'

The Leclair woman cried, 'You got your nerve! After what I been through—'

Metz laughed. 'I've said there are places where women is swell.' He proceeded swiftly. 'When Blondy woke up Damon had the five grand in his fist, but the file was gone. She give me a bell at the Shawl. McFee, you got that Shelldon file, or you know where it is. Better play ball.'

McFee said softly, 'I'm covering you, Joe.' And then, 'You mean, I killed Damon?'

Metz answered carefully, 'Damon don't count now. He isn't going to be found here. It don't matter who killed him. There's plenty boys Melrose can plant when Dietrich is in. If you killed Damon, swell! You know your business. But you better not try bucking Melrose.'

McFee moved some more.

He was in a spot. If Metz was bluffing, a Melrose heel had killed Damon, and the Melrose crowd had the Shelldon file. That would mean McFee knew too much and must become casualty No. 2. If Metz was not bluffing, he probably was convinced McFee had done the job and copped the file. Bad, too. And it left the question: Who shot Damon?

McFee asked, 'Where's Melrose?'

'Aboard Larry Knudson's yacht,' Metz answered smoothly.

McFee crept forward again.

The Leclair woman shrilled, 'Joe! He's coming at you—'

5

Rising straight from his heels, a little to the right of Metz, McFee threw his left to where he thought the man's chin was, landed. Metz' head snapped back. The rest of him followed it. His gun spat flame. McFee steamed past. Metz cracked against the foyer wall.

Metz howled, 'Watch those fire exits!'

'Lights!' another man yelled. 'Where the hell—'

The Leclair woman screamed, 'Backstage—' and then, 'Look out for that red-headed tramp—'

McFee ran towards the north side aisle. McFee knew what he was doing. The switch was in the front of the house, off the backstage, north side. He was depending on the red-headed girl. They had a reasonable chance with the house dark – none if the lights came on.

Someone collided with an aisle seat. McFee jumped the man, struck bone with the nose of his gun. The man fell among the seats. He groaned, then shouted faintly, 'Over here, you birds—'

Metz yelled, 'The other aisle! Gun him, if he jumps an exit— Some'dy find that damned light room—'

McFee found it. Hadn't he been a Gaiety usher when he was a kid? There were steel switch boxes on a wall. The master switch box was largest. He plucked out a couple of fuses. They heard him. They drummed after him. Sets snapped back as someone crossed the house.

McFee cleared the switch room door, a flash beam jumped up the stage stair, pranced around in the wing.

A man howled, 'Now we got the—'

Leclair screamed. 'That red-headed witch—'

McFee ducked across the backstage. The light lost him. A door hinge creaked, and he knew what was troubling Leclair. Very swell!

But the others didn't hear Leclair. They didn't hear the red-headed girl opening the exit door. Somebody monkeyed in the switch room, but the house stayed dark. A couple of men collided in the backstage. McFee wasn't one of them. The light jack-rabbited around the wall, shied at McFee. He chased towards the south wing. A shot came after him.

Metz yelled, 'Jump him, Tony—'

The flash beam plucked Tony Starke out of the north wing. Starke had been a pretty fair heavy, and he owned a gymnasium. He looked tremendous. McFee twisted sidewise and leaned on the canvas drop that shut the backstage off from the house. The canvas was rotten old. It ripped with a thin scream, spraying dust, as McFee fell through it.

Art Kline was on the runway that fronted the orchestra. Pretty nearly as big as Starke, Kline bounced for Joe Metz, at the Spanish Shawl and was famous for his hands. He had broken a man's neck with them. Kline pulled a fast jump over the orchestra and landed on top of McFee. They milled for a moment. Then Metz, coming through the ripped curtain, collided with them, and all three pitched into the orchestra, McFee on top.

Kline conked his head, but it didn't do him any harm. He and Metz held McFee. Metz yelled for the flashlight. They milled some more, bone thudding on bone; then a door opened and they rolled down a short stair under the stage and hit a wall. The place smelled of stale beer and fried onions.

Leclair shrilled, 'That red-headed tramp's gone for the coppers. I'm telling you—'

McFee was getting plenty now. The flash beam came. Monty Welch brought it. Welch was five feet four. He dealt blackjack at the Spanish Shawl and knew when every cop in the city paid his next mortgage installment. Tony Starke rolled in with him, sat on McFee's head.

Metz went through McFee's clothes, then said, 'What you done with that Shelldon file?'

McFee said nothing. He didn't like it under Tony Starke's two hundred and twenty, but he still was figuring on the red-headed girl. The coppers could make it in three minutes flat – if they wanted to.

Monty Welch said in his whispering voice, 'Gimme a cigarette and a match, Art. I'll open his trap—'

The Leclair woman showed up then. Tony Starke put the light on her. She wore an ermine coat pulled tight around her body. Leclair had brought the coat from Broadway. Somebody said she had traded a couple of letters for it. She said very quietly, 'McFee's red-headed friend went for the cops while you birds was playing tag—'

Metz blurted, 'What's that?'

'I been telling you – the tramp that was with him—'

Metz said huskily, 'We got to get outta this.' He sucked in his cheeks. His bulbous temples were wet and gleaming. 'We take McFee. McFee'll talk later. Monty, you jam your gun in his kidneys. Hand it to him if he squawks. Tony, Art, carry Damon. I'll drive.'

Kline and Starke hoisted McFee to his feet. Welch's gun made him step fast. They drummed up the stair. They climbed out of the orchestra, paraded up the center aisle, cut across to the south aisle by the seventh row. It was like a scene from an old Gaiety play.

As they clattered into the side aisle, a police siren wailed somewhere down Carter Street.

Metz said tersely, 'We go through the Palace. Monty, fan that light—' And then, as Welch spread the beam on the aisle floor, 'Cripes!'

They forgot McFee. His toe sent the flash whizzing out of Welch's hand. It shattered against the wall and darkness buried them. McFee sank back into the seat right behind him.

Metz howled, 'Some'dy's been here—'

'I fell over him when I came in,' Starke sobbed.

'Grab McFee—'

But the coppers were hammering on the foyer door, and they hadn't time to look for McFee, Metz said, 'Scram!' They jumped through the fire exit, pushed through the Palace service door. Sam Melrose had taken over the Palace along with the Gaiety.

The coppers were coming down the alley.

McFee crawled out of a seat and spread his hands on the aisle floor, where he had left Damon's body. It wasn't there.

McFee leaned against the wall. He rolled a match in his ear. 'That's funny,' he said.

6

McFee felt a draft on his face. A man carefully let himself into the house. Two other men were behind him. The first man, Pete Hurley, of the homicide squad, spread a flash beam over the aisle floor. Hurley's hard hat sat on the back of his square head and he jiggled a cold cigarette between pouchy lips.

Hurley said bitterly, 'Hello, Handsome.'

'You got a pip this time.' McFee sucked on a loose tooth, felt his jaw. 'Tell one of your boys to fix a light. Here's a coupla fuses.'

One of the men took the fuses, went away.

'Some'dy belled the desk and yelled "Murder at the Gaiety," ' Hurley said querulously. He added cautiously, 'Rance Damon. What's the dope?'

'Sweet,' McFee answered, and stood up. 'A box full of medals for Some'dy, and nob'dy wanting to wear 'em.' Wobbling, he put on his shoes. 'Gimme a cigarette, Beautiful.'

'I ain't looking for medals,' Hurley said harshly. 'Medals ain't safe in this town. Where's Damon?'

'Damon's dead. He went away. Ask Melrose's boys.'

'Melrose's boys?'

'Joe Metz, Art Kline, Monty Welch, Tony Starke. It was good while it lasted.' McFee lighted a cigarette, then spread out his hand. Lights began to go on. Hurley stared at McFee with his bitter, button eyes. McFee added presently, 'Irene Mayo brought you boys.'

'Who's this Mayo queen?'

'A nice little number. She's been in pictures. Likes to pull strings. She wanted Damon to be governor.'

'You got that Shelldon file?'

'I didn't kill Damon, mister.'

Hurley didn't look at McFee, as he said slowly, 'The birds that shot Damon musta got away with him. You say Melrose's boys didn't take him away, so they didn't shoot him. That's reasonable ain't it?' He forced his uneasy, hostile eyes up to McFee's cold grin. 'I said, that's reasonable, ain't it?'

'Anything's reasonable that's got to be,' McFee answered.

Hurley's tone was sullen as he proceeded, 'Melrose's boys is out then. How about that red-headed number. I mean—'

'You mean, did she carry Damon out in her stocking? No, Buttercup, she didn't. And if she didn't she couldn't have rubbed him out. That's reasonable, isn't it?'

Hurley's cigarette became still. 'Mebbe there'll be a coupla medals in this after all—'

McFee said, 'You can always sell 'em for hardware.'

Hurley spread light upon the wet smear Damon's body had left. Sign indicated that the body had been dragged to the fire exit and out into the alley. There the sign ended.

Inside again, Hurley asked McFee, 'Why don't that red-headed dame come back?'

'I guess she'd had plenty. You'll find her at the St. Regis.' He added dryly, 'Melrose's tell you where to find Leclair.'

'I'll find Leclair.' And then, impressively, 'Melrose is aboard Knudson's yacht.'

Hurley followed the blood drop down the aisle. Here and there on the drab wall were imprints of Damon's wet, red hands. They leaped at the eye. They implied a frantic striving, a dreadful frustration. The two dicks tailed Hurley, McFee trailed the three of them, chewing the end of his cigarette. They crossed the backstage, shoved into the dressing room.

Hurley looked the automatic over, put it down. He looked at the glasses and gin bottle, at the upset table lamp, at the squashed tube of crimson grease paint.

'Some'dy better change his shoes,' Hurley muttered.

McFee said casually, 'Leclair's shoes looked clean.'

Hurley stared sourly at the picture album around the walls. 'Burleycue ain't what she was. You need a pair of field glasses to see the jittering toothpicks that prance on the boards nowadays.' Turning to one of his men he said, 'Harry, go give Littner a bell. Tell him he'd better slide over. Tell him—' Hurley slanted his eyes at McFee. 'Tell him we are in a spot.'

Littner was Captain of Detectives.

Hurley chalked crosses on the floor, near the dressing table and close to the couch, to indicate where he and McFee thought Damon and Leclair had stood, when the shot was fired.

Littner and the Chief came first; then Larrabee, the District Attorney, and Atwell, a deputy coroner. Larrabee said it was too bad about Damon.

Pretty nearly everybody said it was too bad and something ought to be done. When Larrabee heard about the Grand Jury Shelldon file he went white around the gills, and shut up. Larrabee was half and half about most things. He had Bright's Disease. That was why he wasn't going to run again. The camera boys stood up their flashlight set. The fingerprint lads prowled around with their brushes and powders. A flock of dicks were detailed to do this and that. Littner turned the pistol over to Walter Griggs, the ballistic expert. The newshawks came.

The Chief said to Littner, 'Melrose is gonna be damn good and sore.'

'He ought to be damn good and glad some'dy else lifted Damon,' Littner muttered.

'You figure he needs an out?'

Littner said cautiously, 'Melrose is aboard Knudson's yacht, isn't he?'

Littner ought to have been Chief of Police.

After a while, McFee said to Hurley, 'I guess I'll go finish my coffee.'

7

McFee walked up Carter to Third, stood there a minute, rolling a match in his ear. The block between Second and Third was full of police and county cars, but the rest of the town looked empty. It was three-fifteen. McFee had been in the Gaiety about two and a half hours. He saw a coupe parked half a block down Third and walked towards it.

Irene Mayo sat behind the wheel, smoking a cigarette. Her eyes were feverish. Her white face was posed above the deep fur of her wrap like a flower in a vase. She said huskily, 'I thought you'd come.'

'It takes a while,' McFee answered. He got in beside her. 'Thanks for giving the cops a bell.'

'Did they hurt you?' She looked intently at him.

'Some'dy sat on my head.'

The red-headed girl let in the clutch. They made a couple of righthand turns then a left.

McFee said, 'Damon sold out, didn't he, sister?'

'Yes—' The word tore itself from Irene Mayo's lips. Her knuckles tightened on the wheel. 'That blonde woman—'

'Hadn't it in him, I guess,' McFee muttered.

She said in a brittle voice, 'He could have been governor. I had what he needed . . . I could have given him—' She shivered, pressed her hand to her throat. 'I don't blame Rance. A man is just so much – no more. But Melrose – Sam Melrose—' She uttered the name as if it poisoned her mouth. 'Melrose knew how to break Rance. And he had Rance shot because he wasn't *sure*—' She stared straight ahead, her eyes as hard as bright new coins. 'I'll make Sam Melrose wish he hadn't come to this town if it kills me to do it.'

They drove some more.

'Some'dy took Damon's body away,' McFee said.

'What did you say?'

McFee told her about it. 'Damon must have been taken after you got away. There was a five minute interval before the cops came.'

'What do the police think?'

'It isn't what they think – this is Melrose's town. They take the position that Melrose didn't have Damon blinked because it wasn't his boys carted Damon's body away. They say that means some'dy else killed Damon.'

'Don't you see?' Her tone was stinging, vicious. 'Those Melrose men had Rance taken while you were talking to that Leclair woman. When the police came, and they couldn't take you with them, they pretended Rance had vanished. They knew you'd tell the police. They knew the police – Melrose's police! – would use it for an "out." McFee—' She gripped his arm, her face terribly white, 'you must see that! You don't believe what the police are only pretending to believe?'

They made a right-hand turn.

McFee put a cigarette in his mouth, said quietly, 'Sister, you better lemme take the wheel. There's a car tailing us. They'll have more power than we have.'

'They can't run us down.'

'They can do anything in this town. And they will, if they think I got what they want. Slide over.'

The girl said cooly, 'Have you got what they want, McFee?'

A pair of white eyes grew large in the rear view mirror, McFee laid one hand on the wheel, slid the other around the girl's hips. His toe lifted her foot from the gas pedal. McFee said harshly, 'Don't be a fool – this is serious.' She yielded then and glided over his lap.

McFee jumped the car forward. It was a handy little bus, but it didn't have the steam. McFee made a left hand turn and they hit a through boulevard. The tail car showed its lights again. The lights grew bigger. A milk truck rattled past.

McFee let the coupe out, but the white eyes swelled.

McFee said, 'This is your coupe?'

'Rance's.'

'Where's your house?'

'Avalon. Eighteen hundred block. Avalon's about a mile beyond the next boulevard stop.'

McFee looked at the girl out of slanted eyes. 'I got a hunch they're out to wreck us. I know those birds. If they ride us down, it'll be as soon as we quit the boulevard.'

Irene Mayo said passionately, 'I don't know what they want, but nothing will make me believe Melrose didn't have Rance killed.'

They approached the cross boulevard, doing fifty or so. The neon lights of an all-night filling station blazed on the opposite corner.

'I'd like to stand those lads on their heads,' McFee muttered. He grinned, but his somber eyes were calculating as they looked at the girl. 'I got a hunch. How much you good for, sister?'

'As much as you are.'

He laughed a little. 'Maybe we could get away, but I doubt it. If we waited somewhere, and phoned for a police bodyguard, they'd jump us before the cops could find us. I don't know but what we hadn't better try to stand 'em on their heads.'

The girl said nothing. McFee ran the car up to the filling station oil pumps. Behind them, the brakes of the pursuing car made a high wailing sound and the car – a rakish black sedan – rocked to a standstill. It had not crossed the intersection.

'What's the street this side of Avalon?'

'Hawthorne.'

'Trees on it?'

'Yes.'

To the white-uniformed, freckle-faced lad who came running up, McFee said, 'Gimme a five-gallon can of crankcase oil – Eastern. Step on it.' McFee took out a jacknife, opened a blade. The lad re-appeared, lugging the can of oil. McFee placed it on the seat, between himself and the red-headed girl. 'Throw in five gallons of gas.' He added to the girl, 'Just to fool those birds,' and drove his knife blade into the top of the can. Ripping around the edge, he muttered, 'This is going to be dirty.'

The girl's eyes became spheres of green light.

Oil slopped onto McFee's clothing, over the girl's wrap. The lad came back, McFee threw ten dollars at him.

'Keep the change, kid. And do this—' McFee impaled him with an oily forefinger. 'Hop your telephone. Call police headquarters. Tell 'em, there's an accident on Hawthorne, north of Grand. Tell 'em to send a riot squad. Tell 'em McFee told you.'

The boy blurted, 'Anybody hurt?'

'There's going to be,' McFee said as he jumped the car into the boulevard.

They hit fifty. The sedan behind them zoomed across the intersection, then settled down to tailing the coop from two blocks back.

Irene Mayo said tersely. 'Avalon – three blocks.'

McFee dropped to thirty. The car behind picked up. McFee made the right hand turn at Hawthorne. The street was narrow, a black tunnel of peppers and eucalypti.

McFee drove half a block, dropping to fifteen. He shifted off the crown of the street. He placed the red-headed girl's right hand on top of the wheel. She stared at him, her mouth a red gash in her white face. McFee bent back the top of the can. He caught the ragged edge nearest him with his left hand, thrust his right under the bottom of the can. The lights behind made a wide arc as the sedan swung crazily into Hawthorne.

Before the lights had quite straightened out, McFee heaved the can over the wheel and dumped the oil onto the crown of the road.

The oil ran in every direction. McFee flung the can into the trees. The sedan came roaring down Hawthorne, huge and devastating behind its tremendous lights. McFee shot the coupe ahead. He abruptly turned into a private driveway, shut off the lights.

The brakes of the big sedan screamed. The car staggered, ploughed towards the wet smear that oozed towards either curb of the narrow street. Someone in the car shouted thickly, hysterically.

The locked wheels of the sedan skidded into the oil.

McFee and Irene Mayo saw a big sedan slide sidewise on tortured rubber. Twice the car cut a complete circle at terrible speed, its lights slicing the darkness; then it leaped the opposite curb and snapped off a street light standard. Glass shattered. A wheel flew somewhere. The huge car lifted itself in a final spasm and fell on its side.

McFee said softly, 'Very swell.'

8

Windows were going up as McFee backed into Hawthorne. He turned on his lights. Somebody yelled at him. At the corner, he made a left hand turn; then a right hand at Avalon. He drove two blocks, and saw the St. Regis, a green light over its entrance, at the next corner. It was a fairly exclusive, small, three-story house with garages. He drove into an open garage.

'Not bad.' He laughed and looked at the girl. She was leaning against his shoulder, very white. 'Oh,' said McFee. 'Well.'

He took out the ignition key. There were five keys on a ring. Sliding out of the coupe, he lifted the girl into his arms and carried her around to the front entrance. No one was about. The trees in the parking threw long shadows after him. A police siren wailed somewhere.

The letter-box directory indicated that Miss Mayo's apartment was No. 305. He carried her upstairs, reminded of an Olga Nethersole play he had seen at the Gaiety years ago. Heavy, wine-colored carpet covered the stairs and halls. Some potted palms stood around and looked at him.

At No. 305, McFee tried three of the keys before he got the door open. A little light from the corridor came in with McFee – enough for him to see a divan in the middle of the living room into which the small entrance hall opened. He laid the girl on it, snapped a floor lamp switch. The room had dim lights, soft rugs, lots of pillows, some books and a couple of pictures. A swell little shack for a lad to hang up his hat in.

One of the girl's green snakeskin slippers had become unbuckled. It fell off. McFee saw a long manila envelope fastened to the lining of her wrap with a safety pin. He chewed his knuckle, then unpinned the envelope. 'Shelldon File' was pencilled on its upper left-hand corner. The envelope was sealed. McFee stared hard at the girl. Her eyelashes rested on the shadows beneath her eyes. Slitting the top of the envelope, he looked into it. His expression became astonished. He smiled crookedly and put the envelope inside his waistcoat.

In the kitchen McFee got a glass of water. When he came back the girl was sitting up.

'How's it coming?' he asked.

'Nicely.' Her eyes were amused but a little cold. 'You must have done a gorgeous Sappho.' She looked at her hands, at her wrap and gown. 'That oil made a horrible mess. Do you suppose they are hurt?'

'You can give the hospital a bell in ten minutes.'

She laughed uneasily. 'Make yourself comfortable while I get into something else.'

McFee was in a mess himself. He lit a cigarette. He began to walk up and down.

An ornamental mirror hung on the wall opposite the bedroom door. The girl had not closed the door and he saw her reflection in the mirror. She stood beside a table, a framed photograph clasped in her hands. Her expression and attitude were tragic and adoring. She pressed the photograph to her lips, held it there. Her slender body drooped. She put the photograph down but continued to stare at it, her fingers pressed against her mouth. The photograph was of Rance Damon.

Irene Mayo slipped out of her green gown, when she reappeared some minutes later her eyes were subtle and untragic, and she wore lounging pajamas of green silk with a flowing red sash. She dropped onto the divan and laid her red head against a green pillow.

'You'd better use the bathroom, McFee,' she told him.

The bathroom was finished in green and white tile and much nickel. He used a monogrammed hand towel on his oil splashed clothes. He washed his hands and face and combed his hair. Stared at his automatic meditatively, then stood it on its nose in his right hand coat pocket.

When McFee showed himself again, Irene Mayo had a bottle of gin and a couple of glasses on a small table.

'Straight is all I can do.'

'You couldn't do better.'

McFee sat down on the girl's left. The liquor made a gurgling sound. She poured until McFee said 'yes,' which wasn't immediately.

As he occupied himself with the glass, a blunt object jammed his ribs. He finished the liquor.

The girl said coldly, 'Your own gun.'

McFee asked, 'What do you want?'

'That envelope.' Her eyes were cold, too. 'McFee, I went through Rance's pockets just before you came back and found me kneeling beside him. He had the Shelldon file. I took it. You have it. I want it back.'

'What you want it for?'

'That's my business.'

'Maybe I want it too.'

'Don't be a fool.' Her cheek bones began to burn. 'I'll kill you if you don't give me that file.'

'What'd the coppers say to that?'

'I'd tell them you wouldn't go home.'

McFee smiled charmingly and unbuttoned his waistcoat. Still smiling, he handed her the envelope and said, 'You better look at the catch.'

Suspicious, she jumped up, backed to the other side of the room, still covering him with the .38, and shook the envelope. Sheets of folded paper slid out, fluttered onto the floor. They were blank.

The girl said furiously, 'McFee, I'll give you just three seconds—'

'Use your bean,' McFee said harshly. 'You saw me unpin that envelope. You know where I been since – the kitchen, the bathroom. I haven't got anything in my clothes. 'If you like, I'll take 'em off. Some'dy's give you the run-around.'

She stared at him, the cold fury in her eyes turning to mortification. 'I didn't look – I took it for granted— What an idiot you must think me!' she wept. And then, stamping angrily, 'How do you explain this?'

McFee said, 'I can think of a coupla answers.' He helped himself appreciatively to the gin. 'Number One: Leclair's putting the buzz on Melrose. She killed Damon, picked the meat out of the envelope, and left those blanks behind. Number Two: Damon had showed Leclair the file, but was trying to sell her the blanks.' McFee set his glass down. 'Here's another one: Mr. X, as the book writers call him, shot Damon and worked the switch. Don't ask me why. There's only one answer, sister.'

'And Sam Melrose knows it!' Irene Mayo declared passionately.

She came towards McFee, her red sash swaying as she walked. Laughing a little, she sat down beside him, handed him the pistol. McFee took the cartridge clip out of his coat pocket, opened the magazine, shot the clip home. He set the safety.

Irene Mayo said, 'Oh! You knew what I would do? You are clever—'

'Just an agency dick trying to get along,' McFee answered softly.

She laid her head on the green pillow, her red mouth smiling.

'I didn't mean to,' she murmured. And then, 'Is your wife home, McFee?'

'Visiting her sister,' he said.

After a while, McFee went away.

Down below McFee hopped the taxi he had called from Irene Mayo's apartment. He told the man to take him to the Manchester Arms, on Gerard Street. It was daylight.

At the Manchester, McFee paid the fare and went into the house, feeling for his keys. They were gone. 'Metz!' he muttered, and explored his other pockets. Some letters and a note book he had had were gone. 'I owe those lads a couple,' he muttered.

McFee got a spare key off the building superintendent and walked up to his apartment on the fourth floor. He let himself into the entrance hall and pushed into the living room.

Joe Metz sat in a chair in front of the door. He had a .38 in his hand.

Metz said, 'Hello, McFee.'

McFee stood quite still. Metz's left cheek was strapped in adhesive tape from eye to mouth. His bulbous forehead was wet. Art Kline came out of the bathroom in his shirt sleeves. He was swart and squat, a barrel of a man. His nose and right forearm were plastered. The door behind McFee closed. Steel prodded his kidneys.

'Don't make any break, sap,' said whispering Monty Welch.

McFee answered, 'I thought I put you lads on ice.'

'You bust Tony Starke's neck,' Metz said.

Welch drove McFee forward. Metz stood up. The whites of his eyes showed. Art Kline shuffled across the room. He carried his hands as if they were paws. His eyes were fixed, reddish, minute.

Metz said, 'Sit down.'

McFee stared at the empty chair. It had wide wings. The three closed in upon him.

'Sit down, McFee.'

The latter whirled quietly and crashed his right into Kline's swart jaw. The blow made a dull chopping sound. Kline hit a sofa against the wall. If he'd had anything less than a horse shoe in his jaw he'd have stayed there, but as the other two jumped McFee he bounced up, shook his head, dived in. McFee took a beating before they slammed him down into the chair. He rocked a moment, then threw himself forward and up. They slammed him back.

Art Kline smashed him terrifically in the mouth. McFee fell against the back of the chair. Metz began to go swiftly, thoroughly, through his clothes.

He said harshly, 'McFee, what you done with that Shelldon file? What we just handed you is pie crust to what you'll get if you don't play ball.'

'I haven't got it,' McFee whispered.

Kline hit him again. McFee's mouth became bloody. He sat very still.

Metz said, 'What you holding out for, goat? This is Melrose's town. You can't buck Sam. Come through, or I'll turn this coupla bear eaters loose.'

Sick and raging, McFee blurted, 'You bat–eyed kite, d'you think I'd be sitting here if I had it? I'd be down at the Trib spilling a story to Roy Cruikshank that'd put you gophers in your holes.'

'Not if you were saving it until you thought you had enough to put the bell on Melrose.' Metz unfolded a handkerchief, wiped his wet forehead, said slowly, 'McFee, you must have that file. And if you have it, you're holding it with a notion of putting the bell on Sam. Nob'dy in this town'll live long enough to do that – I mean it both ways. But Sam wants that indictment killed, election coming on. Ten grand, McFee?'

'Go paddle your drum.'

'Lemme work on him,' Art Kline said. An impediment in his speech gummed up his voice. 'I owe him a couple for Tony.'

He went behind McFee's chair. He laid his tremendous hands on the top of it, flexed his powerful fingers. Whispering Monty Welch sat on the right arm of the chair. His patent leather-shod diminutive feet swung clear of the floor. Welch placed a cigarette between his lips, ignited it with a gem-studded lighter.

McFee waited.

Metz said, 'They got no use for dicks in heaven.'

McFee's mouth twitched. There was sweat in his eyes, on his cheekbones. He suddenly threw himself out of the chair and at Metz. The latter smacked him lightly across the head with his gun. McFee wobbled, fell back.

Metz said, 'I'm waiting.'

McFee did not answer. Welch dragged on his cigarette. The detached expression of his puckish face was unchanged as he held the red end a half inch from McFee's cheek. McFee slowly lifted his head. Art Kline laughed and slapped adhesive tape over McFee's mouth; then he caught McFee's wrists and began to bend his arms over the back of the chair.

Metz said, 'Blow your whistle when it's plenty.'

McFee threw himself around in the chair, but the steam had gone out of him. Metz and Welch held his legs. Kline leaned heavily, enthusiastically, on his arms. A seam in McFee's coat shoulder burst. His sinews cracked. His eyeballs came slowly out of their sockets.

Metz said, 'Well?' anxiously.

McFee mumbled defiantly behind his taped lips.

'Funny about a guy's arm,' Art Kline said.

To his downward pressure he added a sidewise motion. Welch drew his cigarette across McFee's corded throat. McFee's face turned green. His eyes rolled in a hot, white hate.

'This oughta do it,' Art Kline said.

Someone knocked at the door.

McFee fell sidewise in his chair, his arm limp. Welch squeezed out his cigarette. Metz held up a hand, his thin white face oddly disconcerted. The other two nodded slowly. The knocking set up a reverberation in the room.

A soprano voice said lazily, 'This is Roy Cruikshank, McFee. Pete Hurley's with me. The superintendent said you came in ten minutes ago. We are coming in with a pass key, if you don't open up.' Placatingly, 'Now be reasonable, Handsome – we got to get out the paper.' Pete Hurley added querulously, 'I wanna talk to you about that wrecked sedan on Hawthorne. Open the door!'

McFee lifted his head. He clawed at his taped lips, raised up in his chair. Art Kline smacked him down again.

'One peep outta you—'

Metz's agile eyes had been racing around the room. They jumped at Kline. 'Cut that!' he said tersely. And then, in a loud voice, 'I'm coming. We been in a little game.'

Metz' eyes lighted on a tier of bookshelves. On the top shelf were some decks of cards and a box of poker chips. Beside the bookshelves stood a card table. Moving fast, Metz grabbed the table with one hand, cards and box of chips with the other. Monty Welch took them away from him.

'Set 'em up,' Metz said.

In the kitchen on the sink were some glasses and a bottle of gin. Metz carried these into the living room. He placed them on the floor besides the card table, which Welch had set up in front of McFee's chair. McFee stared at Metz ironically. Art Kline stood over him, bewildered. Metz carefully upset the card table, spilling chips and cards. He threw some money on the floor.

Outside, Hurley shouted, 'McFee, I told you t'open the door!' and rattled the handle.

'Maybe he's pulling his pants on,' Roy Cruikshank said patiently.

'Don't get excited.' Metz spoke irritably. 'I'm coming.' He ripped the tape off McFee's lips. 'Tell 'em anything you please – it won't stick. Not in this town, it won't. We got all the alibis we need.' To the other two he said, 'McFee and Art tangled over a pair of jacks, see? Art laid him out.'

Metz poured gin into a glass. He drank half of it, spilled the remainder on the carpet. He wiped his lips on a handkerchief and opened the door.

'Hello, Pete!' Metz said.

'Oh, it's you!' Hurley's bitter button eyes went tight in their sockets. He shoved past Metz, saying, 'Where's McFee?'

Roy Cruikshank tailed him into the living room. Cruikshank was a slouching pink lad in his thirties. He had an egg-shaped stomach, evangelical hands and cynical, indolent eyes.

'Party,' Cruikshank said lazily. 'Well, well.'

Hurley's hostile eyes made their calculations. Art Kline sat on the couch, nursing his jaw. Welch, leaning back in a chair near the table, squeezed five cards in his left hand, lighted a cigarette with his right. McFee's face was a mess.

'What happened, Handsome?' Hurley muttered.

McFee smiled with bruised lips. 'Ask Metz.'

'Art and McFee mixed over a pair of Jacks,' Metz said with annoyed distinctness. 'McFee smacked Art. Art laid him out.'

'How long you been playing?'

'Half an hour.'

Hurley flared out, 'The superintendent told Roy and me—'

'It don't matter what the superintendent told you. McFee's been here half an hour. Coupla days ago, out to the Shawl, McFee said, "Joe, why don't you and the boys drop in for a session some time? If the missus and me are out you'll find the key under the mat." There's a lad for you! So we dropped in tonight – around two. We played rummy until McFee came.'

Hurley looked at Welch and Kline. 'That right?'

'Check.'

'Me, too.' Kline rubbed his jaw. 'That guy packs a cannon in his kick.'

Glinting amusement surfaced the dark violence in McFee's eyes. Hurley put a cigarette in his mouth, jiggled it angrily. Reddening, he said, 'You heard these boys, McFee?'

'Sure!' McFee answered. 'Gimme a drink, some'dy.'

As Cruikshank handed McFee the glass a faint irritability stirred his cynical indolence. 'Sure that's all, McFee?'

'That's all right now,' McFee answered deliberately.

But Hurley had a couple of kicks left. To Metz he said vehemently, 'I want the how of this Gaiety business.'

'Some'dy phoned the Shawl,' Metz replied cautiously. 'Who was it, Art?'

'I dunno.'

Metz waved his hand. 'That's how it is, Pete. Tough, though. Damon was a nice kid. And Melrose is going to be damn good and sore.'

Hurley suddenly became enraged. 'You got your gall sitting there telling me—' He became inarticulate, his face a network of purple veins. 'By God! This town—'

Metz asked quietly, 'What you want to know, Pete?'

Hurley took out a handkerchief, wiped the palm of his hands, put it away. He said huskily, 'I wanna know where you boys were between eleven and one.'

'I'll tell you,' Metz said confidingly. 'We were having a little supper in Sam Melrose's rooms at the Shawl. Art, Monty, Tony, Max Beck, Fred Pope and me. Mabel Leclair put on a shimmy number. She left the Gaiety around eleven. One o'clock, Tony pulled out. He had a date. Art and Monty and me came here.' Metz added lazily, 'Anything else, Pete?'

Hurley's throat sounded dry as he said, 'And that Leclair queen didn't hand Rance Damon five grand for the Shelldon file; and—'

'Why, Pete!'

'—You birds didn't walk Damon away with a hole in his chest—'

Metz asked Welch and Kline seriously. 'Either you boys got Damon in your pockets?' And then, 'Who's been giving you the run-around, Pete?'

Hurley glared at McFee. The latter said nothing. McFee's eyes were hot and violent, but he smiled with his lips and Hurley pulled his own eyes back into his head.

'And you ain't heard Tony Starke bust his neck in a smash on Hawthorne?'

'Gosh, no! How'd it happen?'

Hurley flared out disgustedly, 'Mercy Hospital. He'll live.'

Metz stood up. 'We better go buy Tony a bouquet.' He put on his hat. He buttoned his waistcoat. Art Kline got into his coat and shook down his trousers. Monty Welch carefully smoothed down his hair. Metz smiled. 'Well, I'll be seeing you, McFee. We had a hot party.'

As they reached the door Hurley said sourly, 'The vice detail raids the Shawl tonight. Slattery and his boys. Midnight.'

'Saturday's a swell date to knock over a roadhouse doing our business—'

'We got to make a play, ain't we? The Mayor's coming.'

'Ohhh,' said Metz. 'Hizoner. Well!'

They went away.

9

Roy Cruikshank wrapped his evangelical hands around glassware and poured himself a drink. He set his hat on the back of his pink head. 'Those lads were giving you the works, McFee?'

The latter jeered, 'And why didn't I tell Hurley about it?' He flexed his shoulder muscles, began to walk the floor. 'Why didn't I tell him those pansies tailed Mayo and me in that sedan to Hawthorne Street? Roy, I told Hurley plenty before I left the Gaiety.'

Hurley blew up. 'I mighta called the wagon, sure. And Morry Lasker'd have had 'em bailed out before I'd booked 'em at the desk. If it had come to court – which ain't likely – Metz and his lads'd have brought a sockful of alibis, and Lasker'd have given McFee the haw-haw for his tag-in-the-dark yarn. "Y'honor-gen'lemen-the-jury, the witness admits the only light in the theater was that of an electric torch. How could he positively have identified my clients—" ' Hurley jiggled his cigarette. 'The papers'd pan the cops and the D. A. for not making it stick. And me out airing my pants.'

The Tribune man crooned, 'Now he's getting sore.'

'Whatdayou want for two hundred bucks a month? If I can crack the Melrose drag, fine. If I pull a dud I lose my badge. Lookit Frank Ward. Chased Melrose doing seventy and give him a ticket. Frank lost his job – and five kids.' Hurley jerked his hat over his eyes, stood up. 'The Chief said to me, "Hurley, you're a good copper. But don't get too good." I ain't going to.'

Hurley slammed the entrance door.

Putting a cigarette in the middle of his pink face, Roy Cruikshank said, 'Hurley isn't a bad guy.' He laughed from his belly up. 'Tonight the vice detail raids Melrose's Spanish Shawl. The Mayor goes along. Metz has rolled up the bar and there's checkers in the gambling room. Hizoner drinks his lemonade and makes his little speech, entitled, Everything's Rosy in Our Town. Some'dy ought to give us a new deal.'

McFee went into the bathroom. He swabbed his face with hot water, took a shower. He rubbed his shoulders with linament, got into clean pajamas, a bathrobe. He had a mouse under his left eye. His lips were bruised and broken. The hot violence still glinted on the surface of his eyes.

In the kitchen McFee prepared coffee, ham and eggs and flap-jacks; set the food on a tray with mess-gear. Cruikshank had righted the card table. He was dealing himself poker hands. 'Boy!' said Cruikshank. They ate without talk, McFee believing in food first. Cruikshank was careless with his eggs. His neckties said so.

After they had cleaned up the tray, Cruikshank began to fool abstractedly with the cards. McFee suggested they cut for nickels. Cruikshank thought it a good idea until McFee had won around five dollars; then he muttered sourly, 'I guess I've paid for my breakfast.'

McFee said abruptly, 'Who's the Trib backing for district attorney?'

'The Trib—' Cruikshank cut a ten-spade to McFee's heart-queen. 'What you got on those girls, damn your hide—' He shoved across a chip. 'The Trib – oh, yeah. Why, Jim Hughes, I guess. Jim's a good egg, and he'd give the country a break.'

'Jim isn't bad,' McFee admitted, 'but Luke Addams is better; Luke knows the political set-up. Jim'd have to learn too much.'

'Well, it don't matter who the Trib backs. Melrose has written the ticket – Dietrich. The Mayor endorses Dietrich and it's count 'em and weep.'

McFee stacked chips. 'Dietrich elected'll throw the country Melrose.' He looked at Cruikshank, eyes cold. 'That'll give him the county, City Hall and police machines. Larrabee is soft, but he's got church backing and while he's D.A. he's never been more than half Melrose's man.'

'What's on your mind?'

'I'll tell you.' McFee spoke harshly. 'If Melrose's heels had kept their hands off me this morning, I'd have kept mine in my pants pocket. But they didn't.' His words made a bitter, drumming sound. 'So I'm out to give Melrose a ride.'

'On what?'

'The Damon murder.'

'You think he or his heels killed Damon?'

McFee said softly, 'Can I make it look that way, you mean?'

'You got the City Hall hook-up to beat.'

McFee shuffled the cards. 'Littner might buy a ticket,' he muttered. 'Littner ought to be chief.' He added thoughtfully. 'Littner's going to be Chief.' And then, 'Roy, could you swing the Trib to Luke Addams, if you wanted to?'

'Mebbe.' Cruikshank rubbed his plump hands on his fat thighs. 'But I don't guess I want to. Jim Hughes—'

'Swell!' said McFee. 'Roy, you owe me five ten. I'll cut you for it against Luke Addams for D.A. Five-ten isn't high for a district attorney.'

Cruikshank grinned. 'Cut 'em first.'

McFee turned up a four-diamond.

'If I don't beat that—' Cruikshank exulted.

But his cut was a trey-heart.

'McFee, you lucky stiff, I got a hunch you're going to slam this across.'

McFee said, 'You owe me five-ten, Roy.' He poured a couple of drinks. 'To Luke Addams, the next D.A.'

Cruikshank went away.

At his telephone McFee dialed Dresden 5216. He said, 'Hello, Luke . . . McFee. Pin this in your hat: You are to be District Attorney . . .' Luke Addams laughed. So did McFee.

Then he hung up and went to bed.

McFee got up around twelve and stood under the shower. His eye was bad, his lips were puffy, but he felt better. As he dressed, the telephone rang.

Irene Mayo was calling.

McFee said, 'Oh, pretty good . . . a couple of the boys dropped in. Nothing much . . .' And then, 'How about some lunch, sister? . . . Cato's. Half an hour . . . Right.'

McFee stopped at his office, in the Strauss Building and looked over the mail his secretary had laid on his desk. Out of a white envelope – five-and-ten stock – fell a triangular shaped scrap of drug store paper. On it, in crude characters, was printed:

Sam Melrose got the Shelldon file, you bet.
He's going to work on it. Mr. Inside.

McFee stared at the note. 'Well,' he said finally, and went out.

At Cato's, Irene Mayo waited in the booth McFee usually occupied. She wore a green felt beret, a string of pearls and a knitted green silk suit with white cuffs. Her eyes were smudgy, feverish in her taut face. She smiled, with a slow, subtle curving of her red lips.

McFee said, 'Pretty nice.'

'Not very nice,' she answered. 'Does your eye hurt?'

McFee grinned. 'You ought to see the other lad . . . I suppose you had callers?'

She nodded. 'Captain Littner and Mr. Hurley. They stayed about an hour, but I couldn't tell them anything they didn't know.'

The red-headed girl ordered a roast. McFee said he was on a diet and took turtle soup, planked steak with mushrooms and apple pie. They talked a while. The girl presently fetched an envelope out of her vanity bag.

'That came this morning,' she said.

The envelope was a replica of the one McFee had received. He took a swallow of coffee and shook a scrap of drug store paper out of the envelope. The crude printing on it was familiar.

You tell McFee Melrose got the Shelldon file
at the Spanish Shawl. Mr. Inside.

The girl flared out, 'Of course he's got it. And that means he had Rance shot. McFee—' She laid a cold hand on his, her eyes hot. '—I could kill Melrose – myself. It's in me to do it. Rance meant everything to me – I can't tell you—'

McFee said, 'The Governor's lady.'

She turned white. She whipped up her fork as if she was going to throw it at him. After a long moment she said coldly, 'You mean I didn't love him – that I was just politically ambitious—'

'Oh, you loved him, sister.'

'McFee, you are horrid.' Tears started in her eyes. 'But I don't care what you think. He'd have got there. I could have made him. He had appeal – the public—'

'What about the Leclair woman?' McFee asked.

Irene Mayo answered stonily, 'She didn't count,' and made patterns on the table cloth with her fork. 'I loved him, but – I shouldn't have minded his blonde – much. A man is a man. Only the other thing *really* mattered—' The red-headed girl lifted her eyes to McFee's. 'I am exposing myself, McFee. I did want to be – the Governor's lady. You'll think me merecenary. I don't care. I'd rather be that than dishonest. But Sam Melrose had to—' Her eyelids fell over the hate behind them, as she asked, 'Who do you suppose "Mr. Inside" is?'

'That doesn't make sense.'

'Nothing makes sense.'

'What does he mean by that sentence in your note, "He's going to work on it?" '

'I been thinking about that,' McFee said. 'If Melrose has that Shelldon file he could do one of two things with it: Burn it, or work it over. By work it over, I mean change, substitute, lose in part, cut out, then send the file back with its kick gone. But we still got a good one to answer—' McFee stirred his coffee. 'If Melrose has the file, what's he been chasing you and me all over the lot for?' He added after a moment. 'The vice detail raids the Shawl tonight, by the way.'

This appeared to interest Irene Mayo tremendously, but she stared at McFee silently while he wiped mushroom gravy off his lips and buttered a biscuit. 'You said the Shelldon scandal wasn't big enough, in itself, to pull Melrose down, didn't you?'

McFee nodded. 'You know what happened, don't you? Mike Shelldon was a big shot poker hound. Some'dy bumped off in one of Melrose's joints – Melrose, maybe – but there isn't enough, if y'ask me.'

'Wouldn't there be enough if it was definitely linked with the murder of Rance?'

'Yes.'

'You just said the vice detail was going to raid the Shawl tonight. McFee—' She laid her hand on his. '—if Melrose has that file at the Shawl, and it should be found there – by the police – before witnesses – newspaper men—'

'Swell!' said McFee. 'Some'dy'd have to do something then. But it isn't going to be, sister—'

'You don't know—' Her words came feverishly. 'I'm not the sort of woman to sit down and wait. *I can't!* I've got to do something myself. McFee, take me out to the Shawl tonight. It's Saturday – there'll be a crowd—'

'If Sam has that file out there, you don't suppose it's lying around loose—'

'Of course I don't. But we might get a break. Things do break sometimes – unexpectedly. He knows what a gun is for, doesn't he?' she said, a little wildly. 'He threatened us – we can threaten him – and if the police and some newspaper men are there—' She stared at McFee. She was very pale. She held her napkin in a ball between her clasped hands. 'Not afraid, are you?'

McFee had finished his apple pie, sugared his second coffee.

'Got a hunch?'

'Yes.'

'Well—' His eyes were amused. 'Wrap yourself around that food and I'll give you a bell tonight.'

'McFee, you are a darling!'

'That's better than being Governor,' he said.

After he had taken Irene Mayo to her car, McFee walked back along Third, turned down Carter. Some people were staring vacantly at the Gaiety Theater. A sign in the lobby said; HOUSE CLOSED TODAY. Across the exit alley hung a theater ladder. A cop on guard said, 'Hello, McFee.'

'Dirty job,' McFee replied. He noticed that Maggie O'Day's

hole-in-the-wall was shuttered. 'That's funny,' he muttered. 'What happened to O'Day?'

'Search me,' the cop said. 'I been around Second and Carter twenty years and I never seen that old girl shut up before.'

Rolling a match in his ear, McFee went down Second. He walked seven blocks and turned west on Finch, a street of ramshackle detached houses. Finch had been red light once; now it was colored. McFee stopped in front of a tall house with a crazy porch and a triangular wooden block at the curb. A pickaninny thumbed his nose at McFee.

McFee went along a broken cement walk to a drab side door. Two sloping boards with grooves in them led from the broken walk up to the door sill. McFee knocked. No one came. He was about to knock again when he sniffed the air. His eyes ran down the door. Folded newspaper showed between door bottom and sill. A keyhole was blocked. Moving fast, McFee pinched out his cigarette, picked up a piece of cement and shattered the window with it. He rammed the door with his shoulder. Lock and bolt gave and he fell into the room. A wave of combustible gas forced him back into the open, gagging.

A fat colored woman with a red handkerchief on her hair came up, running. She screamed.

McFee said, 'Shut up. Go telephone the coppers.' The harsh fury in his tones spun her around, goggle-eyed.

McFee drew air deep down into his lungs and plunged into the gas-filled room. He shot up a window, hung his head outside, refilled his lungs. Facing inside he saw a gas heater, its cock wide open. Three cocks of a gas plate in one corner of the room were open. He shut off the gas flow and refreshed himself again.

Maggie O'Day lay in the middle of the floor. She lay on her side. Close against her was the wheel chair she had rolled herself home in for twenty years or more. But the last time she had come home she had come on her crutches.

Rance Damon's body was in the chair.

A rug tucked him into it. The five grand was still in his left hand. His right hung over the side of the chair, clutched in one of Maggie O'Day's weather-beaten bony ones.

McFee bent over the woman. He felt at her heart, lifted an eyelid. 'Tough,' he muttered. He went to the door and filled his lungs.

There were some rag rugs, a day bed, a couple of rocking chairs with antimacassars, a table, some framed pictures; near the gasplate was a wall cabinet. A door that led into the wall had been made tight with newspapers. Sheets of newspaper littered the floor.

A photograph of a large, fleshy, pallid man, still in his thirties, but already gross with high living, lay on the table. It was faded, had been taken perhaps thirty years before. The print had been torn in three, then carefully pieced together with adhesive tape.

McFee muttered, 'The late Senator Gaylord.' He chewed a knuckle, stared at the photograph, then looked at Damon and the woman. He said moodily, 'Poor old girl!'

A bruise discolored Maggie O'Day's left temple. One of her crutches lay on the floor, behind the wheel chair. McFee saw something else then. He saw a red smear some two inches long on a sheet of newspaper on the floor in front of the wheel chair. He picked up the sheet, his eyes fixed and cold.

The smear was crimson grease paint.

McFee inspected Damon's shoes, the old woman's shoes. Neither pair was daubed with grease paint.

Very softly McFee said, 'Pretty!'

A couple of coppers came. An assistant coroner, named Ridley, came.

Presently, Ridley said, 'The old girl's been dead quite a while – ten or twelve hours. She cracked her head when she fell. It must have knocked her cold.'

'Maybe some'dy cracked her first,' McFee said.

'You mean, somebody else turned on the gas?'

10

A couple of hours later, McFee talked with Captain Littner, Chief of the Homicide Squad, in Littner's office, in police headquarters on Greer Street. Littner was a lean hairless man with an oval head and bleak eyes as clear as cold water. He had a political, a cautious mind.

'O'Day had a son,' Littner said. 'Some thirty years ago. But nobody knew – I mean, nobody was *sure* – what became of him. There was a lot of talk. Gaylord—' Littner rubbed his chin, looked at McFee.

'Sure,' said McFee. 'Gaylord. And now we got Melrose. You talked with Leclair yet?'

'Yes.'

'Did she mention alibis?'

'Nine of them.'

'Where'd you see her?'

'Melrose brought her in. He said he left the Scudder yacht late this morning.' Littner was amused. 'He guessed we better close the Gaiety awhile. And anyhow, Leclair was opening a dance act at the Spanish Shawl tonight. He guessed he owed Leclair a statement to the police – oh, beans!' said Captain Littner gently. 'What a town!'

'You ought to be Chief, Littner,' McFee said.

'Yes,' Littner answered carefully. 'We traced that .32 – the one killed Damon. It belonged to Joe Metz.'

McFee exclaimed, 'Now, you don't tell me!'

119

'Joe said he hadn't much use of a .32 and he sold it to Damon in the Press Club, couple of weeks ago. Rance wanted it for someone, Joe said. Joe's got all the witnesses he needs – Carl Reder, Fred Pope, Wade Fiske. They say they saw Damon buy the gun, take it from Metz. Damon paid him fifteen dollars—' Littner smiled coldly. 'Maybe he did.'

McFee said abstractedly, 'Maybe he did, at that.' And then, 'What do you think of this notion Damon's murderer bumped off O'Day because the old girl saw him leave the Gaiety?'

'We have that smear of grease paint.'

'Grease paint isn't easy to clean up,' McFee said, thoughtfully. 'If it's on cloth – any sort of fabric, I guess – it isn't. Now if I'd killed some'dy and stepped in a mess of grease paint, I'd throw my shoes away.'

'Where'd you throw 'em, McFee?'

'Well, I might throw 'em in some'dy's trash barrel. How's that?'

'Not bad.' Littner made a note on a memorandum pad. 'I'll put a detail on trash collection.' He pulled his long jaw down. 'McFee,' he asked, 'what about that red-headed girl?'

'Nice little number.' McFee stood his hat on the back of his head. 'A go-getter, and no better than she ought to be, maybe. Littner, if Leclair had dropped instead of Damon, I'd say Mayo could have done it. But she wanted Damon; she had a notion she could make him governor. Mayo wouldn't have shot Damon.' Littner nodded, and McFee proceeded. 'I got another idea. The vice detail's going to knock over the Shawl tonight – twelve P.M. Melrose'll be there – Metz, Leclair. The Mayor's billed to tell a bed-time story. How about it, Mr. Littner?'

Captain Littner said, 'Beans!' He opened a cupboard in his desk. 'What'll you have, McFee?'

'Rye,' said McFee. 'The trouble with you, Littner, is you don't wisecrack 'em enough. Lookit the Chief now—' He took the glass Littner handed him, pushed his forehead up, pulled it down. 'Littner,' he asked again, 'how'd you like to be Chief?'

'The pay's good.'

'You'd need plenty drag.'

'Yes.' Littner stared at McFee with a flicker of warmth in his eyes. 'Yes, I'd need plenty of drag.'

'Luke Addams is going to be District Attorney,' McFee said. 'We got to elect Luke first.'

'Luke'd be a big help,' Littner admitted.

McFee leaned close again. 'Here's a question: If that Shelldon file should happen to be found in the Spanish Shawl tonight, what'd the Shelldon-Damon tie-up do to the Melrose organization?'

'Everything,' Littner answered drily. 'But it won't be.'

McFee handed Littner the 'Mr. Inside' notes. He told him where he'd got them and watched Littner over the end of his cigarette.

Littner said carefully, 'Maybe I'll drop in at the Shawl around twelve.'
And then, 'Help yourself.'

'Thanks,' said McFee.

It was five o'clock. McFee's car was in a garage on Fourth. He walked
up to Carter, crossed Second. The cop was still on duty in the Gaiety alley.
One of the lobby doors of the theater was open. A man with wide ears and
a thick neck came out.

McFee said, 'Hello, Harrigan.'

'A swell dish you canaries handed me last night,' the house manager said
sourly.

'Lookit the publicity,' McFee told him.

'What the hell! You pull a murder on me and the coppers close the
house. I could have sold out at two bucks a seat if they'd give me a break.'

'Why'n't you talk to Melrose?'

Harrigan muttered uneasily and put a cigar in his mouth. 'Guess it ain't
my picnic.' McFee followed him towards the door and Harrigan said, 'The
show's closed, mister.'

'There's a couple of points I want to check up.'

'Go read a book.'

McFee said, 'There ought to be money in this for the house. If I give
you a slant on what happened you ought to be able to hang an act on it
when the coppers give you the go-sign. It'd sell big.'

Harrigan looked at the end of his cigar. 'A guy's gotta be careful,' he
mumbled; and then, 'All right.'

The backstage was dark. In Leclair's room, McFee turned on a wall
bracket lamp. Light flowed out into the backstage. The couch stood against
the wall. McFee stared at the crosses Hurley had chalked on the floor.

'Leclair was standing farthest from wall and couch,' McFee muttered.
'Damon was close against the couch—'

Harrigan cut in obliquely, 'Leclair was out to the Shawl when Damon –
if it was Damon – rubbed out.'

'Oh, sure,' McFee said solemnly. 'Joe Metz and the boys said so. It was
just a couple of ghosts I saw. Well, Mr. and Mrs. X, then. Mr. X flopped
into Mrs. X's arms. They went down. Got a ball of string, Harrigan?'

The latter found string.

'Stand here,' McFee said, and Harrigan set his No. 10's on the Mr. X
cross. 'Hold this against your chest.'

McFee gave Harrigan the loose end of the string. Unrolling the ball as
he went, he walked some twenty feet into the backstage, stopped and held
the ball of string chest high. He stood on the south edge of the lane of
light. The darkness of the backstage partly concealed him.

'The bullet must have traveled pretty well along the line of the string,'
McFee said. He added drily, 'If there was any bullet—'

Slackening the line, McFee inspected a shallow horizontal groove, about an inch long, in the door jamb. The string had been level with the groove and about six inches to the right of it. McFee stared hard at the groove, twirled a match in his ear.

Backing up again, McFee said, 'Put your dogs on the other cross.'

Harrigan did so and the string grazed the groove. McFee said, 'Swell!' and threw the ball at Harrigan. 'Buy yourself a drink on me.'

'Hey, wait a minute, fellah,' Harrigan yelled. 'You got me on by toes. What's the rest of it?'

McFee said, 'Read it in the papers,' and went out.

At Cato's, McFee ordered a Porterhouse steak smothered in onions. After his third coffee, he drove to his apartment. It was now eight o'clock. He looked up Irene Mayo's number and dialed Spring 2341. There was no response. McFee waited a little, then hung up.

He walked around the room, glaring at the Evening Tribune. The Trib said two killings in twenty-four hours was plenty and something ought to be done. McFee made a ball of the sheet. He carried the breakfast tray in to the kitchen. He put away the card table and poured himself a drink. He tried Irene Mayo's number again. No good.

McFee took a shower and got into his dinner clothes. He had wrecked four black ties when his telephone rang.

'Hello,' McFee said. No one answered. 'Hello, there – McFee talking.'

He heard voices, vaguely familiar, but detached and distant and apparently not addressed to him. He embedded his ear in the receiver and waited, a fixed, hot look in his eyes.

The indistinct muttering continued until a voice suddenly cried, 'You can't keep me here! I know where we are. We are in a house on Butte Street – I saw the name – Butte Street. Butte Street!'

It was Irene Mayo's voice that had ended on that desperate shrill note. Her voice had been thin and distant, but clear. McFee heard that muttering again.

And then, hysterically, 'Don't touch me! I haven't got it – McFee—' A man laughed. A woman laughed.

McFee waited. His forehead was wet. He wiped it with a handkerchief. Gently replaced the receiver, and stood up. At his desk, McFee looked at a city map. He put a gun in his jacket pocket, and went down into the street.

As he got into his car, McFee said softly, 'A house on Butte Street.'

11

McFee drove towards the foothills that threw a possessive arm around the town, on the north. Here the streets went up and down like stair carpets and lost themselves in tangles of oaks and eucalypti. This neighborhood had been built up years before, then forgotten while the town grew westward. Most of the residents were scattered, set in small acreage, and exclusively hedged about. Street lights were few.

Butte, a tag-end street, one block long, ended in a canyon. McFee drove up, then down the street. There were only three houses on it. Two were dark. The third, at the end of the street, was a secretive-looking, one-story, rambling, redwood place. A cypress hedge enclosed the grounds. A side window glowed.

McFee left his car at the corner, across the road from the street lamp, and walked back.

He went up a cinder driveway, saw a garage, half filled by a dark-colored sedan. The lighted side window shone dimly in the black expanse of house and mantling trees. Curtains screened the windows. McFee could not see into the room, but he heard voices.

He heard Joe Metz' voice. He heard Joe Metz say, 'Sister, we just begun to work on you—'

McFee found the back door locked. The house was built on the slope of the canyon. He saw a basement window on his left, below the level on which he stood. The light was on the other side of the house; the wind made a melancholy rustling in the trees. He came to a decision. Holding his soft felt hat against one of the small square panes of the cellar window, he struck the felt sharply with the nose of his gun. The brittle glass broke with a tinkling sound.

His arm inside the window, McFee found the hook. The window swung upward on hinges. McFee threw the beam of his flash inside the cellar room, let himself down into it. He saw a stair, went quietly up it, came to a door. It opened when he turned the handle and pushed against it. He left his shoes on the top step.

McFee found himself in a dark, square hall, redwood timbered. He heard voices, saw an open door with light somewhere beyond it. Through the door he entered a living room with a huge stone fireplace. The light and the voices came from a partly opened door, opposite the one through which he had just come.

As McFee approached this door, Monty Welch whispered, 'Lemme at her, Joe—'

This room was the library. McFee saw Mabel Leclair in a black velvet gown, curled up on a divan, eating chocolates. Metz and Welch were bent over an arm chair in which Irene Mayo strained away from them in an attitude of terror. Joe Metz held her by the arm. Her eyes were enormous, frantic. She whimpered faintly. Her lips were taped. Welch burned a cigarette.

McFee said, 'Quit that, Joe.'

Monty Welch must have heard McFee first. He spun on his heel, white violence bursting through his professional calm. As McFee said 'Joe', Welch fired from the pocket of his dinner jacket. He fired again, lurching toward McFee. The latter aimed, let go. Welch's shoulder bunched up, he screamed and went down. He threshed about, buried his face in the carpet.

Metz stood erect, his hands at his sides. McFee went towards him. Metz did not move or speak. His bulbous forehead gleamed. His lip muscles twitched. McFee took a long stride, a short one, and struck Metz a terrible blow in the mouth. It made a crunching sound and Metz hit the carpet. McFee pulled the adhesive tape from Irene Mayo's lips.

'McFee—' the red-headed girl sobbed. She rocked in the chair, began to rub her wrists.

'Sure,' McFee said. 'Take it easy.'

Welch dragged himself across the floor. McFee toed his gun under the divan. Metz lay groaning. His mouth and the plaster strap on his cheek were a crimson mess. He held a handkerchief against it. Suddenly, he jerked out an automatic. McFee's unshod toe caught his wrist before he could fire. The gun shattered the glass front of a bookcase. McFee raised Metz by his lapels and flung him onto the divan, alongside Mabel Leclair. The Leclair woman screamed and covered her face.

McFee searched all three of them for other weapons, found none.

'What give you the notion Miss Mayo had the Shelldon file, Joe?'

Metz blotted his wet lips, whispered, 'She knows where it is – you, too – one of you—'

McFee cut in softly, 'The gun killed Damon was yours, Joe.'

'I sold it to Damon.' Metz' bruised lips distorted his speech. 'The boys saw me hand it him. I told Littner—'

'How about Damon handing it Leclair?'

The blonde woman opened her mouth, but as McFee looked at her she closed it again with a gasping sound. McFee proceeded. 'You went to Miss Mayo's apartment, I s'pose. That's kidnapping. We'll give Littner a bell.'

The telephone stood on the table. McFee backed towards it. Metz stared after him, his eyes haggard above the red-spotted handkerchief against his lips. The blonde woman wept. Holding his shoulder, Monty Welch struggled to a sitting position, his lips gray.

The telephone was a dial instrument. Several magazines had been inserted under the receiver, so that while the receiver was on the hook, the hook was up. McFee laughed a little and looked at the red-headed girl. She nodded, her eyes hot with hate. As McFee seized the telephone, she got control of herself and caught his arm.

'What's on your mind, sister?'

'McFee, it's our turn now.' She spoke feverishly. 'These people aren't important. Melrose – Sam Melrose *is*. He's at the Shawl. The Leclair woman is opening a dance act there tonight. Well, she isn't—'

'What's that?'

Irene Mayo said deliberately, 'Metz is going to phone Melrose that Leclair is too ill to appear. Shock – anything! And he's going to tell

Melrose her red-headed friend, Zella Vasquez, is on her way out to take Leclair's place. Melrose – no one at the Spanish Shawl has seen me. If Metz telephones Melrose I'm coming he'll accept me as Leclair's friend. Why shouldn't he?' Irene Mayo hammered on the table. 'McFee, you've got to make Metz telephone him—'

'Swell!' McFee said.

'I won't!' Metz shouted thickly. 'By God, if you lay a hand on me—'

McFee jerked him up and shook him into a shivering silence. He walked him backwards, slammed him down beside the table.

He said, 'Metz, since half-past one this morning, you've been rocking the cradle. It's my turn now. Do as I tell you, or I'll spatter you over that wall. Grab that phone and tell Melrose Leclair is sick. Tell him Zella Vasquez, her red-headed side kick, is on her way out. And make it stick!'

Metz' Adam's apple ran up and down his throat. He rubbed his wet palms together, pulled the telephone towards him. He dialed Thorn 99238. He had to do it twice and then, huskily, 'Mr. Melrose – tell him Metz calling.'

McFee stuck his gun into the back of Metz' neck. He didn't say anything. Melrose helloed, and Metz began a pretty good job of doing as he had been told. When he weakened, McFee leaned on his gun and Metz picked up again. Melrose put some question about Zella Vasquez.

Metz answered carefully, 'I dunno, Sam. Leclair says she's good – that oughta be plenty—' The blonde woman made blasphemous noises but subsided when McFee looked at her. Metz proceeded, 'She's on her way, Sam . . .' Metz hung up. 'What Melrose won't do to you for this, mister—'

McFee gave Irene Mayo his gun, said, 'Watch him,' and cut out a length of the telephone cord. He bound Metz' hands and corded them to the straight back of the chair in which he sat. Metz did not resist. His ankles McFee fastened to the legs of the chair with Metz' belt and a couple of handkerchiefs. Metz dripped sweat but said nothing. At the back of the house McFee found some clothesline. He sat Monty Welch on another straight backed chair and roped him to it. Welch had fainted. McFee slammed a third chair down in front of Mabel Leclair.

She screamed, 'You ain't going to tie me up—'

McFee cut in, 'I'll forget you're a lady, if you don't sit in that chair.'

'Forget it anyhow,' Irene Mayo said hotly.

As McFee was tying up the Leclair woman, she flared out, 'Sam Melrose thinks you red-headed Shebas are particular arsenic.'

'He's going to change his mind.'

'You couldn't hold Rance Damon.'

Vivid spots of color on her cheek bones, Irene Mayo slapped the blonde woman hard across the mouth, rocking her head backwards. Mabel Leclair went pale under her make-up, became inarticulate. The red-headed girl was throwing up the gun when McFee said, 'That's plenty, sister.'

McFee found a roll of adhesive tape on the table. He taped the lips of his prisoners. Metz he dragged into the hall, on the heels of his chair, and tumbled into a clothes closet. The door locked, he threw the key into the cellar and put on his shoes, he locked Monty Welch in the pantry; left Mabel Leclair in the library.

Irene Mayo said, 'You do a good job, McFee.'

He nodded. 'That telephone stunt was slick.'

She shuddered. 'I was afraid you were out. They were getting some drinks. I knew it was the only chance— They thought I was shouting at them.'

McFee stared at her. He said slowly, 'Think you can put over that Zella Vasquez number?'

She smiled. 'I've known lots of men, McFee.'

'What you think you going to get out of it?'

'I told you at lunch. If Melrose has that Shelldon file – if I should find it – or the police – You said they were raiding the Shawl—' She clasped her hands, whispered huskily, 'Perhaps I'm a fool, but I can't help it. I can't help feeling something's going to break—'

McFee muttered, 'Let's get at it, then.'

A clock in the hall showed nine-five as they went out.

They walked down Butte Street to McFee's car.

'I want to go home first,' the girl said.

McFee smiled one-sidedly, answered, 'Right.'

At Irene Mayo's apartment, McFee poured himself a drink. He took the glass over to the telephone and called Roy Cruikshank, at the Tribune office, then Littner at headquarters. Ringing off, he pushed his face up and set his glass down. Near the telephone stood a portable typewriter. McFee took a chair and slid paper under the roller. He wrote for about ten minutes, then read what he had written, and put the paper inside his jacket pocket.

Irene Mayo came prancing out of the bedroom. She wore a green silk blouse, a blue velvet bolero, a frothy red skirt and a green sash. She looked like a red-headed Carmen. Snapping her fingers, she fell into McFee's arms. Her green eyes were veiled and humid.

McFee said, 'Very nice,' and kissed her. 'If Melrose don't fall, I'll go peddling fleas to a dog circus.'

It was nine-fifty. McFee drove fast. They took one of the beach boulevards, followed it a while, and turned north. Presently they made a west turn, then a northwest turn into a dirt road that ended in a grove of cypress trees. The trees were on a bluff high above a crashing beach, and garlands of red, green and blue lights hung against them. Crooked in the bright arm of the trees was a sprawling, dark-shingled building with gem-like windows. A horde of cars stood around. Music throbbed. People churned in a splatter of sound and color.

Irene Mayo said, 'I'll go in alone. You come back later—' She added lightly, 'If you care to.'

McFee laughed and let her out. She ran under a canopy of colored lights and vanished through a door. An attendant ran towards McFee's car, but McFee reversed and roared down the road. At the intersection he parked long enough to smoke a couple of cigarettes before he put the car around.

He entered the Spanish Shawl at eleven-five.

12

At one end of the rowdy cafe floor a six-piece colored orchestra – Dutch Louie and his Pals – peddled hot music. The ebony lads looked livid and wet in the overhead yellow lights. A good crowd danced about. The closely regimented tables made a horseshoe about the patch of shining floor. Most of them were taken but Leo Ganns, the head waiter, found McFee one at the lower end of the room.

He ordered broiled lobster and coffee.

The music stopped and the floor emptied. McFee touched a match to a cigarette. The air was heavy with smoke and the odors of food. Some liquor was flowing. Two girls near McFee sat lopsided and very still. Dutch Louie began to shout through a megaphone in his mellow drawl. He ballyhooed one Zella Vasquez, red-headed Spanish dancer, who stood 'em on their ears in Havana, Cuba. 'Yessir, ladies and gem'men, an' if you don't think she's got something you jest gotta have—'

Irene Mayo whirled onto the floor in her Spanish costume. Behind her came a dark, slick-looking number from the Argentine or Chicago, maybe. They did a fox trot, the ebony boys wailing 'My Baby's a Red-head-too.' After that, a tango. Then Irene Mayo went solo and turned in a sweet *la jota Aragonese*. As she frothed past McFee, her eyes bright with fever, rested on him without recognition. She threw herself into the dark number's arms, and the crowd stamped. They did another tango. McFee dug into his lobster. The crowd howled for more and got the hat dance.

Sam Melrose came smiling onto the floor. He was an olive-skinned man with an uneven mouth and grizzled hair parted in the middle. His face was old, his forehead was corded by deep lines that never smoothed out. He was thirty-eight.

The hat dance finished, Irene Mayo pinwheeled towards Melrose. He caught her in his arms, kissed her, and whirled her off through a door. The house yelled its throat dry, but the red-headed girl did not return. The slick-looking number took the bows.

McFee said, 'Not bad,' and finished his coffee.

McFee strolled through a door which opened into a red-carpeted hall, pushed through a door in the wall opposite and joined half a dozen men drinking at a bar. The bar was a swivel arrangement that could be swung into the hall behind it on a couple of minutes' notice.

The barkeep said, 'What'll you have, McFee?'

'Straight.' As the barkeep set up his goods, McFee asked, 'Comp'ny tonight, Ed?'

'I dunno,' the man muttered.

McFee walked into the gaming room, which adjoined the bar. Roulette, black jack and craps were running. There were no windows in the room. The only entrance to it was from the bar. The games were at the lower end of the room, and it was possible to swing a false wall across the tables as quickly as the bar could be made to vanish. The device was superficial, but all the roadhouse ever had needed. Some twenty or thirty people were playing, their voices feverish and blurred. Now and then a word pattern emerged. 'You pick 'em – we pay 'em . . . Get your money down . . . Six . . . point is six . . . twenty-one . . . throws a nine. Take your money . . .'

Art Kline stood near the crap dealer. He looked at McFee, flexed his shoulder muscles, looked away. It was twenty minutes of midnight.

Walking into the hall, McFee glanced down it to where Melrose had his rooms. A woman's voice lifted hysterically for an instant above the harsh overtones of the Shawl. Art Kline stuck his head into the hall. When he saw McFee, he pulled it back. McFee smiled coldly, waited a minute, then went past the bar to a side door.

It was light outside. He walked to the rear of the building. Here it was dark. Trees threw tall shadows. Light came from a curtained window behind some shrubbery. McFee glanced around, then pushed through the shrubbery. It plucked at his face and throat. The window curtains did not quite meet and he was able to see into the room. He saw a soft, intimitate room and a floor with a yellow parchment shade. Irene Mayo reclined in a plush upholstered chair beneath the lamp. Sam Melrose sat on an arm of the chair.

The red-headed girl laughed provocatively. Melrose bent towards her. She pushed him away, her fingers on his lips. They talked a while, Melrose leaning attentively over the girl. McFee heard her slightly hysterical laugh and Melrose's bleak chuckle, but Dutch Louie and His Pals drowned out their conversation.

The room had three doors. One led into the hall, another opened into a small washroom, the third gave entrance from the business office. A red carpet covered the floor. An ornate flat-topped desk stood in one corner, a chair behind it, a cloak tree beside it. On the desk was a wire letter basket.

Melrose got up and went into the business office, closing the door behind him. Irene Mayo came sharply forward onto her feet. She stared at the closed door, an obsessed look on her face. She ran swiftly towards the ornate desk, bent over the wire basket. McFee saw a flat manila envelope in her hand, and muttered, 'Swell!'

Someone behind him said, 'We got you covered, McFee.'

McFee turned slowly, his palms tight against his thighs. Three men in dinner jackets stood on the other side of the shrubbery, guns in their hands. One of them was Art Kline. An ascetic-looking man with disillusioned eyes and a plume of gray hair on his white forehead had addressed McFee. This was Fred Pope, who ran the Red Jacket, a Melrose enterprise.

Their faces gleamed a little. Their shirt fronts stood up like slabs of stone.

Fred Pope said, 'Sam wants to talk to you, McFee.'

'I had a notion he might.'

'Come outta that.'

McFee stepped into the triangular huddle the three men had made of their bodies. They took his gun away from him.

'Straight ahead,' Pope said. 'No monkey business.'

A private door gave them access to the business office. There were comfortable chairs, a couple of mahogany desks, safe, telephone, and a filing cabinet. A desk lamp was lighted. The hall door opened and Sam Melrose entered, a cobwebby bottle in his hands.

When he saw McFee the lines that corded his forehead tightened until they looked like wires embedded in his skull. He set the bottle down, came towards McFee with quiet, quick steps. Fred Pope laughed, dropped into a chair. Kline and the other man laid their backs against the outer wall.

An electric clock on the filing cabinet indicated seven minutes of twelve.

Sam Melrose said, 'McFee, I want that Grand Jury Shelldon file.'

'Don't be a sap.'

'What do you mean?'

'You got it already, Sam.'

'McFee, you been handing my boys that line ever since they ran you down in the Gaiety this morning. I'm damn good and sick of it.' Melrose's flat-surfaced eyes distended coldly. 'But I'll give you a break. You shoved your nose into my business – got what I paid money for. All right – come through with that file and we quit even. You walk outta here. You go home. You forget everything you figured on remembering. And you let my business alone after this. When I get this town like I want it I'll throw some sugar your way. Where you put that file?'

McFee smiled, felt for a cigarette, put it in his mouth. He flipped a match at it. Anger puffed across Melrose's eyes, subsided. The two hard-faced men started forward, but fell back at Melrose's gesture.

The clock showed four minutes of twelve.

McFee said, 'Lemme see, there's a murder tied up with that Shelldon blow-off, isn't there, Sam?'

'I can beat it.'

'What's the idea, then?'

'It looks bad, election coming on. I want it outta the way.'

'Wait a minute, Sam. You got Leclair to make a deal with Damon. Damon is dead. His mother is dead. And the old lady didn't turn on the gas—' McFee paused, considered the other indulgently. 'Can you beat all that, Sam?'

Melrose cut in harshly, 'My boys didn't rub out Damon and his mother.'

'Well, you oughta know. If that Shelldon file don't turn up at the wrong time, maybe the taxpayers'll believe you. It's funny what taxpayers'll believe. But the Damon-O'Day murders and the Shelldon racket'd make a bad combination.' McFee laughed. 'That Shelldon file's getting pretty important, Sam.'

Melrose said, 'Ten grand, McFee?'

'I haven't got it.'

'Listen, mister—' The lines that corded Melrose's frontal bone deepened again. 'I dunno what you playing for, but if it's to put the bell on me you got the wrong cat by the tail. I'm running this town. I'm gonna keep on running it. Nob'dy can get to first base unless I say so. McFee—' he prodded the latter in the chest, '— I want that Shelldon file. If you don't come across my boys'll walk you out and leave you some place.'

The clock said one minute of twelve.

Dragging on his cigarette, McFee muttered, 'Well, I dunno—'

The telephone rang.

Melrose picked it up. He did not remove his eyes from McFee, as he said, 'Melrose talking.' . . . And then, 'Yes, Joe . . . Yes, what's that? . . . McFee – That red-head – His sidekick – But you phoned – What? . . . A frame-up – . . . You dunno . . .' Melrose's violent eyes impaled McFee. The latter stood stiffly, sweat on his temples. Melrose said coldly, 'I got both of 'em here – Oh, McFee'll talk—'

Comprehendingly, Art Kline, Fred Pope and the other man crowded McFee. As Melrose rang off, he said, 'Watch McFee!' and jumped toward his private room, jerked the door open. His eyes were hot when he faced around. 'She musta heard – Fred, that redhead's the Mayo woman. McFee brought her – a frame – Bring her back.'

As Fred Pope went away, Melrose said quietly, 'What's back of this Mayo woman coming here?'

'Some'dy's been kidding you, Sam.'

'You gonna talk?'

'Nothing to talk about.'

'Lemme work on him a while, Boss,' Art Kline said.

It was two minutes after twelve.

McFee shook the sweat out of his eyes. Dutch Louie and His Pals were tearing a staccato jazz out of their horns. The music swelled, filled the house with crashing sound. But McFee could hear the ticking of his watch, the pounding of his heart.

'Listen to the music, Sam,' he said.

Melrose shouted, 'By God, McFee, if you won't talk my boys'll burn it out of your toes—'

McFee struck him in the mouth. As Melrose went backwards, Kline and the other men jumped in. They milled for a minute. McFee got home four or five good ones, but he was taking a beating when the music stopped. The house became completely quiet.

A police whistle shrilled out in the cafe room.

Melrose ejaculated, 'The coppers! I forgot—' And then, 'I'll fix those birds—' He checked himself, said less positively, 'Art, you stay here—'

McFee cut in softly, 'You can't do it.' Melrose glared at him, dabbed a cut lip with a handkerchief. 'Sam, you are in a spot. Littner and Cruikshank are out there. You didn't s'pose I'd walk in here without having my tail covered? I told Littner to look for me.'

'Lotta good that'll do you,' Melrose said harshly. To his men, 'Take McFee down the beach – the shack. Keep him there till I come.'

Art Kline stood behind McFee. 'Get going, sap,' he said, in his gummed-up voice, and shoved metal into McFee's back.

As McFee moved towards the side door, Littner entered.

Melrose's eyes turned white. Kline and the other man stared at him, slid their guns away. Littner looked around with his cold water eyes, rubbed his long jaw.

'Hello, McFee,' he said. 'Sam.'

'Littner,' McFee said.

'Argument?'

'No,' McFee answered. 'Sam bit his lip. He was just going to open a bottle of bubbly.' McFee walked to the desk, picked up the bottle Melrose had placed there. It was moist and cold. 'Seventy-six. Elegant.' He turned to Melrose. 'Got a glass for Littner, Sam?'

Melrose stared at McFee, his flat eyes inflamed. He did not speak. A flood of sound, shot through with panic, filled the house. Women screamed, glassware shattered. Melrose wiped his mouth, felt at his throat, pulled in a long breath. Then he sullenly crossed to the filing cabinet and took three glasses, a corkscrew and a napkin out of the bottom drawer. McFee ceremoniously handed him the bottle. Melrose wiped the top of the bottle, wrapped the napkin around it. The cork popped. Melrose poured unsteadily.

McFee said, 'To the next District Attorney.'

They drank.

Blood from Melrose's cut lip turned the 'seventy-six' pink. He muttered blasphemously, held the napkin against his mouth. McFee hung his arm over Melrose's shoulders. A white heat played across the flat surfaces of Melrose's eyes.

McFee asked, 'You got the Mayor out there, Littner?'

'Yes.'

'Buy him a lemonade before you bring him in. Sam and I got business to do.' McFee slapped Melrose's shoulder affectionately. 'Five minutes, Littner.'

McFee linked his arm in Melrose's. Melrose resisted him a moment, then let the other lead him towards the door of the inner room. Littner's eyes followed them, faintly ironical. Art Kline and his companion glared angry bewilderment.

At the door, McFee said softly, 'Tell your boys this is private, Sam.'

Melrose muttered, 'That stands.'

McFee looked at Littner. 'Maybe you better stick close. Some'dy might take a notion.' Littner nodded.

McFee shut the door.

Melrose's face was yellow and wet. 'What's your proposition?'

14

The room had a secretive intimacy that affronted the uncomplicated McFee, but he marched his somber eyes around it. The washroom door stood ajar. It had been shut when McFee had looked in through the window. His eyes dwelt on it a moment. Then he dug out the 'Mr. Inside' notes and handed them to Melrose. 'Take a look at these.'

Melrose said thickly, 'Would my boys have been tailing you all day, if I had that file here?'

'Sure you haven't got it here, Sam?'

'What you mean?'

McFee said slowly, 'Littner and Roy are here to look for it. It'll make a swell story – if they find it in this room – A swell story, Sam—'

Comprehending, Melrose yelled, 'You planted that file here! You and that readheaded tramp – What you done with it?' He dropped his hand into his jacket pocket. He pushed his face into McFee's, said in a low tone, 'You find that file quick, or take it in the belly.'

'Littner's out there, Sam.'

Melrose breathed hard. He took his hand out of his pocket. He wiped sweat out of his eyes, rubbed his palms together. 'I'll bust you for this, McFee.' His eyes slid desperately around the room – chairs, desk, washroom, carpet.

McFee said, 'Sit tight, Sam, or I'll call Littner.'

Melrose began to walk the floor. He stopped abruptly, came to grips with himself. 'Let 'em find it,' he said huskily. 'I can beat the rap.'

'Think so?' McFee chewed a finger nail. 'Damon wasn't so much, but O' Day was his mother. Nob'dy knew it until today. The old girl had about a million friends in this town and all of 'em are beginning to feel sorry for her. You know what people are when they begin feeling sorry. Think you got enough drag to beat the Damon-O'Day-Shelldon combination?'

'My boys didn't rub out Damon and O'Day.'

'This is politics, Sam.' McFee thumbed a match at a cigarette. 'It isn't what a lad does or don't do – it's what his public'll stand for.'

'How d'I know that file's planted here?'

'Call Littner – you'll know then.'

'You found out who killed Damon?'

McFee answered carefully, 'Maybe.'

Melrose pulled up in front of McFee. 'What you want?'

The racket on the cafe floor had dropped to a backlash of irritation and protest. A door opened. Littner spoke to someone. Joe Cruikshank's soprano answered. The Mayor's platform boom cut in.

McFee said, 'Sam, you been running this town long enough. I'm going to take it away from you.'

'Yes?'

'The Mayor's out there telling everybody what a good guy he is.' McFee spoke softly, pulled out the paper he had typewritten at Irene Mayo's. 'The Mayor's your man. Your money elected him, keeps him in the City Hall. This is an unsigned indorsement of Luke Addams' candidacy for District Attorney—'

'A lotta help that'll give him.'

McFee said gently, 'With the City Hall machine and the newspapers pulling for Addams we got a pretty good chance beating Dietrich. Addams in, we work for a new deal in the police hookup – Littner chief. But that's future. Sam, you are going to tell Hizoner to put his John Henry to this declaration of independence, or I give Littner the go sign.' He smiled. 'How 'bout it?'

Melrose raged, 'I will not!' But he was shaken. 'I'll see you—'

McFee cut in, 'You want Littner to use his search warrant? This is politics. I'm telling you.'

Jerking at his wilted collar, Melrose walked to the window. McFee slanted his eyes at the washroom door. He kept them there until Melrose faced around.

'I can throw plenty sugar your way—'

McFee said, 'You are going to need sugar, Sam.'

Melrose opened his mouth, shut it without saying anything, pressed the heels of his hands into his eyes. When he dropped them, his eyes were crazy, and he came charning towards McFee with his hands clenched. Littner entered just then, a brown paper parcel under his arm. Roy Cruikshank was behind him. The Mayor boomed in the outer room. His handsome, silver head was visible for a moment before Cruikshank closed the door. Melrose shook his head, let his hands fall.

Littner sat down, laid the parcel on the floor beside him. He said nothing. His oval head, his cold water eyes said nothing. Cruikshank put a cigarette in his pink mouth, pulled his hat over his eyes and leaned against the wall.

'Do I get that file?' Melrose asked tonelessly.

McFee said, 'Sorry. We got to have a guarantee the City Hall'll root hard enough.' He added reluctantly, 'But I'll give you a break, Sam. I'll show Littner who killed Damon and his mother.'

Melrose wet his lips. 'All right.' McFee handed him the unsigned indorsement. He read it, turned it over, flared out, 'None of my boys killed Damon. By God, McFee if this is another frame—'

McFee said, 'I never framed anybody, Sam.'

As Melrose went out and shut the door behind him, the Mayor's platform boom ceased. A low-toned, bitter argument began. Melrose's voice whiplashed, 'I'm still running this town, Mr. Mayor.'

McFee sat down. His eyes moved towards the washroom door, remained there a moment, came back. He wiped his face.

Littner said mildly, 'Warm for the time of the year.'

'It's some of that unusual weather,' Cruikshank muttered under his hat brim.

'Maybe Sam'll buy us a highball,' McFee said. He laughed softly, looked at the cherubic Cruikshank, at the politically minded Littner. 'Politics is funny. The lad who don't have to put over more than a couple of dirty ones to pull three good members out the bag has a medal coming to him.'

'Some'dy ought to pin a medal on you, Handsome,' Cruikshank said.

'I'm not through with this town yet.'

Melrose came in then, a dull burn on either wet cheek bone. He handed McFee the indorsement, sat down and shelved his chin on his chest. He did not speak, did not look at McFee. The latter examined the signature. A clock ticked loudly somewhere. In the next room the Mayor was booming, 'Luke Addams is a man in whom I have the greatest confidence. It will be a pleasure—' Dutch Louie and His Pals whipped into a jazz.

Parading his eyes around the room, McFee blinked at the washroom door, let them idle on the ornate desk. He went to the desk, bent over the wire basket and looked through the papers in it. He stood erect and stared at the end of his cigarette. A couple of overcoats hung on the cloak tree, near the desk. McFee put a hand inside one of them and brought forth a long manila envelope with 'Shelldon' penciled in one corner. The envelope was open. He glanced into it.

Melrose lifted his head. Rage had contracted his eye pupils, ground them to points of bitter, fierce light. He did not speak.

McFee handed Cruikshank the Shelldon file and the Mayor's indorsement. 'Stick 'em in the Tribune vault a while,' he said.

'Right,' Cruikshank muttered.

15

Littner gave McFee the brown paper parcel. 'No. 3 trash collection wagon brought them in,' he said.

'Very nice,' McFee answered. He sat down, the parcel on his knees. He looked at his watch. 'Twelve-thirty-five. It's just twenty-four hours since a lady came to see me, at Cato's. She said the lad she was with, Rance Damon, had gone into the Gaiety about an hour before. She said he'd followed Sam Melrose—'

Melrose ejaculated, 'He did not. I was on Scudder's yacht. I got all the alibis—' He stopped there, wiped his mouth on the napkin. 'You birds got nothing on me.'

McFee proceeded softly, 'The lady and I got into the Gaiety. Damon had been shot. He died. Some'dy had stepped on a tube of grease paint. Crimson. Smeared it around. Damon's body walked out. I found it in Maggie O'Day's. Maggie was his mother. She had rolled him home in her wheel chair. Maggie was dead – gas. But there was a bruise on her head. Maybe she fell. Maybe she was slugged. I found a smear of crimson grease paint on a newspaper on the floor. There was no grease paint on Maggie's shoes or Damon's. Very well. I figured this way: The party killed Damon stepped on the tube of grease paint, in the dark, bust it open, got all smeared up. Grease paint is bad. Maggie saw that party beating it out the Gaiety. The party followed Maggie home, to see how come Maggie accused the party of murdering her son and got slugged – with her own crutch, maybe. The gas was to make it look like suicide – grief. The party's shoe smeared the newspaper. The party didn't know it, went away. Now grease paint is hard to clean off fabric goods, and when the party saw what'd happened to a nice pair of shoes it looked like a good idea to get rid of 'em. Sounds easy. Only it isn't. Littner's men found 'em at the city trash collection dump.'

McFee unrolled Littner's brown paper parcel. A pair of green satin pumps fell out. He held one of them up. The sole, instep, and right side of the pump were smeared with crimson grease paint.

Melrose blurted, 'That lets my boys out.'

McFee lighted a cigarette, looked at the match a while. 'I said a lady came to see me at Cato's. She was wearing green satin pumps – these pumps. When I took her home three hours later she was wearing green snakeskin slippers. She beat it out the Gaiety and phoned headquarters around 1:30. I picked her up on Third at 3:15 – nearly two hours. That gave her plenty time to tail Maggie O'Day home, kill her, get back to the car, drive to her apartment – taking the Shelldon file with her – change her shoes, and get back to Third.'

McFee rolled a match in his ear. 'But I couldn't figure out why Irene Mayo killed Damon. Wasn't she going to make him Governor, herself the Governor's lady? So I went back to the Gaiety and ran a string along what looked like the bullet trajectory. There was a horizontal groove in the door jamb level with the line the bullet followed—'

A muffled, sobbing sound interrupted McFee and terminated in a wail of despair. McFee wiped his face and throat with a handkerchief. A bitter, silent moment went by.

McFee said deliberately, 'Irene Mayo wrote those "Mr. Inside" notes. She planted that Shelldon file here because Melrose's blonde had taken Damon with five grand. She wasn't with Damon last night. She tailed him down to the Gaiety. Melrose wasn't there. Slick little number. She tried to pull a fast one at her apartment this morning with a "Shelldon" envelope full of blanks. Said she'd found it on Damon while I was in Leclair's room. Said it had fooled her. Well, she pretty near fooled me.' McFee stared gloomily at his cigarette. 'Damon must have given her that gun – Metz' gun. She didn't intend to kill him – the lad she was going to make Governor. No. She fired at Leclair. Because Leclair was gumming up the works. You can't figure women. The bullet richochetted from the door jamb, took Damon—'

That tortured cry came again, McFee got up, walked towards the washroom door.

A pistol shot reverberated in the room.

McFee took three strides forward. The door leaned open. He caught the redheaded girl in his arms. He carried her to a chair, laid her in it. Littner, Melrose, Cruikshank stood around. People came rushing in, the Mayor booming . . .

McFee said, 'I had a notion she'd do it.' And then, huskily, 'I never was much of a lad for hanging a woman.'

DOUBLE CHECK
THOMAS WALSH

Nightmare in Manhattan, Thomas Walsh's first novel, one of the most exciting police novels ever written, was rightly awarded the Edgar Allan Poe Award by the Mystery Writers of America as the Best First Mystery of 1950.

Walsh, however, had been writing for the pulps since 1933, and then wrote numerous stories for such better-paying 'slicks' as *Collier's* and *The Saturday Evening Post*, as well as numerous contributions to *Ellery Queen's Mystery Magazine*. He won his second Edgar for the short story 'Second Chance' in 1978.

When his prize-winning novel was made into a motion picture in the same year in which it was published, the title was changed to *Union Station*, clearly New York's Grand Central Station under a pseudonym. It was well-adapted from the printed page to the screen, losing none of its tension. The entire plot occurs within a 48-hour period and the notion of a deadline looming, while now a cliché of thriller movies, was still fresh when Walsh (1908–1984)) wrote this, the first of his eleven novels.

He wrote a half-dozen stories for *Black Mask* in the 1930s, and 'Double Check' was the first; it appeared in the issue of July 1933.

DOUBLE CHECK

THOMAS WALSH

Devine was a small, slender man, thin-featured, and quick of manner. His hair and the wisp of mustache on his upper lip were deep black. His sharp eyes, wrinkled at the corners, watched the man across from him with a mixture of anxiety and forced lightness as he spoke.

'You must understand that I'm not taking it seriously,' he said.

Flaherty nodded. He knew the type – money, position, pride and a manner that told nothing whatsoever of the man himself.

The banker's low voice went on more rapidly:

'I received the first letter two weeks ago. After that they kept coming at intervals of two or three days. Of course I paid them no attention – men in my profession are constantly getting letters of this type. Cranks, most of them. But yesterday they put in a phone call here to my office; it was then that I decided to send for the police. Professional advice, you know—' He smiled faintly with an uncertain upward curl of the lips.

Flaherty nodded. 'The right thing to do,' he said. 'Have you got the letters?'

Devine turned slightly in his chair, pressing one of the white-disced buzzers at his side. 'Why, no. Unless Barrett – my secretary – kept them. I didn't imagine—'

A tall man with gray eyes, gray clothes, grayish-brown hair, came noiselessly through the door. He stared coldly at Flaherty after a brief nod.

'No,' he answered, when Devine repeated the question. 'Sorry – I threw them in the waste-paper basket; in fact, it seemed the best place for that kind of rubbish. I had no idea they were necessary.'

Flaherty's lean young face soured. Snobby guy, he thought. 'You should have saved them. Sometimes there's a lot to be got out of stuff like that. Hold any more.' He turned back to Devine. 'What did the phone call say?'

'It came in about noon. When I picked up the receiver there seemed to be two voices at the other end. But they were speaking too far away from the instrument for me to make out the words. Oh, yes – I think I got one; something like Ginger or Jigger. I took it for one of the men's names. When I said hello a voice replied: "We're not fooling. Have the money by noon Thursday. No police. If you're ready to pay put an ad in the *Morning*

Herald to Charlie. We'll let you know what to do with it." Then they hung up.'

'That all?' Flaherty asked, shortly. At the banker's nod he rose and gripped his hat. 'Don't do anything until you hear from me; I'll phone you tonight. We might have to put that ad in the morning paper to get them. There's nothing to worry about.'

Devine's thin features broke in a smile he couldn't quite control; his tongue tipped out nervously for an instant. 'I'm not afraid, of course. I have no intention of paying. They can't frighten me like they would a little shopkeeper. I'll leave it in your hands, Mr. eh – Flaherty.'

Flaherty didn't like that eh stuff so much as he went out. He slammed the door behind him and passed through the outer offices of the First Commercial Bank to the shaded crispness of a late September afternoon. His dark, small eyes flickered right and left along the street. Nothing to stuff like that, usually. Still—

He handed in his report at headquarters and was going down the stairs from the chief's office when he met Mike Martin coming up. Mike was big and paunchy, with a gruff voice and hands like fleshed mallets. Beside the younger, slimly muscled Flaherty he resembled a fat pug next a whippet.

Flaherty grabbed his arm and drew him into a niche by the elevator shaft. 'Just the man, Mike. You're working with me on an extortion case. Old man's say-so.'

'The old man's getting' smart,' said Mike. 'He musta wanted someone with brains on the job.'

'Yeh,' said Flaherty. 'And he thought you'd pick up a little experience. It's Conrad Devine, head of the Commercial Bank.'

Mike took a cigarette from Flaherty's pack and puffed slowly.

'Devine?' he said. 'They're not picking smart. There's talk the Commercial's about to crash.'

Flaherty grunted. 'What bank ain't?' he said. 'They called him up yesterday. He says he heard one of the names – it sounded like Jigger to him.'

Mike spat thoughtfully into the corner of the wall. 'Jigger? That might be Jigger Burns – been pretty quiet for a while now. But he don't figure in a case like this.'

Flaherty said: 'That's the way I got it. This ain't the Jigger's line. But anything'll do these days.'

'Let's see,' said Mike. 'Jigger's a peter man – expert on nitro. He's cracked enough jackboxes to blow us to hell.' He stared at Flaherty wide-eyed, without seeing him. 'I saw him in Joe's place Monday night – fourteen minutes to eight. He was wearin' a blue suit, white spats, yella gloves—' Mike stopped admiringly. 'Yella gloves! The old lady bought me some last Christmas, but I'm damned if I could ever wear 'em. I had to tell her they were lost. He was talkin' to Johnny Greco.'

'You're fading,' said Flaherty. 'I didn't hear you mention his tie. What you got on Johnny Greco?'

'Tough,' said Mike, spitting again. 'Thirty-five; five feet eight; one sixty on the hoof; dark hair and eyes; scar on right eyebrow. Up twice for assault – once for homicide. Acquitted – no witnesses. He—'

'Can it,' said Flaherty. 'I know the ginny. Davis brought him in on a loft job last week, but had to drop him on a writ. He plays around with a Polack girl at the *Esplanade*. We could stop there this evenin' and pick him up.'

Mike looked at his watch. 'Make it nine,' he said. 'The old lady's havin' company, and she'll want me around for a bit.'

'Run along,' said Flaherty bitterly. 'They oughta put married coppers on desk duty, with aprons and bibs. I'll bet you look sweet with a baby blue dishtowel spread on that belly of yours. What do you use to make your wash so white, Mr. Martin?'

'Honest to gawd,' Mike scowled, 'some day, Flaherty, I'm gonna lay you like a rug.'

The long vertical sign threw a rush of dirty yellow light across the pavement. The lettering winked on and off rapidly: *Esplanade – Dancing 25c.*

Two dusty, fly-spattered doors gave into a hallway with shabbily carpeted stairs leading up. A quick rush of music, undertoned by voices and sudden, whirled-away gusts of laughter, swept against his ears as Flaherty stepped in, holding the door back for Mike Martin. Flaherty was neat and slender in a brown suit and wine-colored tie; behind him Mike was in gray, unpressed and shiny. His tie was crooked and his soft collar folded up in clumsy flabs.

Flaherty gritted his teeth. 'You're the type, fella; watch the girls fightin' for you when we get upstairs. By —— a blind man miles off could tell you were a copper.'

'They could,' said Mike. 'The old man mighta wanted a cop on the job as well as a jiggollo. If I'd had my good suit back from the tailor's—'

'Yeh,' said Flaherty. 'I'll work inside. Stick by the door, Mike, and try to hide behind a cuspidor. Come on.'

Mike followed slowly up behind his partner's quick legs. At the stairhead Flaherty tossed a quarter to a girl in a window, and was passed through the turnstile by a tall, pimply faced man with glasses. A small anteroom, lit dimly by wall clusters of frosted red bulbs, and furnished with stuffed lounges and wood-backed settees, opened before him; past this the larger space of the ballroom spread from side to side of the building.

Flaherty pushed his way slowly along the side, looking over the crowd. He came back to the door, went around a second time, a third. After he smoked a cigarette and danced once with a plump brunette he walked out to where Mike was waiting in a chair near the door.

'No luck,' he said. 'Johnny and the Jigger aren't showing. Maybe they will be in later. We'd better stick.'

Mike nodded. Time passed slowly. Now and again men came up the stairs and pushed through the turnstile, greeting the pimply faced guardian as they passed. Flaherty grew restless, lit one cigarette from another, took a few quick puffs and quenched them in the sand bowl at his feet.

They had been waiting almost an hour when a little sallow-faced man came up the stairs and went past them to the men's room. Mike jerked his head.

'Joey Helton, Flaherty. We can give him a try.'

Flaherty nodded and followed him across the room to the door. Inside, the little man was washing his hands at the sink. He didn't turn as they entered but jumped quickly when Mike said: 'Hello, Joey.' The sharp rat's eyes flickered from one to the other, narrowed and beady.

Flaherty said, smiling thinly: 'Hello, Joey. We got some news for Johnny the Greek. Seen him lately?'

'I ain't,' said the little man. 'What's the news?'

'He's been left a dirty pair of socks,' said Flaherty. 'We wanta see him about washin' them up. Try to remember, Joey.'

The little man snarled suddenly. 'To hell with you!' He stepped by them with a quick twist of his body for the door.

Flaherty's arm yanked him back, thrust the small body against the sink. 'Easy, Joey. Three months without a sniff would soften you up.'

Joey glanced at Mike's stony face, licked his lips weakly. He said: 'All right. I don't know nothin' about the Greek; he's been comin' here pretty often, and hangin' out with that Polish skirt. That's all I see.'

'That's all I want,' said Flaherty. 'You're a good boy, Joey. When you go out step up to the Polack and say something. But nothin' about this. Got it?'

'Yeh,' said Joey. He straightened his tie sullenly and went out. A second later they followed.

Flaherty reached the edge of the dance-floor a yard behind the little man. He watched him thread a way through the crowd, stop before a tall blonde girl near the front. She nodded, turned away, and Joey went on again.

Flaherty went back to Mike. 'I'm gonna call Devine,' he said. 'Stick here.'

'Okey,' said Mike. 'I'll wait.

Flaherty went past the ticket-taker to a phone booth at one side. He thumbed through the book, got his number, dropped a nickel in the box. When he announced himself a man's voice said: 'Just a moment, sir.' He was trying to get a cigarette from his pack with one hand when a quick, staccato voice broke metallically in the earpiece.

'Mr. Flaherty?' Flaherty grinned a little; there was no eh stuff this time. Devine's voice quivered and ran up swiftly, like a child's. 'I've got another message – by phone. They threaten to kill me tonight. They found out about you. My——! You must get out here at once. If they—'

Flaherty got out his cigarette and scraped a match against the side of the booth. He said: 'Don't get excited. We'll have some men out there in ten minutes, maybe less. They're trying to scare you into it. Don't worry.'

He hung up. Scared as hell now, but tough enough this afternoon when the steam wasn't on. No guts, that kind. . . .

Mike was waiting for him. 'Wanta hop out to Devine's?' Flaherty said. 'Pick up a man on your way. He's got the jitters – thinks they're gonna spot him tonight. I'll stick here; maybe I can get something from the Greek's girl. Call me when you get there.'

Mike said: 'Okey,' and went out towards the stairs. Flaherty stepped on to the dance-floor and looked about. The girl Joey Helton had spoken to was off at one side, in a row of chairs reserved for hostesses. Flaherty walked across the floor and stopped before her. 'Dancing this one?' he asked.

She nodded, looked up without interest. When the music started they glided out to the floor. She was as tall almost as Flaherty, with blonde, short-clipped hair, and a heavy sensuous mouth. Her eyes were dark blue, thick-lidded.

They danced on without speaking. When the number was over, Flaherty said: 'Thanks. You can step, sweetheart. Have the next?'

She responded with a faint shrug of her bared shoulders. The lights dimmed down and a young man in the band laid aside his instrument, began to croon in a sleepy voice through a small megaphone.

She had a firm, supple curved body. She kept her head turned, eyes over his shoulder. He shifted, tightened his hold.

'You're nice,' he said. 'Me, I think so. Too nice to waste your time on greaseballs.'

She didn't say anything for a moment; then she spoke from the side of her mouth, not turning her head. 'Greaseballs?' she said.

'Sure,' said Flaherty. 'You know who I mean. The little ginny I saw you dancing with last night.'

Her face swung up to his, whiffing with it a cheap reek of perfume across his nostrils. There was a faint mocking gleam under her mascaraed lashes.

'I was not here last night.' Her voice was low, husky, with a thin blur of accent.

Flaherty laughed. 'Musta been the night before. I see you with him a lot. Steady?'

She shrugged, humming the song the band played, deep in her throat.

'I get breaks like that,' Flaherty said. 'Any chance of ditchin' him for dinner tonight?'

'No,' she said. 'I got a sick mother.'

'I know the song,' Flaherty answered. 'The old man ain't so well and you're keepin' the kid sister in a convent. All right, girlie; I'll see you again.'

When the music was over he let her go back to her seat. She was meeting someone, probably; he'd have to take a chance on that being Johnny Greco. He resigned himself to wait, looking at his watch. Twenty minutes past ten; Mike's call would be due now.

He walked out to the anteroom and smoked a cigarette. When the phone in the booth tinkled he went across and into it before the pimply faced man could turn.

'Hello,' he said.

'Flaherty?' Under Mike Martin's furred voice pulsed a ripple of excitement. 'Better get out here quick, boy. Some laid a pineapple in Devine's car. The chauffeur and him was blown to hell not five minutes ago.'

Flaherty got a taxi at the corner and stared tense-eyed into the darkness during the ten-minute ride. What was coming off? Johnny Greco was no fool; neither was Jigger Burns. Bumping a guy was a dough job – they weren't in it for fun. Devine hadn't come through – they didn't give him time. Force of example, so that the next heavy man they touched wouldn't squawk? That, maybe. He wondered what Mike had seen.

The cab swung into the quiet darkness of Magnolia Avenue. Three blocks farther on, a knot of people huddled together under the pale glint of a street lamp. Lights gleamed from houses all about; hastily clad people grouped in doorways, called to each other in shrill tones from window to window.

Flaherty got out and paid the driver. 'Wait ten minutes,' he said.

Devine's house was set back from the road on a low terrace. Flaherty saw it as a large three-story building, with a curve of graveled driveway leading whitely up across the dark lawn. A thick hedge banked it on the street side; when Flaherty cut in through this on the driveway a uniformed figure stepped out before him. He was fishing for his badge when Mike Martin came out from the shadows.

'All right, Smith,' he said. 'Get the crowd away. It's up here, Flaherty.'

They went up in silence to the top of the hill. Lights poured from the ground-floor windows, sending a flood of illumination across grass and shrubbery. Ragged curtain ends fluttered out through the smashed panes; the stoop to the porch sagged drunkenly, half of it toppled on its side and resting on the earth. The porch itself had been a Colonial affair, tall, white, with slim pillars and a curved portico. Three of the pillars were snapped off in the center, and at the right end a segment of roof hung down like a misshapen curtain.

The car squatted before the house, a foot away from the stoop. In the light it was a twisted and charred mass of grayish metal. The top was blown off, and fragments of glass from its windows littered the ground with little silver shreds of light. At the side nearest Flaherty the metal warped outward in a great hole.

'It's a morgue job,' said Mike. 'You couldn't identify either of them with a microscope.'

Flaherty bent and looked inside. When he straightened, his face was grayish. 'Cripes!' he said.

'Yes,' said Mike. 'Messy, hah?'

'Did you see it go up?'

Mike spat and nodded. 'We'd just got here,' he said. 'I grabbed Smith at the station and we came out in the flivver. I didn't see anybody in the street. I told Smith to wait and crossed over. Then I saw a little guy in a top hat come down the stoop and get into the car.'

Flaherty scowled at his feet. 'Devine,' he said. 'I thought the damn' fool would know enough to stick inside.'

'I heard the starter begin to purr – just for a second. Then I felt the pineapple bust loose. I didn't see anything – it slammed me back through the bushes like I was a laundry bag. When I got up here it was all over.'

Flaherty lit a cigarette and tossed the match in the grass. For a second the flame scooped his lean, sharp face out of the shadow.

'They might have had it wired to the motor. But then why the hell didn't it blast out comin' from the garage? What was the chauffeur doin'? Did he leave the bus at all after bringin' it out?'

'I don't know,' Mike answered. 'I haven't had time to talk to the servants. They're so scared they're blubberin'. They got an English butler in there you should see, Flaherty. Gawd! He'll give the laundry a job this week.'

'See what the chauffeur was doin'.' Flaherty said. 'You might get a tip questionin' the people around here. I'm goin' back for Johnny Greco and the Jigger. This is where the nitro came in, Mike.'

Blocks distant a siren screamed. Flaherty tossed aside his cigarette.

'That's probably the old man. Devine was a big shot in this burg; he'll wanta know how come. I'll leave you get the congrats, Mike. So–long. I'll phone you at headquarters later.'

Mike cursed bitterly. 'You yella—' he said. 'The old man will save some for you. I'll see to that.'

At the corner Flaherty's taxi swerved to avoid the police car, then straightened out along Magnolia Avenue. They made good time; it was ten minutes past eleven by Flaherty's watch when they pulled up before the *Esplanade*.

The crowd inside was thicker, gayer, noisier. Flaherty sifted through the mob, passed to the anteroom, came back to the dance-floor. The blonde was nowhere in sight. He went out to the gate; to the pimply faced man on duty he said: 'Where'd the tall blonde go? That Polack girl—'

The man shrugged. 'She left ten minutes ago.'

Flaherty cursed. 'Where does she live?' he snapped.

'I'm not runnin' that kind of place,' pimply face said. Behind the lenses his eyes were small and guarded. 'There's plenty of blondes in there, guy.'

Flaherty yanked him around; he said, hard-eyed: 'Where does she live?'

Pimply face licked his lips uncertainly and then shot out his jaw. 'What you lookin' for, guy? Trouble? I told you—'

'Yeh,' said Flaherty. 'I heard you the first time. I guess you ain't got the records. You're in a spot, fella. You know the regulations on joints like this.'

Pimply face tried to hold his stare and failed. He said sullenly: 'Sure I got the records. Wait a minute. I'll see.'

He went across to the window, spoke to the girl inside, and came back with a small white filing slip in his hand. 'Anna Brinski – 213 Allington Place,' he said, raising his eyes furtively to Flaherty's. 'What's the trouble? Any—'

Flaherty let his words drift out without answering. He took the stairs three at a step and turned left at the door. Four blocks over, Allington Place emptied into the avenue: a narrow, darkly lit thoroughfare, with two parallel rows of cheap brownstone tenements leading down. He found 213 by counting off six houses from the corner; the numbers over the door, faded by time and weather, were indistinguishable in the gloom.

In the vestibule he struck a match, passing the flame over the bells. He read near the end: Anna Brinski, Apt. 43. The door swung back at his touch, admitting him to a narrow hall, palely lit.

He went up on his toes, two steps at a time, without sound. A radio moaned harshly in one of the flats, squawked with a sudden inrush of static as he passed; he caught fragments of voices, snores, the lingering thick odor of fried fish.

At the top of the flight a single bulb glowed weakly, shedding a wan light over the apartment doors. There were six on each floor; the one numbered three was in an angle near the front. When he got to the fourth landing Flaherty stopped and listened; he could hear nothing but the high querulous voice of a drunken woman below.

His footsteps patted on the oilcloth, slid off into the darkness with low echoes. He rapped sharply, twice, on the door of 43 – there was no bell.

After a minute of quietness someone said inside: 'Who's there?'

Flaherty said hoarsely: 'Anna? Johnny sent me over. He can't meet you tonight. He's bein' tailed.'

She said something short, bitterly. Flaherty grinned. When the door opened a crack he laid his body against it and pushed.

The room inside was brightly lit. There was a day-bed at one end, not yet made up, a messy dressing-table across from it, a tall floor-lamp with a torn shade near the window. The air was drenched with the brassy smell of burnt out cigarettes. Clothes littered the couch, poured over on to the floor; an open suitcase lay on the small center-table.

'So you're goin' away,' said Flaherty, leaning against the door. 'You shoulda let me know, Anna.'

Her hair was down, stuck with curlers; she was wearing a sleazy dressing-gown. She smiled softly, but her eyes kept the same.

'The cheap bull,' she said. 'Where do you think?'

'No fun,' said Flaherty. 'I'm asking, Anna.'

He locked the door behind him and went across to the hall at one end that led into the tiny kitchenette and bath. Both were empty.

He grinned coming back. 'So Joey Helton squeaked to you after all. We'll have to mark him up a point.'

She sat down on the couch and picked a cigarette from the heavy bronze smoking-stand at the side. 'What do you want?' she said.

'Nothin' much,' said Flaherty. 'Where were you gonna meet Johnny Greco?'

She shrugged. Her gown slipped down and she pulled it up, lazily, with one hand. 'I don't know him – this Johnny.'

Flaherty's eyes narrowed. 'You're wastin' your time on that stuff, sister. Where were you to meet him?'

She stared down at the cigarette in her hand without answering. Flaherty turned away from her and walked over to the suitcase. He thumbed through the flap in the top. He picked up the garments one by one, felt them through, dropped them to the floor. Her eyes changed color, darkened, in the cone of light from the lamp. She spat out something that Flaherty couldn't understand.

He stared at her for a second. 'Don't say it in English,' he said. 'I'm the kind of guy that hasn't got any chivalry.'

When the bag was empty he went over to the couch and reached down for the pocket-book she had tried to hide with her back. As he bent for it she was on him like a tigress, without warning. He snapped his elbow up under her chin, felt the jarring click of teeth coming together as her knee shot up viciously to his stomach, stabbing him with pain. He grabbed her wrist; his grasp tightened, twisted until she moaned suddenly and went soft in his arms. He dropped her roughly to the couch and picked up the bag.

'Any more?' he asked.

She lay staring up at him, her eyes blazing. After a minute Flaherty turned his attention to the bag. Two folded pink strips of paper were on top; he shook them out, dropping his eyes along the lines. 'Los Angeles!' He whistled. 'Gettin' out far, weren't you? The other one for Johnny—' He put them in his pocket. 'Get dressed, kid; I'm gonna take you for a little ride downtown. I know a couple of guys there that have the knack of getting' questions answered.'

She sat up sullenly, rubbing her wrists. He tossed her a dress from the heap and fished in his pockets for his cigarettes. He was taking them out when knuckles rapped quickly on the door.

Half into the dress she stopped, looked up. Her mouth opened. Flaherty's grasp yanked her head back in an instant.

'Quiet,' he said softly. 'It'll be better for you later, Anna.'

The knuckles rapped again. In two steps Flaherty was by the door, swinging it back, hidden as it came. Anna stood motionless by the couch.

A tall, gray-clad man entered, his head jerking forward as he saw her. He spoke quickly, without breath. 'Anna! It's all set. I—'

He might have heard Flaherty breathe. In the quick twist of his head under a lowered hat brim Flaherty could see nothing but lips and a sharp chin. He said, pushing the door to behind him: 'Drop it, guy.' The other snarled, his eyes wavering for an instant to Anna.

'You dirty little—'

Flaherty shot as the man's gun came out, dropping him limply, suddenly, like a pricked balloon. The short, sharp crash of the gun echoed back from the walls to a beating silence. Flaherty heard faintly the drunken woman still quarreling as he bent over the body.

'You've killed him,' said Anna. Her voice was quiet enough. She stood by the bronze stand, the cigarette in her fingers drifting smoke lazily across her face.

Flaherty said nothing. He gripped the man's shoulders and swung him around back to Anna for a brief moment. At the sound of her rush behind him he straightened too late. On one knee as he brought the gun up he saw the light glinting dully on the edge of the bronze base. Then it crashed down in a vicious arc, before the dark glitter of her eyes. Flaherty fell forward across the dead man, his gun dropping from his hand, his mind whirling and lost in red-streaked confusion.

He was pulled back to consciousness slowly by a throbbing agony over his left ear. When he opened his eyes the light pierced them like tiny knives driving into his skull. He pushed the body away from him, got to his knees, his feet, stood swaying unsteadily as he looked around.

The lights in the room were still lit, but it was very quiet. Anna, of course, was gone. He went out to the kitchen and put his head under the faucet, letting the water pour coldly over his cheek. The skin was unbroken, but there was a lump that felt like an apple where the blow had landed.

After a minute he felt better; he dried off his face and returned to the living-room, looking at his watch. Quarter past twelve. He hadn't been out long; half hour maybe – not more. He gripped the dead body and swung it over on its back.

He found himself looking at the thin, pale face of Barrett, the banker's secretary. There was a hole just over the bridge of his nose. Flaherty squatted on the floor, resting his body on his clenched hands. Barrett!

It came clearer to him in a while. Barrett and Anna – the two of them had framed it from the start. Then where did Johnny Greco and the Jigger come in? Had Anna been using Barrett all the time, ready to ring in the other two for the big prize?

He cursed his aching head. This mixed it up worse than ever. If Barrett was the brains he wouldn't have stood for the blow-up – not without the money. He'd be in a game like this once, for big stakes – but he wasn't the kind to risk it as a steady racket. He hadn't the guts. Then why had Devine been killed without a chance to get the money?

Flaherty couldn't figure it. Unless there was something more, something in back, something he hadn't come upon— He pushed back the dead man's coat and turned out his pockets. A wallet, dark leather, well used; a few bills, a letter, some cards; a slip of white paper, without inscription, marked in hasty handwriting – 1934. That was all.

He put the paper in his pocket, picked up the gun, and rose. He closed the door behind him, leaving the lights still lit and the dead eyes of Barrett staring glassily at the ceiling. The hall was pretty quiet as he descended. He wondered if anyone had heard the shot. Taken it for backfire if they had; it wouldn't be healthy to meddle in a joint like this.

He turned left on the pavement and headed for the avenue, grateful for the cool night air that swept over his forehead. He had almost reached the corner when a car turned in. It raced along smoothly, slowed as it passed him. He had an instant's warning in the split-second glitter of steel from the seat.

At his side a row of ashcans flanked the dark space of an area. He dropped to the ground, rolled over, heard the ting of the bullets, sharp and vicious, as they hit the metal cans. He turned quickly in the narrow space, fired twice. The car flashed under the lamps like a black monster, spitting four more stabs of orange from its side before it rounded the corner at the far end and roared away.

Windows slammed up and a man's voice shouted hoarsely. Flaherty rose from his shelter, brushing his pants carefully. It was getting hot now. They'd come back for him, sure enough; if he'd been out five minutes longer, there'd be two stiffs up there now instead of one. Why? What was coming off, so important that they had to get him out of the way?

It was Anna, of course. She was the only one who knew where he was. She had told Johnny, and he came back to finish the job. The game wasn't over yet, then. And whatever was going to happen they were afraid he would spoil – they thought that somehow, somewhere he'd gotten a tip. What the hell could it be?

It worried Flaherty. Did they take him for a sucker, potting at him like that? What was under his double-blanked eyes that he couldn't see?

Farther down the avenue there was an all-night drug-store. Flaherty went in and called headquarters; after a minute he was connected with Mike Martin.

He said: 'Meet me at the corner of Lynch and Holland as soon as you can make it. Things are popping, Mike.'

Outside again he waited in the darkened entrance of a jewelry store. Lynch Street, a thoroughfare of office buildings and stockbrokers' firms, stretched dark and silent before him, its blackness interspersed by scattered yellow pools from street lamps. The black bulk of Devine's bank squatted back from the pavement a half block away. Flaherty lit a cigarette and scowled at it. Things had moved fast in ten hours. Now—

A dull monstrous boom, a roll of thunder in a confined space, crashed in one wave down the avenue. A golden flare burst up and expired in an instant behind the glass doors of the Commercial bank.

Flaherty raced up the street, bringing his gun loose. A block away he heard the shrill pipe of a police whistle, and closer at hand the rasping squeal of car brakes. He swung around to see Mike Martin hop off a taxi running-board and rush to him across the sidewalk.

'Take the front,' snapped Flaherty. 'Don't go in. They've not had time to scatter.'

He raced around the side of the building over the grass plot that rimmed it. A door gaped open in the rear, with the red bulb of a night-light on top. In its glow Flaherty saw that the yard, rimmed by a high stone fence in back, was empty. They had to get out the front way then, or around by the grass plot. And they couldn't have, yet. They were bottled.

He got inside, keeping to the shadows. A heavy puff of smoke was rising slowly from the center of the building's long room; as he advanced cautiously it thinned, faded slowly against the high stone ceiling. Between the bookkeepers' desks in back and the glass partitioned cashiers' cages in front there was a wide, iron-gated alcove. The gate was open now, with the sprawled figure of a man before it.

Flaherty was motionless in the shadow, listening. He could hear nothing. Queer, this— They must have known the explosion would be heard, must have known—

After an irresolute moment he stepped over the dead man and into the lighted alcove, automatic ready before him. The huge steel door of the vault was flung outward against the wall, the center of it torn and twisted like paper by the charge. Flaherty gave it a glance and then went back to the watchman, rolling him over. An old, wizened face, not much expression now, a bullet hole through the back of his head. Flaherty got up and went softly to the back door.

Mike stood in the shadows outside, dropping his raised arm when he saw Flaherty.

'The man on beat came up. I left him at the front. See anything, Flaherty?'

Flaherty took a second before answering. 'The watchman's stiff, Mike. He's been dead at least an hour. And the vault's been cleaned of cash.'

'Hell,' said Mike. 'They couldn't have cleaned it; they didn't have time.'

'No,' said Flaherty. 'They didn't have time, Mike – that's the funny part.'

After a second he continued: 'We haven't figured the thing right from the start. There's something in back of this we're not even sniffing. It don't hang together the way it is. If they wanted to rob the bank what did they kill Devine for? He wasn't in the way.'

'I don't get you,' said Mike. 'It's open and shut to me. They bump off Devine but don't get the money. All right – they figure they're in and they might as well get somethin' out of it, so they lam back here and blow the vault. Jigger's opened ones a lot tougher than this cheesebox.'

Flaherty said: 'That's one way, Mike. But why did they clean the vault first and then blow it? That's the only answer – we both know they didn't have time after the charge went off. A guy would do that just for one reason; to make it look—' He stopped. After a breath he said: 'Oh!' softly, and whistled.

Mike moved restlessly. 'What the hell you getting' at?'

'I was just wonderin',' said Flaherty, 'how tall Jigger Burns is.'

'He's a little guy. Not much over five five.'

Flaherty grunted. 'It's beginnin' to fit.' From his upper vest pocket he took a small slip of paper and held it out to Mike. After a minute Mike handed it back. '1934? Don't mean nothin' to me.'

Flaherty rapped out briefly the events of the night. When he had finished Mike said: 'The secretary, hah? I'll be double damned.'

'We ain't got much time. What do you think that number means?'

Mike pushed back his hat. 'A street number, d'ye think—'

'Yeh,' said Flaherty, 'only there ain't a street name on it. It might be a post-office box only there ain't no key. Maybe it's next year.'

Mike stirred uneasily. 'Lay off,' he said. 'Some day, honest to gawd, I'm gonna lay you like a rug.'

Flaherty said: 'I found it on Barrett's body. What's he carryin' it around for? Because it's something important – something he mustn't forget. Take it that way. Then he probably got to meet someone there tonight – they haven't much time – at 1934. It wouldn't be a street number; he'd know the house, and wouldn't hafta mark the number down on paper. You can't run out and hire a house in the middle of the night. Besides the getaway has to be fast, so it would be somethin' they could hire any time and leave when they wanted. What's left? A hotel room?'

'I was gonna say it,' Mike answered. 'If it's a hotel there's only two in town high enough for a number like that: The *Sherman* and the *Barrisford*.'

Flaherty crushed the slip in his pocket. 'There'll be a squad along any minute. Stay till they slow, Mike. Let them go through the place – they won't find anything. Then hop over to the *Sherman*; that's the nearest and busiest. The clerk'll know if I'm upstairs. If I'm not, try the *Barrisford*.'

He left Mike and walked swiftly to the corner after a word to the policeman in front. Three blocks up and two over he entered the lobby of the hotel *Sherman*. From the restaurant in back, swift syncopated strains of dance music floated out, but the lobby itself was almost deserted.

The clerk at the desk was a slight, superior-looking person with a pale face and exquisite hands. When Flaherty flashed the badge his lower lip dropped. He said: 'Oh – oh! Really, I hope—'

Flaherty fumbled for the paper. 'You have nineteen floors, haven't you?'

The clerk looked relieved. 'No,' he said. 'There are only eighteen. Of course—'

Flaherty stopped searching; he cursed and chewed his lip while the little man eyed him apprehensively. 'How tall's the *Barrisford*?' he snapped.

'Sixteen, I believe. I know we're the biggest in town. Eight hundred rooms—'

Flaherty got out the paper and looked again. No mistake: 1934. That settled that. Telephone number – safe deposit vault, maybe? But how—

The clerk cleared his throat nervously. 'It's funny,' he said. 'I don't know whether you— You see, we have to be careful, there are so many superstitious people. We haven't a floor numbered thirteen – we skipped it. Thirteen is fourteen and so on. We really have only eighteen floors though our room numbers run up to nineteen. Now if you—'

Flaherty, turning away, whirled back. 'Who's in 1934? Get it quick. I want the key.'

The clerk jumped at his voice. He came back from the inner office holding a key, his eyes worried.

'A gentleman registered this evening for that room – a Mr Walker. Is there anything wrong? I can't let you have this without our man—'

Flaherty reached over and grabbed the key. 'Who's your house dick – Gilmour? Send him up as soon as you locate him. Tell him to be careful – it won't be a picnic. There'll be shooting.'

He headed across the lobby while the clerk said: 'Oh – oh,' faintly.

At the top floor Flaherty left the elevator and stepped into a long red carpeted corridor, empty and brightly lit. He looked at the room numbers and swung to his left.

Nineteen thirty-four was near the end of the hall. He stood outside, listening. No sound . . . He fitted the key in the lock and twisted the knob an inch at a time, softly. A tiny line of blackness appeared at the crack and Flaherty bent double, slipped through in a flash, silently.

Darkness netted him in, diffused faintly by two windows at the far side. He made out the dim white splotch of a bed to his right – nothing more in the light-blurred focus of his gaze. Nothing happened. He stood motionless an instant, surprised and uneasy, before turning to the wall for the light switch.

The faintest flicker of darkness moved from his left – in the same instant he felt a thin rush of air, and something hard, sharp-edged, crashed viciously into his wrist, knocking his gun to the floor. He dropped, feeling for it, as the lights overhead snapped on. A woman's leg flicked past his hand, kicking the revolver across the rug. Someone said in a soft, oily voice: 'Hold it, Flaherty.'

Flaherty got up slowly to his knees, his lips pressed tight against the pain in his wrist. There were three people in the room: Anna, behind him and to his left, Johnny the Greek near the door, automatic in hand, and a slender small man in a chair, bound to it and gagged.

Johnny's face, edged with a bluish bristle of beard, twisted in a leer. 'Smart guy, Flaherty. Too bad we was expectin' you. Next time you're in a lobby look around. There's telephones.'

'I shoulda thought of a lookout,' said Flaherty. 'But this don't help you, Johnny; I got the joint tied up in a knot. The outside's lousy with cops.'

Johnny sneered. 'Sez you. That stuff don't go, dick – you came into the lobby alone. Your pals'll be along, but that'll be too late to do you any good. We're about through here.' His eyes flickered to Anna. 'Behind him, kid.' To Flaherty he said: 'Get over to that chair, snappy.'

Flaherty went over slowly and sat down, watching his face. There wasn't a chance. Johnny stared at him through narrow lids, his eyes small and hard like balls of black glass. Killer's eyes . . .

'I'll have to get some towels,' Anna said. 'They'll do for his arms.' She moved back of him towards the bathroom.

The little man made sounds under his gag. Flaherty looked at him and saw a large head with blond, oddly streaked hair, pale eyes, clean shaven upper lip.

'What you want?' snarled Johnny. The sounds continued. He dropped one hand and loosened the gag. 'Spit it quick, fella.'

The little man breathed hoarsely once or twice before speaking. He looked at Flaherty and quickly away. His words were rapid, imploring.

'You've got the money – give me a chance to get free. I'll leave you downstairs. If he knows who I am—'

'I know you're Conrad Devine,' said Flaherty. He was stalling for time. Where the hell were Gilmour and Mike Martin? If he could keep them here five minutes— 'You shaved off your mustache and blondined your hair – not a very good job, but good enough to fool anybody who thought you were dead. And who wouldn't?'

The little man snarled savagely; he said to Johnny: 'You see?'

'Sure,' said Flaherty. 'Your bank was on the rocks and you didn't have a nickel to save it. You thought you'd get what you could, so you framed this little racket with Barrett. The fact that you two birds got where you did in a bank is a laugh.

'Barrett knew Anna through going to the dance hall, and she got you in with Jigger Burns. You let Jigger in on it for a cut – you needed him for the bombs. You figured everything was as safe as Gibraltar—

'When I phoned tonight you made out you were scared, asked me to come right out. You cooked up some story for Jigger Burns – you were about the same size – and sent him out to your car when you saw the police flivver arrive. Fitted in one of your top hats, I was supposed to recognize your figger – I'd be too far away to see the face – watch you blown to hell, and give you a perfect alibi. Even the cops wouldn't be dumb enough to suspect a dead man.

'You mentioned Jigger to me at your office so I'd be lookin' for him. That made everything hotsy-totsy: you'd be livin' in another town with enough dough to last you the rest of your life, the police would be lookin' for a guy that was in a thousand bits, and I'd be left holdin' the bag. Yeh—'

Johnny said: 'That ain't such a bad idea, Flaherty. I like to see cops holdin' the bag. We'll give you a start, Devine – but no breaks, guy! Let him loose, Anna.'

There was a sudden quick flicker in Devine's eyes, instantly hid. Flaherty seeing it, said nothing. Anna came over in a moment with the towels and knelt behind Flaherty, pressing his arms together.

Flaherty continued to talk, while Devine stretched himself with a long sigh and went over to the bed, watched carefully by Johnny.

'I got the lead at your bank,' Flaherty droned on. 'The vault was blown after the money was taken. Why? To make it look like a strong-arm job. Whoever pulled it got in the back door with a key, murdered the watchman, and opened the vault with the combination. Then they set the time bomb and beat it. I got to thinkin' about you then, Devine. You had the keys and knew the combinations. There was talk your bank was crackin'; the body in the car couldn't be identified. You didn't have any notes to show me – you were too smart to rib them yourself—'

'Shut up,' snarled Johnny. 'Got him fast, Anna?'

Flaherty laughed. 'And at the end they gypped you, at that. When you got the dough and came back here to lie low for a couple of days before headin' out, the girl friend and Johnny fix you like a baby and take away the candy. Hell—'

The banker's pale eyes were slits of ice. His lips were frozen in a wrenched smile. 'You're very clever,' he said.

Anna yanked the toweling tight. As she began to fasten the knot Flaherty flexed his arms, pushing her backward to the floor. Johnny came forward a step, not watching Devine, his eyes vicious. 'Once more and I drop you, guy.'

Flaherty got it then, watching the set, pinched-in face of Devine as his hand dropped to his overcoat pocket. Johnny had frisked him; had he frisked the topcoat on the bed? The damn' fool – Flaherty got his weight on his toes, ready to leap.

'Yeh,' said Johnny. 'Be a good boy. You ought—'

Anna screamed suddenly, seeing the sudden bulge in the banker's pocket.

'Johnny! He—'

Johnny whirled, opening his mouth. The shot came before he could speak. He gave a puffy, choked grunt, fell flatly to the floor.

At the report Flaherty flung himself face downward behind the bed. Johnny was on the other side, moaning, his gun a foot away from his clenched hand. Flaherty wriggled forward, stretched his arm, grabbed the butt as darkness fell at a click over the room.

There was a rush of feet in the hall and confused shouts. Someone lunged furiously at the door; Flaherty heard Mike Martin's bull voice roaring.

Devine fired twice. The bullets dug splinters from the floor, flung them in Flaherty's face. Flaherty didn't shoot; he crouched back, watching the far wall.

In the darkness Anna kept screaming shrilly, terribly. There was a rustle of motion, a scraping, a sudden rush, before the pale square of the window on the far side was darkened by a slender figure. Flaherty could see it very clearly. He fired once.

The door to the hall crashed back, and a slit of light melted instantly into the greater brilliance of the ceiling bulbs. Mike was by the switch, covering the room. In the doorway stood Gilmour, the house detective, his fat face pale and flabby. 'What the hell!' he said.

Flaherty got to his feet. 'It's all right,' he said. 'The party's over, fella.'

In the center of the room Anna was on her knees over Johnny, sobbing. The Greek didn't seem badly hurt; he sat up and stripped off his bloody coat, cursing sullenly under Gilmour's revolver.

On the other side a breeze from the open window puffed the curtains lightly past the figure of Devine that lay half across the sill. It didn't move.

Flaherty went over and lifted it back from the fire-escape, then reached out and pulled in the yellow leather bag Devine had pushed before him. Under two shirts on top, crisp piles of greenbacks were stacked row on row to the bottom.

Flaherty grunted, caressed them a second with his long fingers. 'What a haul,' he said. 'And I'd have to be a copper.'

Mike Martin's puffy red face showed over his shoulder. 'What's all the shootin', Flaherty? Who the hell is that?'

'Ain't you heard?' said Flaherty. 'It's Santa Claus.'

Mike cursed. 'Honest to gawd,' he said, 'some day, Flaherty, I'm gonna lay you like a rug.'

THE CITY OF HELL!

LESLIE T. WHITE

Barely remembered today, Leslie T. White (1901–1967) was a lifelong member of the law enforcement community, beginning as a ranger on some of the large private estates that dotted the landscape in the California of the early part of the 20th century.

He moved to jobs in the sheriff's office and police department before becoming one of a few highly paid investigators attached to the District Attorney's office in Los Angeles, where he became a largely self-taught expert in fingerprinting, electronic eavesdropping, trailing suspects, photography and other nascent tools of crime fighters.

He had headline-making experiences in the tong wars, battles with communists, helping to solve the Doheny murder mystery, and numerous other major criminal activities in California. These experiences served as the basis for his autobiography, *Me, Detective*, and such novels as *Homicide* (1937), *Harness Bull* (1937) and *The River of No Return* (1941).

His 1943 novel *5,000 Trojan Horses*, was filmed in the same year by Warner as *Northern Pursuit* with a screenplay by Frank Gruber; it was directed by Raoul Walsh and starred Errol Flynn. Ten years later, *Harness Bull* was made into the famous motion picture *Vice Squad* (released in Great Britain as *The Girl in Room 17*) with a screenplay by Lawrence Roman; it was directed by Arnold Laven and starred Edward G. Robinson.

'The City of Hell!' was first published in *Black Mask* in October 1935.

THE CITY OF HELL!

LESLIE T. WHITE

The piercing screams of a woman filled the awed hollow of silence left void by the chatter of a sub-machine-gun and acted as a magnet of sound to suck the big squad car to the scene. Even before the police driver braked the hurtling machine to a full stop, Duane and Barnaby debouched from either side of the tonneau, balanced a moment on the running-boards, and hit the pavement running. Then while the doughty sergeant restrained the hysterical mother, Captain Barnaby went down on his baggy knees beside the broken little body.

It lay across the curb, feet and knees in the street, rag-covered torso flattened on the sidewalk: a tot of three, chubby, with light olive skin and eyes black as a starless night. There were three welling holes staggered across the tiny back and from somewhere beneath rivulets of scarlet inched along the dusty cement like accusing tentacles. A chubby little fist moved convulsively, aimlessly. Barnaby laid one of his great calloused hands over the baby hand, squeezed it, then looked up.

A sea of sullen faces met his frowning gaze; haunted faces with frightened eyes that stared. They formed a thick circle around him, ringing him in with the dead baby, with Sergeant Duane and the crazed mother whose agonized wails stabbed his consciousness.

'What happened here?' he demanded. 'Come on, can't anybody speak?'

He saw they were afraid; their silence showed that. They stared dully at him, then looked at each other. It made him mad. He rocked back on his haunches and grabbed the arm of a little urchin of some eight years.

'You saw it, kid,' he snapped. 'Tell me about it!'

The youngster squirmed, rolled his eyes and, when he saw he could not escape, opened his mouth to speak. A sudden wild shriek from the hysterical woman froze the words in his tiny throat. Barnaby turned his head and met Duane's eyes.

'Take her inside!' he commanded.

As Duane dragged the woman away, the cop on the beat panted up; a moment later the police driver joined them. They drove back the sickened audience and Barnaby once more turned his attention to his child witness.

'Now tell me what happened, kid,' he urged quietly.

159

Sweating and trembling the little chap stuttered out a vivid word-picture of the tragedy. Barnaby absorbed it in dribbles, disconnected fragments that years of bitter experience had taught him to assemble. . . .

A group of children had been playing in the street, happy to be free of school. They hadn't heard the big car until it was almost on them. Then, laughing, they had darted for the sidewalks. Nipper was the dead baby's name. There had been a man walking along the sidewalk in front of little Nipper; it was apparent that he was the object of gunfire. But he had vanished between two buildings just before the hail of lead came to chatter little Nipper's life away. The car hadn't stopped; nobody had taken the number. It had all taken place so quickly. . . .

Captain Barnaby released his grip and the little boy shot from his hand like a freed arrow to vanish into the black maw of a tenement. Barnaby rose, removed his battered fedora and combed his unruly hair with gnarled fingers. His lips moved in a bitter curse that was half prayer. Then the ambulance swerved around a nearby corner, so he left the broken baby and tramped into the house where he had seen Duane take the mother.

He had no trouble locating the room on the third floor; he simply charted his course by the compass of sound. He made his way up finally to stop at the entrance of the poverty-stricken room.

Duane stood with his back to the door, one hip resting against a square table, fists doubled, his face turned towards the sobbing woman in a chair. On one side of her stood a tall, gaunt man, his features twisted in grief as he sought to console her. Opposite was an aged woman whose snow white hair and dark skin reminded Barnaby of looking at a negative. He squared his shoulders and barged inside.

Duane turned, saw him. 'It's their only kid,' he jerked. 'They don't know a thing about it, except that their kiddie's gone.'

Barnaby swore softly, turned to the trio. 'We're the police . . .' he began, but stopped at a scream from the mother.

She jerked out of her seat and faced him, wild-eyed, savage.

'Police!' she shrieked in his face. 'You're just like the gangsters wat kill my baby! You know who did it, but you won't do nothin'! We're only poor people, nobody care if my baby . . .' Her voice trailed into a sob and the gaunt man pulled her back into the chair.

Barnaby swiveled and walked into the corridor. At the head of the stairs, the man overtook him.

'Captain,' faltered the man, 'could you just forget what my wife says? She ain't in no condition. . . . I'm workin' for the city, see, an' I can't afford to lose my position 'cause she lose her head. . . .' He stopped in anxious embarrassment.

Barnaby turned slowly and gave him a cold stare. 'Your wife's opinion of the police of this particular town,' he growled, 'is about the same as mine.' Without enlarging on the statement, he left the astonished man and clumped down the three flights to the street below. Duane caught up with him when he reached the squad car. They seated themselves in the tonneau and Barnaby waved the driver into motion.

He was silent a long time, then he said: 'I wish some of the sob-sisters that romance about these damn' killers could have seen that! You know me, Sam, I'm not sentimental, but there was an awful loneliness about that poor little kid. Damn!'

Sergeant Duane passed a rough palm over his bald head. 'It was probably some of Swarm's boys after one of Antecki's mob. Not that it helps us much with not a shred of evidence to go by.'

Barnaby nodded stolidly. For several minutes he was lost in thought; at length he spoke.

'They didn't get the guy they came for, so they'll be back. Perhaps if we cruise around—'

Duane shrugged. 'You're the doctor,' he grumbled, 'but I can't see what good it'll do. We don't know 'em, an' if we did we couldn't make it stick.'

Barnaby called to the driver. 'Hey, Murray, cruise around this district for a while. Take it easy, but be ready to roll when I bellow.' He leaned back against the cushions and began to muse aloud: 'We got a hell of a department, Sam! I been on it a long while; I didn't know a department could get so rotten.'

'It's no worse than the other departments,' Sam Duane growled. 'They take their orders from the grafters just like we gotta.'

Barnaby sighed, then asked: 'Their only kid, you said?'

'Yeah. The father drives a garbage truck for the city – that's what he made the crack about – scared of losing his job. The old woman is the granny. Didja see how she took it?'

Barnaby nodded sourly. 'I didn't like it. I hate to see people act like they *had* to take stuff like that. Poor devils! We got a hell of an outfit, Sam.'

'Funny, but suppose we did run in those killers – a jury'd probably turn 'em loose.'

'If they ever got to a jury,' Barnaby said insinuatingly.

Duane stiffened. 'You mean—? Oh, hell, Skipper, you can't pull that these days! Those lads have connections.'

Barnaby growled deep in his throat, fished out his pipe and began to tamp tobacco into the bowl. He puffed it alight, then slumped back into one corner of the seat, staring into the darkness. Duane followed his example and in a grim silence, the big squad car prowled the streets.

It was Barnaby who spotted the sedan rolling past at an intersection. He stiffened, nudged Duane and taking the briar from his teeth, pointed with the stem. Sergeant Duane slid to the edge of his seat.

'*Hoods . . . !*'

The Skipper gave a short brittle laugh. He jammed the pipe into a pocket, leaned over the front seat and gave the driver his instructions:

'Murray, slam that sedan into a lamp-post; I don't give a damn if you have to wreck us, don't let 'em get away.'

The police chauffeur nodded without turning his head. He shifted into second, depressed the accelerator and caromed diagonally across the intersection. The siren gave one throaty snarl as he rammed the sedan over to the curb.

The other driver made no attempt to elude detention. He braked sharply to avoid a crash and thrust his head out the window.

'Hey, what's the idea . . . ?' he began, stopping when he saw Barnaby swing out of the police car, gun in hand.

Duane followed and threw a beam from his flash into the closed car. There were two men in the rear seat.

Barnaby yanked open the rear door. 'File out,' he ordered curtly, gesturing with his gun.

The pair in the back seat hesitated, then the larger of the two, a big blond man, grinned insolently, tilted his hat to a rakish angle and climbed to the street. His companion, a stocky fellow, followed scowling.

'You, too,' Barnaby growled at the driver, and that worthy grudgingly complied.

The big man yawned. 'What is this, Cap, a pinch?'

Barnaby caught him by the shoulder and spun him around. 'Keep your mouth shut, Ritter,' he barked. 'We'll start off with a frisk.' He ran practiced hands over the man's body and found a snub-nosed .38 in a shoulder harness.

'I gotta license to pack that rod,' Ritter offered, by way of explanation. 'Don't get ideas, copper.'

Duane searched the other pair. 'Clean!' he reported disappointedly.

Barnaby inclined his head towards the tonneau. 'Frisk the heap,' he growled, keeping his eyes on the big man. 'An' who are these muggs?' he demanded of the latter, indicating the two other hoods.

Ritter grinned. 'I suppose you got a warrant to search our car, Cap?' He ignored the question.

Barnaby's eyes glowed. 'I don't need a warrant to frisk a load of rats.'

Ritter shrugged. '*No?* Then maybe they changed the Constitution since lunch time. My mouthpiece told me then. . . .'

Duane came running around the back of the sedan. He had a sawed-off shot-gun in his hands.

'The car was clean,' he snapped, 'but I found this in the gutter. They must have heaved it out when we stopped 'em.'

Ritter smiled maliciously. 'You'll have a hell of a time proving. . . .'

Barnaby hit him alongside the jaw, knocking him over the left-front fender. 'You damned . . . !'

Duane caught his arm. 'Easy, Cap, easy!' Lowering his voice, he added, 'We ain't got a thing on 'em!'

The man came up massaging his jaw. 'That'll cost you your job, flat-foot!'

Barnaby shook his arm free of Duane and started another swing, but Ritter stumbled hastily out of range. The captain flexed his fingers and backed up a stride. 'All right,' he rasped. 'Pile in!' He waved them into the squad car with his gun.

The trio climbed into the rear seat. Barnaby ordered the police chauffeur to drive the sedan while Duane piloted the official car. Then he took his place in the front, sitting sidewise so he could cover the cargo of hoods in the rear.

Ritter made one more prophecy. 'You can't lock us up in this town, flat-foot!'

He was right. They had barely reached Central Station when a criminal lawyer named Hymie Croker magically appeared armed with writs of *habeas corpus*. The three guns swaggered from the station, free, and from the shadow of the sergeant's desk, Captain Barnaby and Sergeant Duane watched in sullen silence.

When they had gone, Duane commented: 'It's sure a swell system, Skipper. Not much like it was twenty years ago, when my old man was chief.'

'Mike Duane was a man,' Barnaby snarled through clenched teeth. 'He'd have fired us if we'd brought those hoods in without first beatin' 'em so they couldn't walk. We haven't got a chief no more, we got a puppet. To hell with it, I'm goin' to bed!' He turned, slapped open the swinging doors and barged out into the night.

A court appearance in the morning and a lengthy conference with a deputy prosecutor after that, kept Captain Barnaby away from Headquarters until late the following afternoon. When he finally strode into the station, the desk sergeant flagged him.

'Chief Grogan wants to see you, Captain. He left orders to shoot you right up the moment you came in.'

Barnaby bobbed his rugged head, turned and tramped up the stairs to Grogan's office on the second floor. He was admitted at once.

Chief of Police Grogan squatted behind a desk, his broad back to the windows. His full, moon-shaped face was an apoplectic purple and his heavy jowls welled over the tight collar band of his tunic as though it strangled him. He had a small, querulous mouth that was permanently puckered as though he was just about to whistle. What hair he had left was gray and he wore it plastered sidewise across his pate in a vain attempt at deception. His thick hands toyed with an onyx lighter.

'You wanted to see me?' Barnaby asked.

Grogan nodded sourly. 'Sit down,' he commanded; and as Barnaby complied, he rose to his feet and began to pace the stuffy office. He made two complete circuits, then jerked to a stop and glared down at the Captain.

'What in hell kind of a cop are you?' he roared. 'I understand you stopped a carload of citizens last night without a damn' bit of evidence, beat up one of the men for no good reason and then didn't have enough facts even to lock them up!'

Barnaby's eyes narrowed.

'You understand wrong,' he retorted dryly. 'I stopped a sedan of professional hoods for a frisk. A rat named Ritter, an ace gunman of Coxy Swarm's, got tough, so I slapped him. Ritter had a gun. . . .'

'. . . for which he has a permit,' cut in Grogan. 'By what authority did you search that machine?'

What little warmth remained in Barnaby's eyes faded abruptly. 'By what right, you ask? D'you know what happened down there last evenin'? A child was cut down by a mob of killers! They was tryin' to knock off another hood an' this kid of three took it instead.'

Grogan made a disgusted motion with his big hand. 'A *wop* kid!'

'He lived an' breathed,' Barnaby said slowly. 'He died because we coppers tolerate a lot of rats in this town.'

The Chief's mouth shrank. 'Captain Barnaby,' he rasped, 'you're relieved of your command immediately. You are suspended for ten days, after which you will report in uniform to night patrol duty in a suburban precinct.'

Barnaby ran his tongue around the inside of his cheek. 'I see. I rate this demotion because . . .'

'Because of conduct unbecoming an officer of the law; because you violated the laws you are sworn to uphold; because you have a vicious temper and beat up citizens; because . . .'

Barnaby stood up, lifted a restraining hand. There was fire glowing in the caverns under his shaggy brows.

'Grogan, you're a blustering *dummy*. You mouth a lot of words but you're tryin' this act because Coxy Swarm ordered to you to get rid of me. Ritter told me this was comin'.'

The Chief swelled his chest. 'Wait a minute, Captain Barn . . .'

The older copper interrupted him. 'Shut up! You can take your crooked graft–eaten force an' go straight to hell with it.' With an explosive oath, he swiveled and stalked out of the room.

He went down to the street and began to walk. Sweat stood out on his corrugated forehead; sweat of rage. Then as time passed and his temper cooled, he began to realize the cold truth.

He had *quit!*

Quit! That meant he wasn't a copper anymore! Or did it? Twenty years

– no, it was longer than that; it was twenty-six years next June that he came to the Department. Hell, he'd headed the Homicide Squad for nearly a decade. He spread his big hands before him – with battered knuckles, calloused palms. His quizzical eyes stole to his heavy feet. Not a copper . . . ? That was a laugh!

He had *quit!*

What was wrong? It hadn't been like that in the old days! Sure, there was graft – you can't change human nature entirely – but small stuff that meant little, not this wholesale business. But murder was murder and the old laws of war or peace always offered safety to women and babies. Was it the laws, the tricks the crooks' shysters were skilled in under the guise of legality? Was it the way they were enforced, or the present administration?

Grogan had accused him of unbecoming conduct. What in hell had he done to rate that? Slap a baby killer? Was *that* unbecoming of an officer? The Old Man had called him a law violator! Huh! What was he paid a salary for?

Unable to find the answers to his muttered queries, Barnaby shrugged and raised his chin. Darkness had settled over the city; street lights sputtered into being. He glanced at a corner post and found himself in the district where Sam Duane lived. . . .

Cold sweat dampened his collar. Had Sam got it, too? Sam had a wife and family . . . ! Barnaby fished out a handkerchief and daubed his face. He'd better have a talk with Sam. It was one thing for Barnaby to throw up his job, he had no one to worry about. Somehow he'd just never found the time to get married. It wasn't that he hadn't wanted to – he had. He wanted a real home, loved kids, but a copper doesn't get much time for courting women – not the kind he'd want to mother his kids.

It took him ten minutes to reach the shabby little duplex that Sam Duane called home. A woman admitted him. Her wan features were wrinkled and worn, her body shapeless, and her head wore a crown of pale silver, but to Barnaby, Molly Duane was still the golden-locked colleen she had been the day she married Sam. One look at her patient face warned him.

She smiled and inclined her head to a curtained opening.

'Sam's in the parlor. Go right in, Clyde.'

Barnaby squared his shoulders, swung on his heel and pushed into the room.

Sam Duane was sitting in a decrepit rocker, his stockinged feet on the windowsill, his chin resting on his chest, clamping his briar between his teeth. He spoke without turning his head.

'H'lo, Skipper. I hoped you'd drop in.'

Barnaby pulled up a chair without invitation and straddled it. He probed through his pockets for his own pipe, found it and rapped it against the heel of his palm.

'Grogan haul you up?' he asked with studied casualness.

Duane bobbed his bald head. 'Yep. Back to the *goats* with a *log* of wood.' Which is a copper's descriptive phrase to explain that he was transferred to the suburbs to swing a club as he patrolled a foot beat.

'You quit, eh?' Duane added.

Barnaby thumbed tobacco into his pipe. 'Yeah, I . . .' He stopped as the front door-bell whirred. He heard Molly pad down the corridor, heard the door creak open, then the booming voice of Dennis Hallahan flooded the small home.

Sam lifted his chin. 'Come on in, Denny,' he invited. Simultaneously the curtains were brushed aside and Hallahan and another dick named Louis Forsythe came in. The parlor seemed crowded.

Hallahan and Forsythe belonged to the same breed as Duane and Barnaby; born coppers, disillusioned, bitter, but patriotic to a losing cause – *justice*. To describe them would be to describe any typical old harness bull. Big men, with wide hunched shoulders, powerful biceps and cold, neutral eyes. They hold their heads a certain way after some twenty years of forced aggressiveness, a sort of cross between a Seville bull and an English bull dog. Their mouths grow straight and thin from cynicism, faces furrow and seam from the sight of constant tragedy. They grow to look alike, to think alike, to act alike. . . . A grand breed – a vanishing race.

That was Barnaby, that was Duane, and Hallahan, and Forsythe!

'You gave Grogan some good advice, Clyde,' Hallahan commented. Hallahan had retired a year ago; Forsythe was due to take his pension in another eight months.

Barnaby nodded. 'I couldn't help myself,' he explained slowly. 'The sight of him sittin' there, a beefy, blusterin' figurehead . . . well, somethin' snapped inside of me and . . . I quit!'

Hallahan sighed. 'It's too damn' bad you threw away your pension. This town needs men like you! The city's in a hell of a shape; the criminal element are in power. What this town needs is a new department. Why a half-dozen old timers could clean this rat's nest up in forty–eight hours! Why, I remember when Old Mike Duane was chief we . . .'

He droned on, but ex-Captain Barnaby was not listening.

'. . . *old timers could clean this rat's nest up in forty–eight hours!*'

Old timers? He raised smoldering eyes and looked into the dim-lit faces around him. *Forty-eight hours?* Two days! And why not?

Forsythe was talking when Barnaby held up a commanding hand for silence. Forsythe paused. . . .

Barnaby's voice knifed the sudden hush. 'Dennis, could *you* an' *me* raise a few old timers for a clean-up?'

No one spoke for nearly five minutes. These were not impulsive youngsters; these were veterans. They knew the seriousness of the suggestive question; knew the potential dynamite packed into the simple phrase.

Hallahan spoke first, almost defensively, for he remembered it was his own words that prompted the query.

'You mean, Clyde, to gun out these hoods?'

Barnaby leaned forward and his voice took on a saw-edge. 'I mean to form a real department, to investigate, to convict, to execute.' The idea assumed shape as he spoke. 'To clean up; to deal out, not shyster's law, but justice. Every one of you boys knows the problem – it isn't enough to find out who commits crime, it's to make a jury believe it. *We* know the guilty ones, the thieves, the killers, and the grafters, but we can't do anything about it. Hallahan, you're a widower, independent – what do you think?'

Hallahan leaned back in his chair, his eyes watching the blue spiral of smoke that eddied ceilingward from his corncob.

'To deal out justice, not law,' he mused absently. Then a laugh rang from his throat and he sat very straight.

'Think?' he roared. 'I think it's a hell of a good idea! You an' me. . . .'

'Count me in,' Forsythe interrupted.

Hallahan shook his head. 'No, Louis, not you. There's your pension to think about. You'd lose that. An' of course Sam is out, too. We can't use married men with families that might suffer.'

Barnaby nodded in accord. 'That's right,' he growled. 'We'll get no thanks if we succeed. If we fail. . . .' He made an eloquent gesture with his big hands.

Duane never moved his head, but his voice roared out.

'*Molly . . . !*'

Steps sounded in the hallway and a moment later, Molly Duane's head appeared in the opening.

'Yes, Sam?'

Sam turned his face towards her. 'Molly,' he said quietly, 'the boys are going to form an unofficial police department. They're goin' to clean up this town, gun out baby killers an' the like. They may get themselves killed, Molly. What do you think about it?'

She hesitated just an instant, then: 'And you want to go with them, Sam?' she whispered.

Barnaby cut in. 'That's out! Sam ain't gonna do no such a damn' fool thing. Why it's practically suicide an' . . .'

In the wan light, they saw her smile. 'If Sam wants to go, he can,' she told them firmly. 'Our babies are all grown and have families of their own; they don't need us now. It sounds like a mighty good thing. I've confidence in Sam and I can go to the children if anything should . . . well, *happen*.'

'Thanks, Molly,' Duane said huskily.

She went away.

'Four of us should be enough,' Sam Duane went on quietly. 'An' since we'll need a Chief, I suggest Clyde.'

Hallahan stared for a minute at the drapes, still swaying from Molly Duane's passing. Then a deep sigh escaped him. 'What a woman,' he whispered, then added with a deeper growl: 'I think that's another damn' swell idea. What do you say, Louis?'

Forsythe got up and walked over to the telephone. 'Just a minute,' he begged. 'I got just one job to do before I take orders from our new Chief.' He dialed a number, waited until the receiver made a metallic noise, then began:

'Hello, Grogan? This is Lieutenant Forsythe. Well, get this straight the first time, you thick-headed —— ——'

Hallahan's explosive laughter drowned Forsythe's words.

'Louis,' Hallahan boomed, 'is resigning!'

At exactly eleven thirty, 'Big Dutch' Ritter was comfortably ensconced at a ring-side table in *La Parisienne Café* in company with his swart body-protector, Whisper Rieg, affectionately known as 'The Scourge', and a pair of blonde entertainers. The redoubtable Ritter paused in the middle of a humorous tale when his alert eyes glimpsed the bulky figure of Barnaby and Duane bearing across the polished dance-floor towards his table. He had just time to remark out of the corner of his mouth that, 'this ought to be good,' when Barnaby reached his side.

'All right, Ritter, you're comin' with us!'

'The Scourge' slid to his feet, but made no overt move when he caught the imperceptible shake of his boss' head. Ritter grinned, tilted back in his chair and eyed the two veterans.

'Don't clown, Cap. Sit down an' have a drink. I heard you got canned.'

One of the girls tittered nervously; perhaps she thought Skipper Barnaby didn't look like a man to fool with. She started up from her chair.

Barnaby glanced sidewise as Duane; their eyes met. 'Okey, Sam!' he rasped: and made a dive for Ritter.

Rieg tried to earn his salary; he went for his gun. But big Sam Duane's persuader thudded behind his left ear and he immediately lost all interest in the encounter. Before he hit the polished floor, Duane caught him, slung him over his shoulder.

But 'The Scourge' didn't know anything about it.

Barnaby's dive carried the now startled Ritter to the floor. He made a vague motion in the general direction of his arm-pit but all it earned him was a stunning blow on the jaw from one of the copper's massive fists. The 'ace' mobster stole a hasty glance at his assailant towering above him . . . and surrendered.

He was rudely yanked erect, a steel bracelet bit into his right wrist and by it, he was unceremoniously dragged out of the café in the wake of the well-burdened Duane. And no one interfered with their going. Ritter balked outside when he saw that the car awaiting him was not an official machine – Ritter had learned that a ride in a regular police car invariably terminated at Police Headquarters where one of the mob's shysters would be waiting to spring him.

But his obstinacy was short-lived. Barnaby mouthed an expressive oath, then half-threw, half-kicked him into the rear seat where he was at once handcuffed to the unconscious 'Scourge'.

The car swung into motion.

Duane drove, eyes glued on the road ahead, mouth tightened. Barnaby sat sidewise on the seat beside him, his left elbow resting on the back seat, his bitter gaze riveted on the pair in the rear. In his right hand, he cradled a long night-stick; it swayed suggestively in his restless grip.

Ritter saw the stick, remembered the car, and stark terror gripped him. Some of the angry color seeped from his avaricious features, leaving them the shade of stale dough.

'Wait a minute, Barnaby,' he jerked. 'You can't do this!'

Barnaby's mocking laughter hit him like a blow. There was no mirth in the sound, rather a menace. . . .

'But this ain't official!' protested Ritter.

The doughty veteran sneered. 'Sure it's official, you rat. You got me canned from one police force, but I got on another. You're arrested, Ritter; you'll get a trial all legal-like. But you won't have no crooked lawyers, Ritter.'

The gunman's eyes protruded. 'Another police force?' he gasped. 'What city hired you? Where are you takin' us . . . ?'

'To a city where you belong, Ritter – *The City of Hell!*'

Duane toured around several blocks, crossing his own trail to make sure they had no tail, then satisfied at last there was no one following, he cut rapidly across the city to the warehouse district. He came to an abandoned loft building, circled it twice, finally to stop in a pool of black shadow. As he stepped out one side of the car, Barnaby went out the opposite side.

'All right, Ritter,' Barnaby growled, opening the rear door. 'Pile out.' Duane turned the beam of his flash in the tonneau.

Rieg had regained part of his sense. He sat blinking at the light. Ritter shrank back into the seat, but when Barnaby hit him across the shins with the night-stick, he bounced to the edge of the seat and filed out, dragging the still dazed Rieg with him.

Ritter said: 'On the level, Cap, ain't there some way we can square this beef. I'll see you get your old job back an' . . .'

Barnaby stiffened, his thin smile widened into a wolfish grin.

'So you can get me my old job back, eh?' he whispered softly. His voice changed abruptly to a savage growl. 'Why you lousy . . . !'

Smack! It was only an open-handed slap, but it floored the astonished Ritter and he, in turn, pulled 'The Scourge' down with him.

It was Duane who prodded them erect. He motioned them to follow the big form of Barnaby who was striding through the darkness. The reflected light of his flash painted him in eery shadow; he loomed there like some fabled giant.

'I wouldn't irritate him,' Duane suggested mildly. 'He's in good humor now, but he might get peevish.'

Ritter shuddered and hurried in Barnaby's wake.

Barnaby's course led him through long-deserted rooms, down a dusty stairway to a basement. He explored the filth-laden floor for a few minutes until he found a heavy iron plate set flush with the cement. He scuffed dirt away from an iron ring, hooked his fingers through it and lifted the lid, disclosing a black hole that vanished into the bowels of the earth.

He leaned forward and rapped briskly on the rim of the hole with a night-stick. The noise echoed out of the blackness to be followed by a ponderous silence. . . .

Abruptly, as from a great distance, the sound of a tapping came to them; an echo, as it were, of Barnaby's own raps.

Barnaby prodded Ritter with the club. Duane unlocked the cuffs.

'Get down, muggs,' he ordered; and when he saw them hesitate, added, 'get, or I'll heave you down!'

They went . . . down a rusty ladder, into the arms of Hallahan and Forsythe.

Barnaby came down last, pulling the iron cover in place after him. When he reached the bottom, he grinned.

'Ritter, meet the new police department; coppers of *The City of Hell!*'

Duane swung his light so it illuminated the others. 'Any luck?' he asked.

'Plenty!' chortled Hallahan. 'Come on.'

He led the way down a great brick tube about twelve feet in diameter. The concave floor was slimy and a thin trickle of filthy water crawled along the middle. The wan glow of the flashlights showed dripping walls and on several occasions, huge bats swept squealing at the heads of the grim paraders.

Suddenly Rieg shrieked in terror.

'Something stabbed my ankle!' he wailed.

Barnaby grunted. 'Rats! Big sewer rats. Better stick close; they'll attack a single man.'

Rieg huddled closer.

The tunnel branched abruptly. Hallahan, leading, swung off. A hundred yards farther along, he turned the beam of his light on an opening several feet above the floor of the main tube. He nodded to the others and climbed the iron rungs to disappear into the cave-like hole.

At a prod from Barnaby's night-stick, Ritter and his trembling companion, followed.

They found themselves in a square, windowless room. It was like the dungeon of some medieval castle. In the center was a crude table, rotten with age. Along two of the walls were winches. A candle was stuck in a whiskey bottle. Hallahan lighted it and extinguished the flash. Hidden drafts made the single flame flicker and ghostly shadows danced on the brick walls.

Hallahan seated himself at the table. He took a small note-book from his pocket, fingered the stub of a pencil and looked at Barnaby.

'Have you told him, Chief?'

Barnaby shook his head. 'You're the *judge*,' he remarked.

Hallahan nodded soberly and turned to the gaping prisoners. He surveyed them for a while, then began to speak in a slow, judicial tone.

'You're in the court of a new order, boys,' he told them. 'Chief Barnaby called it *The City of Hell*. Up above, you crooks run things; your boss makes and breaks judges, coppers, politicians. You and your lawyers rule the courts, the city government, the law. Well, we've started a new city down here. This old sewer is a monument to the system; it was built years ago by a bunch of crooked grafters and had to be abandoned because it wouldn't work. For nearly three decades it's been a breeding place for rats so we figgered this was a good place to bring you birds. Now you're under arrest and you'll get a fair trial. First we want you to take the stand an' tell us . . .'

'Aw, cut out this baloney!' Ritter sneered. 'What the hell do you think you're settin' yourself up to be? We'll stand trial whenever we have to, in a court of law – what's this farce anyway? You guys gone goofy?'

Hallahan sighed patiently. 'The Constitution guarantees every citizen the right of trial by jury, but the Constitution was made before your breed came into existence; it was intended to protect decent citizens from oppression. Since you're not a decent citizen, Ritter, you an' "The Scourge" can't expect that sort of protection. We want you to tell us the truth about that baby killin' last night.'

Ritter stiffened. 'I'll be damned if I will! Come on with your rough stuff. I can take it!'

Hallahan nodded. 'That's been the trouble up above. The cops beat up you guys but it didn't work because the human body can only absorb just so much punishment an' after that you don't feel it. We got a better stunt.' He swung his gaze on Forsythe. 'Lieutenant, lock up the prisoners!'

Forsythe strode willingly out of the shadows and clamped a big hand on each of the two crooks.

'Gladly, *Your Honor*.' He jerked them around and started for the door, then paused in front of Duane. 'Sam, would you take that club an' beat off the rats until I chain these muggs to the floor?'

Duane hefted a club. 'Sure,' he agreed.

'The Scourge' leapt sidewise. 'Rats! Good God! You can't do that! We'd be eaten alive!'

Forsythe jerked him towards the opening. 'That's your funeral; you heard the Judge's orders.'

Rieg continued to struggle. 'No, no, I tell you!'

Barnaby strode over and caught 'The Scourge' by the neck. He hustled him through the opening into a smaller tunnel. As the flash sent an explorative beam ahead, large gray shapes scurried into the deeper shadows where twin eyes glowed in the darkness at the human intruders.

Ritter snarled through his teeth. 'Shut up, Rieg! It's a bluff!'

Barnaby snorted but made no reply. He threw the squirming gunman to the slimy floor, snapped a cuff on his wrist and hooked the other end to an iron ring sunk in the floor. 'The Scourge' sobbed brokenly, but Ritter kept his nerve up.

'Swarm will take care of you finks!' he prophesied grimly.

Barnaby wiped his hands together. 'An' these wharf rats will take care of you. That makes it even.' He started to leave the cavern, but Rieg's cry stopped him.

'You're murderin' me!' he shrieked.

Barnaby wagged his gray head. 'No Whisper, you're commitin' suicide. If you talk, you got a fightin' chance. For instance, if you was to tell us who ordered you killers out. . . .'

'I can't!' screamed 'The Scourge'.

Barnaby shrugged and passed through the opening. He heard Ritter's husky tones pleading, cajoling Rieg to keep up his nerve. Then a rat must have bitten 'The Scourge' for he uttered one long wail of terror.

'Listen to reason, in God's name!' he howled.

Barnaby paused, winked to Forsythe, then called back. 'Give us names, Whisper, not an argument.'

'Swarm. . . .'

Coxy Swarm leaned forward, his elbows propped on the arms of his chair, and his cold fish-eyes focused on the slender little man striding up and down the room.

'If Rieg and Ritter had been snatched by some of the other boys it would be my job, Hymie,' he growled. 'But you're paid a damn' good salary to act as the mouthpiece for this outfit, and when the cops grab two of my best boys, it's *your* job to see they get sprung. I'm waiting for service.' The cold cigar on one side of his thin-lipped mouth crawled up at an aggressive angle.

The little lawyer stopped, combed his black tousled hair with nervous fingers, then made a futile gesture with his hands.

'But I tell you, Coxy,' he shouted, after the manner of a man who has been repeating the same explanation over and over, 'these two men, Barnaby and Duane, are not with the police department! I did what you asked and had them demoted, but they got tough and quit. But in spite of that, I have assistants staked out at every precinct station within fifty miles of here. So far, these ex-cops haven't taken Ritter and Rieg to a jail. If they do, I'll spring 'em; I can get any man I want released from any jail in this county. But, Coxy, be reasonable! I can't get a man out of jail when he hasn't been put in!'

A tall, gangling hood sitting near the door spoke. 'You don't suppose these cops took the boys for a ride, do you?'

Lawyer Croker stiffened to his full five feet four inches. 'They wouldn't dare!' he shouted. 'I'd have them broke!'

Swarm jerked the cigar out of his mouth, glanced at the cold ash and hurled it from him with an oath. He reached a big hand into a niche in the wall beside him and grabbed a telephone. Then he called an unlisted number.

'Judge Tweedie? Listen, Tweedie, this is Swarm. Two dumb cops named Barnaby and Duane snatched a pair of my best boys, see. I want those flat-feet nailed to the cross! Get in touch with the foreman of your Grand Jury and have 'em bring in an indictment first thing in the morning. No, don't wait until morning to call the foreman, do it right now. I don't give a damn if it is nearly midnight! Maybe we can smoke that pair out in the open with an indictment, but if my boys find 'em in the meantime, you won't need to bother with the Grand Jury. Goodbye!' He waited for no answer, but hung up.

He let his eyes wander over the assembled group. Besides Croker the lawyer, five of his ablest lieutenants sat quietly in a semi-circle, awaiting his orders. Despite his rage, he felt a suffusion of pride creep over him. These were not the beetle-browed gorillas of fiction; these men were well educated – with the exception of Gebardi, an importation from Sicily – and versed in modern business administration. They could organize a union, break a strike, control a voting precinct, or examine a company's account books with equal facility. And what was even more important, they could and would carry out his orders without question.

'Miller,' he said finally, to the lanky hood by the door, 'take Gebardi and find out if either Duane or Barnaby's got a wife. If so, grab her and take her up to the farm. Gebardi'll know how to make her talk. But don't actually kill her because we might need her to write a note to her husband.'

Croker wiped sudden sweat from his face. 'I can save you time,' he wheezed. 'This guy Barnaby is not married, but Duane is. He lives on

Becker Street, the third duplex from the corner of Hansard Avenue. His wife's name is Molly. Duane's nuts about her.'

Miller stood up, motioned to Gebardi and adjusted his fedora. 'That'll help, Hymie. If she knows where her old man is we'll make her tell us. If she don't,' he shrugged grimly, 'it'll be tough on her.' With Gebardi at his heels, he went out.

Lawyer Hymie Croker's mouth opened and closed in a quick, nervous smile. He wiped the moist handkerchief over his face and sought to conceal the involuntary shudder that shook his slender frame. Croker belonged to that peculiar breed of jackal who could cheerfully frame an innocent man into the penitentiary, or even to the gallows, and feel no pang of conscience. He could advise his assorted clients on the slickest manner of evading the laws; even assist them in their work under the cloak of his profession. But when he stood in the presence of violence, the yellow stripe that lined his back widened until he trembled.

Swarm took a fresh cigar from his vest pocket, ripped off the end with his teeth and set it on the table before him. 'I can't exactly figure this out,' he mused, scowling. 'There's just a chance that these two cops took the boys for a buggy ride. But it don't look that way; they took too much of a chance in snatching them out of *La Parisienne*. At least a hundred people saw them do it.'

'Perhaps they wanted to make 'em talk,' suggested a mobster named Haight.

Croker answered that one. 'Talk? What for? Grogan takes his orders from me and Judge Tweedie has the Grand Jury in tow. Tweedie'll have the Grand Jury return an indictment as Coxy told him to do and Barnaby and Duane will be in jail. I can promise you service along that line.' He used the handkerchief again.

'Anyway,' drawled a big man, 'they couldn't make Ritter talk. He can take it.'

Swarm shrugged. 'Hymie's right. There's nobody for them to tell anything to. You're right about Ritter, Slade, but I got my doubts if Rieg could keep his mouth shut under pressure. "The Scourge" is mean as hell with a gun in his hand, but . . .' He shrugged and pulled his chair closer to the table. 'Well, sit down, Hymie, and we'll have a round of stud.'

Croker prodded a chair into position with his foot. 'I'll sit in until Miller and Gebardi call back. We ought to hear from them within half an hour.'

About forty minutes later, Haight quit the game and walked to the door of the office. He mumbled something about a drink and went out, only to reappear about a minute later with his face the color of damp cement.

Swarm frowned, slowly put down his cards, started to push back his chair. 'Well, what in hell's the matter with you?'

Haight made a vague motion with his head towards the darkness behind. 'Gebardi . . . !'

The way he said it brought them to their feet in unison, but Swarm was the first man to reach the crumpled body of his ace executioner.

Gebardi was quite dead. He lay across the curb, his bloody knees in the gutter, his torso sprawled across the sidewalk. A nearby street lamp loaned ghastly shadows to the scene. The corpse looked like a great black spider which had been stepped on.

Swarm cursed, shot a quick glance up and down the street. It was practically deserted; the body could have lain there but a few minutes.

'Come on,' he snarled. 'Carry it inside.'

Three of the men grabbed their erstwhile companion and whisked him inside the office. From a closet, Swarm took out a large rubber sheet and spread it on the floor. They dumped the battered remains of Gebardi on to this. It was then that Swarm glimpsed the folded piece of paper pinned to the dead man's chest.

He retrieved it and moved closer to the light. Examination disclosed the obvious fact that the paper had been clipped from an advertisement in a newspaper. It simply stated in large black type:

Sure Cure for Rodents!

That was all.

'And Miller . . . ?' gasped Croker. 'They've grabbed Miller!'

Swarm crushed the clipping in the palm of his fist. 'Every one of you birds get out and see what you can find. Get your boys moving. I want these two crazy cops dead by daylight.' As the men started for their haunts, he swung on Croker.

'Have you got your car with you, Hymie?'

The lawyer nodded. 'I told my driver to wait around the corner.'

Swarm nodded impatiently. 'Okey. Now you beat it to Grogan. Tell him to find Barnaby and Duane before morning, or there'll be another Chief of Police in this damn' town!' He made a gesture of dismissal and the lawyer waited no longer. He scooped up his hat and cane and fled the office. And the last thing he saw as he went out was the bloody corpse of the late Antonio Gebardi spread-eagled on the rubber sheet.

Although the night air was cold, Attorney Croker was sweating when he rounded the corner and headed for the shelter of his own limousine. He rapped his cane sharply against the running-board to awaken the driver who sat slumped over the steering wheel, opened the door himself and climbed into the tonneau. Then he picked up the speaking tube and issued his orders.

'Central Police Station, Gunner; and step on it!'

As the big machine got into motion, he relaxed against the soft cushions and lighted a cigarette. He shuddered involuntarily as he recalled the finding of Gebardi; he couldn't stand blood or physical torture. He felt his stomach knotting and knew he was in for another attack of indigestion. He inhaled deeply, letting the smoke dribble through his nostrils. . . .

And then he suddenly became aware that the limousine had drawn up in front of a small, darkened drug-store!

Disdaining to use the speaking tube, he jumped forward to the edge of his seat, jerked open the glass window that separated the tonneau from the driver's compartment and shouted:

'What's the meaning of this, Gunner? Didn't I tell you to hurry! I . . .' The words froze in his throat.

For the driver turned abruptly. Instead of the battered, familiar features of his own chauffeur, Gunner McSpadden, he found himself staring at the rugged, leathery face of old Dennis Hallahan.

Hallahan shoved back the chauffeur's cap so that the visor would not shield his features. He was grinning, but somehow, Croker could read no mirth in the expression.

The dapper little lawyer carried a gun by way of ornamentation. Now, as he suddenly recalled the picture of Gebardi, half-chewed with slugs, fear gripped him and he made a vague pass for his own weapon. But he didn't complete the movement. The door jerked open and the enormous bulk of Lieutenant Forsythe crowded into the tonneau beside him.

'Hello, Hymie,' Forsythe said, and the tinge of his voice matched Hallahan's smile. 'We want to have a nice long chat with you.' He picked up the speaking tube and gave his orders. 'Home, James, and don't spare the nags.'

Lawyer Croker knew the meaning of the word *fear*. Sheer panic gripped him; sweat dampened his clothing in one awful rush; he went sick.

'Where are you taking me?' he screamed, struggling forward in his seat.

Forsythe grabbed him by the collar and jerked him back so hard his spine quivered.

'To your home town, Hymie; *The City of Hell!*'

He laughed, but Hymie Croker didn't hear him. Hymie Croker had fainted. . . .

Judge Alexander Z. Tweedie looked like a judge even arrayed in his pajamas. His leonine head was crowned with a silver mane which he brushed straight back. His eyes were hidden in shadowed caves, guarded by bushy brows and out front, a pair of nose glasses acted as a barricade. His skin was rugged, seamed, and he had the kind of a jaw that is popularly supposed to denote great strength of character – but which does nothing of the kind. In his younger days, Alexander Tweedie had wanted to be an actor; his father wanted him to be a lawyer. Now he was both. He made a successful politician because he was a good actor, looked the part he chose to play, and knew how to obey orders. He was an impressive, judicial fraud.

At twelve-thirty at night, he sat closeted in his study with William Greeves, foreman of the Grand Jury. Greeves was a slight figure, nearly bald, who wore thick lensed glasses and suffered from an inferiority complex. His appointment to the Grand Jury had been one of the greatest surprises in his life; now he spent most of his time attempting to convince himself, as well as a rather cynical wife, that it came as a reward for his business sagacity and his civic loyalty. What made him of value to the powers-that-be, was the fact that he honestly believed in himself. He was still dizzy from his sudden exaltation and was pathetically grateful to Judge Tweedie, whom he knew was responsible for the appointment.

Tweedie ran his long fingers through his showy mane and peered over his glasses into the anxious features of his guest.

'Greeves,' he boomed, 'I called you here so that we could be ready to act first thing in the morning. This is . . . well . . . almost a crisis in our city. These two ex-policemen have run amuck. I know them both; hard, calloused brutes who hesitate not at all to kill.'

'Just what have they done?' William Greeves wanted to know.

'Done!' Judge Tweedie looked sad. He took off his nose-glasses and rapped on the desk between them. 'They have murdered a young Italian, they have kidnaped at least three other young men and now . . .' he paused to let the full import of his words soak in, '. . . . they have apparently kidnaped one of the cleverest and finest members of our bar.'

'Why?' asked Greeves.

'Retaliation! These two policemen were demoted. None of us is safe as long as they are free. It will hasten the end of this reign of terror if we act in unison.' A happy thought came to him so he added: 'You or I may be next, Greeves! Think of that!'

William Greeves thought and didn't like the image his mind conjured. 'I'll attend to it first thing in the morning,' he assured his mentor. 'We'll put through an indictment at once.' He scooped up his hat, carefully placed it on his head and offered his hand.

'Good night, Your Honor.'

Tweedie unlimbered from his chair, rose with studied dignity, and grasping the proffered hand with one of his own, he put the other hand on Greeves' shoulder.

'It is only by putting our shoulders to the wheel together, Greeves, will we succeed in our efforts to make our city the fairest in the land.'

The foreman of the county Grand Jury nodded; he was visibly impressed. Tweedie held onto his hand and steered him to the front door.

'Good night, Greeves,' he said, and closed the door.

He smiled then and turning, started for the stairs. He was tired and anxious to return to the bed he had so recently deserted. But halfway down the hall, he heard a hesitant knock on the door. He frowned impulsively, about faced and walked back. Greeves had probably forgotten something, he decided, and by the time he folded his hand around the knob, his face was set in a benign smile.

He opened the door . . . and the smile died.

Captain Clyde Barnaby's massive bulk filled the opening. Without pausing for an invitation, he pushed the jurist back into the house, entered and heeled the door shut.

'You're invited to a party, Judge,' Barnaby leered. 'You don't need to dress, but let's go back to your study so's we can get some papers. We want to play some games.'

Tweedie struck an attitude. 'This is an outrage, sir! I'll have you arrested and . . .'

Barnaby tapped him on his inflated chest with a stubby forefinger. 'Now, listen to me, you old fraud. You do as I say an' you won't get hurt, but one peep out of you an' I'll knock you colder than Little America.' He caught Tweedie by the arm, spun him around and gave him a hard push in the general direction of the study.

He turned when they got into the study. Barnaby softly closed the door, leaned against it.

'Now, Judge,' he suggested slyly, 'fill up a brief-case with a lot of printed forms, writs, warrants, complaints, search-warrants, forthwith subpoenas and whatever else you have. Also don't forget your seals, pen, and other apparatus.'

'Why this is ridiculous!' protested Tweedie, giving an excellent imitation of outraged dignity.

Barnaby sighed, fished a blackjack from the recesses of his baggy side-pocket and dangled it from his right thumb. Some of the apoplectic color went out of Tweedie's face. He tightened the cord of his bathrobe, grabbed a brief-case from a nearby desk and began to jam it with papers. His fingers trembled so that he had trouble securing the straps.

'Now,' said Barnaby, 'you'll come with me . . . quietly.'

Tweedie hesitated. 'And if I refuse . . . ?'

The captain shrugged indifferently. 'You go in either case; it's merely a choice of whether you come with your eyes open or . . . closed.'

'May I have the opportunity to clothe myself?'

'You don't need no more clothes,' Barnaby assured him dryly, opening the hall door. 'You look funny enough the way you are.'

Something akin to a sob escaped the jurist's lips, but he took the lead without further protest and stalked down the corridor. At a nod from the copper he opened the front door and stepped out into the night. Barnaby fell in step beside him and together they strode to the sidewalk, where a car awaited them.

Tweedie recognized Duane behind the wheel. He muttered something and stumbled into the tonneau. Half-in, he suddenly saw the slender figure huddled in a corner of the seat.

It was William Greeves.

The bitter night wind whipped Judge Tweedie's flimsy garments, but the judge was not cold . . .

He was scared.

It was the strangest court proceedings ever held in the long annals of legal history! Perhaps the most amazing feature of it all was that the idea was born, not in the cunning brain of a criminal lawyer, but in the honest heads of four old harness bulls. The courtroom was in the bowels of the earth, an abandoned sewer, and the city was directly overhead. Barnaby sat in the middle of a long, improvised table. At one end sat his Honor, Judge Alexander Z. Tweedie, garbed in striped pajamas and a dark blue bathrobe; at the other end, William Greeves shivered on a small soap-box chair.

The room was more like a dungeon than a courtroom, and the crude lighting fixtures – beer-bottles and candles – sent jumpy little shadows carousing around the bat-infested ceiling. There was only one door – a sort of arch – and on either side of this stood Hallahan and Duane. Forsythe was down with the prisoners.

Then Captain Clyde Barnaby began to speak.

'Greeves,' he addressed himself to the little man, 'we believe you are merely a fool, not dishonest. Like a lot of business men, you think you can dabble in politics with no experience whatever, trusting to your limited judgement of men to carry you through. We brought you here for two reasons, first, to use you for the ends of justice and because we believe you really would do the thing we are going to do if you had the knowledge and the strength. You keep your eyes and ears open and you'll learn more about politics in the next thirty minutes than you ever dreamed of knowing. If you play smart, you can have the glory of this clean-up and perhaps get to be governor of the State on the strength of it; who knows? However, you have little choice; if you interfere, we'll . . .' He paused significantly, fixed his steely eyes on the slack-jawed Greeves.

'I won't interfere!' promised Foreman Greeves.

Barnaby swung towards the jurist. 'An' you, you graftin' old scoundrel, we ought to send you to the Federal pen. We got enough evidence already to do just that, but we feel we can use you more profitably. That's your luck just so long as you obey orders. When we're finished, you, like Greeves, will be regarded as a civic benefactor.'

'What,' shivered Tweedie, and not from the cold, 'do you want?'

'In the first place,' Barnaby went on, 'we want you to declare this a real court of law.'

'But . . . but *jurisdiction* . . .' protested Tweedie.

Barnaby nodded. 'We got the answer to that one. This place is within the city limits; a city goes *down* as well as up. You declare this a legal court and hear testimony and admit evidence. The first thing we want are some nine or ten subpoenas and a dozen or so blank warrants of arrests. That will erase any possible charges cropping up later.'

'You . . . you damned blackguards!' choked Tweedie. 'I refuse!'

Barnaby sighed. He glanced at Duane. 'Sergeant, will you take the judge into the next chamber and . . . well . . . *talk* to him privately!'

Duane grinned pleasantly, unlimbered a short length of rubber-hose from under his coat and strode forward. Tweedie gulped, shrank back against his chair.

It was Greeves who made him pause.

The little foreman sat on the edge of his chair, eyes bulging. 'Just . . . just a minute!' he begged with a courage that must have surprised even himself; it would assuredly have amazed his wife. 'Just what are you men trying to do?'

Barnaby frowned, squinted with one eye. He stopped Duane's advance with a motion of one hand, then he studied William Greeves for a full three minutes of absolute silence. At length he spoke:

'All right, Greeves, that's a fair question. This city up above has been slowly worked into the hands of grafters, hoodlums, mobsters and professional killers: in a word, the machine has it by the throat. Chief of Police Grogan – we have him a prisoner, by the way – takes his orders from Coxy Swarm, our local Al Capone. Tweedie here, heads the Grand Jury, tells you fellows what he wants done, but he gets his orders from much the same source. The whole mess is so rotten it stinks, yet the way it's tangled, there's no way of unraveling it except by cleaning it out wholesale. Since it would be impossible to do that by any known regular means, we've improvised our own system. We've got the key man of every crooked outfit in the city, got 'em here under chains and handcuffs. We've got Hymie Croker, the mouthpiece of Swarm and the other mobs; we got Grogan, head of the police department; we got Tweedie, senior judge of the bench and head of the local bar association.'

'What good will that do you?' Greeves asked in a strangely awed tone.

'Plenty. When Tweedie declares this a legal court of law, we'll issue search-warrants, go through the homes, the offices and the safe deposit vaults of these grafters. We'll find enough evidence so that the courts up above will have to act to save their own faces; if they refuse, we'll step into a Federal court and indict the whole outfit with a Federal Grand Jury.'

Greeves was very white of face. 'Is . . . is that the true state of affairs?' He looked from one grim face to the other and his shoulders came back.

'I see it is,' he declared harshly. 'I've been a fool, a . . . a . . . damn' fool! You show me some proof of your statements, something *I* can act on, and you won't need to go before any Federal Grand Jury!'

Barnaby grinned. 'We'll show you,' he promised.

Greeves looked sternly at Tweedie. 'Judge, as Foreman of the Grand Jury, I demand that you sift the evidence these officers produce!'

Tweedie's skin was yellow. 'These men are renegades,' he stormed. 'They are no longer officers of the law!'

Barnaby snorted. 'Dennis,' he commanded, 'bring Grogan in, will you?'

Hallahan vanished, to reappear a few minutes later with Chief Grogan in tow. Grogan was indignant, to say the least, and tough.

Barnaby looked at him. 'Grogan, take your choice; you either reinstate the four of us to our commands, or we'll produce the contents of your safe deposit box to the Federal District Attorney.'

Grogan tensed himself. 'What do you know about my safe deposit box?'

Barnaby grinned. 'Which'll it be?'

Grogan glanced furtively at Greeves, winced and looked at Tweedie. What he saw there failed to reassure him.

'Okey,' he agreed reluctantly, 'you're back.'

Hallahan shoved him over to the table. 'Put that in writing, Grogan.' As Grogan reached for a pen, Barnaby suggested:

'You might add that we are conducting a special investigation into municipal graft at the instigation of the Grand Jury and Judge Alexander Tweedie.' He turned to the two men at the table. 'How about that, Greeves? And you, Judge?'

'Excellent!' snapped Greeves, wiping his face. 'If you can only prove . . .' His voice trailed, died.

Tweedie swallowed, combed his white mane, and nodded. 'You may use my name, Captain Barnaby,' he agreed with a sigh.

Grogan glanced from one strained face to the other. Then he bent over the paper and wrote rapidly. When he finished, Barnaby picked up the document, read it with a growing smile, and nodded to Hallahan.

'Take the Chief out, Dennis, and bring up the shyster.'

As Hallahan went out with Grogan, Barnaby said to the others:

'You'll listen to the conversation to come. If you feel we have a case, you can act; if you don't, you are at liberty to refuse. This may not be strictly admissible testimony, but I wager you'll feel justified in voting for an indictment and in giving us warrants to proceed with our investigations.'

Hallahan appeared at the doorway and thrust Croker into the center of the room. The little lawyer stumbled, caught his balance and glared at Barnaby. He opened his mouth to speak, then, apparently for the first time, saw Tweedie and Greeves. His jaw sagged, his eyes bulged and he looked sick. Before he could recover his surprise, Barnaby took over the command.

'Croker, you're in a court of law. You know these gentleman at the table with me, so I can skip the introductions and get down to business. You are not only a criminal lawyer, you are a lawyer-criminal! The present charge against you is conspiracy to commit murder.'

'You're crazy!' screamed the attorney. 'What kind of a frame-up is this?'

'This is no frame,' Barnaby went on smoothly. 'The day before yesterday, Swarm sent three of his boys out to gun a rat from the Antecki mob. You were in on that plot and advised the men to drop the machine-gun into the river at the completion of the crime. Instead of the hood, however, a little kid was murdered, an innocent bystander. You've got that crime on your hands, as well as others, Croker. What have you to say?'

'I say you're nuts!' shouted Croker, waving his arms. 'You can't prove a damn' thing!' He swung on the white-haired jurist. 'You can't get away with this, Tweedie! I'll have . . .'

The Honorable Tweedie was caught between two fires, but he scented the direction of the wind and proved his diplomacy.

'Are those things true, Counselor?' he demanded heavily.

Croker gasped. 'You can't get away with this!' he reiterated, but his tone was beginning to lack conviction.

Greeves asked: 'Can you prove . . . ?'

Barnaby grunted. 'One of the guns – a hood named Rieg – confessed to the whole thing. He told us Swarm ordered them out after a conference with Croker.'

'You tortured Rieg!' Croker interrupted hysterically. 'You can't use that kind of testimony . . .'

'He talked,' Barnaby went on grimly. 'After they killed the baby, they threw the machine-gun over the West bridge so that it couldn't be traced and then went back with a sawed-off riot-gun to complete the job. Well, we fished the machine-gun out of the river. We can now definitely tie up that job to Swarm and Ritter with the help of a ballistician – the guy that can tell which gun fired which bullet.

'Now that dead baby stands over this whole proceedings. Rieg's testimony isn't enough to circumvent a lot of legal red-tape, but he did tell me where to find evidence. Croker's got a safe deposit box in the First National Bank under the name of Peter Hoople. I want a search warrant, or better still, a forthwith subpoena and have the contents of that box brought before you men. That will supply us with priceless data to continue our work. What do you say?'

Croker became shrieking. 'You can't do this!' he wailed. 'It isn't legal! I'll bring charges against you that will . . .'

Barnaby made an imperceptible motion with his hand. Hallahan stepped up and drove his fist against Croker's jaw. The lawyer folded like a carpenter's rule.

Tweedie daubed his face. 'This is irregular . . .' he began helplessly.

Greeves' features were tense. 'I demand that you issue the subpoena as Captain Barnaby requests, Judge Tweedie! And have you any more witnesses, Captain?'

Barnaby nodded. 'Plenty,' he promised; then to Hallahan. 'Take Croker away and bring on another.'

Tweedie gulped. 'Where is this going to end, Captain?'

'It's going to end, Judge, when I get enough evidence to smear over every court in this county; when you and the rest of the judicial trained-seals *have* to act to save your own hides; when I have the necessary evidence to get a warrant and go legally gunning for Coxy Swarm and Dave Antecki. Not that I care for your flimsy warrants; I just don't want those rats to die martyrs. It'll soon be daylight, Judge, and when the banks open, I want my boys there with warrants and subpoenas signed by *you*.'

Skipper Barnaby had his wish. In a variable night of hell, a scared jurist and a dumfounded juror listened to the whines and sobs, the lies and ratting of gunmen and thieves. And later, when Forsythe, Hallahan and Duane began to bring back the evidence they claimed by search warrants, the work began in deadly earnest. In the case of Croker's safe deposit box, claimed by a forthwith subpoena, a representative of the bank came with the evidence. He was amazed and terrified when Hallahan steered him into the subterranean courtroom, but after a talk with Greeves, he fell into the spirit of the thing. Barnaby commandeered him to examine accounts.

It was late afternoon when the work was finally completed. Gaunt, haggard, weary, but very game, Greeves pushed aside the papers before him and looked at Barnaby.

'This is incredible! It will shake the city to its very foundations! At least a score of the biggest names in local politics will go to the penitentiary!'

Barnaby nodded heavily. 'And now for the real job.' He turned to Hallahan. 'Bring in "The Scourge".'

Rieg was brought in to stand in fear before the grim board. All his bravado was gone, leaving a spineless, trembling rat.

Barnaby glared at him for a full minute before speaking. Then he began:

'Rieg, I'm turning you loose!'

Greeves burst out: 'But he'll warn the gang . . .'

'That's just what I want him to do,' Barnaby stopped him, and continued speaking to the startled gunman, 'I want you to tell Coxy Swarm that Clyde Barnaby, Dennis Hallahan, Sam Duane and Louis Forsythe are coming to get him. Tell him we have warrants for not only his own person, but for every man in his gang. You can assure him from me that if he submits peaceably to arrest, we will take him alive . . . and hang him later. Now get out!'

Rieg bolted, uninterrupted. He left behind him a void of startled silence. Greeves broke in:

'You deliberately warned Swarm! You've provoked a fight!'

Barnaby pushed himself erect. 'I hope I did,' he growled savagely. 'I can still see that little kid!'

*

Dave Antecki was a mobster of the old school. He was built close to the ground, with a flat face to match his figure. He was called Dave the Ape, but never in his presence; he had a blow-torch personality.

Dave the Ape made no pretension as to his headquarters. Where Swarm picked the quiet seclusion of the city's finest residential quarter, Antecki preferred the section that spawned him. As a thin front, he ran a small beer-parlor. It was a tough joint, with a tough clientele; the music was discordant, but it was loud; the food came in quantity rather than quality.

Antecki was seated at his favorite table, in the lee of the trap-drummer, eating a raviola dinner in company with a flousy blonde. She was as loud as the music and as coarse as the food, but she was young and big-chested and that was all that interested Dave the Ape. He had unbuttoned his vest in anticipation of some heavy eating, when one of his trusted henchmen came up to the table.

'Dave, Coxy is on his way over here!'

Antecki gagged, belched and sat very stiff. '*Him* . . . ? Comin' *here?*' Assured that his man was in earnest, he shouted, 'He wants trouble, eh? All okey. Call in the boys. . . .'

The informer shook his head. 'He don't want no trouble, Dave. He's in a jam . . . we all are. Somebody's snatched Chief Grogan . . .'

'*Grogan?*' Antecki gasped.

'An' Judge Tweedie an' Hymie Croker, an' Ritter an' . . .'

Dave the Ape stopped him. 'Somebody's crazy!' he growled, 'but if this is a frame, we'll be ready. Get Tony an' Perez to get behind them palms on either side of the dance-floor with the choppers. I'll meet Swarm right here.'

The blonde with the big chest and the willing way started to get up. 'Well, thanks for the salad, Dave, an' so long. I just remembered I got to see a man about a dog some place.'

'What's the matter, Amy, scared?'

'Uh-huh,' demurred the charmer, 'just my stomach. I can't stand the taste of hot lead.' She tossed him a kiss and moved away. Antecki might have stopped her, but at that moment, a stir near the entrance attracted his attention.

Swarm stepped into the big room, followed closely by five men. Their hands were all in plain sight, obviously so. Swarm took his bearings, glanced around the place and saw Antecki standing beside his table. He raised his right hand like an Indian and walked quickly across the room. As his men fell in behind him, a half dozen of Antecki's boys converged from various parts of the room.

Swarm paid no attention to them, nor did he offer to shake hands with Dave the Ape. He said:

'Hello, Dave. Can we talk some place?'

Antecki's eyes strayed casually in the direction of his machine-gunners, and nodded.

'Sure, sit down; we're as good here as any place. These are all my boys.'

Swarm dropped into a chair and motioned his men to do likewise. They all sat down and carefully placed their hands on the tables.

Swarm spoke again.

'Do you know Captain Barnaby and Sergeant Duane?'

Antecki nodded. 'Sure. Cops. I heard you got 'em fired.'

'They quit,' Swarm corrected him. 'Well, they've snatched about five of my best boys and killed at least one.'

'You want me to take my hair down an' have a good cry, perhaps?'

'The only reason I came to you, Dave,' Swarm snapped pointedly, 'is because we're in a spot. It ain't only my boys, but Croker, Tweedie, every key man in the machine is snatched. Maybe the Federals are behind this, but we got to find that out.'

'*We* . . . ?'

'Yes, *me!* Maybe it'll interest you to know that Grogan's gone, too. That leaves *you* in a hole, Dave.'

Antecki made no admissions. He massaged his heavy jowl thoughtfully, a little stupidly. He had paid well for protection and it never occurred to him that any force on earth could disrupt the *whole* machine. His own lawyer had advised him he was safe from prosecution as long as he paid his tribute.

Rieg came stumbling into the place at that moment.

Swarm swore. 'Rieg . . . ?' and the others just stared.

Rieg picked up a glass of red wine that still stood in front of Antecki's plate, emptied it down his throat and stared wild-eyed at the group.

'Barnaby is comin' for you, Coxy!' he choked.

Swarm smiled grimly. 'Where you been?'

In halting, broken phrases, 'The Scourge' mouthed out the story of what had happened to him from the moment big Clyde Barnaby had snatched him from the table in *La Parisienne* until his release. He told them about Tweedie, about Greeves and about Hymie Croker. He choked out the story of the warrants, of the bank secrets and of the work of the bank's representative.

'It ain't legal!' shouted Dave the Ape.

Rieg gave him a sour glance. 'He's got enough to send us all to the gallows!'

Swarm reached over and caught 'The Scourge' by the throat. 'You ratted, Rieg! You must have . . . !'

Rieg's protestations of innocence did him no good. At a sign from Swarm, two men rose and grabbed Rieg by the arms.

Swarm nodded his head towards the door. 'He ratted, boys,' was all he said, but that was sufficient. The pair started out, dragging the snivelling gun-man between them.

At that moment, a man appeared at the door.

'A coupla cops!' he shouted. 'A guy named Barnaby says he's comin' in after Swarm an' you, Dave!'

Antecki stood up. 'There ain't no damn' cop alive what can take me outa my own place! You can beat it out the back way, Swarm. I got two tommy-guns in this room. . . .'

Swarm smiled a little thinly. 'Just two dumb flatfeet and no witnesses. We'll see this out right now, Dave.' He gestured for his boys to spread out.

In a great semi-circle they lined the end of the big room facing the double entrance-doors. Antecki took out his gun and held it under a napkin atop the table. Swarm slid his automatic into a side pocket and kept his hand glued to the butt.

In silence they waited.

And abruptly the silence was broken by the voice of Captain Barnaby. He was calling from beyond the doors.

'I got warrants for you muggs,' came the unseen voice. 'Come out with your hands in the air.'

Antecki and Swarm exchanged glances. Swarm answered for them both.

'Come in and take us, flatfoot!'

As though operated by unseen hands, the wide, double-doors swung outward. The waiting audience tensed themselves for sudden action . . . then stared unbelievingly at the apparition that met their slitted eyes.

About fourteen men came through the door in one thick mass; not fourteen coppers, but men they knew well, all handcuffed together in a giant ring, backs to the middle. Ritter, Miller, Hymie Croker, Grogan . . . and about eight more ace-mobsters. Like children playing ring-around-the-rosy, their hands were joined in a protecting band, a human barricade. . . .

And in the middle of this trembling stockade, stood Captain Barnaby and Dennis Hallahan with riot-guns in their hands.

'Drop those guns, Coxy, an' you too, Dave!' commanded Barnaby coldly.

Croker cried like a burnt child. 'Don't shoot, Coxy! We'll all be killed!'

Barnaby and Hallahan advanced with terrible finality, prodding the human fence ahead.

'Come an' get in the game, boys,' Barnaby jeered. 'We'll have a good dance.'

Antecki glanced around the room. 'Stop where you are!' he yelled. 'I got machine-guns on you!'

Barnaby mocked him. 'Don't shoot, Dave! You'll cheat the State out of a hangin'! Put down your guns an' come out with your hands in the air. Do what I tell you! We're comin' for you!' He advanced slowly, grimly.

The mobsters stood, uncertain. Swarm was backed up against the slight rise of the orchestra dais; Antecki waited in front of the bass drum. At the first indication of trouble, the colored musicians had vanished.

Swarm tried guile. 'You can't take us, Barnaby. We won't be bluffed!'

The circle drew closer, Barnaby hurled a taunting laugh. 'I could kill you from here, Coxy, but I want you alive. I want to see you sweat in death row, I want to see you dance on the gallows and watch them open you up in the morgue. I want . . .'

It was Antecki that gave way first. He screamed a foreign oath, threw aside the concealing napkin and shouted to his gunners:

'Tony, Perez! Let 'em have it!' Then he fired point blank into the approaching mass. . . .

All hell broke loose! With the deafening chatter of the twin machine-guns, came the screams of stricken men. And then it seemed that the stuttering crash of the Tommies was double in volume. Barnaby and Hallahan dropped in unison. Croker, his head almost torn away by the stream of lead, fell across Barnaby. But Hallahan had time to send Antecki into eternity before the corpse of Miller pinned him down.

The chaos of sound ceased as abruptly as it had started. No gun thunder now, only gurgling sobs and low, throaty curses. And then Sam Duane's voice filled the hall.

'Are you all right, Skipper?'

Barnaby pushed the body of the lawyer off him and lifted his head. The place was in shambles. He glanced back at the doorway. Duane and Forsythe loomed in the opening, each with a smoking sub-machine-gun in their hands. He rose, looked down at Hallahan.

Hallahan sat up, pulled himself erect.

Duane and Forsythe, white of features, came over. 'It went off on schedule,' Sam Duane said through clenched teeth. 'I never want another experience like that, though.'

Barnaby shrugged. 'It saved the State a lot of money an' the taxpayers have earned a little consideration. That's literally getting' two birds with one stone.'

Forsythe put his gun on the table and wiped his face. 'We didn't have much to do,' he told Barnaby. 'Those two gunmen of Antecki's went crazy. They cleaned the decks of everything that was standing and then we finished them.'

Barnaby walked over to the dais. Antecki had fallen backwards and was sitting in the middle of the giant bass drum.

Duane said: 'Look, Skipper, seems like Swarm was tryin' to run away.'

Barnaby turned. Coxy Swarm lay across the edge of the dais, feet and knees on the dance-floor, tuxedoed torso flattened on the dais itself. There were three welling holes across his back and blood seeped over the polished floor.

Skipper Barnaby sighed. 'It took a guidin' hand to put a finish like that,' he growled, a touch of reverence in his tone. 'Destiny, I reckon some 'ud call it.'

'Hows that?' Hallahan wanted to know.

'That's just the way that little kid got it,' Barnaby grunted, and turned away.

RED WIND
RAYMOND CHANDLER

One could easily make the argument that Raymond Chandler (1888–1959) was the greatest writer who ever sold a story to a pulp magazine, and I would further make the case that he was one of the half-dozen great American writers of the 20th century.

An oil company executive until the Great Depression caused the industry to collapse, he sold his first short story in 1933 at the age of 45. Less popular than either Carroll John Daly or Dashiell Hammett, he did not achieve fame until the publication of his first novel, *The Big Sleep*, in 1939 after having produced 20 novellas for *Black Mask* and other pulps.

Few authors in any genre matched Chandler's prose, which employed the use of metaphor and simile in a masterly way. The poet W.H. Auden described his books as 'works of art' rather than escape literature. Among his most important contributions to detective fiction may be his definition of what a private eye should be, as he wrote in 'The Simple Art of Murder' for *The Atlantic Monthly* in December, 1944. He compared him to a modern knight.

'Down these mean streets a man must go who is not himself mean, who is neither tarnished nor afraid. The detective in this kind of story must be such a man. He is the hero, he is everything. He must be a complete man and a common man, and yet an unusual man. He must be, to use a rather weathered phrase, a man of honor.'

'Red Wind' was first published in *Dime Detective* in January 1938.

RED WIND

RAYMOND CHANDLER

There was a desert wind blowing that night. It was one of those hot dry Santa Anas that come down through the mountain passes and curl your hair and make your nerves jump and your skin itch. On nights like that every booze party ends in a fight. Meek little wives feel the edge of the carving knife and study their husbands' necks. Anything can happen. You can even get a full glass of beer at a cocktail lounge.

I was getting one in a flossy new place across the street from the apartment house where I lived. It had been open about a week and it wasn't doing any business. The kid behind the bar was in his early twenties and looked as if he had never had a drink in his life.

There was only one other customer, a souse on a bar stool with his back to the door. He had a pile of dimes stacked neatly in front of him, about two dollars' worth. He was drinking straight rye in small glasses and he was all by himself in a world of his own.

I sat farther along the bar and got my glass of beer and said: 'You sure cut the clouds off them, buddy. I will say that for you.'

'We just opened up,' the kid said. 'We got to build up trade. Been in before, haven't you, mister?'

'Uh-huh.'

'Live around here?'

'In the Berglund Apartments across the street,' I said. 'And the name is Philip Marlowe.'

'Thanks, mister. Mine's Lew Petrolle.' He leaned close to me across the polished dark bar. 'Know that guy?'

'No.'

'He ought to go home, kind of. I ought to call a taxi and send him home. He's doing his next week's drinking too soon.'

'A night like this,' I said. 'Let him alone.'

'It's not good for him,' the kid said, scowling at me.

'Rye!' the drunk croaked, without looking up. He snapped his fingers so as not to disturb his piles of dimes by banging on the bar.

The kid looked at me and shrugged. 'Should I?'

'Whose stomach is it? Not mine.'

The kid poured him another straight rye and I think he doctored it with water down behind the bar because when he came up with it he looked as guilty as if he'd kicked his grandmother. The drunk paid no attention. He lifted coins off his pile with the exact care of a crack surgeon operating on a brain tumor.

The kid came back and put more beer in my glass. Outside the wind howled. Every once in a while it blew the stained-glass door open a few inches. It was a heavy door.

The kid said: 'I don't like drunks in the first place and in the second place I don't like them getting drunk in here, and in the third place I don't like them in the first place.'

'Warner Brothers could use that,' I said.

'They did.'

Just then we had another customer. A car squeaked to a stop outside and the swinging door came open. A fellow came in who looked a little in a hurry. He held the door and ranged the place quickly with flat, shiny, dark eyes. He was well set up, dark, good-looking in a narrow-faced, tight-lipped way. His clothes were dark and a white handkerchief peeped coyly from his pocket and he looked cool as well as under a tension of some sort. I guessed it was the hot wind. I felt a bit the same myself only not cool.

He looked at the drunk's back. The drunk was playing checkers with his empty glasses. The new customer looked at me, then he looked along the line of half-booths at the other side of the place. They were all empty. He came on in – down past where the drunk sat swaying and muttering to himself – and spoke to the bar kid.

'Seen a lady in here, buddy? Tall, pretty, brown hair, in a print bolero jacket over a blue crêpe silk dress. Wearing a wide-brimmed straw hat with a velvet band.' He had a tight voice I didn't like.

'No, sir. Nobody like that's been in,' the bar kid said.

'Thanks. Straight Scotch. Make it fast, will you?'

The kid gave it to him and the fellow paid and put the drink down in a gulp and started to go out. He took three or four steps and stopped, facing the drunk. The drunk was grinning. He swept a gun from somewhere so fast that it was just a blur coming out. He held it steady and he didn't look any drunker than I was. The tall dark guy stood quite still and then his head jerked back a little and then he was still again.

A car tore by outside. The drunk's gun was a .22 target automatic, with a large front sight. It made a couple of hard snaps and a little smoke curled – very little.

'So long, Waldo,' the drunk said.

Then he put the gun on the barman and me.

The dark guy took a week to fall down. He stumbled, caught himself, waved one arm, stumbled again. His hat fell off, and then he hit the floor with his face. After he hit it he might have been poured concrete for all the fuss he made.

The drunk slid down off the stool and scooped his dimes into a pocket and slid towards the door. He turned sideways, holding the gun across his body. I didn't have a gun. I hadn't thought I needed one to buy a glass of beer. The kid behind the bar didn't move or make the slightest sound.

The drunk felt the door lightly with his shoulder, keeping his eyes on us, then pushed through it backwards. When it was wide a hard gust of air slammed in and lifted the hair of the man on the floor. The drunk said: 'Poor Waldo. I bet I made his nose bleed.'

The door swung shut. I started to rush it – from long practice in doing the wrong thing. In this case it didn't matter. The car outside let out a roar and when I got onto the sidewalk it was flicking a red smear of taillight around the nearby corner. I got its license number the way I got my first million.

There were people and cars up and down the block as usual. Nobody acted as if a gun had gone off. The wind was making enough noise to make the hard quick rap of .22 ammunition sound like a slammed door, even if anyone heard it. I went back into the cocktail bar.

The kid hadn't moved, even yet. He just stood with his hands flat on the bar, leaning over a little and looking down at the dark guy's back. The dark guy hadn't moved either. I bent down and felt his neck artery. He wouldn't move – ever.

The kid's face had as much expression as a cut of round steak and was about the same color. His eyes were more angry than shocked.

I lit a cigarette and blew smoke at the ceiling and said shortly: 'Get on the phone.'

'Maybe he's not dead,' the kid said.

'When they use a twenty-two that means they don't make mistakes. Where's the phone?'

'I don't have one. I got enough expenses without that. Boy, can I kick eight hundred bucks in the face!'

'You own this place?'

'I did till this happened.'

He pulled his white coat off and his apron and came around the inner end of the bar. 'I'm locking this door,' he said, taking keys out.

He went out, swung the door to and jiggled the lock from the outside until the bolt clicked into place. I bent down and rolled Waldo over. At first I couldn't even see where the shots went in. Then I could. A couple of tiny holes in his coat, over his heart. There was a little blood on his shirt.

The drunk was everything you could ask – as a killer.

The prowl-car boys came in about eight minutes. The kid, Lew Petrolle, was back behind the bar by then. He had his white coat on again and he was counting his money in the register and putting it in his pocket and making notes in a little book.

I sat at the edge of one of the half-booths and smoked cigarettes and watched Waldo's face get deader and deader. I wondered who the girl in the print coat was, why Waldo had left the engine of his car running outside, why he was in a hurry, whether the drunk had been waiting for him or just happened to be there.

The prowl-car boys came in perspiring. They were the usual large size and one of them had a flower stuck under his cap and his cap on a bit crooked. When he saw the dead man he got rid of the flower and leaned down to feel Waldo's pulse.

'Seems to be dead,' he said, and rolled him around a little more. 'Oh yeah, I see where they went in. Nice clean work. You two see him get it?'

I said yes. The kid behind the bar said nothing. I told them about it, that the killer seemed to have left in Waldo's car.

The cop yanked Waldo's wallet out, went through it rapidly and whistled. 'Plenty jack and no driver's license.' He put the wallet away. 'O.K., we didn't touch him, see? Just a chance we could find did he have a car and put it on the air.'

'The hell you didn't touch him,' Lew Patrolle said.

The cop gave him one of those looks. 'O.K., pal,' he said softly. 'We touched him.'

The kid picked up a clean highball glass and began to polish it. He polished it all the rest of the time we were there.

In another minute a homicide fast-wagon sirened up and screeched to a stop outside the door and four men came in, two dicks, a photographer and a laboratory man. I didn't know either of the dicks. You can be in the detecting business a long time and not know all the men on a big city force.

One of them was a short, smooth, dark, quiet, smiling man, with curly black hair and soft intelligent eyes. The other was big, raw-boned, long-jawed, with a veined nose and glassy eyes. He looked like a heavy drinker. He looked tough, but he looked as if he thought he was a little tougher than he was. He shooed me into the last booth against the wall and his partner got the kid up front and the bluecoats went out. The fingerprint man and photographer set about their work.

A medical examiner came, stayed just long enough to get sore because there was no phone for him to call the morgue wagon.

The short dick emptied Waldo's pockets and then emptied his wallet and dumped everything into a large handkerchief on a booth table. I saw a lot of currency, keys, cigarettes, another handkerchief, very little else.

The big dick pushed me back into the end of the half-booth. 'Give,' he said. 'I'm Copernik, Detective Lieutenant.'

I put my wallet in front of him. He looked at it, went through it, tossed it back, made a note in a book.

'Philip Marlowe, huh? A shamus. You here on business?'

'Drinking business,' I said. 'I live just across the street in the Berglund.'

'Know this kid up front?'

'I've been in here once since he opened up.'

'See anything funny about him now?'

'No.'

'Takes it too light for a young fellow, don't he? Never mind answering. Just tell the story.'

I told it – three times. Once for him to get the outline, once for him to get the details and once for him to see if I had it too pat. At the end he said: 'This dame interests me. And the killer called the guy Waldo, yet didn't seem to be anyways sure he would be in. I mean, if Waldo wasn't sure the dame would be here, nobody could be sure Waldo would be here.'

'That's pretty deep,' I said.

He studied me. I wasn't smiling. 'Sounds like a grudge job, don't it? Don't sound planned. No getaway except by accident. A guy don't leave his car unlocked much in this town. And the killer works in front of two good witnesses. I don't like that.'

'I don't like being a witness,' I said. 'The pay's too low.'

He grinned. His teeth had a freckled look. 'Was the killer drunk really?'

'With that shooting? No.'

'Me too. Well, it's a simple job. The guy will have a record and he's left plenty prints. Even if we don't have his mug here we'll make him in hours. He had something on Waldo, but he wasn't meeting Waldo tonight. Waldo just dropped in to ask about a dame he had a date with and had missed connections on. It's a hot night and this wind would kill a girl's face. She'd be apt to drop in somewhere to wait. So the killer feeds Waldo two in the right place and scrams and don't worry about you boys at all. It's that simple.'

'Yeah,' I said.

'It's so simple it stinks,' Copernik said.

He took his felt hat off and tousled up his ratty blond hair and leaned his head on his hands. He had a long mean horse face. He got a handkerchief out and mopped it, and the back of his neck and the back of his hands. He got a comb out and combed his hair – he looked worse with it combed – and put his hat back on.

'I was just thinking.' I said.

'Yeah? What?'

'This Waldo knew just how the girl was dressed. So he must already have been with her tonight.'

'So, what? Maybe he had to go to the can. And when he came back she's gone. Maybe she changed her mind about him.'

'That's right,' I said.

But that wasn't what I was thinking at all. I was thinking that Waldo had described the girl's clothes in a way the ordinary man wouldn't know how to describe them. Printed bolero jacket over blue crêpe silk dress. I didn't even know what a bolero jacket was. And I might have said blue dress or even blue silk dress, but never blue crêpe silk dress.

After a while two men came with a basket. Lew Petrolle was still polishing his glass and talking to the short dark dick.

We all went down to Headquarters.

Lew Petrolle was all right when they checked on him. His father had a grape ranch near Antioch in Contra Costa County. He had given Lew a thousand dollars to go into business and Lew had opened the cocktail bar, neon sign and all, on eight hundred flat.

They let him go and told him to keep the bar closed until they were sure they didn't want to do any more printing. He shook hands all around and grinned and said he guessed the killing would be good for business after all, because nobody believed a newspaper account of anything and people would come to him for the story and buy drinks while he was telling it.

'There's a guy won't ever do any worrying,' Copernik said, when he was gone. 'Over anybody else.'

'Poor Waldo,' I said. 'The prints any good?'

'Kind of smudged,' Copernik said sourly. 'But we'll get a classification and teletype it to Washington some time tonight. If it don't click, you'll be in for a day on the steel picture racks downstairs.'

I shook hands with him and his partner, whose name was Ybarra, and left. They didn't know who Waldo was yet either. Nothing in his pockets told.

TWO

I got back to my street about 9 P.M. I looked up and down the block before I went into the Berglund. The cocktail bar was farther down on the other side, dark, with a nose or two against the glass, but no real crowd. People had seen the law and the morgue wagon, but they didn't know what happened. Except the boys playing pinball games in the drugstore on the corner. They know everything, except how to hold a job.

The wind was still blowing, oven-hot, swirling dust and torn paper up against the walls.

I went into the lobby of the apartment house and rode the automatic elevator up to the fourth floor. I unwound the doors and stepped out and there was a tall girl standing there waiting for the car.

She had brown wavy hair under a wide-brimmed straw hat with a velvet band and loose bow. She had wide blue eyes and eyelashes that didn't quite reach her chin. She wore a blue dress that might have been crêpe silk, simple in lines but not missing any curves. Over it she wore what might have been a print bolero jacket.

I said: 'Is that a bolero jacket?'

She gave me a distant glance and made a motion as if to brush a cobweb out of the way.

'Yes. Would you mind – I'm rather in a hurry. I'd like—'

I didn't move. I blocked her off from the elevator. We stared at each other and she flushed very slowly.

'Better not go out on the street in those clothes,' I said.

'Why, how dare you—'

The elevator clanked and started down again. I didn't know what she was going to say. Her voice lacked the edgy twang of a beer-parlor frill. It had a soft light sound, like spring rain.

'It's not a make,' I said. 'You're in trouble. If they come to this floor in the elevator, you have just that much time to get off the hall. First take off the hat and jacket – and snap it up!'

She didn't move. Her face seemed to whiten a little behind the not-too-heavy make-up.

'Cops,' I said, 'are looking for you. In those clothes. Give me the chance and I'll tell you why.'

She turned her head swiftly and looked back along the corridor. With her looks I didn't blame her for trying one more bluff.

'You're impertinent, whoever you are. I'm Mrs. Leroy in Apartment Thirty-one. I can assure—'

'That you're on the wrong floor,' I said. 'This is the fourth.' The elevator had stopped down below. The sound of doors being wrenched open came up the shaft.

'Off!' I rapped. 'Now!'

She switched her hat off and slipped out of the bolero jacket, fast. I grabbed them and wadded them into a mess under my arm. I took her elbow and turned her and we were going down the hall.

'I live in Forty-two. The front one across from yours, just a floor up. Take your choice. Once again – I'm not on the make.'

She smoothed her hair with that quick gesture, like a bird preening itself. Ten thousand years of practice behind it.

'Mine,' she said, and tucked her bag under her arm and strode down the hall fast. The elevator stopped at the floor below. She stopped when it stopped. She turned and faced me.

'The stairs are back by the elevator shaft,' I said gently.

'I don't have an apartment,' she said.

'I didn't think you had.'

'Are they searching for me?'

'Yes, but they won't start gouging the block stone by stone before tomorrow. And then only if they don't make Waldo.'

She stared at me. 'Waldo?'

'Oh, you don't know Waldo,' I said.

She shook her head slowly. The elevator started down in the shaft again. Panic flicked in her blue eyes like a ripple on water.

'No,' she said breathlessly, 'but take me out of this hall.'

We were almost at my door. I jammed the key in and shook the lock around and heaved the door inward. I reached in far enough to switch lights on. She went in past me like a wave. Sandalwood floated on the air, very faint.

I shut the door, threw my hat into a chair and watched her stroll over to a card table on which I had a chess problem set out that I couldn't solve. Once inside, with the door locked, her panic had left her.

'So you're a chess player,' she said, in that guarded tone, as if she had come to look at my etchings. I wished she had.

We both stood still then and listened to the distant clang of elevator doors and then steps – going the other way.

I grinned, but with strain, not pleasure, went out into the kitchenette and started to fumble with a couple of glasses and then realized I still had her hat and bolero jacket under my arm. I went into the dressing room behind the wall bed and stuffed them into a drawer, went back out to the kitchenette, dug out some extra-fine Scotch and made a couple of highballs.

When I went in with the drinks she had a gun in her hand. It was a small automatic with a pearl grip. It jumped up at me and her eyes were full of horror.

I stopped, with a glass in each hand, and said: 'Maybe this hot wind has got you crazy too. I'm a private detective. I'll prove it if you let me.'

She nodded slightly and her face was white. I went over slowly and put a glass down beside her, and went back and set mine down and got a card out that had no bent corners. She was sitting down, smoothing one blue knee with her left hand, and holding the gun on the other. I put the card down beside her drink and sat with mine.

'Never let a guy get that close to you,' I said. 'Not if you mean business. And your safety catch is on.'

She flashed her eyes down, shivered, and put the gun back in her bag. She drank half the drink without stopping, put the glass down hard and picked the card up.

'I don't give many people that liquor,' I said. 'I can't afford to.'

Her lips curled. 'I supposed you would want money.'

'Huh?'

She didn't say anything. Her hand was close to her bag again.

'Don't forget the safety catch,' I said. Her hand stopped. I went on: 'This fellow I called Waldo is quite tall, say five-eleven, slim, dark, brown eyes with a lot of glitter. Nose and mouth too thin. Dark suit, white handerkerchief showing, and in a hurry to find you. Am I getting anywhere?'

She took her glass again. 'So that's Waldo,' she said. 'Well, what about him?' Her voice seemed to have a slight liquor edge now.

'Well, a funny thing. There's a cocktail bar across the street . . . Say, where have you been all evening?'

'Sitting in my car,' she said coldly, 'most of the time.'

'Didn't you see a fuss across the street up the block?'

Her eyes tried to say no and missed. Her lips said: 'I knew there was some kind of disturbance. I saw policemen and red searchlights. I supposed someone had been hurt.'

'Someone was. And this Waldo was looking for you before that. In the cocktail bar. He described you and your clothes.'

Her eyes were set like rivets now and had the same amount of expression. Her mouth began to tremble and kept on trembling.

'I was in there,' I said, 'talking to the kid that runs it. There was nobody in there but a drunk on a stool and the kid and myself. The drunk wasn't paying any attention to anything. Then Waldo came in and asked about you and we said no, we hadn't seen you and he started to leave.'

I sipped my drink. I like an effect as well as the next fellow. Her eyes ate me.

'Just started to leave. Then this drunk that wasn't paying any attention to anyone called him Waldo and took a gun out. He shot him twice' – I snapped my fingers twice – 'like that. Dead.'

She fooled me. She laughed in my face. 'So my husband hired you to spy on me,' she said. 'I might have known the whole thing was an act. You and your Waldo.'

I gawked at her.

'I never thought of him as jealous,' she snapped. 'Not of a man who had been our chauffeur anyhow. A little about Stan, of course – that's natural. But Joseph Coates—'

I made motions in the air. 'Lady, one of us has this book open at the wrong page,' I grunted. 'I don't know anybody named Stan or Joseph Coates. So help me, I didn't even know you had a chauffeur. People around here don't run to them. As for husbands – yeah, we do have a husband once in a while. Not often enough.'

She shook her head slowly and her hand stayed near her bag and her blue eyes had glitters in them.

'Not good enough, Mr. Marlowe. No, not nearly good enough. I know you private detectives. You're all rotten. You tricked me into your apartment, if it is your apartment. More likely it's the apartment of some horrible man who will swear anything for a few dollars. Now you're trying to scare me. So you can blackmail me – as well as get money from my husband. All right,' she said breathlessly, 'how much do I have to pay?'

I put my empty glass aside and leaned back. 'Pardon me if I light a cigarette,' I said. 'My nerves are frayed.'

I lit it while she watched me without enough fear for any real guilt to be under it. 'So Joseph Coates is his name,' I said. 'The guy that killed him in the cocktail bar called him Waldo.'

She smiled a bit disgustedly, but almost tolerantly. 'Don't stall. How much?'

'Why were you trying to meet this Joseph Coates?'

'I was going to buy something he stole from me, of course. Something that's valuable in the ordinary way too. Almost fifteen thousand dollars. The man I loved gave it to me. He's dead. There! He's dead! He died in a burning plane. Now, go back and tell my husband that, you slimy little rat!'

'I'm not little and I'm not a rat,' I said.

'You're still slimy. And don't bother about telling my husband. I'll tell him myself. He probably knows anyway.'

I grinned. 'That's smart. Just what was I supposed to find out?'

She grabbed her glass and finished what was left of her drink. 'So he thinks I'm meeting Joseph. Well, perhaps I was. But not to make love. Not with a chauffeur. Not with a bum I picked off the front step and gave a job to. I don't have to dig down that far, if I want to play around.'

'Lady,' I said, 'you don't indeed.'

'Now, I'm going,' she said. 'You just try and stop me.' She snatched the pearl-handled gun out of her bag. I didn't move.

'Why, you nasty little string of nothing,' she stormed. 'How do I know you're a private detective at all? You might be a crook. This card you gave me doesn't mean anything. Anybody can have cards printed.'

'Sure,' I said. 'And I suppose I'm smart enough to live here two years because you were going to move in today so I could blackmail you for not meeting a man named Joseph Coates who was bumped off across the street under the name of Waldo. Have you got the money to buy this something that cost fifteen grand?'

'Oh! You think you'll hold me up, I suppose!'

'Oh!' I mimicked her, 'I'm a stick-up artist now, am I? Lady, will you please either put that gun away or take the safety catch off? It hurts my professional feelings to see a nice gun made a monkey of that way.'

'You're a full portion of what I don't like,' she said. 'Get out of my way.'

I didn't move. She didn't move. We were both sitting down – and not even close to each other.

'Let me in on one secret before you go,' I pleaded. 'What in hell did you take the apartment down on the floor below for? Just to meet a guy down on the street?'

'Stop being silly,' she snapped. 'I didn't. I lied. It's his apartment.'

'Joseph Coates'?'

She nodded sharply.

'Does my description of Waldo sound like Joseph Coates?'

She nodded sharply again.

'All right. That's one fact learned at last. Don't you realize Waldo described your clothes before he was shot – when he was looking for you – that the description was passed on to the police – that the police don't know who Waldo is – and are looking for somebody in those clothes to help tell them? Don't you get that much?'

The gun suddenly started to shake in her hand. She looked down at it, sort of vacantly, and slowly put it back in her bag.

'I'm a fool,' she whispered, 'to be even talking to you.' She stared at me for a long time, then pulled in a deep breath. 'He told me where he was staying. He didn't seem afraid. I guess blackmailers are like that. He was to meet me on the street, but I was late. It was full of police when I got here. So I went back and sat in my car for a while. Then I came up to Joseph's apartment and knocked. Then I went back to my car and waited again. I came up here three times in all. The last time I walked up a flight to take the elevator. I had already been seen twice on the third floor. I met you. That's all.'

'You said something about a husband,' I grunted. 'Where is he?'

'He's at a meeting.'

'Oh, a meeting,' I said, nastily.

'My husband's a very important man. He has lots of meetings. He's a hydroelectric engineer. He's been all over the world. I'd have you know—'

'Skip it,' I said. 'I'll take him to lunch some day and have him tell me himself. Whatever Joseph had on you is dead stock now. Like Joseph.'

'He's really dead?' she whispered. 'Really?'

'He's dead,' I said. 'Dead, dead, dead. Lady, he's dead.'

She believed it at last. I hadn't thought she ever would somehow. In the silence, the elevator stopped at my floor.

I heard steps coming down the hall. We all have hunches. I put my finger to my lips. She didn't move now. Her face had a frozen look. Her big blue eyes were as black as the shadows below them. The hot wind boomed against the shut windows. Windows have to be shut when a Santa Ana blows, heat or no heat.

The steps that came down the hall were the casual ordinary steps of one man. But they stopped outside my door, and somebody knocked.

I pointed to the dressing room behind the wall bed. She stood up without a sound, her bag clenched against her side. I pointed again, to her glass. She lifted it swiftly, slid across the carpet, through the door, drew the door quietly shut after her.

I didn't know just what I was going to all this trouble for.

The knocking sounded again. The backs of my hands were wet. I creaked my chair and stood up and made a loud yawning sound. Then I went over and opened the door – without a gun. That was a mistake.

THREE

I didn't know him at first. Perhaps for the opposite reason Waldo hadn't seemed to know him. He'd had a hat on all the time over at the cocktail bar and he didn't have one on now. His hair ended completely and exactly where his hat would start. Above that line was hard white sweatless skin almost as glaring as scar tissue. He wasn't just twenty years older. He was a different man.

But I knew the gun he was holding, the .22 target automatic with the big front sight. And I knew his eyes. Bright, brittle, shallow eyes like the eyes of a lizard.

He was alone. He put the gun against my face very lightly and said between his teeth: 'Yeah, me. Let's go on in.'

I backed in just far enough and stopped. Just the way he would want me to, so he could shut the door without moving much. I knew from his eyes that he would want me to do just that.

I wasn't scared. I was paralyzed.

When he had the door shut he backed me some more, slowly, until there was something against the back of my legs. His eyes looked into mine.

'That's a card table,' he said. 'Some goon here plays chess. You?'

I swallowed. 'I don't exactly play it. I just fool around.'

'That means two,' he said with a kind of hoarse softness, as if some cop had hit him across the windpipe with a blackjack once, in a third-degree session.

'It's a problem,' I said. 'Not a game. Look at the pieces.'

'I wouldn't know.'

'Well, I'm alone,' I said, and my voice shook just enough.

'It don't make any difference,' he said. 'I'm washed up anyway. Some nose puts the bulls on me tomorrow, next week, what the hell? I just didn't like your map, pal. And that smug-faced pansy in the bar coat that played left tackle for Fordham or something. To hell with guys like you guys.'

I didn't speak or move. The big front sight raked my cheek lightly almost caressingly. The man smiled.

'It's kind of good business too,' he said. 'Just in case. An old con like me don't make good prints, all I got against me is two witnesses. The hell with it.'

'What did Waldo do to you?' I tried to make it sound as if I wanted to know, instead of just not wanting to shake too hard.

'Stooled on a bank job in Michigan and got me four years. Got himself a nolle prosse. Four years in Michigan ain't no summer cruise. They make you be good in them lifer states.'

'How'd you know he'd come in there?' I croaked.

'I didn't. Oh yeah, I was lookin' for him. I was wanting to see him all right. I got a flash of him on the street night before last but I lost him. Up to then I wasn't lookin' for him. Then I was. A cute guy, Waldo. How is he?'

'Dead,' I said.

'I'm still good,' he chuckled. 'Drunk or sober. Well, that don't make no doughnuts for me now. They make me downtown yet?'

I didn't answer him quick enough. He jabbed the gun into my throat and I choked and almost grabbed for it by instinct.

'Naw,' he cautioned me softly. 'Naw. You ain't that dumb.'

I put my hands back, down at my sides, open, the palms towards him. He would want them that way. He hadn't touched me, except with the gun. He didn't seem to care whether I might have one too. He wouldn't – if he just meant the one thing.

He didn't seem to care very much about anything, coming back on that block. Perhaps the hot wind did something to him. It was booming against my shut windows like the surf under a pier.

'They got prints,' I said. 'I don't know how good.'

'They'll be good enough – but not for teletype work. Take 'em airmail time to Washington and back to check 'em right. Tell me why I came here, pal.'

'You heard the kid and me talking in the bar. I told him my name, where I lived.'

'That's how, pal. I said why.' He smiled at me. It was a lousy smile to be the last one you might see.

'Skip it,' I said. 'The hangman won't ask you to guess why he's there.'

'Say, you're tough at that. After you, I visit that kid. I tailed him home from Headquarters, but I figure you're the guy to put the bee on first. I tail him home from the city hall, in the rent car Waldo had. From Headquarters, pal. Them funny dicks. You can sit in their laps and they don't know you. Start runnin' for a streetcar and they open up with machine guns and bump two pedestrians, a hacker asleep in his cab, and an old scrubwoman on the second floor workin' a mop. And they miss the guy they're after. Them funny lousy dicks.'

He twisted the gun muzzle in my neck. His eyes looked madder than before.

'I got time,' he said. 'Waldo's rent car don't get a report right away. And they don't make Waldo very soon. I know Waldo. Smart he was. A smooth boy, Waldo.'

'I'm going to vomit,' I said, 'if you don't take that gun out of my throat.'

He smiled and moved the gun down to my heart. 'This about right? Say when.'

I must have spoken louder than I meant to. The door of the dressing-room by the wall bed showed a crack of darkness. Then an inch. Then four inches. I saw eyes, but didn't look at them. I stared hard into the bald-headed man's eyes. Very hard. I didn't want him to take his eyes off mine.

'Scared?' he asked softly.

I leaned against his gun and began to shake. I thought he would enjoy seeing me shake. The girl came out through the door. She had her gun in her hand again. I was sorry as hell for her. She'd try to make the door – or scream. Either way it would be curtains – for both of us.

'Well, don't take all night about it,' I bleated. My voice sounded far away, like a voice on a radio on the other side of a street.

'I like this, pal,' he smiled. 'I'm like that.'

The girl floated in the air, somewhere behind him. Nothing was ever more soundless than the way she moved. It wouldn't do any good though. He wouldn't fool around with her at all. I had known him all my life but I had been looking into his eyes for only five minutes.

'Suppose I yell,' I said.

'Yeah, suppose you yell. Go ahead and yell,' he said with his killer's smile.

She didn't go near the door. She was right behind him.

'Well – here's where I yell,' I said.

As if that was the cue, she jabbed the little gun hard into his short ribs, without a single sound.

He had to react. It was like a knee reflex. His mouth snapped open and both his arms jumped out from his sides and he arched his back just a little. The gun was pointing at my right eye.

I sank and kneed him with all my strength, in the groin.

His chin came down and I hit it. I hit it as if I was driving the last spike on the first transcontinental railroad. I can still feel it when I flex my knuckles.

His gun raked the side of my face but it didn't go off. He was already limp. He writhed down gasping, his left side against the floor. I kicked his right shoulder – hard. The gun jumped away from him, skidded on the carpet, under a chair. I heard the chessmen tinkling on the floor behind me somewhere.

The girl stood over him, looking down. Then her wide dark horrified eyes came up and fastened on mine.

'That buys me,' I said. 'Anything I have is yours – now and forever.'

She didn't hear me. Her eyes were strained open so hard that the whites showed under the vivid blue iris. She backed quickly to the door with her little gun up, felt behind her for the knob and twisted it. She pulled the door open and slipped out.

The door shut.

She was bareheaded and without her bolero jacket.

She had only the gun, and the safety catch on that was still set so that she couldn't fire it.

It was silent in the room then, in spite of the wind. Then I heard him gasping on the floor. His face had a greenish pallor. I moved behind him and pawed him for more guns, and didn't find any. I got a pair of store cuffs out of my desk and pulled his arms in front of him and snapped them on his wrists. They would hold if he didn't shake them too hard.

His eyes measured me for a coffin, in spite of their suffering. He lay in the middle of the floor, still on his left side, a twisted, wizened, bald-headed little guy with drawn-back lips and teeth spotted with cheap silver fillings. His mouth looked like a black pit and his breath came in little waves, choked, stopped, came on again, limping.

I went into the dressing room and opened the drawer of the chest. Her hat and jacket lay there on my shirts. I put them underneath, at the back, and smoothed the shirts over them. Then I went out to the kitchenette and poured a stiff jolt of whiskey and put it down and stood a moment listening to the hot wind howl against the window glass. A garage door banged, and a power-line wire with too much play between the insulators thumped the side of the building with a sound like somebody beating a carpet.

The drink worked on me. I went back into the living room and opened a window. The guy on the floor hadn't smelled her sandalwood, but somebody else might.

I shut the window again, wiped the palms of my hands and used the phone to dial Headquarters.

Copernik was still there. His smart-aleck voice said: 'Yeah? Marlowe? Don't tell me. I bet you got an idea.'

'Make that killer yet?'

'We're not saying, Marlowe. Sorry as all hell and so on. You know how it is.'

'O.K., I don't care who he is. Just come and get him off the floor of my apartment.

'Holy Christ!' Then his voice hushed and went down low. 'Wait a minute, now. Wait a minute.' A long way off I seemed to hear a door shut. Then his voice again. 'Shoot,' he said softly.

'Handcuffed,' I said. 'All yours. I had to knee him, but he'll be all right. He came here to eliminate a witness.'

Another pause. The voice was fully of honey. 'Now listen, boy, who else is in this with you?'

'Who else? Nobody. Just me.'

'Keep it that way, boy. All quiet. O.K.?'

'Think I want all the bums in the neighborhood in here sightseeing?'

'Take it easy, boy. Easy. Just sit tight and sit still. I'm practically there. No touch nothing. Get me?'

'Yeah.' I gave him the address and apartment number again to save him time.

I could see his big bony face glisten. I got the .22 target gun from under the chair and sat holding it until feet hit the hallway outside my door and knuckles did a quiet tattoo on the door panel.

Copernik was alone. He filled the doorway quickly, pushed me back into the room with a tight grin and shut the door. He stood with his back to it, his hand under the left side of his coat. A big hard bony man with flat cruel eyes.

He lowered them slowly and looked at the man on the floor. The man's neck was twitching a little. His eyes moved in short stabs – sick eyes.

'Sure it's the guy?' Copernick's voice was hoarse.

'Positive. Where's Ybarra?'

'Oh, he was busy.' He didn't look at me when he said that. 'Those your cuffs?'

'Yeah.'

'Key.'

I tossed it to him. He went down swiftly on one knee beside the killer and took my cuffs off his wrists, tossed them to one side. He got his own off his hip, twisted the bald man's hands behind him and snapped the cuffs on.

'All right, you bastard,' the killer said tonelessly.

Copernik grinned and balled his fist and hit the handcuffed man in the mouth a terrific blow. His head snapped back almost enough to break his neck. Blood dribbled from the lower corner of his mouth.

'Get a towel,' Copernik ordered.

I got a hand towel and gave it to him. He stuffed it between the handcuffed man's teeth, viciously, stood up and rubbed his bony fingers through his ratty blond hair.

'All right. Tell it.'

I told it – leaving the girl out completely. It sounded a little funny. Copernik watched me, said nothing. He rubbed the side of his veined nose. Then he got his comb out and worked on his hair just as he had done earlier in the evening, in the cocktail bar.

I went over and gave him the gun. He looked at it casually, dropped it into his side pocket. His eyes had something in them and his face moved in a hard bright grin.

I bent down and began picking up my chessmen and dropping them into the box. I put the box on the mantel, straightened out a leg of the card table, played around for a while. All the time Copernik watched me. I wanted him to think something out.

At last he came out with it. 'This guy uses a twenty-two,' he said. 'He uses it because he's good enough to get by with that much gun. That means he's good. He knocks at your door, pokes that gat in your belly, walks you back into the room, says he's here to close your mouth for keeps – and yet you take him. You not having any gun. You take him alone. You're kind of good yourself, pal.'

'Listen,' I said, and looked at the floor. I picked up another chessman and twisted it between my fingers. 'I was doing a chess problem,' I said 'Trying to forget things.'

'You got something on your mind, pal,' Copernik said softly. 'You wouldn't try to fool an old copper, would you, boy?'

'It's a swell pinch and I'm giving it to you,' I said. 'What the hell more do you want?'

The man on the floor made a vague sound behind the towel. His bald head glistened with sweat.

'What's the matter, pal? You been up to something?' Copernick almost whispered.

I looked at him quickly, looked away again. 'All right,' I said. 'You know damn well I couldn't take him alone. He had the gun on me and he shoots where he looks.'

Copernik closed one eye and squinted at me amiably with the other. 'Go on, pal. I kind of thought of that too.'

I shuffled around a little more, to make it look good. I said, slowly: 'There was a kid here who pulled a job over in Boyle Heights, a heist job. It didn't take. A two-bit service station stick-up. I know his family. He's not really bad. He was here trying to beg train money off me. When the knock came he sneaked in – there.'

I pointed at the wall bed and the door beside. Copernik's head swiveled slowly, swiveled back. His eyes winked again. 'And this kid had a gun,' he said.

I nodded. 'And he got behind him. That takes guts, Copernik. You've got to give the kid a break. You've got to let him stay out of it.'

'Tag out for this kid?' Copernik asked softly.

'Not yet, he says. He's scared there will be.'

Copernik smiled. 'I'm a homicide man,' he said. 'I wouldn't know – or care.'

I pointed down at the gagged and handcuffed man on the floor. 'You took him, didn't you?' I said gently.

Copernik kept on smiling. A big whitish tongue came out and massaged his thick lower lip. 'How'd I do it?' he whispered.

'Get the slugs out of Waldo?'

'Sure. Long twenty-two's. One smashed a rib, one good.'

'You're a careful guy. You don't miss any angles. You know anything about me? You dropped in on me to see what guns I had.'

Copernik got up and went down on one knee again beside the killer. 'Can you hear me, guy?' he asked with his face close to the face of the man on the floor.

The man made some vague sound. Copernik stood up and yawned. 'Who the hell cares what he says? Go on, pal.'

'You wouldn't expect to find I had anything, but you wanted to look around my place. And while you were mousing around in there' – I pointed to the dressing room— 'and me not saying anything, being a little sore, maybe, a knock came on the door. So he came in. So after a while you sneaked out and took him.'

'Ah,' Copernik grinned widely, with as many teeth as a horse. 'You're on, pal. I socked him and I kneed him and I took him. You didn't have no gun and the guy swiveled on me pretty sharp and I left-hooked him down the backstairs. O.K.?'

'O.K.,' I said.

'You'll tell it like that downtown?'

'Yeah,' I said.

'I'll protect you, pal. Treat me right and I'll always play ball. Forget about that kid. Let me know if he needs a break.'

He came over and held out his hand. I shook it. It was as clammy as a dead fish. Clammy hands and the people who own them make me sick.

'There's just one thing,' I said. 'This partner of yours – Ybarra. Won't he be a bit sore you didn't bring him along on this?'

Copernik tousled his hair and wiped his hatband with a large yellowish silk handkerchief.

'That guinea?' he sneered. 'To hell with him!' He came close to me and breathed in my face. 'No mistakes, pal – about that story of ours.'

His breath was bad. It would be.

FOUR

There were just five of us in the chief-of-detective's office when Copernik laid it before them. A stenographer, the chief, Copernik, myself, Ybarra. Ybarra sat on a chair tilted against the side wall. His hat was down over his eyes but their softness loomed underneath, and the small still smile hung at the corners of the clean-cut Latin lips. He didn't look directly at Copernik. Copernik didn't look at him at all.

Outside in the corridor there had been photos of Copernik shaking hands with me, Copernik with his hat on straight and his gun in his hand and a stern, purposeful look on his face.

They said they knew who Waldo was, but they wouldn't tell me. I didn't believe they knew, because the chief-of-detectives had a morgue photo of Waldo on his desk. A beautiful job, his hair combed, his tie straight, the light hitting his eyes just right to make them glisten. Nobody would have known it was a photo of a dead man with two bullet holes in his heart. He looked like a dance-hall sheik making up his mind whether to take the blonde or the redhead.

It was about midnight when I got home. The apartment door was locked and while I was fumbling for my keys a low voice spoke to me out of the darkness.

All it said was: 'Please!' but I knew it. I turned and looked at a dark Cadillac coupe parked just off the loading zone. It had no lights. Light from the street touched the brightness of a woman's eyes.

I went over there. 'You're a darn fool,' I said.

She said: 'Get in.'

I climbed in and she started the car and drove it a block and a half along Franklin and turned down Kingsley Drive. The hot wind still burned and blustered. A radio lilted from an open, sheltered side window of an apartment house. There were a lot of parked cars but she found a vacant space behind a small brand-new Packard cabriolet that had the dealer's sticker on the windshield glass. After she'd jockeyed us up to the curb she leaned back in the corner with her gloved hands on the wheel.

She was all in black now, or dark brown, with a small foolish hat. I smelled the sandalwood in her perfume.

'I wasn't very nice to you, was I?' she said.

'All you did was save my life.'

'What happened?'

'I called the law and fed a few lies to a cop I don't like and gave him all the credit for the pinch and that was that. That guy you took away from me was the man who killed Waldo.'

'You mean – you didn't tell them about me?'

'Lady,' I said again, 'all you did was save my life. What else do you want done? I'm ready, willing, and I'll try to be able.'

She didn't say anything, or move.

'Nobody learned who you are from me,' I said. 'Incidentally, I don't know myself.'

'I'm Mrs. Frank C. Barsaly, Two-twelve Fremont Place, Olympia Two-four-five-nine-six. Is that what you wanted?'

'Thanks,' I mumbled, and rolled a dry unlit cigarette around in my fingers. 'Why did you come back?' Then I snapped the fingers of my left hand. 'The hat and jacket,' I said. 'I'll go up and get them.'

'It's more than that,' she said. 'I want my pearls.' I might have jumped a little. It seemed as if there had been enough without pearls.

A car tore by down the street going twice as fast as it should. A thin bitter cloud of dust lifted in the street lights and whirled and vanished. The girl ran the window up quickly against it.

'All right,' I said. 'Tell me about the pearls. We have had a murder and a mystery woman and a mad killer and a heroic rescue and a police detective framed into making a false report. Now we will have pearls. All right – feed it to me.'

'I was to buy them for five thousand dollars. From the man you call Waldo and I call Joseph Coates. He should have had them.'

'No pearls,' I said. 'I saw what came out of his pockets. A lot of money, but no pearls.'

'Could they be hidden in his apartment?'

'Yes,' I said. 'So far as I know he could have had them hidden anywhere in California except in his pockets. How's Mr. Barsaly this hot night?'

'He's still downtown at his meeting. Otherwise I couldn't have come.'

'Well, you could have brought him,' I said. 'He could have sat in the rumble seat.'

'Oh, I don't know,' she said. 'Frank weighs two hundred pounds and he's pretty solid. I don't think he would like to sit in the rumble seat, Mr. Marlowe.'

'What the hell are we talking about anyway?'

She didn't answer. Her gloved hands tapped lightly, provokingly on the rim of the slender wheel. I threw the unlit cigarette out the window, turned a little and took hold of her.

When I let go of her, she pulled as far away from me as she could against the side of the car and rubbed the back of her glove against her mouth. I sat quite still.

We didn't speak for some time. Then she said very slowly: 'I meant you to do that. But I wasn't always that way. It's only been since Stan Phillips was killed in his plane. If it hadn't been for that, I'd be Mrs. Phillips now. Stan gave me the pearls. They cost fifteen thousand dollars, he said once. White pearls, forty-one of them, the largest about a third of an inch across. I don't know how many grains. I never had them appraised or showed them to a jeweler, so I don't know those things. But I loved them on Stan's account. I loved Stan. The way you do just the one time. Can you understand?'

'What's your first name?' I asked.

'Lola.'

'Go on talking, Lola.' I got another dry cigarette out of my pocket and fumbled it between my fingers just to give them something to do.

'They had a simple silver clasp in the shape of a two-bladed propeller. There was one small diamond where the boss would be. I told Frank they were store pearls I had bought myself. He didn't know the difference. It's not so easy to tell, I dare say. You see – Frank is pretty jealous.'

In the darkness she came closer to me and her side touched my side. But I didn't move this time. The wind howled and the trees shook. I kept on rolling the cigarette around in my fingers.

'I suppose you've read that story,' she said. 'About the wife and the real pearls and her telling her husband they were false?'

'I've read it,' I said, 'Maugham.'

'I hired Joseph. My husband was in Argentina at the time. I was pretty lonely.'

'*You* should be lonely,' I said.

'Joseph and I went driving a good deal. Sometimes we had a drink or two together. But that's all. I don't go around—'

'You told him about the pearls,' I said. 'And when your two hundred pounds of beef came back from Argentina and kicked him out – he took the pearls, because he knew they were real. And then offered them back to you for five grand.'

'Yes,' she said simply. 'Of course I didn't want to go to the police. And of course in the circumstances Joseph wasn't afraid of my knowing where he lived.'

'Poor Waldo,' I said. 'I feel kind of sorry for him. It was a hell of a time to run into an old friend that had a down on you.'

I struck a match on my shoe sole and lit the cigarette. The tobacco was so dry from the hot wind that it burned like grass. The girl sat quietly beside me, her hands on the wheel again.

'Hell with women – these fliers,' I said. 'And you're still in love with him, or think you are. Where did you keep the pearls?'

'In a Russian malachite jewelry box on my dressing table. With some other costume jewelry. I had to, if I ever wanted to wear them.'

'And they were worth fifteen grand. And you think Joseph might have hidden them in his apartment. Thirty-one, wasn't it?'

'Yes,' she said. 'I guess it's a lot to ask.'

I opened the door and got out of the car. 'I've been paid,' I said. 'I'll go look. The doors in my apartment are not very obstinate. The cops will find out where Waldo lived when they publish his photo, but not tonight, I guess.'

'It's awfully sweet of you,' she said. 'Shall I wait here?'

I stood with a foot on the running board, leaning in, looking at her. I didn't answer her question. I just stood there looking in at the shine of her eyes. Then I shut the car door and walked up the street towards Franklin.

Even with the wind shriveling my face I could still smell the sandalwood in her hair. And feel her lips.

I unlocked the Berglund door, walked through the silent lobby to the elevator, and rode up to Three. Then I soft-footed along the silent corridor and peered down at the sill of Apartment 31. No light. I rapped – the old light, confidential tattoo of the bootlegger with the big smile and the extra-deep hip pockets. No answer. I took the piece of thick hard celluloid that pretended to be a window over the driver's license in my wallet, and eased it between the lock and the jamb, leaning hard on the knob, pushing it toward the hinges. The edge of the celluloid caught the slope of the spring lock and snapped it back with a small brittle sound, like an icicle breaking. The door yielded and I went into near darkness. Street light filtered in and touched a high spot here and there.

I shut the door and snapped the light on and just stood. There was a queer smell in the air. I made it in a moment – the smell of dark-cured tobacco. I prowled over to a smoking stand by the window and looked down at four brown butts – Mexican or South American cigarettes.

Upstairs, on my floor, feet hit the carpet and somebody went into a bathroom. I heard the toilet flush. I went into the bathroom of Apartment 31. A little rubbish, nothing, no place to hide anything. The kitchenette was a longer job, but I only half searched. I knew there were no pearls in that apartment. I knew Waldo had been on his way out and that he was in a hurry and that something was riding him when he turned and took two bullets from an old friend.

I went back to the living room and swung the wall bed and looked past its mirror side into the dressing room for signs of still current occupancy. Swinging the bed farther I was no longer looking for pearls. I was looking at a man.

He was small, middle-aged, iron-gray at the temples, with a very dark skin, dressed in a fawn-colored suit with a wine-colored tie. His neat little brown hands hung slimply by his sides. His small feet, in pointed polished shoes, pointed almost at the floor.

He was hanging by a belt around his neck from the metal top of the bed. His tongue stuck our farther than I thought it possible for a tongue to stick out.

He swung a little and I didn't like that, so I pulled the bed shut and he nestled quietly between the two clamped pillows. I didn't touch him yet. I didn't have to touch him to know that he would be cold as ice.

I went around him into the dressing room and used my handkerchief on drawer knobs. The place was stripped clean except for the light litter of a man living alone.

I came out of there and began on the man. No wallet. Waldo would have taken that and ditched it. A flat box of cigarettes, half full, stamped in gold: 'Louis Tapia y Cia, Calle de Paysandú, 19, Montevideo.' Matches from the Spezia Club. An under-arm holster of dark-grained leather and in it a 9-millimeter Mauser.

The Mauser made him a professional, so I didn't feel so badly. But not a very good professional, or bare hands would not have finished him, with the Mauser – a gun you can blast through a wall with – undrawn in his shoulder holster.

I made a little sense of it, not much. Four of the brown cigarettes had been smoked, so there had been either waiting or discussion. Somewhere along the line Waldo had got the little man by the throat and held him in just the right way to make him pass out in a matter of seconds. The Mauser had been less useful to him than a toothpick. Then Waldo had hung him up by the strap, probably dead already. That would account for haste, cleaning out the apartment, for Waldo's anxiety about the girl. It would account for the car left unlocked outside the cocktail bar.

That is, it would account for these things if Waldo had killed him, if this was really Waldo's apartment – if I wasn't just being kidded.

I examined some more pockets. In the left trouser one I found a gold penknife, some silver. In the left hip pocket a handkerchief, folded, scented. On the right hip another, unfolded but clean. In the right leg pocket four or five tissue handkerchiefs. A clean little guy. He didn't like to blow his nose on his handkerchief. Under these there was a small new keytainer holding four new keys – car keys. Stamped in gold on the keytainer was: Compliments of R.K. Vogelsang, Inc. 'The Packard House.'

I put everything as I had found it, swung the bed back, used my handkerchief on knobs and other projections, and flat surfaces, killed the light and poked my nose out the door. The hall was empty. I went down to the street and around the corner to Kingsley Drive. The Cadillac hadn't moved.

I opened the car door and leaned on it. She didn't seem to have moved, either. It was hard to see any expression on her face. Hard to see anything but her eyes and chin, but not hard to smell the sandalwood.

'That perfume,' I said, 'would drive a deacon nuts . . . no pearls.'

'Well, thanks for trying,' she said in a low, soft vibrant voice. 'I guess I can stand it. Shall I . . . Do we . . . Or . . . ?'

'You go on home now,' I said. 'And whatever happens you never saw me before. Whatever happens. Just as you may never see me again.'

'I'd hate that.'

'Good luck, Lola.' I shut the car door and stepped back.

The lights blazed on, the motor turned over. Against the wind at the corner the big coupe made a slow contemptuous turn and was gone. I stood there by the vacant space at the curb where it had been.

It was quite dark there now. Windows, had become blanks in the apartment where the radio sounded. I stood looking at the back of a Packard cabriolet which seemed to be brand new. I had seen it before – before I went upstairs, in the same place, in front of Lola's car. Parked, dark, silent, with a blue sticker pasted to the right-hand corner of the shiny windshield.

And in my mind I was looking at stomething else, a set of brand-new car keys in a keytainer stamped: 'The Packard House,' upstairs, in a dead man's pocket.

I went up to the front of the cabriolet and put a small pocket flash on the blue slip. It was the same dealer all right. Written in ink below his name and slogan was a name and address – Eugénie Kolchenko. 5315 Arvieda Street, West Los Angeles.

It was crazy. I went back up to Apartment 31, jimmied the door as I had done before, stepped in behind the wall bed and took the keytainer from the trousers pocket of the neat brown dangling corpse. I was back down on the street beside the cabriolet in five minutes. The keys fitted.

FIVE

It was a small house, near a canyon rim out beyond Sawtelle, with a circle of writhing eucalyptus trees in front of it. Beyond that, on the other side of the street, one of those parties was going on where they come out and smash bottles on the sidewalk with a whoop like Yale making a touchdown against Princeton.

There was a wire fence at my number and some rose trees, and a flagged walk and a garage that was wide open and had no car in it. There was no car in front of the house either. I rang the bell. There was a long wait, then the door opened rather suddenly.

I wasn't the man she had been expecting. I could see it in her glittering kohl-rimmed eyes. Then I couldn't see anything in them. She just stood and looked at me, a long, lean, hungry brunette, with rouged cheekbones, thick black hair parted in the middle, a mouth made for three-decker sandwiches, coral-and-gold pajamas, sandals – and gilded toenails. Under her ear lobes a couple of miniature temple bells gonged lightly in the breeze. She made a slow disdainful motion with a cigarette in a holder as long as a baseball bat.

'We-el, what ees it, little man? You want sometheeng? You are lost from the bee-ootiful party across the street, hein?'

'Ha-ha,' I said. 'Quite a party, isn't it? No, I just brought your car home. Lost it, didn't you?'

Across the street somebody had delirium tremens in the front yard and a mixed quartet tore what was left of the night into small strips and did what they could to make the strips miserable. While this was going on the exotic brunette didn't move more than one eyelash.

She wasn't beautiful, she wasn't even pretty, but she looked as if things would happen where she was.

'You have said what?' she got out, at last, in a voice as silky as a burnt crust of toast.

'Your car.' I pointed over my shoulder and kept my eyes on her. She was the type that uses a knife.

The long cigarette holder dropped very slowly to her side and the cigarette fell out of it. I stamped it out, and that put me in the hall. She backed away from me and I shut the door.

The hall was like the long hall of a railroad flat. Lamps glowed pinkly in iron brackets. There was a bead curtain at the end, a tiger skin on the floor. The place went with her.

'You're Miss Kolchenko?' I asked, not getting any more action.

'Ye-es. I am Mees Kolchenko. What the 'ell you want?'

She was looking at me now as if I had come to wash the windows, but at an inconvenient time.

I got a card out with my left hand, held it out to her. She read it in my hand, moving her head just enough. 'A detective?' she breathed.

'Yeah.'

She said something in a spitting language. Then in English: 'Come in! Thees damn wind dry up my skeen like so much teesue paper.'

'We're in,' I said. 'I just shut the door. Snap out of it, Nazimova. Who was he? The little guy?'

Beyond the bead curtain a man coughed. She jumped as if she had been stuck with an oyster fork. Then she tried to smile. It wasn't very successful.

'A reward,' she said softly. 'You weel wait 'ere? Ten dollars it is fair to pay, no?'

'No,' I said.

I reached a finger towards her slowly and added: 'He's dead.'

She jumped about three feet and let out a yell.

A chair creaked harshly. Feet pounded beyond the bead curtain, a large hand plunged into view and snatched it aside, and a big hard-looking blond man was with us. He had a purple robe over his pajamas, his right hand held something in his robe pocket. He stood quite still as soon as he was through the curtain, his feet planted solidly, his jaw out, his colorless eyes like gray ice. He looked like a man who would be hard to take out on an off-tackle play.

'What's the matter, honey?' He had a solid, burring voice, with just the right sappy tone to belong to a guy who would go for a woman with gilded toenails.

'I came about Miss Kolchenko's car,' I said.

'Well, you could take your hat off,' he said. 'Just for a light workout.'

I took it off and apologized.

'O.K.,' he said, and kept his right hand shoved down hard in the purple pocket. 'So you came about Miss Kolchenko's car. Take it from there.'

I pushed past the woman and went closer to him. She shrank back against the wall and flattened her palms against it. Camille in a high-school play. The long holder lay empty at her toes.

When I was six feet from the big man he said easily: 'I can hear you from there. Just take it easy. I've got a gun in this pocket and I've had to learn to use one. Now about the car?'

'The man who borrowed it couldn't bring it,' I said, and pushed the card I was still holding towards his face. He barely glanced at it. He looked back at me.

'So what?' he said.

'Are you always this tough?' I asked. 'Or only when you have your pajamas on?'

'So why couldn't he bring it himself?' he asked. 'And skip the mushy talk.'

The dark woman made a stuffed sound at my elbow.

'It's all right, honeybunch,' the man said. 'I'll handle this. Go on.'

She slid past both of us and flicked through the bead curtain.

I waited a little while. The big man didn't move a muscle. He didn't look any more bothered than a toad in the sun.

'He couldn't bring it because somebody bumped him off,' I said. 'Let's see you handle that.'

'Yeah?' he said. 'Did you bring him with you to prove it?'

'No,' I said. 'But if you put your tie and crush hat on, I'll take you down and show you.'

'Who the hell did you say you were, now?'

'I didn't say. I thought maybe you could read.' I held the card at him some more.

'Oh, that's right,' he said. 'Philip Marlowe, Private Investigator. Well, well. So I should go with you to look at who, why?'

'Maybe he stole the car,' I said.

The big man nodded. 'That's a thought. Maybe he did. Who?'

'The little brown guy who had the keys to it in his pocket, and had it parked around the corner from the Berglund Apartments.'

He thought that over, without any apparent embarrassment. 'You've got something there,' he said. 'Not much. But a little. I guess this must be the night of the Police Smoker. So you're doing all their work for them.'

'Huh?'

'The card says private detective to me,' he said. 'Have you got some cops outside that were too shy to come in?'

'No, I'm alone.'

He grinned. The grin showed white ridges in his tanned skin. 'So you find somebody dead and take some keys and find a car and come riding out here – all alone. No cops. Am I right?'

'Correct.'

He sighed. 'Let's go inside,' he said. He yanked the bead curtain aside and made an opening for me to go through. 'It might be you have an idea I ought to hear.'

I went past him and he turned, keeping his heavy pocket towards me. I hadn't noticed until I got quite close that there were beads of sweat on his face. It might have been the hot wind but I didn't think so.

We were in the living room of the house.

We sat down and looked at each other across a dark floor, on which a few Navajo rugs and a few dark Turkish rugs made a decorating combination with some well-used overstuffed furniture. There was a fireplace, a small baby grand, a Chinese screen, a tall Chinese lantern on a teakwood pedestal, and gold net curtains against lattice windows. The windows to the south were open. A fruit tree with a whitewashed trunk whipped about outside the screen, adding its bit to the noise from across the street.

The big man eased back into a brocaded chair and put his slippered feet on a footstool. He kept his right hand where it had been since I met him – on his gun.

The brunette hung around in the shadows and a bottle gurgled and her temple bells gonged in her ears.

'It's all right, honeybunch,' the man said. 'It's all under control. Somebody bumped somebody off and this lad thinks we're interested. Just sit down and relax.'

The girl tilted her head and poured half a tumbler of whiskey down her throat. She sighed, said, 'Goddam,' in a casual voice, and curled up on a davenport. It took all of the davenport. She had plenty of legs. Her gilded toenails winked at me from the shadowy corner where she kept herself quiet from then on.

I got a cigarette out without being shot at, lit it and went into my story. It wasn't all true, but some of it was. I told them about the Berglund Apartments and that I had lived there and that Waldo was living there in Apartment 31 on the floor below mine and that I had been keeping an eye on him for business reasons.

'Waldo what?' the blond man put in. 'And what business reasons?'

'Mister,' I said, 'have you no secrets?' He reddened slightly.

I told him about the cocktail lounge across the street from the Berglund and what had happened there. I didn't tell him about the printed bolero jacket or the girl who had worn it. I left her out of the story altogether.

'It was an undercover job – from my angle,' I said. 'If you know what I mean.' He reddened again, bit his teeth. I went on: 'I got back from the city hall without telling anybody I knew Waldo. In due time, when I decided they couldn't find out where he lived that night, I took the liberty of examining his apartment.'

'Looking for what?' the big man said thickly.

'For some letters. I might mention in pasisng there was nothing there at all – except a dead man. Strangled and hanging by a belt to the top of the wall bed – well out of sight. A small man, about forty-five, Mexican or South American, well-dressed in a fawn-colored—'

'That's enough,' the big man said. 'I'll bite, Marlowe. Was it a blackmail job you were on?'

'Yeah. The funny part was this little brown man had plenty of gun under his arm.'

'He wouldn't have five hundred bucks in twenties in his pocket, of course? Or are you saying?'

'He wouldn't. But Waldo had over seven hundred in currency when he was killed in the cocktail bar.'

'Looks like I underrated this Waldo,' the big man said calmly. 'He took my guy and his pay-off money, gun and all. Waldo have a gun?'

'Not on him.'

'Get us a drink, honeybunch,' the big man said. 'Yes, I certainly did sell this Waldo person shorter than a bargain-counter shirt.'

The brunette unwound her legs and made two drinks with soda and ice. She took herself another gill without trimmings, wound herself back on the davenport. Her big glittering black eyes watched me solemnly.

'Well, here's how,' the big man said, lifting his glass in salute. 'I haven't murdered anybody, but I've got a divorce suit on my hands from now on. You haven't murdered anybody, the way you tell it, but you laid an egg down at police Headquarters. What the hell! Life's a lot of trouble, anyway you look at it. I've still got honeybunch here. She's a white Russian I met in Shanghai. She's safe as a vault and she looks as if she could cut your throat for a nickel. That's what I like about her. You get the glamor without the risk.'

'You talk damn foolish,' the girl spat him.

'You look O.K. to me,' the big man went on ignoring her. 'That is, for a keyhole peeper. Is there an out?'

'Yeah. But it will cost a little money.'

'I expected that. How much?'

'Say another five hundred.'

'Goddam, thees hot wind make me dry like the ashes of love,' the Russian girl said bitterly.

'Five hundred might do,' the blond man said. 'What do I get for it?'

'If I swing it – you get left out of the story. If I don't – you don't pay.'

He thought it over. His face looked lined and tired now. The small beads of sweat twinkled in his short blond hair.

'This murder will make you talk,' he grumbled. 'The second one, I mean. And I don't have what I was going to buy. And if it's a hush, I'd rather buy it direct.'

'Who was the little brown man?' I asked.

'Name's Leon Valesanos, a Uruguayan. Another of my importations. I'm in a business that takes me a lot of places. He was working in the Spezzia Club in Chiseltown – you know, the strip of Sunset next to Beverly Hills. Working on roulette, I think. I gave him the five hundred to go down to this – this Waldo – and buy back some bills for stuff Miss Kolchenko had charged to my account and delivered here. That wasn't bright, was it? I had them in my briefcase and this Waldo got a chance to steal them. What's your hunch about what happened?'

I sipped my drink and looked at him down my nose. 'Your Uruguayan pal probably talked curt and Waldo didn't listen good. Then the little guy thought maybe that Mauser might help his argument – and Waldo was too quick for him. I wouldn't say Waldo was a killer – not by intention. A blackmailer seldom is. Maybe he lost his temper and maybe he just held on to the little guy's neck too long. Then he had to take it on the lam. But he had another date, with more money coming up. And he worked the neighborhood looking for the party. And accidentally he ran into a pal who was hostile enough and drunk enough to blow him down.'

'There's a hell of a lot of coincidence in all this business,' the big man said.

'It's the hot wind,' I grinned. 'Everybody's screwy tonight.'

'For the five hundred you guarantee nothing? If I don't get my cover-up, you don't get your dough. Is that it?'

'That's it,' I said, smiling at him.

'Screwy is right,' he said, and drained his highball. 'I'm taking you up on it.'

'There are just two things,' I said softly, leaning forward in my chair. 'Waldo had a getaway car parked outside the cocktail bar where he was killed, unlocked with the motor running. The killer took it. There's always the chance of a kickback from that direction. You see, all Waldo's stuff must have been in that car.'

'Including my bills, and your letters.'

'Yeah. But the police are reasonable about things like that – unless you're good for a lot of publicity. If you're not, I think I can eat some stale dog downtown and get by. If you are – that's the second thing. What did you say your name was?'

The answer was a long time coming. When it came I didn't get as much kick out of it as I thought I would. All at once it was too logical.

'Frank C. Barsaly,' he said.

After a while the Russian girl called me a taxi. When I left, the party across the street was doing all that a party could do. I noticed the walls of the house were still standing. That seemed a pity.

SIX

When I unlocked the glass entrance door of the Berglund I smelled policeman. I looked at my wrist watch. It was nearly 3 A.M. In the dark corner of the lobby a man dozed in a chair with a newspaper over his face. Large feet stretched out before him. A corner of the paper lifted an inch, dropped again. The man made no other movement.

I went on along the hall to the elevator and rode up to my floor. I soft-footed along the hallway, unlocked my door, pushed it wide and reached in for the light switch.

A chain switch tinkled and light glared from a standing lamp by the easy chair, beyond the card table on which my chessmen were still scattered.

Copernik sat there with a stiff unpleasant grin on his face. The short dark man, Ybarra, sat across the room from him, on my left, silent, half smiling as usual.

Copernik showed more of his big yellow horse teeth and said: 'Hi. Long time no see. Been out with the girls?'

I shut the door and took my hat off and wiped the back of my neck slowly, over and over again. Copernik went on grinning. Ybarra looked at nothing with his soft dark eyes.

'Take a seat, pal,' Copernik drawled. 'Make yourself to home. We got pow-wow to make. Boy, do I hate this night sleuthing. Did you know you were low on hooch?'

'I could have guessed it,' I said. I leaned against the wall.

Copernik kept on grinning. 'I always did hate private dicks,' he said, 'but I never had a chance to twist one like I got tonight.'

He reached down lazily beside his chair and picked up a printed bolero jacket, tossed it on the card table. He reached down again and put a wide-brimmed hat beside it.

'I bet you look cuter than all hell with these on,' he said.

I took hold of a straight chair, twisted it around and straddled it, leaned my folded arms on the chair and looked at Copernik.

He got up very slowly – with an elaborate slowness, walked across the room and stood in front of me smoothing his coat down. Then he lifted his open right hand and hit me across the face with it – hard. It stung but I didn't move.

Ybarra looked at the wall, looked at the floor, looked at nothing.

'Shame on you, pal,' Copernik said lazily. 'The way you was taking care of this nice exclusive merchandise. Wadded down behind your old shirts. You punk peepers always did make me sick.'

He stood there over me for a moment. I didn't move or speak. I looked into his glazed drinker's eyes. He doubled a fist at his side, then shrugged and turned and went back to the chair.

'O.K.,' he said. 'The rest will keep. Where did you get these things?'

'They belong to a lady.'

'Do tell. They belong to a lady. Ain't you the lighthearted bastard! I'll tell you what lady they belong to. They belong to the lady a guy named Waldo asked about in a bar across the street – about two minutes before he got shot kind of dead. Or would that have slipped your mind?'

I didn't say anything.

'You was curious about her yourself,' Copernik sneered on. 'But you were smart, pal. You fooled me.'

'That wouldn't make me smart,' I said.

His face twisted suddenly and he started to get up. Ybarra laughed, suddenly and softly, almost under his breath. Copernik's eyes swung on him, hung there. Then he faced me again, bland-eyed.

'The guinea likes you,' he said. 'He thinks you're good.'

The smile left Ybarra's face, but no expression took its place. No expression at all.

Copernik said: 'You knew who the dame was all the time. You knew who Waldo was and where he lived. Right across the hall a floor below you. You knew this Waldo person had bumped a guy off and started to lam, only this broad came into his plans somewhere and he was anxious to meet up with her before he went away. Only he never got the chance. A heist guy from back East named Al Tessilore took care of that by taking care of Waldo. So you met the gal and hid her clothes and sent her on her way and kept your trap glued. That's the way guys like you make your beans. Am I right?'

'Yeah,' I said. 'Except that I only knew these things very recently. Who was Waldo?'

Copernik bared his teeth at me. Red spots burned high on his sallow cheeks. Ybarra, looking down at the floor, said very softly: 'Waldo Ratigan. We got him from Washington by Teletype. He was a two-bit porch climber with a few small terms on him. He drove a car in a bank stick-up job in Detroit. He turned the gang in later and got a nolle prosse. One of the gang was this Al Tessilore. He hasn't talked a word, but we think the meeting across the street was purely accidental.'

Ybarra spoke in the soft quiet modulated voice of a man for whom sounds have a meaning. I said: 'Thanks, Ybarra. Can I smoke – or would Copernik kick it out of my mouth?'

Ybarra smiled suddenly. 'You may smoke, sure,' he said.

'The guinea likes you all right,' Copernik jeered. 'You never know what a guinea will like, do you?'

I lit a cigarette. Ybarra looked at Copernik and said very softly: 'The word guinea – you overwork it. I don't like it so well applied to me.'

'The hell with what you like, guinea.'

Ybarra smiled a little more. 'You are making a mistake,' he said. He took a pocket nail file out and began to use it, looking down.

Copernik blared: 'I smelled something rotten on you from the start, Marlowe. So when we make these two mugs, Ybarra and me think we'll drift over and dabble a few more words with you. I bring one of Waldo's morgue photos – nice work, the light just right in his eyes, his tie all straight and a white handkerchief showing just right in his pocket. Nice work. So on the way up, just as a matter of routine, we rout out the manager here and let him lamp it. And he knows the guy. He's here as A. B. Hummel, Apartment Thirty-one. So we go in there and find a stiff. Then we go round and round with that. Nobody knows him yet, but he's got some swell finger bruises under that strap and I hear they fit Waldo's fingers very nicely.'

'That's something,' I said. 'I thought maybe I murdered him.'

Copernik stared at me a long time. His face had stopped grinning and was just a hard brutal face now. 'Yeah. We got something else even,' he said. 'We got Waldo's getaway car – and what Waldo had in it to take with him.'

I blew cigarette smoke jerkily. The wind pounded the shut windows. The air in the room was foul.

'Oh, we're bright boys,' Copernik sneered. 'We never figured you with that much guts. Take a look at this.'

He plunged his bony hand into his coat pocket and drew something up slowly over the edge of the card table, drew it along the green top and left it there stretched out, gleaming. A string of white pearls with a clasp like a two-bladed propeller. They shimmered softly in the thick smoky air.

Lola Barsaly's pearls The pearls the flier had given her. The guy who was dead, the guy she still loved.

I stared at them, but I didn't move. After a long moment Copernik said almost gravely: 'Nice, ain't they? Would you feel like telling us a story about now, Mis-ter Marlow?'

I stood up and pushed the chair from under me, walked slowly across the room and stood looking down at the pearls. The largest was perhaps a third of an inch across. They were pure white, iridescent, with a mellow softness. I lifted them slowly off the card table from beside her clothes. They felt heavy, smooth, fine.

'Nice,' I said. 'A lot of the trouble was about these. Yeah, I'll talk now. They must be worth a lot of moey.'

Ybarra laughed behind me. It was a very gentle laugh. 'About a hundred dollars,' he said. 'They're good phonies – but they're phony.'

I lifted the pearls again. Copernik's glassy eyes gloated at me. 'How do you tell?' I asked.

'I know pearls,' Ybarra said. 'These are good stuff, the kind women very often have made on purpose, as a kind of insurance. But they are slick like glass. Real pearls are gritty between the edges of the teeth. Try.'

I put two or three of them between my teeth and moved my teeth back and forth, then sideways. Not quite biting them. The beads were hard and slick.

'Yes. They are very good,' Ybarra said. 'Several even have little waves and flat spots, as real pearls might have.'

'Would they cost fifteen grand – if they were real?' I asked.

'Sí. Probably. That's hard to say. It depends on a lot of things.'

'This Waldo wasn't so bad,' I said.

Copernik stood up quickly, but I didn't see him swing. I was still looking down at the pearls. His fist caught me on the side of the face, against the molars. I tasted blood at once. I staggered back and made it look like a worse blow than it was.

'Sit down and talk, you bastard!' Copernik almost whispered.

I sat down and used a handkerchief to pat my cheek. I licked at the cut inside my mouth. Then I got up again and went over and picked up the cigarette he had knocked out of my mouth. I crushed it out in a tray and sat down again.

Ybarra filed at his nails and held one up against the lamp. There were beads of sweat on Copernik's eyebrows, at the inner ends.

'You found the beads in Waldo's car,' I said, looking at Ybarra. 'Find any papers?'

He shook his head without looking up.

'I'd believe you,' I said. 'Here it is. I never saw Waldo until he stepped into the cocktail bar tonight and asked about the girl. I knew nothing I didn't tell. When I got home and stepped out of the elevator this girl, in the printed bolero jacket and the wide hat and the blue silk crêpe dress – all as he had described them – was waiting for the elevator, here on my floor. And she looked like a nice girl.'

Copernik laughed jeeringly. It didn't make any difference to me. I had him cold. All he had to do was know that. He was going to know it now, very soon.

'I knew what she was up against as a police witness,' I said. 'And I suspected there was something else to it. But I didn't suspect for a minute that there was anything wrong with her. She was just a nice girl in a jam – and she didn't even know she was in a jam. I got her in here. She pulled a gun on me. But she didn't mean to use it.'

Copernik sat up very suddenly and he began to lick his lips. His face had a stony look now. A look like wet gray stone. He didn't make a sound.

'Waldo had been her chauffeur,' I went on. 'His name was then Joseph Coates. Her name is Mrs. Frank C. Barsaly. Her husband is a big hydroelectric engineer. Some guy gave her the pearls once and she told her husband they were just store pearls. Waldo got wise somehow there was a romance behind them and when Barsaly came home from South America and fired him, because he was too good-looking, he lifted the pearls.'

Ybarra lifted his head suddenly and his teeth flashed. 'You mean he didn't know they were phony?'

'I thought he fenced the real ones and had imitations fixed up,' I said.

Ybarra nodded. 'It's possible.'

'He lifted something else,' I said. 'Some stuff from Barsaly's briefcase that showed he was keeping a woman – out in Brentwood. He was blackmailing wife and husband both, without either knowing about the other. Get it so far?'

'I get it,' Copernik said harshly, between his tight lips. His face was still wet gray stone. 'Get the hell on with it.'

'Waldo wasn't afraid of them,' I said. 'He didn't conceal where he lived. That was foolish, but it saved a lot of finagling, if he was willing to risk it. The girl came down here tonight with five grand to buy back her pearls. She didn't find Waldo. She came here to look for him and walked up a floor before she went back down. A woman's idea of being cagey. So I met her. So I brought her in here. So she was in that dressing room when Al Tessilore visited me to rub out a witness.' I pointed to the dressing-room door. 'So she came out with her little gun and stuck it in his back and saved my life,' I said.

Copernik didn't move. There was something horrible in his face now. Ybarra slipped his nail file into a small leather case and slowly tucked it into his pocket.

'Is that all?' he said gently.

I nodded. 'Except that she told me where Waldo's apartment was and I went in there and looked for the pearls. I found the dead man. In his pocket I found new car keys in a case from a Packard agency. And down on the street I found the Packard and took it to where it came from. Barsaly's kept woman. Baraly had sent a friend from the Spezzia Club down to buy something and he had tried to buy it with his gun instead of the money Barsaly gave him. And Waldo beat him to the punch.'

'Is that all?' Ybarra said softly.

'That's all,' I said licking the torn place on the inside of my cheek.

Ybarra said slowly: 'What do you want?'

Copernik's face convulsed and he slapped his long hard thigh. 'This guy's good,' he jeered. 'He falls for a stray broad and breaks every law in the book and you ask him what does he want? I'll give him what he wants, guinea!'

Ybarra turned his head slowly and looked at him. 'I don't think you will,' he said. 'I think you'll give him a clean bill of health and anything else he wants. He's giving you a lesson in police work.'

Copernik didn't move or make a sound for a long minute. None of us moved. Then Copernik leaned forward and his coat fell open. The butt of his service gun looked out of his underarm holster.

'So what do you want?' he asked me.

'What's on the card table there. The jacket and hat and the phony pearls. And some names kept away from the papers. Is that too much?'

'Yeah – it's too much,' Copernik said almost gently. He swayed sideways and his gun jumped neatly into his hand. He rested his forearm on his thigh and pointed the gun at my stomach.

'I like better that you get a slug in the guts resisting arrest,' he said. 'I like that better, because of a report I made out on Al Tessilore's arrest and how I made the pinch. Because of some photos of me that are in the morning sheets going out about now. I like it better that you don't live long enough to laugh about that baby.'

My mouth felt suddenly hot and dry. Far off I heard the wind booming. It seemed like the sound of guns.

Ybarra moved his feet on the floor and said coldly: 'You've got a couple of cases all solved, policeman. All you do for it is leave some junk here and keep some names from the papers. Which means from the D.A. If he gets them anyway, too bad for you.'

Copernik said: 'I like the other way.' The blue gun in his hand was like a rock. 'And God help you, if you don't back me up on it.'

Ybarra said: 'If the woman is brought out into the open, you'll be a liar on a police report and a chisler on your own partner. In a week they won't even speak your name at Headquarters. The taste of it would make them sick.'

The hammer clicked back on Copernik's gun and I watched his big finger slide in farther around the trigger.

Ybarra stood up. The gun jumped at him. He said: 'We'll see how yellow a guinea is. I'm telling you to put that gun up, Sam.'

He started to move. He moved four even steps. Copernik was a man without a breath of movement, a stone man.

Ybarra took one more step and quite suddenly the gun began to shake.

Ybarra spoke evenly: 'Put it up, Sam. If you keep your head everything lies the way it is. If you don't – you're gone.'

He took one more step. Copernik's mouth opened wide and made a gasping sound and then he sagged in the chair as if he had been hit on the head. His eyelids dropped.

Ybarra jerked the gun out of his hand with a movement so quick it was no movement at all. He stepped back quickly, held the gun low at his side.

'It's the hot wind, Sam. Let's forget it,' he said in the same even, almost dainty voice.

Copernik's shoulders sagged lower and he put his face in his hands. 'O.K.,' he said between his fingers.

Ybarra went softly across the room and opened the door. He looked at me with lazy, half-closed eyes. 'I'd do a lot for a woman who saved my life, too,' he said. 'I'm eating this dish, but as a cop you can't expect me to like it.'

I said: 'The little man in the bed is called Leon Valesanos. He was a croupier at the Spezzia Club.'

'Thanks,' Ybarra said. 'Let's go, Sam.'

Copernik got up heavily and walked across the room and out of the open door and out of my sight. Ybarra stepped through the door after him and started to close it.

I said: 'Wait a minute.'

He turned his head slowly, his left hand on the door, the blue gun hanging down close to his right side.

'I'm not in this for money,' I said. 'The Barsalys live at Two-twelve Fremont Place. You can take the pearls to her. If Barsaly's name stays out the paper, I get five C's. It goes to the Police Fund. I'm not so damn smart as you think. It just happened that way – and you had a heel for a partner.'

Ybarra looked across the room at the pearls on the card table. His eyes glistened. 'You take them,' he said. 'The five hundred's O.K. I think the fund has it coming.'

He shut the door quietly and in a moment I heard the elevator doors clang.

SEVEN

I opened a window and stuck my head out into the wind and watched the squad car tool off down the block. The wind blew in hard and I let it blow. A picture fell off the wall and two chessmen rolled off the card table. The material of Lola Barsaly's bolero jacket lifted and shook.

I went out to the kitchenette and drank some Scotch and went back into the living room and called her – late as it was.

She answered the phone herself, very quickly, with no sleep in her voice.

'Marlowe,' I said. 'O.K. your end?'

'Yes . . . yes,' she said. 'I'm alone.'

'I found something,' I said. 'Or rather the police did. But your dark boy gypped you. I have a string of pearls. They're not real. He sold the real ones, I guess, and made you up a string of ringers, with your clasp.'

She was silent for a long time. Then, a little faintly: 'The police found them?'

'In Waldo's car. But they're not telling. We have a deal. Look at the papers in the morning and you'll be able to figure out why.'

'There doesn't seem to be anything more to say,' she said. 'Can I have the clasp?'

'Yes. Can you meet me tomorrow at four in the Club Esquire bar?'

'You're really rather sweet,' she said in a dragged out voice. 'I can. Frank is still at his meeting.'

'Those meetings – they take it out of a guy,' I said. We said goodbye.

I called a West Los Angeles number. He was still there, with the Russian girl.

'You can send me a check for five hundred in the morning,' I told him. 'Made out to the Police Relief Fund, if you want to. Because that's where it's going.'

Copernik made the third page of the morning papers with two photos and a nice half-column. The little brown man in Apartment 31 didn't make the paper at all. The Apartment House Association has a good lobby too.

I went out after breakfast and the wind was all gone. It was soft, cool, a little foggy. The sky was close and comfortable and gray. I rode down to the boulevard and picked out the best jewelry store on it and laid a string of pearls on a black velvet mat under a daylight-blue lamp. A man in a wing collar and striped trousers looked down at them languidly.

'How good?' I asked.

CHAPTER IX: THE GIRL WITH THE CRIMINAL MIND

When The Flame didn't speak, I tried:

'You didn't bring me here to fill me up on Communism?'

And she laughed.

'No – hardly. That wouldn't be fitting in me. Communism is a hatred of the poor for the rich – not simply an envy. But—' She stepped quickly forward and laid both her hands on my shoulders. 'I had to see you again,' she said, and those brown eyes sparkled as she looked up at my face. 'Sometimes I wonder if it's just my pride that you're the only man I wanted, that I couldn't have – and then I hate myself. Other times I wonder if it's that thing we read about in best sellers, and laugh secretly at. Simply love. Funny. You're the only man who ever—'

'Let's not go into that, Florence.' I took her hands off my shoulders. 'Let me tell you it's far harder not to love you than it would be to love you. There's your life and mine. I wouldn't have the right to ask any woman to share mine and—'

'Stop!' and the youth went out of her face and the woman crept in. 'I made an agreement with you. Anyway, I made it with myself. I'd go straight. And I did. I went straight, though every cop in New York was trying his damnedest to drag me back into the life again. The joke of it, Race! They pulled me out of twenty dollar a week jobs, where the chance to rob the cash till might bring me a few dollars. Me. The Flame! Whose advice – or even suggestion – was bid for in the thousands. And what right had they? I've never done a stretch – never even seen the inside of stir. And they rode me, Race. Didn't want to let me take twenty dollars for ten to twelve hours work a day.'

She laughed now, and I didn't like her laugh.

'They even had me tossed out of jobs where the boss was paid to take me on. A bought position in a sixth grade store. Even the slimy employment agents, who send you to a job or hire you for one, take it out of a girl's pocketbook or her body. Yes, I found the same graft in the East Side sweat shops. All my life the law has taken things from me – even to that real love in the orphanage, when I was a child. A memory. The one decent thing in my life. But why try to make you understand? Honesty? Why, honesty is simply avoiding or evading the law. You can buy a job in the city today – from the position of the meanest worker on the city dump, to a judgeship of even the higher courts. Well – I'm through.'

'Easy does it, Florence.' I knew what a woman she was when she worked herself up into one of these fits.

'Easy does it! That's what you tell me. But through the months you let me sit night after night in this lonely room. I loved you then. Maybe I love you now. I don't know. But I hate myself for it. I had you come tonight because I thought – well – just pride. I looked at myself in the glass. I'm still The Flame. I've still got the same active – and, yes – maybe criminal mind; still the same beautiful body. You can't deny that. Now – what do you want me to do with it. Sit here and rot it out in this dirty dive? Sit here – for what? So that you can come in to me during my old age, and tell me that you've bought me a bid to the poorhouse? The poorhouse! Why, you've even got to have money or influence to get into it.'

I'd seen The Flame bad before, but never quite like this. Rudolph Myer was right. I shouldn't have come. But still, if I had known the truth – known exactly how I was going to find her – I'd have come anyway, I suppose. But I simply said:

'I didn't think you wanted me, Florence.'

'That's a lie,' she said, very calmly. More dangerous for that calm I thought. 'That's a lie, Race. You knew I wanted you – and I wanted you tonight. I wanted to look at you again. I've been living in a dream, but Myer let me know the truth. You bought and paid for half the rotten jobs I worked on. He didn't tell me in so many words. He didn't have to. And, Myer—' she stopped, flashed those bright, keen eyes on me now. 'Well?'

And that 'Well?' was a stickler, you got to admit.

'Florence—' I tried the 'soft words turneth away wrath' business. 'Why don't you be a good sport? You and I have played the game together – faced death together. Just a couple of good pals. I've got some money. Let me give you a stake, until—'

'Just chums!' And her laugh was like finger nails along a wall. 'I suppose you'd want me to show you a good behavior card every month; report in person to Rudolph Myer once a week; hit the sawdust trail and shake a tambourine down in the Bowery! And all this while you go around with a gun in your hand and the peculiar idea of personal ethics which allow you to knock over some gunman and trust to the city to give him a decent burial. No – I don't want your money. When I take something I give something in return for it, and—'

'Such as this.' My hand had fallen upon the table and rested on a small object that dug into my palm. I picked that thing up now and held it out to The Flame. I'm no jeweller, you understand, but the thing I held was a ring – and the diamond in it was large and real.

'Yes.' The Flame cocked up her chin. 'Such as this.' She snatched it from me, looked at it a moment and shoved it onto a finger. 'Such as this. You want to know why I brought you here tonight? Well – I wanted to tell you this. I wanted to look at you again and know. Now – I'm through. The city doesn't want honest citizens. There are dicks right on the Force today who opened car doors for me and touched their hats when they knew I was riding high in the rackets, who have insulted me when I was straight. Politicians – public office holders – and perhaps even a big criminal lawyer, who you—' She stopped dead, pulled open the drawer of her desk and tossed a roll of bills out to me. 'That evens it up. There's every penny,

'I'm sorry, sir. We don't make appraisals. I can give you the name of an appraiser.'

'Don't kid me,' I said. 'They're Dutch.'

He focused the light a little and leaned down and toyed with a few inches of the string.

'I want a string just like them, fitted to that clasp, and in a hurry,' I added.

'How, like them?' He didn't look up. 'And they're not Dutch. They're Bohemian.'

'O.K., can you duplicate them?'

He shook his head and pushed the velvet pad away as if it soiled him. 'In three months, perhaps. We don't blow glass like that in this country. If you wanted them matched – three months at least. And this house would not do that sort of thing at all.'

'It must be swell to be that snooty,' I said. I put a card under his black sleeve. 'Give me a name that will – and not in three months – and maybe not exactly like them.'

He shrugged, went away with the card, came back in five minutes and handed it back to me. There was something written on the back.

The old Levantine had a shop on Melrose, a junk shop with everything in the window from a folding baby carriage to a French horn, from a mother-of-pearl lorgnette in a faded plush case to one of those .44 Special Single Action six-shooters they still make for Western peace officers whose grandfathers were tough.

The old Levantine wore a skull cap and two pairs of glasses and a full beard. He studied my pearls, shook his head sadly, and said: 'For twenty dollars, almost so good. Not so good, you understand. Not so good glass.'

'How alike will they look?'

He spread his firm strong hands. 'I am telling you the truth,' he said. 'They would not fool a baby.'

'Make them up,' I said. 'With this clasp. And I want the others back, too, of course.'

'Yah. Two o'clock,' he said.

Leon Valesanos, the little brown man from Uruguay, made the afternoon papers. He had been found hanging in an un-named apartment. The police were investigating.

At four o'clock I walked into the long cool bar of the Club Esquire and prowled along the row of booths until I found one where a woman sat alone. She wore a hat like a shallow soup plate with a very wide edge, a brown tailor-made suit with a severe mannish shirt and tie.

I sat down beside her and slipped a parcel along the seat.

'You don't open that,' I said. 'In fact you can slip it into the incinerator as is, if you want to.'

She looked at me with dark tired eyes. Her fingers twisted a ~
that smelled of peppermint. 'Thanks.' Her face was very pale.

I ordered a highball and the waiter went away. 'Read the papers?'
'Yes.'

'You understand now about this fellow Copernik who stole your act?
That's why they won't change the story or bring you into it.'

'It doesn't matter now,' she said. 'Thank you, all the same. Please –
please show them to me.'

I pulled the string of pearls out of the loosely wrapped tissue paper in
my pocket and slid them across to her. The silver propeller clasp winked in
the light of the wall bracket. The little diamond winked. The pearls were
as dull as white soap. They didn't even match in size.

'You were right,' she said tonelessly. 'They are not my pearls.'

The waiter came with my drink and she put her bag on them deftly.
When he was gone she fingered them slowly once more, dropped them into
the bag and gave me a dry mirthless smile.

I stood there a moment with a hand hard on the table.

'As you said – I'll keep the clasp.'

I said slowly: 'You don't know anything about me. You saved my life
last night and we had a moment, but it was just a moment. You still don't
know anything about me. There's a detective downtown named Ybarra, a
Mexican of the nice sort, who was on the job when the pearls were found
in Waldo's suitcase. That is in case you would like to make sure—'

She said: 'Don't be silly. It's all finished. It was a memory. I'm too
young to nurse memories. It may be for the best. I loved Stan Phillips –
but he's gone – long gone.'

I stared at her, didn't say anything.

She added quietly: 'This morning my husband told me something I
hadn't known. We are to separate. So I have very little to laugh about
today.'

'I'm sorry,' I said lamely. 'There's nothing to say. I may see you
sometime. Maybe not. I don't move much in your circle. Good luck.'

I stood up. We looked at each other for a moment. 'You haven't touched
your drink,' she said.

'You drink it. That peppermint stuff will just make you sick.'

I stood there a moment with a hand on the table.

'If anybody ever bothers you,' I said, 'let me know.'

I went out of the bar without looking back at her, got into my car and
drove west on Sunset and down all the way to the Coast Highway.
Everywhere along the way gardens were full of withered and blackened
leaves and flowers which the hot wind had burned.

But the ocean looked cool and languid and just the same as ever. I drove
on almost to Malibu and then parked and went and sat on a big rock that
was inside somebody's wire fence. It was about half-tide and coming in.

The air smelled of kelp. I watched the water for a while and then I pulled a string of Bohemian glass imitation pearls out of my pocket and cut the knot at one end and slipped the pearls off one by one.

When I had them all loose in my left hand I held them like that for a while and thought. There wasn't really anything to think about. I was sure.

'To the memory of Mr. Stan Phillips,' I said aloud. 'Just another four-flusher.'

I flipped her pearls out into the water one by one at the floating seagulls.

They made little splashes and the seagulls rose off the water and swooped at the splashes.

WISE GUY

FREDERICK NEBEL

Few pulp writers were as prolific as Frederick Nebel (1903–1967), who wrote several long-running series, mainly in *Black Mask* and its closest rival, *Dime Detective*, in a career that essentially ended after a single decade (1927–1937). His crimefighting heroes are tough and frequently violent, but they bring a strong moral code to their jobs, and a level of realism achieved by few other pulp writers.

Homicide Captain Steve MacBride, who is as tough as they come, and his ever-present sidekick, *Free Press* reporter Kennedy, who provides comedy relief in most of the 37 stories in which they appear, was a *Black Mask* fixture for nearly a decade.

Donny 'Tough Dick' Donahue of the Interstate Agency, with 21 adventures, all in *Black Mask*, ran from 1930 to 1935; a half-dozen of the best were collected in *Six Deadly Dames* (1950).

The stories featuring Cardigan, an operative for the Cosmos Detective Agency, nearly fifty in all, ran from 1931 to 1937 in the pages of *Dime Detective*; the best of them were published in *The Adventures of Cardigan* (1988).

Both of Nebel's novels were filmed: *Sleepers East* (1933) in 1934 and *Fifty Roads to Town* (1936) in 1937.

'Wise Guy,' a MacBride and Kennedy story, was first published in *Black Mask* in April 1930.

WISE GUY

FREDERICK NEBEL

An alderman who does not want to play Gangland's racket calls
for help of Capt. Steve MacBride.

Alderman Tony Maratelli walked up and down the living-room of his
house in Riddle Street. Riddle was the name of a one-time tax
commissioner. Maratelli was a fat man, with fat dark eyes and two
generous chins. His fingers were fat, too, and the fingers of one hand were
splayed around a glass of Chianti, from which at frequent intervals he took
quick, sibilant draughts. Now an Italian does not drink Chianti that way.
But Maratelli looked worried. He was.

The winter night wind keened in the street outside and shook the
windows in a sort of brusque, sharp fury. Riddle Street is a dark street.
Also a windy one. That is because one end of it disembogues into River
Road, where the piers are. One upon a time Riddle Street was aristocratic.
Then it became smugly middle–class and grudgingly democratic. Then
proletariat. Other streets around it went in for stores and warehouses and
shipping offices. But Riddle Street clung to its brownstone fronts and its
three-step stoops. It was rated a decent street.

Maratelli stopped short as his five-year-old daughter bowled into the
room wearing a variety of night attire known as teddy bears.

''Night, poppa.'

Maratelli put down the glass of Chianti, picked up the baby and
bounced her playfully up and down on the palms of his fat hands.

'Good–night, angel,' he said.

His wife, who was taller than he, and heavier, came in and smiled and
held out her arms.

'Give her to me, Tony,' she said.

'Yes, mama,' said Maratelli. 'Put her to bed and then close that door.
Captain MacBride will be here maybe any minute.'

'You want to be alone, Tony, don't you?'

'Yes, mama.'

She looked at him. 'It's about . . .'

'Yes, mama. Please take angel to bed and then you, too, leave me alone.'

'All right, Tony.' She looked a little sad.

He laughed, and his ragtag mustache fanned over his mouth. He pinched the baby's cheeks, then his wife's, then marched with her to the inner door. They went out, and he closed the door and sighed.

He went over to the table, picked up the glass of Chianti and marched up and down the room. His broad, heavy shoes thumped on the carpet. He wore a henna-colored shirt, a green tie, red suspenders and tobacco-brown pants. His shoes creaked.

When the bell rang, he fairly leaped into the hallway. He snapped back the lock and opened the door.

'Ah, Cap! Good you come!'

MacBride strolled in. He wore a neat gray Cheviot overcoat, a flap-brimmed hat of lighter gray. His hands were in his pockets and he smoked a cigar.

'Slow at Headquarters, so I thought I'd come down.'

'Yes – yes – yes.'

Maratelli closed the hall door. The lock snapped automatically. He bustled into the living-room, eyed a Morris chair, then took a couple of pillows from the lounge, placed them in the Morris chair and patted hollows into them. He spread his hands towards the chair.

Have a nice seat, Cap.'

'Thanks.'

'Give me the overcoat and the hat.'

'That's all right, Tony.'

MacBride merely unbuttoned his coat, sat down and laid his hat on the table. He was freshly shaven, neatly combed, and his long, lean face had the hard, ruddy glint of a face that knows the weather. He leaned back comfortably, crossing one leg over the other. The pants had a fine crease, the shoes were well polished, and the laces neatly tied.

'Chianti, Cap?'

'A shot of Scotch'd go better.'

'Yes – yes – yes!'

Maratelli brought a bottle from the sideboard, along with a bottle of Canada Dry.

'Straight,' said MacBride.

Maratelli took one with him, said, 'Here's how,' and they drank.

MacBride looked at the end of his cigar.

'Well, Tony, what's the trouble?'

The wind kept clutching at the windows. Maratelli went over and tightened a latch. Then he pulled up a rocker to face MacBride, sat down on the edge of it, lit a twisted cheroot and took a couple of quick, nervous puffs. He stared vacantly at MacBride's polished shoe.

Finally – 'About my boy Dominick.'

'H'm.'

'You know?'

'Go on, Tony.'

'Yes – yes. Look, Cap, I'm a good guy. I'm a good wop. I got a wife and kids and business and I been elected alderman and – well, I'm a pretty good guy. I don't want to be on no racket, and I don't want any kind of help from any rough guys in the neighborhood. I been pestered a lot, Cap, but I ain't gonna give in. I got a wife and kids and a good reputation and I want to keep the slate what you call pretty damn clean. Cap, I ask you to come along here tonight after I been thinking a lotta things over in my head. I need help, Cap. What's a wop gonna do when he needs help? I dunno. But I ask you, and maybe you be my friend.'

'Sure,' said MacBride. 'Get it off your chest.'

'This wop – uh – Chibbarro, you know him?'

'Sam Chibbarro?'

'Yes – yes – yes.'

'Uhuh.'

'Him.'

'What about him?'

Maratelli took a long breath. It was coming hard, and he wiped his face with his fat hand. He cleared his throat, took a drink of Chianti and cleared his throat again.

'Him. It's about him. Him and my boy Dominick. You know my boy Dominick is only twenty-one. And – and—'

'Going around with Chibby?'

'Yes – yes. Look. This is it, and Holy Mother, if Chibby knows I talk to you—' He exhaled a vast breath and shook his head. 'Look. I have lotsa trucks, Cap, being what I am a contractor. I have ten trucks, some big, some not that big. Chibby – uh – Chibby he wants my trucks for to run booze at night!'

MacBride uncrossed his legs and put both heels on the floor. He leaned forward and, putting the elbow of one arm on his knee, jack-knifed the other arm against his side. His eyes, which had a windy blue look, stared point-blank at Maratelli.

'And you?'

'Well—' Maratelli sat back and spread his hands palmwise and opened his eyes wide – 'me, I say no!'

'How long has this been going on?'

'Maybe a month.'

'And Dominick. Where does he come in?'

Maratelli fell back in his chair like a deflated balloon. 'That is what you call *it*, Cap. He is very good friends. He thinks Chibby is a great guy. He says I am the old fool.'

MacBride looked at the floor, and his eyelids came down thoughtfully; the ghost of a curl came to his wide mouth, slightly sardonic.

Maratelli was hurrying on – 'Look, Cap. My Dominick is a good boy, but if he keeps friends with that dirty wop Chibbarro it is gonna be no good. I can't stand for it, Cap. And what can I do with Dominick? He laughs at me. Puts the grease on his hair and wears the Tuxedo and goes around with Chibby like a millionaire. Dominick has done nothing bad yet, but if this Chibby— Look, Cap, whatcha think I'm gonna do?'

MacBride sat back. 'Hell, Tony, I've had a lot of tough jobs in my day, but you hand me a lulu. It's too bad. You've got my sympathy, and that's no bologney. I'll think it over. I'll do the best I can.'

'Please, Cap, please. Every night Dominick goes out with Chibby. Dominick ain't got the money, so Chibby he pays the bills. And where do they go? Ah – the *Club Naples*, and places like that, and women – Holy Mother, it ain't good, Cap! My wife and my baby – I ask you, Cap, for my sake.'

'Sure, Tony.'

MacBride stood up.

Maratelli stood up, his breath whistling in his throat. 'But if Chibby knows I speak to you—'

'He won't,' clipped MacBride.

He buttoned his coat, put on his hat and shoved his hands into his pockets. 'I'll be going.'

'Have another drink.'

'Thanks – no.'

Maratelli let him out into the street and hung in the doorway.

'Night, Cap.'

'Night, Tony.'

MacBride was already swinging away, his cigar a red eye in the wind.

II

Jockey Street was never a good street. It was the wayward offspring of a wayward neighborhood. Six blocks of it made a bee line from the white-lights district to the no-lights district, and then petered off into the river.

The way was dark after the third block, except for a solitary electric sign that winked seductively in the middle of the fourth. It projected over the sidewalk, and the winking, beckoning letters were painted green:

L   U

C   B

N A P L E S

MacBride did not come down from the bright lights. He came up from River Road, up from the bleak, unlovely waterfront. He still walked with his hands in his pockets, and the wind blew from behind, flapping his coat around his knees.

A man in a faded red uniform with tarnished gold braid stood in front of the double doors. As MacBride drew near, the man reached back and laid his hand on the knob. He opened the door as MacBride came up, and MacBride went inside.

The ante-room was quite dim, and the sound of a jazz band was muffled. To the right was a cloak-room, and the girl came over to take MacBride's coat. But MacBride paid no attention to her. A man came forward out of the dim-lit gloom, peering hard. He wore a Tux, and he had white, doughy jowls and thin hair plastered back, and he was not so young.

'Your eyesight bad, Al?' chuckled MacBride.

'Oh . . . that you, Cap?'

'Yeah.'

'Cripes, I'm glad to see you, Cap!'

He grabbed MacBride's hand and wrung it. MacBride stood still, slightly smiling, his face in shadow, and Al laughed showing a lot of uncouth teeth.

This was Al Vassilakos, a Greek who went over big with the wops and who was on speaking terms with the police. Mike Dabraccio really started the joint, a couple of years ago, but Mike talked out of turn to the old Sciarvi gang, and Sciarvi told Mike to go places. Al was instated by Sciarvi himself, and when Sciarvi got himself balled up – and subsequently shot – in a city-wide gang feud, Al carried on with the club. He'd kept clean since then, but Sam Chibbarro, called Chibby, was back, and MacBride had his doubts.

It looked as if Al was a little put out at MacBride's imperturbable calm.

'You – you looking for some guy, Cap?'

'No. Just wandering around, Al. How's business?'

'Pretty good.'

'Mind if I sit inside?'

'Glad to have you, Cap.'

MacBride took off his overcoat and his hat and gave them to the girl. Al walked with him across the ante-room and opened a door. A flood of light and a thunder of jazz rushed out as MacBride and Al went in. Al closed the door and MacBride drifted over to a small table beside the wall and sat down. Al signaled to a waiter and motioned to MacBride.

'Snap on it, Joe. That's Captain MacBride from Headquarters. Don't give him none of that cheap alky.'

'Okey, boss.'

Al went over and put his hands palm-down on the table and asked, 'How about a good cigar, Cap? And I've got some good Golden Wedding.'

'All right, Al – on both.'

'Hey, Joe! A box of Coronas and that bottle of Golden Wedding. Bring the bottle out, Joe.'

'Okey, boss.'

'Anything you want, Cap, ask me. I'll be outside. I gotta be outside, you know.'

'Sure, Al.'

Vassilakos went out to the ante-room, but he still looked a bit worried.

It didn't take long for MacBride to spot Sam Chibbarro. Chibby was at a big table near the dance-floor. Dominick was there, too. And MacBride picked out Kid Barjo, a big bruiser swelling all out of his Tux. There were some women – three of them. One had red hair and looked rather tall. Another had hair black as jet pulled back over the ears. The third was a little doll-faced blonde and she was necking Dominick. MacBride recognized her. She was Bunny Dahl, who used to hoof with a cheap burlesque troupe and was for a while mama to Jazz Millio before Jazz died by the gun. The whole party looked tight. A lot of people were there, and many of them looked uptownish.

This Club Naples was no haven for a piker. A drink was two dollars a throw, and the *couvert* four. If a hostess sat down with you, your drink or hers was three dollars a throw, and her own drinks were doctored with nine parts Canada Dry. A sucker joint.

Joe brought the bottle of Golden Wedding and a fresh box of cigars. MacBride took one of the cigars, bit off the end, and Joe held a match. MacBride puffed up and Joe went away, leaving the Golden Wedding on the table. MacBride poured himself a drink and watched Chibby and his crowd making whoopee.

Presently Kid Barjo got up, wandered around the table and then flung his arms around Bunny Dahl. Dominick didn't like that, and he took a crack at Barjo, and Chibby stood up and jumped between them. Bunny thought it was a great joke, and laughed. Chibby dragged Barjo to the other side of the table and made him sit down. Barjo was cursing and looking daggers at Dominick.

The jazz band struck up, and Chibby took the red-haired girl and pulled her out to the dance-floor. Barjo sulked and Dominick seemed to be bawling out Bunny. Then Bunny got up in a huff and hurried through a door at the other end of the cabaret. Barjo jumped up and followed her. Dominick took a drink and lit a cigarette and turned his back on the door. But he kept throwing looks over his shoulder. Finally he got up and went through the door, too, not so steady on his feet.

MacBride took another drink and sat back. When the dance was over Chibby and the red-haired girl came back to the table, and Chibby looked around and asked some questions. He shot a look towards the door, cursed and went through it.

MacBride leaned forward on his elbows and watched the door. The jazz band cut loose, and the saxophone warbled. The two girls at Chibby's table were both talking at the same time, and both of them looked peeved. The small dance-floor was jammed.

Joe came over and said, 'Everything okey, Cap?'

'Yeah,' said MacBride, watching the door.

'Maybe you'd like a nice sandwich? Al told me to ask you.'

'No, Joe.'

'Okey, Cap.'

'Okey.'

Joe turned, swooped down on a table that had been temporarily abandoned by two couples. He swept up four glasses that were only half empty, swept out, and came back with four full ones. He marked it all down on his pad. A gyp-joint waiter has no conscience.

The drummer was singing out of the side of his mouth, '*Through the black o' night, I gotta go where you go.*'

Chibby came out of the door. He was frowning. He walked swiftly to his table, clipped a few words to the girls. They started to get up. He snapped them down. Then he turned and headed towards the ante-room.

'Hello, Chibby,' said MacBride.

Chibbarro jerked his head around.

'Jeeze ... well, hello, MacBride! Where'd you come from?'

'I've been here – for a while – Chibby.'

'Yeah?'

'Yeah.'

'Hell ... ain't that funny!'

'Funny?'

'Yeah, I mean funny I didn't see you.'

'That is funny, Chibby.'

'Yeah, it sure is. See you in a minute, Cap.'

Chibby hurried out to the ante-room. MacBride turned his head and looked after him. Chibby looked over his shoulder as he pushed open the door. MacBride squinted one eye. His lips flattened perceptibly against his teeth, and one corner of his mouth bent downward. A curse grunted in his throat, behind his tight mouth. He looked back towards the door at the other end of the dance-floor.

The two girls who had been sitting at Chibby's table were now walking towards the ante-room. MacBride watched them go out. A frown grew on his forehead, then died. Joe came in from the ante-room and stood with his back to the door. He was looking at MacBride. His face was a little pale. He backed out again.

MacBride turned in time to see the door swing shut, but he did not see Joe. He stood up and took a fresh grip on his cigar. He walked towards the door and shoved it open. He stood with the light streaming down over his shoulders.

'Goin', Cap?' asked Al Vassilakos.

MacBride let the door shut behind him. 'Where's Chibby?'

Al was standing in the shadows, his face a pale blur. 'I guess he went, Cap.'

'Where're those two women were with him?'

'They . . . all went, Cap.'

The red end of MacBride's cigar brightened and then dimmed.

'Al, what the hell's wrong?'

'Wrong? Well, hell, I don't know. They just went out.'

MacBride turned and pushed open the door leading into the cabaret. He strode swiftly among the tables, crossed the dance-floor and went through the door at the farther end. This led him into a broad corridor. He stopped and looked around, one eye a-squint. He pushed open a door at his left. It was dark beyond. He reached for and found a switch; snapped on the lights. The room was well-furnished – but empty.

When he backed into the corridor, Al was there.

'What the hell, Cap?'

'Don't be dumb!'

MacBride went to the next door on the right, opened it and switched on the lights. It, too, was empty. He came back into the corridor and bent a hard eye on Al.·Then he pivoted and went on to the next door on the left. He opened it and turned on the lights. He looked around. It was empty. There was an adjoining room, with the door partly open.

'Jeeze, Cap, what's the matter?'

'Pipe down!'

MacBride crossed the room and pulled the door wide open. He felt a draught of cold night air. He reached around and switched on the lights in the next room.

A table was overturned.

Kid Barjo lay on the floor with a bloody throat.

'H'm,' muttered MacBride, and turned to look at Al.

The Greek's jowls were shaking.

MacBride took a couple of steps and bent down over Kid Barjo. He stood up and turned and looked at the Greek.

'Dead, Al. Some baby carved his throat open.'

'My God Almighty!' choked Al.

MacBride spun and dived across the room to the open window. He looked out. An alley ran behind. He jumped out and ran along, followed a sharp turn to the right. He saw that the alley led to the street. He ran down it and into Jockey Street. There was no one in sight.

He entered the Club Naples through the front door and returned to the room where the Greek was still standing. He looked at a telephone on the wall.

'Listen, Al. Did Chibby make a call in the lobby?'

'I – I—'

'Come on, Al, if you know what's good for you.'

'I think he did.'

'Okey. He called whoever was in here when he knew I was outside and they breezed through this window. And you've been stalling, you two-faced bum!'

'So help me, Cap—'

'Can it! There's one of three people killed this guy.'

'Jeeze!'

The Greek fell into a chair, stunned.

MacBride called Headquarters.

Outside in the cabaret the drummer was singing, '*That's what you get for making whoope-e-e-e!* . . .'

Out in the street the green sign blinked seductively:

L   U

C   B

N   A   P   L   E   S

III

Sergeant Otto Bettdecken was eating a frankfurter and roll when MacBride barged into Headquarters followed by Moriarity and Cohen, and Kennedy of the *Free Press*.

MacBride said, 'Otto, that guy's full name was Salvatore Barjo; age, twenty-six; address, the Atlantic Hotel. Stabbed twice in the front of the neck.'

Bettdecken filled out a blue card and his moon face clouded. 'Crime of passion, Cap?'

'Ha!' chirruped Kennedy.

'We don't know yet,' said MacBride. 'The morgue bus picked the stiff up and I closed the joint for the night.'

'How about the Greek?'

MacBride shrugged. 'He's free. I want to give him some rope first. He ain't tough enough to worry about. He came across with the names of the three broads. Mary Dahl – the one they call Bunny; there was a red-head named Flossy Roote, and the other broad, the one that was originally with Barjo – she's Freda Hoegh. Flossy's this guy Chibbarro's woman, and I understand Freda's a friend of Bunny's. Chibby lived with Flossy in a flat at number 40 Brick Street. We went down there, but of course they weren't there. I parked Corson on the job. Freda and Bunny have a flat at number 28 Turner Street, but they haven't shown up either. I put De Groot on that job. No doubt they're hiding out, along with Dominick Maratelli.'

Bettdecken shook his head. 'This'll drive Tony crazy.'

'Yeah,' said MacBride, and headed for his office.

Moriarity and Cohen and Kennedy trailed after him, and MacBride got out of his overcoat and hung it up. He started a fresh cigar and took a turn up and down the room.

Kennedy leaned against the wall and tongued a cigarette from one side of his mouth to the other.

'That guy Barjo always was a bum welter anyhow.'

MacBride snapped, 'Which is no reason why he should be knifed in the throat! And this young Dominick—'

'A wise guy,' drawled Kennedy. 'A young wop just out of his diapers and trying to be a man about town. I know his kind. In fact, I know Dom. Flash. Jazz. He's not the only slob this jazz racket has taken for a buggy ride. And take it from me, old tomato, he's not going to get out of this with a slap on the wrist.'

Moriarity said, 'The thing is, after all your gas, Kennedy, who – who *did* poke Barjo in the throat?'

'Well, first the broad – this Bunny Dahl – goes in,' said Kennedy. 'Then Barjo. Then Dominick. Well – I'd say Dominick.'

'Nix,' popped Ike Cohen, swinging around from the window.

'No?'

'The broad,' said Cohen. 'The other guys were just covering her. Cripes, from what Cap says, they were all pretty tight. And the broad, having not much brains, would be the first to pull a dumb stunt like that. What do you say, Cap?'

'Not a hell of a lot,' growled MacBride. 'I'll leave the theory to you bright boys. I'm just waiting till we nail one of those babies. But as for the broad rating no brains, I don't know. And I don't see where Dominick rates big in brains, either.'

Moriarity sat on the desk, dangling his feet. He said, 'Anyhow, I'm inclined kind of to think it was the broad. It looks like a dizzy blonde's work.'

Kennedy laughed wearily. 'Well, if it was, Mory, we'll have a nice time in Richmond City. All the sob-sisters will sharpen up their pencils. Bunny will put a crack in her voice and try to look like a virgin that this guy Bario tried to ruin. "I did it to save my honor!" Like that. As if she ever had any honor. Listen, I saw that little trollop in a burlesque show one night, down never the river and—'

'All right, all right,' horned in MacBride. 'We can imagine.'

'Anyhow,' said Kennedy, 'I'll bet it wasn't the broad.'

The papers had it next morning. Dominick Maratelli's name was prominent – 'wayward son of Alderman Antonio Maratelli.'

MacBride, who had gone home at two, was back on the job at noon. There were reports on his desk, but nothing of importance. Chibbaro and Dominick and the three girls were still missing, and none of them had been to their flats following the murder.

The city was being combed thoroughly by no less than a dozen detectives, and every cop was on the lookout too. The fade-away had probably been maneuvered by Chibby. MacBride thought so, anyway, and it struck him as a pretty dumb move on Chibbaro's part. For why should Chibby entangle himself in a murder with which, apparently, he was not vitally concerned?

Tony Maratelli blundered into Headquarters a little past noon. He was shaking all over. He was hard hit.

'Cap, for the love o' God, what am I gonna do?'

'You can't do a thing, Tony.'

'Yes, yes. I mean – but I mean, can't I do something?'

'No. Calm yourself, that's all. Dominick's in Dutch, and that's that. I can't save him, Tony.'

'But, Holy Mother, the disgrace, Cap! And my wife, you should see her!'

'I know, I know, Tony. I'm sorry as hell for you and the wife, but the kid pulled a bone, and what can we do?'

Tony walked around the office and then he sat down and put his head in his hands and groaned. MacBride creaked in his chair and looked at Tony and felt sorry for him. Here was a wop who had kept his hands clean and tried to attach some dignity to his minor office. His record was a good one. He was a good husband, a square shooter and a conscientious alderman. But what mattered all that to the public when his son ran with a bum like Chibbarro and got mixed up in a drunken brawl that terminated in the killing of Kid Barjo the popular welter?

'You go home, Tony,' said MacBride. 'There's nothing to do but hope for the best.'

Tony went home. He dragged his feet out of Headquarters, and he looked dazed. This was tragedy, no less. It was the tragedy of a good man tainted by the blood of his kin. And it is the warp and woof of life; you can't choose your heritage, nor can you choose your offspring. A man in public office is a specimen eternally held beneath the magnifying glass of public opinion, and public opinion can metamorphose a saint into a devil.

The police net which MacBride had caused to be flung out, seemed not very effective. Three days and three nights passed. No one was apprehended. Kid Barjo was buried, and Moriarity and Cohen attended the funeral – not from any feeling of sorrow or respect for the newly dead. But – sometimes – killers turn up when the dead go down. That was one of the times they didn't.

At the end of a week the *News-Examiner* printed a neatly barbed editorial relative to the inability of certain police officials to cope with existing crime conditions. The innuendo was thrown obliquely at MacBride, who took it with a curse. The editorial made much of the fact that a representative of the law had been in the Club Naples at the time of the killing. . . .

'Of course I was there,' MacBride told Kennedy. 'But I had no reason to suppose that a murder was in the wind. Drunks will be drunks, and I give any guy a decent break.'

'Some folks think you're getting soft, Cap,' smiled Kennedy.

'Yeah?'

'Yeah.'

MacBride creaked in his chair and wagged a finger at Kennedy. 'You tell those – folks, Kennedy, that I'm just as tough today as I was twenty years ago.'

'Have you seen any more of Tony Maratelli?'

'No – not since the day after the killing. I told him to go home and calm down.'

There was a knock on the door, but before MacBride could reply, it burst open and Sergeant Bettdecken stood there, a banana in one hand and his face all flushed.

'God, Cap, I just got a call from Scofield! There's hell in Riddle Street. Uh – the front of Tony Maratelli's house been blown off!'

'Ain't that funny?' said Kennedy. 'We were just talking about him.'

MacBride bounced out of his chair and reached for his hat and coat.

IV

There was a crowd in Riddle Street.

The night was dark, but the red glow of the burning house lit up part of the street. Fire engines were there, and hose lay like great black serpents in the lurid glow, and the black rubber coats and helmets of firemen gleamed as they shot water into the flames.

The water fell back into the street and froze and glazed the pavements. Behind the fire lines stood men pointing and talking; and there were women with shawls around their heads and with coats flung hastily over night-dresses. There were a few women with children in arms.

A sleek red touring car with a brass bell on the cowl drove up and the fire chief, white-haired beneath his gold-braided cap, got out and looked up at the flames and had a few words with a lieutenant.

Part of the house wall caved in with a muffled roar, and dust and smoke billowed, and some of the onlookers cried out. A couple of patrolmen kept walking up and down and pushing back those who tried to edge in beyond the lines.

MacBride arrived in a police flivver driven by Hogan. Kennedy was in the back seat with him. MacBride got out and shoved his hands into the pockets of his neat gray cheviot and looked around and then spotted Patrolman Scofield. Scofield came over and saluted and MacBride asked:

'Where's Tony?'

'In that house across the street – number 55.'

'Anybody hurt?'

'Tony got a bash on the head, that's all. His wife wasn't hit, but she's pretty hysterical.'

'Where were you when this place was blown?'

'Three blocks up River Road. I heard it and came on the run.'

'I'll take a look at Tony.'

He went into number 55. The hall-door was open, and there were some people in the hall. The sitting-room was off to the right, and MacBride saw a white-coated ambulance doctor sitting on a chair and listlessly smoking a cigarette. Tony was sitting on another chair wrapped in a heavy bathrobe and staring into space. His wife was sitting on a cot, holding her baby in her arms and moaning and rocking from side to side. Several women were grouped around her, trying to comfort her, and one held a glass of water.

MacBride drifted into the room, looked everybody over with quick scrutiny, and then went over and stood before Tony. After a moment Tony became aware of his presence and looked up and tried to say something, but he could only shake his head in dumb horror. MacBride took one hand out of his pocket and laid it on Tony's shoulder and pressed the shoulder with brief but sincere reassurance.

'Snap out of it, Tony.'

'Holy Mother. . . . Holy Mother. . . .'

'I know, I know. But snap out of it. You're alive. Your wife and baby're alive.'

'Like – like the end of the world. . . .'

MacBride caught his toe in the rung of a chair and slewed it nearer. He sat down and took a puff on his cigar and then took the cigar from his mouth and braced the hand that held it on his knee.

'You've got to snap out of it, Tony. . . .'

Tony winced. 'Out of bed I was throwed . . . out of bed . . . like—' He groaned and put his hands to his head.

MacBride looked at the cigar in the hand on his knee and then looked up at Tony. 'Were you asleep when it happened?'

'Yes . . . I was asleep. The wall fell in. . . .'

'Did you get any warning before-hand? I mean, was there any threatening letter?'

'No – no.'

'Well, try to snap out of it, Tony. I'll see you again.'

MacBride got up and put the cigar back in his mouth and his hands back in his pockets. He looked around the room, his windy blue eyes thoughtful. Then he went out into the hallway and so on out into the street. He stood at the top of the three stone steps and watched the firemen pouring water into the demolished house. The flames had died, but the water was still hissing on hot beams.

Kennedy came out of the crowd, his face in shadow but the red end of a cigarette marking out his mouth. From the bottom of the steps he said:

'Now why do you suppose they chucked a bomb at Tony's house, Cap?'

'Who chucked a bomb?' said MacBride.

'Are we thinking about the same guys?'

MacBride went down the steps. 'Yeah, I guess so. But I don't know why.'

'Let's go back to Headquarters and get a drink.'

'I'm hanging around a while,' said MacBride.

Half an hour later water stopped pouring into the ruins. The firemen began to draw in the hose. The front of the building had disappeared. You could look into the lower and upper stories and see the debris.

MacBride went over and had a few words with the chief. He borrowed a flashlight from one of the firemen and went up the blackened stone steps. He climbed over the broken door and swung his flash around. He stepped from one broken beam to another and finally reached the living-room. The floor was slushy with black ashes that had been soaked by the water. The smell was acrid. He looked at the chair wherein he had sat one night and talked with Tony. It was burnt and broken.

He proceeded over fallen plaster that was gummy beneath his feet and reached a stairway. He climbed this and came to the floor above. The white beam of his flash probed the tattered darkness. Overturned chairs, beds soaked with water and blackened with soot. Tony's home in ruin. . . . He sighed.

There were three bedrooms, and he went from one to another, and looked around and meditated over several things, and then he went down by the cluttered stairway and worked his way back to the street.

He returned the flashlight to the fireman and said, 'Thanks.'

He stood on the curb, his chin on his chest and his hands in his pockets. Presently he was aware of Kennedy standing beside him.

'Where've you been, Cap?'

'Places,' said MacBride.

'What did you see?'

'Things.'

V

Tony Maratelli stood by the window of number 55 Riddle Street and looked across at the epitaph of his home.

It was not a pleasant sight, in the sharp clear light of a winter morning. He could see the broad bed wherein he and his wife were used to sleeping; the smaller bed in another room wherein his daughter had narrowly escaped death; the other room and the other bed that were Dominick's. . . .

Tony looked sad and haggard, and when a fat man looks haggard it is in a way pathetic. A couple of men were already at work removing the debris from the sidewalk, and a policeman walked back and forth, guarding what remained of Tony's possessions.

Of course, mused Tony, he would have a nice house again, somewhere. He had plenty of money. But – that house was an old one, and he had lived there for fifteen years – first as tenant, then as owner. It had been one of the milestones of his success as a building contractor. Wherefore its ruin made him feel sad. He pulled his heavy bathrobe tighter about his short, adipose body and sniffed.

He saw MacBride come down the opposite side of the street, pause to have a talk with the patrolman on duty, then run his eyes over the ruined house. Tony's eyes steadied. He licked his lips. MacBride was his friend, but. . . .

The captain turned abruptly and crossed the street. Tony waited for the sound of the doorbell. It came. Mrs. Reckhow, who had been good enough to give him and his family shelter overnight, appeared from another room.

But Tony said, 'It's for me, Mrs. Reckhow, thanks.'

'All right, Mr. Maratelli,' she said, and disappeared.

Tony went out into the hall and opened the door and MacBride said, 'Morning, Tony,' and walked in.

They came back into the living-room and MacBride took off his hat, looked at it, creased the crown and then laid the hat on a table.

'How you feeling, Tony?'

'Not so good. I feel rotten, Cap. Yeah, I feel rotten.'

His black hair was tousled about the ears and he needed a shave and his jowls seemed to hang forlornly towards his shoulders.

MacBride, who had had only six hours sleep, looked fresh and vigorous. He went over by the window and looked at the men working on the sidewalk and then he turned around and looked at Tony.

'Tony,' he said, and looked at the floor, pursing his lips.

'Uh?' came Tony's voice from somewhere in the roof of his mouth.

'Tony . . . about Dominick.'

Tony wiped a hand in front of his face as though he were brushing away a spider-web. 'Uh . . . you found him?'

'No.'

'Oh . . . I thought you found him.'

'No, I didn't find him.'

'Oh.' His voice was weary, coming out like weary footsteps.

MacBride brought his eyes up from the floor and fastened them on Tony's eyes and seemed to screw down the bolts of his gaze with slow but sure precision.

'We'd better talk plain, Tony.'

Tony's eyes glazed and seemed to stare as though at something beyond MacBride's shoulder.

'Plain,' said MacBride, his voice going down.

'Well. . . .' Tony shrugged and looked around the room as if there was something there he wanted.

MacBride clipped, 'How long was Dominick in your house before they blew the front off?'

Tony muttered, 'Holy Mother!' and sat down heavily in a chair.

'How long, Tony?'

'Look, Cap! Could I go and give my boy up when he come to me for protection, crying like a baby? Could I? Didn't my wife she plead with me, too? But she did not have to plead, no. Dominick is my son, my flesh and blood, and if his father will not give him protection, who will? He is only the boy, Cap! He—'

'Now, wait a minute, Tony,' broke in MacBride. 'I can guess all that. What I want to know is, how long was he there?'

'Three days – just three days. But – I couldn't go tell you, Cap! The boy he ask me to protect him. He is sorry. He is sorry he got mixed up with that Chibby. He didn't do nothing, Cap. He didn't kill that box-fighter—'

'Who did?'

'I don't know.'

'Tony. . . .'

'Please to God, I don't know!'

A muscle jerked alongside MacBride's mouth. 'Dominick knew! He told you!'

'No – no!'

'Tony' – MacBride's voice was like a keen wind far off – 'Tony, I've given you every break I could. I know you're a good guy – the best wop I've ever known. But – you've got to come clean. Listen to me: I'm being razzed for that killing. You know why – because I happened to be in Al's joint when these bums got soused and Barjo got knifed. But aside from that – even if I wasn't razzed – I'd want the killer just the same—'

'But Dominick he didn't kill—'

'Don't go over that. He must have told something. What did he tell you?'

Tony spread his arms and looked as if he were going to cry. 'Noth-ing, Cap.' And he kept wagging his head from side to side. 'Didn't I keep asking him? Sure. Didn't I beg him to tell me? But he don't tell. He just say he didn't kill Barjo – and he swear by the cross and kiss it. Cap, please to God, that is the truth!'

MacBride took one hand out of his pocket and rubbed his jaw and put the hand back into his pocket again. A flush of color was in his lean hard cheeks, and there was a cool subdued fury lurking in his wide direct eyes. His voice became almost laconic:

'All right, then. He was in your house. When did he get away?'

'It must have been when the fire started. I heard him yell from the other room, and then he was gone when I got there. He must have run right out. And now – now, where is he?'

'That's what I'm trying to find out. I knew he'd been there when I poked around after the fire. He must have left in a hurry. His dress shirt and his studs were on the dresser, and his Tux was hanging on the wall. That's why I knew he'd been home.'

'Yes, he didn't go out once. He was . . . afraid.'

'Sure.'

'And now—'

His life,' put in MacBride, 'won't be worth two cents if Chibby and his crowd find him. That's why I want to know where he is. He must have run out on the crowd and come home. They're afraid he'll spring something. That's why they crashed your house.'

Tony rocked back and forth. 'And if I knowed where he is, Cap, sure I'd tell you. I don't want my boy murdered. God, if I only knowed where he is!'

'Listen,' said MacBride, 'where are you going from here?'

'I think we'll go to a hotel. The Maxim, yes.'

'Okey. But remember – if Dominick gets in touch with you, tell me right away. The only safe place for him is in the jail.'

'Jail!'

'Now calm yourself. Jail – yes. Let me know when you get in The Maxim.'

'Yes.' He got up, wobbling about. 'Cap, you're my friend, ain't you?'

'Yeah, sure, Tony.'

'Thanks, Cap – thanks!' His breath wheezed. 'My poor wife, she is all bust up.'

'Well, you're not helping her any by slopping all over the place. Buck up. Get a shave. Don't crack up like a damn' hop-head. For crying out loud!'

He laughed bluntly and slapped Tony on the back and went out.

VI

Moriarity and Cohen were trying to get a kick out of playing two-handed Michigan when MacBride breezed into the office. They looked up once and then went on playing while MacBride got out of his overcoat. He came over and sat down and said:

'Deal me a hand.'

Cohen said, 'Well, how'd you make out?'

'Yes and no. Tony doesn't know a damned thing. But Dominick did come back to his house. He breezed when the place was blown.'

'And didn't the kid tell his old man anything?' asked Cohen.

'No.'

Moriarity said, 'What makes you think Tony was playing ball?'

'I just know it.'

Moriarity laughed. 'Maybe you are getting soft, Cap.'

'Lay off,' said MacBride. 'Tony's a square wop.'

'Then why the cripes didn't he tell you his kid was home?'

MacBride looked at his cards. 'You haven't got a kid, have you?'

'Not that I know of.'

Cohen laughed. 'There's a wisecrack for you, Cap!'

MacBride put four chips on the queen. 'Then you wouldn't know, Mory, why the old wop didn't tell me. But he's square.'

'Oh, yeah,' sighed Moriarity.

'Go ahead,' said MacBride, 'razz me. I can stand it. If I took you guys and the newspapers seriously I'd jump in the river as a total loss. But you're all just a bad smell to me.'

Moriarity laughed. 'Poor old Cap!'

'Can that, too! And listen, you gumshoes. We want Dominick. He's lone-wolfing it somewhere. Even you, Mory, would realize that after he left Chibby's crowd and went back home, he wouldn't dare show his mug again with the crowd. You'd realize that, Mory – any dumb-bell would.'

Cohen said, 'Chew on that, Mory.'

'And,' said MacBride, 'we want Dominick before Chibby or one of his guns nails him. They're after him; you can bet your shirt on that. He knows something, and they're after him.'

'At least,' said Moriarity, 'it crimps Kennedy's idea that Dominick killed Barjo. I still say it was the broad.'

Cohen snapped, 'Hey, you, it was me first had the idea it was the broad.'

'All right, grab the gold ring, guy – grab it.'

'My idea may be crimped,' said Kennedy, a new voice in the doorway. 'But if it was the broad, why the hell should Chibbarro be going to such great pains to keep Dominick and the three girls and himself out of sight?'

'Now you've asked something, Kennedy!' chopped off MacBride.

Kennedy strolled in and said, 'All right, Mory. I was wrong, let's say, on picking Dominick as the killer. I was wrong. Now, you bright young child, *why* is Chibbarro playing hide-and-seek?'

Mory put on a long face. 'Well, if the broad was his friend—'

'Bologney!' chuckled Kennedy. 'She was just a broad. Chibby wouldn't waste a sneeze on her if there wasn't a reason. If she killed Barjo, and there wasn't a good reason for his trying to hide her, that bum would have come right out and told Cap what she'd done. But he *had* to save her – *for a reason*. That's how much you know, Mory.'

MacBride had to chuckle, and he looked at his right-hand men. 'Boys, you're both good cops. In a fight, you're the berries. But take my advice and don't try to figure things out too closely. Not when this wiseacre Kennedy is roaming about.'

'I'll put your name in the paper twice for that tomorrow,' said Kennedy. 'But get Dominick, and make him talk. I'm not saying the broad killed Barjo. I'm saying that *if* she killed him, then there's something bigger behind this job than just a ham welter getting a knife in his gizzard.'

'Kennedy,' said MacBride, 'sometimes you're a pain in the neck, but today you're an inspiration.'

'Three times in the paper tomorrow, Cap. Two more cracks like that and I'll see about getting you a headline.'

'And another crack like that, Kennedy, and I'll plant my foot in your slats.'

'Ah, well,' grinned Kennedy, 'boys will be boys. How about a drink?'

MacBride dragged out a bottle of Dewar's.

VII

In a way of speaking, Dominick Maratelli was between the devil and the deep sea. That is reckoning, of course, on the conjecture of MacBride that Dominick had dropped the mob and that the mob was seeking him. The mob . . . and the law.

Moriarity and Cohen worked overtime on the hunt. Precinct plain-clothes men worked too. And uniformed cops.

It was believed that when Dominick took hasty flight from the bombed house, he was broke. A man must eat. He must sleep somewhere. It was winter, and streets and alleys do not make comfortable lodgings.

Nor was MacBride idle. He too, roamed the streets and made inquiries at lunch-rooms, speakeasies; and most of his roaming was done during the dark hours. He went alone, looking into the twenty-five-cent-a-night flop-houses, conning the bread-lines in North Street.

There was no clue yet as to the whereabouts of Chibby and the three girls. And MacBride was eternally aware of the fact that Dominick's life depended on who found him first. Tony kept calling constantly . . . but there was no news.

And in the middle of the next week there was an article in the papers relative to the fact that Antonio Maratelli had resigned as alderman. Of course, the political powers that be had asked him to resign – a request that was by way of being a threat. Tony made no kick. He was more interested in saving his son.

Kennedy said, 'If you ask me, Cap, that young wise guy Dominick deserves to be bumped off. There his old man got a nice political job, and was kind of proud of it, and then this young pup pulls a song and dance that the old man has to pay for. The reward of virtue is most certainly a kick in the pants.'

MacBride tightened his jaw a little harder and continued to roam the streets. . . .

There was a black cold night when he wandered into a dark windy street and saw a familiar green sign blinking seductively:

L U

C   B

N A P L E S

As he drew nearer, he could hear the uniformed doorman beating cold feet on the cold pavement.

MacBride came up in the shadow of the houses and the doorman reached back for the doorknob. He did not recognize MacBride until the captain's foot was on the step, and then he seemed to hesitate in perplexed indecision.

MacBride looked at him and said, 'Well?'

'Oh . . . hello, Cap. Didn't recognize you.' He opened the door.

MacBride walked into the dim, stuffy ante-room and stood just inside the door and looked around. The coat-room girl came over but MacBride shook his head and she recognized him and bit her lip and retreated back into the gloom. A stiff white shirt-front came out of another corner of the gloom, and a voice said:

'Well, buddy?'

'I'm MacBride.'

'Oh . . . yeah.'

'Where's Al?'

'I'm Patsy. It's all right. What can I do for you?'

'Get me Al.'

'Well, he ain't here right now.'

'Where is he?'

'I dunno. He went out about an hour ago. If you want to wait for him – there's a little room off here.'

'I don't want to wait for him.'

'Well, I'm sorry, Cap.'

Muffled was the racket of the jazz band.

MacBride turned and pulled open the door and stepped out and looked up and down the street.

The doorman was gone.

MacBride's hands were in his pocket, and the hand in his right pocket closed over the butt of his gun. He moved towards the narrow alley that flanked one side of the building and led to the courtyard in the rear. He looked down it and he flexed his lips and then he entered the alley and walked lightly but rapidly.

He reached the courtyard in the rear. He saw a door and a lighted window, but the shade was drawn down. He moved towards the door and grasped the knob and turned it and the door gave and opened on a crack. He pushed it wide and stepped into a corridor that was dimly lighted by shaded wall lights. He had been in this corridor once before. He closed the door behind him.

From the door farthest away on the right he saw Dominick step out, and behind him the doorman and Al Vasilakos. He started to rap out a command, but Dominick, who was on the point of making for the rear door, saw him and spun and ran in the opposite direction.

'Hey, you!' shouted MacBride.

He barged down the corridor past Al and the doorman. Through the door at the end he burst into the noisy cabaret. The jazz band was hooting and people were dancing. Dominick was running alongside the tables and making for the front. MacBride sailed after him, and the jazz band petered off and the dancers stopped and stared with amazement. MacBride bowled over a drunk that teetered into his path and reached the door to the ante-room six jumps behind Dominick. The door banged in his face, and as he flung it open he saw the front door slam shut.

He streaked through the ante-room and cannoned out in the cold dark street. He heard running footsteps and saw Dominick heading for River Road. MacBride took up the chase and pulled his gun out of his pocket.

'Hey, you, Dominick!' he shouted.

But Dominick kept running.

They were nearing River Road when MacBride raised his gun and fired a high warning shot. He saw Dominick duck and run closer to the shadows of the houses. He fired another shot, bringing it closer but still reluctant to kill.

Suddenly beneath the arc-light that stood on the corner of Jockey Street and River Road, he saw a uniformed policeman appear. At the same time Dominick cut across to the opposite side of the street. The policeman crossed too, to head him off, and then Dominick swerved back into the center of the street and turned around, ran this way and that, and finally stopped and crouched.

MacBride reached him first and clipped, 'Now put your hands up, kid!'

I – I'll—'

'You'll shut up! Is that you, Zeloff? Frisk him. I don't think he's got anything, but frisk him.'

Patrolman Zeloff went through Dominick quickly and deftly. 'Naw, not a thing, Cap.'

MacBride took out manacles and locked Dominick's hands behind his back. Then he shoved his gun back into his pocket. Dominick was shivering with the cold. He wore no overcoat.

MacBride said, 'Zeloff, go back to the Club Naples and pinch Al and bring him to Headquarters. I'll take this bird along in a cab.'

'Okey, Cap.'

'And close the joint.'

'Sure.'

MacBride grabbed Dominick's arm and walked with him towards River Road.

'For cripes sake, Cap, listen. Al hasn't done a thing—'

'Shut up. *Hey, taxi!*'

VIII

The light with the green shade hung over the shiny flat-topped desk and the light umbrellaed outward over the desk and included in its radiance Dominick and MacBride, who sat and faced each other across the desk.

Dominick was thin and a black stubble was on his face and black circles were beneath his eyes, but there was also black mutiny in his eyes. He had on a shirt beneath his thin coat, but no collar, and his black hair was rumpled but still a bit shiny from the last application of hair oil.

'You,' said MacBride, 'you caused all this.'

'Well, why the hell bring it up?'

'I intend bringing it up and up. You're just a wise guy who tried to run with big, bad boys. You worried hell out of your father and mother. Because of you your father's house was blown up. Because of you your father lost his aldermanic job. Now what the hell kind of a break do you suppose you deserve?'

'Did I ask for a break? Did I?'

'Of course not. But you're expecting one. What I want to know is, who killed Barjo?'

'I don't know.'

'You mean you don't feel like telling me.'

'About that.'

MacBride leaned forward and put his elbows on the table and drew his brows close down until they almost met at the top of his nose. 'Dom, my boy, you're going to spring what you know.'

'Like hell I am.'

'Like hell you are.'

'Listen, you. I didn't kill Barjo. You've got nothing on me – not a thing! I didn't kill him.'

'Why did you drop out of sight?'

'That's my business.'

'Why did you sneak home and hide away?'

'That's my business too.'

MacBride put his voice down low. 'We know of course that Chibby is after you.'

'You don't know anything.'

MacBride snapped, 'Listen to me, you little two-tongued dago! I'm giving your old man a break. I'm trying to give you a break – not because I like you – but because I like your old man! As for you, I think you're a lousy pup! But get this – get it! – I want Chibby or one of the broads was on that party the night Barjo got knifed. I don't care what the hell one I get, I want one of them! And you – you're going to play ball with me or, by cripes, I'll whale hell out of you!'

'I'm not playing ball!' rasped Dominick. 'I was on that party, I know that. But I didn't do a thing to anybody. And I ain't going to squeal!'

'You poor dumb slob!' MacBride half rose out of his chair and planted his palms on the desk. 'Don't you realize that Chibby wants to blow your head off? Don't you realize that we're the only guys can save you?'

Dominick was biting his lip and his black eyes were jerking back and forth across the desk. He shook his head. 'I – I ain't going to say a thing.'

The door opened and Patrolman Zeloff shoved in Al Vassilakos. 'There he is, Cap.'

'Okey, Zeloff. Hello, Al. What the hell are you looking all hot and bothered about?'

'This – this is a dirty trick, Cap!'

'Is it? Listen to me, Al. I've given you all the breaks you're going to get. You were harboring a fugitive from the law.'

'I wasn't!' choked the Greek. 'So help me, I wasn't. This guy came to me and asked me to give him some jack so he could blow the town. He didn't have no jack. I gave him hell for coming around.'

Dominick cut in, 'He didn't do anything, Cap. I went there and asked him for some jack, just like he said.'

'Sure,' said Al, waving his hand. 'See?'

'All right, all right,' said MacBride. 'I see. But you've always tried to kid me, Al, and you'll warm your pants here a while. I don't like your joint. You're two-faced as hell. And I don't like you. Zeloff, put this guy in the cooler for a while.'

'Okey, Cap.'

'Aw, say, Cap,' said Al, 'give me a break.'

'Break? I'm through giving guys breaks.'

'Aw–'

'Come on, you!' snapped Zeloff, and pulled Al out into the hall.

MacBride swung around in his chair, sitting bolt upright, and threw his gaze across the desk like two penetrating beams of blue fire.

'You see the kind of a palooka you went to looking for help! The first yap out of him is to save his own face!'

'Well, d' you see me yapping?'

'Dominick . . .' MacBride said the word with deadly softness as he leaned back. 'Dominick, I warn you, you're in for a beating if you don't come across. I don't care if you are Tony's son. I'm trying to give you a break, but maybe I'll have to break you first. You can be nice . . . or I can be – nasty. Do you get me?'

Dominick drew his face up tightly and pinched his brows down over his midnight eyes. 'You can't lay a hand on me!'

'I don't – personally. I've got men who do it for me.'

'Yah, you're just the bull-dozing cop I heard you were! Just a big flat-foot! Just a big, loud-mouthed tough guy!'

'Just,' said MacBride, 'that.'

Dominick jumped up, a lean shaft of vibrating dark fire. 'You won't beat me! You won't! By God Almighty . . . you *won't.*'

'Unless you play ball.'

The telephone bell rang. MacBride picked up the instrument.

'Captain MacBride talking,' he said. 'Yeah, Mory . . . What? . . . No, no; go ahead. . . .' He listened, his eyes narrowing 'What's that address? . . . Yeah; 22 Rumford Street. Okey. I'll shoot right down.'

He slammed the telephone back to the desk and went to the door and yelled down the corridor. A reserve came on the run.

'Shove this guy in a cell, Mike. I got a date with a good break.'

He piled into his overcoat, grabbed his hat and went out into the central room. He called Hogan, and Hogan ran out to get the police flivver. MacBride was waiting for him on the sidewalk.

IX

Rumford Street is on the northern frontier of the city. It is a hilly street, climbing up from Marble Road. A drab street, walled in by three-and four-story rooming-houses. Ordinarily a peaceful neighborhood.

The police flivver swung off Marble Road and labored up the grade. When it was half way up MacBride saw an ambulance and a small group of people.

'That's it, Hogan.'

'Yeah.'

The flivver drove up behind the ambulance, and MacBride got out and saw a patrolman and the patrolman saw him and saluted.

'Second floor, Cap.'

'Right.'

MacBride entered the hall door and climbed the dusty narrow staircase. On the second landing he saw light streaming out through a door, and a policeman was standing in the door. He saw MacBride and stepped aside, and MacBride went into a small living-room.

Kennedy was sitting on a chair with his feet on a table and his hands clasped behind his back. Cohen was walking back and forth taking quick drags on a cigarette.

'Hello, Cap,' he said, and jerked his head towards the next room.

But MacBride had caught sight of a doctor and a couple of uniformed patrolmen and Moriarity standing beside a bed, and there was a pulmotor working. He caught sight, too, of a girl's legs protruding from a nightgown, and then Moriarity turned around and saw him and shrugged and came out.

'It's Bunny Dahl,' he said.

'What happened?'

'Gas.'

'What – suicide?'

'Dunno. Ike and me stopped in a speakeasy just around on Marble Road. Kennedy was there, and we were just about to start a card game when Patrolman Cronkheiser came busting in looking for a telephone. It seems he was walking his beat down Rumford Street when a woman ran out hollering for help. She lives next door. She'd smelt gas and got up and went out in the hall, and then when she knocked on this door and got no answer she ran out and hollered and Cronkheiser came up and busted in. Bunny was laying on the floor, by one of them gas heaters – there it is.'

'How is she?'

'Pretty rotten. They want to try the pulmotor because they think she may pass out before they reach the hospital.'

MacBride went in and looked at her and then came back into the other room.

'Queer,' he said.

'Yeah,' said Kennedy. 'Looks as if she got cold feet.'

MacBride said nothing for a minute, and then he said, 'I got Dominick.'

Kennedy's feet fell down from the table. 'Things come in bunches, like bananas, don't they? Where'd you get him?'

'Club Naples. He was feeling Al for some jack when I wandered in. I got Al, too. I don't like that two-faced Greek. I'm going to get something on him yet.'

'Did he say anything?' asked Moriarity.

'No. The kid's got spirit. He won't squeal. But – he'll have to. Even if we have to beat him.'

MacBride turned and looked into the other room and then he rubbed his hand slowly across his jaw. The doctor looked over his shoulder and beckoned, and MacBride came in and stood beside the bed.

'She's trying to say something, Captain.'

'What's she trying to say?'

'About a chap named Chibby.'

'Oh . . . Chibby.'

MacBride sat down on the edge of the bed and took out a pencil and an old envelope. 'Bunny,' he said. 'What's it all about, Bunny?'

'Chibby . . . did it . . .'

'How?'

'He got me drunk . . . then he tied a rag around my mouth . . . so I couldn't yell . . . then he held my head down by the gas stove . . .'

'H'm.' One side of MacBride's mouth drew down hard. He leaned closer. 'Bunny, where is he?'

'I don't know. . . . Al knows.'

'Why did he do this to you, Bunny?'

'Because I knew he . . .' Her voice trailed off.

The doctor said, 'We'd better try getting her to the hospital. She hasn't got much of a chance.'

'Okey.' MacBride stood up. He went back into the other room and said, 'Ike, I want you to go to the hospital with Bunny and hang around and see if she says anything more. Mory, you come with me to Headquarters. Al is in for hell.'

He went out into the hall and down the narrow dusty stairs. Moriarity followed him, and Kennedy trailed along behind. They all climbed into the flivver, and Hogan started the motor and they drove off.

X

MacBride had removed his hat, but his overcoat was still on and his hands were in his pockets. His face was gray and hard like granite, and his eyes were like blue cold ice, and he stood with his feet spread apart and his square jaw down close to his chest.

Kennedy sat on the desk with his feet on a chair and his elbows on his knees and his hands loosely clasped. Moriarity stood with his back to the radiator and a dead cigarette hanging from one side of his mouth.

Al Vassilakos sat in the swivel-chair with the light streaming brightly into his white puffed face. It was a face that seemed to have been crudely molded out of dough. His knees were pressed together and his toes were turned in and pressed hard against the floor, and his pudgy hands gripped the arms of the swivel-chair.

MacBride said, 'You know where Chibby is, Al.'

'So help me, Cap—'

'Shut up! You know where he is. I want to know where he is.'

'Uh – honest, Cap—'

'Shut up! There's no time for stalling. You've been playing me for the fool and I'm sick of it. I want to know where Chibby is. I'll give you one minute to come across.'

He took his left hand out of his pocket and crooked his arm and stared down at the watch on his wrist.

Al gripped the arms of the chair harder with his pudgy hands. His toes screwed against the floor. His white stiff shirt-front moved up and down jerkily. His lower lip, which had been caught under his teeth, flopped out and gleamed wet, and his nose wrinkled and his eyes bulged wildly. His breath was beginning to grate in his throat. His body was straining in the chair, and the chair creaked, and he was stretching his throat in his tight stiff collar, as if fighting for breath. Sweat burst out on his forehead and gleamed like globules of grease, and his whole face, that had been dead like dough, began to twitch and convulse as agitated nerve muscles raced around beneath his skin.

MacBride looked dispassionately at the watch on his wrist. Kennedy seemed interested in his hands. Morarity's eyes were hidden behind shuttered lids, but he was staring at Al.

MacBride shoved his hand back into his pocket. 'Minute's up, Al.'

Kennedy looked up from his hands.

Al strained harder in his chair, his white face ghastly in the light that poured down upon it.

'Well, Al? . . .' MacBride drew his lips flat back against his teeth.

Al choked. 'No-no!'

MacBride walked to the door and opened it and called, 'Hey, Mike!'

He came back into the room and after a while a patrolman came in buttoning his coat.

'Mike,' said MacBride, 'take this guy upstairs and put him over the hurdles. You, too, Mory.'

The policeman and Moriarity heaved Al out of the chair and dragged him out of the room. Al was blubbering and breaking at the knees.

MacBride closed the door and sat down in the swivel-chair. Kennedy lit a cigarette and shot smoke through his nostrils.

'Bunny sure got hell, didn't she, Cap?'

'Yeah. It's like that song about what you get for making whoopee.'

'I wonder what's behind this. I wonder why Chibby tried to bump off the broad. Maybe *he* killed Barjo.'

'Maybe.'

They didn't talk much. MacBride started a cigar and sat back in his chair, and after a while Kennedy got down from the desk and wandered about the room.

Half an hour later the door opened and Moriarity stood there. He carried his coat under his arm.

'Okey, Cap.'

'Yeah?'

'Yeah. Chibby's hiding out at 95 Hector Street with about six other guns.'

'All right, Mory. Put your coat on.'

XI

It was a big, powerful touring car that left Headquarters and droned through the dark streets. Hogan was at the wheel. Beside him sat Moriarity and MacBride. In the rear were five policemen and Kennedy. It was half-past two in the morning. The dark streets were empty, and the big car plunged from one into another, and the men in the back swayed from side to side as the car bent sharply around corners.

'This is Hector,' said Hogan.

'What's the number?' asked MacBride.

'The numbers begin here,' said Kennedy. 'That 95 should be about three blocks down.'

MacBride said, 'Pull up about a block this side, Hogan.'

'Okey.'

The car slowed down and rolled along leisurely, and presently Hogan swung into the curb and applied the brake.

MacBride got out first and looked up and down the street. The policemen got out and stood around him, and their badges, fastened to the breasts of their heavy blue overcoats, flashed intermitttently.

'It must be on the other side of the street,' said MacBride. 'Come on.'

They crossed the street and walked along close to the houses. The houses were set back from the sidewalk and fronted by iron fences, and just behind the fences were depressions and short flights of stone steps that led down to the basement floors. The street lights were few and far between, and the windows of the houses were darkened.

MacBride was saying, 'We'll try to get in through the cellar.'

They reached number 95 and went in through the gate and crowded noiselessly down the stone steps until their heads were level with the sidewalk. There were two windows, without shades, and the windows were dirty.

'They're supposed to be on the top story,' whispered Moriarity.

'And it's four stories,' muttered MacBride. 'Let's try the windows.'

They tried them, but the windows were locked. MacBride stood for a moment thinking. Then – 'There's no fire-escapes in front. They must be in the rear. Let's find a way to the rear. The next block.'

They came back to the sidewalk and walked on, took the next left turn and then turned left again into the street that paralleled Hector. MacBride counted the houses.

'You might have noticed,' said Kennedy, 'that 95 was the only four-storied house. The others were three.'

'It should be about here,' said MacBride.

He mounted the steps and rang the bell. After a few minutes the door opened and an old woman wearing a nightcap looked out.

'Madam,' said MacBride, 'we're from Police Headquarters. We'd like to pass through your house so that we can get to the one behind it in Hector Street.'

'What's the trouble?'

'We're looking for someone.'

'Well – well – all right. But waking an old woman up on these cold nights . . .'

'I'm very sorry, madam.'

She led them through the hall and opened a door in the rear that led into a small yard. Beyond the yard was a low board fence. Beyond the fence was the back of the four-storied house.

'Thank you, madam,' said MacBride.

'It's all right, but with my sciatica . . .'

MacBride and the cops and Kennedy passed out into the yard. MacBride scaled the fence and dropped down into the other yard, and the others were close behind.

'There's the fire-escape,' he said, and walked towards it.

He was the first to go up. Whatever may be said of him, good or bad, he never hung back in the face of impending danger. If he planned a dangerous maneuver, he likewise led the way, remarking, with ironic humor, that he carried heavy insurance.

He climbed quite noiselessly, and the men were like an endless chain behind him, a dark chain of life moving up the metal ladders. The windows they moved past were black as black slabs of slate. The skirts of their long blue coats swung about their knees as the knees rose and fell with each upward step.

MacBride went slower as he neared the top landing. He stopped and looked back down over the line of men, and right behind him was Patrolman Haviland, and behind Haviland was Patrolman Kreischer, who was getting on in years. And looking at them, MacBride felt a little proud of them.

He looked upward and climbed slowly, and Haviland came up to crowd on one side of him and Kreischer came up to crowd on the other side. They all had their guns out. MacBride had his out, too, but he reached over and took Haviland's nightstick.

He looked at the window, and then he raised the heavy stick and smashed the glass. He struck four times, and then plunged in through the yawning aperture.

Somewhere in the darkness there was a shout. A split-second later a gun boomed and a flash of fire stabbed the darkness and a bullet slammed into the window frame. MacBride fired around the room and lunged across the floor. He heard a man scream. If he could find a door, then he could find a light-switch, he reasoned.

Someone cannoned into him, and MacBride crashed against the wall. A gun exploded so close to his face that the smoke made him choke. He ducked and sprang away and banged into another twisting body, and ducked away again. He brought up suddenly against a door and then he groped around for the light-switch. He could not find it. A body hurtled against him with such force that the captain went down.

Somebody pulled the door open, and the dim light from the hall filtered in. Two or three forms dived out through the door. MacBride leaped up and lunged towards the door and collided with another man who was trying to get out. Both went down under a rush of four policeman who had not time to recognize MacBride. MacBride disentangled himself in a hurry and heaved up as Haviland was on the point of swinging his nightstick.

'Hey!' shouted MacBride.

'Oh . . . you, Cap!'

Another man came barging out of the door behind a flaming gun, and one of the bullets put a hole through MacBride's new hat but did not budge it the fraction of an inch. Kreischer fired three times, and the man threw up his hands and screamed, and the momentum of his dive carried him over the banister and crashing down to the hall below.

And in the hall below the cops who had run down were fighting with the men who had opened the door and sought to escape. Somebody in the room had found the light-switch – it turned out to be Kennedy – and the light revealed two gangsters lying dead on the floor and Kennedy mildly scratching his nose, as though he were trying to figure out why the men did not get up.

MacBride ran to the head of the stairs and saw the spurts of gunfire below. He forked the banister backward and slid down with lightning-like speed. He flew off the end and did a backward somersault, and as he was getting up Patrolman Mendelwitz toppled over him groaning and then slid to the floor like a bag of wet meal.

The fighting moved down the next stairway, and MacBride went after it, and Kreischer and Haviland came pounding down behind him. MacBride, going down the staircase, stumbled over a body, but caught hold of the banister and steadied himself. It was the body of a gangster.

MacBride looked over the banister and saw three gangsters backing towards the next landing below. He climbed over the banister, hung out a bit and then dropped. It was a fall of about fifteen feet, and MacBride landed on somebody's shoulders and created a new panic. He saw one of the other gangsters swing towards him, and he recognized Sam Chibbarro, and Chibarro recognized him. The gunman swung his rod towards MacBride's head, but another body sailed down from above and crashed Chibbarro to the floor. It was Kennedy, unarmed, but effective, nevertheless. The third gangster turned and ran for the head of the next staircase, and Haviland fired along the banister and got him in the side and the gangster fell against the wall and then slid down to the floor.

Chibbarro flung off Kennedy and bolted, but MacBride, having knocked his own man out, dived for Chibbarro and caught him by the tail of the coat. Chibbarro cursed and tried to get out of his coat, and then he pivoted and his gun swung close. MacBride let go of the coat-tail and caught Chibbarro's gun hand as the gun went off. The shot walloped the floor, and then MacBride swung Chibbarro's arm up and backward and clouted him over the head with the barrel of his own gun. Chibbarro went down like a felled tree.

Kreischer came up on the run, big-footed, and then stopped and watched Chibbarro fall. Then he looked at MacBride and grinned with his beet-red face.

'*Himmel!*' he said.

'I guess that's that, Fritz,' said MacBride. 'Hey, Haviland, how is Mandelwitz?'

'He's laying back here and cursing like hell.'

'Okey. Then he's all right. Harrigan, find a telephone and call the hospital and then call the wagon. Hey, Sokalov, for God's sake, don't keep pointing that gun this way! It's all over. Put it away.'

'All right. . . . I forgot, Cap.'

MacBride looked around and saw Kennedy leaning against the wall and lighting a cigarette. Kennedy's hat was twisted sidewise on his head, and two buttons were gone from his coat, and his face was dirty. He looked comical. MacBride chuckled bluntly.

'How come you're alive, Kennedy?'

'There is a Providence,' said Kennedy with mock gravity, 'that watches over fools, drunks and bum reporters.'

'I always said you were a bum reporter,' put in Moriarity.

Kennedy spun away his match. 'Imagine a guy like that!'

XII

Dawn was breaking, but the light in the office still streamed down over the flat, shiny desk.

Chibbarro sat in a chair within the radius of the light, his hair plastered down over his ears and forehead and a streak of dried blood on his cheek. His brows were bent, and he scowled at the top of the flat shiny desk.

Moriarity stood with his back to the radiator, and Kennedy had reversed a chair and now straddled it with his arms crossed on the back and his chin on his crossed arms.

MacBride sat in the swivel-chair and looked at Chibbarro.

'You did wrong, Chibby,' he said, 'to come to Richmond City. It's a tough town.'

'Tough hell!'

'Tougher than you are, Chibby. I always wondered why you came here. I'm wondering now why you tried to kill Bunny Dahl.'

'She was a chicken-hearted broad!'

'Bad . . . doing what you did, Chibby.'

Chibbarro took out his handkerchief and blew his nose. 'I been framed all around. That boy scout Dominick—'

'Didn't spring a thing.'

'Bah!'

'It was Al.'

'The lousy pup!'

MacBride leaned back and put his hands behind his head. 'So you didn't kill Barjo.'

'No, of course I didn't kill him! D' you think I'm a fool, to put a knife in a guy at a souse party?'

'I didn't think you were so much of a fool. But why did you try to put Bunny out of the way?'

Chibbarro turned his back on MacBride. 'You can ask my lawyer all them things.'

'That's all right by me, Chibby. But it won't help your case.'

The door opened and Ike Cohen walked in. 'Hello, Cap – Mory – Kennedy.' He looked at Chibbarro. 'Hello, Chibby, you small–time greaseball!'

'Go to hell!' said Chibbarro.

'Funny, you are!'

MacBride said, 'What news, Ike?'

'The frail just died.'

Chibbarro looked up with a start, and his dark eyes widened and horror bulged from the pupils. Then he pulled his face together and crouched sullenly in the chair.

Cohen drew a folded piece of paper from his pocket and handed it to MacBride.

'She regained consciousness long enough to spring this, Cap. It's signed by her and witnessed by the doctor and me.'

MacBride unfolded the paper and spread it on the desk. He read it over carefully, then settled back in his chair holding it in one hand.

'Listen to this, gang,' he said, and read aloud:

' "I killed Salvatore Barjo. He was drunk. He followed me into a room in the Club Naples and tried to attack me. I picked up a paper cutter that was laying on the table and stabbed him. Then Dominick came in. Then Chibby came in. Chibby cursed hell out of me, and Dominick yelled at him and said I had to be got out of the jam. Chibby said like hell. Then I said he'd get me out of it or I'd tell what I knew about him. That's why he got me out of it. So we hid out. Then Dominick and Chibby got in a fight and Dominick skinned out. He was a good guy, Dominick. He didn't know what Chibby had up his sleeve. He thought Chibby was just a bootlegger.

' "Then Chibby got his gang together and they hunted for Dominick to bump him off before the cops got him. Chibby thought Dominick knew more than he did. Chibby came here from Chicago. He was one of the Rizzio gang, and he came here to work up a white slave trade. He got me to work with him, and in the month here I helped him get twelve girls for houses in Dayton and Columbus. That was his real racket, but he wanted to try booze on the side, and he wanted to be friends with Dominick because his old man was alderman, and that might help.

' "When we heard the cops had Dominick I wanted to go to Headquarters and get him out. I was sick of the whole rotten business. Chibby swore he'd kill me, and I dared him. I said I was going, and that I'd say nothing about him. But he didn't believe me. He got me tight and then he shoved my head down by the gas-heater. I guess he always was a bum." '

'Hell's bells!' said Kennedy.

MacBride dropped the letter to the desk and got up and walked around the room.

'So that was it, Chibby,' he said. 'White slaving, eh?'

Chibbarro stared darkly at the shiny top of the desk.

MacBride said, 'And you only protected the girl because you knew it was the only way of protecting yourself. God, but you're a louse!'

'Imagine this guy wanting a lawyer!' said Moriarity.

'Yeah,' said Cohen. 'Ain't he the optimistic slob?'

MacBride picked up the telephone and called a number. After a moment he said, 'Hello, Tony. This is MacBride. . . . Now hold your horses. We've got the kid here. . . . Yeah, yeah, he's all right, and he'll get out after a while. . . . What's that? . . . No, I'm not going to comfort him. I'll leave that to you. If he was my kid I'd fan him. . . . All right, come around when you feel like it.'

He put down the telephone and sighed and stared at it for a long moment.

Kennedy pulled a photograph out of his pocket and stared at it.

'She wasn't such a bad-looking frail.'

MacBride looked at him. 'Where'd you get that?'

'In her bedroom. We'll smear it on the front page of the noon editions.'

MacBride went to the window and looked out and saw the red sun coming up over the rooftops. And it occurred to him, without any blur of sentimentality, that Chibby and Dominick and Al were small-timers, and that the girl – this Bunny Dahl – had been stronger than all of them put together.

Kennedy was saying, 'It's tough the way sometimes a broad has to die to get her picture in the paper.'

MURDER PICTURE
GEORGE HARMON COXE

It can be no surprise that George Harmon Coxe (1901–1984) began his career as a newspaperman, since his two major literary creations, Jack 'Flashgun' Casey (mostly known as 'Flash' Casey) and Kent Murdock were both photojournalists.

Casey came first, created for *Black Mask* in 1934. A secondary character here to young reporter Tom Wade, he quickly moves to the fore, accompanied by his young sidekick on a regular basis. There were more than 20 'Flash' Casey stories and five novels.

Murdock, very much like Casey but not as tough or violent, made his debut the following year in the novel *Murder with Pictures* (1935). Although Casey is the better-known character, Murdock appeared in many more novels (21 in all), the first of which was filmed in 1936 with Lew Ayres playing the hero.

One unusual aspect of both series is that most of the adventures feature private detectives but, unlike virtually all other fiction in *Black Mask* and the other pulps, they are bad guys, frequently hired by villains to protect their evil interests.

While the earliest stories are much in the Carroll John Daly school of shoot first, ask questions later, they soon became more cerebral, especially the Murdock tales, as murders and their solutions tended to involve technological devices rather than merely a bullet in the skull.

'Murder Picture' was first published in *Black Mask* in the issue of January 1935.

MURDER PICTURE

GEORGE HARMON COXE

Casey, ace photographer of the *Globe*, Flash Casey, as everyone from the copy boy to Captain Judson of the Homicide Squad called him, stood scowling down at a photographic enlargement spread on the table before him.

Big shoulders hunched above his lean waist, reddish hair ruffled, eyes narrowed and frowning, he cursed in a steady monotone of disgust.

The little man at the corner desk, busy making records of his prints, stopped work long enough to glance over at the big cameraman and grin.

'Whatsa bellyache, Flash?'

'Plenty,' Casey growled. He rapped a big, bony fist on the barely dried photo. 'Here I get an inside tip on that racetrack layout raid and me and Wade crash in just as they are pulling it. I shoot one – this one.' The fist rapped again. 'Then Haley and his pals throw us out. I knew there must be something more we missed, so I duck in a back way and shoot another through the washroom door, and this time the cops steal the plate off me before they put me out again.'

'Well, ain't that one you got any good?'

'A pip, but that other one musta—'

'Hell,' the little man said, fretfully, 'Blaine don't *have* to know there was another one, does he?'

A slow grin drove the scowl from Casey's homely, strong features.

'You're saying something, Tim. He don't *have* to – unless he asks me. Guess I better get it in to him.'

He gathered up the print and started towards the door.

'And tell him how good it is,' the little man jeered. 'Aw, you guys make me—'

The jangling telephone bell cut him off.

Casey, passing it, took up the receiver.

'Yeah – Casey.'

The voice of Lieutenant Logan of the Homicide Squad answered him.

'Listen, Flash. I just talked with Haley. He tells me you sneaked into the washroom of that race-track dive.'

'What about it?'

269

'Did you come across the airshaft – from the Blue Grass Products office?'

'Yeah, but—'

'I'm down there now. I want to see you.'

'When? I'm busy and—'

'I don't care a damn whether you're busy or not. Get out here right away or I'll send somebody after you.'

Casey said: 'Aw—' and pronged the receiver.

His eyes were thoughtful as he walked into the city room, but lighted up as he approached the city editor.

Casey said: 'Boy, this is a honey,' and laid the eight by ten photographic enlargement on Blaine's desk.

The city editor pushed up in his chair, slid his forearms across the desk top and glanced at the print. It was an exceptionally clear reproduction of the interior of a race-track layout, taken a few seconds after the police had staged a raid an hour previous.

The camera had caught the major part of the room, with its blackboards, loud speaker, cashier's cage; most of the milling crowd of forty or fifty people, half of them women. Casey, a look of satisfaction on his thick face, leaned down and pointed to specific features of the picture, as though he was afraid Blaine would miss them.

'There's Captain Judson,' he said, 'and Haley, the louse.' He moved his forefinger to a stocky man with a white, fatty face who was just coming out of a door on which the word, *Men*, was barely legible. 'And get a load of Mike Handy.'

Casey's forefinger moved to a smartly dressed and obviously frightened lady who had thrown one arm around the neck of a plump young man with a tiny mustache: Lee Fessendon, son of the new owner of the *Globe*, brother of the managing editor. A fellow who, though married, continued to retain his reputation of man–about–town.

'Young Fessendon.' Casey's voice was humorously disgusted. 'Takin' an afternoon off.' He straightened up, grunted. 'Made a hell of a fuss about it, wanted the plate.'

Blaine leaned back in his chair and his clasped hands made a cradle for the nape of his neck.

'This all you took?' he said finally.

'It ain't all I took.' Casey's mouth dipped at the corners and his brows knotted in a scowl as he thought of the second picture he had taken, of the trouble he had surmounted to get it.

'But it's all I got,' he growled. 'Haley and a couple of his dicks took the other one away from me.'

His brows flattened out. 'But what's the matter with that one? It's exclusive – and it's good, ain't it?'

'Very good,' said Blaine sardonically. 'Very good indeed; only we can't use it.'

'Can't use it?' Casey exploded. 'Who says we can't?'

Blaine would have been poor copy for the movies. He did not look the part. He was too well dressed, and he had no eyeshade. Slender, distinguished looking with his prematurely gray hair, he had a lean, hawk-like face and small gray eyes that met Casey's in a cold, contemptuous stare.

'I do,' he said, and his voice was thin, abrupt.

'Oh.' Casey's eyes narrowed. 'So that's how it is?' He thrust his hands deep in his trousers pockets, brought his chin down on his chest and surveyed Blaine from under bushy brows. 'If anybody'd told me this an hour ago, I'd called him a liar.'

'Told you what?' said Blaine irritably.

Casey made no direct answer. Leaning stiff armed on the desk, he made a bulky figure with a thick, upward-arching chest, and tousled hair that was peppered with gray at the temples and too long at the back. A squarish face, set, thin-lipped now, held dark eyes that were narrowed and smoldering.

'The only thing I ever liked about you,' he said flatly, 'was that you played ball. You protected confidential channels, but you never squashed a story or picture because it was about a friend of somebody's Aunt Emma. But Fessendon's got your number, huh? When he cracks the whip—'

'You interest me,' sneered Blaine.

Casey pointed at the picture on the desk. 'Lee Fessendon got caught out of school with one of his women. He's scared to take a bawling out from his wife, huh?'

He made noises in his throat and shook his head. 'He tried to talk me out of the plate down there in the hall. But you – you have to humor the boss' brother, huh?'

'Finished?' purred Blaine. And when Casey remained silent, 'Satisfied now, are you?'

He leaned forward in his chair, smiled a smile that held no mirth, spoke in a voice that was brittle.

'I don't have to make explanations to a camera. But sometimes I like to humor you, Flash. And I'm going to tell you the answer to this one; because you amuse me, and because it helps illustrate my original and permanent contention – that you are a thick-headed sap.'

Blaine reached for one of the telephones on the desk, spoke a few words. When he looked back at Casey, he said:

'You sneaked this picture over on Captain Judson. And the reason we are killing it, sweetheart, is because Judson called Fessendon and told him if we printed it he'd close us out at Headquarters for a month.'

'Judson called—' Casey broke off and a slow flush crept into his lean cheeks. His widened eyes looked chagrined, incredulous.

In another moment, J. H. Fessendon, brother of Lee, son of the new owner, and managing editor of the *Globe*, swung through the doorway of a corridor behind the desk. He accepted the photograph from Blaine with a manicured hand, studied it.

Casey's flushed face knotted in a scowl as he watched Fessendon. He did not like him or his pseudo go-getter methods. A plump, baldish man of forty-five: pink skin that looked as if a massage was part of his daily ritual; expensive tweeds, tailored with a tight vest and waistband, as though to control and mold the paunch.

'Yes – yes.' Fessendon said crisply. 'This must be the one. Too bad we can't use it. Where's the plate?' He glanced at Blaine, who eyed him narrowly, then at Casey. 'Get the plate, Casey.'

Casey fastened contemptuous eyes on Blaine, wheeled and left the desk. In the photographic department, he asked Tom Wade if he had made an extra print. Wade said he had, and Casey growled:

'Swell. I'll paste it in my diary.' At the doorway, he turned. 'Put it in my desk.'

Fessendon was pacing back and forth beside Blaine's desk, followed by surreptitious glances from the crew in the 'slot', the half dozen rewrite men scattered about the city room. Casey handed Fessendon the plate, and he held it up to the light. Grunting in approval, he struck the glass against the corner of the desk. The plate shattered in a dozen pieces. Then Fessendon tore up the print.

'Got to make sure,' he said easily, picking up the pieces and dropping them in a wastebasket, 'got to make sure, you know.'

Blaine turned in his chair and watched Fessendon through the doorway, as did every other eye in the room. When he turned back, he met Casey's humid, searching gaze for a moment, and his face flushed. Then he busied himself with some copy, said:

'Don't stand there gawking. If you got legitimate shots we'd have something to print.'

Casey opened his mouth and rage kept it open. But he did not speak. He could not think of the right thing to say.

2

Tom Wade was talking on the telephone when Casey returned to the anteroom of the photographic department and slid into the chair behind his desk. He lit a cigarette, puffed once, then let it hang from his half opened lips.

The hot anger which streaked through his brain when Fessendon smashed the plate was a smoldering, cancerous growth now. A heaviness that was a mixture of dejection and disappointment weighed upon him. It was not so much the loss of the plate; that had happened before; it was the way Blaine had let him down – and Fessendon's gesture, as though he could trust neither Casey nor the city editor.

Wade talked for nearly five minutes longer, and when he hung up Casey told him what had happened.

'It's like I told you before,' he finished. 'The sheet's goin' to seed since Fessendon bought it. And I still think Lee is the guy that gyped us out of the shot. He probably called Blaine and Blaine gave me the song about Judson—'

'That don't sound like Blaine to me,' Wade said slowly.

'And Fessendon,' Casey rasped. 'Bustin' the plate like we was crooks or something.' He began to curse, and after a moment said: 'Who the hell were you talkin' with so long?'

'Alma Henderson.'

'That tramp that was—'

'Wait a minute!' Wade's voice was unnaturally harsh. A blond, round-faced youth with a guileless manner and a happy-go-lucky philosophy, Wade's ordinarily good-natured face was now flushed, his blue eyes snapping.

'Oh,' said Casey and his brows came up. 'So that's the way it is.'

'No,' Wade said doggedly, flushing at his burst of temper, 'but she's no tramp. She's a good kid and—'

Casey's mind flashed back to the raid. To get the second picture, the one Haley had taken, he and Wade had crashed into the office of the Blue Grass Products, which was separated from the race-track room by an airshaft. Casey had been in the building before, knew there was an airshaft and had crossed this to get to the men's room of the gambling hall.

Alma Henderson was apparently in charge of the Blue Grass office. It had surprised Casey that Wade knew her, because heretofore the youth had but little time for women. But Casey, intent on getting another picture, dismissed his curiosity and had left Wade arguing with the girl while he crossed the airshaft with his camera.

He said: 'She's a good kid, huh? Okey. But she works for the Blue Grass outfit, and Moe Nyberg runs it. A cheap tout, a first-class thug. Why, the heel; everything he touches stinks. He's probably hooked up with that race-track dive, now that I think of it. And he plays with Mike Handy who runs the biggest gyp stable in the East. So what does that make this Henderson dame?'

'What the hell?' Wade flung out. 'A girl's got to eat.'

'All right, all right. I don't care. I got troubles of my own.'

Casey lit another cigarette, puffed at it until his head was shrouded in blue. But it wasn't all right. Wade was impulsive, and he had a lot to learn.

To get mixed up with any woman connected with Nyberg might put him on the skids.

He said: 'What did she want?'

'She wants me to come over to her place.'

'What for? She knows you're workin', don't she?'

'She's got a story.' Wade said jerkily. 'She wouldn't tell me over the phone, but she says it's a job for the cops.'

'Hah!' rasped Casey. 'Then why don't she go down to Headquarters and spill it?'

'Here's why.' Wade took a newspaper from his desk, opened it, pointed to a single column head on page 12.

Casey read:

GIRL PRISONER FLEES DOCTOR

Brought to the State Hospital in East Concord Street for a physical examination, Miss Mary Merkle, 21, serving a sentence at the Reformatory for Women until 1937, escaped today from the office of Doctor . . .

Casey looked up. 'I told you she was a tramp.'

Wade flushed. 'You're wrong, Flash. She gave me part of the story over the phone. She came down from Vermont three years ago. She got mixed up in a bad crowd, there was a raid, she had no near relatives—'

Wade went on with his story and Casey looked at the date line of the paper. May 17th.

'When she escaped,' Wade went on, 'she had no place to go, so she looked up one of the guys she used to know and he got her a job with Moe Nyberg. If she goes to the cops with her story, bingo. Back to the Reformatory.'

'That's probably where she belongs,' growled Casey, and was half ashamed of his words when he saw the hurt look in Wade's eyes.

'She's scared, Flash. And' – Wade hesitated, caught his lower lip between his teeth – 'I think she wants me to help her out of town.'

'You're nuts,' Casey said. He looked at the youth, read correctly the stubborn set of the jaw. He spread his hand wearily, said:

'Listen. I gotta go back to Roxbury and see Logan. Something's up. You can go with me. And after that I'll go and see this Henderson dame with you.'

Wade shook his head. 'She told me to hurry.'

'But—' snorted Casey.

'Wait.' Wade backed towards the door and his voice was a bit thick. 'She's depending on me, says I'm the only one in town she can trust. I told her I'd come and I'm not letting her down – not even for you.'

Casey blew out his breath. Guileless as hell. And just as stubborn. Sold on the girl – or her story. He said:

'What's her address?'

'Seven sixty-three Pratt Street.'

Casey smiled then and the smile was genuine, tinged with a certain admiration for the youth's earnest loyalty. He said: 'Okey, give it a whirl. Only watch your step and remember she works for Moe Nyberg.'

When Wade went out, Casey shrugged and picked up his camera and platecase. 'I'd better take 'em,' he said half aloud. 'Logan sounded tough.'

Fifteen minutes later, Casey set his camera and case on the floor in front of a door whose upper panel of frosted glass bore the inscription: *Blue Grass Products*, and scowled.

The transverse corridor on the third floor of the ancient and deserted looking office building was empty, ominously quiet, lighted by a single bulb at the far end. A half dozen doors, with upper panels of glass, gave on the hall, and in each case they were dark. The one in front of him was dark, and this he could not understand.

Where the hell was Logan?

Casey sucked at his upper lip, pushed his hat forward and scratched his shaggy nape. He swept the tails of his topcoat aside as he jammed his fists on his hips; then he yanked the hat brim down, said: 'Nerts,' and banged his fist on the doorframe.

He waited a moment, banged again. Then, although he heard no sound, he happened to glance at the doorknob. It was turning slowly.

Doubt, chilled and gripping, reared up in his brain. He reached quickly for the platecase, but as he straightened up, prepared to retreat, the door came open a three-inch crack.

Casey froze there, an open-mouthed, wide-eyed statue. Surprise, momentary panic, riveted his gaze on that vertical strip of blackness, on the muzzle of a gun which had been thrust forward in the opening so that the dim light of the hall caught the round barrel, burnished it.

For a second or two there was no sound but the sharp suck of Casey's breath as it caught in his lungs. Then the door swung open and a low, matter-of-fact voice said:

'Okey, Flash. Come on in.'

Casey exhaled noisily and stepped forward with sweat breaking out on his forehead. The lights of the room went on. Logan moved out of the doorway and Casey cursed, said: 'Why you louse!'

He stopped in front of Logan, glared at him, and the lights of the room glistened on the thin film of moisture on his forehead.

'You louse! You scared hell out of me.'

'Couldn't be helped,' said Logan flatly, making no apology.

'Ah—' Casey brushed his forehead, pushed back his hat. 'You knew I was comin'. You called me up, didn't you? What the hell do—'

'I knew you were coming,' said Logan holstering his gun, 'but I'm hopin' we might get some other callers.'

Something in Logan's cold abrupt tone caught and held Casey's interest. It was no gag, that gun business. Logan was in dead earnest. And when he got that way—

Casey glanced around. From where he stood, the office was as he remembered it; long, well furnished with a flat-topped desk, a typewriter desk, leather upholstered chairs. The doorway on the right, apparently leading to a connecting office, had been closed this afternoon. It was open now and two detectives stood in the doorway.

Casey recognized the short, stocky fellow with the red face and the heavy chain draped across his bulging vest as Sergeant Manahan. The other fellow was from Headquarters, too, but he did not know his name. He said:

'Well, what's the act for?'

Logan took him by the arm, walked him out of the entryway so that he could get a full view of the room. Then Casey saw the man on the floor.

Between the little entryway and the cubbyhole, with its washstand and window giving on the airshaft, was a closet. The door of this was open, and the body of a man, lying on his stomach, his face cocked to one side, was half in, half out of the closet, as though he had fallen out when the door was opened.

He was well dressed, his oxford gray topcoat looked new and his shoes were polished. From what Casey could see, the fellow appeared to be about thirty-five, dark-haired, average height. Now there was a definite stiffness about the still form, and in the back a reddish blotch fused with the gray fabric of the coat.

Casey looked at Logan. 'Who is he?'

'Grady. A private dick from New York.'

'Shot in the back?'

'Twice – from close range.'

'Where do I come in?' asked Casey, frowning.

'That's what I want to know,' said Logan. 'I want to know all about the horseplay you staged here this afternoon. I may be wrong. But I think this guy was in that closet – dead – when you were in this room.'

Casey's eyes widened. He stared at Logan, said: '——— !' Then he thought about the Henderson woman, and Wade, and some of the color oozed from his face.

'Then she saw it!' he wheezed huskily. 'She must've seen it. And it was a plant. That's why she wanted Wade.'

'Keep your pants on,' Logan said bruskly, 'and start at the beginning.'

3

Lieutenant Logan, sitting on the massive, flat-topped desk at the end of the room, his arms angling out beside him, propping him up, was a well built fellow with black hair and eyes. About Casey's age, he had a flair for clothes. His linen was immaculate, so was his police record. Right now he wore spats – and nobody said anything about them either.

'Wait a minute,' he said when Casey told him about the girl – and the telephone call which had summoned Wade. 'At the beginning. How'd you get here, what'd you do – everything. I want it all.'

Casey glared at Logan for a moment, then spoke in thick jerky tones.

'I got the tip from Gerry at Headquarters. When Wade and I got downstairs Judson and Haley and their gang were just gettin' ready to start. We went up the stairs and when they broke down the door I went in behind the cops. I got one picture, then Judson threw me out.'

Casey cursed at the thought, continued rapidly.

'I knew there was an airshaft some place around so Wade and I cut down this other hall. I figured it oughtta be about there, so we crashed in here; didn't know what it was but took a chance.

'The Henderson dame was alone here. She gave us an argument, looked scared as hell, but Wade talked to her and—'

'The closet was closed,' Logan said.

'Yeah,' chafed Casey, 'so was this other door – to the next office. And anyway I opened the window' – he pointed to the frosted glass pane in the wall of the cubbyhole – 'and saw that the window across the shaft was part-way open.'

He stepped towards a wide shelf which lay on iron brackets on one wall of the cubbyhole. 'The dame was arguing all the time, but I found out this shelf was loose, I shoved it across the shaft and it just reached. So I took the camera and slid across. It was the men's room.'

'Anybody in it?' asked Logan.

'No. And I went through to the hall, got one picture. But Haley saw me, caught me before I could reach the door. He and a couple of those thugs you call detectives took the plate away from me.'

'Did you come back here?'

'Yeah, but' – Casey's thick face cracked in a scowl – 'the place was closed.'

'Hah!' snapped Logan. 'Then what?'

'I couldn't figure it,' Casey went on, still scowling, 'but I finally found Wade downstairs. He said that the girl was afraid Nyberg might get sore, and it was time to close up anyway, so she chased him out of the office and locked up.'

Casey shook his head. Logan waited silently.

'It sounded screwy at the time, but I had other things on my mind. Anyway she wanted Wade to take her downstairs – said she was afraid the cops might think she had been in the gambling place. So Wade took her downstairs. He was out on the street when I found him – the crazy fool. He said a car with a couple tough-looking eggs came along and the dame got in and left him standing there.'

'That's all, huh?' Logan asked.

'That's all that happened to me, yeah.'

'All right.' Logan pushed back his gray felt, pursed his lips, finally said: 'It begins to add up. Now I'll tell you my side.

'You're about the only button pusher I know that's satisfied to take pictures and leave the police work for the cops. And that's important this time – because there's no pictures – no story – tonight. We're gambling that the killers might come back for the body *if they think the kill is covered*.'

Logan watched Casey drop into a chair, then continued.

'Grady was working for three or four race-tracks – the stewards or something. Remember that stink about the horse doping ring a couple years or so ago?' Casey nodded and Logan said: 'The Feds were in on that. This is something new.

'Grady was about ready to crack this ring until Dopey Donlan got knocked off a couple days ago.'

'He was in it?' Casey asked.

'Yeah. And that's why he was killed. Because the big shots were afraid he'd squawk under pressure. He's a hophead and he probably would.

'But Grady had some dope on that kill. I didn't know a thing about it till last night. Grady worked under cover until he came down to Headquarters and told me what he had. He said he thought he'd be ready for the showdown today. But you know these private dicks. Afraid we'd steal his stuff. Wouldn't spill a thing till he was ready.'

Logan shrugged. 'Well, he was ready this afternoon. He was the guy that tipped us off to this joint. He had the man he wanted. When he pulled the raid, Judson was to pinch the killer – or the big hot, or somebody.'

Logan slid off the desk and walked over to the body.

'What an idea. He's cleaned. Nothing on him but his clothes. If he hadn't come to see me last night, we'd have a hell of a time identifying him at all.'

'How'd you get wise he was here,' said Casey, taking out a cigarette and trying to get his mind off Wade.

'Haley found some blood in that washroom across the way. He found some – just a spot or two – on the window sill. He remembered you being there, looked around, tumbled to this office. But it was locked. I came down. We found him in the closet.'

Casey stood up, began to pace the floor. 'Then somebody got him into the washroom from the race-track dive, or followed him in, put the slug on him and' – he stopped, turned to glance at the wide shelf he had used – 'and slid his body across here.'

'Yeah,' said Logan. 'And you and Wade busted in. The killers might've been in this next office. The girl had to get Wade out. That's why she got him to go downstairs with her.' Logan's voice got thin, thready.

'That's why we're waiting. If they aren't wise they'll come back for the

body – I hope. That must've been their original plan – to leave it here till tonight. No word got out of this. Judson, Haley, the examiner and us are the only ones that know about it.

'We've got a guy that tried to get in that washroom about three or four minutes before the raid. He says the door was locked, that he watched it from then on till the raid. Nobody came out. So that must've been the time that Grady got it. Somebody got wise to him – but they couldn't know about the raid. It just happened to break right after they'd killed him and—'

Logan broke off in surprise as Casey spun towards him with a thick, throaty curse.

'The picture!' Casey's eyes got bright and glaring. 'The one I took first. That's it. I caught Handy with the camera, *caught him coming out of the washroom a couple seconds after the raid*. He must've been in there when the door was locked, and—'

'Wait a minute!' rapped Logan, and grabbed Casey. 'What picture – what the hell you talking about?'

Casey told him then. Described the picture he had taken in short, clipped sentences. But he could not keep still when he talked. He had to walk, keep moving, because of the thought that festered in his brain and gave him no peace.

'It's gotta be that way. And the girl knew Grady was dead – in that closet. She musta told Nyberg and—'

'We got word out to pick Moe up,' Logan interrupted. 'We had Handy – and let him go.'

'They must've made that Henderson tramp get Wade out to her place,' Casey rushed on, 'so they could put the pressure on him. Maybe force him to get that place. Only—'

Casey broke off and went slack-jawed.

'Only what?' rapped Logan.

'Only there ain't any plate. Blaine – Fessendon, the —— !' Casey explained what had happened. 'Those hoods won't believe the kid when he tells 'em it's smashed.'

Logan jerked Casey around. 'Take it easy. You got too much imagination. That girl might be on the level. And Wade. Hell, with his kind of dumb luck—'

He broke off as Casey jerked loose and started for the door. He leaped after the big photographer, caught him again.

'Where you goin'?'

'I'm goin' to that girl's place and—'

'No you're not.' Logan's chin jutted out and his brows drew down. 'You're goin' down to the *Globe* with me and get that picture first. After that we'll go.'

Casey put balled fists on his hips and leaned forward so that his chin was three inches from Logan's nose.

'I am, huh?' he grunted.

'It's a murder picture,' said Logan. 'With that and this other guy's testimony about the washroom, and the M.E.'s verdict to the time of death—'

'And Judson callin' in, sayin' we can't print it,' flared Casey.

'I don't know about Judson, but—' Logan began.

'And Blaine,' grated Casey. 'If he'd had his way there wouldn't be any picture. But there is; I held out on him. And you oughtta be ——damn' glad I did. You can have it. But I'm not gonna waste time goin' to the office now; and you're not gonna take me down till I find that girl.'

Anger flooded Logan's face and he started to speak. For just a moment he met Casey's burning stare; then he backed a step and threw up his hands.

Those black eyes of Logan's could see beneath many surfaces; and when Casey spoke like that you believed him. Logan believed him now. And strangely enough, his lips twitched in a flicker of a smile.

'If that's the way it is,' he said caustically, 'I guess I'd better go with you.' Turning to Manahan he added: 'Call Judson. Get a couple more men up here. You may get action yet. But if word of this gets out I'm gonna beat the hell out of you, personally.'

He grabbed Casey, who had already shouldered his platecase, said: 'The kid'll be okey as long as the kill is covered. But that girl. We can use her.'

Pratt Street is a narrow offshoot of Massachusetts Avenue. The sidewalks are narrow and made to look more so because the apartments, seedy looking three and four-story brick structures, jammed close together, are all set right out to the edge of the legal building line.

Seven sixty-three, in the middle of the block, had but two characteristics to distinguish it from its adjoining neighbors and those across the street: its number, and the name *Edgemere*, painted in gilt across its single door.

The tunnel-like entryway was so dark Logan had to strike a match to inspect the name cards above the mailboxes along the right wall. 'This is the place, all right,' he said. 'Alma Henderson – 3-C.'

The inner door was unlocked and the air here seemed hot and stuffy after the chilled sweep of the night outside. They climbed silently, Logan in the lead, and the soft pounding of a steam radiator on the second floor paced their steps up the last flight of stairs.

Three-C was on the right, rear. Logan knocked once, turned the knob. The door was not locked and as he opened it, Casey grunted impatiently and pushed him into the lighted room. Logan took two steps and stopped short and stiff, so that Casey ran into him and heard him breathe a curse.

Casey looked over his shoulder and saw why. Alma Henderson was on

the floor by a wide-open window. A crumpled heap of arms and legs and orange dress.

Casey closed the door softly, and automatically. Logan started across the room. Casey remained where he was, glanced about and became vaguely aware of a cheaply furnished living-room that tried hard to be smart.

Then, because a new indefinable sense of fear reached at his nerve ends with icy fingers, he called: 'Wade!' and was instantly aware of the hollowness of his voice, and the absurdity of the act. Wade was not here. Because if he were here—

'Shot her in the back, too,' Logan said bitterly.

Casey lurched across the room. He looked down at the lifeless figure of a girl who was tall, and young, and slender – too slender, and had nice hands. Even in death her face held a youthful prettiness that makeup could not hide.

His gaze held by the discoloured spot in the left side of that orange dress, Casey continued to stare at Alma Henderson. But after a moment he was not conscious of what he saw. It was a mental picture that sickened him and he put his thoughts into words.

'She saw Grady killed. She had to go, but before that they got her to spot Wade.'

'That puts the weight on your picture,' Logan said slowly. 'It's not as good as the girl, but she can't testify.'

'Suppose Wade saw her get it?' Casey spoke as though talking to himself. 'You know how that sets him up.'

'If he's not here, he's still alive.'

'You look around then,' Casey muttered. 'I'll stay here.'

'Sure,' said Logan, moving away. 'It's gonna be a pleasure to meet up with these guys. In the back. And it looks like she might've been trying to open that window.' He cursed softly. 'It's kinda screwy. It don't look like a planned kill.'

Casey backed away a step, lifted his head and looked out the window. City lights from beyond suffused the drab sky and made a dirty blue background for the rear rooflines of houses in the next block, for spindly antennae, and a pot-bellied water-tower. A sound of movement behind him flicked his eyes away from the somber picture and he turned.

A man stood beside the doorway to the inner hall. A stocky man with a twisted grin on his broad, sallow face. He had a small automatic in his right hand.

Then Logan came into the room. He had his hands raised shoulder high, and he walked slowly. Behind him came a thin, hollow-chested, ratty-looking youth who held the muzzle of his gun stiffly against Logan's back.

'Just be nice,' the stocky man said. 'Both of you.'

4

The tableau held motionless a second or two; then the thin man's glance slid sidewise to Casey and he jabbed with his gun, spoke to Logan.

'So it's gonna be a pleasure to meet up with us, huh?' He chuckled but his lips were sneering. 'Well, the pleasure's all yours. How do you like it?'

Casey felt a thickness in his throat and he cleared it with a grunt, said: 'Where's Wade?' ominously.

'Who's Wade?' asked the stocky man and cocked one eyebrow in an expression of mock concern.

'You know who,' said Casey huskily and slid one foot forward across the rug.

'Hold it!' clipped the stocky man. 'We know how we stand, and if you think you can crowd us, you're nuts.'

Casey stopped with his left foot advanced. He was a good eight feet from Logan, ten feet or more from the stocky man. He'd never get that far, and he knew it. He had no weapon, and there was nothing he could get his hands on – except the vase on the gateleg table, and that was back by the wall.

The stocky man pocketed his gun, moved towards the telephone stand near the doorway to the inner hall, said: 'Get him away from that phone. I'd better find out what we do with these punks.'

The thin man marched Logan forward three steps, and as they stopped Casey watched the lieutenant. The handsome face was set now, and there was a tight, pinched smile on his lips. The smooth skin at his cheekbones was stretched like a banjo head, but it was the eyes that held Casey's gaze.

There was an intense gleam in their dark depths, and, as Casey watched, he saw one lid pull down in a slow, deliberate wink. The lid remained narrowed.

Casey knew then that Logan was going to fight for it. He weighed their chances and then forgot about that angle. He would be ready when Logan moved. He waited.

The stocky man had dialed a number and was talking in low, jerky tones.

'One of 'em's that picture-taker; the other acts like a cop . . . . Yeah . . . . Yeah. Because we couldn't get out. We didn't lock the door, and these muggs bust in with only one knock. We couldn't make the back door, so we ducked in the bedroom. Sure. But what do we do with 'em?'

He was silent for a moment after that: then he said: 'Okey. Yeah.'

Casey did not see the fellow hang up, because his eyes were still on Logan. But he heard the click of the receiver. And at that instant, Logan acted.

His movement was a peculiar, spinning maneuver that should have been

awkward, but wasn't. The spin was catlike in its quickness, compact, and to the right.

As he moved his right fist swung down from the shoulder height, smashed on the thin man's gun wrist. The automatic spun from the fellow's grasp, skidded towards Casey. Then Logan completed the spin as his left came up and around in a looping hook.

Casey went into action as he heard the smack of fist on jawbone. One step brought him over the fallen automatic. As he stooped, a slanting, corner-of-the-eye picture presented the stocky man straightening from the telephone table, clawing at his pocket.

The automatic was cool in Casey's hot fingers. As he snatched it up he went to one knee and swung his arm over. He saw the sweep of the stocky man's gun, caught sight of the muzzle. Then the roar in his ears, the slap of recoil in his wrist told him the shot was his own.

The gun barrel that threatened him wavered, dipped. The automatic began to slide from limp fingers. Then Casey raised his eyes. The man's mouth was open, quivering. There was a bluish hole over the one eye. He put one hand on the telephone table. The hand slipped off and he went over, crashing down with the table and the instrument under him.

Logan blew out his breath and let go of the unconscious gunman he had been holding for a shield. The fellow thudded down on his haunches, toppled over on his side. Logan pulled the telephone out from under the stocky man's body and slipped the receiver into place before he spoke.

'I coulda smacked this egg before,' he said grimly. 'Only I thought maybe we could learn something from the phone call.'

Casey had straightened up. Logan stepped over, took the gun away from him. He turned it over in his hands thoughtfully, and looked at Casey's with eyes that were speculative.

'You're handy with that thing. How'd you learn to put 'em where you want 'em?'

'In France,' said Casey absently. 'I was a sergeant, and a .45 was the only gun I had. I did some practicing.'

He went across to the davenport and sat down, his mind relieved of the necessity of action, returning once more to Wade. Then the thin man stirred on the floor. Casey watched him until he sat up. He stepped towards the fellow, jerked him to his feet and jammed him back against the wall.

'What'd you do with Wade?'

The thin man's eyes showed fear, but his lips tightened. Casey grunted, hauled off and threw a looping right that landed flat-handed against the side of the man's head and knocked him down.

Casey pulled the fellow up again. He repeated the question and when he got no answer, repeated the dose. The fellow began to curse in a whining, yet vicious voice. Logan said: 'Lay off.'

Casey knocked the man down again. The side of the face was beet-red now, but he was otherwise unmarked. 'Where's Wade?' He shook the fellow. 'What'd you do with him?'

This time the answer blurted in his face.

'They took him out. Buck'n me stuck around to search the place, to see if there was anything around that might—'

'Who took him out?'

The man seemed to flinch, but his teeth bared and clenched.

'Where'd they take him? Where is he now?'

'Go to hell! I won't—'

Casey lost his temper then. The right came over again, but this time the hand was a fist and it landed on the side of the jaw. The fellow stiffened and he was still stiff when he hit the floor. Casey started after him again, then Logan yanked him back, spun him around.

'I told you to lay off.'

'We gotta find Wade,' rasped Casey.

'Yeah. Sure. But you mark that guy all up and I'll get blamed for it, and we won't get a chance to work him over. It takes more than a wallop to make some guys talk.'

'Well?' Casey's eyes got bright and glaring and his voice was thick. 'What do we do, sit here and wait for something to happen?'

'You get down to the *Globe* and camp on the picture. I'll be down after it inside of ten minutes – just as soon as I can get somebody to take over here.'

He picked up the telephone, barked a number. Casey, scowling, hesitant, watched Logan until the lieutenant said: 'Go on get the hell out of here.'

Casey's eyes slid to the girl in the orange dress, with the stain on the back. Then he turned quickly and left the room.

It was not until Casey reached the *Globe* that he remembered his camera in the rumble seat of the roadster, remembered that he had it with him all the time, and that he had taken no pictures in Alma Henderson's apartment.

Ordinarily this would have rankled; his pride in his work would have taunted him. To have a chance like that and get no pictures. This time he did not seem to care. And it was not entirely that the affair was to be kept quiet for a while. The answer, he told himself, was that he did not give a damn whether he got exclusive pictures or not. What the hell good did it do to break your neck for pictures for a lug like Fessendon? And Blaine. In a mind that was already harassed with thoughts of Wade, there was room for further doubt and uncertainty. It wasn't like Blaine to let even the managing editor pull a stunt like breaking that plate.

To Casey, Blaine had always been the sort of fellow who would quit a job, rather than compromise with his duty or his scruples. And quitting would entail no hardship. He was the best desk man in the city – could get a job in any office.

Casey took the photograph from his desk, studied it. Then, cursing softly, he went down to the photo-engraving room, spoke to a sturdy looking man in blue jumpers and shirt sleeves.

'This is the only print Mac. I've gotta turn it over to the police, so make me a cut of it, will you, just in case this gets lost?'

Mac said sure, and Casey waited while the fellow set up the print and made his negative. As he returned the picture he said:

'What size you want it?'

'Same size, I guess.'

'What'll I do with the cut?'

'Oh—' Casey hesitated, not caring particularly what was done with it. All he wanted was to have something to fall back on, some margin of safety in case something happened to the print. Blaine or no Blaine, he was going to hang on to it, until Handy and Nyberg were rounded up, until he found Wade. 'Just pull a proof and keep it on hand for me,' he finished.

5

Casey was slouched down behind his desk when Logan came in five minutes later. The lieutenant took the print, scanned it eagerly.

'It's gonna help,' he said. 'And it's about all we got, because I couldn't find anyone in that gambling take that remembered seeing anyone come out of that washroom.'

'What're you gonna do?' Casey asked morosely.

'I've got that skinny guy outside. I'm takin' him down to work over.'

'Well damn you, Logan, put on the pressure! He knows where Wade is – make him talk and hurry it up!'

'I'll crack him,' Logan said resentfully. 'Hang on till you hear from me.'

When the lieutenant left an office boy stuck his head in the doorway. 'Hey, Flash. There's a guy here wants to see you.'

'Tell him I'm busy,' grunted Casey.

The boy went out. But he came back a few minutes later, said: 'That guy won't go,' apologetically. 'He says Wade told him to come and see you, that Wade owes him for the trip an—'

'Jeeze!' Casey's eyes widened in sudden hope and amazement. 'Get him up here!'

The taxi-driver, a beetle-browed husky, came in a moment later and immediately took the offensive.

'Somebody owes me some dough,' he barked. 'I want it.'

'Maybe you'll get it,' said Casey. 'Where's Wade?'

'I drove him to Pratt Street. He told me to wait, but he acted kinda nervous about something. He started in the house, then came back and said that if he didn't come out in half an hour I was to come to you and tell you, that you'd pay.'

'Nervous, huh?' wheezed Casey. 'Boy, am I glad I threw a little scare into him before he left.'

The driver blinked, said: 'What?' and Casey snapped:

'Never mind – never mind.'

'Well,' the driver shrugged, 'anyway, he came out about twenty minutes later – with a couple guys I'd seen go in before. But he didn't come near my cab. They got in another bus. Well, it shaped up kinda screwy to me so I followed that other car. Then I came back here. I been waiting for—'

Casey blew out his breath and a tight smile pressed his lips against his teeth. 'Where'd they go?'

The driver gave an address on Alson Street, and Casey said:

'Did you see 'em go in the place?'

'No. I didn't want to stop. But I saw 'em get out of the car before I turned the next corner. Now how about my dough? It's two–forty, waitin' time and all.'

Casey took out a five-dollar bill, and as he passed it to the driver his brain focused on one thought. He knew where Wade had been taken. He might have been moved since; he might not be there now. But it was a red hot lead.

The driver said: 'I can't change that.'

'Who said anything about change?' snapped Casey. Then, before the driver could do more than grin, the telephone rang. Casey answered it and a harsh baritone said:

'Casey?'

'Yeah.'

'You got a picture of that raid this afternoon. The kid buddy of yours says it hadn't been developed when he left the office. Is it still that way?'

Casey was not long in making up his mind. Wade, knowing no one would believe him if he said the plate was smashed – that would be too much like a stall – had sold somebody on the idea that the plate had not been developed.

'Sure.' Casey hunched forward, then, seeing the taxi-driver edging towards the door, he motioned him to wait. 'What about it?'

'I want it, that's all.'

'Who's talking?' Casey, grasping for some idea, tried to stall.

'Don't give me that,' rasped the voice. 'You got the plate. I want it. And if I get it, the kid'll be okey.'

'What's all the fuss about?' Casey made his voice bored, indulgent. 'You can have the plate if that's the way it is. We weren't gonna use it anyway. I'll bring it out myself if you say so.'

'You'll do as I say if you know what's good for the kid.'

'Sure,' said Casey.

'Then shut up and listen. You say the plate hasn't been developed. Okey I'll believe you because if you cross me, it's your tough luck, not mine. I'll have somebody pick up that plate. Don't try to tip off the cops, don't worry about havin' this call traced because it's a pay-station. If we get the plate and things are on the level, we'll have it developed. If it's the right one, the kid'll be okey.

'We'll hold him for a few days – to make sure you don't shoot off your mouth about this – and let him go. But try anything screwy – give me the wrong plate – and do you know what'll happen to this guy Wade?'

'I can guess,' said Casey bitterly.

'And with your experience you oughtta be pretty close.'

Casey glanced up at the taxi-driver and the germ of an idea caught in the recesses of his brain, expanded. He pulled a pad of paper across the desk, began to write hurriedly – a note to Potter, a leg man, telling him to take Casey's roadster and go to the Alson Street address the taxi-driver had given him, and wait outside.

He could take no chances on that angle. That address had to be watched – until he could get in touch with Logan – and Potter could do that much anyway.

'What's to prevent me from callin' the cops and have 'em here waiting for your hoods when they come for the plate?' he said into the phone as he wrote.

'Just this. If my plan is okey – and I don't miss many – my men are outside your door waiting for you right now.

'I'm timin' it close. You've got thirty seconds to go out, get them – without an argument – and let one of them speak to me. I'll hold the phone for that thirty seconds. Don't hang up, because if you do; if I don't hear from my men; if they don't come back – I know I've got to run for it, and I won't be takin' the kid. Now make up your mind, and step on it. I'm startin' to count.'

Casey put the receiver on the desk and jumped to his feet. The sweat was creeping out on his forehead now, because he knew the man on the telephone was speaking the truth. The idea was thought out in detail. It was wild, but that voice made it convincing.

In the interval that he stepped towards the taxi-driver, he thought of many things. He had – Wade had – from now until a fake plate was developed. Blaine – Fessendon, damn them, had ruined forever any possibility of bargaining with the real plate.

Logan had the picture. It might convict Handy. But that would be damn' small satisfaction to Wade. It was too late for Grady, the private dick; for Alma Henderson. But Wade—

Casey grabbed the driver's arm, spoke in a hoarse whisper. 'Take this note out to the city room. Find Potter. I don't know where he is, but find him. Give him this note. Then go out and wait for me. I'm gonna need you.'

He gave the driver a shove, waited until he disappeared down the corridor; then he walked quickly along the same path, stepped into the noisy, light-flooded city room.

Two men stepped close to him. One was tall, foppishly dressed, handsome in a thin, swarthy way. He had a mustache and he smiled as he spoke, and showed large, even teeth.

'You got a phone call for us?'

Casey glanced at the other man, saw that he was a long-armed, puffy-eared fellow with a bullet head and no neck; then he said:

'Yeah. Step on it, will you?'

'After you,' the swarthy man said.

Casey led the way. The men had apparently been warned to try no rough tactics. That alone showed how surely the layout had been planned. If they carried guns, they did not show them.

They hurried down the corridor to the deserted anteroom, and the idea in Casey's head, in full bloom now, put a grim smile on his lips, hope in his heart. Potter could go to Alson Street. Wade had been taken there from the Henderson woman's place; he was not necessarily there now. But if Potter covered that address, if he, Casey, could follow these hoods . . . .

He grunted softly. He had pulled a stunt like that once, gone through a window to an adjoining two-story roof. And that taxi guy should be outside. He'd had some such half-baked idea when he told him to wait. The hoods would take the plate to the boss. If they went to Alson Street, he'd be sure; if not, he'd at least have two chances – and this time he could overlook neither.

The swarthy man said: 'Watch him Russo,' and bent down to lift the receiver.

'Hello. Yeah – this is Jaeger. Yeah, looks okey to me. Sure, I know what to do.'

He hung up, smiled at Casey, and there was something hard, merciless in the smile.

'Let's have the plate.'

Casey went to his platecase, took out a plate-holder which held one unexposed plate.

Jaeger took it, slipped it into his pocket. 'Okey. I like the way you're behavin'. See if you can keep it up.' He turned to Russo. 'Get goin'. Out in the hall and see that she's clear.'

Russo went out, and Jaeger said, 'I'll lock the door from the outside. Don't make too much noise – too soon.' He stepped to the telephone and a vicious yank ripped the cord from the box at the baseboard. He did the same with the instrument across the room. Then he took the key from the door and went out.

*

Casey waited until the key clicked in the lock. Then he yanked open the drawer of his desk. Reaching far back, he drew out his .38 automatic, slipped it into his pocket. Then he crossed the anteroom to a green-shaded window and threw it open.

He'd hoped they'd forget the telephones. Then he could have called Logan, tipped him off. Well, Logan could get in on it later. Right now, and for the first time, he had something he could sink his teeth into, something tangible to work on. He had played his hand the only way he knew how, and the time left him depended on how soon that plate was developed. He did not think any more about Wade, because nothing but action could save him now, and Casey knew it.

He went through the window, and the staggered line of the downtown city looked as if it had been cut out of stiff black cloth and hung there against the muddy blue of the sullen sky.

Casey clung to the window sill a moment with his fingertips, to steady himself, let go. He hit the gravel roof one story below, hit on his heels and went over backward. The fall shook him, but that was all, and he rolled to his knees, ran towards the fire-escape at the rear of the building.

Less than a minute later he was back on the street, huddled in the darkened doorway of a music shop, watching the *Globe* entrance. Jaeger came out first with Russo at his heels. They crossed the street to a small sedan.

Casey sidled down along the building front. He had already located his taxi. And as soon as the sedan pulled out from the curb, he was on the running-board, pounding the dozing driver, who shook himself, scowled at Casey, said:

'What the hell's the—'

'Follow that sedan,' barked Casey, swinging open the rear door.

'Oh,' growled the driver. 'It's you, huh?' He stepped on the starter, craned his neck to get a look at the sedan as he shifted into low. 'What's all this screwy followin' about?'

'About five bucks for you.' Then, crisply, 'Find Potter?'

The cab roared into the street and the driver said: 'Yeah,' and cramped the wheel for a U turn. The clock above Park Street said 11:55. There was enough traffic to screen them, but not enough to confuse their quarry with any other car.

The sedan had turned right at Boylston; the lights changed as the cab approached them, but they got a green arrow and made the turn. The theater front on the left was dark; beyond the high spiked fence on the right, the Common looked even darker. Casey leaned forward, knocked on the glass and the driver slid back the partition.

'Not too close, but if they give you the slip—'

'Give who the slip?' The driver snorted contemptuously. 'Don't be crazy.'

Casey grunted, took the gun out of his pocket and inspected the clip. He slipped off the safety, fondled the cold bulk of the automatic, let it rest gently in his palm. When he looked out the window again the railroad yards were slipping by on the left, and the sedan was a block and a half ahead.

They crossed the avenue, and Casey's brain fought with questions and answers. When he looked up again it was because the cab had started to slow. He saw then that the sedan was slanting in towards the curb, still a block and a half ahead. Then he saw his roadster – at least he thought it was a roadster. Yeah. They were on Alson Street.

The cab slowed still more and Casey said: 'Keep going, you mugg. Right on by 'em! Don't slow down!'

He slouched on the seat as soon as he saw the two men leave the sedan and cross the sidewalk. When the cab passed the apartment house he called to the driver.

'Take another street, turn right, go around the block.' He slid up on the seat, got out at the corner beyond the sedan a minute or so later. He gave the driver the promised five dollars, added: 'I'll remember you. You got what it takes.'

Casey spun about before the driver could thank him. As he turned into Alson Street he moved warily, and his eyes sought the shadowed niches and areaways.

Alson Street was not much different from Pratt Street. It was a little wider, and on one side, the opposite side from Casey and the parked sedan, there were some remodeled brownstone fronts. The apartments on the near side of the street were a little taller, a little more flossy and pretentious than that of Alma Henderson's; but the reputations were about the same.

The roadster was parked nearly to the next corner, but Potter stepped from the shadows directly across the street from the sedan. Casey crossed to him and pulled him back into the areaway which had concealed him.

Potter said: 'What's up?' He was a stringy, long-necked fellow who wore glasses and a perpetually tired look. 'I parked the roadster down the street a ways, because I wasn't sure just what you wanted me here for.'

'It's just as well,' said Casey and took out the automatic.

'Hey!' wheezed Potter.

'Wade's in that apartment,' Casey muttered, and went on with a brief story of what had happened. 'I got you to help because I wanted to check on this address, and because no matter what happens, there's gonna be a sweet story for some guy.'

'But why don't you get Logan—'

'That's your job,' clipped Casey. 'For all I know they might try to develop that plate inside – might be developing it now. So find a phone. There's a drug-store two blocks down. Tell Logan the set-up. He oughtta get out here pretty damn' fast.'

'But what—' stammered Potter. 'You ain't goin' up there and try to shoot it out with those hoods alone?'

'I hope not,' Casey said grimly. 'I'm gonna try and stall, throw a bluff – till Logan gets here. He'll know how to handle it; only if the shooting starts, I'm not gonna be empty handed.'

Casey had left the *Globe* without his topcoat. Now he took the .38, reached around and stuck it down inside his pants, right in the small of his back. The pressure of his belt held the gun securely; the coat, draped from the shoulders, showed no suspicious bulge. He started across the street.

6

The foyer of the apartment house was U shaped and the single, self-operated elevator door was directly opposite the entrance. Casey stopped in front of it, realizing that he did not know where Jaeger and Russo had gone.

He muttered, 'No one's been in or out of here since they came. They mustta left the elevator where they got off,' and started up the stairs.

There was no elevator at the second floor; none at the third. He found it waiting on the fourth. He thought: 'It's after twelve. I'll try every place with a light in it.'

Eight doors opened from the wide, deserted hall. Casey started at the front, dropping to his knees at each door and peering at the bottom crack. The first three were dark. At the fourth – the second door on the right – a hairline of yellow met his gaze.

Casey put his ear close to the keyhole. A subdued murmur of voices reached him, unexcited. He straightened a little, drew a long, silent breath, glanced, unconsciously, back over his shoulder, then bent to the keyhole again.

He felt that he could wait a few minutes, give Logan that much time. Not too long, for if the plate could not be developed here, they wouldn't waste much time in taking it where it could be, and Casey had to stall them here if he was to count on Logan's help. The slow minutes dragged. Casey tried to estimate their number; tried once to reach his watch, but gave it up in preference to keeping his ear glued to the keyhole. Finally he straightened, took a deep breath and knocked.

After a moment a voice said: 'Who is it?'

Casey grunted and his lips pressed into a weird, tight smile. The palms of his hands were damp, but he wiped them on the sides of his coat.

He said: 'Santy Claus.'

The knob turned slowly, but the door opened in a jerk that flung it wide. Jaeger and Russo stood to one side, their automatics leveled at Casey's stomach. Beyond, Moe Nyberg stood behind Wade, held him by

291

the coat collar and pressed a gun in his back. Over by the windows stood Mike Handy.

Casey felt no fear now. No surprise. Rather a tense grim satisfaction gripped his brain. But after that first glimpse of the occupants of that room, he went into his act. Surprise flooded his face, choked his voice.

'Hey,' he wheezed. 'What the hell?'

'Get in here!' clipped Jaeger.

Casey stepped across the threshold and Russo shut the door.

'How'd you get here?' jerked Nyberg.

'He followed us,' said Jaeger. 'He must've—'

'Followed you?' croaked Casey, licking his lips. 'No. Honest to gawd. I didn't know—'

'It's a plant!' growled Handy, starting forward. 'Look in the hall.' He turned and looked out the windows at the street below.

Russo opened the door, peered out, said: 'Naw. It's clear.'

Handy said: 'Clear outside too,' and relaxed.

Nyberg purred: 'You'd better spill it, Flash. And you'd better make it good. How did you find us?'

Casey was stuck here, and he knew it. To tell the truth about either Wade's taxi-driver, or his following the two gunmen would probably scare Handy into moving them out of the apartment – before Logan could get there.

So he let his imagination go, and made up his story as he went along. How logical it sounded did not particularly bother him; he wanted to make it interesting – and take plenty of time.

'A taxi guy told me,' he said nervously. 'Wade said he took the Henderson woman downstairs after the raid, and a couple tough looking muggs picked her up. Well, he was stuck on the girl; see? And he thought something might be up. But he couldn't run out on me, so he got a taxi-driver to follow this other car and find out where these two guys went.

'When the cabby came back to the office, Wade was out. He got worried about his pay so he looked me up. I took care of the fare and he gave me this address – just before you two came to the *Globe*.' He nodded at Russo and Jaeger. 'Maybe you saw him go out and—'

'Go on!' pressed Nyberg ominously.

'Well,' Casey shrugged. 'I wasn't sure of the set-up so I thought I'd do some checking.'

'Oh,' grunted Nyberg. He looked relieved and loosed his hold on Wade.

Casey, apparently still bewildered, glanced around. Jaeger brushed his mustache with an index finger and smiled again. Nyberg pushed Wade down on the divan. He was a sturdily built fellow, Nyberg. Bald, greasy-looking, with a heavy red nose and a thick-lipped mouth. His dress was slovenly, his fingernails dirty. Casey met his shrewd stare for a moment, then glanced at Handy.

Mike Handy looked worried. There was a film of moisture on his fatty face, and his eyes, which were black and seemed all iris, shifted nervously from the door to the windows beside him. The fingers of his other hand, which hung loosely at his side, moved spasmodically.

Wade said: 'You were wrong about her, Flash.'

Casey did not answer, or look at Wade. He gave no sign that he had heard, because he did not want to let on what he knew – not yet.

Then Handy said: 'Let's get out of here. I don't like it. If we get caught in here—' He moved to a chair and picked up his black topcoat.

Nyberg nodded and stepped towards Wade. And Casey felt his nerves grow taut. They couldn't leave. Logan would never find them. He decided to tell what he knew – all of it. Gambling that his revelations would hold attention, postpone the present plan.

'How was I wrong about her?' he growled, and turned on Wade. 'She got you to her place so these guys could take you, didn't she? She put you on the spot and—'

'So—' breathed Nyberg, 'this surprise business was an act? You know about that, huh?'

'Sure,' said Casey and made his voice confident, aggressive. 'I oughtta. I was there when we trapped your other two hoods – in fact, I shot the stocky guy right over the eye. He's in the morgue now.'

'She didn't spot me,' Wade said, and Handy's gasp was a background for his words.

Casey felt the sudden tenseness in the room, but he watched the young photographer. Wade was sitting on the divan with his elbows on his knees and his head down. His voice was listless; so was his attitude. He acted as though he did not care what happened, and Casey knew, in such condition, he could get little help from Wade in a showdown.

'She was on the level,' Wade went on. 'You know why she chased me out of the office this afternoon? Because these guys – all but Handy – were in the next room. She was scared – for me, and for herself. She got me out and hoped to run for it.

'But these two guys' – he nodded at Jaeger and Russo – 'ran down the back way and picked her up. She told 'em I didn't know a thing. Then, when she called me at the *Globe*' – Wade hesitated, continued wearily – 'that was okey. Only—'

'To hell with all this crap,' barked Nyberg. 'What else do you know, smart guy?'

'Plenty,' said Casey and grinned deliberately. 'I know about Dopey Donlan, and the private dick, and the dope ring you were promoting at the tracks, and how you hooked that up with that track gambling outfit that got raided.'

'You spoke your piece, smart guy,' Nyberg said and his thick lips twisted in a mirthless smile, 'and now you're in it up to your neck. You're gonna find out just how it feels.'

Handy put on his coat. 'Let's get out of here. There's something screwy about this. I don't like it.'

The sweat was on his forehead again and his lip trembled. 'You, Russo, put the gun on the kid. Nyberg, Jaeger, watch Casey. Better search him first.' He waited while Jaeger patted Casey's pockets, and Casey held his breath and stuck out his stomach, stuck it out and leaned so that his back arched slightly and the unbuttoned coat hung out and away from the gun.

'We'll take 'em out,' Handy went on. 'If this plate is okey, I'm set.'

'You're set?' sneered Nyberg. 'How about me – the rest of us.'

'Well,' flared Handy. 'I was in that raid this afternoon. Lucky they let me go after I paid the fine. If anybody'd seen me come out of that washroom—'

'Nerts!' said Nyberg. 'I'm getting' sick of your angles. Why all the panic? Why don't we knock these guys off right here and now?'

'No – no,' said Handy, and his voice was shrill. 'Take them out. I pay you plenty. I want a chance to get this plate developed, get an alibi.'

'You're with us,' snapped Nyberg contemptuously, 'and here's once you stay with us. I'm beginnin' to hate guys like you – all mouth and no guts.' He stepped to Wade, yanked him to his feet. 'Come on, Kid.'

Casey waited there by the door. He was glad now that he had put on the bluff. It had worked longer than he expected. But was it long enough? He couldn't tell. It was hard to judge time in this kind of a spot. And you could say things awfully quick. How much time had he killed? Five – six minutes. More, he hoped.

Russo had stepped over behind Wade. Handy opened the door and looked into the hall. Nyberg and Jaeger came alongside of Casey and he felt the guns in his side.

Casey made one more attempt to stall. 'Say.' He let the fear come into his voice. 'What're you gonna do. You can't—'

'Who can't,' sneered Nyberg. 'You know what we're gonna do – so quit stallin'. You can take it, can't you? Or is all these things I've heard about you just a lot of hot air.'

He dug his gun into Casey's ribs, and they went out into the hall. Handy, and Wade and the bull-necked Russo; then Casey and Nyberg and the grimly smiling Jaeger.

7

The elevator was still waiting in the hall. On the silent downward trip, Casey tried to map out some logical course of action. Logan had not arrived. Otherwise he would have been waiting in the hall.

The elevator door slid open and they started across the narrow, dimly lighted foyer. Casey felt the reassuring pressure of his gun in his back. He thought he could get to it. But there were three other guns – and there was Wade.

The kid did not know about Casey's gun. He would have no tip-off to a plan, even if Casey had one. And if the heat went on—

Handy paused after they went through the inner doors. There, in the imitation marble entryway, he said:

'It's too risky – six of us piling in that little sedan. Besides, we've used it twice today – we might get picked up. We'll just walk down the street easy-like. I've got a car in a garage around the corner.'

He hesitated and the dim light from the foyer, sifting through the glass doors, made his fatty face jaundiced and shiny with moisture. He made one more plea.

'I'll make it a grand more apiece if you'll let me—'

This time it was Jaeger who voiced his contemptuous opinion. 'I'll string with Nyberg. It'll be worth my grand to see you play ball.'

Handy opened the outer door without answering. Nyberg said: 'Keep your hands down and walk nice, guys.'

Handy kept well in the lead, but the rest of them fanned out on the wide sidewalk. Casey cast a quick glance up and down the street and a blanket of dejection settled down upon him. His roadster was parked in the same spot, but the street was deserted. Logan had not—

Then he saw Potter.

At first there was but a blacker blotch in the shadows of that entryway across the street. Then the blotch took shape. It was Potter all right, his stringy height identified him. He was on the sidewalk now, and he was starting across the street.

Casey sucked in his breath and held it. His glance slid sidewise. Wade was about an arm's length away, on his left, the curb side; beside, and slightly behind, walked Russo. Holding the same position – beside and a pace behind – Nyberg and Jaeger flanked Casey.

Casey had wanted to wait as long as he could in the hope that Logan might come. And if he did not come, that gun was the last resort.

He and Wade? Well, they were in it: they had to take a chance, accept the risk. But Potter, the crazy fool: it was no affair of his. And he was married and—

'Moe!' Jaeger's voice was soft, jerky. 'There's a guy comin' across the street.'

'Let him come,' said Nyberg hoarsely. 'If he horns in we might just as well shoot the works and—'

Then Potter, now halfway across the street, said: 'Hey!'

It was absurd, that word. And Potter's act, although he may not have known it, was suicidal. Casey inwardly cursed it as such. Yet that soft call undoubtedly gave him a second to get set, because every man but himself glanced at Potter as he spoke.

Casey leaned to the left and made a vicious backhand swipe with the flat of his hand. He caught Wade alongside the face and the force of the blow knocked him off his feet, so that he fell over against Russo, carrying him to his knees. At the same instant, Casey's right hand reached for the gun in his back.

He forgot Wade as he spun about and his fingers found the butt of the automatic, but he was aware that somebody was fighting in the gutter. Then he had the gun free, up, and squeezed the trigger, twice, rapidly.

Nyberg's body jerked. Beside him and two feet away a flash of orange exploded and Casey felt something slice between his ribs and his left arm.

The slug, the flash of flame, came from Jaeger's gun. And as he fired, the fellow stepped behind Nyberg's sagging body, intent on using it as a shield.

Casey's finger already tensed for a third shot when he saw what he faced. He had but little time to act, and he did as impulse commanded. He ducked his head and half dived forward so that his shoulder crashed into Nyberg's stomach.

They went down, all three of them. And Jaeger was underneath. He was cursing now and so was Casey, although he did not know it. For a moment or so the three men were a tangle of arms and legs, and as they scrambled there, Casey thought he heard the shrill scream of a siren.

Then Jaeger rolled clear, rolled clear and came to his knees. Casey's right hand was partly pinioned by the now limp weight of Nyberg's body. He yanked at the wrist, felt the gun come free. But his eyes had never left Jaeger, and he knew he was too late.

The fellow's teeth flashed in some reflected ray of the street light, and the gun leveled as Casey tried to swing up his hand in time. A hundredth part of a second maybe; no longer than that. But Casey looked down the muzzle of that gun and his muscles tensed for the shock.

Somebody said: 'You ———!'

The crash of the gun wiped out the phrase, pounded at Casey's right ear, half deafened him. And he could not understand it because he had seen no flash from that gun muzzle.

A car roared past. Jaeger, still on his knees, began to tip over, half on his face, half on his side. When his shoulders hit the sidewalk Casey looked around. Potter was standing three feet away. His right hand was still stiffly extended – and there was a gun in it.

Casey blew out his pent-up breath and spun about on his knees. Handy was fifty yards away, racing madly for the corner, his coat-tails flying. A touring car swung into the curb beside him.

There was a shouted command, another. Handy raced on, swerving towards an entryway. The car kept pace. Then flame streaked through the night and two sharp cracks slapped down the street, reverberating from the brick walls. Handy took three more steps at breakneck speed. He stumbled; he slid forward on his face like Rabbit Maranville stealing home.

8

Captain Judson put his fists on his hips and said: 'You get in the damnedest messes.'

'It took you long enough to get here,' Casey said grimly.

Logan was looking down at Nyberg. Wade sat on the curb. Potter still held the gun. He lifted his arm, stared at the automatic, dropped the arm again. He kept doing it, as though he could not believe he had used it. And all the time he was saying: 'Jeeze – jeeze,' in thick, hushed tones.

There were two police cars in the street now, and overhead windows were up, and heads and shoulders in whitish nightclothes hung on the sills.

Logan said: 'Looks like the only guy left is Russo.' He stared at the bullet-headed fellow who stood flanked by two plain-clothesmen. 'How did we miss him?'

Casey had told what had taken place in the apartment, finished with: 'Don't ask me. I only knocked Wade into him. After that—'

'You damn' near knocked me out,' Wade said. 'I thought he was gonna let me have it. He could have easy enough. But I guess Potter—' he broke off.

Potter coughed, spoke apologetically. 'They were both on the ground, but I saw this guy start to swing his gun around, so I kicked him in the head and took it away from him.' He hesitated, looked at Casey. 'Then when I saw how you were fixed – well, I had to let him have it.'

'You had to do it, huh?' Casey said, and grinned wryly. 'I guess it's a break for me you felt that way about it.'

'I never shot anyone before,' Potter said. 'I was afraid I'd miss. I got as close as I could.'

Logan said: 'You newspaper guys do pretty well for amateurs.'

Casey looked down at Nyberg, cursed once, said: 'I'm glad I got that —— anyway.'

An ambulance pulled into the curb. Then Casey realized that he was shivering, that he had no coat. And his side was smarting; he thought his undershirt was wet. He told Logan about it and one of the internes started to take him into the apartment house foyer.

Casey turned to Wade. 'Come on, snap into it. My camera's down in my roadster. Get busy.'

Judson watched the interne strap up Casey's side. The wound was superficial, grazing the ribs and cutting a shallow, two-inch furrow in the flesh.

Casey glanced up at Judson and let his voice get disgusted. 'What a help you turned out to be.'

Judson scowled. 'What's the matter with you?'

'Was that picture I got this afternoon a break for you?'

'Sure it was a break. That tipped the business. We'd got Handy eventually – on that alone.'

'Yeah,' fumed Casey. 'But if you'd had your way there wouldn't been any picture. I just happened to hold out that print.' He snorted disdainfully. 'Callin' up the office and tellin' 'em we can't print it.'

'Who called up?'

'You did.'

Judson's eyes widened, then narrowed. His voice had a humorous undertone.

'Maybe a scratch on the ribs makes you slug-nutty or something. You talk that way. Hell' – he grunted, pulled at his nose – 'Whenever you steal a picture on me I don't want printed I won't call the office. I'll take it away from you myself – like Haley did with your second one.'

Casey scowled for a moment; then his eyes got sultry and he said: 'Oh,' softly.

Wade took six pictures. Casey had the three plate-holders in his pocket when they went into the *Globe* city room. Blaine was at the desk.

Casey who had been talking to Wade all the way in, pulled him to a stop before they crossed the room. 'Listen, Kid. Shake it off. I know how you feel. And if it helps any, you were right, and I was wrong, like most wise guys are.

'She wasn't a tramp – she just ran with tramps. She had two strikes on her, just working for a guy like Nyberg. That's not your fault.'

'But if I could have helped her or—'

'Sure, I know.' Casey pulled Wade across the room. 'We did the best we could. After all, she sorta put you on the spot by even callin' you to her place. But she was level with you and she did what she could with what she had to do with.'

'I guess you're right,' Wade said and seemed to shrug off some of his dejection. 'Only I sorta liked her.'

Blaine leaned back in his chair and his eyes were cold and unsmiling. Casey said: 'Did Potter phone in the story?'

'Yes.'

'Well, I got a story you're gonna hear and—'

'And I've got one for you,' snapped Blaine. 'You're fired!'

Casey's jaw dropped, and Wade stiffened and froze there.

'Fired?' Casey swallowed, and amazement gave ground slowly before his anger.

He choked on a curse and had a hard time getting his words out. Not because he was fired. That had happened before. What threw him off stride was that Blaine had stolen his thunder, had taken the offensive right out of his hands.

'All right,' he clipped. 'I'm fired. One of your ideas huh?'

'It was Fessendon's idea,' said Blaine. He lifted some copy paper from a halftone cut. Beside the metal plate was a proof. The proof was of the picture Casey had given Logan. 'I think this cut came up from the engraving room by mistake, but Fessendon saw the proof. You held out on him, huh?'

'And a damn' good thing I did,' flung out Casey. He put both hands on the desk top and leaned on them. He held that position while he told Blaine the whole story about that picture, what it meant to the police, how it had been used to bargain with and the reason he had had a halftone made.

There was a peculiar gleam in Blaine's eyes now. Casey saw it, but he could not fathom it. It was hard, intent, yet there seemed to be something in the background. It couldn't be humor – a grim sort of humor—

Casey flung aside the thought, and with this mental effort some of his rage evaporated. That first hot burst at Blaine's announcement came from impulsive reaction; but as the true character of the situation, as the underlying significance of the city editor's attitude dawned upon him, a new kind of anger fastened itself upon him. Anger that was logical and mixed with weariness, disillusionment, resentment.

This feeling was strange to Casey, strange but not hard to understand. He had been going at top speed since four-thirty that afternoon. The past five hours had been crammed with action, and death, and a nerve-wracking tension that centered around the safety of Tom Wade.

Perhaps it was this strain that brought about that hollow feeling of discouragement; it might have been that he was tired, that his head ached, or that the wound in his side had left him weakened. More probably it was because Blaine had let him down. Blaine, the sharp-tongued, unsympathetic driver – who always backed up his men.

'All right,' Casey said finally. 'I'll be glad to go.' His voice was husky, a bit scornful now, his smoldering anger and resentment tinging each word.

'I only stuck here because you had something on the ball, and because I always thought you were on the level. I had you figured for the one newspaperman in town who would print the news as he saw it and not let some fat-headed guy with a lot of money call you.

'But if Fessendon's got you, if you can't take it, if you're gonna do what he says and like it' – Casey breathed deeply, tightened his lips – 'why, that's okey with me. I knew damn' well I had the right dope when you pulled that Judson gag. But I never thought you were a liar.'

'Who's a liar? What about Judson?' said Blaine, and his voice got thin.

'Just like I said. He didn't call here and tell you or Fessendon to kill that picture. I asked him.'

'He didn't—' Blaine got up slowly, menacingly and leaned across the desk.

'It was that skirt-crazy Lee Fessendon that—'

Blaine spun about and started through the doorway behind his desk. Casey followed him, still talking. And Wade, goggle-eyed and with nothing else to do, tagged behind. Blaine moved to Fessendon's office with stiff-kneed strides, threw open the door.

Fessendon looked up from his desk, started to smile. The smile faded when Blaine spoke.

'You said Judson told you we had to kill Casey's picture.'

'He – he did,' said Fessendon, avoiding Blaine's stare.

'Casey says Judson said no such thing.'

'Well,' Fessendon stood up and his pink face got red and scowling. 'Are you going to take his word against mine?'

'Any time,' rapped Blaine, 'and anywhere. I told you when I stayed on here I'd run this sheet my way or not at all. You framed up the Judson gag because neither you – nor your kid brother had guts enough to stand up and—'

'You can't talk that way to me,' stormed Fessendon.

'You hear me, don't you?'

Fessendon took a menacing step forward. 'I'm running this paper. Suppose Lee did call me up and tell me about that picture? I don't take orders from you, Blaine, and—'

'You said it.' Blaine's lip curled. 'Maybe you take them from that jelly-kneed brother who was afraid to face a bawling out from his wife.'

'You're fired,' shouted Fessendon.

'That makes two of us,' said Blaine.

'Three,' piped up Wade.

'And I have one thing more to toss in the pot,' Blaine rapped. 'Plenty of fellows think I'm a slave driver; I don't doubt they hate my guts. But I've had one sort of a reputation. I played the game and I played it square. Casey's the first man that ever said I wasn't on the level: the first guy that ever called me a liar – and I can't blame him.

'I hate a liar, too, Fessendon. I hate a double-crosser. And that's what you are, a lousy, lying, double-crossing——!'

Fessendon hit Blaine then. Hit him back of the ear and Blaine went down. Casey cursed and stepped forward, but Blaine sat up, said: 'You stay out of this.'

He got to his feet and deliberately repeated his opinion. Fessendon, his face a livid mask, swung his right. This time Blaine was ready. He said: 'I thought so,' as he moved inside that right and jabbed his left to Fessendon's stomach.

Fessendon gasped and he seemed to gag as he crumpled. Then Blaine crossed his right. It landed flush and it straightened Fessendon before it dropped him.

Blaine backed away, turned at the door. Casey and Wade followed him out. Blaine went to his desk, opened the bottom drawer, took out a brief case and systematically packed it with his personal belongings. He closed all the drawers, stepped over to the clothes-tree and got his hat and coat. As he stepped past the grinning Casey and the open-mouthed Wade, he turned, spoke irritably:

'Well, come on, you big ox. Don't stand their gawking.'

In the hall Casey said: 'Did Fessendon tell you to fire me?'

'Sure,' said Blaine, punching the elevator button. 'If I hadn't he would have.'

'But you knew I had some redhot plates of that—'

'I didn't *know* you had 'em,' said Blaine. But you generally pull something out of the hat, and I wanted to fire you before you showed them to me. Then you could take them down the street to the *Express* or *Mirror* – not that you need anything to bargain with.'

Blaine muttered a soft curse. 'You got a dirty deal from Fessendon, but you ought to be glad you're out. I was all washed up with him anyway, after he broke that plate – as if we were a bunch of blackmailers. But he just came in his office about ten minutes ago, and I was going to be nice about it and give him two weeks' notice.'

Casey's broad face was cracked in a wide grin that would not come off. He was no longer tired. It was good to be free of Fessendon, to know that Blaine was level, that Wade was okey. He released a sigh of satisfaction and relief, said:

'Well, where we goin' now?'

'I'm gonna call up Gilman at the *Express* and see if he wants a city editor and a couple of cheap cameras. But first' – the elevator door opened and Blaine stepped in – 'we'll stop at Steve's and have a couple to celebrate on.'

Casey said: 'You think of things.'

Wade grunted sardonically, said: 'The idea is okey so long as I don't get stuck with short beers.'

THE PRICE OF A DIME

NORBERT DAVIS

When Raymond Chandler, not a young man, decided to try to write for the pulps, one of the stories that most impressed him was 'Red Goose' by Norbert Davis. Years later, he reread it and wrote, in a letter, that it was not as good as he remembered it, but still very good, and that he had never forgotten it.

Davis (1909–1949) was one of the few writers who attempted to blend fast-moving violence and whimsy in his stories, the humor being an element that so displeased the great *Black Mask* editor, Joseph T. Shaw, that he published only five stories by the prolific author.

With his fiction selling easily to most of the major pulps, Davis graduated with a law degree from Stanford but never bothered to take the bar exam. His work also made it onto the pages of the higher-paying 'slick' magazines (so-called because of their shiny paper) like *The Saturday Evening Post*, and into book form. Two of his novels, both featuring Doan (a private eye whose first name is never mentioned) and Carstairs (a gigantic Great Dane who is his constant companion), *The Mouse In the Mountain* (1943) and *Sally's In the Alley* (1943), are hilarious adventures that nonetheless have their share of violence, mostly presented as harmless fun.

'The Price of a Dime' is the second story about Ben Shanley and was initially published in *Black Mask* in April 1934.

THE PRICE OF A DIME

NORBERT DAVIS

Shaley was sitting behind the big desk in his private office. He had his hat on, pushed down over his forehead, so that the wide brim shaded his hard, narrowed eyes, his thin, straight nose. He had an opened penknife in his hand, and he was stabbing the soft wood of a drawer of the desk in an irritated way.

There was a sudden shrill scream from the outer office.

Shaley started. He scowled at the door.

In the outer office a chair tipped over with a crash. There was another scream, louder than the first one.

Shaley tossed his penknife on the desk and got up.

'She'll drive me crazy one of these days,' he muttered, heading for the door in long-legged strides.

He banged the door open, looked through into the outer office.

Sadie, his secretary, was scuffling with a fattish blonde woman. Sadie had the woman by the shoulders, trying to push her through the door into the corridor. The blonde woman's face was puffy, tear-stained. She had a desperately hopeless expression. She was the one who was doing the screaming.

Sadie had her sleek, dark head down, pushing determinedly, but the blonde woman's weight was too much for her.

Shaley said: 'Well?' in an explosively angry voice.

Both women turned on him. Sadie got started first.

'You told me you didn't want to see anybody this morning, and she wanted to see you, and I told her you couldn't see her, and she wouldn't go away, and so I tried to put her out, and she started to scream.' Sadie said this all in one breath.

The blonde woman sniffed a little. 'I've got to see you. I've got to see you, Mr. Shaley. It's about Bennie. I've got to see you.'

'All right, all right,' Shaley said helplessly. 'All *right!* Come on in here.'

'But you told me—' Sadie protested.

'Will you kindly sit down and get to work?' Shaley asked in an elaborately courteous voice.

Sadie blinked. 'Yes, Mr. Shaley,' she said meekly.

Shaley jerked his head at the blonde woman. 'Come in.' He shut the door of the private office again, pointed to a chair. 'Sit down.' He walked around his desk, sat down in his chair, and dropped his hat on the floor beside him. He frowned at the blonde woman. 'Now what is it?'

She was dabbing at her puffy eyes with a handkerchief that was a moist, wadded ball. 'I'm sorry I screamed and acted that way, Mr. Shaley, but I had to see you. Bennie told me to see you, and he's in bad trouble, and so I *had* to see you.'

'Who's Bennie?'

The blonde woman looked surprised. 'He's my brother.'

'That makes it all clear,' said Shaley. 'Does he have a last name?'

'Oh, sure. Bennie Petersen.' The blonde woman looked like she was going to start to cry again. 'He told me you knew him. He told me you'd help him. He's a bellboy at the *Grover Hotel.*'

'Oh,' said Shaley understandingly. 'Bennie Peterson, huh? That little chiseler—' He coughed. 'That is to say, yes. I remember him. What's he done now?'

'The blonde woman sniffed. 'It wasn't his fault, Mr. Shaley.'

'No,' said Shaley. 'Of course not. It never is his fault. What did he do?'

'He just lost a dime, Mr. Shaley. And now Mr. Van Bilbo is going to have him arrested.'

Shaley sat up straight with a jerk. 'Van Bilbo, the movie director?'

She nodded. 'Yes.'

'Van Bilbo is going to have Bennie arrested because Bennie lost a dime?'

'Yes.'

'Hmm,' Shaley said, scowling. 'Now let's get this straight. Start at the beginning and tell me just what happened – or what Bennie told you happened.'

'Well, Bennie took some ginger ale up to a party on the seventh floor of the hotel. This party tipped him a dime. Bennie was coming back down the hall to the elevator. He had the dime in his hand, and he was flipping it up in the air like George Raft does in the movies. But Bennie dropped the dime on the floor. He was just leaning over to pick it up when Mr. Van Bilbo came out of one of the rooms and saw him, and now he's going to have Bennie arrested.'

Shaley leaned back in his chair. 'So,' he said quietly. 'The old dropped dime gag. Bennie dropped a dime in front of a keyhole, and he was looking through the keyhole for the dime, when Van Bilbo caught him at it, huh?'

She shook her head. 'Oh, no! Bennie wouldn't look through a keyhole. He wouldn't do a thing like that, Mr. Shaley. Bennie's a good boy. Our folks died when we were young, and I raised him, and I know.'

Shaley studied her calculatingly. She really believed what she was saying. She really believed that Bennie was a good boy.

'All right,' Shaley said gently, smiling at her. 'Forget what I said. Of course Bennie wouldn't peek through a keyhole. What did he tell you to say to me?'

'He told me to tell you to go to Mr. Van Bilbo and tell him that it was all right. That Bennie was Mr. Van Bilbo's friend, and that they could get together on this matter and fix it all up. Bennie said you'd understand.'

Shaley nodded slowly. 'Oh, yes,' he said meaningly. 'I understand all right. Where is Bennie now?'

'He's hiding so the police won't find him. He told me not to tell anybody where he was.'

Shaley smiled at her. 'I can't help him unless I know where he is.'

'Well . . .' Her voice broke a little. 'You *are* his friend, aren't you, Mr. Shaley? You *will* help him, won't you? Just this time, Mr. Shaley, please. He promised me he'd never get into trouble again.' She stared at him anxiously.

'I'll help him,' Shaley said.

She sighed, relieved. 'He's hiding in a boarding-house. I don't know the street address, but you can easily find it. It's a big white house with a hedge around it, and it's right in back of the Imperial Theater in Hollywood. He's going by the name of Bennie Smith.'

'I'll find him,' said Shaley. 'Where can I get hold of you?'

'I work in *Zeke's Tamale Shop*. On Cahuenga, north of Sunset.'

'I know the place,' said Shaley, standing up. He went over and opened the door. 'Don't worry about it any more. I'll fix things up for you.'

She fumbled with the worn bag she was carrying. 'I drew my money out of the bank this morning, Mr. Shaley. I can pay you. I'll pay you right now.'

'Forget it,' Shaley said, uncomfortably. 'I'll send you a bill. And don't give Bennie any of that money. I'll take care of him.'

He stood in the doorway and watched her go through the outer office and out the door into the corridor.

Sadie looked over one slim shoulder at him, with a slight hurt expression.

'I heard what you said to her,' she stated, nodding her sleek head. 'And you told me just this morning that you weren't going to take any more customers unless they paid you in advance.'

'Phooey!' said Shaley. He slammed the door shut and went back and sat down behind his desk.

He picked up the penknife and stared at it thoughtfully.

'I'll fix him up, all right,' he said sourly to himself. 'I'll wring the little cuss' neck. Picking me to be the stooge in a blackmailing squeeze.'

He began to stab the drawer again with the penknife, scowling.

Suddenly the penknife stopped in mid air. Shaley sat still for several seconds, his eyes slowly widening.

He said: 'My gawd!' in a thoughtfully awed voice. He sat there for a while longer and then yelled: 'Sadie!'

Sadie opened the door and looked in. 'What?'

'Listen, there was a murder in some hotel around here about a week back – some woman got herself killed. What hotel was it?'

'The *Grover*,' said Sadie.

Shaley leaned back in his chair. He smiled – a hard, tight smile that put deep lines around his mouth. He said: 'So,' in a quietly triumphant voice.

'I read all about it in the paper,' said Sadie. 'The woman's name was "Big Cee". She was mixed up with some gangsters or something in Cleveland, and the police thought she came out here to hide, and that some of the gangsters found her. The papers said there were no clues to the murderer's identity. Mr. Van Bilbo, the movie director, read about her death, and he felt sorry for her, and he paid for her funeral. I think that was very nice of him, don't you, Mr. Shaley? A woman he didn't know at all, that way.'

'Yes,' said Shaley. 'It was very nice of Mr. Van Bilbo. Go away now. I want to think.'

Sadie slammed the door. Shaley picked his hat up off the floor and put it on, tipping it down over his eyes. He slid down in his chair and folded his hands across his chest.

After about ten minutes, he reached out and took up the telephone on his desk and dialed a number.

A feminine voice said liltingly: 'This is the *Grover* – the largest and finest hotel west of the Mississippi.'

Shaley said: 'Is McFane there?'

'Yes, sir. Just a moment, sir, and I'll connect you with Mr. McFane.'

Shaley waited, tapping his fingers on the desk top.

'Hello.' It was a smoothly cordial voice.

Shaley said: 'McFane? This is Ben Shaley.'

'Hello there, Ben. How's the private detecting?'

'Just fair. Listen, McFane, have you got a bellhop around there by the name of Bennie Petersen?'

'We did have. The little chiseler quit us last week without any notice at all. Just didn't show up for work. He in trouble?'

Shaley said: 'No. Uh-huh. I was just wondering. He quit right after that murder you had, didn't he?'

'Yes, come to think—' McFane stopped short. 'Hey! Are you digging on that?'

'No, no,' Shaley said quickly. 'I was just wondering, that's all.'

'Listen, Ben,' McFane said in a worried tone. 'Lay off, will you? We spent a thousand dollars' worth of advertising killing that in the papers. It gives the hotel a bad name.'

'You got it all wrong,' Shaley said soothingly. 'I'm not interested at all. I was just wondering. So long, McFane, and thanks.'

'Wait, Ben. Listen, I'll make it worth your while – I'll retain—'

Shaley hung up the receiver. He walked quickly out of the private office.

'If a guy by the name of McFane calls,' he said to Sadie, 'tell him I just left for Europe. I'll call you in an hour.'

'From Europe?' Sadie asked innocently.

Shaley went out and slammed the door.

The high board fence had once been painted a very bright shade of yellow, but now the paint was old and faded and streaked. It was peeling off in big patches that showed bare, brown board underneath.

Shaley parked his battered Chrysler roadster around the corner and walked back along the fence. There was a group of Indians standing in a silent, motionless circle in front of the big iron gate. They all had their arms folded across their chests. They all wore very gaudy shirts, and two of the older ones had strips of buckskin with beads sewn on them tied around their heads.

They didn't look at Shaley, didn't pay any attention to him.

Shaley walked up to the iron gate and peered through the thick, rusted bars. There was a car – a yellow Rolls-Royce – parked in the graveled roadway. The hood was pushed up, and two men were listening to the engine.

'If that's what you call a piston slap,' one said, 'you should be chauffeuring a wheelbarrow.'

Shaley said: 'Hey, Mandy.'

The man straightened, turned around. He was short, dumpy. He was wearing golf knickers and a checked sweater and checked golf hose and a checked cap. He had a round, reddish face sprinkled with brown spots. He was chewing on the stub of a cigar, and tobacco juice had left a brown trail from the corner of his mouth down his chin. He stared at Shaley without any sign of recognition.

'Let me in, Mandy,' Shaley requested.

Mandy strolled up to the gate, looked at Shaley through it.

'I don't suppose you'd have a pass, would you?'

Shaley said: 'Come on, Mandy. Let me in. I want to talk to you.'

'Huh!' said Mandy. He opened the gate grudgingly.

Shaley slipped inside, and Mandy slammed the gate with a clang.

'Go ahead and talk,' he invited. 'It won't do you any good. I won't buy anything.'

Shaley looked at the other man meaningly. This one wore a plum-colored military uniform with silver trimmings. He looked as a motion picture director's chauffeur should look. He was thin and tall with a swarthily dark face and a small black mustache. He had his military cap tipped at a jaunty angle.

He stared from Mandy to Shaley, then shrugged his thin shoulders.

'Excuse me,' he said. He slammed the hood down and got into the front seat of the Rolls and backed it up the road.

'Pretty fancy,' Shaley said, jerking his head to indicate the chauffeur and the car.

'He gripes me,' Mandy said sourly. 'I liked old Munn better.'

'Why all the war-whoops outside?' Shaley asked.

'Extras. Waitin' to be put on. We ain't gonna shoot any exteriors today. We're shootin' a saloon scene. I told 'em that six times, but you can't argue with them guys. They just grunt at you.'

'How's Van Bilbo coming since he's been producing independent?'

Mandy shrugged. 'Just fair, I think we got a good one this time – forty-niner stuff.'

They were silent, watching each other warily.

Shaley said suddenly: 'Who was Big Cee, Mandy?'

'Huh?' Mandy said vacantly.

Shaley didn't say anything. He squatted down on his heels and began to draw patterns in the dust with his forefinger.

After a while, Mandy said bitterly: 'I mighta known you'd get on to that. You find out everything, damn you.'

There was another silence. Shaley kept on drawing his patterns in the dust.

'Her name was Rosa Lee once,' Mandy said sullenly. 'She worked with the old man on some serials way back in '09 or '10.'

Shaley drew in a long breath. 'So,' he said quietly. He stood up. 'Thanks, Mandy.'

'Don't you try any of your sharp-shooting on the old man!' Mandy warned ferociously. 'Damn you, Shaley, I'll kill you if you do!'

Shaley grinned. 'So long, Mandy.' He opened the gate and slipped outside.

Mandy put his head through the bars. 'I mean it now, Shaley. You try anything funny on Van Bilbo, and I'll kill you deader than hell!'

Shaley went into a drug-store on Sunset and called his office.

'Anybody call me?' he asked, when Sadie answered the telephone.

She said: 'Yes, Mr. Shaley. That man McFane called three times. He seems to be mad at you. He swore something terrible when I told him you'd gone to Europe. And that woman called – that woman that was here this morning and didn't pay you any money.'

'What'd she want?'

'She wanted to thank you for getting Bennie that job in Phoenix.'

'For what?' Shaley barked.

'For getting Bennie that job in Phoenix.'

'Tell me just what she said,' Shaley ordered tensely.

'She called just a little while ago. She said she wanted to thank you. She said the man you had talked to had called her up and told her that he would give Bennie a job in a hotel in Phoenix, and that she had told the man where Bennie was so the man could go and see him about the job.'

Shaley stood there stiffly, staring at the telephone box.

'Hello?' said Sadie inquiringly.

Shaley slowly hung up the receiver, scowling in a puzzled way.

'Good gawd!' he said to himself suddenly in a tight whisper.

He banged open the door of the telephone booth and ran headlong out of the drugstore.

Shaley parked the Chrysler with a screech of rubber on cement. He got out and walked hurriedly along the sidewalk, along a high green hedge, to a sagging gate. He strode up an uneven brick wall, up steps into a high, old-fashioned porch.

A fat man in a pink shirt was sitting in an old rocker on the porch with his feet up on the railing.

'Where's Bennie Smith's room?' Shaley asked him abruptly.

'Who?'

'Bennie Smith?'

'What's his name?' the fat man inquired innocently.

Shaley hooked the toe of his right foot under the fat man's legs and heaved up. The fat man gave a frightened squawk and went over backwards, chair and all. He rolled over and got up on his hands and knees, gaping blankly at Shaley.

Shaley leaned over him. 'Where's Bennie Smith's room?'

'Upstairs,' the fat man blurted quickly. 'Clear back. Last door on the left.' He wiped his nose with the back of his hand. 'Gee, guy, no need to get so hard about it. I'd 'a' told you. I was only fooling. No need to get so rough with a fellow.'

Shaley was running across the porch. He went in the front door into a dim, moist-smelling hall with a worn green rug on the floor. He went up a flight of dark, carpeted stairs, along a hall.

The last few steps he ran on his toes, silently. He had his hand inside his coat on the butt of the big .45 automatic in his shoulder-holster.

He stopped in front of the last door on the left, listening. He pulled out the automatic and held it in his hand. He knocked softly on the door with his other hand.

There was no answer.

Shaley said: 'Bennie,' and knocked on the door again.

He turned the knob. The door was locked.

Working silently, Shaley took a ring of skeleton keys out of his left-hand coat pocket. The lock was old and loose. The first key turned it.

Shaley pushed the door open cautiously, standing to one side.

He drew in his breath with a hissing sound.

Bennie was lying on the bed. He looked very small and thin and young. In death his face had lost some of its sharpness, its wise-guy cynicism.

He had been stabbed several times in his thin chest. The bed was messy.

Shaley shut the door very quietly.

Shaley turned off of Sunset and drove up Cahuenga. He parked the Chrysler and walked slowly across a vacant lot towards a long, shack-like building that had a big red Neon sign on top of it that said: *Zeke's.*

Shaley walked around to the back and knocked on the door.

An angry voice from inside said: 'How many times must I tell you bums that I can't give you no hand-outs until after the rush—' The man opened the door and saw Shaley. He said: 'Oh! Hello, Mr. Shaley.' He was a short, fat man with a round face that was shiny with perspiration. He wore a white chef's cap.

Shaley craned his neck, peering in the door. He could see into the interior of the dining-car. Bennie's sister was standing at the cash register, joking with a policeman and a man in a bus driver's uniform.

'What's the matter, Mr. Shaley?' the short man asked.

Shaley nodded his head to indicate the blonde woman. 'Her brother has just been murdered.'

The short man said: 'Bennie?'

'Yes.'

'Oh, ——!' said the short man. 'And she thought he was the grandest thing that ever lived.'

'You'll have to tell her,' Shaley said.

'Me? Oh, —— no! No. I don't want to. You tell her, Mr. Shaley.'

Shaley said: 'I can't.'

The short man stared at him. 'I got to tell her. And she thought he was so swell. She gave him most of her wages.' He rubbed his hand across his mouth. 'Oh, ——! That poor kid.'

Shaley turned around and walked away. He was swallowing hard.

When Shaley came up and peered through the big iron gate, Mandy and the chauffeur were looking into the engine of the Rolls-Royce much in the same attitude as before.

'It's a wrist-pin,' Mandy said. 'I'm telling you it's a wrist-pin.'

Shaley said: 'Mandy.'

Mandy came over and opened the gate. 'You're like a depression,' he told Shaley sourly. 'Always popping up when people don't expect you. What do you want now?'

'I want to see Van Bilbo.'

'He's in his office. They're just gettin' ready for some re-takes on that saloon scene. What's the matter with you, anyway?'

Shaley said: 'I just saw a kid that was murdered. He was a little rat and a chiseler and a liar, but he had a swell sister. She trusted me, and I let her down. I'm going to talk to Van Bilbo and then I'm going to start something. Stick around.'

He walked along the road, his feet crunching in the gravel.

The chauffeur looked at Mandy. 'Screwy?' he inquired.

Mandy was squinting at Shaley back. He shook his head slowly.

'No. He gets that way when he's mad. And when he's mad, he's a great big dose of bad medicine for somebody.'

Shaley turned around the corner of a barn-like building and was in a short dusty street with false-fronted sets on each side. There were board sidewalks and a couple of big tents that had saloon signs in front of them.

There were saddled horses tied to a long hitching-rack. There were men in fringed buckskin suits with coonskin caps and long rifles, and men in big sombreros wearing jingling spurs on their boots and big six-shooters in holsters at their waists, and men clad in black with high stovepipe hats. There were girls in low-necked dresses, and girls in calico and sun-bonnets.

A man up on a wooden tower that held an arc lamp was yelling angrily at a man on the ground, who was yelling back at him just as angrily. Two carpenters were having a loud argument in front of a saloon door. Another man had a long list in his hand and was running around checking up on the costumes of the extras. At the side of the street three men had a camera apart, examining its interior gravely.

Shaley walked along the middle of the street, went into a small wooden office building at the far end. He walked down a dusty corridor, knocked on a door that had a frosted glass panel with a crack in it running diagonally from corner to corner.

A voice said: 'Come in.'

Shaley opened the door and went into a small, cubby-hole of an office.

Van Bilbo was sitting behind the desk. Van Bilbo was a small, thin man. He was bald, and he wore big horn-rimmed glasses that gave him an owlish look. He always reminded Shaley of a small boy making believe he was grown up.

'Hello,' he said shyly, peering over his glasses at Shaley.

'Do you remember me?' Shaley asked.

Van Bilbo shook his head, embarrassed. 'I'm sorry. I meet so many people . . . I don't remember. . . .'

Shaley shut the door and sat down in a chair. 'I'll tell you a story – a true one. One time there was a man who was a racetrack driver. He cracked up badly, and his nerves went haywire. He couldn't drive any more. He

313

came out to Hollywood, hoping to find something to do. He didn't. He went broke. One day he was standing outside a studio. He'd pawned everything he owned but the clothes he wore. He was hungry and sick and pretty much down. While he was standing there a director came along. The director gave that man a ten–dollar bill and told him to go get something to eat. He gave the man a work–slip and let him work as an extra for a month, until he got on his feet again. I was that man, and you were the director. I don't forget things like that.'

Van Bilbo made flustered little gestures. 'It – it was nothing . . . I don't even remember. . . .'

'No,' said Shaley. 'Of course you don't. You've helped out plenty that were down and out and plenty that were in trouble – like Big Cee.'

Van Bilbo repeated: 'Big Cee,' in a scared voice.

Shaley nodded. 'That wasn't very hard to figure out, knowing you. She used to work for you a long time ago. She was in a jam. She called on you to help her out, and you did. She was running a joint in Cleveland. She got in wrong with some politicos, and they closed up her place. She was sore. She got hold of some affidavits that would look mighty bad in a court record. She skipped out here, intending to hide here and shake the boys back in Cleveland down for plenty. But they didn't want to play that way. They sent a guy after her, and he biffed her.'

Part of this Shaley knew, and part he was guessing; but he didn't have to guess very much; with what he knew, the rest was fairly obvious.

Van Bilbo was staring at the door with widened eyes. Shaley turned to look.

A shadow showed through the frosted glass – a hunched, listening shadow.

Shaley slid the .45 out of his shoulder–holster and held it on his lap, watching the shadow. He went on talking to Van Bilbo:

'That was what happened and everything would have been closed up now and over with, only you and a bellhop, by the name of Bennie, put your fingers in the pie. Big Cee got scared somebody might be after her, and she called you in and gave you the affidavits to keep for her. Bennie saw you leaving her room, and, being a chiseler by trade, he got the idea that he might shake you down a little. He was curious about Big Cee, and he kept on watching the room. He saw the murderer go in and out. Then when he found out Big Cee had been knocked off, Bennie thought he was on easy street for fair.'

Shaley paused, watching the shadow. The shadow was motionless.

'Bennie planned to put the squeeze on both you and the murderer. He made a bad mistake as far as the murderer was concerned. This murderer wasn't the kind of a boy to pay hush money. He's a dopey and a killer. Bennie found that out and went undercover while he tried to get in touch with you through me. The murderer was looking for Bennie. In the first place, Bennie knew too much, and in the second place the murderer didn't want Bennie putting the squeeze on you for fear you'd get scared and turn those affidavits over to the police.'

The shadow was moving very slowly, getting closer to the door.

Shaley went on quickly: 'The murderer was trailing Bennie's sister, trying to locate Bennie. He trailed the sister to me. He used my name to get the sister to give him Bennie's address. He killed Bennie. But he hasn't got those affidavits yet, and he wants them. He paid your chauffeur to quit, so he could get his job and be close to you without anybody getting suspicious. Come on in, baby!'

The glass panel of the door suddenly smashed in. An arm in a plum-colored uniform came through the opening. A thin hand pointed a stubby-barreled revolver at the two men inside.

Shaley kicked his chair over backwards just as the revolver cracked out. Shaley's big automatic boomed loudly in the small room.

There was the pound of feet going quickly down the hall.

Shaley bounced up, kicked his chair aside, jerked the door open.

The thin form in the plum-colored uniform was just sliding around the corner at the end of the hall. Shaley put his head down and sprinted.

He tore out through the door into the street in time to see the plum-colored uniform whisk through the swinging doors of the saloon.

Extras stared open-mouthed. A man with two heavy six-guns and a fierce-looking mustache was trying to crawl under the board sidewalk. One of the dance-hall girls screamed loudly.

Shaley started across the street. There was a little jet of orange flame from the dimness behind the swinging doors. The crack of the revolver sounded slightly muffled.

The horses tied to the hitching-rack reared and kicked, squealing frantically.

Shaley trotted across the dusty street. He had one hand up to shield his eyes from the glare of the sun. He had his automatic balanced, ready, in the other hand.

He got to the swinging doors, pushed them back.

The place was fixed up as a dance-hall and saloon. There was a long bar and a cleared space for dancing with a raised platform for the fiddler at the far end.

Shaley ducked suddenly, and a bullet from the back window smashed into the wall over his head.

He ran across the room and dived headlong through the window. He saw that he had made a mistake while he was still in mid-air. The man in the plum-colored uniform hadn't run this time. He had decided to make a fight of it. He was crouched under the window.

Shaley tried to turn himself around in the air. He hit the ground on one shoulder and rolled frantically. And as he rolled, he caught a glimpse of a thin, swarthy face staring at him over the barrel of a stubby revolver.

There was a shot from the corner of the building. The man in the plum-colored uniform whirled away from Shaley, snarling.

Mandy was standing there, dumpily short, cigar still clenched in his teeth. He had a big, long-barreled revolver in his hand. As the man in the plum-colored uniform turned, Mandy pointed the revolver and fired again.

The man in the plum-colored uniform shot twice at him, and then Shaley's heavy automatic boomed once.

The man in the plum-colored uniform gave a little gulping cry. He started to run. He ran in a circle and suddenly flopped down full-length. The plum-colored uniform was a huddled, wrinkled heap on the dusty ground.

Shaley got up slowly, wiping dust from his face. Heads began to poke cautiously out of windows, and excited voices shouted questions.

Van Bilbo came running – a small, frantic figure with the horn-rimmed glasses hanging from one ear. He ran up to Mandy, pawed at him.

'Are you hurt? Are you hurt, Mandy?'

Mandy said: 'Aw, shut up. You're like an old hen with the pip. Of course I ain't hurt. That guy couldn't shoot worth a damn.' He pushed Van Bilbo away.

Shaley said to the people who came crowding around: 'This man is a dope fiend. He went crazy and suddenly attacked Mr. Van Bilbo. You can all testify that I shot in self-defense.'

Mandy was pushing away through the crowd. Shaley followed him.

'Mandy,' Shaley said.

Mandy turned around.

'Give me that gun,' Shaley demanded and jerked the revolver out of Mandy's hand.

It was a single-action six-shooter. Shaley opened the loading gate, spun the cylinder. He punched out one of the loaded cartridges and looked at it.

The cartridge had no bullet in it. It was a blank.

'I thought so,' said Shaley. 'You grabbed this one off one of the extras. You damn' fool, you stood out there in the open with a gun full of blank cartridges and let that monkey shoot at you, just to give me a chance at him. That's guts, Mandy.'

'Aw, nerts,' said Mandy uncomfortably. 'I just didn't think about it, that's all. He got old Munn's job and I didn't like him anyway.'

Shaley glanced over where the whiskered man with the two big six-guns was just appearing from under the board sidewalk.

'There's a guy that thought, all right.'

Mandy scowled—

'Oh, them!' He spat disgustedly. 'Them heroes of the screen ain't takin' no chances gettin' hurt. It'd spoil their act.'

CHICAGO CONFETTI
WILLIAM ROLLINS, JR.

William Rollins, Jr. (1897–1950) may at first glance appear to be just another standard pulp writer, working for a penny a word, as hard-boiled writers so often did in the 1920s and '30s. But there are more than a few points of unusual interest about him.

Although born in Massachusetts, he fought for the French in World War I, and his best-known novel, *The Ring and the Lamp* (1947), is set shortly after World War II – in Paris.

His first novel, *Midnight Treasure* (1929) featured a boy, much in the tradition of Huckleberry Finn, who helps solve a mystery in an adult novel. Rollins also wrote three stories for *Black Mask* in the 1920s featuring Jack Darrow, a 16-year-old crime-solving hero, when it was all but engraved in marble that children had no place in the hard-boiled fiction of the pulp magazines.

He also received acclaim for his novels that would be sure to make most readers take notice, including from the *Saturday Review of Literature* (stating that '*Treasure Island*'s best moments are rather pastoral' compared to the tension of *Midnight Treasure*); from the *Boston Transcript* (which claims that *The Obelisk* 'often equals the best of Joyce'); and from Lillian Hellman (who hailed *The Shadow Before* as 'the finest and most stimulating book of this generation').

'Chicago Confetti' first appeared in the March 1932, issue of *Black Mask*.

CHICAGO CONFETTI

WILLIAM ROLLINS, JR.

'Henry Fuller murdered? Sure, I know it!'

I looked at him over my cigar. I don't like cigars, but all dicks, public and private, are supposed to wear them; and far be it from me not to have the right office furnishings when a prospective client comes in.

'Sure, I know it!' I said again, taking the weed out of my mouth for a bit of fresh air. 'Don't you suppose I take the *Times* and read the tabloids?'

'Well,' he said, 'you see I'm his nephew.' He said it quiet, like he'd been used to being the old man's nephew all his life; which I suppose he was. But to me it was like the lad's telling me he was Santa Claus.

I stood up quick, and gave Santa a cigar from the other box. Then I sat him down in a deep seat that's hard to get out of, and looked him over.

Considering he'd basked in the light of twenty million all his life, he didn't have such a healthy tan. One of the studious kind, with goggles that made him look nearer forty than the thirty which I suppose he was. Thin light hair, thin body, thin-colored blue eyes . . . and yet, looking them over as he started talking, I got the feeling that, if necessary, he could lay down his 'Iliad', or whatever it was that guy Joyce wrote, and get to business. He was talking business now as he leaned over my desk – business that I like to hear.

'You see, Mr. Warren,' he explained in a slow voice, 'the police are doing the best they can—'

'The police,' I muttered, waving them aside. That's part of my business.

'Exactly. The police. But the family decided we wanted to leave no stones unturned to discover the – the—'

'——' I helped him.

'Exactly. The —— that – that—'

'Bumped him off,' I finished.

'Exac—' He hesitated, frowning. 'Well, not exactly "bumped". There were no bruises on the body. He was shot with a revolver.'

'I know. In his own apartment. Monday evening about eight o'clock. Nobody present. You see,' I explained, 'crime news is this biddie's society page. And you want—?' I raised my eyebrows questioningly.

'Your help, if we can have it.'

319

'Hmm.' I picked up a note book and studied its blank pages. Having just started in on my own, this was my first prospect. I nodded thoughtfully; shut the book and looked up. 'Good,' I told him. 'And now as to terms.'

Coleman Fuller (that's what his card said; but it hadn't meant anything to me when I first read it) stood up.

'If you can drive around with me to Mr. Bond's – that's our family lawyer – we can fix that satisfactorily, I think,' he said.

I glanced at the clock.

'How's half an hour?' I asked; then, when he nodded: 'I got a little business to transact. That's Harley Bond, in the United Trust Building?'

'The same.' He bowed and crossed to the door. I stopped him as he opened it.

'By the way, Mr. Fuller,' I said; 'how'd you happen to come to me? Satisfied customer, I suppose?'

He smiled, a little self-consciously.

'Well – not exactly,' he murmured; 'you see – well, my cousin George and I looked through the book, under detective agencies, and we flipped a coin – that was George's idea – to see whether we'd start at the top or bottom. The Z's won, and yours was the first.' He laughed, sort of embarrassed, bowed again and went out.

I gave him time to get to the street and then jumped up, clamped on my hat and went out to the corner quick lunch, where I transacted my business. I was eating light those days. Fifteen minutes later I was in my snappy second-hand bus (I'm not telling what make; but it will rattle up to sixty) and in another ten minutes I was walking through the Gothic lobby of our latest Cathedral of Business. And there I meet young Professor Fuller himself again, standing at the foot of the elevators and talking to the dizziest blonde that never glorified the American girl.

He looked sort of flustered.

'On time, I see, Mr. Warren,' he murmured; and he said something to the girl that I didn't hear, lifted his lid, and stepped into the elevator. I nearly lost the car looking after her as she went out. She wasn't hiding much, and I didn't blame her.

'Charming girl,' said Mr. Student as we shot up; 'just an – er – acquaintance.'

'Well,' I shot back, stepping out at the thirteenth; 'she may be an acquaintance to you, but if I had your luck in knowing her, she'd either be a friend or an enemy.' We walked down the corridor, and in a couple of minutes I was standing before Harley Bond, Attorney-At-Law, and one of the stiffest priced ones in our town.

I'd seen him before, of course, in and out of court – a small terrier sort of man of about forty-five. This was the first time I'd seen him so near to, though; and as he looked at me, across his desk as big as a banquet table, I noticed the little bags under the eyes I'd missed before, and I figured Mr. Bond liked his liquor, and liked it long. He had a pleasant smile, though.

'Glad to know you, Mr. Warren,' he said in that easy drawl of his that made such a hit in court. He stretched out his hand. 'I've got to admit that if the family here had consulted me,' he added as we shook, 'I would have recommended a better known agency, but—'

'We've never had a failure yet,' I broke in.

His eyes twinkled at that.

'I figured as much,' he said. Harley Bond was nobody's fool. 'However,' he sat upright, becoming serious, 'now you're hired, let's get down to business. First—'

'—the terms,' I finished for him.

His lips formed in a silent whistle at that.

'I see a successful future ahead of you, Mr. Warren,' he murmured. 'The terms, however, have already been fixed by Mr. Carl Fuller, Mr. Henry's eldest brother. Ten thousand dollars to whomever finds and successfully proves the guilt of the murderer. To be paid on the sentencing.'

I nodded shortly and mentally waved the lunchroom goodbye. Then I turned to minor details.

There was little known about the murder, it seems, other than what the papers had stated. Henry Fuller had gone to his apartment, 38 Bradford Street, at seven-thirty Monday evening, to dress for dinner. At eight-thirty his valet, who had been on an errand for him (he had a dozen alibi witnesses) returned, to find him dead, shot through the heart. A doctor was called, who put the time of death at eight o'clock. Henry Fuller was unmarried. So far as was known he had no enemies.

'And the will?'

Mr. Bond coughed.

'The will divided the property equally among his two sisters and two of his three brothers,' he replied. 'The third – John – had not been on the best of terms with him. Mr. John is – er—' Again the lawyer coughed, 'the father of Mr. Coleman here.'

I turned to our young student, who so far had said nothing. He nodded solemnly.

'Exactly,' he murmured. 'But I, myself, have been on the best of terms with Uncle Henry for over a year now. I think, if he had lived a little longer, he would have – well, er—'

'I see,' I delicately finished for him. 'But he didn't, so you're out of luck.' I stood up. 'And now, Mr. Bond, I'll take a look around. You might give me the names and addresses of a few bereaved friends and relatives before I go,' I added.

I looked them up that afternoon, all the unfortunate kinfolk who were going to divide twenty million among them following the unhappy death of old Fuller. I didn't expect to find anything, and that's what I found. It wasn't till early the next afternoon that I got around to the valet.

Jobson was his name. He was still sticking around the old man's apartment, with the consent of the relatives, squeezing the last hour out of free lodgings until the advanced rent was used up and he'd have to move into cheaper quarters.

The building itself was a dingy affair, the kind only a millionaire can afford to live in, long, four storied, on an old aristocratic street. I had a job routing out the elevator-boy-of-all-work from where he was sleeping in an alcove by the switchboard, but at last I found him, and after a ten-minute ride up three flights, I stumbled along the dark corridor, discovered the right door, and finally was standing in the presence of the formidable Mr. Jobson himself.

He sat me down very politely when he found what I wanted; sat my one hundred and seventy pounds on the flimsiest gilded chair in all that gilded drawing-room, so he had the drop on me from the start.

'Anything I can do to help solve this horrible affair, sir, I'll be delighted to do,' he rumbled, standing over me. 'But, unfortunately, I am completely in the dark—'

'It seems to have been a dark night all around,' I interrupted him.

He bridled at that.

'I have alibis, sir!' he declared; 'at least a dozen people—'

I flapped my paw.

'Save your alibis until you're accused of something,' I said. 'I just dropped in for a pleasant little chat.'

Well, we talked about art and literature and one thing and another, but I wasn't getting any news that I'd come for, and I was just about to let up on him and lift anchor – when I settled back again.

I'd caught him looking at the clock.

Now there are ways of looking at a clock, and then there are ways.

Well, I kept him there for another twenty minutes, and at the end of that time he was as nervous as a débuting opera singer with the hiccoughs. At last he couldn't stand it any longer.

'I'm sorry, Mr. Warren,' he said, 'but I must put off this pleasant conversation till another time. You see, I – I've an engagement with a—' he leered; 'you understand, sir, don't you!'

I jumped up.

'I sure do,' I answered. 'You should have told me before. I have those engagements myself sometimes.' And I gave him leer for leer. In another minute I had shaken hands with him and watched the door shut tight; and the moment the latch clicked, I was sliding across the hall to the elevator, where I rang the bell and kept my finger on it till I heard the bang of the metal door below. Even then I wasn't comfortable.

'Anybody on the switchboard downstairs?' I asked the boy as he opened the door for me.

'Nobody, sir. Just me,' he replied.

I nodded. I was safe there, anyhow. And if Jobson went out or anybody came in to keep an appointment, I could spot them from that little alcove.

'Listen, son,' I said, as we gently parachuted down to bottom, 'they seem to give you a lot of jobs to tend to around here.'

'They do that, all right,' the boy grumbled. He opened the door. I passed out and waited for him.

'I guess an extra ten spot wouldn't look bad to you, hah?' I said as he settled down by the board.

He eyed me funny.

'Well . . . ' he murmured. I patted him on the shoulder.

'Don't worry; nothing like that, buddy. I just want to take your switchboard job off your hands a few minutes.' I pulled my hat over one eye and set my jaw in the proper fashion, and the kid got it right away.

'You're a dick!' he whispered, all eyes. Then his glance dropped to the roll that was coming out of my pocket, and he slipped off his seat and gave me the switchboard. I pulled on the earphones and waited. I know how to run a board; a good dick has to know a lot of things. Even being an expert window-washer comes in handy because – but you've read all about that.

Then came the first call. Mrs. Winslow's maid wanted those lamb chops right away, and wanted them in a loud voice; and then in a lower voice she added: 'bring them around yourself, Tony dear, if you can.' Then came the second call on the heels of that one, and Hattie Somebody and I learned all about what the doctor thought of Jessie's kidneys. He didn't think they were so hot, Jessie was glad to tell us; and I was beginning to be afraid I'd pulled a boner – that either Jobson was going out or somebody was coming calling (in which case I'd hear the ring for the elevator) when a third call was put in.

'Duval 8390.' That was Jobson's deep voice; there was no mistaking it.

I plugged in, passed on the call, and waited. Not long. I heard a receiver come off. Then:

'Hello.' A woman's voice.

'Is this Miss Kelly?'

'Yes.'

'This is Jobson. You know – Jobson.'

'Yes.' Short, noncommittal.

'I wanted to know is – is you know – there?'

'No, he isn't.'

'Well, get ahold of him right away. Right away, you understand?'

'Yes.'

'And tell him not to come around here. It's dangerous. You understand?'

323

'Yes.'

'Tell him to meet me at the hotel there. At that room – what's the number?'

'311.'

'311. In about an hour. You understand?'

'Yes. I'll tell him.' Her receiver went down, and his after it. I pulled out the plugs, and plugged in central.

'Listen, operator,' I said when she answered. 'Give me the address of Duval 8390, like a good girl, will you? I know it's a hotel.'

'Sorry, sir,' came the mechanical answer, 'but we're not allowed—'

'I know, I know, honey,' I cut in; 'but be big hearted just for once, will you? You see, I just got a tip that my wife and another chap—'

I heard her giggle. A moment's wait. Then:

'Duvaal, a-it – thrrree – noine – O, is the *Stopover Inn*, sir, on the Eastern Highway.'

I let out a noiseless whistle. I don't think I even thanked her. I was thinking just one thing. I was thinking that I was going to earn that ten grand – if I ever got it.

For the *Stopover Inn*, on the Eastern Highway, was the hangout of the Lewis gang!

I canned the whistle, hopped up, and patted the boy on the head.

'Nice boy,' I said; 'you'll be a millionaire some day,' and passed him the ten. Then I went back to my room, packed my bag with things I didn't need and was on my way.

The *Stopover Inn* is about ten miles out, and when I swung around the last corner, a flivver was just drawing up and I saw Jobson get out. I tore on past, interested in the scenery across the road, drove on for another mile, and then turned back.

I parked my car near Jobson's, got out, dragged out my suitcase, and walked into the small dirty lobby. There was just a dumb-looking, pimpled-face boy behind the desk, and I was glad of that.

'Room,' I snapped. 'Top floor, where I won't get the traffic so much. I've got a lot of heavy sleeping to do.' One glance had already told me there were only three floors to the place; ten rooms to a floor, five front, five back.

The boy stared at me stupidly.

'You got to wait for Miss Kelly to get back,' he drawled without moving his lips; why use your lips when your nose will do? 'She's upstairs.'

But Miss Kelly was just whom I didn't want to see, she or anybody else who might ask questions, aloud or to themselves. I wanted to hold that off as long as I could. I glanced at the keyboard at my side. 311's key was missing from its hook; but most of the other keys were there.

'Baloney,' says I, like I meant it. 'I'm not waiting for Miss Kelly or anybody else. I just come in from five hundred miles.' Luckily my car was turned the right way if they investigated. I glared at him. 'I don't want Miss Kelly, I want sleep! You understand? Here!' I made a dive for the key of 313, which was near me. 'Show me a room!'

But the boy's hand was on the rack nearly as soon as mine.

'That room's taken,' he said, mighty quick for him. 'I'll show you a room.' He took the key of 317 and came out from behind the desk. He almost fell over my suitcase as he shambled towards the stairs. I picked up the valise and followed his shuffling steps.

The two flights of stairs were narrow, dark and dirty, and so was the corridor at the head of the second flight. But both stairs and corridors were carpeted so thick you couldn't hear your own footfalls; which had its uses and had its drawbacks. The boy showed me my room, a narrow back room with one window, and started off again. He was so dumb he didn't even fool with the shades till I came across with a tip.

'Here,' I said, as I slipped him a quarter; 'and I don't want to be disturbed. I'm sleeping through twenty-four hours.' I slammed the door and noisily locked it, and gave him two minutes before I softly turned the key again, opened the door and stepped outside.

It was always night in that windowless corridor, but it wasn't any Gay White Way. One gasjet burned in the middle, and even that looked pretty discouraged. I locked my door from the outside, and walked down the hall – I didn't have to tiptoe on that thick carpet – to the last back corner room, number 311.

There were two voices inside, a woman's and a man's; but I didn't stop to listen. I moved back to the room beside it, number 313. I listened there a second; then I pulled out a pass key.

Yes, it was unoccupied. A regular cheap hotel room, that was mostly bed. The bed used to be brass. You could tell that by the bits that glittered here and there over the rough rusty iron. There was one window that faced a large but mangy orchard in back, and one stiff-backed chair. I noiselessly pulled the chair over to the door that connected with 311, but which was locked with its keyhole stuffed. Then I sat down and waited.

I heard the woman speak. She must have been standing near the outer door, talking to somebody back in the room.

'Well, when he comes, I'll send him right up,' she was saying. She had a nice, musical voice. I figured it must be Miss Kelly. 'I called him right after you phoned. He ought to be here any minute.'

There was a grunt right beside me. Jobson must be lying on the bed. The door opened and closed. I couldn't hear her feet as she walked away, past my door, down the hall.

A half an hour passed, with nothing more exciting than an occasional creak of the springs as Jobson twisted on the bed. I made myself as comfortable as I could on that lousy chair and waited; I think I even dozed once or twice. Then, all at once, I was sitting upright, ears cocked I heard the click of the outer doorknob in the next room.

Jobson sat up on the bed; I could hear the springs creak.

'Well,' he grunted, 'you took long enough getting here.'

There wasn't an answer until the door was shut and the key creaked in the lock. Then a low voice mumbled something I couldn't hear.

'Uh-huh,' Jobson answered; 'well, that's all right. Now let's get down to business.' And with that he moved off the bed and I heard him thump across the room, probably to a chair near the other bird. I pulled my own chair even closer to the door and stuck my ear against it. Then I got down on my knees and tried my ear at the key hole. I even took a chance at pulling out the wadding, but that wouldn't work. And all I got for my pains was a thick mumbling conversation.

True, now and then I caught bits of conversation, and they were interesting listening, though it was always Jobson's voice, never the other guy's.

'How much?' he said, once. 'Well, give me ten grand and little Freddie Jobson will be just a memory to you from then on.'

I pulled one of my silent whistles at that. 'Trying to blackmail the Lewis gang?' I thought: 'I can think of safer things than that – like sleeping on railroad ties.' Another time he said something about poor, dead Mr. Fuller, and his tone of voice brought to mind the bereaved relatives. And then came the fast one.

I heard him jump up, like he was sore.

'Listen, brother,' he says, forgetting discretion; 'don't pull that line on me. I might not have been there when you bumped him off, but I was listening in when you was there that same afternoon. And I heard him speak about the hundred grand the gang was trying to hold him up for. And I heard you say: "Listen," I heard you say; "I think I can show them the light if you give me fifty thousand – personally." And then: "I'll be around to get your decision shortly before eight." I wonder he didn't take a shot at you then, instead of waiting till you got back to try it, like you said. How would that story sound before a jury, brother? Hah? *And how would it sound if the gang heard about it?*'

So! I smiled to myself. *That* was why Jobson dared try blackmail! It wasn't the gang he had to face, but somebody connected with it who had tried to double-cross them! And right then there's the little buzz of a telephone in their room.

I glanced around the room here while I heard one of them thump across the floor. There wasn't any phone here; probably 311 was used for business conferences only, and the only connecting phone was in that room. I heard Jobson's voice muttering something into the mouthpiece. Then he slammed down the receiver with a vicious jerk.

'Listen!' he said in a hoarse whisper, and I could almost see him whirl around to his companion. 'She says to tell you the cops are on their way upstairs! I must have been shadowed, and – and – for —— sake, I can't be found talking to you! *Hide, man! Hide!*'

And then, for the first time, I heard the other guy's voice; just a half dozen low words:

'Just a second. I want to tell you. . . .' His voice became a mumble; then a whisper; then I couldn't hear it at all, and I figured he must be hiding. And he only had a minute to do it before I heard the thump of two or three men's feet coming along the hall. Oh, yes, I could hear it. It takes more than a thick carpet to deaden the step of a good bull.

They passed my door, went on to the next, and rapped, short and sharp. I heard steps cross the room, heard the key turn in the lock and the door open. And then I got a jolt.

A deep voice spoke, and I recognized it right away for Police Sergeant Rooney's.

'Well,' he says; 'so here's our little bird! You was right after all, Mr. Bond!'

And I heard Bond say in that slow drawl of his:

'Oh, I knew we'd find him, all right, Sergeant!' And I sat back and scratched my head.

So Bond was doing a little detective work on the quiet, was he! Taking a crack at that ten grand reward himself! I set my lips tight. I didn't know how he'd trailed Jobson here – unless by the bull stationed outside the apartments on Bradford Street – and I didn't give a damn; but when they brought that other bird – the guy what had done the shooting – before the Captain, little Percy Warren (Yeah, that's the name!) would be tripping alongside them, ready to put in part claim for the bonus! There are ethics in every trade, and Harley Bond was going to stick to lawyering, or I'd know the reason why! But I wasn't feeling so cheerful while I sat there listening to Jobson's pulling his sob stuff.

'Why, I wasn't doing nothing, Mr. Bond! I just came around here because—' And Bond cuts in:

'Nobody's accusing you of doing anything, Jobson,' he says; 'I just wanted to have a little talk with you to see if you knew anything more about this affair; and I asked the sergeant to come along and—'

And just then a truck went rumbling by; and though it was on the other side of the inn, it shut off all connections with the next room. Before the air cleared and I could tune in again it was all over.

'Well, come along!' Rooney snaps.

I stood up, ready to join the party and do a little arguing; and then I stopped short. Had they found the other guy – the bird that did the dirty work? They'd had time, maybe, to dig him out from wherever he was hiding; but how did I know they knew he was there in the first place? I crossed the room softly, slipped my key in the lock, turned it, and waited.

If they had the killer with them, that was my tough luck; if they didn't, it was Bond's. I'd produce him in my own good time, when the lawyer wasn't around to split the bonus.

I listened while they piled out the door and locked it behind them; waited while they tramped past my door. Then I opened up a crack and peeked.

There were four of them going down the hall. I could just make them out as they passed under the gasjet: the sergeant, another cop, Bond, and Jobson – and nobody else! I chuckled to myself, apologized to Lady Luck, and shut the door quick; for just then I spotted a girl down the hall ahead of them. Miss Kelly, probably.

I locked the door, pulled the key out, and slipped across to the window. With that girl out there, the hall wasn't safe. I pulled the window way up, gentle, and stuck my head out.

It wasn't easy going. I planked my toes on a little ledge, pressing them tight against the side of the house; and I edged along, quiet as I could until I had my hand on the window-sill of 311.

In a split-second I had my gun out, pointing up. I was a pretty target if the killer had heard me or came wandering my way, but I figured I'd get the first crack, if he stuck his head out.

He didn't, though; so I eased up above the water-line, leveled my gun on the sill. Then I shifted my grip from my hand to my elbow, jerked back the curtain and looked, my finger quivering on the trigger.

There wasn't anybody in the room; at least in sight. In another second I was over the sill and inside.

It was a bigger room than the others, several chairs, a table, a bed – I slid across to the bed and pulled a quick old maid; but nobody was hiding there. I crossed to the door. Then I swung around and went over to the window on the side of the building and looked out.

There was a maple there, reaching to the roof. One branch stuck out, almost to the window. It wasn't a hefty branch; I'd hate to shinny down it, and I'd just put on an act myself that wasn't so bad. But I figured a slim active guy could manage it, if it was that or the chair.

He *could* have done it; but— I stood a minute, staring out the window. There was something wrong, somewhere; something that didn't fit into the picture. I turned back, stared at the floor, thinking. I stooped to look under the bed again, just to satisfy myself.

'Well? Lose something?'

I whirled around. A girl was standing in the doorway. That had been a fast one! I sauntered towards her.

'Just a hairpin. It doesn't matter.'

She forced a little grin at that – nice lips, they were; but her eyes watched me pretty hard through a pair of horn-rimmed glasses. And now her smile got a little curl to it as she walked in to meet me.

'What did you want it for? Clean a pipe, or just pick a lock?' She halted behind a chair, rested her elbows easily on the back of it, and looked me up and down. 'I suppose you know you made a mistake and got in the wrong room?' she said.

I sat down on the bed, took out my cigarettes and lit one, pretty slow, giving her look for look. I was stalling for time. I wanted to size her up, get what there was to get from her; and at the same time I was trying to put together a little puzzle that was working in my mind. She wasn't hard to look at, for all the glasses and her hair twisted in a knot at the back of her head like a biddy's on Monday morning. Somehow she looked familiar, but I shoved that off; I can only work on one thing at a time.

I said:

'You're half right on your supposition, Miss Kelly.'

Her eyebrows rose at that.

'Miss Kelly, eh? Pleased to meet you, Mr.—'

'Burns. William J.'

She had to laugh.

'You don't go in for false whiskers like most of them, do you?' she said. Then, going back: 'So I'm half right, am I? And as this is the wrong room, I take it you didn't make a mistake in getting into it.'

'Good for Vassar!' I applauded; then I got serious. 'How long have you been working here, Miss Kelly?' I asked. Not that I wanted an answer. I was busy thinking.

'Let's see your tin medal before you start the third degree,' she answers, coolly. 'And while you're about it,' she drawled, when I didn't make a move, 'you might tell me how you happened to get in this locked room. It'd make interesting reading.'

I looked up at her quick. I'd got hold of something.

'Do you know Jobson?' I demanded.

'Let's see the medal.' She flicked a fly carelessly off her cheek.

'Do you know Jobson?' I repeated it in a monotone.

She was tapping her toe, easy, looking bored-like at the ceiling.

'Let's see the medal.'

And then, in the same monotone:

'Do you know a murderer was in this room with him?'

She forgets the ceiling at that. Her eyes shot down to mine, big and startled behind her glasses. I could see the color draw out of her cheeks.

'*You saw – a murderer – here?*' she almost whispered.

'I'm not saying what I saw.' I leaned forward, studying her a moment. She wasn't faking that horror; that was easily seen. But I wasn't worrying about that right now. I had a theory, and I was taking a long shot at it.

'Miss Kelly,' I said, slowly and distinctly; 'you were in the hall after the cops left with Jobson and another chap – Mr. Bond, the lawyer?'

She hesitated a moment. She swallowed hard; then she nodded, without speaking.

'Now!' I snapped; 'answer me this, and answer me *right!* Did you see another man sneak out of here after they left?'

Again she gave me a long hard stare, like she was doing a lot of thinking. Then, finally, she nodded.

'Yes, I did,' she said, low. 'I thought he was one of the party, so—'

I waved explanations away.

'Never mind that,' I said; but I felt a quick thrill. It looked like my guessing was coming out right. 'What did he look like?' I asked.

'A medium, thin fellow; white face, big nose; sort of mean little eyes—'

That was a description of Spike Lewis himself. I jumped up.

She drew in her breath. Then she went on. 'Listen. I've tended to my own business so far. But I can learn a lot of interesting news if I want to, and in quick time.' She thought a moment. 'Where are you going to be at eight o'clock?' she asked at last.

'Who knows? Maybe in the morgue with the unidentified bodies.'

She tossed off a polite smile, and then was all serious.

'Listen. Take this number.' I pulled out my note book. 'Ashley 2836. That's a long way from here. I wouldn't dare give you this number. Phone that number at eight, sharp. If I'm not there, I haven't any news for you. If I have, I'll be there.' She stuck out her hand, pal fashion, looking me in the eye. 'And I think I'll be there,' she finishes.

We shook.

'Good enough for you, Miriam!' I says, starting down the hall. 'I'll give you a ring.'

I was half way down the next flight when I heard her call. I looked up, and saw her grinning over the banister.

'Believe it or not,' she calls, softly, 'it's Desdemona!' Two minutes later I was in my car and bowling towards town.

I was pretty well pleased with myself as I tore along. I was damned certain who the killer was now; all I had to do was catch him, and catch him with the goods. That may sound hard, and I knew it wasn't going to be any cinch. But Percy Warren wasn't being paid easy money for an easy job. When I reached town, I turned off the highway and slowed her up a bit. Then I sat up with a bang.

'Why, you ham sleuth you!' I muttered to myself.

Here I'd been handing myself orchids for snappy thinking. And if I was right, it meant that Jobson, instead of being safe in jail, held as material witness, suspicious character, or whatever the temperamental captain decided on, it meant he'd probably been freed to get himself murdered! I was only about ten blocks from the Bradford Street apartments, but I swung up to the curb by a drug-store, vaulted out, and ran inside to a phone booth.

Jobson answered after a minute's ringing. I breathed a sigh of relief when I heard his voice.

'Listen, Jobson,' I said when I'd told him who I was, 'are you alone there?'

He hesitated long enough so that I knew the answer.

'Yes, I am,' he growled.

'All right,' I snapped; 'have it your way. But answer me this: did your little playmate come up the elevator with you, or did he sneak in some other way?'

I heard him suck in his breath. Then he turned and whispered something to somebody. I climbed inside the mouthpiece. There wasn't any time for fooling.

'Jobson!' I called. '*Jobson!*'

He came back at that.

'What is it?' he says, sulkily.

'Listen, Jobson,' I says, sharp and quick. 'You're playing with dynamite! You get out of that apartment *right away, you understand?* That guy's going to—' I stopped.

There was a curious dull *plop!* in my ear.

'Jobson!' I called.

Silence. Then a far-away sounding thud.

'*Jobson!*'

A second I stood listening to nothing. Oh, I knew the truth, all right, but I just hung on, listening. And then, all at once, I *wasn't* listening to nothing.

I was listening to somebody breathing, close to the phone, somebody who was listening back at me. I slammed down the receiver, ran out to the car, and started her with a jerk, and in two or three minutes I was in the lobby of the Bradford Street apartments.

The overworked elevator boy was sitting on a stool in the elevator.

'Listen, kid,' I says, shaking him to wake him up. 'Shoot me up to the third, as fast as this hearse can go!' And then, after he'd got it running: 'And give me a pass key to the Fuller apartment!' I was afraid maybe mine wouldn't work. 'Snappy!'

I left him staring after me as I loped around the corner of the corridor. Another minute and I'd opened the apartment door and locked it behind me. Then I took a few steps into the front room, and stopped.

He was dead all right. His big hulk of a body lay sprawling on the floor below the telephone, where that gun with its silencer had dropped him. I noticed the receiver was back on the hook, though. And Jobson hadn't done that.

I knelt down and took a quick look at him. But before I did, I knew Mr. Jobson had gone where all good blackmailers go, and in a second I was on my feet again. I hadn't hoped to be able to help him, and I didn't expect to find the killer around. But I did hope, if I scared him away soon enough, to find some sign of the bird's job, so as to be able to nail it on him. I gave the telephone receiver the once-over.

Right away I could see it was wiped clean as a Wall Street sucker. I gave the room a quick look. I didn't expect to find a special brand of cigarette butts tucked away in dark corners; if there was anything at all, it would be right under my eyes. And it wasn't there. I moved down the carpeted corridor, off which were the rooms.

The first three were bedrooms. I hardly gave them a look. Then the bathroom; then the dining-room. I opened the door at the end of the corridor.

Here was the kitchen. There was a door open across, and a dark stairway, leading down, probably, to the tradesmen's entrance. I figured that's how the killer got in. There weren't any doormen at that entrance. I looked around, and gave one of those Percy Warren whistles.

There were two empty glasses on the table, and a beer bottle beside them. They'd been talking it over here before I called. Here was how I would nail my friend – good ole finger prints!

I crossed the kitchen floor and reached for the glasses, planning to lift them by sticking my fingers inside.

'All right. Stick them up – *and don't turn around!*'

I stuck them up. That deep hoarse voice meant business. I heard him take a step back.

'All right. Turn and look. Then turn front again.'

I gave a look around.

There wasn't anybody in sight. But there was the muzzle of a gun sticking out the end of the corridor. That was all I could see, and that was all he meant for me to see. Just to show he wasn't playing.

'Are you looking front now?' the voice snapped.

'Yep.'

I heard him cross the kitchen, catlike, till he was at the opposite wall.

'Now turn and walk down the corridor – *slow!*'

I turned and crossed to the corridor. I heard him come after me as I started down it. I reached the bathroom.

'Stop!'

I stopped.

'Right hand down – *slow!* Reach around for the key. Got it? Now put it in this side the door.'

I followed instructions. He was close behind me now.

'Get in there. Cross to the window, hands up!'

I crossed to the window. The door slammed and the key clicked.

I didn't even bother to turn. I threw open the window, looked out, and gave a laugh. What a mistake that baby had made! In another second I was outside and running down the fire-escape.

There was an alley leading from the foot of the stairs to the street. It was surrounded on three sides by the apartment, and the only trouble was the tradesmen's stairway led to another block. But I tore on down the stairs and down the alley, and almost ran into the dick that was keeping an eagle eye on the apartment.

He was leaning against the side of the building at the head of the alley, and I reckon the sound of my feet woke him up. He stepped out to block my way.

'What's the big rush, buddy?' he says.

'Want to be on time for church,' I snarled; 'out of my way, flatfoot!'

But he grabbed me by both arms.

'Now listen, Major,' he said, soft-like, 'you don't want to run like that, it's bad for the heart. And besides, I'd love it a lot if you'd just stick around a bit, so's we can get acquainted,' and a lot of soft soap like that that the old-time dick pulls before he slaps you down; and I had to argue with him and show him everything but my baby pictures before he let up on me.

And by that time my killer probably was home and had his two beer glasses tucked safe in bed. I made a couple of observations on the bull's ancestors and walked around to Bradford Street; and just as I was passing the front of the apartment, a car drew up. I turned and looked.

Coleman Fuller was climbing out. He gave me a salute.

'Coming or going, Mr. Warren?' he asked. 'I was just going up to see Jobson.'

I looked him over quick.

'He's something to see,' I said, 'if you like them dead.'

His mouth and eyes opened wide at that.

'Dead?' he whispered. 'You don't mean—'

'Don't I, though! Go up and take a look at him. And while you're about it, you might phone headquarters. I've kept it a little secret so far because I haven't time to go down and fill out questionnaires, like they'd want me to. I've got a job on my hands.'

But he grabbed my arm as I was starting off.

'Was it the same man that killed my uncle?' he asked, all breathless.

'Same and identical.'

'And – and do you know yet who it was? Have you any idea?'

I tipped him a wink.

'There's a little birdie been flitting around my ear the last couple of hours,' I said. I started to go on, but he was keen for more dope. 'Listen,' I said, 'if things go right, I'll know more about it tonight. Maybe I'll even have a little surprise package to bring you afterwards.'

'Tonight?' He stared at me. Then: 'Where are you staying?' he suddenly said.

I thought quick, then decided it wouldn't do any harm.

'*Stopover Inn*, on the Eastern Highway.'

'*Stopover Inn?*' he gasped. 'But isn't that—'

'Yep,' I cut in. 'The hangout of the wild and wicked Lewis gang.'

He thought that over. Then he looked at me funny and said: 'Are you going there – all alone?'

'What do you want to know that for?' I asked.

He looked away.

'I just – it's rather dangerous going there alone, isn't it?' he murmured.

I started off.

'Don't you worry about that,' I told him. 'That's your Uncle Dudley's business. Just you have that ten grand ready, or else a first class undertaker.' I left him there, hopped into Lizzie, and started off. I wanted to be alone to think something over, for I'd just seen a bright light. Seeing Nephew Coleman had done that.

Desdemona. Take off those glasses, fluff up that knotted hair, throw a few glad rags on her in place of that starched dress, and what have you? You have a lady I'd seen just once before, and then only for a second.

And what did that prove?

I took that thought into a restaurant and chewed on it along with an extra tough steak. It might not prove so much, and then again it might prove a hell of a lot. The more I thought of it, the more I leaned towards the latter idea. It was just short of eight o'clock, and jumping up, I paid my check, went out to the nearest drug-store, and put in a call.

Desdemona herself answered the phone.

'Listen, Mr. Warren.' She spoke in a whisper, her lips close to the mouthpiece. 'I've learned something. I know who did it and I know where to find him. Have you got a car?'

'She's champing right outside here.'

'Well, listen. Can you drive out now and get me? I'm on Milton Boulevard in a drug-store. Number 1038.'

I whistled.

'That's a hell of a long ways out, Juliette,' I said.

'Well,' she answered, 'if you're interested in landing this fish—'

'Right you are!' I cut in. 'I'll motor right along. But listen, lady!' I added quick. 'You park yourself there, understand? Maybe I'll put in a call or two for you on the way!' And I hung up, went out and whipped up the steed.

While I bowled along at a good pace, I kept my eyes peeled, watching particularly the traffic coming the other way. It must have been two miles out that I realized I was nobody's fool.

The car – a high-powered bus – was coming slow. Over the headlights I could just make out a half dozen men's heads, all turned to peer at the traffic going my way. Then they came alongside me.

I just had time to see six pair of eyes staring at me, to see one thin white face with a long nose – the face of Spike Lewis that decorates the front page of our papers so often – to hear a quick exclamation from all of them. Then they were way behind me, and I was working Elizabeth up to sixty. I gave a quick glance around.

The big car was swinging around. I turned front and tended to business.

The traffic was medium thick about now. For a couple of miles there weren't any side streets, so the cars were buzzing right along, with nothing to hinder them. But I got Elizabeth going full steam and left the most of them pretty much standing still. After a minute or two I gave another look behind me.

Boy, was that bus eating up the road! In that quick eyeful I could see it charging down on me, a powerful looking baby, with a half dozen heads peering forward. I had the same chance of pulling away from her as if I was on foot with the gout. But I tore on for a bit longer.

Then I eased up, as much as I dared. Fifty. Forty-five. Forty. I can hear those lads now, roaring behind me. I saw one long chance, and I took it.

The road was clear all around me, except for a car ahead. I eased her some more, until I could near feel the hot breath of that bus, so to speak, on the back of my neck. Then, all at once, I clamped down on clutch and brake.

It all happened in a flash. There was a *zipp!* as that juggernaut went shooting past; six tense faces turned towards me; the loud *crrrackrackrack!* of a machine-gun and a *plop!* as the tail end of the burst hit my fender. I went shooting in a crazy wide arc across to the left hand side of the road, up on the sidewalk, passing the lamppost on the wrong side; but not before, from the corner of my eye, I saw the poor innocent bozo in the car that was ahead of mine, suddenly slump in his seat.

I came down off the sidewalk – lucky it was low here – without stopping, and gave a look around. The car with the dead man had crashed into another, and the crowds were already pulling up to see the fun. Nobody noticed me; if they did, I suppose they figured I was getting out of the way and that it was the dead man they wanted. The juggernaut was probably a mile away by now, and I figured it would keep right on going. I glanced at a house number.

1104. I'd come a bit beyond where I was heading for. In another minute I was drawing up at the drug-store number 1038 and climbed out.

Desdemona Kelly met me at the door, pale and fidgety.

'You got here all right, I see,' she said in a low voice.

I hauled up the eyebrows in the right fashion.

'Why shouldn't I?' I asked.

'Why – I just thought – it seemed like I heard some shooting up the line,' she answered, weaklike.

'Oh that.' I shrugged. 'Just some Chicago confetti. It seems they were after a guy in the car ahead of me – and got him. Got his wife and baby too,' I added, to make the story good.

Desdemona turned all white at that.

'The wife and baby?' she whispered.

I led her out to the car.

'Why not?' I murmured. 'The baby might shake a rattle at them. Brave lads like that can't take chances.' I steered her in, climbed inside myself, and we started off for town. I passed her a fag and we both lit up.

'Mr. Warren,' she said, slow and low, 'I suppose you think I'm as good as a – as a murderer.'

'Depends on how good the murderer is,' I answered, easy, snapping my butt into the street.

'You think,' she went on, 'I worked this racket.'

'Do I?' I murmured. 'Tell us some more, Portia.'

'What you going to do?' she asked, after about a mile.

'Eat, dance, then back to the *Stopover Inn* a day or two—'

She sucked in her breath quick.

'Ain't you – ain't you—' she commenced; and then she stopped.

'Afraid of meeting some of the boys?' I finished. 'That's just what I'm hoping for. You see, Jessica, it just happens that I've got information that Lewis – or whoever the hell did the killing – was trying to double-cross the gang. That's why he bumped old Fuller off!'

She stared at me hard at that. Somehow it seemed that her face – under the drug-store blush – went white again. She didn't say a word. Just looked and looked at me.

We got back to the *Stopover* and found the place all dark. Desdemona slipped out the car first to get the lay of the land, claiming she didn't want to be seen in my company. Then she came back to the door, wig-wagged me an 'all's well,' and I climbed down and went in after her. There was one green-shaded lamp lighted in the lobby, over the desk, and the pimpled-faced lad was sprawled under it, fast asleep.

Desdemona turned with her finger to her lips.

'Good night,' she whispered; blew me a kiss, and disappeared in a back room. I waded up the dark stairs, two flights, turned down the corridor to room 317. I shut and locked the door, and then pulled it open without bothering to turn the key back.

The bolt had been taken out of the lock.

'Oh, ho!' thought I; 'there've been villains at work!' And I shut the door and shoved the flimsy washstand in front of it, just in case. I pulled out my little toy, gave it a quick loving once-over, and stuck it back in my pocket.

Then I stood before the window, stripped to the waist, slipped on my pajama jacket, turned out the light, and got dressed again. After which I went over to the open window and looked out.

It was mighty dark outside, but not so dark that I couldn't make out something I'd noticed this afternoon – a little roof, about two feet wide (probably over a bay window below) running from just beneath my window to the window of 319. It was a flat roof, I found when I stepped outside; it was mighty simple to slip over to the next room. I pulled open that window, soft and wary. I stood a second, out of gun range, ears cocked. Then I climbed inside.

I slipped over to the bed, ran my hand lightly over it. It was empty. I'd been pretty sure the room wasn't taken. According to the keys on the board downstairs, I seemed to be about the only guest in the hotel. I crossed to the door, settled myself and waited.

I must have waited half an hour. I know I heard a clock somewhere outdoors strike two, and I must have waited ten minutes after that. Then, mighty faint, I heard something. I put my ear to the floor and listened.

It made all the difference in the world when I did that. I could feel the vibrations, and it sounded like three or four people must be sneaking up the corridor, along that thick carpet. I waited there a minute, ready to shoot into action. Then, all at once, I got puzzled.

I was hearing those sneaky steps, coming nearer. But I was hearing something else, too – or feeling its vibrations. It was a tiny vibration, coming right from the long board where my ear was.

I was sitting up like a flash, gun ready, pointed back into the room. Somebody was stealing across the floor towards me.

I got up to a crouch; edged along farther into the room, all set to jump to one side if the door opened. I must have made about a yard. Then a hand reached out and touched me softly on the face.

I don't know why I didn't fire. I reckon instinctive knowledge came with the feel of that soft hand. But that trigger was as near in action as I'd ever like to have it in somebody else's hand.

I heard her suck in her breath.

'Mr. Warren,' she whispered.

'Present. Ready for all comers.'

'I was hoping you'd go back to your room before they came. Get back in the corner, for —— sake!'

'I'm pretty well set, thanks.'

But now her voice was terrified, and no acting. I could tell that, even in the dark.

'*Please!*' she breathed; 'in the corner; for my sake!'

'Well . . . anything for a lady, Orphelia.' I slunk back.

'*And don't show yourself!*' I heard her hand softly turn the knob, just as there was a little grating sound in the next room – my washstand being pushed back. The door of this room opened, and a faint path of gaslight shot inside. She stepped to the doorway, blocking it.

'Well! What the hell are you birds doing around here?' Her voice was low, but cutting.

I heard a deep voice mutter something.

'Yeah?' she answered. 'Well, you guessed wrong. Yes, I know' – she broke in quick on the guy – 'but, you damned fool, don't you know he's got half a dozen playmates hanging round outside?'

That seemed to get them. There was a bit more mumbling; then I heard them slink away. She closed the door and stood there a second, looking my way, I guess. I stepped out.

'Rosalind,' I said, 'my family thanks you. To tell the truth, we never trusted you much before; but—'

'Yeah?' she said, kind of rough. 'Stow that. And go back bye-bye quick.'

'First, though, the reward,' I said; and I caught her and kissed her, a real two bits kiss.

She didn't push me away. She stood there a bit, after I was through, and I could hear her breathing heavy.

'You're a nice boy,' she said at last, way low. 'Why don't you quit this dick racket, and get out of this hotel – *now!*'

'Lady,' I whispered, 'the charm of your company—'

But I could hear her turning away.

'All right,' she cut in, nonchalantly. 'Do your window climbing act and get under the sheets.' She opened the door and shut it after her; and in another minute I was in and out the windows, and had settled myself for the night.

I figured afterwards it must have been four o'clock when I snapped awake. I sat upright (I'd been sitting on the floor, against the wall) and listened. He was coming now – the guy I'd been laying for. I watched where I knew the door was when I dozed off.

There was a little wait. Then it came again – the faint *squeak* of the rollers under the washstand as it was being moved. And now I could see a tiny slit of light showing where the opening door was. I got to my knees, crawled over to a point of vantage, and waited.

The slit grew wider. The light from the hall seemed almost bright, after the dead darkness. The stand squeaked, stopped; squeaked, stopped.

I waited till the door was open six inches. Then I stood up.

Plop!

The slug from the silenced gun dug into the wall back of me. With one gesture I swung around to the window, fired, and dropped.

The room rang with the shot for a while, and when it died away everything was still. The door and the stand didn't move any more; it didn't have to. Whoever had been shoving there had done his job.

Like a damned fool, I'd kept my eyes peeled on that door, just like they planned. And meanwhile the bozo himself had fired from the window; and now he was inside with me.

I softly drew myself up, ready, and then didn't move. He didn't move, either. We were both waiting. All at once there was a little clatter by the opposite wall.

Even while I pulled the trigger, I knew I was pulling my second boner. I know when somebody tosses a pencil across the room. It was just instinct, I guess, that made me fire. Right away something bit my shoulder, burning it. I rolled under the bed while the report was still whooping around. I figured he must be somewhere at the other end of it. I lay there, listening. My arm stung a little. Not much.

I guess I must have Indian blood in me. A gravestone is a noisy, nervous animal, compared to what I was. I did a little necessary breathing – not much – and that was all. The second hand went tearing round and round somebody's clock. It was his move first.

Probably he thought at last he must have got me. Anyhow, he moved a bit. Not three feet from me.

I let him have it.

By the time the noise died away, I heard them running up the stairs and along the corridor. I rolled from under, and when I got to my feet they were tumbling in the room – a whole army, it sounded like. When they lighted the light, though, I saw there were only four. Sergeant Rooney and three bobbies. Yes, and Coleman Fuller, standing there, white as a sheet.

I said:

'Have you got the girl?'

It seems they met her coming down on their way up. She stepped in, under escort, when I spoke.

'You nearly pulled a fast one, Desdy,' I said, 'when you got my eyes on that door you were pushing open. But then, you deserved that break, after the help you gave me.'

She gave me a gum-chewing look. I wasn't a nice boy now.

'What do you mean, help you?' she said.

'Why, by keeping the gang out of talking – and shooting – distance from me when I told you I might spread the news your boy friend double-crossed them. If they could pop me at a bowing distance – like in a passing car – well and good; but it was better to leave the near-at-hand job to the boy friend himself, and keep the others away, wasn't it!'

She started to speak; stops; looks sidewise at Fuller; then back at me.

'What makes you think he's my boy friend?' she asked sullenly.

'Just clever deduction,' I answered, modestly. 'It took me a while to recognize you, with your glasses and fancy get-up, as the dame I'd seen talking with young Mr. Fuller here in the United Trust lobby—' (I heard Fuller mutter: 'my ——!') – but then, when you were so quick to remember seeing somebody – Spike Lewis, or anybody else – steal down this hall, after Sergeant Rooney here and Bond and Jobson left, it was easy to see you were protecting one special guy. I was already pretty sure who the killer was, though,' I finished. 'Let's give credit where credit is due.'

Rooney let out a strong Anglo-Saxon word at that.

'What's this?' he said, staring at me. 'The killer was hiding in that room when we was there?'

I shook my head.

'Only half right, Sergeant,' I answered. 'He was in the room with you. But he wasn't hiding.'

'He wasn't hid—? He was in the—?' Rooney gawked at me like one of us is nuts. 'Well, who the—' he stuttered; 'where—?'

'All answered with one dramatic gesture, Sergeant,' I cut in. And I gave the bed a pull, rolling it a couple of feet towards the door.

Harley Bond was curled up behind the head. He wasn't dead. But he was sleeping peacefully, and wasn't apt to wake up for some little time.

I got my blood money when the jury's foreman said the harsh words. Police Captain Starr was there when they handed it to me, and he gave me a pat on the head.

'It was easy enough, Captain,' I answered; downcast eyes go well at headquarters, particularly if you're a private dick. 'I was stumped for a while, because I figured Bond came into the room along with the police. A bunch of trucks came by just then, so I couldn't hear much. But then I figured that what I *did* hear didn't prove he wasn't there right along, talking with Jobson.'

The captain shook his head slowly.

'He was a wise baby, that lad,' he muttered. 'Strange how a man of his capabilities could get into a jam like this. But that's the way of it, I suppose,' he said, turning philosopher. 'Got doing business for a gang, saw how easy money could be pulled by playing between the gang and their sucker and was caught with the goods.

'Might have gone panicky; might have thought he was ruined unless he could stop the sucker talking. Anyway he pulled it. Then there was Jobson.

'He knew Jobson was being shadowed, so he phoned us he was meeting him to learn what he could, and for us to call around in half an hour and he'd tell us what he learned. Had himself protected coming and going.' The captain stood up. 'A wise baby,' he said, half to himself; 'about as wise as they make them.'

I folded my check carefully.

'*Pretty* wise, Captain,' I agreed. I looked lovingly at the piece of paper in my hand. 'But not the wisest, Captain,' I cooed softly, 'not the wisest.'

I turned to Coleman Fuller as we went out of the station. 'As for you, Mr. Fuller,' I said, 'I suppose when you learned I was going out to the *Inn* alone your motherly instinct made you sneak out the police force to protect me.'

'Exactly,' he said nodding solemnly.

'And I suppose,' I went on, 'if the sergeant had appeared too soon and copped the prize himself, you know what would have happened to you?'

He nodded again, just as solemn. I looked him over, wondering if he was human.

'And I suppose,' I said, 'you know what a low-brow like me wants to do when he's come into a juicy bit of money?'

'Exactly,' he murmured. He reached in his pocket and pulled out a full pint flash, and after I took a good pull at it, he finished it off himself. 'That,' he said, 'is just about enough to last us till we reach the nearest speak.'

I looked him over again; and I liked his looks.

'Exactly,' I said.

TWO MURDERS, ONE CRIME
CORNELL WOOLRICH

Only Edgar Allen Poe ranks with Cornell Woolrich (1903–1968) as a creator of heart-stopping suspense, and Poe produced relatively little compared with the prolific poet of darkness.

A sad and lonely figure (he dedicated books to his hotel room and to his typewriter), Woolrich is the greatest noir writer who ever lived, in spite of stylistic failings that include so much purple prose that, in the hands of a lesser writer, would make one wince. His use of coincidence, too, made believable or unnoticed because of the break-neck thrill ride of his stories, is unmatched by any author with the exception of the unreadable Harry Stephen Keeler.

In addition to hundreds of stories, mainly written for the pulps, Woolrich produced such classic novels of suspense as *The Bride Wore Black* (1940), filmed in 1968 by Francois Truffaut, and *Black Alibi* (1942), filmed the following year by Jacques Tourneur as *The Leopard Man*. The most famous film made from his work is Alfred Hitchcock's *Rear Window* (1954), based on a short story written under the pseudonym William Irish. Among numerous other Irish works to be filmed are the noir classic *Phantom Lady*, filmed by Robert Siodmak in 1944, two years after book publication, and *Deadline at Dawn*, directed by Harold Clurman in 1946, also two years after book publication.

'Two Murders, One Crime' was first published in the July 1942 issue of *Black Mask* under the title 'Three Kills for One.'

TWO MURDERS, ONE CRIME
CORNELL WOOLRICH

That night, just like on all the other nights before it, around a quarter to twelve Gary Severn took his hat off the hook nearest the door, turned and said to his pretty, docile little wife in the room behind him: 'Guess I'll go down to the corner a minute, bring in the midnight edition.'

'All right, dear,' she nodded, just like on all the other nights before this.

He opened the door, but then he stood there undecidedly on the threshold. 'I feel kind of tired,' he yawned, backing a hand to his mouth. 'Maybe I ought to skip it. It wouldn't kill me to do without it one night. I usually fall asleep before I can turn to page two, anyway.'

'Then don't bother getting it, dear, let it go if you feel that way,' she acquiesced. 'Why put yourself out? After all, it's not that important.'

'No it isn't, is it?' he admitted. For a moment he seemed about to step inside again and close the door after him. Then he shrugged. 'Oh well,' he said, 'I may as well go now that I've got my hat on. I'll be back in a couple of minutes.' He closed the door from the outside.

Who knows what is important, what isn't important? Who is to recognize the turning-point that turns out to be a trifle, the trifle that turns out to be a turning-point?

A pause at the door, a yawn, a two-cent midnight paper that he wouldn't have remained awake long enough to finish anyway.

He came out on the street. Just a man on his way to the corner for a newspaper, and then back again. It was the 181st day of the year, and on 180 other nights before this one he had come out at this same hour, for this same thing. No, one night there'd been a blizzard and he hadn't. 179 nights, then.

He walked down to the corner, and turned it, and went one block over the long way, to where the concession was located. It was just a wooden trestle set up on the sidewalk, with the papers stacked on it. The tabs were always the first ones out, and they were on it already. But his was a standard size, and it came out the last of all of them, possibly due to complexities of make-up.

The man who kept the stand knew him by his paper, although he didn't know his name or anything else about him. 'Not up yet,' he greeted him. 'Any minute now.'

Why is it, when a man has read one particular paper for any length of time, he will refuse to buy another in place of it, even though the same news is in both? Another trifle?

Gary Severn said, 'I'll take a turn around the block. It'll probably be here by the time I get back.'

The delivery trucks left the plant downtown at 11:30, but the paper never hit the stands this far up much before twelve, due to a number of variables such as traffic-lights and weather which were never the same twice. It had often been a little delayed, just as it was tonight.

He went up the next street, the one behind his own, rounded the upper corner of that, then over, and back into his own again. He swung one hand, kept his other pocketed. He whistled a few inaccurate bars of *Elmer's Tune*. Then a few even more inaccurate bars of *Rose O'Day*. Then he quit whistling. It had just been an expression of the untroubled vacancy of his mind, anyway. His thoughts went something like this: 'Swell night. Wonder what star that is up there, that one just hitting the roof? Never did know much about them. That Colonna sure was funny on the air tonight.' With a grin of reminiscent appreciation. 'Gee I'm sleepy. Wish I hadn't come out just now.' Things like that.

He'd arrived back at his own doorway from the opposite direction by now. He slackened a little, hesitated, on the point of going in and letting the paper go hang. Then he went on anyway. 'I'm out now. It'll just take a minute longer. There and back.' Trifle.

The delivery truck had just arrived. He saw the bale being pitched off the back to the asphalt; for the dealer to pick up, as he rounded the corner once more. By the time he'd arrived at the stand the dealer had hauled it onto the sidewalk, cut the binding, and stacked the papers for sale on his board. A handful of other customers who had been waiting around closed in. The dealer was kept busy handing them out and making change.

Gary Severn wormed his way in through the little cluster of customers, reached for a copy from the pile, and found that somebody else had taken hold of it at the same time. The slight tug from two different directions brought their eyes around toward one another. Probably neither would have seen the other, that is to look at squarely, if it hadn't been for that. Trifle.

It was nothing. Gary Severn said pleasantly, 'Go ahead, help yourself,' and relinquished that particular copy for the next one below it.

'Must think he knows me,' passed through his inattentive mind. The other's glance had come back a second time, whereas his own hadn't. He paid no further heed. He handed the dealer his nickel, got back two cents, turned and went off, reading the headlines as he went by the aid of the fairly adequate shop-lights there were along there.

He was dimly aware, as he did so, of numbers of other footsteps coming along the same way he was. People who had just now bought their papers as he had, and had this same direction to follow. He turned the corner and diverged up into his own street. All but one pair of footsteps went on off the long way, along the avenue, died out. One pair turned off and came up this way, as he had, but he took no notice.

He couldn't read en route any more, because he'd left the lights behind. The paper turned blue and blurred. He folded it and postponed the rest until he should get inside.

The other tread was still coming along, a few yards back. He didn't look around. Why should he? The streets were free to everyone. Others lived along this street as well as he. Footsteps behind him had no connection with him. He didn't have that kind of a mind, he hadn't led that kind of a life.

He reached his own doorway. As he turned aside he started to drag up his key. The other footsteps would go on past now, naturally. Not that his mind was occupied with them. Simply the membranes of his ears. He'd pulled out the building street-door, had one foot already through to the other side. The footsteps had come abreast—

A hand came down on his shoulder.

'Just a minute.'

He turned. The man who had been buying a paper; the one who had reached for the same one he had. Was he going to pick a quarrel about such a petty—?

'Identify yourself.'

'Why?'

'I said identify yourself.' He did something with his free hand, almost too quick for Gary Severn to take in its significance. Some sort of a high-sign backed with metal.

'What's that for?'

'That's so you'll identify yourself.'

'I'm Gary Severn. I live in here.'

'All right. You'd better come with me.' The hand on his shoulder had shifted further down his arm now, tightened.

Severn answered with a sort of peaceable doggedness, 'Oh no, I won't go with you unless you tell me what you want with me. You can't come up to me like this outside my house and—'

'You're not resisting arrest, are you?' the other man suggested. 'I wouldn't.'

'Arrest?' Severn said blankly. 'Is this arrest? Arrest for what?'

A note of laughter sounded from the other, without his grim lips curving in accompaniment to it. 'I don't have to tell you that, do I? Arrest for murder. For the worst kind of murder there is. Murder of a

police-officer. In the course of an attempted robbery. On Farragut Street.'
He spaced each clipped phrase. 'Now do you remember?'

Arrest for murder.

He said it over to himself. It didn't even frighten him. It had no
meaning. It was like being mistaken for Dutch Schultz or – some sort of a
freak mix-up. The thing was, he wouldn't get to bed until all hours now
probably, and that might make him late in the morning. And just when he
was so tired too.

All he could find to say was a very foolish little thing. 'Can't I go inside
first and leave my paper? My wife's waiting in there, and I'd like to let her
know I may be gone for half an hour or so—'

The man nodded permission, said: 'Sure, I'll go inside with you a
minute, while you tell your wife and leave your paper.'

A life ends, and the note it ends on is: 'Can I go inside first and leave my
paper?'

On the wall was a typical optician's sight-chart, beginning with a big
beetling jumbo capital at the top and tapering down to a line of
fingernail-size type at the bottom. The detectives had been occupied in
trying themselves out on it while they were waiting. Most, from a distance
of across the room, had had to stop at the fourth line below the bottom.
Normal eyesight. One man had been able to get down as far as the third,
but he'd missed two of the ten letters in that one. No one had been able to
get down below that.

The door on the opposite side opened and the Novak woman was
brought in. She'd brought her knitting.

'Sit down there. We'd like to try you out on this chart, first.'

Mrs. Novak tipped her shoulders. 'Glasses you're giving out?'

'How far down can you read?'

'All the way.'

'Can you read the bottom line?'

Again Mrs. Novak tipped her shoulders. 'Who couldn't?'

'Nine out of ten people couldn't,' one of the detectives murmured to the
man next to him.

She rattled it off like someone reading a scare-head. 'p, t, b, k, j, h, i, y,
q, a.'

Somebody whistled. 'Far-sighted.'

She dropped her eyes complacently to her needles again. 'This I don't
know about. I only hope you'll gentlemen'll going to be through soon.
While you got me coming in and out of here, my business ain't getting my
whole attention.'

The door opened and Gary Severn had come in. Flanked. His whole life
was flanked now.

The rest of it went quick. The way death does.

She looked up. She held it. She nodded. 'That's him. That's the man I saw running away right after the shots.'

Gary Severn didn't say anything.

One of the detectives present, his name was Eric Rogers, he didn't say anything either. He was just there, a witness to it.

The other chief witness' name was Storm. He was a certified accountant, he dealt in figures. He was, as witnesses go, a man of good will. He made the second line from the bottom on the chart, better than any of the detectives had, even if not as good as Mrs. Novak. But then he was wearing glasses. But then – once more – he'd also been wearing them at the time the fleeing murderer had bowled him over on the sidewalk, only a few doors away from the actual crime, and snapped a shot at him which miraculously missed. He'd promptly lain inert and feigned death, to avoid a possible second and better-aimed shot.

'You realize how important this is?'

'I realize. That's why I'm holding back. That's why I don't like to say I'm 100% sure. I'd say I'm 75% sure it's him. I got 25% doubts.'

'What you'd *like* to say,' he was cautioned, 'has nothing to do with it. Either you are sure or you aren't. Sureness has no percentages. Either it's one hundred or it's zero. Keep emotion out of this. Forget that it's a man. You're an accountant. It's a column of figures to you. There's only one right answer. Give us that answer. Now we're going to try you again.'

Gary Severn came in again.

Storm moved his figures up. '90% sure,' he said privately to the lieutenant standing behind him. 'I still got 10% doubt left.'

'*Yes* or *no?*'

'I can't say no, when I got 90% on the yes-side and only—'

'YES or NO!'

It came slow, but it came. It came low, but it came. 'Yes.'

Gary Severn didn't make a sound. He'd stopped saying anything long ago. Just the sound of one's own voice, unheard, unanswered, what good is that?

The detective named Rogers, he was there in the background again. He just took it in like the rest. There was nothing he felt called on to say.

The news-dealer, his name was Mike Mosconi, set in jackknife position in the chair and moved his hat uneasily around in his hands while he told them: 'No, I don't know his name and I'm not even sure which house he lives in, but I know him by sight as good as you can know anybody, and he's telling the truth about that. He hasn't missed buying a paper off me, I don't think more than once or twice in the whole year.'

'But he did stay away once or twice,' the lieutenant said. 'And what about this twenty-second of June, is that one of those once or twices he stayed away?'

The news-dealer said unhappily, 'I'm out there on the street every night in the year, gents. It's hard for me to pick out a certain night by the date and say for sure that that was the one out of all of 'em— But if you get me the weather for that night, I can do better for you.'

'Get him the weather for that night,' the lieutenant consented.

The weather came back. 'It was clear and bright on the twenty-second of June.'

'Then he bought his paper from me that night,' Mike Mosconi said inflexibly. 'It's the God's honest truth; I'm sure of it and you can be too. The only one or two times he didn't show up was when—'

'How long did it take him to buy his paper each time?' the lieutenant continued remorselessly.

Mike Mosconi looked down reluctantly. 'How long does it take to buy a paper? You drop three cents, you pick it up, you walk away—'

'But there's something else you haven't told us. At what time each night did he do this quick little buying of the paper? Was it the same time always, or did it vary, or what time was it?'

Mike Mosconi looked up in innocent surprise. 'It was the same time always. It never varied. How could it? He always gets the midnight edition of the *Herald-Times*, it never hits my stand until quarter to twelve, he never came out until then. He knew it wouldn't be there if he did—'

'The twenty-second of June—?

'Any night, I don't care which it was. If he came at all, he came between quarter of and twelve o'clock.'

'You can go, Mosconi.'

Mosconi went. The lieutenant turned to Severn.

'The murder was at ten o'clock. What kind of an alibi was that?'

Severn said in quiet resignation, 'The only one I had.'

Gates didn't look like a criminal. But then there is no typical criminal look, the public at large only thinks there is. He was a big husky black-haired man, who gave a misleading impression of slow-moving genial good-nature totally unwarranted by the known facts of his career. He also had an air of calm self-assurance, that most likely came more from a lack of imagination than anything else.

He said, 'So what do you expect me to say? If I say no, this ain't the guy, that means *I* was there but with someone else. If I say yes, it is him, that means the same thing. Don't worry, Mr. Strassburger, my counsel, wised me up about the kind of trick questions you guys like to ask. Like when they want to know "Have you quit beating your wife?"'

He looked them over self-possessedly. 'All I'm saying is I wasn't there myself. So if I wasn't there myself, how can there be a right guy or a wrong guy that was there with me? *I'm* the wrong guy, more than anybody else.' He tapped himself on the breast-bone with emphatic conviction. 'Get the right guy in my place first, and then he'll give you the right second guy.'

He smiled a little at them. Very little. 'All I'm saying, now and at any other time, is I never saw this guy before in my life. If you want it that way, you can have it.'

The lieutenant smiled back at him. Also very little. 'And you weren't on Farragut Street that night? And you didn't take part in the murder of Sergeant O'Neill?'

'That,' said Gates with steely confidence, 'goes with it.'

Gates got up, but not fast or jerkily, with the same slowness that had always characterized him. He wiped the sweat off his palms by running them lightly down his sides. As though he were going to shake hands with somebody.

He was. He was going to shake hands with death.

He wasn't particularly frightened. Not that he was particularly brave. It was just that he didn't have very much imagination. Rationalizing, he knew that he wasn't going to be alive any more ten minutes from now. Yet he wasn't used to casting his imagination ten minutes ahead of him, he'd always kept it by him in the present. So he couldn't visualize it. So he wasn't as unnerved by it as the average man would have been.

Yet he was troubled by something else. The ridges in his forehead showed that.

'Are you ready, my son?'

'I'm ready.'

'Lean on me.'

'I don't have to, Father. My legs'll hold up. It ain't far.' It was made as a simple statement of fact, without sarcasm or rebuke intended.

They left the death cell.

'Listen, that Severn kid,' Gates said in a quiet voice, looking straight ahead. 'He's following me in in five minutes. I admit I did it. I held out until now, to see if I'd get a reprieve or not. I didn't get the reprieve, so it don't matter now any more. All right, I killed O'Neill, I admit it. But the other guy, the guy with me that helped me kill him, it wasn't Severn. Are you listening? Can you hear me? It was a guy named Donny Blake. I never saw Severn before in my life until they arrested him. For ——'s sake, tell them that, Father! All right, I'm sorry for swearing at such at time. But tell them that, Father! You've got to tell them that! There's only five minutes left.'

'Why did you wait so long, my son?'

'I told you, the reprieve – I been telling the warden since last night. I think he believes me, but I don't think he can get them to do anything about it, the others, over him – Listen, *you* tell him, Father! You believe me, don't you? The dead don't lie!'

His voice rose, echoed hollowly in the short passage. 'Tell them not to touch that kid! He's not the guy that was with me—'

And he said probably the strangest thing that was ever said by a condemned man on the way to execution. 'Father, don't walk any further with me! Leave me now, don't waste time. Go to the warden, tell him—!'

'Pray, my son. Pray for yourself. You are my charge—'

'But I don't need you, Father. Can't you take this off my mind? Don't let them bring that kid in here after me—!'

Something cold touched the crown of his head. The priest's arm slowly drew away, receded into life.

'Don't forget what you promised me, Father. Don't let—'

The hood, falling over his face, cut the rest of it short.

The current waned, then waxed, then waned again—

He said in a tired voice, 'Helen, I love you. I—'

The hood, falling over his face, cut the rest of it short.

The current waned, then waxed, then waned again—

They didn't have the chart on the wall any more. It had done them poor service. The door opened and Mrs. Novak was ushered in. She had her knitting with her again. Only she was making a different article, of a different color, this time. She nodded restrainedly to several of them, as one does to distant acquaintances encountered before.

She sat down, bent her head, the needles began to flicker busily.

Somebody came in, or went out. She didn't bother looking.

The toecaps of a pair of shoes came to a halt just within the radius of vision of her downcast eyes. They remained motionless there on the floor, as though silently importuning her attention. There wasn't a sound in the room.

Mrs. Novak became aware of the shoes at last. She raised her eyes indifferently, dropped them. Then they shot up again. The knitting sidled from her lap as the lap itself dissolved into a straight line. The ball of yarn rolled across the floor unnoticed. She was clutching at her own throat with both hands.

There wasn't a sound in the room.

She pointed with one trembling finger. It was a question, a plea that she be mistaken, but more than anything else a terrified statement of fact.

'It's him – the man that ran past by my store – from where the police-officer—!'

'But the last time you said—'

She rolled her eyes, struck her own forehead. 'I know,' she said brokenly. 'He looked *like* him. But only he looked *like* him, you understand? This one, it *is* him!' Her voice railed out at them accusingly.

'Why you haf to bring me here that other time? If you don't, I don't make such a mistake!'

'There were others made the same mistake,' the lieutenant tried to soothe her. 'You were only one of five or six witnesses. Every one of them—'

She wouldn't listen. Her face crinkled into an ugly mask. Suddenly, with no further ado, tears were working their way down its seams. Somebody took her by the arm to help her out. One of the detectives had to pick up the fallen knitting, hand it back to her, otherwise she would have left without it. And anything that could make her do that—

'I killed him,' she mourned.

'It wasn't you alone,' the lieutenant acknowledged bitterly as she was led from the room. 'We all did.'

They seated Donny Blake in a chair, after she had gone, and one of them stood directly behind it like a mentor. They handed this man a newspaper and he opened it and held it spread out before Blake's face, as though he were holding it up for him to read.

The door opened and closed, and Storm, the chartered accountant, was sitting there across the room, in the exact place the Novak woman had been just now.

He looked around at them questioningly, still unsure of just why he had been summoned here. All he saw was a group of detectives, one of them buried behind a newspaper.

'Keep looking where that newspaper is,' the lieutenant instructed quietly.

Storm looked puzzled, but he did.

The detective behind the chair slowly began to raise it, like a curtain. Blake's chin peered below first. Then his mouth. Then nose, eyes, forehead. At last his whole face was revealed.

Storm's own face whitened. His reaction was quieter than the woman's had been, but just as dramatic. He began to tremble right as he sat there in the chair; they could see it by his hands mostly. 'Oh my God,' he mouthed in a sickened undertone.

'Have you anything to say?' the lieutenant urged. 'Don't be afraid to say it.'

He stroked his mouth as though the words tasted rotten even before they'd come out. 'That's – that's the face of the man I collided with – on Farragut Street.'

'You're sure?'

His figures came back to him, but you could tell they gave him no comfort any longer. 'One hundred percent!' he said dismally, leaning way over his own lap as though he had a cramp.

'They're not altogether to blame,' the lieutenant commented to a couple of his men after the room had been cleared. 'It's very hard, when a guy looks a good deal like another, not to bridge the remaining gap with your own imagination and supply the rest. Another thing, the mere fact that we were already holding Severn in custody would unconsciously influence them in identifying him. We thought he was the guy, and we ought to know, so if we thought he was, he probably was. I don't mean they consciously thought of it in that way, but without their realizing it, that would be the effect it would have on their minds.'

A cop looked in, said: 'They've got Blake ready for you, lieutenant.'

'And I'm ready for him,' the lieutenant answered grimly, turning and leading the way out.

The doctor came forward, tipped up one of Blake's eyelids. Sightless white showed. He took out a stethoscope and applied it to the region of the heart.

In the silence their panting breaths reverberated hollowly against the basement walls.

The doctor straightened up, removed the stethoscope. 'Not very much more,' he warned in a guarded undertone. 'Still okay, but he's wearing down. This is just a faint. You want him back?'

'Yeah,' one of the men said. 'We wouldn't mind.'

The doctor extracted a small vial from his kit, extended it toward the outsize, discolored mass that was Blake's nose. He passed it back and forth in a straight line a couple of times.

Blake's eyelids flickered up. Then he twitched his head away uncomfortably.

There was a concerted forward shift on the part of all of them, like a pack of dogs closing in on a bone.

'Wait'll the doc gets out of the room,' the lieutenant checked them. 'This is our own business.'

Donny Blake began to weep. 'No, I can't stand any more. Doc,' he called out frantically, 'Doc! Don't leave me in here with 'em! They're killing me—!'

The doctor had scant sympathy for him. 'Then why don't you tell 'em what they want to know?' he grunted. 'Why waste everyone's time?' He closed the door after him.

Maybe because the suggestion came from an outsider, at least someone distinct from his tormentors. Or maybe because this was the time for it anyway.

Suddenly he said, 'Yeah, it was me. I did. I was with Gates and the two of us killed this guy O'Neill. He horned in on us in the middle of this uncut diamond job we were pulling. He didn't see me. I came up behind him while he was holding Gates at the point of his gun. I pinned him to the wall there in the entrance and we took his gun away from him. Then Gates said, 'He's seen us now,' and he'd shot him down before I could stop him. I said, 'He's still alive, he'll tell anyway,' and I finished him off with one into the head.'

He covered his face with palsied hands. 'Now I've given it to you. Don't hurt me any more. Lemme alone.'

'See who that is,' the lieutenant said.

A cop was on the other side of the door when it had been opened. 'The D.A.'s Office is on the phone for you, lieutenant. Upstairs in your own office.'

'Get the stenographer,' the lieutenant said, 'I'll be right back.'

He was gone a considerable time, but he must have used up most of it on the slow, lifeless way he came back. Dawdling along. He came in with a funny look on his face, as though he didn't see any of them any more. Or rather, did, but hated to have to look at them.

'Take him out,' he said curtly.

No one said anything until the prisoner was gone. Then they all looked at the lieutenant curiously, waiting for him to speak. He didn't.

'Aren't you going to have it taken down, lieutenant, while it's still flowing free and easy?'

'No,' the lieutenant said, tight–lipped.

'But he'll seal up again, if we give him time to rest—'

'We're not going to have a chance to use it, so there's no need getting it out of him.' He sank deflatedly onto the chair the prisoner had just been propped in. 'He's not going to be brought to trail. Those are the orders I just got. The D.A.'s Office says to turn him loose.'

He let the commotion eddy unheard above his head for a while.

Finally someone asked bitterly, 'What is it, politics?'

'No. Not altogether, anyway. It's true it's an election year, and they may play a part, but there's a lot more involved than just that. Here's how they lined it up to me. Severn has been executed for that crime. There's no way of bringing him back again. The mistake's been made, and it's irretrievable. To bring this guy to trial now will unleash a scandal that will affect not only the D.A.'s Office, but the whole Police Department. It's not only their own skins, or ours, they're thinking of. It's the confidence of the public. It'll get a shock that it won't recover from for years to come. I guess they feel they would rather have one guilty criminal walk out scot-free than bring about a condition where, for the next few years, every time the law tries to execute a criminal in this State, there'll be a hue and cry raised that it's another miscarriage of justice like the Severn case. They won't be able to get any convictions in our courts. All a smart defense lawyer will have to do is mention the name of Severn, and the jury will automatically acquit the defendant, rather than take a chance. It's a case of letting one criminal go now, or losing dozens of others in the future.' He got up with a sigh. 'I've got to go up now and get him to sign a waiver.'

The handful of men stood around for a minute or two longer. Each one reacted to it according to his own individual temperament. One, of a practical turn of mind, shrugged it off, said: 'Well, it's not up to us – Only I wish they'd told us before we put in all that hard work on him. Coming, Joe?'

Another, of a legalistic turn of mind, began to point out just why the D.A.'s Office had all the wrong dope. Another, of a clannish turn of mind, admitted openly: 'I wouldn't have felt so sore, if only it hadn't happened to be a police sergeant.'

One by one they drifted out. Until there was just one left behind. The detective named Rogers. He stayed on down there alone after all the rest had gone. Hands cupped in pockets, staring down at the floor, while he stood motionless.

His turn of mind? That of a zealot who has just seen his cause betrayed. That of a true believer who has just seen his scripture made a mockery of.

They met in the main corridor at Headquarters a few hours later, the detective and the murderer who was already a free man, immune, on his way back to the outer world.

Rogers just stood there against the wall as he went by. His head slowly turned, pacing the other's passage as their paths crossed. Not a word was exchanged between them. Blake had a strip of plaster along-side his nose, another dab of it under his lip. But Gary Severn was dead in the ground. And so was Police Sergeant O'Neill.

And the little things about him hurt even worse. The untrammelled swing of his arms. The fastidious pinch he was giving his necktie-knot. He was back in life again, full-blast, and the knot of his necktie mattered again.

He met the detective's eyes arrogantly, turning his own head to maintain the stare between them unbroken. Then he gave a derisive chuckle deep in his throat. It was more eloquent, more insulting than any number of words could have been. 'Hagh!' It meant 'The police – hagh! Their laws and regulations – hagh! Murder — hagh!'

It was like a blow in the face. It smarted. It stang. It hurt Rogers where his beliefs lay. His sense of right and wrong. His sense of justice. All those things that people – some of them anyway – have, and don't let on they have.

Roger's face got white. Not all over. Just around the mouth and chin. The other man went on. Along the short remainder of the corridor, and out through the glass doors, and down the steps out of sight. Rogers stood there without moving, and his eyes followed him to the bitter end, until he was gone, there wasn't anything left to look at any more.

He'd never be back here again. He'd never be brought back to answer for that one particular crime.

Rogers turned and went swiftly down the other way. He came to a door, his lieutenant's door, and he pushed it open without knocking and went in. He put his hand down flat on the desk, then he took it away again.

The lieutenant looked down at the badge left lying there, then up at him.

'My written resignation will follow later. I'm quitting the force.' He turned and went back to the door again.

'Rogers, come back here. Now wait a minute – You must be crazy.'

'Maybe I am a little, at that,' Rogers admitted.

'Come back here, will you? Where you going?'

'Wherever Blake is, that's where I'll be from now on. Wherever he goes, that's where you'll find me.' The door ebbed closed, and he was gone.

'Which way'd he go?' he said to a cop out on the front steps.

'He walked down a ways, and then he got in a cab, down there by the corner. There it is, you can still see it up ahead there, waiting for that light to change—'

Rogers hoisted his arm to bring over another, and got in.

'Where to, cap?'

'See that cab, crossing the intersection up there ahead? Just go which ever way that goes, from now on.'

Blake left the blonde at the desk and came slowly and purposefully across the lobby toward the overstuffed chair into which Rogers had just sunk down. He stopped squarely in front of him, legs slightly astraddle. 'Why don't you get wise to yourself? Was the show good? Was the rest'runt good? Maybe you think I don't know your face from that rat-incubator downtown. Maybe you think I haven't seen you all night long, everyplace where I was.'

Rogers answered quietly, looking up at him. 'What makes you think I've been trying for you not to see me?'

Blake was at a loss for a minute. He opened his mouth, closed it again, swallowed. 'You can't get me on that O'Neill thing. You guys wouldn't have let me go in the first place, if you could have held me on it, and you know it! It's finished, water under the bridge.'

Rogers said as quietly, as readily as ever, 'I know I can't. I agree with you there. What makes you think I'm trying to?'

Again Blake opened and closed his mouth abortively. The best answer he could find was, 'I don't know what you're up to, but you won't get anywhere.'

'What makes you think I'm trying to get anywhere?'

Blake blinked and looked at a loss. After an awkward moment, having been balked of the opposition he'd expected to meet, he turned on his heel and went back to the desk.

He conferred with the blonde for a few minutes. She began to draw away from him. Finally she shrugged off the importuning hand he tried to lay on her arm. Her voice rose. 'Not if you're being shadowed – count me out! I ain't going to get mixed up with you. You should have told me sooner. You better find somebody else to go around with!' She turned around and flounced indignantly out.

Blake gave Rogers the venomous look of a beady-eyed cobra. Then he strode ragingly off in the opposite direction, entered the waiting elevator.

Rogers motioned languidly to the operator to wait for him, straightened up from his chair, ambled leisurely over, and stepped in in turn. The car started up with the two of them in it. Blake's face was livid with rage. A pulse at his temple kept beating a tattoo.

'Keep it up,' he said in a strangled undertone behind the operator's back.

'Keep what up?' answered Rogers impassively.

The car stopped at the sixth and Blake flung himself off. The door closed behind him. He made a turn of the carpeted corridor, stopped, put his key into a door. Then he whirled savagely as a second padded tread came down the corridor in the wake of his own.

'What d'ye think you're going to do,' he shrilled exasperatedly, 'come right inside my room with me?'

'No,' Rogers said evenly, putting a key to the door directly opposite, 'I'm going into my own room.'

The two doors closed one after the other.

That was at midnight, on the sixth floor of the Congress Hotel. When Blake opened the door of his room at ten the next morning, all freshly combed and shaven, to go down to breakfast, it was on the tenth floor of the Hotel Colton. He'd changed abodes in the middle of the night. As he came out he was smiling to himself behind the hand he traced lightly over the lower part of his face to test the efficacy of his recent shave.

He closed the door and moved down the corridor toward the elevator.

The second door down from his own, on the same side, opened a moment or two after he'd gone by, before he'd quite reached the turn of the hall. Something made him glance back. Some lack of completion, maybe the fact that it hadn't immediately closed again on the occupant's departure as it should have.

Rogers was standing sidewise in it, back to door-frame, looking out after him while he unhurriedly completed hitching on his coat.

'Hold the car for me a sec, will you?' he said matter-of-factly. 'I'm on my way down to breakfast myself.'

*

On the third try he managed to bring the cup up to its highest level yet, within an inch of his lips, but he still couldn't seem to manage that remaining inch. The cup started to vibrate with the uncontrollable vibration of the wrist that supported it, slosh over at the sides. Finally it sank heavily down again, with a crack that nearly broke the saucer under it, as though it were too heavy for him to hold. Its contents splashed up.

Rogers, sitting facing him from a distance of two tables away, but in a straight line, went ahead enjoyably and calmly mangling a large dish of bacon and eggs. He grinned through a full mouth, while his jaws continued inexorably to rotate with a sort of traction movement.

Blake's wrists continued to tremble, even without the cup to support. 'I can't stand it,' he muttered, shading his eyes for a minute. 'Does that man have to—?' Then he checked the remark.

The waiter, mopping up the place before him, let his eye travel around the room without understanding. 'Is there something in here that bothers you, sir?'

'Yes,' Blake said in a choked voice, 'there is.'

'Would you care to sit this way, sir?'

Blake got up and moved around to the opposite side of the table, with his back to Rogers. The waiter refilled his cup.

He started to lift it again, using both hands this time to make sure of keeping it steady.

The peculiar crackling, grating sound caused by a person chomping on dry toast reached him from the direction in which he had last seen Rogers. It continued incessantly after that, without a pause, as though the consumer had no sooner completed one mouthful of the highly audible stuff than he filled up another and went to work on that.

The cup sank down heavily, as if it weighed too much to support even in his double grasp. This time it overturned, a tan puddle overspread the table. Blake leaped to his feet, flung his napkin down, elbowed the solicitous waiter aside.

'Lemme out of here,' he panted. 'I can still feel him, every move I make, watching me, watching me from behind—!'

The waiter looked around, perplexed. To his eyes there was no one in sight but a quiet, inoffensive man a couple of tables off, minding his own business, strictly attending to what was on the plate before him, not doing anything to disturb anyone.

'Gee, you better see a doctor, mister,' he suggested worriedly. 'You haven't been able to sit through a meal in days now.'

Blake floundered out of the dining room, across the lobby, and into the drugstore on the opposite side. He drew up short at the fountain, leaned helplessly against it with a haggard look on his face.

'Gimme an aspirin!' His voice frayed. 'Two of them, three of them!'

*

'Century Limited, 'Ca-a-awgo, Track Twenty-five!' boomed dismally through the vaulted rotunda. It filtered in, thinned a little through the crack in the telephone-booth panel that Blake was holding fractionally ajar, both for purposes of ventilation and to be able to hear the despatch when it came.

Even now that he had come, he stayed in the booth and the phone stayed on the hook. He'd picked the booth for its strategic location. It not only commanded the clock out there, more important still it commanded the wicket leading down to that particular track that he was to use, and above all, the prospective passengers who filed through it.

He was going to be the last one on that train. The last possible one; and he was going to know just who had preceded him aboard, before he committed himself to it himself.

It was impossible, with all the precautions he had taken, that that devil in human form should sense the distance he was about to put between them once and for all, come after him this time. If he did, then he was a mind-reader, pure and simple; there would be no other way to explain it.

It had been troublesome and expensive, but if it succeeded, it would be worth it. The several unsuccessful attempts he had made to change hotels had shown him the futility of that type of disappearance. This time he hadn't made the mistake of asking for his final bill, packing his belongings, or anything like that. His clothes, such as they were, were still in the closet; his baggage was still empty. He'd paid his bill for a week in advance, and this was only the second day of that week. He'd given no notice of departure. Then he'd strolled casually forth as on any other day, sauntered into a movie, left immediately by another entrance, come over here, picked up the reservation they'd been holding for him under another name, and closed himself up in this phone-booth. He'd been in it for the past three-quarters of an hour now.

And his nemesis, meanwhile, was either loitering around outside that theatre waiting for him to come out again, or sitting back there at the hotel waiting for him to return.

He scanned them as they filed through in driblets; now one, now two or three at once, now one more again, now a brief let-up.

The minute-hand was beginning to hit train-time. The guard was getting ready to close the gate again. Nobody else was passing through any more now.

He opened the booth-flap, took a tight tug on his hat-brim, and poised himself for a sudden dash across the marble floor.

He waited until the latticed gate was stretched all the way across, ready to be latched onto the opposite side of the gateway. Then he flashed from the booth and streaked over toward it. 'Hold it!' he barked, and the guard widened it again just enough for him to squeeze through sidewise.

He showed him his ticket on the inside, after it was already made fast.

He looked watchfully out and around through it, in the minute or two this took, and there was no sign of anyone starting up from any hidden position around the waiting rooms or any place near-by and starting after him.

He wasn't here; he'd lost him, given him the slip.

'Better make it fast, mister,' the guard suggested.

He didn't have to tell him that; the train didn't exist that could get away from him now, even if he had to run halfway through the tunnel after it.

He went tearing down the ramp, wig-wagging a line of returning redcaps out of his way.

He got on only by virtue of a conductor's outstretched arm, a door left aslant to receive him, and a last-minute flourish of tricky footwork. He got on, and that was all that mattered.

'That's it,' he heaved gratifiedly. 'Now close it up and throw the key away! There's nobody else, after me.'

'They'd have to be homing pigeons riding a tail-wind, if there was,' the conductor admitted.

He'd taken a compartment, to make sure of remaining unseen during the trip. It was two cars up, and after he'd reached it and checked it with the conductor, he locked himself in and pulled down the shade to the bottom, even though they were still in the tunnel under the city.

Then he sank back on the upholstered seat with a long sigh. Finally! A complete break at last. 'He'll never catch up with me again now as long as I live,' he murmured bitterly. 'I'll see to that.'

Time and trackage ticked off.

They stopped for a minute at the uptown station. There was very little hazard attached to that, he felt. If he'd guessed his intentions at all, he would have been right at his heels down at the main station, he wouldn't take the risk of boarding the train later up here. There wouldn't be time enough to investigate thoroughly, and he might get on the wrong train and be carried all the way to the Mid-West without his quarry.

Still, there was nothing like being sure, so after they were well under way again, he rang for the conductor, opened the door a half-inch, and asked him through it: 'I'm expecting to meet somebody. Did anyone get on just now, uptown?'

'Just a lady and a little boy, that who—?'

'No,' said Blake, smiling serenely, 'that wasn't who.' And he locked the door again. All set now.

Sure, he'd come out there after him maybe, but all he, Blake, needed was this momentary head-start; he'd never be able to close in on him again, he'd keep it between them from now on, stay always a step ahead.

They stopped again at Harmon to change to a coal-powered engine. That didn't bother him, that wasn't a passenger-stop.

There was a knock on the compartment-door, opposite West Point, and dread came back again for a moment. He leaped over and put his ear to it, and when it came again, called out tensely, making a shell of his two hands to alter his voice: 'Who is it?'

A stewardess' voice came back, 'Care for a pillow, sir?'

He opened it narrowly, let her hand it in to him more to get rid of her than because he wanted one. Then he locked up again, relaxed.

He wasn't disturbed any more after that. At Albany they turned west. Somewhere in Pennsylvania, or maybe it was already Ohio, he rang for a tray and had it put down outside the locked door. Then he took it in himself and locked up again. When he was through he put it down outside again, and locked up once more. That was so he wouldn't have to go out to the buffet-car. But these were just fancy trimmings, little extra added precautions, that he himself knew to be no longer necessary. The train was obviously sterile of danger. It had been from the moment of departure.

Toward midnight, way out in Indiana, he had to let the porter in to make up the two seats into a bed for him. He couldn't do that for himself.

'I guess you the las' one up on the whole train,' the man said cheerfully.

'They all turned in?'

'Hours ago. Ain't nobody stirring no mo', from front to back.'

That decided him. He figured he may as well step outside for a minute and stretch his legs, while the man was busy in there. There wasn't room enough in it for two of them at once. He made his way back through sleeping aisles of green berth-hangings. Even the observation-car was empty and unlighted now, with just one small dim lamp standing guard in the corner.

The whole living cargo of humanity was fast asleep.

He opened the door and went out on the observation platform to get a breath of air. He stretched himself there by the rail and drank it in. 'Gee,' he thought, 'it feels good to be free!' It was the first real taste of freedom he'd had since he'd walked out of Head—

A voice in one of the gloom-obscured basket-shaped chairs off-side to him said mildly, 'That you, Blake? Been wondering when you'd show up. How can you stand it, cooped up for hours in that stuffy two-by-four?' And a cigar-butt that was all that could be seen of the speaker glowed red with comfortable tranquillity.

Blake had to hang onto the rail as he swirled, to keep from going over. 'When did you get on?' he groaned against the wind.

'I was the first one on,' Rogers' voice said from the dark. 'I got myself admitted before the gates were even opened, while they were still making the train up.' He chuckled appreciatively. 'I thought sure *you* were going to miss it.'

He knew what this was that was coming next. It had been bound to come sooner or later, and this was about the time for it now. Any number of things were there to tell him; minor variations in the pattern of the adversary's behavior. Not for nothing had he been a detective for years. He knew human nature. He was already familiar with his adversary's pattern of behavior. The danger-signals studding it tonight were, to his practised eye, as plainly to be read as lighted buoys flashing out above dark, treacherous waters.

Blake hadn't sought one of his usual tinselled, boisterous resorts tonight. He'd found his way instead to a dingy out-of-the-way rat-hole over on the South Side, where the very atmosphere had a furtive cast to it. The detective could scent 'trap' a mile away as he pushed inside after him. Blake was sitting alone, not expansively lording it over a cluster of girls as was his wont. He even discouraged the one or two that attempted to attach themselves to him. And finally, the very way in which he drank told the detective there was something coming up. He wasn't drinking to get happy, or to forget. He was drinking to get nerve. The detective could read what was on his mind by the very hoists of his arm; they were too jerky and unevenly spaced, they vibrated with nervous tension.

He himself sat there across the room, fooling around with a beer, not taking any chances on letting it past his gums, in case it had been drugged. He had a gun on him, but that was only because he always carried one; he had absolutely no intention of using it, not even in self-defense. Because what was coming up now was a test, and it had to be met, to keep the dominance of the situation on his side. If he flinched from it, the dominance of the situation shifted over to Blake's side. And mastery didn't lie in any use of a gun, either, because that was a mastery that lasted only as long as your finger rested on the trigger. What he was after was a long-term mastery.

Blake was primed now. The liquor had done all it could for him; embalmed his nerves like novocaine. Rogers saw him get up slowly from the table. He braced himself at it a moment, then started on his way out. The very way he walked, the stiff-legged, interlocking gait, showed that this was the come-on, that if he followed him now, there was death at the end of it.

And he knew by the silence that hung over the place, the sudden lull that descended, in which no one moved, no one spoke, yet no one looked at either of the two principals, that everyone there was in on it to a greater or a lesser extent.

He kept himself relaxed. That was important, that was half the battle; otherwise it wouldn't work. He let him get as far as the door, and then he slowly got to his feet in turn. In his technique there was no attempt to dissimulate, to give the impression he was *not* following Blake, patterning his movements on the other's. He threw down money for his beer and he put out his cigar with painstaking thoroughness.

The door had closed behind the other. Now he moved toward it in turn. No one in the place was looking at him, and yet he knew that in the becalmed silence everyone was listening to his slow, measured tread across the floor. From busboy to tawdry hostess, from waiter to dubious patron, no one stirred. The place was bewitched with the approach of murder. And they were all on Donny Blake's side.

The man at the piano sat with his fingers resting lightly on the keyboard, careful not to bear down yet, ready for the signal to begin the death-music. The man at the percussion-instrument held his drumstick poised, the trumpeter had his lips to the mouth-piece of his instrument, waiting like the Angel Gabriel. It was going to happen right outside somewhere, close by.

He came out, and Blake had remained in sight, to continue the come-on. As soon as he saw Rogers, and above all was sure Rogers had marked him, he drifted down an alley there at that end of the building that led back to the garage. That was where it was going to happen. And then into a sack, and into one of the cars, and into Lake Mich.

Rogers turned without a moment's hesitation and went down that way and turned the corner.

Blake had lit the garage up, to show him the way. They'd gotten rid of the attendant for him. He went deeper inside, but he remained visible down the lane of cars. He stopped there, near the back wall, and turned to face him, and stood and waited.

Rogers came on down the alley, toward the garage-entrance. If he was going to get him from a distance, then Rogers knew he would probably have to die. But if he let him come in close—

He made no move, so he wasn't going to try to get him from a distance. Probably afraid of missing him.

The time-limit that must have been arranged expired as he crossed the threshold into the garage. There was suddenly a blare of the three-piece band, from within the main building, so loud it seemed to split the seams of the place. That was the cover-up.

Rogers pulled the corrugated tin slide-door across after him, closing the two of them up. 'That how you want it, Blake?' he said. Then he came away from the entrance, still deeper into the garage, to where Blake was standing waiting for him.

Blake had the gun out by now. Above it was a face that could only have been worn by a man who has been hounded unendurably for weeks on end. It was past hatred. It was maniacal.

Rogers came on until he was three or four yards from him. Then he stopped, empty-handed. 'Well?' he said. He rested one hand on the fender of a car pointed toward him.

A flux of uncertainty wavered over Blake, was gone again.

All Rogers said, after that, was one thing more: 'Go ahead, you fool. This is as good a way as any other, as far as we're concerned. As long as it hands you over to us, I'm willing. This is just what we've been looking for all along, what's the difference if it's me or somebody else?'

'You won't know about it,' Blake said hoarsely. 'They'll never find you.'

'They don't have to. All they've got to do is find you without me.' He heeled his palms toward him. 'Well, what're you waiting for, I'm empty-handed.'

The flux of uncertainty came back again, it rinsed all the starch out of him, softened him all up. It bent the gun down uselessly floorward in his very grasp. He backed and filled helplessly. 'So you're a plant – so they want me to do this to you – I mighta known you was too open about it—'

For a moment or two he was in awful shape. He backed his hand to his forehead and stood there bandy-legged against the wall, his mind fuming like a seydlitz-powder.

He'd found out long ago he couldn't escape from his tormentor. And now he was finding out he couldn't even kill his tormentor. He had to live with him.

Rogers rested his elbow in his other hand and stroked the lower part of his face, contemplating him thoughtfully. He'd met the test and licked it. Dominance still rested with him.

The door swung back, and one of the gorillas from the club came in. 'How about it, Donny, is it over? Want me to give you a hand—'

Rogers turned and glanced at him with detached curiosity.

The newcomer took in the situation at a glance. 'What're ya, afraid?' he shrilled. 'All right, I'll do it for you!' He drew a gun of his own.

Blake gave a whinny of unadulterated terror, as though he himself were the target. He jumped between them, protecting Rogers with his own body. 'Don't you jerk! They *want* me to pull something like that, they're *waiting* for it, that's how they're trying to get me! It didn't dawn on me until just now, in the nick of time! Don't you see how he's not afraid at all? Don't you notice how he keeps his hands empty?' He closed in on the other, started to push him bodily back out of the garage, as though it were his own life he was protecting. It was, in a way. 'Get out of here, get out of here! If you plug him it's me you kill, not him!'

The gun went off abortively into the garage-roof, deflected by Blake's grip on his wrist. Blake forced him back over the threshold, stood there blocking his way. The gorilla had a moment or two of uncertainty of his own. Blake's panic was catching. And he wasn't used to missing on the first shot, because he was used to shooting down his victims without warning.

'I've drawn on him now, they can get me for that myself!' he muttered. 'I'm gonna get out of here—!' He suddenly turned and went scurrying up the alley whence he'd come.

The two men were left alone there together, the hunter and the hunted. Blake was breathing hard, all unmanned by two close shaves within a minute and a half. Rogers was as calm as though nothing had happened. He stood there without moving.

'Let him go,' he said stonily. 'I don't want him, I just want you.'

Rogers sat there on the edge of his bed, in the dark, in his room. He was in trousers, undershirt, and with his shoes off. He was sitting the night through like that, keeping the death-watch. This was the same night as the spiked show-down in the garage, or what there was left of it. It was still dark, but it wouldn't be much longer.

He'd left his room door open two inches, and he was sitting in a line with it, patiently watching and waiting. The pattern of human behavior, immutable, told him what to be on the look-out for next.

The door-opening let a slender bar of yellow in from the hall. First it lay flat across the floor, then it climbed up the bed he was on, then it slanted off across his upper arm, just like a chevron. He felt he was entitled to a chevron by now.

He sat there, looking patiently out through the door-slit, waiting. For the inevitable next step, the step that was bound to come. He'd been sitting there like that watching ever since he'd first come in. He was willing to sit up all night, he was so sure it was coming.

He'd seen the bellboy go in the first time, with the first pint and the cracked ice, stay a minute or two, come out again tossing up a quarter.

Now suddenly here he was back again, with a second pint and more cracked ice. The green of his uniform showed in the door-slit. He stood there with his back to Rogers and knocked lightly on the door across the way.

Two pints, about, would do it. Rogers didn't move, though.

The door opened and the boy went in. He came out again in a moment, closed it after him.

Then Rogers did move. He left the bed in his stocking feet, widened his own door, went 'Psst!', and the boy turned and came over to him.

'How much did he give you this time?'

The boy's eyes shone. 'The whole change that was left! He cleaned himself out!'

Rogers nodded, as if in confirmation of something or other to himself. 'How drunk is he?'

'He's having a hard time getting there, but he's getting there.'

Rogers nodded again, for his own private benefit. 'Lemme have your passkey,' he said.

The boy hesitated.

'It's all right, I have the house-dick's authorization. You can check on it with him, if you want. Only, hand it over, I'm going to need it, and there won't be much time.'

The boy tendered it to him, then showed an inclination to hang around and watch.

'You don't need to wait, I'll take care of everything.'

He didn't go back into his own room again. He stayed there outside that other door, just as he was, in undershirt and stocking feet, in a position of half-crouched intentness, passkey ready at hand.

The transom was imperfectly closed, and he could hear him moving around in there, occasionally striking against some piece of furniture. He could hear it every time the bottle told off against the rim of the glass. Almost he was able to detect the constantly-ascending angle at which it was tilted, as its contents became less.

Pretty soon now. And in between, footsteps faltering back and forth, weaving aimlessly around, like those of someone trying to find his way out of a trap.

Suddenly the bottle hit the carpet with a discarded thud. No more in it. Any minute now.

A rambling, disconnected phrase or two became audible, as the tempo of the trapped footsteps accelerated, this way and that, and all around, in blundering search of a way out. 'I'll fool him! I'll show him! There's one place he can't – come after me—'

There was the sound of a window going up.

Now!

Rogers plunged the passkey in, swept the door aside, and dove across the room.

He had both feet up on the windowsill already, ready to go out and over and down. All the way down to the bottom. The only thing still keeping him there was he had to lower his head and shoulders first, to get them clear of the upper pane. That gave Rogers time enough to get across to him.

His arms scissored open for him, closed again, like a pair of pliers. He caught him around the waist, pulled him back, and the two of them fell to the floor together in a mingled heap.

He extricated himself and regained his feet before the other had. He went over, closed and securely latched-down the window, drew the shade. Then he went back to where the other still lay soddenly inert, stood over him.

'Get up!' he ordered roughly.

Blake had his downward-turned face buried in the crook of one arm. Rogers gave him a nudge with his foot that was just short of a kick.

Blake drew himself slowly together, crawled back to his feet by ascending stages, using the seat of a chair, then the top of a table next to it, until finally he was erect.

They faced one another.

'You won't let me live, and you won't even let me die!' Blake's voice rose almost to a full-pitched scream. 'Then whaddya *after?* Whaddya *want?*'

'Nothing.' Rogers' low-keyed response was almost inaudible coming after the other's strident hysteria. 'I told you that many times, didn't I? Is there any harm in going around where you go, being around where you are? There's plenty of room for two, isn't there?' He pushed him back on the bed, and Blake lay there sprawled full-length, without attempting to rise again. Rogers took a towel and drenched it in cold water, then wound it around itself into a rope. He laced it across his face a couple of times, with a heavy, sluggish swing of the arm, trailing a fine curtain of spray through the air after it. Then he flung it down.

When he spoke again his voice had slowed still further, to a sluggard drawl. 'Take it easy. What's there to get all steamed-up about? Here, look this over.'

He reached into his rear trouser-pocket, took out a billfold, extracted a worn letter and spread it open, holding it reversed for the other to see. It was old, he'd been carrying it around with him for months. It was an acknowledgment, on a Police Department letterhead, of his resignation. He held it a long time, to let it sink in. Then he finally put it away again.

Blake quit snivelling after awhile, and was carried off on the tide of alcohol in him into oblivion.

Rogers made no move to leave the room. He gave the latched window a glance. Then he scuffed over a chair and sat down beside the bed. He lit a cigarette, and just sat there watching him. Like a male nurse on duty at the bedside of a patient.

He wanted him alive and he wanted him in his right mind.

Hatred cannot remain at white heat indefinitely. Neither can fear. The human system would not be able to support them at that pitch, without burning itself out. But nature is great at providing safety-valves. What happens next is one of two things: either the conditions creating that hatred or fear are removed, thus doing away with them automatically. Or else custom, familiarity, creeps in, by unnoticeable degrees, tempering them, blurring them. Pretty soon the hatred is just a dull red glow. Then it is gone entirely. The subject has become *used* to the object that once aroused hatred or fear; it can't do so any more. You can lock a man up in a room even with such a thing as a king cobra, and, always provided he isn't struck dead in the meantime, at the end of a week he would probably he moving about unhampered, with just the elementary precaution of watching where he puts his feet.

Only the lower-voltage, slower-burning elements, like perseverance, patience, dedication to a cause, can be maintained unchanged for months and years.

One night, at the same Chicago hotel, there was a knock at the door of

Rogers' room around six o'clock. He opened it and Blake was standing there. He was in trousers, suspenders, and collarless shirt, and smelling strongly of shaving tonic. His own door, across the way, stood open behind him.

'Hey,' he said, 'you got a collar-button to spare, in here with you? I lost the only one I had just now. I got a dinner-date with a scorchy blonde and I don't want to keep her waiting. By the time I send down for one—'

'Yeah,' Rogers said matter-of-factly, 'I've got one.'

He brought it back, dropped it in Blake's cupped hand.

'Much obliged.'

They stood looking at one another a minute. A tentative grin flickered around the edges of Blake's mouth. Rogers answered it in kind.

That was all. Blake turned away. Rogers closed his door. With its closing his grin sliced off as at the cut of a knife.

A knock at the door. A collar-button. A trifle? A turning-point? The beginning of acceptance, of habit. The beginning of the end.

'This guy's a dick,' Blake confided jovially to the redhead on his left. 'Or at least he used to be at one time. I never told you that, did I?' He said it loud enough for Rogers to hear it, and at the same time dropped an eyelid at him over her shoulder, to show him there was no offense intended, it was all in fun.

'A dick?' she squealed with mock alarm. 'Then what's he doing around you? Aren't you scared?'

Blake threw back his head and laughed with hearty enjoyment at the quaintness of such a notion. 'I used to be in the beginning. I'd have a hard time working up a scare about him now, I'm so used to him. I'd probably catch cold without him being around me these days.'

Rogers swivelled his hand deprecatingly at the girl. 'Don't let him kid you. I resigned long ago. He's talking about two years back, ancient history.'

'What made you resign?' the other girl, the brunette, began. Then she checked herself. Blake must have stepped warningly on her toe under the table. 'Let it lie,' he cautioned in an undertone, this time not meant for Rogers to hear. 'He don't like to talk about it. Probably—' And he made the secretive gesture that has always stood for graft; swinging his thumb in and out over his palm. 'Good guy, though,' he concluded. Rogers was looking off the other way. He smiled to himself at something out on the dance-floor just then. Or maybe it wasn't out on the dance-floor.

'Let's break it up,' Blake suggested, as one co-host to another. 'This place is going stale.'

The waiter came up with the check, and Blake cased his own billfold, down low at his side. 'I'm short again,' he admitted ruefully.

'Let's have it, I'll pay it for you,' Rogers, who had once been a detective, said to the man he considered a murderer. 'We can straighten it out between us some other time.'

Rogers, paring a corn with a razor-blade, looked up as the familiar knock came on his door. 'That you, Donny?' he called out.

'Yeah. You doing anything, Rodge?'

They were Donny and Rodge to each other now.

'No, come on in,' Rogers answered, giving the razor-blade a final deft fillip that did the trick.

The door opened and Blake leaned in at an angle, from the waist up. 'Fellow I used to know, guy named Bill Harkness, just dropped in to the room. Haven't seen him in years. We been chewing the rag and now we're fresh out of gab. Thought maybe you'd like to come on over and join us in a little three-handed game, what d'ya say?'

'Only for half-an-hour or so,' Rogers answered, shuffling on the sock he had discarded. 'I'm turning in early tonight.'

Blake withdrew, leaving the door ajar to speed Rogers on his way in to them. He left his own that way too, opposite it.

Rogers put out his light and got ready to go over to them. Then he stopped there on the threshold, half in, half out, yawned undecidedly, like someone else once had, one night a long time ago, on his way out to get a midnight edition of the paper.

He didn't have to be right at his elbow every night, did he? He could let it ride for one night, couldn't he, out of so many hundreds of them? He'd be right across the hall from them, he could leave his door slightly ajar – He was tired, and that bed looked awfully good. He was a human being, not a machine. He had his moments of let-down, and this was one of them. Nothing was ever going to happen. All he'd managed to accomplish was play the parole-officer to Blake, keep him straight. And that wasn't what he'd been after.

He was about to change his mind, go back inside again.

But they'd seen him from where they were, and Blake waved him on. 'Coming, Rodge? What're you standing there thinking about?'

That swung the balance. He closed his own door, crossed over, and went in there with them.

They were sitting there at the table waiting for him to join them. This Harkness struck him as being engaged in some shady line of business. But then that was an easy guess, anyone on Blake's acquaintance-list was bound to be from the other side of the fence anyway.

'Pleased to meet you.'

'Likewise.'

He shook hands with him without demur. That was a thing he'd learned to do since he'd been around Blake, shake hands with all manner of crooks.

Blake, to put them at their ease together, trotted out that same worn theme he was so fond of harping on. 'Harkness don't wanna believe you used to be a dick. Tell him yourself.' He told it to everyone he knew, at every opportunity. He seemed to take a perverse pride in it, as though it reflected a sort of distinction on him. A detective had once been after him, and he'd tamed him into harmlessness.

'Don't you ever get tired of that?' was all Rogers grunted, disgustedly. He took up his cards, shot a covert glance at Blake's friend. 'No folding money, only nickels and dimes.'

Blake took it in good part. 'Ain't that some guy for you?'

The game wore on desultorily. The night wore on desultorily along with it. Just three people at a table, killing time.

Harkness seemed to have a fidgety habit of continually worrying at the cuff of his coatsleeve.

'I thought they quit hiding them up there years ago,' Blake finally remarked with a grin. 'We're not playing for stakes, anyway.'

'No, you don't get it, there's a busted button on my sleeve, and it keeps hooking onto everything every time I reach my arm out.'

Only half of it was left, adhering to the thread, sharp-pointed and annoying as only such trivial things are apt to be. He tried to wrench it off bodily and it defeated him because there wasn't enough of it left to get a good grip on. All he succeeded in doing was lacerating the edges of his fingers. He swore softly and licked at them.

'Why don't you take the blame coat off altogether? You don't need it,' Blake suggested, without evincing any real interest.

Harkness did, and draped it over the back of his chair.

The game wore on again. The night wore on. Rogers' original half-hour was gone long ago. It had quadrupled itself by now. Finally the game wore out, seemed to quit of its own momentum.

They sat there, half-comatose, around the table a moment or two longer. Rogers' head was actually beginning to nod. Harkness was the first one to speak. 'Look at it, one o'clock. Guess I'll shove off.' He stood up and got back into his coat. Then he felt at the mangled thatch the game had left in its wake. 'Got a comb I can borry before I go.'

Blake, mechanically continuing to shuffle cards without dealing them any more, said: 'In that top drawer over there,' without looking around. 'And wipe it off after you use it, I'm particular.'

The drawer slid out. There was a moment of silence, then they heard Harkness remark, 'Old Faithful.'

Rogers opened his heavy-lidded eyes and Blake turned his head. He'd found Blake's gun in the drawer, had taken it out and was looking it over. 'Ain't you afraid of him knowing you've got this?' he grinned at Blake.

'Aw, he's known I've had it for years. He knows I'm licensed for it, too.' Then he added sharply, 'Quit monkeying around with it, put it back where it belongs.'

'Okay, okay,' Harkness consented urbanely. He laid it down on the bureau-scarf, reached for the comb instead.

Blake turned back again to his repetitious card-shuffling. Rogers, who was facing that way, suddenly split his eyes back to full-size at something he saw. The blurred sleepiness left his voice. 'Hey, that busted button of yours is tangled in the fringe of the scarf, I can see it from here, and the gun's right on the edge. Move it over, you're going to—'

The warning had precisely a reverse effect. It brought on what he'd been trying to avoid instead of averting it. Harkness jerked up his forearm, to look and see for himself; anyone's instinctive reflex in the same situation. The scarf gave a hitch along its entire length, and the gun slid off into space.

Harkness made a quick stabbing dive for it, to try to catch it before it hit the floor. He made it. His mind was quick enough, and so was his muscular coordination. He got it on the drop, in mid-air, in the relatively short distance between bureau-top and floor. But he got it the wrong way, caught at it in the wrong place.

A spark jumped out of his hand and there was a heavy-throated boom.

Then for a minute more nothing happened. None of them moved, not even he. He remained bent over like that, frozen just as he'd grabbed for it. Rogers remained seated at the table, staring across it. Blake continued to clutch the cards he'd been shuffling, while his head slowly came around. Rogers, at least, had been a witness to what had happened; Blake had even missed seeing that much.

Harkness was moving again. He folded slowly over, until his face was resting on the floor, while he remained arched upward in the middle like a croquet-wicket. Then he flattened out along there too, and made just a straight line, and lay quiet, as though he was tired.

Rogers jumped up and over to him, got down by him, turned him over. 'Help me carry him over onto the bed,' he said, 'It musta hit him—' Then he stopped again.

Blake was still stupidly clutching the deck of cards.

'He's gone,' Rogers said, in an oddly-blank voice. 'It musta got him instantly.' He straightened up, still puzzled by the suddenness with which the thing had occurred. 'I never saw such a freaky—' Then he saw the gun. He stooped for it. 'What did you leave it lying around like that for?' he demanded irritably. 'Here, take it!' He thrust it at its owner, and the latter's hand closed around it almost unconsciously.

Blake was finally starting to get it. 'A fine mess!' he lamented. He went over to the door, listened. Then he even opened it cautiously, looked out into the hall. The shot apparently hadn't been heard through the thick walls and doors of the venerable place they were in. He closed it, came back again. He was starting to perspire profusely. Then, as another thought struck him belatedly, he took out a handkerchief and began to mop at himself with something akin to relief. 'Hey, it's a good thing you were right in here with the two of us, saw it for yourself. Otherwise you might have thought—'

Rogers kept staring down at the still figure, he couldn't seem to come out of his preoccupation.

Blake came over and touched him in anxious supplication on the arm, to attract his attention. 'Hey, Rodge, maybe you better be the one to report it. It'll look better coming from you, you used to be on the force yourself—'

'All right, I'll handle it,' Rogers said with sudden new-found incisiveness. 'Let's have the gun.' He lined his hand with a folded handkerchief before closing it on it.

Blake relinquished it only too willingly, went ahead mopping his face, like someone who has just had the narrowest of narrow escapes.

Rogers had asked for his old precinct number. 'Give me Lieutenant Colton.' There was a moment's wait. He balanced the instrument on one shoulder, delved into his pockets, rid himself of all the paper currency he had on him. He discarded this by flinging it at the table, for some reason best known to himself.

In the moment's wait, Blake said again, mostly for his own benefit: 'Boy, it's the luckiest thing I ever did to ask you in here with us to—'

Rogers straightened slightly. Three years rolled off him. 'Eric Rogers reporting back, lieutenant, after an extended leave of absence without pay. I'm in room Seven-ten at the Hotel Lancaster, here in the city. I've just been a witness to a murder. Donny Blake has shot to death, with his own gun, a man named William Harkness. Under my own eyes, that's right. Orders, lieutenant? Very well, I'll hold him until you get here, sir.' He hung up.

Blake's face was a white bubble. It swelled and swelled with dismay, until it had exploded into all the abysmal fright there is in the world. 'I wasn't near him! I wasn't touching it! I wasn't even *looking*! I was turned the other way, with my back to— You know that! Rogers, you know it!'

Rogers kept holding his own gun on him, with the handkerchief around it. 'Sure, I know it,' he agreed readily. 'I know it and you know it, we both know it. You hear me say it to you now, freely, for the last time, while we're still alone here together. And after this once, neither God nor man will ever hear me say it again. I've waited three years, seven months, and eighteen days for this, and now it's here. You found a loophole once. Now I've found a loophole this time. Your loophole was to get out. My loophole is to get you back in again.

'Listen to me so you'll understand what I'm doing, Blake. You're going to be arrested in a few more minutes for murder. You're going to be tried for murder. You're going to be – if there's any virtue left in the laws of this State – executed for murder. They're going to call that murder by the name of this man, Harkness. That's the only name that'll be mentioned throughout the proceedings. But the murder you're really about to be arrested, tried, and electrocuted for will be that of a man whose name won't appear in it once, from first to last, from beginning to end – Police Sergeant O'Neill. *That's* the murder you're going to die for now!

'We couldn't get you for the one you did commit. So we'll try you for another you didn't commit and get you for that instead.'

THE THIRD MURDERER
CARROLL JOHN DALY

It doesn't take a genius to recognize that there are better airplanes than the ones flown by the Wright Brothers, but they were there first, assuring themselves of an important place in history.

The same holds true for Carroll John Daly (1889-1958). There have been many practitioners of the hard-boiled private eye story who are far superior to Daly, but he was the first, inventing the form nearly three-quarters of a century ago with a story titled 'Three Gun Terry' featuring private investigator Terry Mack. The story appeared in *Black Mask* in the issue of May 15, 1923, and served as the prototype for all the tough, wise-cracking private dicks who followed.

The first story featuring Race Williams, his most famous character, soon followed with the publication of 'Knights of the Open Palm' in *Black Mask* on June 1, 1923. When he followed with another Race Williams story, 'Three Thousand to the Good', in the July 15, 1923 issue, Daly had created the first series hard-boiled private eye in fiction.

While in no way a distinguished literary performer, the relentless narrative drive of Daly's fiction made him one of the highest paid pulp writers for a quarter of a century, so popular that it was widely reported that his name on the cover automatically increased sales of the issue by 15%. *The Third Murderer* was originally serialized in *Black Mask* (June–August 1931) as *'The Flame' and Race Williams*.

THE THIRD MURDERER

CARROLL JOHN DALY

CHAPTER I: A THREAT TO KILL

I didn't like his face and I told him so.

He was handsome enough in a conceited, sinister sort of way. And the curve to the corner of his mouth was natural too – but more pronounced now by the involuntary twitching of his upper lip; a warning that a lad is carrying too much liquor and is getting to the stage where he'll slop over. Which is his own business, of course, and not mine – except when that lad decides to slop over on me.

'You don't like my face, eh?' Pale blue eyes narrowed. The skin on his forehead contracted and formed little ridges up close to the heavy blackness of his hair. The quivering lips turned into a sneer. Maybe you couldn't call that leering, threatening face natural – but you couldn't exactly call it acting either. Perhaps it would be best to say that it had started with acting years back and was more a habit now than either a natural contortion or a voluntary set-up. Something that came with long practice.

I looked at the clock above the bar. It lacked ten minutes to the half hour and five minutes past the hour I was to meet Rudolph Myer, criminal lawyer and the best mouthpiece in the city of New York – that is, for my purpose. 'Criminal lawyer' is right. Just 'criminal' might fit him. But then, if he is most times only a half block ahead of the District Attorney's office, he holds that lead – and on three different occasions had made monkeys out of the bar associations when he was brought up on charges of 'unethical practice'. Which any one has to admit is hardly a malicious way of classing jury fixing, wholesale perjury, and even extortion.

But I could use Myer at times, when some overzealous gunman got the idea that he could draw a little quicker than I, and later his relatives or friends found out that he couldn't. After such bits of shooting Rudolph Myer was the best man in the world to get me out of stir on a Habeas Corpus writ, and the best man also to keep me out. But back to the lad leaning against the bar in the Golden Dog Night Club, who was playing the game of 'Who can Make the Funniest Faces?' and winning in a gallop.

Now, the time – and Myer's promise that he would put something interesting in my way – sort of toned down my childish impulse to play 'ugly looks' with the youth who had missed his forte in life and should have been an impersonator instead of a racketeer.

So I moved down the bar, pretended that I didn't see him lift his glass and follow me, and also ignored the bartender's pantomime, which was to indicate to the youthful wise-cracker that he was holding a roman candle in his hand, with the wrong end up. Which was sound advice – even if I didn't fancy the bartender butting into my affairs.

'You're a smart guy, ain't ya?' His elbow crooked on the bar and his cheek went into his open palm. 'Race Williams – Private Investigator. Just a dirty dick, that's all you are. And you don't like my face. Well – a lot of people don't like to see it when they've got cause to fear it.' He paused a moment, licked at his lips, smiled sort of pleasantly to himself – then opened his eyes a bit and fairly glared at me like an animal, his lips slipping back.

'You read the papers. Be careful you don't look a Gorgon in the face – and die.'

'Well – it's ugly enough,' I told him. 'Why don't you take it down to Headquarters and use it to frighten policemen?'

'Yeah – yeah?' He wasn't the sort of a guy who went in for light banter – not him. He took himself very seriously. 'Yeah?' he said again, and then, 'Well – it's been down to Headquarters many times – see? And no dick dared to lay a fist on it. They didn't "third degree" me, buddy – not me, a Gorgon.'

'Been stealing milk cans?' I raised my voice, for his was fairly loud now and others were listening. Maybe I'm not so hot at the repartee, but talking around this lad was like talking around a clothing store dummy. I knew him, of course. Eddie Gorgon, who had more than once beaten the rap for murder.

'Milk cans!' he said. 'Not me.' And when some one laughed he lost his head slightly and cut loose. 'The yellow dick, Williams,' he raised his head for the few others to get the remark, 'let's his moll hide out in a dirty dump. When she was making the grade and turning over the big shots he lived off her and—' My hand shot up and fastened on the lapels of his coat. I jerked him straight and gave him the office.

'If you don't want that face of yours mussed up for a change, why—' and as too many others were taking an interest I tried hard and got a smile over, though I was boiling. 'Since I never trail with a woman I guess you've got your dates mixed or you're thinking of yourself,' I finished. There was a chance for him to pull back, but he didn't take it.

'Face mussed up!' he repeated, in what he considered great sarcasm. He rather liked his twisted map, I guess. 'Don't trail with women! You? No – not with women who can't pay their way – and your way. No women! Why, all the boys on the Avenue know about The Fla— Take your dirty hands off'a me.' He jerked free, and throwing open his coat let me see the gun beneath his armpit. 'You'd like a name for her? You'd like to muss the face of Eddie Gorgon? You'd like to chuck the front that you have the guts to cross me – Joe Gorgon's brother?' A slight pause as he shoved his face out. 'Well – the little moll was called The Flame – Florence Drummond. The Girl with the Criminal Mind. The—'

And I pasted him. Maybe I lost my head. Maybe I didn't. Certainly though, there was nothing definite in my mind when I let him have it. Maybe I should have provoked him into drawing a gun. Maybe it would have saved a lot of later unpleasantness. But it's not what you should have done that counts in life. It's what you do. And truth is truth. I had nothing in my mind but his glaring eyes and protruding chin and quivering lips. If I had any desire at all, it was to shut his lying, foul mouth – and perhaps that's even stretching the truth a little. The desire, after all, was just to sock him.

Now I won't say that he was 'out' before he hit the floor, though I like to think that he was. No, he wasn't dead – just out. To put it simply: I landed flush on his protruding button and – and he hit the floor like a thousand of brick. Maybe, if he hadn't landed on his thick head he would have been badly hurt. As it was, he stretched himself out on his back and listened to the birdies chirp.

But one birdie chirped a final message to Eddie Gorgon as he opened his eyes and looked dazedly around. That birdie was yours truly – Race Williams. I simply bent over him.

'All right, Eddie,' I told him pleasantly. 'You've made your next to last crack about The Flame, in this life. Remember that. The next one is your last.'

'I'll kill you for this. I'll kill you for this,' he said over and over again, in a dazed sort of way. But though I lingered by his side for a moment he made no effort to reach for his gun.

People were gathering now. The manager had run in from the main dining room, two burly waiters behind him. I didn't expect trouble – but then I'm always ready for it, so I sort of got my back to the wall and stood smiling at the manager.

The manager looked from me to the still prostrate Gorgon. It wasn't a memory that would linger pleasantly in his mind. Eddie Gorgon was a big shot, with his brothers behind him. But then, I was something of a big shot, with nothing but myself behind me – or maybe a gun or two, though they're generally before me.

I think the manager would have decided in my favor, for I was on my feet and the more immediate danger. But he didn't have to decide. The crowd sort of fell back. A giant of a man had entered the doorway. There was something of resemblance between him and the man on the floor. Eddie Gorgon was sort of a replica of the big man in the doorway, though the face of the reclining gunman was younger and less lined. It was also less controlled. Yep, I knew the big bozo. Joe Gorgon, the active member of the feared and fawned upon Gorgon brothers. Joe Gorgon, New York's most deadly racketeer, most politically prominent – and reputed to be one of the fastest-drawing gunmen in the country's greatest city – or out of it, for that matter.

Well – maybe he was. I stood, so, with my back against the wall. If he was sure that he was faster than I, here was his chance to prove it. I don't give way to any man when it comes to pulling rods. That's my living. If it's going to be my death – well – I folded my arms and waited.

I think that he saw me but I can't be sure. At least, he never looked straight at me. I stood my ground while he went over and knelt beside his brother. There was nothing to read in his hard cruel face, with the small nervous little eyes. But he didn't have to worry if his brother was alive or dead. Already Eddie Gorgon was sitting up, and the curses died on his lips as he looked into the hard, unsympathetic face of his elder brother, Joe.

And that was all of that picture. Fingers fell upon my arm.

'Come, come—' said a soft, persuasive voice. 'Don't be mixing yourself up in some common brawl that don't concern you. We don't want to be over-conspicuous here tonight. At least, not yet.'

I shrugged my shoulders and followed Rudolph Myer through the narrow hall, out into the cloak room, and so to the main dining room. It was a cinch he hadn't seen the little byplay. And it was a cinch I wasn't going to mention it to him. He might be of a nervous temperament, and consider it not altogether conducive to a long life and the pursuit of happiness.

CHAPTER II: AT THE GOLDEN DOG

'Mussy bit of a row inside,' Rudolph Myer jerked his thumb back toward the bar when we had taken seats in the almost deserted dining room. 'Looked like big Joe Gorgon crossing the—. But, there – I've got a job for you.'

'Never mind that yet, Myer.' I dismissed that topic for the time being. 'What's new of The Flame? Still going straight?'

'Still – an hour ago, anyway. But she don't fancy the "honesty is the best policy" racket, I guess. I don't think it's the money, Race; the drudgery of the work; the law stepping in and tipping her boss off that she's got a record, every time she lands a job. The girl's got the stuff in her. I think it's the excitement; the lure of danger; the control of men, she misses. Imagine her keen, active, if criminal, mind now solving the length of a bolt of silk! Though – damn it – the cheapness of her rooms, after being used to every luxury in life, should be enough to throw her. It's like me, Race. Maybe I wouldn't be honest if—. What are you grinning at?' He broke off suddenly.

I didn't tell him. Rudolph Myer was a queer duck and the crookedest lawyer in the city. Which is some record, no matter how you look on lawyers. But I dismissed the 'honest', knowing how touchy he was on that subject.

After all, honest lawyers are useless lawyers – at least, in the underworld. And Rudolph Myer was anything but useless. So I took the talk back to The Flame again.

'How about her estate – her mother's end of it, after her stepfather, Lu Roper, died?'

'Look here!' Rudolph Myer let the fingers of both his hands meet at the tips as he placed his elbows on the table. 'I've done a bit of legal work for you, Race. We've been friends, and – listen. What do you really know about The Flame – Florence Drummond? Oh, I only did what you've asked me to do – helped her get jobs so that she could live honest – but as a lawyer of course I learned things. I had to, in trying to get her a bit of Mrs. Drummond's money in Philadelphia. But Mrs. Drummond wasn't her mother, Race. Mrs. Drummond simply adopted The Flame a great many years ago from an orphanage outside of Harrisburg. Things were sort of sloppy in those days. The legal papers for adoption never went through properly. Besides which, Lu Roper, her guardian, used what he could get his hands on. But he was a gangster and a killer, and got shot before they could roast him. No, there was little money for The Flame – besides which, she didn't even fancy my taking an interest in her. At least, lately.' He looked toward the ceiling.

'Well—' I stroked my chin and feigned an indifference concerning The Flame I did not feel, 'she's a good kid, Myer. She did me a good turn. Get her another job – good pay. Make it look natural. I'll foot the bills.'

'Yeah—' His shrewd, sharp eyes danced. 'You should know her best, Race. Yet you seem to be the only man who ever knew her who thinks she's feeble minded. I warned you it wouldn't work.'

'What? She knows that I—'

'Maybe.' He shrugged. 'Read that.' He shoved a note across to me. It was not sealed. I took out the single folded sheet. It read simply enough.

'Race:—

 You must see me tonight. This is not a plea. Perhaps you owe me that much. I'll expect you at one o'clock exactly. Climb four flights – second door left – rear. Apt. 5-C.

 I am halfway between the girl and the woman you knew.

                                                THE FLAME.'

'I am halfway between the girl and the woman you knew.'

That final line was perfectly clear to me. I thought back to my first meeting with Florence Drummond. The wistful, child-like girl who might have been just out of boarding school. And then the times when she was the hard, cruel woman of the world, taking on ten years – her mind shrewd, her every action alert, her face stony and cold – a leader and organizer of criminals. The death of Lu Roper in the Pennsylvania station, back in the Tags of Death affair! The steady hand as she killed the man to save my life; her fight in the underworld, against the distorted brain of the man known as The Angel of the Underworld, in his mad, fantastic, yet almost real grasping for a single Power. Of the night she destroyed that collection of evidence that would set the streets of the lower city aflow with blood; of her disappearance into the maelstrom of a great city; her fight now to go straight.

I looked up at Rudolph Myer, and in my mind was the question: When The Flame wrote that note to me, did she love me – or did she hate me? And I—. Well – The Flame was her name. Given to her because men were attracted to her as the moth to a flame. And again my knowledge that to love The Flame – for a man to hold The Flame in his arms – was to die. Call it superstition if you like. But those who had held her had died. As well to call it a superstition to believe that if you look down the loaded end of a six-gun and press the trigger you're apt to be amazed at the results.

'You read this?' I asked, for Rudolph Myer was watching me closely.

'Why not?' he said. 'It was open. A confidence between lawyer and client. And if you seek legal advice, it is – Don't go.'

'Why?'

'Because,' he said very slowly, as he lit a cigar, 'The Flame is a very remarkable woman. You will either hold her in your arms and die, or—' He shrugged his shoulders. 'But after all that might be the way. A lovely woman! I am sometimes glad that the lure of the flesh does not appeal to me.'

'And how does she stand toward me now?' I wasn't paying much attention to Rudolph's chatter. Greed, I believed, was his single passion.

'I think – as she writes. Halfway between love and hate, with your presence there tonight to decide. But I've got something more important for you – or at least, something that may be important. Look here!' He placed his hand in his pocket, drew forth a long thick envelope and handed it across the table to me.

This time I had to break the seal. And inside the envelope were five one hundred dollar bills.

'From a client,' said Rudolph Myer. 'The fee for keeping a closed mouth and escorting an individual from – from one destination to another.'

'And the client?' I fingered the bills. They were new and fresh.

'Proposes to remain incognito.' The shoulders hunched again. 'But if you recognize his features – I can not prevent that. I might add,' he winked broadly at me, 'that I knew him at once. And to miss this opportunity might be the mistake of your life.'

'Might?'

'Yes – might. The thing might go no further, of course. There is that possibility. Your name is in his head. His task is a tremendous one. But there are times when even a man whose pen is weighty enough finds the gun a much surer weapon. At least, tonight he needs the service of a bodyguard.'

I fingered through the bills a moment, tucked them carefully into the envelope again and handed it back to Rudolph Myer.

'It's not enough,' I told him. 'I'll want a thousand for the job.'

No, I wasn't greedy, but I knew Rudolph Myer. I thought this client, who had consulted him, had paid more than that – told him to offer me more than that. Rudolph would certainly subtract a good commission for himself.

He saw my reasoning too, for he nodded his understanding as he waved away the proffered envelope.

'It's a small job, Race. I told him five hundred wasn't enough to interest you, but he wouldn't pay more. "I'm not thinking of the five hundred," he said, "and if Race Williams is the kind of a man I think he is and some have described him, neither will he. It's small work – half an hour by a man's side, with the chances a hundred to one that nothing will happen. I don't believe Williams is a grafter, like other private detectives in the city. But he may get out of this the biggest thing in his career. Myer, I could hire a half dozen strong armed men tonight – trusted men – for less than half that sum. Don't tell Williams this, but I'm paying five hundred dollars for the opportunity to look him straight in the eyes and read what's behind them – and judge."'

'Yeah?' Somehow I believed that Myer hadn't got much out of it for himself after all. 'What do you think?'

Myer hesitated a moment.

'I think this man could offer you certainly the biggest case of your career – and certainly too, if not the most hopeless one, the most dangerous. If I were you I'd cop off the five hundred, tip my hat to the gentleman in question and leave him flat. I'll be waiting here until you come back.'

'Here? Why?'

'Well—' said Myer, 'I'm acting for – shall I say "our" client, and expect to be paid my regular fee. I've engaged this table for the evening. There will be interesting people at the adjoining table – or so I understand. I think you'll be asked to deliver a message to one of them, and I shall report his reactions to that message.'

'Then what?' I was growing interested. Mysteries are all right in books, but you don't meet so many in real life. Besides, I like guys who give you straight talk. And when Myer didn't say anything, I said:

'I'm going to meet The Flame by one o'clock, you know.'

Rudolph Myer snapped out his watch.

'It's twenty minutes to eleven. You're to meet – er – our client at eleven. He promises to keep you only half an hour. You'll be back here before twelve, and on your way as soon after as you wish.'

I nodded at that. 'But – how come this man picks you to pick me? Why don't he come straight to me?'

'I'll tell you this much. More, I'd consider betraying the interest of a client; and at present it's to my best interest not to. This client came to me, spoke of my familiarity with the underworld, and asked me to deliver a message to a certain party.'

'And the party was—?'

'That you will probably learn later.'

'And the message?'

'That I didn't find out. The name of the party who was to be the recipient of that message was quite sufficient for me. Even though I didn't learn the contents of that message, my – or rather – our client was honest enough to tell me that the delivery of that message would gain the animosity of the greatest menace in the city of New York. I like money. But I like life better. I turned him down flat.' Rudolph Myer grinned across at me. 'But I did tell him there was only one man fool enough to take the chance. Of course, Race, I named you.'

'And then?'

'He walked about a bit and said, "I have thought of him. I have often thought of Williams." And half to himself, "But if it had to come out, I wonder how the papers and the people – and even the officials – might take it."'

'Tell me some more.'

'That is all. Name yourself a good price if you go on with the thing. But make no promises until you are sure of the circumstances. And get yourself a job chasing pickpockets before you decide to cross the man our client names.'

Now, if Rudolph Myer had not wanted me to mix myself up in this thing he couldn't have gone about it in a worse way. I may be fussy about the cases I take and don't take, and where the lack of money won't always keep me out of a job – the lack of danger might. When I get mixed up in a case I like things to happen.

When there was no more to come out of Myer I grabbed up my hat, was rather amazed at the place I was to meet my unknown client – which was in front of a drug store – and with a final sentence to Rudolph Myer, left the table.

'See you some more,' was all I said.

At the main street door of the dining room I met the head waiter, and parted company with a yellow boy that brought a smile to his face. And when you can buy a smile out of Russett, the head waiter at the Golden Dog, you've spent some real money.

'Who'll be the party at the next table to Mr Myer tonight?' I asked him. I don't invest money in smiles alone. I like talk.

'Tonight!' Russett looked down at the bill in his hand before he spoke. 'Tonight – and most every Monday night – who else but Mr. Gorgon – Mr. Joseph Gorgon.'

'Ah – yes,' was all I said. But I must have liked it, for I repeated that bit of eloquence, 'ah – yes' to myself again as I sought the street.

The Gorgons, for some time prominent in the city of New York, were suddenly shoving themselves into my life – or perhaps, to be more exact – I was shoving myself into their lives. But, any way you take it – things looked promising. That is, if you look on sudden and violent death as promising.

CHAPTER III: THE MAN OF VENGEANCE

I bought a paper as I rode down town in the subway. Things certainly were breaking wide open in our peaceful city. One more city magistrate had been forced to resign from office. The Grand Jury had indicted two others, and the name of a Supreme Court judge was featured pretty conspicuously in the latest investigation – featured with an indifference to a libel suit that bespoke great confidence on the part of the *Morning Globe*.

And once again on the first page was the picture of Joe Gorgon, with the caption below it. TWENTY YEARS AGO HE SOLD PEANUTS. TODAY DOES HE SELL JUDGESHIPS?

And through the story was a rehash of the several examinations of Joe Gorgon: The rise of the Gorgon brothers to fortune, if not exactly fame; how Joe Gorgon, back in the days when his name was Gorgonette, had pushed himself up to the leadership of the old Gorilla Bridge Gang, when his younger brother, Eddie, was running barefoot in the streets of New York.

The article went on more or less sarcastically about the unfortunate 'breaks that young Eddie Gorgon was getting in life' according to his brother Joe. Twice Eddie had actually been indicted for murder, and to the knowledge of the newspapers Eddie was questioned on half a dozen crimes of extreme violence. But how many times the hand of the law, hampered by criminal magistrates, crooked politics and the brotherly love of Joe Gorgon, had been stayed, was beyond the record of that newspaper.

'Investigations may come and magistrates may go, but the rule of Joe Gorgon in the city of New York is still with us. But where his brother, Eddie, is constantly in trouble, the breath of scandal has not blown upon Joe Gorgon – at least, not hard enough to blow him into a prison cell, where he undoubtedly belongs.'

That was headline stuff. I skipped to the column heads. One, at least, was good for a grin and reminded me of Eddie Gorgon's last laugh, about looking a Gorgon in the face and dying.

LATEST EAST SIDE GUN-MURDER RECALLS COLUMNIST'S STORY OF THREE GORGON BROTHERS.

And the reporter here had played upon his imagination a bit, but made a rather plausible story for the public at that. He dished up first the article written by a well known columnist comparing the Gorgons to the old myth, and Hawthorne's immortal tale of how Perseus was sent out by the wicked king to bring back to him the head of one of the Gorgons, three winged monsters with claws of bronze and serpents for hair. In this article the writer had nicely called the Gorgon brothers monsters with claws of gold, whose many hairs were the gangsters, crooked public servants and racketeers whom they controlled. But the old Greek myth said that to look a Gorgon in the face meant that the one who looked would turn to stone – or die.

And, continued the story, Eddie Gorgon had certainly stared long enough at Butch Fitzgerald, in an East Side dive, to fulfill the old myth. It is sufficient to say that Butch Fitzgerald had died – been shot to death on Delancey Street. Though Eddie Gorgon presented indisputable evidence that at the time he was visiting friends in New Bedford, Massachusetts, there are many who would bet their last nickel that Eddie Gorgon had a face, if not a hand, in the murder.

But the article, in conclusion, said that the enterprising columnist, not forgetting that the old myth and Hawthorne's tale consisted of three Gorgons, had gone out and not only hunted himself up another Gorgon brother, but had interviewed that brother, Professor Michelle Gorgon, a quiet man surrounded by his books. 'An artist and a scholar, whose collection of first prints is the envy and admiration of both amateur and professional collectors. If Michelle Gorgon feels the notoriety which his brothers have given his name, he keeps it well buried inside him. But it is rather well known that neither Joe nor Eddie often visit their brother's apartment atop one of Park Avenue's most pretentious dwellings.

'It would be a queer trick of fate if this educated and quiet, soft spoken Michelle Gorgon after all turned out to be the fine Italian hand that has guided his brothers up the ladder of doubtful fame. For, after all, to talk with Joe Gorgon leaves one with the impression that despite his rather forced smoothness of surface, his Gorilla days are not far behind him.'

Of course I had heard that story before. Just the fanaticism of a columnist, but maybe very real to Eddie Gorgon or his brother, Joe. After all, I've often said that crooks are like children at play. Anything that stimulates or satisfies their vanity is quickly grabbed at. Yep, I could very easily see them coddle to that Gorgon myth, rather than resent it. And certainly Eddie Gorgon had told me that to look at a Gorgon meant death. And certainly Eddie Gorgon had glared me down. But then, if I remember Hawthorne's tale of the GORGON'S HEAD, Perseus had used a sword, and I – well – I go in heavy for guns, and I'm still alive to tell you that a forty-four in the hands of a man who knows how and has the will to use it takes a lot of glaring down – even from a Gorgon. But I shrugged my shoulders, folded up my paper, and stepping out on the subway platform climbed to the street above.

I met my man – or rather, he met me. I was hardly out of the subway station before he walked straight up to me.

'Race Williams.' He eyed me closely from under his gray felt hat. Keen, sharp, hard eyes. But I gave him look for look. And I didn't know him. That is, I did and didn't. His face was familiar. But we'll simply say that he was about forty-five; clear, weather beaten skin; piercing, cold, but honest eyes – and the chin of a fighter. Not pugnacious, you understand more, determined, ambitious. A go-getter, and what I liked mostly – not a guy to be sidetracked from his purpose.

He had a way of talking straight talk.

'You will not, of course, presume on my identity. If you discover it, forget it. I shan't go into details about your qualifications. I believe in laying my hand on men personally. If I'm fooled, I want to fool myself. I don't want to blame any one but myself. You have been paid for this job tonight. If it is my pleasure, afterwards, I want you to forget this – this incident. That's agreeable, of course.'

'Suits me.' I was trying to place him, but couldn't. This much I felt. I had spotted that map in a daily paper – and not so long since either. But I shrugged my shoulders. If he wanted it strictly business he could have it his way.

He led me to a car, threw open the door and watched me climb in.

'I shall drive,' he said. 'You shall watch that we are not followed. I am putting a great confidence in you.'

'Okay!' was the best I gave him as he slid behind the wheel.

'You are not a very talkative man.'

'It's your racket.' I shrugged.

'Yes – my racket.' And he seemed to think aloud, as Rudolph Myer had described it. 'Entirely my racket.' And then, with a half turn of his head toward me, 'I am placing in your hands tonight the life of a man. Maybe, the life and honor of a great many men. What do you say to that?' He fairly snapped the last words at me. I didn't like it. I didn't like his attitude. He was treating me like an ordinary gunman – the gunman the papers sometimes painted me.

'You're trying to buy a lot of silence in New York for five hundred dollars,' was what I said to that.

He sort of jumped the car around the corner.

'If a man's honor is for sale, I could never raise a sufficient sum to bid for his silence against—' He hesitated, and then, 'I am not buying your silence, Mr. Williams. It is my understanding that it is not for sale. I'm paying you for your time – and your courage, which I understand is for sale. I back my judgment of character rather than my bank balance.' I think that he smiled. 'Perhaps it's less altruistic and laudable when I confess that my bank balance, compared with my judgment, is negligible. I must confess that I picked you first from – well – if not exactly hearsay, from the opinion of another.'

'Rudolph Myer.' I smiled a bit.

He smiled too. A hard sort of smile.

'You believe that?' he asked.

'Well – Myer told me so.'

'Quite so. I told him that.' He nodded, pulled the car up by the iron fence of St. – well – I'll just say, a well known city hospital, and leaving it there in the dark walked by my side to a small gate.

We passed slowly into the hospital, down the dimly lit corridor, ignored the elevator and climbed to the second floor. There another long corridor, a turn to the left, through a curtain into a dark alcove at the end – and a man who had been sitting beside a partly open door jumped to his feet, and with a hand to his hip swung and faced us.

I got a jolt out of that. The man, in plain clothes, was Detective Sergeant O'Rourke, of the New York City police.

'A police case.' I guess the words were jarred out of me, and probably not in an enthusiastic voice. The police don't often want me in with them – and I don't want them in with me. Fair is fair! Now, was it simply to identify a man that I was there? I turned to my guide and client. Let the police fight their own battles! They do everything to hamper mine. Five hundred dollars to identify a suspect that the police couldn't lay a finger to! Well – I'd tell this lad where he got off. But I didn't tell him. He was talking.

'Detective Sergeant O'Rourke,' he said very slowly, 'is off duty tonight. That is, off regular police duty.'

O'Rourke was all right. It wasn't working with him I objected to. In fact, I'd go a long way for O'Rourke any time – and had. And O'Rourke would go a long way for me – and maybe, after all, he had. But, as I said, I swallowed my hasty words. I would see what broke.

A white clad nurse opened a door for us, stepped quickly aside, sniffed once – then bowed and left the room. Another nurse, who was sitting by the side of the single bed, rose as we passed behind the screen and I looked at the man on the bed.

He was very old, I thought. His hair was gray. But it was the corrugated skin of his sunken cheeks, the deep lines that set off vividly the hollows that were his eyes. Emaciated parchment covered the single hand upon the white sheet; thick, purple ridges ran from his fingers to his wrist, to lose themselves in the sleeve of the snowy white hospital night shirt.

'You don't know that man?' my client asked me. And there was nothing of anxiety or hope in his voice. It was simply a question; an ordinary question he might ask any one. So he hadn't brought me there for the purpose of identification, for he hardly looked at me when I shook my head.

The old eyes opened. Burning, colorless orbs, except that they shone like two coals of fire. My unknown client stepped to the bed and took him by the hand. The old man clutched the hand frantically, dragging his other with a great effort from beneath the clothes. Eyes alight with both fear and fever burnt from those hollows as his fingers clutched that single strong hand in a grip of terror.

My client spoke.

'It is all right, my friend. I have come back as I promised. I have come to take you away from here. Take you where you'll be comfortable.' And as the eyes still burned steadily – terror and horror in their flaming depths, but no recognition – my client leaned down and barely whispered, 'Take you to a place where you will find safety – safety and vengeance.'

'Vengeance! That is it. That is it. That is what you promise me.' There was a decided foreign accent to the old man's words, that was not hidden by the thickness of his voice as he pulled himself up in the bed and kissed that hand he held over and over. 'Vengeance!' he said again. 'The soul of Rose Marie cries out for vengeance. It is years ago – many. They feared me then. I am not so young now. The Devil. Yes, that was it. They called me The Devil. And now—' And he fell back on the bed, muttering to himself 'prison' and 'sickness' and 'silence.' That was all I could understand.

It was at that moment that the nurse who had left the room came back with a doctor. An elderly gentleman who, from his dignity and bearing, was evidently the big medical shot at the hospital.

'I have waited for your return.' The doctor snapped out his watch as he spoke. 'Not simply to advise you, but to warn you. The patient will get better here, with proper care, the right nourishment, and – and less disturbances. If you move him there is the possibility – I'll say more – the gravest probability that he will die.' And at the request of my unknown client he dismissed the nurses.

'I understand and appreciate your interest.' My boss had some dignity of his own when he wished to use it. 'Let me assure you, Doctor, that you have done all that your professional ethics demand – even as your deepness of human feeling dictates. Let me assure you again that for this man to remain here means almost certain death. No.' He raised his hand. 'I have said more than I should, now.'

'But an ambulance, surely?'

My client hesitated a moment, and then:

'I am afraid not. Too many would know – and to drive it myself would create hospital talk. No.' And suddenly and abruptly, 'You will kindly ask the nurses to return and make the patient ready to travel.'

'But my dear sir, it is a question of human life, and—'

'You are not going to dispute my authority.' A hand went into his pocket and came out with a folded sheet of paper.

'No – no.' The doctor turned slightly sulky. 'I took the trouble to check you up more fully on that this evening from the district attorney's office.'

'From the district attorney, himself – personally?'

'No. From the district attorney's office.'

'You've been a fool.' My client exploded slightly for the first time, and then calmer, 'or perhaps I have. But let me assure you that the importance of the man being moved is now even graver. You will call the nurses – at once. Any delay on your part is hampering the cause of justice.'

'It's kidnaping,' the doctor mumbled. Looked again at the document which my client held in his hand before him, and finally went to the door.

'Kidnaping, certainly – but official kidnaping.' And as the nurses came into the room, 'You will do me the kindness, Doctor, to tell me just how long ago you telephoned to the—' with a glance at the nurses, 'officials.'

'Shortly. Perhaps an hour ago. The thing worried me. I—. Can't you wait a minute, sir? The whole thing is unseemly – inhuman – and without precedent in the hospital.'

'So – they suggested that you hold the man. Not by force, Doctor – not by official authority – but, let us say, by diplomacy.'

And he had the doctor. He squirmed beneath those eyes – the accusation in the man's face. But years and breeding will tell. Dignity won out and the doctor gave him eye for eye.

'And what if they did, sir? It was most natural. You are not hinting that the district attorney's office of New York City would enter into a conspiracy with me to hamper, as you put it, the cause of justice – or that they are not acting in this situation in good faith! I believe, sir, were it as you have hinted, the word would be "crooked".'

'Not "crooked", Doctor. Let us say "a hurt pride" – "a false ambition" – or perhaps just the word "politics". A word with you in private?'

And I was out of it. But the doctor was a more friendly man when, ten minutes later, we descended to the basement of the hospital in the slowly moving elevator, while Detective Sergeant O'Rourke held the limp, unconscious body of a little old man in his strong arms.

As we passed that main floor I breathed easier. Not in fear or even excitement, you understand. Perhaps in relief. For, after all, the game as I play it is always in the interest of my client. And the man who moved so quickly by the open steel work of the old elevator shaft door was John H. Holloway, an assistant district attorney of the city of New York.

CHAPTER IV: NOT BAD SHOOTING

Now, one thing seemed certain. My client was quite a lad, any way you look at it. If he put something over on the hospital and walked out with a patient he was a high class criminal, which I didn't for an instant believe – even if the presence of O'Rourke didn't eliminate such a possibility. Detective Sergeant O'Rourke was known in the city as 'The Honest Cop'. Which being an honest cop was the reason for his still being a sergeant, despite his recognized courage and ability that should have entitled him to an Inspector's shield.

But whoever my client was, he was a big shot in his own field. Big enough evidently to keep the district attorney's office from crossing him – at least, in an official capacity. I was getting a bit interested, also I was taking an interest in this lad's map again. It was familiar all right – but not from life, I thought again, but from the newspapers. The newspapers! I liked the taste of that and spun it around on my tongue. It would be worth recalling later.

There we were, out in the hospital grounds. My client leading, O'Rourke following, with the unconscious burden, and I bringing up the rear. Nothing exciting? Maybe not. Yet to me there was a feeling of tension in the air – pending disaster. This client of mine walked with such a steady, almost grim step of determination. If ever a lad had set himself one tough task to bring to a conclusion, this was the bozo.

Tall buildings all around us, the dull lights of the hospital behind us. The outline of the white coated doctor, who stood in the doorway rubbing his chin and moving his lips as if he talked. Nothing but the quiet, somber, and somewhat iodoformed air of a summer night in an orderly city hospital. Yet, for all that, I swung a gun from under a shoulder holster beneath my right arm and stuck it in my jacket pocket.

We made a little gate and came out on the street, perhaps half a block from where our car was, for we had entered by a different gate.

Right behind the car was another, a closed car – parked. We had to pass it to reach our own. It didn't have such a sinister appearance. My client plodded straight on, but O'Rourke slowed up a minute and spoke to me.

'Don't be too free and easy with them guns of yours now, Race. Tonight, it looks like diplomacy. That boat there behind our car is from the district attorney's office. I'd hate to be recognized on this job, but the city's rotten with racketeering graft, or—' And he jostled the human burden in his great arms as he pulled his slouch hat down over his eyes.

Did instinct warn me of danger as we turned on that sidewalk and started toward the car parked so close behind ours? No, I guess it wasn't just instinct. I'm always ready for danger, and there was something wrong about that car. I could see behind the wheel. No well trained police chauffeur sat straight and stiff, ready and waiting. No uniformed man leaned against the car or paced the sidewalk behind it.

One thing I did know. My client wasn't anxious to have the district attorney's office in on his little adventure tonight. And the district attorney's office would like very much to be in on it – that is, without seeming to force their presence. It would be simple then for a man to crouch low in the rear of that apparently deserted car, and then follow us. And my boss got the same idea, for he paused suddenly – waved O'Rourke to stand back, and turned toward that car.

A strange thing happened. The red rear light on that car went off – the brake light. You'd hardly have noticed it but for the fact that a moment before I had been looking aimlessly at the make of the car, wondering if it came to a dash through the city streets, if we'd be able to lose it.

The tiny rear light remained. The red brake light, just below it, had gone out. That meant one thing only. Some one crouched in the front of that car had released his foot or his hand from the brake pedal. Why?

An auto horn screeched suddenly, down the block behind us. A motor raced as a car started in second speed far down the street. O'Rourke turned quickly, facing the sudden screech of the siren. Of course my client reacted in the same manner as did O'Rourke. Just as he stretched out his hand and grasped the open window edge of the car, he straightened, turned his head and looked down the street.

But not me. Gangsters don't announce themselves in that style – at least, if they're making an attack. And if it were the police, the job to assure them of our respectability must come from my client or O'Rourke. As for me – I kept my eyes trained straight on that parked car; the front window. The siren and the racing motor would not distract my attention, if that was its purpose – and it was.

It happened. I won't say it was expected, or even what I was looking for. But then, I won't say it was unexpected. Not unexpected, because in plain words – I don't allow the unexpected to happen, if I can prevent it.

A face bobbed up in that car window. A dark coated arm shot above the half open glass, and the heavy bore of a nickel plated six-gun was smacked right against the side of my client's head. I saw the flashing eyes, the set chin, the thick sensuous lips of the gunman, and knew that the rod he held was, at that distance, heavy enough to blow my client's head to pieces. I knew too that the hand that held that gun was steady, and that the thick lips were cruel. My client turned his head suddenly and looked straight into the weapon which in the fraction of a second would carry death. And—. But why go into it?

I simply raised my right hand slightly, closed my finger upon the trigger and shot the gunman smack through the side of his head. Hard? Cold blooded? Little respect for life? Maybe. But after all, it didn't seem to me to be the time to argue the point with the would-be killer. Remember – I was some twenty feet from him – and shooting at an angle.

The gun crashed to the step of the car. The gunman jumped back. And as I ran around the rear of that car he tumbled to the street and lay still. It was a cinch that he had the door open behind him. It was a cinch too that the car which shot up the street was neither a police car nor that of attacking gangsters. It was simply the get-away car for the man who had attempted the life of my client – for it half slowed, swerved to avoid the body in the street, and as its headlight played upon the dead white face, shot away up the block.

I didn't run out and take pot shots at the fleeing car, but made sure that the gunman had been alone. I jerked out my pocket flash, and with that in one hand and my gun in the other, looked the car over. The gunman had been there alone – that is, as far as life was concerned. But in the back of the car lay the body of the chauffeur. The job was a quiet one. Some one had stuck a knife in his heart and twisted it around. There was a welt on his forehead, too, from a blackjack, the butt of a gun, or some other blunt instrument. He had been knocked out, then, before he was killed.

A brutal bit of work certainly. But maybe necessary from the gangster's point of view. You can't tell how long a guy will stay 'out' from a smack on the head. And the waiting killer couldn't know how long it would take for my client to appear on the street.

O'Rourke had laid his human burden against the stone wall surrounding the hospital and was taking a look-see into the car with me.

'It's Conway,' he said, and his voice shook slightly. 'A good boy. Only taken off his beat three weeks ago and assigned to the district attorney's office. Been married two months, on the strength of the promised promotion. It's a tough break for a guy – a tough break for a cop. And the lad you – you gave it to. Just another gangster. A lad that Joe Gorgon's gotten out more than once.'

'Joe Gorgon's some guy.' I put the flash back in my pocket. 'But I'd like to see him get his friend out of this mess.' And in what I think was justifiable pride, 'It wasn't a bad shot, O'Rourke.'

'No—' said O'Rourke, 'it wasn't. I turned just in time to see you give it to him. He had it coming.'

'You'll make a good witness when—' I straightened suddenly as a police whistle came from down the block. 'Do I have to explain this, and—'

'You won't have to worry this time, Race. Colonel—' he stopped suddenly. 'Our man's a big shot. He—. But it looks like all hell's going to break loose in the city. Like—'

'Our last case together. The Angel of the Underworld – and Power.' I helped him out.

'No.' O'Rourke shook his head. 'For that was a man who looked for power – who grasped it, too, in rather a fantastic way. But here is Power already established. Nothing fantastic. A reality of money and greed, tearing into the bowels of a great city. Influence – justice—'

'You're talking like a book,' I told him. 'Let's think of this present mess, and—'

But my client, who O'Rourke called Colonel had already broken into life. He came around from the off side of the car, where he no doubt had been examining the stiff and getting a justifiable and personal kick out of it. Anyway, he had snapped back into life. I saw him talking to O'Rourke just before the harness bull came up the street.

'Just a coincidence that you were here,' I heard him say, as he turned quickly from O'Rourke and picked up the unconscious old man from the grass beside the wall. 'And if that doesn't go over—' a moment's pause, and very slowly, 'But mine is an authority that will carry far.' And this time in determination, and nothing slow about it, 'To the Mayor of the city itself, if it must be – though notoriety is the last thing we wish. Foul murder has been—. Come!' He turned to me, and half staggered down the street with the sick man in his arms.

'I'll take the boy friend.' I nudged his arm. He seemed very shaky – his face very white. The old man was a load for him.

'No – no.' He half wiped at his forehead, jarring the man, who muttered something unintelligible. 'It's better so – much better so.' A pause as I opened the door of his car for him. 'I didn't think they'd go as far as that with me – with me.'

CHAPTER V: LET THE DEAD REST

O'Rourke was talking to the harness bull down the block when the Colonel took the wheel and despite my efforts to get him to let me handle the car, we pulled from the curb.

'It was horrible,' he said. 'He died – his face not a foot from mine. I saw the light go out of his eyes.'

'Pretty bit of shooting, eh?' I leaned back in the rear seat and braced the sick man's head against my shoulder. Personally, I didn't see anything to grumble about. Things had broken good – for him.

'It was awful – terrible.'

'Yeah?' This lad riled me. 'Let me tell you something, friend. You got the finest bit of shooting you'll ever get – at any price. And when I think of a job like that for five hundred smackers I could burst out crying.'

Maybe I was a bit sore. But then, wouldn't you be? I pride myself on doing my work well. And though there was nothing really remarkable about the shooting itself – the circumstances sort of being in my favor – it had taken quick thinking. The real artistic end of it was not in the bullet beside the gunman's ear, but in the fact that I was in a position to put that bullet there. Another lad – especially the sort of talent the Colonel would get from a private detective agency – would have needed a search warrant to find his gun at the right moment.

'It isn't you,' the Colonel said. 'But that he should die like that, my eyes on his eyes and—'

'Next time keep your eyes closed then,' I snapped at him.

'I'm not blaming you—' he started.

And that was enough. The old boy had let his head sink down so that it rested on my knees, which gave me a chance to lean forward and spill my stuff close to my client's ear.

'Let me tell you this. A split second's delay in that bit of gun-play, and – bing! there'd be some one to say "Doesn't the Colonel look natural?" You got me into it. You brought me along. If you were aiming on committing suicide, so that the insurance companies would call it homicide, you should have told me so.' And waxing just a bit sarcastic now, 'You misrepresented the job – or at least Myer did for you. You got your life saved and a lad knocked over for five hundred dollars.'

'I never expected it. Never thought they'd dare. It couldn't have been the old man, Giovoni, they wanted to kill. They couldn't have known. It must have been me. But – I'll pay you more. What you wish – what you charge for—'

'A flat rate for a corpse, eh? Well – I took the five hundred and I'll call it a day, unless unpleasant complications arise. It was your party – your fun – and you've got to foot the bills.'

'I shouldn't mind.' He was nodding his head now, as he narrowly missed a cruising taxi. 'I've been through it all – in the war. But here, in the city streets – sudden and violent death!'

'Then don't stick your face into the business end of strange guns,' I told him. I was a bit hot under the collar as I ducked another look back over my shoulder to be sure we weren't tailed.

You've got to admit I had a right to feel sore. Here I was, due for a pat on the back – or several pats for that matter, and this lad was crabbing and throwing the 'human life' stuff into my face. What did he want me to do? Break down and run to the district attorney's office with a confession? If ever a lad needed one good killing, that gunman was the lad. I started to rake it into the Colonel again – and stopped dead. It took his mind off his driving – at least I thought it did, for he dashed toward the curb and a pole – and finally stopped before a large house on an up-town side street. There was a name that stretched across between the entrances of two houses. I didn't get the lettering then.

The occupants of those two combined houses were more or less expecting us, for the Colonel had hardly climbed the stone steps and pressed the bell when two men in white coats came down the steps, bearing a stretcher. They made quick work of the old guy, Giovoni, in the back of the car. He was muttering now, and breathing sort of heavy. It didn't take a minute to place him on that stretcher and carry him inside.

I climbed out of the car and walked up and down a bit, as the Colonel followed them inside. There was a round shouldered, mustached gent who stood by the door as the stretcher bearers passed. You didn't need three guesses to tell you that he was a doctor – The Doctor.

From the sidewalk it was easy to lamp the name across the two buildings. ELROD'S PRIVATE SANITARIUM it read. But I didn't need that bit of information to wise me up that it was a Quack House.

I spent my time killing butts and looking the street over, but it was a cinch we hadn't been followed. Twenty minutes passed, and one of the white coated stretcher bearers came down the steps and asked me to go inside. I did that little thing. Entered the hall, turned left and stepped into a large waiting room, where the Colonel and the lad I had spotted for the boss sawbones were chewing the fat over a bottle which stood on a table. The white coated stretcher bearer closed the door, leaving himself on the outside.

'Mr. Williams – Doctor Elrod.' The Colonel smiled as the Doctor and I shook hands. Doctor Elrod was a harmless, slightly bent, calm little man, with the professional grin of confidence perpetually stamped on his good natured face. I passed him up and listened to the Colonel.

'I have told Doctor Elrod a little – just a little of our experience and strain of this evening. The Doctor was in the war with me.' The Colonel emptied his glass, lifted the bottle, poured himself out another hooker, shoved the bottle toward me and indicated a glass with his free hand.

'What's this for?' I looked at the liquor. It said 'Genuine Bourbon' on the outside of the bottle.

'It's been a trying evening,' said the Colonel, 'and I've been a little severe with you.' He shoved a glass across the table now. 'You'll need something to steady your nerves. I think I have – have further work for you.'

I shoved the bottle back across the table to him. He was the army man again, I thought. Severe – kindly – patronizing. I didn't like it. And I'm not a guy to nurse a thing. I gave him what was on my chest.

'You couldn't be severe with me,' I told him, and meant it. 'You're not big enough.' And letting him down on that, 'Nor is any one else. And I haven't any nerves. Some day maybe I'll drink with you. But liquor comes under the head of pleasure with me – not business. It's not that the stuff would bother me any,' I threw in, for I didn't like the way he nodded his head. 'It's the psychological effect. I like to feel that when a guy,' and I looked at the Doctor and toned my line down a bit, 'falls down, he didn't collapse through the neck of a bottle I'd been handling.'

'The Doctor's as right as they make them.' The Colonel nodded. 'We've discussed you together, Mr. Williams. Now – well – I wonder about those nerves. I'm sure the Doctor would like to—. Rather – in a professional way, it would be interesting to study your reactions to sudden – sudden danger.'

And Doctor Elrod had quickly and perhaps nervously stepped forward and clutched at my wrist. I could see the watch in his hand.

I jerked myself free and stepped back a bit. I didn't like it. I spoke my piece.

'The Doctor,' I said sarcastically, 'can experiment with rabbits and guinea pigs. I'm not playing either tonight. Science, Colonel, can not play a part in a man's – well – a man's guts. The Doctor wasn't there tonight to hold my hand or feel my pulse.' And suddenly, 'If you must have a demonstration—' I snatched up the bottle of liquor, poured the small glass full to the very brim, and sticking it on the back of my outstretched hand, held it so. Never a drop of the 'perfect stuff' fell to the floor to eat a hole in the rug.

'You can laugh that off,' I told him, 'if you're bent on some low scientific relief.'

And he did. I liked the look in the Colonel's eyes then. Maybe not admiration exactly – rather, call it good sportsmanship. But he only nodded, winked once at the Doctor, knocked off his drink, and taking me by the arm walked to the outer door.

'You will guard the patient well, Doc,' he threw over his shoulder. 'Your medical skill is not half as important as the secrecy of the man's whereabouts. I—' and turning suddenly to me, 'Good God! Williams – I never thought to tell you – to ask you. We might have been followed.'

'We were not followed,' I told him flat. 'You can kiss the book on that.'

'Ah – yes, yes.' And as we went down the steps and climbed into the car, 'I was upset, Williams. Very much upset. You could not have acted differently, of course. Indeed, if you had, I—'

'Would have been as stiff as a mackerel.' I finished for him. There was no use to let him minimize the part I had played.

'Yes – exactly.' He was thoughtful now. 'I have a family back in Washington; a responsibility which makes me think that perhaps—' and straightening as he climbed in behind the wheel and I shoved in along side of him, 'But I'll see the thing through to the end – and I apologize for my rudeness. My—. There!' He stretched out a hand and gripped mine. 'You saved my life tonight, and there are no two ways about that.'

'Okay—' I told him. 'Forget it. Let the dead rest. You paid for it. It was part of the job.' Funny. When you get credit you don't want it, and when you don't get it you're sore as a boil.

We drove for several blocks without a word. Then:

'I think I'll drive you home with me. I have a job that it's almost suicide to give a man.'

I smiled at him, and chirped:

'The suicide clause has run out on all my insurance policies. Besides which, I'm considered a bad risk, anyway, now. So—'

'Williams,' he said very slowly, 'in some respects you are a very remarkable man.'

Well – he wasn't the first one who had given me that line. But somehow I liked it. He didn't strike me as a guy who went in much for the old oil.

CHAPTER VI: A THOUSAND DOLLAR MESSAGE

His house proved the regulation brown stone front – just a copy of the private hospital affair, a shade closer to the center of things in the city.

He let us in with a key, carefully closed the heavy front door and pushed me quickly before him up the stairs to the floor above.

'I have taken this house for my stay in the city,' he said, as we climbed to the first landing. 'Just a man and his wife to look after me. An elderly, not over bright couple, who are long since in bed.'

A pause as we passed along a narrow hall, and he stood with his hand upon a door knob – a key turning the lock with his other hand.

'I think I shall take you quite a bit into my confidence, Williams. Yes – quite a bit. But come in.'

He threw open the door and we entered a comfortable living room facing on the street.

'You'll excuse me just a moment.' He walked to a door in the rear of that room, inserted a key in the lock and went on talking before unlocking it. 'Make yourself quite comfortable there. I have a—. Well – a man is waiting for me behind this door. One who might grow alarmed – greatly alarmed – if he heard us talking here. I must ease his mind.'

He spun the key, pushed the door open just far enough to admit his body, and slid himself through the narrow aperture, disappeared and—.

The door opened wide this time, and the Colonel was back in the living room again looking quickly around. He opened a closet, the key of which was in the lock; then without a word ducked quickly back into the bedroom again. For it was a bedroom. I could see the bed plainly now – an open window, too, across the room from it.

'What's the matter?' I spoke close to the door, my gun half drawn. Even the most particular movie director would have been satisfied with the perplexed, excited emotion his face was registering.

'Nothing – nothing. It's just my nerves, I guess.' The Colonel blocked my way for a moment, then with a jerk to his shoulders stood aside and pointed into the bedroom. 'He's gone,' he said. 'I've searched the room. There's—. And he used the lamp cord – the wiring – to lower himself to the alley.' He pointed excitedly to the length of wire that was twisted around the bed post and hung over the window-sill.

'Yes.' I saw that. The house was old – there was only one electric floor plug and that was across the room, so there was a generous length of wire needed to reach the lamp. The wire was made of heavy rubber. I leaned out the window and pulled it in. Offhand, I'd say that it reached within – well – ten feet of the ground. Not much of a drop for a man of average height. But my flash, cutting a ray of light into the blackness below, disclosed the fact that whoever had left that room was certainly not lying on the flagging below. I ran the light along the alley a bit, and found it as empty as a country constable's helmet.

'It's your show.' I turned to the Colonel. 'It wasn't much of a place to lock a guy up in anyway, unless he was hog tied – which—'

'There was no man a prisoner in this room.' He had a way of pushing his chin forward and his neck back when he hit his dignity. 'That is, an involuntary prisoner.' He amended his last statement slightly. 'Poor – poor, unfortunate creature.'

'I don't want to stick my nose into your affairs,' I said, 'But I don't go in for riddles either. Wise me up or drop the subject. I don't care which.'

'The man in this room,' the Colonel broke in, 'was the man who brought me the information about Giovoni – the old man in the hospital. It was worth his life if certain parties discovered it.'

'Oh. A squealer – a rat. A—'

'No.' The Colonel shook his head. 'Not in that sense, for I paid him nothing. I would trust you with his name, but that would be breaking a confidence. I promised him secrecy. He came here of his own accord, a withered, sickly, drug addict. He had no money, no friends, and he would not tell me who sent him. At one time he was useful to a certain – a certain trio of criminals. And then the drug. Once a relief from the nightmare of his life; now, to still the craving of his body – and the fear of his mind. He had been useful before; now he feared that he was to be killed. Not because he had ever betrayed these murderers, but because he knew something. Something that he was afraid they might read in his eyes, or that he might let slip in a drug-crazed moment. Yes, he feared death – murder.'

'Sure. Some one was going to put him on the spot.' I nodded. It may have been a rather new and unique procedure to the Colonel, but to me it was an old racket – a natural one. A member of a gang no longer able to hold up his end. Body and mind weakened, and the gang afraid that if he was dragged over the coals at police headquarters – denied his drug – he would talk.

But the Colonel was talking again.

'Yes – on the spot. That's why he told me what he did. He wanted protection; protection I could have given him. Tomorrow I would have put him where they could not find him. In fear that they would get him, he came to me. Now – in fear that he was not safe here, he has lost himself in a great city.'

'It all depends on who THEY are,' I suggested. This running up and down an alley after another guy's hat was beginning to lose its interest.

'Ah!' The Colonel stroked his chin, pushed me into the living room, indicated a chair and sat down across from me. I took the cigar he offered me, shoved it into my pocket, and lit a cigarette.

'Mr. Williams,' the Colonel said very slowly, as he drummed on the arm of his chair, 'would you like to see the city purged of vice and crime – racketeers, and most of all, corrupt officials – crooked magistrates. Yes, and even members of the higher courts perhaps? For the hand of graft can find its way into the pockets of the mighty. It is bad indeed when greed and ambition enter the same brain.'

He was so serious that I tried not to smile as he went on.

'You are a good citizen – a staunch citizen. Wouldn't you like to feel that you played an important part in cleansing New York's cesspool – wouldn't you?'

'At the right price?' I looked straight at him.

His dignity hit him again. The outward chin – the backward neck. I killed his words.

'Before you go on with your altruistic oration, let me spill a bit of chatter.' I leaned forward and gave him what was on my chest. 'I daresay there isn't a big shoe manufacturer who wouldn't want to see every child in the country wear a pair of his shoes – but he don't give them away. Henry Ford would like to see every man, woman and child sporting a Ford coupe – but he don't give them away. It's business with them. When these men are called upon to give to charity, they make out a check. You never saw John D. Rockefeller alleviate the suffering of the unemployed by giving each one of them ten gallons of gas. But he has given away more money for charitable purposes than any man in the country.

'Now – if you want a man hunter, I'm open for such work. And I expect to get paid for it. If a contractor builds a small house he gets a small sum. If he builds an apartment––. Well – that's me. I'll take small pay for a small job and big pay for a big job. If you're raising a fund to help clean up the city and want me, as a good citizen, to contribute to it – all right. I'll give you a check, and expect to see ninety per cent of the money go back into that cesspool you were speaking so elegantly about.

'I'm no amateur detective. I'm a hard working, private investigator. I won't take a job that isn't straight and don't interest me. I may be just a common gunman in your estimation, but I'm a big shot in my own – my own line. At least, others think enough of me to pay me well. I don't know your racket, but I know mine. There. That's a chestful for me, but it's gospel. At least I've made myself clear – that I'm not doubling for a Saint Patrick and driving the snakes out of New York.'

'Yes,' he said slowly, 'you've made yourself clear. But I expect to pay you. You're a very conceited man, Race Williams.' And more slowly even, 'Undoubtedly a very courageous one also. The man I will want you to face – the man I will want you to deliver a message to is a man who has crushed every one who has stood in his way, politically or financially – and though I can not prove it, I believe that behind him is the greatest villain – the greatest murderer – the––. Here!' He took a folded bit of paper and threw it into my lap.

'Just what price does a big shot like you want, to deliver that message to Joe Gorgon? Stop!' His hand went up as I read the single line on the paper. 'The message means nothing to you. But, as God is my judge, I believe that Joe Gorgon would murder, without a moment's hesitation, the man who delivered that message to him – if he believed, as he must believe, that that man was familiar with its significance.'

'Just hand this to Joe Gorgon – nothing more?'

'No. Repeat the message to him tonight. Say it as if you were giving him some information. Say it loud enough for his friends to hear. Oh – they won't understand it. Then report to me his reactions to the message.'

'Don't you think I'll be blasted right then and there?' I couldn't help but be sarcastic.

'No, not then and there. Not you – after what I saw tonight.' And his face paled slightly, in memory of the dead gunman, I thought.

'And that's all you want me to do? When is the message to be delivered?'

'At once – at the Golden Dog. Mr. Myer is keeping the table for your return.'

I looked down at the message again. It seemed simple enough. Cryptic, perhaps. I was thinking of my knocking Eddie Gorgon about, just for amusement. Now – well – this little bit of by-play would only accentuate the animosity of the Gorgons. Besides which, I'd be paid for a hatred that I had already acquired under the head of pleasure.

'And that ends my job?' I asked.

'I hope not. If things are as I believe, I will be able to employ you in the biggest case of your career. The anger of the Gorgons won't matter to you then. It will already be established after you deliver—. But here. It is not fair – it is not right. You are a man whose business brings him into queer places; the blackness of dismal, deserted city streets in the late hours. Come! Give me back the message. I forget that you saved my life tonight.'

But I closed my fist about that bit of paper as I came to my feet.

'Friend,' I told him, 'I'll hurl this message into the teeth of the devil himself for one thousand dollars.'

'Yes, yes – I believe that you would.' And suddenly, 'Done! For after all it is a great step toward a glorious accomplishment. Here.' He took my hand, pressed it a moment and then dragged open a drawer.

I counted the money and pushed it into my pocket. He went on.

'There will be five hundred more if you do it knowingly! As if the message means as much to you as I hope it will to Joe Gorgon – or the man behind Joe Gorgon. The Third Gorgon. Doctor Michelle Gorgon.'

'And that's the whole show?' I asked him, as we left the room and descended the stairs together.

'No. I would like, if possible, to know where Joe Gorgon goes after you deliver that message.'

'I can arrange that.' I was thinking of my assistant, Jerry. A product of the underworld – a boy I could always count on.

'Good!' said the Colonel. 'Telephone me here, then.' And he gave me his phone number. 'And, Mr. Williams – would you be willing to,' and he smiled, 'at a price, of course, work for me? Work for the overthrow of the Gorgon brothers? Work silently and secretly, to get evidence against them – rid the city of their presence? A big job, a hard job, and a job that must be accomplished before the opposing political forces appeal to the governor for another investigation of the racketeering. One man is responsible for it all – you know that.'

'You mean Joe Gorgon?' I nodded. Yes, I thought I knew that.

'No—' he said. 'I mean Doctor Michelle Gorgon. Neither Joe Gorgon nor his racketeers take a step that is an important step without its having been ordered by his brother, Doctor Michelle Gorgon. And Doctor Michelle Gorgon buys judgeships, has crooked officials appointed, and fixes juries. Yes, he is the brains that directs the hands of murderers.'

'I've heard that too. But I don't know if I fully believe it.'

'Well – fully believe it now. For if you don't, you too may be caught in—. But, there – I can count on you.'

'Yes.' I tossed my cigarette out in the street, for we stood on the steps of the house now. 'But just how do you fit?'

'That—. Well – it might break a confidence. But be sure that I hold the interests of the people, the honest public officials; the citizens who would wish to see their own forces – their own elected officials, their own law and order clean out the menace before outsiders are brought in.'

'Why not come down to cases?' I looked at him under the brim of the slouch hat I jerked onto my head.

'Yes, yes.' He seemed to think a moment. And then suddenly gripping my hand, 'Deliver this message. Then I'll see if you still feel – feel that I have a right to ask you to work with me, since they will suspect – yes, know – that you have taken sides with the enemy.'

I grinned at that one. But I saw his point, even if it did sound silly.

'All right,' I said simply. 'You want to see if I still have the stomach for it. You've been reading your Hawthorne again. THE GORGON'S HEAD. To look a Gorgon in the face is to die! And it would be useless for you to come to terms with a man who is about to do that. Yep – you can't make a deal with a dead man.'

And before he could find an answer to that one I was down the steps, after flinging my final line.

'Joe Gorgon will get your message – and it's the easiest thousand dollars I ever earned.'

And I was gone. Swinging down the street – breathing deeply of the cool summer air.

When I finally found a taxi I looked again at the message I still held in my hand, stamping the words into my mind.

'THE DEVIL IS UNCHAINED,' read the message. And I wondered. Was the devil the little sick old man, Giovoni, we had left at Elrod's Private Sanitarium? And if so, would he throw fear into the heart of a Gorgon – the city's biggest racketeer? Joe Gorgon. Absurd? Maybe. But I remembered once, when the accusing words of a ten year old child sent a shrewd, intelligent man to the chair for murder. 'Out of the mouths of babes and old men come—' And though it don't seem to be quoted just right, it might make a deal of sense at that.

CHAPTER VII: A BIT OF MURDER

But I didn't drive straight to the Golden Dog, for I had plenty of time to put on my act for Joe Gorgon and still meet The Flame. I went smack to the Morning Globe office. I knew the man who'd be on the desk at that hour and I'd done a bit of thinking.

They work fast in newspaper offices. They have to. I was turned loose in the morgue, with a man who knew his pictures. Ten minutes later I was staring into the face of the man known as the Colonel. That set chin and those determined eyes stood out in that photo. There was quite a bit to read about him. His war record; his marriage; and his wonderful accomplishments in the army intelligence department.

His full name was Charles Halsey McBride, and he had graduated from college with a deputy Police Commissioner of the city of New York. A commissioner who was taking his job seriously and raising hell all up and down the line, for he was a wealthy man who had the money to do it with and even the backing of the Commissioner – at least, that was the rumor.

'Sure,' said the newsman, chewing what he must have thought was a cigarette. 'McBride's done some good work, though he blew up in the Chicago investigation. Too much notoriety, I guess, though he never made a squawk. There was talk of the government sending him into New York, but on account of his friendship with the Deputy Commissioner it might make hard feelings. At present, I think he's got a leave of absence, though there's a rumor he's working secretly for Washington on the Power Trust. It's unconfirmed though, and we don't know where he is. But city rackets are out of his line. Trusts – big business – mergers – and oil investigations are his meat. He's got a brain in his head, but you can't sit down in a courtroom behind locked doors and hang murders on lads who have witnesses kidnaped or killed – intimidate witness, who won't dare talk – and hire others to do their killing; others, who don't know for sure who really paid them to do—' The phone rang. 'But McBride isn't the lad for that kind of job. It doesn't call for sharp questions from behind a desk.'

'No,' I said, 'it doesn't.' But I was rather thoughtful at that, as I left the chap to his phone and departed.

Colonel McBride! Here was a lad who didn't intend to sit behind his desk and listen to big guys explain their positions through the mouths of clever and high paid lawyers. This lad had guts – and sense, I thought, when he took me on. But it was a cinch he hadn't come on orders from

Washington. If he had, it would have been in the papers. Then, who was behind him? Certainly he wasn't doing this on his own initiative – besides, Detective Sergeant O'Rourke was taking orders from him – and what's more, Colonel McBride had authority. But – he had said that he wished to clean up the city – the Gorgon brothers – before outside authority stepped in. It might be possible that he was working for the Commissioner himself – privately and secretly, until the time to strike came – building up an evidence that would stand the gaff of a jury trial.

And I didn't feel that I had broken a confidence by looking him up. He knew who he was hiring. I had a right to know for whom I was working. A lad in my position can't tell what might be put over on him. I wouldn't even put it past certain officials to try and frame me. But – I had other things to think of. Jerry, the boy who worked for me, would have to be reached and be outside the Golden Dog to tail Joe Gorgon.

After giving Jerry a jingle at my apartment, I drove up town and entered the Golden Dog at exactly seven minutes after twelve o'clock.

Rudolph Myer had something under the table that wasn't ginger ale. He was pounding nervously on the table, but bobbed up straight as I entered the room.

And at the next table was Joe Gorgon with four other men. His great bulk was shoved far back in the chair, his knees crossed, his thumbs stuck in the armholes of his vest, and a cigar protruding from the corner of his mouth. The other four men I knew. One was a ward leader, called Jamison, and beside him my little playmate, Eddie Gorgon. The other two guys' faces were familiar. One, a fairly well known lawyer – and the other, well – just a face. I couldn't place the name of either.

Joe Gorgon didn't see me. His mind was suddenly occupied by the entrance of Billy Riley, one of the three biggest political leaders in the city.

I heard Gorgon call to Riley as he passed the table, and what's more, Riley was nearer to Gorgon than to me. It was a cinch that Riley heard him. It was a cinch too that Riley didn't want to hear him. Like most of us, Riley liked to claim the acquaintance of well-known men – influential men. But Joe Gorgon was getting himself just a bit too well known. Yet Riley didn't have the stomach to turn him down flat. Money flowed from Joe Gorgon's pocket like from the United States mint – and Riley had a fondness for money.

Jamison, the ward leader, looked up quickly – questioningly, from Joe Gorgon to Billy Riley. I read, just as well as Joe Gorgon did, what was in his mind. Perhaps Jamison didn't word it as the book of etiquette might, but in his own way Jamison sensed that Joe Gorgon was getting 'the cut' direct.

'Riley! Riley!' And Joe Gorgon was on his feet with a rapidity that was astounding in one of his size. Two steps he took, and clutched Riley by the arm. Riley turned, and his smile of greeting was nervous – strained.

'Join us for a few minutes.' Joe Gorgon made no effort to keep the conversation private. But there was nothing in his voice but hearty good fellowship.

'Can't, Joe.' And Riley nearly choked over the name. A moment's hesitation, and when Joe Gorgon still held his arm but said nothing, Riley stammered, 'Got a party waiting—' and then something low.

'Nonsense. Everybody's got time for Joe Gorgon.' And Joe clapped a great hand down on Riley's shoulder. 'Friends of mine always have time to join me.' A moment's pause, and again, 'Always – while they're friends.' And the last just reached me as I passed to the next table and flopped down beside Rudolph Myer. But I did see that Billy Riley wasn't so big but that he took the chair Joe Gorgon pushed out for him.

Eddie Gorgon looked around and saw me. His sullen eyes flashed into life – his left hand gripped the table cloth – his right hand slipped beneath his armpit. There was a cut on the side of his mouth. I liked that. I smiled over at him. The hot blood went to his head. He came suddenly to his feet and stood so.

An outside influence had come between Eddie Gorgon and me. The head waiter called out. A heavy-set waiter laid down a tray and hurried to the table of Joe Gorgon. But the running, shabby little form was there before him. An emaciated, wild-eyed man, twitching, gripping fingers that stretched quickly out as he fell to his knees and clutched Joe Gorgon by the coat. Joe Gorgon looked from the crouching figure to his brother, Eddie. Eddie nodded, turned quickly and disappeared toward the bar.

The kneeling man cried out.

'Don't let them kill me! Don't let them kill me! Don't have me—'

And Joe Gorgon was on his feet. His two hands stretched out and gripped the kneeling man by the collar. Seemingly without effort he jerked him to his feet, held him so – tightly, and stared into that drawn, unshaven face.

I knew the lad. A harmless, half crazy little snowbird in the underworld. Just 'Toney' they called him. If he had any other name I hadn't heard it. But he spoke no more. Whether the grip on his collar was so tight as to cut off his speech, or whether the glaring, staring narrow eyes of Joe Gorgon cowed him I couldn't judge. It was all over in a matter of seconds. Joe Gorgon thrust the man roughly into the hands of two waiters, with the single statement:

'Some bum, I guess. I don't know him.' But his eyes followed the whining, crouching, helpless body as the two waiters half carried, half dragged him from the room. And, somehow I wondered if the fantastic newspaper story of the Gorgon myth had – had—. But Joe Gorgon was seated now, and Rudolph Myer was talking – saying the thing that was on my mind.

'Did you see him stare at that man? Did you see the glare in his eyes? A superstitious lot, these warm-blooded people. I tell you, Race, Joe Gorgon was marking that poor unfortunate for death. Not consciously, perhaps – just that he half believes in his own power. Did you hear what the man said? His final words? "Don't have me – killed" was what he would have said. I saw it in his eyes, before fear kept the words from his lips. And Joe Gorgon. He's a man, Race – a brute without pity – without fear – without nerves. See him now. No emotion of any kind.'

'Well—' I came to my feet, grinning at Myer. 'We'll see if we can't knock a bit of emotion into him.'

'You're not – not now!' Myer half leaned forward to clutch at my coat, thought better of it and watched me cross to the other table. I made a hit too as I approached. Billy Riley smiled uncertainly. Jamison gulped his drink. Joe Gorgon turned and looked lazily up at me.

'You – Gorgon!' I flipped a finger against Joe's chest. 'I want a word with you.'

'And you are—?' He pretended not to know me.

'Williams – Race Williams.' I fell into his humor. I didn't intend to cross him or rile him. I wanted him in an open, happy mood. I wanted the emotions, if any, that came from my message to start from scratch.

'Williams?' He seemed to think, then grinned at the others. 'Not the boy detective?'

'Exactly. It's nice, Mr. Gorgon, to think that you remember me. I'm flattered indeed.' And I grinned like a school boy who has gulped his cake in one swallow and not burst before the horrified gaze of the principal.

Joe Gorgon frowned slightly. I wasn't one to take anybody's lip, and Joe Gorgon knew it. Or if he didn't know it, Eddie must have told him. Then I guess his own conceit got the better of him, and he figured out that he and Eddie were two different people and that I'd think twice before I tried that game on him. For his frown disappeared and he smiled, his huge head bobbing up and down.

'Well—' he looked around to see that the others appreciated his high class humor, 'let us hear what you have to say. Surely I shouldn't mind. Already one of your breed – at least, one who sells his information to the highest bidder – has—. But, come – don't stand there grinning like an ape.'

'I've got a message for you.' And I leaned down suddenly, twisted my lips slightly, and shot the words at him like any gangster, with deep secret meaning behind them.

'Joe Gorgon,' I said, 'The Devil is Unchained.'

Now, there didn't seem to me much sense in the words, or much for a man to get gaga over. But they paid a grand to deliver and therefore must carry some weight. And they did. If ever a lad got a thousand dollars' worth out of a message, that lad was my client. Those words wiped the smile off Joe Gorgon's face like you'd run a vacuum cleaner over it. There was a sudden quick flash of bright red to his heavy jowls, that gave place almost at once to a dull white. His right hand stretched out and gripped at the table. He half came to his feet, and sank back again – reached for his untasted cup of coffee, slopped it over his vest, set it down again, and gave the sickest smile that ever a gangster pulled off.

'All right, Mr. Joe Gorgon.' I guess there was elation in my voice. 'Laugh that one off – or play the look of death, and—' I stopped dead and jerked erect. From outside on the street came a shot; another – half a dozen in quick succession, with the rapidity of machine gun action. People jumped to their feet. I stepped back from the table. Billy Riley had taken Joe Gorgon by the arm. People were going toward the door. The head waiter was trying to tell the customers in a high pitched voice that a tire had exploded, and urging them to keep their seats or they'd give the place a bad name. A bad name for the Golden Dog! Not bad comedy, that.

Some one pushed the head waiter in the stomach and walked out the door. Others hesitated. The music broke into life, and I stepped out on the street. A few buildings down the block a tiny crowd had gathered. They were standing around something on the sidewalk. A harness bull was ordering them back. Another was running up the street, and a man in his shirt sleeves stood in a doorway, wildly blowing a police whistle.

From the small private entrance to the Golden Dog came two men. Joe Gorgon walked by himself, though the man beside him – Billy Riley – held his arm. I saw Gorgon wave him aside as he climbed into a taxi, but I saw something else with a grin of satisfaction. Another taxi pulled suddenly from the curb down the street. Through the back window a hand waved to me. Like his namesake in the papers, my boy – Jerry – was also on the job.

I moved toward the ever thickening crowd, pushed my way by a couple of people, grunted as the back of a man half blocked my vision, ran smack into a policeman, and got a look at the dead man on the sidewalk.

It was Toney, the little sleigh rider who had sought Joe Gorgon's protection a short fifteen minutes before. And now – well – he had more holes in him than a sieve. He must have had his back to the gun, and spun when he fell. For plainly in the bright light from the jeweler's window his face stood out. There was no doubt of his identity.

CHAPTER VIII: FOOTSTEPS ON THE STAIRS

Well – that was that. A man had looked a Gorgon in the face and died – or a Gorgon had looked a man in the face and the man had died. Take it any way you wish. Not much loss to the community certainly. Toney had been a shrewd, clever little gangster. A sure shot to gay-cat a job or listen to conversations, or get his nose in wastepaper baskets before the city wagons carted them away. Now – I shrugged my shoulders. It was a cinch that Toney had outlived his usefulness to Joe Gorgon, and his weakening mind and body had become a danger. Anyway, it don't take much reasoning to say that he was dead. No one would deny that.

I pushed back through the crowd, walked up the street, paused before a United Cigar store and snapped my fingers. What had Joe Gorgon said to me there in the Golden Dog? Words that hadn't seemed to make sense at the time. He had said, 'Let us hear what you have to say. Surely I shouldn't mind. Already one of your breed, at least one who sells his information to the highest bidder, has—' And then he broke off. What did he mean? Toney – Toney was selling information to some one – and Eddie Gorgon had left the restaurant to—. Well – Toney had died within a very few minutes. Toney, who had begged Joe Gorgon not to kill him. Toney, a drug addict who—

I shrugged my shoulders. There are times when I don't need a brick building to fall on my head to wise me up to things. And if my thought wasn't true, there was no harm in it. But – I went straight into the cigar store, stepped into a pay telephone booth, and parting with a nickel called the number Colonel McBride had given me.

He answered almost at once. I told him how well his money was spent, and of the tumble Joe Gorgon had taken out of his message.

'By the way,' I said casually, 'the man – the one that dropped out of your bedroom window tonight. He didn't happen to be a shabby little Italian, not too young, a worn blue suit, yellow brown shoes, a gray flannel shirt none too clean, no tie – and answering to the name "Toney"?'

'I – why do you ask?' But the answer to my question was in the tone of his voice.

'Because,' I said, 'you were right about his fearing death. He was killed tonight. Less than five minutes ago, half a block from the Golden Dog.' And I told him about Toney coming to the table.

'He was mad – drug crazed – to go to Joe Gorgon. You think—'

'You can't get a jury to convict on a thought,' I told him. 'But Eddie Gorgon left his brother's table a few minutes before the murder occurred.'

'Good God! that is terrible – terrible.'

'This old man – Giovoni. How important is he to you?'

'He means, perhaps everything – at least, at present. I have a man in Italy investigating the—' and he bit that off. 'But Giovoni is safe. Let me know as soon as you can where Joe Gorgon went when he received that message.'

'Yeah. Want me to keep an eye on Giovoni?'

'No, no – that would be the worst thing you could do. Don't go near El – that place. The man is perfectly safe now.'

Silence on both sides – then he said:

'That's all!'

And we both hung up.

It lacked a half hour before I was to meet The Flame – but then, perhaps the hour had been suggested by Rudolph Myer because of my other engagement, which he had planned. But I was anxious to get back to my apartment and hear Jerry's report as to where Joe Gorgon went in such a hurry.

I won't say I reasoned things out as I rode down town in the taxi. Not me. Reason only too often confuses, especially when you've got little to reason on – not reason with. But thoughts would flash through my mind, and I let them swing along.

The message I had delivered to Joe Gorgon was a knock-out, certainly. No one would deny that. The biggest racketeer in the city had come very close to taking a nose dive. A few words had brought fear to the man who 'feared nothing'. Perhaps it was that he feared nothing physically, but the mental reaction to my few words was—

I tapped on the window. We were perhaps a block and a half from The Flame's address. The taxi pulled to the curb. I stepped out and paid the lad off. One thing in my mind. Was The Flame with me or against me when she sent that note? Anyway, I'd look the block over before meeting her. Not very trusting? Maybe not. Oh – I'll admit it's nice, noble, and high minded to have a trust in your fellow man – or fellow woman for that matter. But it's not exactly healthy in my line of work.

The main street was more or less deserted – just one car. But it stood out in such a neighborhood. A high priced, high powered boat, with a uniformed chauffeur at the wheel. Still, a guy gets used to seeing stranger things than that on the city streets. I passed it up, turned the corner and entered the side street, where according to the number The Flame should live.

Perhaps I got a gulp when I walked past her number. It was a shabby, dreary looking apartment house. Rather hard to connect The Flame up with it. You sort of seemed to think of her with all that was beautiful and, maybe, expensive.

So far I spotted nothing that looked like a trap. I peered into doorways, paced down past half a dozen houses, turned quickly, walked straight to The Flame's apartment house, found the door unlocked – so ignoring the bells, slid into the dimly lit lower hall and started up those stairs.

Started up – and stopped dead. And just when I stopped, or just after I stopped – feet a floor above stopped. Not imagination, that. Not—

I went on. Slowly mounting the stairs. Good sense of hearing – instinct? Call it what you will, but something told me that feet preceded me up those stairs – feet that kept a flight ahead of me. Feet that had been coming down when mine started up, and now stepped carefully back up those stairs – in tune with my own footfalls.

I didn't stop to listen any more. I listened without stopping. Some of my steps I made heavy, some I made light. Sometimes I increased my speed, and it threw the other lad – whoever he was – off his stride. He couldn't keep step with me, and two or three times I heard him plainly on the flight above. He was still steadily increasing his speed as I advanced, and I don't believe I gained a step on him.

Then I tried a light whistle – started an air – broke off in the middle of it and heard his running feet stop, and again try to step with mine.

All right. While he retreated there was no danger. He didn't intend to attack me, then. So I started up the third flight, ever watching above for glaring eyes or a threatening form. But none came. Distinctly I heard old boards creak down that hall. A dull sound as if a foot struck against wood, and a door closed as I reached the landing, turned on the fourth floor and mounted the final flight.

In the dim light I made out apartment 5-C. Listened just a moment, before I knocked on the door. I shrugged my shoulders. After all, it wasn't an inviting neighborhood. There was no reason to connect up the slinking, retreating figure with my visit to The Flame. No reason at all. Yet – I did.

The door opened and I saw her again. There was a hesitancy in her manner which was new to The Flame.

'You – Race. You're early. Just a minute.' She closed the door quickly as I entered, left me – so – in the small hall, slipped quickly down the narrow passage and disappeared from view.

I followed her of course – quickly – silently. She slipped through worn, old curtains, and almost ran across the room. But I reached the curtains in time to see her sweep a bundle of bank notes from the table into a drawer – and something else. Something that glittered, and clinked in the drawer before it snapped shut.

'Now—' She turned, stopped dead when she saw that I was already in the room, half glanced toward the table, shrugged her shoulders and smiled.

'Same old trust in The Flame, eh, Race? Well – what do you think of my diggings – my outfit – the reward of honesty?' And in a mock sort of sincerity, 'Honesty – the one thing that the rich leave for the poor to fatten on.'

I didn't like her mood, so I waited and looked the room over. Things were old and worn, but the place was spotless. The skirt and jacket she wore might have passed for a fashion picture until she got near the light. Then the cheapness of the material forced itself on you in spite of the aristocratic carriage. And as I looked at her I thought of her final sentence in that note. Certainly she was halfway between the girl and the woman.

as nearly as I can figure it out, that you spent to keep my brain straight and my body—' She shrugged her shoulders, stepped back and looked at me.

'You don't like that line, do you?'

'No—' I said, 'I don't. It's cheap stuff. And by "a criminal lawyer" you don't by any chance refer to Rudolph Myer?'

She laughed. But she ignored my question.

'I've tasted the virtue of poverty and didn't find it palatable. Now — I'm through. I've a chance. I'm going to take it.' She looked straight up into my eyes, and those brown glims of hers were brilliant. 'And I'm not starting over. I'm not building up something. I'm to meet a mind that is like mine — brilliant, quick, active. I'm starting in again. Starting in at the top of the ladder.'

'Yeah?' I pulled a butt, stuck a match to the end of it and took a chestful of smoke. 'I'm sure glad, Florence, that you're not overmodest about your own abilities.' And as she just looked at me, 'Well' — you didn't bring me here to walk up and down my vest and dig your heels in at each button, did you?' And when she still played the looking game — the brilliance fading from her eyes and a shrewd, speculative cunning creeping in, I forgot the 'you catch more flies with molasses than with vinegar' and opened up like a valedictorian.

'Kid,' I told her, 'you've got guts or you haven't got guts. There are no two ways about that. You can't play the game if you can't stand the gaff. I—' And suddenly, seeing the woman of the night — the Girl with the Criminal Mind — creep into her face, I lost my nerve or made a stab at bringing to the surface the good that I knew — or maybe felt — or maybe only thought — was in The Flame. 'Look here, Florence'. 'I'll play along with you. We'll meet occasionally. We'll have dinner together. We'll come up here afterwards and—'

'And you'll explain to me the virtues of honest living?' She snapped in on me, and the eyes blazed again. 'I've told you I'm through. I am giving you a break. After tonight — 'The Flame lives again. The Girl with the Criminal Mind takes her place on Broadway. And the police and the rotten officials, who thought my reign was over through lack of guts — not being able to stand the gaff — will bow and scrape again.'

I reached out and placed my hands upon her shoulders. She swung slightly, raised those small delicate hands with the quick, living fingers toward me — swayed once, I thought — and maybe only thought — then with a quick jerk she tore my hands from her shoulders.

A simple movement mine — a quick movement hers. But — well — we all have our moments. Weak or strong, I won't try to lay a name to that one. I'll simply say that The Flame was a very beautiful woman. I'll simply say that experience had taught me that to love The Flame was to die, and for a split second I didn't care. Maybe she lost her chance; maybe I'm wrong, and I simply lost mine. Maybe, again, I stood on the brink of disaster and

413

was saved. Anyway, she spoke her piece. I'll give her credit for saying what was on her mind, so that there was no misunderstanding it.

'Race,' she said, 'you can't help me and you can't hurt me. But I can hurt you. I want one favor from you – one last thing I'll ask. You've often said you owe me something.'

'Yes,' I told her very seriously, 'I do. If ever you need me I'll come to you.' I stood watching her now as I finished very slowly. 'Even knowing that I may be walking to – into—– Well – I'll come. That much you can count on. I'll come.'

'And come armed?' There was a sneer in her voice.

'Yes – and come armed,' I told her. 'A guy may be willing to be a fool, but draws the line at being a damned fool.'

'Well—' she said, 'I'm willing to cry quits. You owe me nothing. I owe you nothing. Just one promise I want. That – for two—' and stopping and looking at my face, 'that for two weeks you'll enter into no case – no matter what the inducement – no matter what the incentive.'

I thought a moment, and then:

'I'm crossing your plans – your crooked plans?'

'Yes,' she said very slowly, 'you're crossing my plans – my crooked plans.'

Another moment of thought. A straight look into those brown, hard eyes, and I gave her a direct answer.

'I won't do it.' That was flat. My ethics may be warped, my ideas twisted, but there's no guy who can say I don't like my own game, and don't play that game as I see it.

'All right?' she snapped suddenly. 'You've had your warning – or rather, should I say – your notice.' And with the slightest twist to those thin, delicate lips, 'I suppose you still think – or still say – you'll come to me when I need you – if I need you.'

I looked her smack in the eyes.

'I still say I'll come to you if you need me – if you send for me.' And very slowly, 'And I still say that I'll come armed.'

'That's a threat.' She jerked up her chin.

'You can take it as you please. I'll pay my debt. For no man can tell when The Flame will be a good citizen – a fine woman. But no man can tell either when—'

'She'd lead Race Williams to – to his death, eh? That's what you want to say, isn't it?'

'Maybe.' I guess my smile was sort of dead. I won't say that I loved The Flame. But I will say that I admired her. Certainly, if she was built to do great wrong, she might just as well be built to do great good. You see, the dual personality doesn't fit in with my practical nature. I always sort of look on it as synonymous with 'two faced'. That is, that it's an outward change, and doesn't really take place in the individual – but only in the

mind of some one who knows the individual. In plain words, there were times when I thought The Flame was all bad, and the good – that youthful, innocent sparkle – was put on to fool others. But fair is fair. There were times also when I felt that The Flame was really all good, and the hard, cruel face – that went with the woman of the night – was put on to hide the real good in her.

There we were, facing each other in that small, sparsely furnished room. The Flame with her back to the curtain by the window, and me with my back against a bare wall, my right hand thrust indifferently into a jacket pocket.

The Flame bit her lip, and emotions you couldn't lay a finger to ran over her beautiful face. I didn't bite my lip. I waited. A long minute passed – feet seemed to creak on the worn stairs outside – steal along the hall and stop by the door of apartment 5-C. Just seemed to, you understand. That don't mean it was nerves on my part. I haven't any. But I have got a keen pair of ears. Ears that weren't sure that the sounds – the faint, almost imperceptible sounds they caught – weren't from the natural, but eerie creakings of an old structure. Let us just say that I liked my back against the wall.

The Flame seemed to be listening too. After a bit, she spoke quickly and hurriedly.

'I've played the game as I've seen the game. I've given you your chance. Now—' she spread out her hands, and her voice was raised – at least, it was shriller, 'you stand in my way, Race Williams, and I'll – I'll – by God! I'll crush you.'

There was a curve to the corner of her mouth, a narrowness to those brown eyes from which the sparkle of youth was entirely missing. There was almost a sneer in her words – but certainly there was a threat to them.

'All right,' I told her. 'We've played the game together and we've played it as opponents. I haven't squawked yet, and I won't squawk now. I—'

And I broke off suddenly. A knock, not too loud and not too low, upon the outside apartment door.

I swung quickly, half stepped toward that door – and stopped.

'Don't!' The Flame clutched me by the arm. 'I – It's better not to have it known you came here. Please! The fire-escape. It's the top floor – a single flight to the roof. Please, Race. It means more than you think, to me.'

'Then it's not war yet.' I smiled at her now, took a few steps forward, threw back the tiny curtain, flipped the window open higher, and took a last glance over my shoulder at The Flame, who stood there uncertain – at least, seemingly uncertain – for it's hard to believe that The Flame could be uncertain about anything. So I'll just say that she stood there in the center of the room.

With half an eye on that small, aristocratic right hand of hers with the long tapering fingers, I threw up a leg and placed a foot on the window sill – and stepped back into the room again. I was looking straight into the sneering eyes and twisted lips of the gangster, Eddie Gorgon – but, much worse, I was also looking straight into the mean, snubbed nose of a forty-five automatic.

As I stepped back, Eddie Gorgon quickly slipped through the window I had so accommodatingly raised for him, and stood with a look of triumphant hatred on his face.

CHAPTER X: THE TRAP IS SPRUNG

There was no excuse for it. I wasn't proud of myself at that moment. Certainly I didn't trust The Flame, but at the same time I didn't expect – even if she did decide to hate me – that she'd shove me on the spot so quickly. Truth is truth. I didn't trust The Flame. Hadn't trusted her when I came. But a mind like The Flame's doesn't lead a man to a trap in her own apartment. And the reason why isn't 'good ethics' or even 'good sportsmanship'. It's just common sense. Even in a city where gang murders have ceased to be front page news it's not quite safe to decorate your own room with a corpse.

Now, as I say, the thing was surprising – but not unexpected. And maybe 'unexpected' is not the correct word there. Maybe it might be a better choice of words to say that I was simply not unprepared for such an emergency. If I happened to be looking down the nose of Eddie Gorgon's gun, my gun was drawing a bead some place along about the center of Eddie Gorgon's stomach. And my finger too was tightening upon the trigger as I raised my jacket pocket slightly and picked out the spot where any ordinary man, according to Gray's Anatomy, would wear his heart.

I won't mince words. And I won't say that there aren't heroes in the pictures, and in real life too, for that matter, who can knock a gun out of a man's hand even when shooting from a jacket pocket. I can do it myself – probably could have done it right then. But 'probably' isn't enough. And where a bullet through Eddie's arm or leg would have been noble and high minded, it wouldn't have interfered with the quick pressure of his finger upon the trigger of his automatic.

No. I know gangsters. I knew Eddie Gorgon. There was death in those bloodshot eyes. Bum hooch in them too, but I didn't get that then – and his twisted lips were cut and raw, where I'd leaned on him a few hours before.

But truth is truth. I was going to kill Eddie Gorgon – kill him before he killed me. Nothing saved him now but his tongue, which licked at his lips

– and his eyes, that gloated before he talked. He was a lad who liked to shoot a little bull before he shot an enemy – especially when he had that enemy covered.

I wasn't worried. A single roar, a prayer for the dead, and the stiff on the slab in the morgue would be labeled EDDIE GORGON. Eddie Gorgon, the racketeer who had beaten his last rap. I like to see a lad go out with a gun in his hand – a gun gripped tightly in a dead hand. It has a soothing effect on a jury.

Eddie didn't say, 'Throw up your hands.' He was lucky there. Those simple words would have been the same as the medical examiner's signature on his death certificate, though he didn't know that.

'So,' and there was a sort of snap to Eddie's lips when he spoke, 'I was right about the dame and you. She's to step out again – so you're back. And I was right about myself too. Me – Eddie Gorgon. There ain't a guy living who's mussed up Eddie Gorgon and lived to tell about it. The boys will know who done you in. The boys'll know why. They'll say it took a Gorgon to step in and smack a gun against Race Williams's chest and blow hell out of him.' The grin went, the gun came forward more menacingly. His face shot closer to mine, and his whisky sodden breath made halitosis seem like a rare perfume from the Orient.

'Don't move!' Eddie almost spat the words as I half drew my face back. 'I want you to know the truth before you go out. I've not only taken your life but I've taken your dame. The Flame won't be sorry for the message she sent me that you were coming here. She'll be Big Time now. No one will bother Eddie Gorgon's woman.' And with a sneer or a leer – or just a twisted pan, call it what you will, Eddie sputtered on. 'She's a neat piece of goods, Race – but they don't come too good for Eddie Gorgon. A guy's life and a guy's woman! Well – it ain't so bad for a bust in the mouth when I wasn't looking. I guess, Race—'

My finger tightened upon the trigger, hesitated a moment, and I shot the words through the side of my mouth at The Flame.

'Is what this rat says true? I don't mind the trap so much.' I half shrugged my shoulders and glued my eyes on his finger that held the trigger of the automatic. 'But I do think you might have grabbed yourself off a pickpocket, or even a stool-pigeon. Besides which—'

'All right – now,' Eddie Gorgon horned in. I had seen the sign in his face while I talked. Just the lust to kill, that so many gangsters work up with dope, or hatred, or passion – but which Eddie Gorgon didn't need to work much in order to bring it to the surface. He was an alley rat; a great guy to hide behind an ash can and shoot a lad in the back. A great guy to—

But no more words. He was a killer. And my finger started to close upon the trigger of my gun. Just a sudden tightening, and—

I held back, my finger half closed, my eyes glued on Eddie's gun. The Flame spoke.

'He lies, of course. Eddie, drop that gun!' There was the single movement of The Flame's right hand, a flash of nickel and ivory, and the girl had jammed a gun against the racketeer's ribs. There was nothing of fear or desperation or hysteria in her action or her words. Just that single movement – and the slightest grunt from Eddie. He didn't have to look down to know. And what's more, he didn't look down.

The sudden impulse to raise my left hand and twist the gun from his died without a movement. I'll give Eddie credit for that much. He wasn't the movie villain, who, at the first disturbance or even suggestion to look up, lets his gun be taken from him. It takes time, you know, to raise your hand and grab a gun – a second or two. And a second or two may not be much time in life, but it is an eternity in death. Even a novice can close his finger upon a gun trigger in a second. But as I said, Eddie knew his stuff. He saw the danger – from me more than The Flame, and cried out his warning.

'Don't you make a move, Race, or I'll plug ya. The girl ain't got the guts to put a Gorgon on the spot. She ain't—'

'Drop your gun, Eddie.' The Flame's voice was hard and cold. 'The Flame fears neither man nor devil, and that last, I guess, throws in a Gorgon. I'd rub you out like a dirty mark. Where do you get that stuff about me? Where—'

'You! What did you bring me here for? Why did you send for me?' His gun dropped from close to my head to my chest, and flattened there. 'Why, I was smack on the fire-escape.' And half incredulous – half pleading, 'What's eatin' ya, kid? Didn't I set you up handsome? Didn't I get you rocks and—'

'You! You talk too much. You bought my mind, not—' She laughed. 'The Flame your woman! Drop that gun.'

'Not me.' Eddie Gorgon jabbed the gun harder against my chest. 'You ain't still got a yen for this yellow dick, eh? I drop my gun, get knocked over, and you send me a wreath!'

'Talk sense, Eddie.' The Flame seemed to try to reason now. 'Suppose I did send for you. I didn't expect you to come up here to my rooms; to have the police drag me over the coals just when I'm ready to step out again. And, you—'

'Me!' said Eddie. 'They can't do nothing to me. I'm a Gorgon. Why, kid, I have an alibi that—'

'Would roast me,' she cut in, and her voice was hard again. 'I tell you, Eddie, if you press that trigger—'

A soft voice broke in from the little hallway.

'Race Williams will shoot suddenly from his right jacket pocket, and be a very much honoured newspaper hero.' And as my finger half closed, the mellow voice went on, 'No, no – Williams. I am sure things should be done more amicably. The gun, Eddie – on the floor – at once!' And in a sudden

change of tone that was as metallic as a cheap phonograph, 'Drop that gun – Edward!'

Eddie's gun smacked to the floor, like you'd knocked it from his hand with a crowbar. Mine came from my pocket and pounded against the chest of Eddie Gorgon. For the time I had forgotten that knock upon the door. Now – I didn't turn. I didn't need to. Some one stood in the doorway, and that some one undoubtedly had me covered.

CHAPTER XI: THE THIRD GORGON

The voice behind me went on – soft, persuasive, almost like a woman's, but with a sinister meaning to it that belied the words themselves.

'That's a good boy – a fine boy. You are impetuous, Eddie – and I am afraid you have been drinking. You will stand back – so – close to the wall.' Eddie moved as if a hand directed him. 'And you, Florence, will lay your gun there upon the table. Mr. Williams, of course, will keep his. It is his trade. I am afraid he is not so susceptible to suggestion. But I am sure he is not so religiously fanatical as to object if I paraphrase even so great a book as the Bible. "Those that live by the sword shall perish by the sword." Which, I suppose, if we had a more modern version would go for guns too.'

Feet moved now – slow moving feet. Both Eddie Gorgon and The Flame were unarmed. Eddie Gorgon was leaning against the wall, breathing heavily, but not watching me. Rather, the slow moving feet – and I could just see the shadow cast upon the floor.

I swung quickly and faced the man. Maybe I knew – and maybe I didn't. Here was the man who hobnobbed with greatness. Here was the man whom a few felt, and fewer mentioned, as the secret power of Joe Gorgon. The man who called judges by their first names, and political leaders by their last. One who had written books on civil and criminal law, though he had never practiced law. But I'll give you the eyeful as I caught it.

In the first place, he was not armed. There was a thin, Malacca cane over his left arm, a gray glove upon his right hand, and its mate clutched in the fingers of that hand. His muffler, slightly open at the neck, disclosed the whiteness of a boiled shirt. And his braided trouser legs added assurance to the impression that he was in evening dress. But his face got you, and the eyes in that face held you – held you in spite of the shadow thrown on them by his black felt hat.

His face was as white as marble, and his eyes such a deep dark blue that at first glance you'd almost think they were black. There was not a single bit of color in his face and his nose was sharp and straight, his lips a single, thin red line. His eyes didn't blink when they looked at me. They just regarded me fixedly; too alive to be compared to glass. Watched me from between heavy lashes that didn't flicker. The whole outline of his face and perfection of his features couldn't be compared to a portrait because of the unnatural whiteness of his skin – and the living fire of his eyes.

I hadn't seen him often – few saw him often. And his picture never graced the papers. But somehow I knew that I was looking into the granite-like countenance of the Third Gorgon, Doctor Michelle Gorgon.

None of us spoke for a moment. Eddie leaned against the wall and stared at the man who, through some freak of Nature, was his brother. The Flame looked at him too, studied him, I think. Maybe I was wrong, but I did get the impression that she had never seen him before – despite the fact that he had called her Florence.

And the Third Gorgon spoke.

'I am not sure,' he said very slowly, 'but I feel that at least one of you, and perhaps all of you, owe me a debt of gratitude. But we'll skip that. It savors too much of our criminal courts. Plenty of knowledge but not enough evidence.' He paused a moment, sniffed at the air, let those flickerless eyes rest on his brother, and half bowed to me.

'We must bow to you, Williams, as the physical dominance in this room – perhaps, thanks to me. Fine wines warm a man's blood and make more active his brain. Poor liquor, even when taken by another, nauseates me. I know you, of course – have read about you and seen your picture in the papers. I understand you do not go in for murder.' A moment's pause, and his head cocked sideways as he put those eyes on me. 'That – that is true?'

'It depends on what you call murder.' Somehow I couldn't feel exactly at ease with this guy.

He shook his head.

'Ah, no. No – not at all. My ideas of murder are not entirely expounded in my books. They are private thoughts and opinions which must be withheld for the public good. And I will not say murder in the legal sense, for if I've followed your exploits correctly you have not obtained your ethics from the criminal code.'

'Well – get to the point. What's on your chest?'

His thin lips dropped slightly, and just for the fraction of a second those eyelids flickered before he spoke.

'You disappoint me, Williams. You really disappoint me.' And with a sudden snap, 'I am speaking of the putrid condition of the air, caused by the presence of my brother. Will you stand in the way of his departure? In plain words – he is unarmed. Are you bent on murdering him?'

'There's the police.' Maybe I was sparring for time. 'He attempted my life, you know.'

'Come – come, my dear Williams.' Doctor Gorgon seemed annoyed, and then he smiled – only his lips moving. 'But you joke.' He turned and

looked at The Flame. He stepped close to her. For a minute he stood so –
then his hand went beneath his coat, and despite the fact that he was
sideways to me I half raised my gun. But when he withdrew his hand it
held nothing more dangerous than a pair of nose glasses attached to a very
thin black ribbon.

He placed the glasses upon his nose, leaned forward and stooped – for
he was close to a head above The Flame. Then he raised his hand and
removed his hat.

If The Flame resented his attitude she did not show it. I saw her little
head bob up – those brown eyes, hard and cold, stare back into his. Then
he turned to Eddie Gorgon, half impatiently.

'You may go, Eddie.' And with a raise of his hand as Eddie started to
say something sulkily, 'Tut – tut, boy. He shan't kill you, you know. And
if he intended to, he would hardly do it in my presence.' And when Eddie
still held his ground, 'That will be all, Edward. Not by the window, you
scamp.' He crossed the room quickly this time, patted Eddie on the back as
he half pushed him toward the door. 'I am sure that Williams realizes there
is a lady present and will not object to your leaving us.'

I didn't object. Maybe I realized there would have been nothing to do.
That is, nothing to do but lay a chunk of lead in Eddie's carcass or call the
police. But one thing I did get, and that was that Eddie Gorgon feared that
affected 'Edward' of his brother's more than even my gun.

'Affected'. Well – I'll withdraw that word. No— Damn it. One thing
that Doctor Gorgon got over to me, even if I don't get it over to others,
was his sincerity – or perhaps, just his own belief in himself. He sure was
the white haired boy, though now that his hat was off, there was just the
glimmer of gray in the jet blackness of his hair. The first few strands of it,
which hung near his forehead.

The Flame looked quickly up at me as Doctor Gorgon followed his
brother to the hall. I smiled back at her. Not a pleasant smile, maybe – but
one of confidence. There was a peculiar look in her eyes. A questioning,
uncertain look.

'Well—' she said at length – while the hollow, whispered, inaudible
tones of conversation came from the little hall, 'why don't you say
something? Don't stand there looking accusingly at me. I—. What right
have you? Why—. Well – say something!'

And I did.

'He travels farthest who travels alone.' I did a bit of quoting myself, like
the Doctor. 'And that probably goes for traveling fastest too. Your friend,
the Doctor, noticed the gun in my pocket, which covered his brother.' And
after a pause, 'I wonder if you did, and if you were protecting Eddie or
me.'

'You think I brought you here to – to your death? Well – why don't you
say so?'

'Should I?' I shrugged my shoulders. 'Is it necessary? Rudolph Myer said I was the only one who took you for being weak minded. At least, Eddie was here – said you sent for him, and you didn't deny it. That he muffed the works by acting too soon, and – perhaps – talking too much, isn't your fault. But you certainly picked yourself a fine little playmate, when you did decide to—'

'Race,' she said very slowly, 'you and I can't fool ourselves any longer. At least, I can't fool myself. I've never posed as being good. Quite the contrary. To hear you talk you'd think I had suddenly changed. Just one thing. You don't believe I led you into a trap tonight?'

I sort of laughed.

'What else could I—'

'The same old song.' She came close to me, put those glims on me. 'Always accusing – never believing. Come—' I let her get close to me, let her place her hands on my shoulders – even let her slip them back about my neck and onto the back of my head.

'Come—' she said again, 'you don't believe it. Yes or no.'

'Yes—' I said, 'I do believe it. You can't come the "kid act" on me any longer. You can't—'

'You fool,' she whispered hoarsely, looking toward the door. 'I never ate my heart out because I couldn't get you – have you. I could have had you whenever I wanted you – you or any other man. But I wanted you to want me, too. Don't you see? I didn't want you like the others. I could always have made you – can make you love me. Because – well – look here.'

That little body of hers was close to me. Warm breath was on my cheeks, hands pressed the back of my head. I just grinned down at her, lifted my hands slowly to take hers from about my neck – and she did it. One quick movement; one quick jerk – lips that touched mine; a breath that seemed to go deep into my body; a burning in my forehead; a quick, dizzy rush of blood – and her eyes, flaming and soft, and—. Oh, hell – it happened. Just for a second – maybe a split second – I crushed The Flame to me, held her so – then thrust her from me, flinging her half across the room. A chair turned, spun a moment, and toppled to the floor.

CHAPTER XII: QUEER TALK

Had I lost my head? I don't know. Why lie about such things? Yet—. Maybe I hadn't been carried away by her presence—. But The Flame was beautiful; The Flame was—. Why shouldn't a man hold a beautiful woman?

I leaned against the wall and looked at her. She was smiling at me. What was in her mind? Here was a wonderful woman. No – something else struck me then. The line I had just pulled on her. 'He travels farthest who travels alone.' And she was coming across the room to me.

The woman! No – the woman was gone now. It was the girl, Florence Dummond. The sparkle of youth in her eyes – a softness – a realness that made me rub my hand across my glims and blink.

'You're right, Race. Maybe, after all—' She stopped dead, and straightened. The hall door closed. Soft, slow feet – and Doctor Michelle Gorgon was in the room.

He ignored my presence completely – went straight to Florence, lifted both her hands in his and stared at her without a word. And The Flame looked back at him. Nothing of anger, just a straight look from clear deep eyes. No color came into her cheeks; no embarrassment to those great brown orbs.

'So you are The Flame. The Girl with the Criminal Mind. Do you know that you are a very fortunate young lady? Very fortunate indeed. I think that I could like you a great deal. I—'

'Doctor Gorgon,' I crossed the room, 'Miss Drummond has had a very trying evening as it is. I think perhaps we will call it a night.'

He was very tall. He turned his head slowly and looked back over his shoulder at me. For some time he regarded me fixedly with those unblinking blue eyes.

There was nothing of anger in them – nothing even of hostility. More annoying for lack of either, I guess. He looked like a scientist studying some bug. And, damn it all – what's more, he looked natural. Not as if he was affecting it, but as if he really meant it. As if he were trying to be – well – not polite – say, tolerant – and hide from me the fact that he regarded himself very much my superior.

'I wonder,' he said at length, 'if you know exactly who I am.'

'Yes—' I said, 'I do. And it don't mean a thing to me. And I wonder if you know exactly who I am and—'

'And that it will mean quite a bit to me?' I think that he smiled – at least, his lips parted. 'I am afraid, Race Williams, that you mean very little to me. To my brothers – yes. Their blood is hot, and the brute strength of the beast is dominant in them. But I am very sure that in you I would find little to worry about. I am afraid I have little interest in the physical. I abhor, as I said, firearms – shrink most appallingly from violence, and physical exertion of any kind incapacitates me for days. You don't go in for murder, you see – and where I must bow most humbly to your physical superiority, it wouldn't really interest me personally. No – you can not mean anything to me. You—' he paused a moment, and I saw his eyes rest upon the overturned chair, move quickly from The Flame to me, and then he said, 'Well – perhaps you may mean something to me, but not in the sense you believe.'

He certainly could talk. There were no two ways about that. And what's more, he could read what was on my mind – or, maybe, written upon my face. Anyway, I did have it in my mind to show him something of the physical that would surprise him. He looked big and strong enough not to be playing the woman.

'Really, Williams, I am sure you do not intend to use physical violence – at least, in the presence of a lady. You—'

'Doctor,' I told him, 'you may be hot stuff with Eddie and a few other bar flies. And you may stand in with certain big men – and it may even be true what's hinted; that you – well – that you're the Third Gorgon that I'd always looked on as sort of an underworld myth until you stared Eddie down. But if you are the big guy behind the political racket, the judgeship scandal racket, and even the murder racket – well – drop Miss Drummond's hands, or I'll throw you down the stairs.'

He didn't get mad – which made me just a bit madder.

'I wonder if you would,' he said slowly. 'It might be interesting and—' He shook his head. 'No – no, we anticipate things.' But he dropped The Flame's hands.

'I think you had better go, Race,' The Flame said.

'Not me,' I told her. 'I'll wait until the Doctor decides to make an "out" – which will be soon, I'm sure.'

'Don't be a fool.' But there was more of interest in The Flame's face than anger. 'I – I won't need you.'

'Good God!' I didn't like that 'I kissed you and got you' look in her eyes and I let her know it. 'I wasn't thinking of you – but myself,' I told her. Which was true. And I looked at Michelle Gorgon when I got off that last crack – and wondered. Yep, here was a lad I didn't understand, and what I don't understand I don't like.

'But Doctor Gorgon has something to say to me. Something that I'd like very much to hear.' And she didn't put those glims of hers on him like she did when she wanted to swing a lad her way. She looked him straight in the eyes – clear, interested – more than interested. Deeply anxious.

'In his way Williams is right.' Doctor Gorgon nodded condescendingly. 'We must see life – or even death – through the brain that is given us. I do not think, dear lady, that I need say more than I have already said to you. I will not say that you have been foolish, for I do not know the thoughts that that mind of yours might carry. Certainly, not what others might read there. But let us say that if you are not correcting an error, you are making a change of plans.' He walked to the table where the money The Flame had tossed there for me still laid. He ran his fingers through the bills, looked at The Flame, jerked open the drawer, and without hesitation lifted out some bills and some jewelry – held them out, so, to The Flame.

'This is all?' he asked.

'No—' The Flame pointed to the ring on her finger.

'I see,' he said. 'I will take it. No – just throw it there on the table. You understand, even though it all comes from the same treasury, it is better that it is returned to the – the sender. For it was his thought, you see – and I am afraid, not exactly a business one.'

'The money on the table,' The Flame spoke very slowly, 'belongs to Mr. Williams.'

'Seven hundred dollars.' This time Michelle Gorgon's eyebrows moved slightly. 'Well – comparisons might be odious. This is yours, Mr. Williams?' He held the bills out to me.

I was just about to knock them from his hand when The Flame spoke.

'Surely, Race,' she said. 'If later events prove unpleasant to you, you're not planning on throwing that in my face.'

I took the money and shoved it into my pocket. I didn't like the present racket. I felt stupid standing there with the gun in my hand, but I was still standing there – and stupid or not stupid, I shoved that gun into my jacket pocket and still kept my hand on it.

Very methodically Michelle Gorgon searched through the drawer of that table, found an envelope, studied its size a moment, then put the money and the jewelry into it, added something from his own wallet and carefully sealed it. Then he crossed again to The Flame and started in with his line as he looked steadily at her and ignored me.

'You are a very beautiful woman – that is, to any man. To me, now – if your limbs were twisted things; your face a hideous death mask, you would still be a very beautiful woman – if those eyes remained untouched. The eyes, my dear, are the peepholes to the inner beauty of the mind. I wonder if you understand me. Understand why I verbally maim your beautiful body.'

'I think I do,' said The Flame. 'I think – I do.'

'And you do not mind?'

'No—' she said. 'I do not mind.'

'I am not playing at the magician, then. The mystery of whose tricks are known only to himself.'

'No—' she said. 'I understand you fully.'

I had stood enough of being made monkeys out of, and I let them know it.

'Well – I don't understand,' I said. 'And now, Doctor, you and I are on our way. If you don't believe in the physical, here's your chance.'

He turned, thrust the envelope toward me and said:

'I wonder if you would care to return this envelope to its rightful owner.'

'No—' said The Flame. 'He'd – he'd kill him, or be killed.'

'I think not,' said Michelle Gorgon. 'But even so,' he shrugged his shoulders, 'the one is a cross which I am beginning unwillingly to bear – and the other—' he looked at me hard now – and I glared back at him, 'a threatening menace on the horizon. Maybe an imaginary menace,' and turning from me to The Flame – and back to me again, 'perhaps a real one whom—' A pause, and suddenly, before I could get a word in, 'Will you, or will you not return these – this envelope to its sender.'

I took the envelope and shoved it carelessly into my pocket.

'Yes—' I said, 'I will. Who is the man?'

'Eddie Gorgon.' There was a slight chuckle. The arm that I had half raised, to bring down on his shoulder was caught, and I was walking from the room with Doctor Michelle Gorgon.

I didn't break away. I didn't twist my arm free and hurl him across the room. Somehow I felt silly enough. Somehow, kid like and foolish like, I wanted to carry the thing off as well as he did. Here was a lad who talked and talked, and said nothing. Or did he say a lot, and I didn't have the wits to get it? But he never threatened – never raised his voice in anger. Treated me in rather good natured contempt – and, to myself, I wondered if we'd been alone would it have been the same. Wouldn't I have just hauled off and cracked him one, or—? But there's not much pride in that thought.

And The Flame. Damn The Flame. I wondered if she knew how I felt. That was what hurt the most – that was what cut. Yep, The Flame was laughing at me. Not out loud. Not in a way you could notice even. Maybe she wasn't even laughing at me. But that will give you an idea of the way I felt. These two seemed to have reached an understanding which I did not get, though I heard every word.

This Third Gorgon – this wop with the white skin and the steady, unblinking eyes, the soft voice and—. Damn it, he didn't seem like a wop – didn't seem like anything but what he represented himself to be – a—. But that's what I was representing him to be. Certainly he had done something to The Flame – reached some understanding with her.

Mind you, a guy can feel stupid, silly, and what have you, and still not walk up in front of a machine gun and wait for the gunman to turn the crank.

I let Doctor Gorgon hold his elbow crooked beneath my arm. One reason was because of The Flame. The other because he had taken my left elbow and my right hand still held the gun. Why hadn't he grabbed at that right arm? Then I'd have some excuse to hit him one.

CHAPTER XIII: JUST ANOTHER WOP

Now, in the outer hall I jerked my arm free, twisted Michelle Gorgon slightly and none too gently, and slapped my gun against his side. Maybe he wasn't any gangster – maybe he didn't tote a gun. But the lower city just reeked with the rumor that, if the truth were told, Doctor Michelle Gorgon had put more men on the spot, big guys, racketeers, than any gang leader that ever putrified our city. It was even rumoured that a noted jurist had dined with Michelle Gorgon at his home the night of his disappearance.

But back to facts as I knew them and concerned me personally. Eddie Gorgon had gone out in that hall a short while before. The hall was dimly lit, but enough to see plainly our two figures walking down those stairs, and distinguish one from the other. Besides which, I hadn't and wouldn't search Michelle Gorgon. Oh – not that I believed all that talk about his not carting a gun – though certainly he hadn't produced one when he entered The Flame's apartment. But – I just couldn't search him. That superior air of his! I'd show him I didn't care if he carried a gun or not. If he did, and wanted to use it on me, that was his privilege.

No, it wasn't because of him personally, that I shoved a gun against his side. It was because of the gang he represented, ruled, through his brothers – or maybe just his brother, Joe – for Eddie could only be counted on to shoot a guy through the back at three paces.

'You know, Williams, you are not a very trusting soul,' Michelle Gorgon said to me as we went down those stairs. 'A gun in my side, now. I abhor the melodramatic – sudden death by violence except of course in the abstract.'

I didn't exactly get that one, so I let it ride. Later, I got the impression that by 'abstract' he meant he killed his enemies without being present in person – just his mind controlling and directing the hand of the one he selected to do his murdering for him.

My gun clamped against his side, though, was paying a few dividends. For, late as the hour was, Doctor Gorgon hummed softly as he descended the stairs, and once a lump of blackness which might have been a shadow or the lurking body of a gunman, seemed to fade back into the darkness. Of course, shadows don't make boards creak, as they fade away. But, again, the house was old, and I wasn't in a particularly good humor.

When we stepped out on the pavement a Rolls Royce stood before the building. A man wrapped in a great coat swung open the car door as I caught the initials in gold stamped upon it. Another, at the wheel, brought the engine into life – though that part I guessed at, for you hardly heard it purr.

'I'll take you home, of course,' he told me, as I hid the gun partly under my coat as we neared the car door. 'Not just courtesy, my dear Williams – not just because you were about to suggest any such procedure – but because your life is very dear to me tonight. I wouldn't have anything happen to you while with me, or just after leaving me. You see, the police – or at least one imaginative policeman has taken quite an interest in me. It is a help, of course. It is convenient to know that, when anything unpleasant happens that might be laid to the interests of my brother, Joe, through the watchfulness of our great police system suspicion can not direct its unpleasant breath upon me.'

I was willing to go with him, all right. And as I got into the car and sat down beside him, he said – and there was little of humor in his voice – rather, he seemed to think he was stating a great universal truth.

'Yours is rather a silly position tonight – now. Like the man who held the lion by the tail and was both afraid to hang on and afraid to let go.' He raised the speaking tube. 'Park Avenue, and home,' he said.

Michelle Gorgon dropped the tube.

'Do you know, Williams, that doesn't seem quite courteous; that you should see me home instead of my seeing you? But a strange fancy struck me. I would like you to pay me a visit – like to talk with you. You wouldn't consider it venturesome to visit me – now – at this late hour? I think that maybe I can interest you.' And as he rambled on I began to like it better – feel better toward him. I just leaned back and listened. Sometimes these lads who talk, no matter how clever they are, say something – say something they shouldn't. Yet, never for a moment did I forget that Michelle Gorgon was a big man. Not one seeking power, but one who had obtained it. And even in the underworld, even in crooked politics, you don't talk yourself to the top – or, at least, if you do – you talk yourself out again. Now – why was he dragging me along? Why did he take such an interest in me?

And once he cut in quickly in his ramblings.

'Are you listening to me?'

'Who could help it?' I answered, for there had been an irritable note in his voice, and I rather liked it. So, I thought, there is a way to get under that skin of his. And with that thought I felt better. Funny. I encouraged him to talk now.

'Why do you want me to visit you – and why should I?'

'Because I will interest you. As to your safety. If you were my most feared enemy, my home would be the safest spot for you in the whole city of New York. The police watch it occasionally. One policeman in particular. And I think, while I'm on the subject, I'll tell you his name. It amuses me and helps establish my reputation, this interest in me. My life is an open book. The police see me come and go. But my mind is closed to all but myself. Silly, this following me about, watching my home. And how long do you think it would take me to stop it – have this busy-body removed from the Force? Just long enough to lift a phone and put a word in the ear of the right party. You might tell my shadow that. I believe you know him. His name is Detective Sergeant O'Rourke, an efficient officer. I should hate to see him removed from duty. You might tell him that, any day, I may grow tired of his attentions. And when that day comes, it will be too late for Sergeant O'Rourke. You see, it will be greatly to his advantage to grow tired of me before I grow tired of him.'

'Yeah. I'll tell him when I see him, Doctor. This is your place?'

I was just a bit surprised. We had drawn up before one of the finest apartment houses on Park Avenue. No rendezvous of gangsters, this.

'You hardly expect hidden passageways here, and secret methods of disposing of bodies.' He smiled. 'As to sub-cellars – well – my quarters are thirty-three stories above the street. There are thirty-two to the building.

'You are on the roof?' I asked.

'On the roof. One might fall off, of course. But even one with your love of violence can see the danger to me in that. Really, it is possible – but a man would have to be most desperate, and greatly in fear of – of you. No, no—' this as we walked into the spacious hall and entered an elevator. 'Death must have its part in life, even in my life, Williams. But it must be smoothed over, and distant – seen, as I said, in the abstract. In plain words. If one annoys, it is better to have him removed through, shall I say – suggestion?'

We sped quickly to the roof, walked down a corridor. Gorgon stopped before a heavy door, waited several seconds, then placed a key in the lock and swung the door open. And as we walked across the wind-swept roof, beneath the brightness of the stars, toward that California bungalow, he chatted on.

'You see, Williams, why I might go a long way not to give all this up. The Italian emigrant has gone far in your city – risen perhaps by the customs your laws so agreeably set out for him. In your city – my city – a man first must banish conscience. Second, create a mind without a body, without emotions.'

We had crossed the roof now, passed under a canopy by the small trees between giant plants. There was real grass, clipped as smooth as a putting green, a tiny fountain, and the ripple of falling water against the slight night wind.

There were three steps of fancy brick and we were on the small porch. A single twist of the door knob – no waiting this time – and I followed Doctor Gorgon into a large, square hall.

He tossed his coat and stick onto a high backed chair, placed his hat upon them, and motioned me to do the same with my hat. But the night was not cold. I wasn't sporting a top coat. My felt hat had cost me twelve bucks – I'd keep it with me. It wouldn't be at all surprising if I had to leave the house of Michelle Gorgon in a hurry.

But he was persistent, and I wasn't going to be small about it. I let him take the hat from me and place it on the chair.

'A social call, Williams – and let us hope, a friendly call. A hat upon your knee would break the illusion and savor distinctly of the law, the police, at least, as we know the police detective in books and plays. Come, I never keep the servants up. I have always felt rather mentally above the teeming millions of the city. This home of mine is perhaps the realization in a material way of my mental attitude. In here – we will be quite alone.'

He walked across the generous hall to a smaller hall, and across that narrow stretch through curtains, and stood aside for me to precede him, as he held a door open.

I didn't like it but I couldn't see any harm in it. My hand was still in my jacket pocket; the Doctor's body so close to mine that I pushed against it as I passed, and just stepped far enough into that room to—. And I drew a surprise.

It was a library. Expensively bound volumes, deep, soft chairs, heavily curtained recesses before windows. But I saw none of that then. I was looking at the figure of a woman in a large chair, the rug hiding her limbs and body to well above the waist. The neck was long and slender, but there were discolorations upon it – heavy, purplish-yellow stretches, which covered the face as well. Patches of skin that seemed to have long since healed, after a burn.

And the woman's hand. I saw her left hand stretched out upon the rug. Twisted, sort of inhuman fingers, thin, emaciated, crippled arm. And Doctor Gorgon had stepped into the room beside me. He too saw the woman.

Yep – you could knock him. He was no superman at that moment. Chalk white, his face may have been before – perhaps it couldn't get any whiter – but at least it took on a new hue. A yellowish white of milk, with blotches in the perfect skin. Blotches like the curdling of milk, just as it turns sour. One hand went under his collar and pulled at it as his mouth hung open. For nearly a minute he looked at the woman. And so did I.

And I was onto Doctor Michelle Gorgon. I thought, too, as I watched his face that perhaps I was the only one in the whole city who was onto him. For that minute, maybe less, he was just what I had placed him for – Eddie for – Joe Gorgon for. Doctor Michelle Gorgon was just a wop, just a human, physical, rotten bit of the life he controlled and stood above. A racketeer, a gangster, a slimy underworld rat. Believe me, for that best part of sixty seconds he did more tricks with his pan than our greatest actor ever pulled off in a Doctor Jekyll and Mr. Hyde performance.

His mouth opened, his lower lip hung down. Little bubbles of saliva gathered as he tucked his lip in and pulled at it with his upper teeth. He didn't speak. Not quite. One read, though, all the foul words he would have said if he could have spoken when he desired. But in a moment of mental strain and physical reaction he got hold of himself. Yet, his voice trembled when he finally spoke to the woman.

'What are you doing here? How dare you come, and—' He swung suddenly on me. 'Outside,' he said. 'In the hall. Outside, Williams!'

Outside it was. It wasn't my party. The heavy door leading to that little hall nearly took my arm off as he closed it and clicked the key. One thing I had seen before that door got me. That was the woman's eyes. Deep brown they were. Mysterious, living, beautiful eyes, like—. And I took a gasp. Like The Flame's. Like—. And the words of Doctor Gorgon popped into my head, chased one another around and formed a picture. A woman with a maimed, twisted body. Nothing but her eyes; nothing—

And from behind that locked door the woman cried out— Shrill, piercing. A scream of terror, even horror.

'No – God! No. He must never see me like this. I won't come again. I swear I won't. I wanted a glass – a mirror.' A sound like an open palm against a face and the cry of the woman. 'Help – he's going to kill me.' And this time the voice died, as if a hand stilled it. Not a hand across the mouth – but a sudden gurgling sound to the stilled voice, as if fingers had clutched at her throat – followed by the sound as if bodies struggled, or one body moved heavily.

I lifted my hand and knocked upon the door. A moment of silence followed my knock. Then I struck the door again. And when I say 'struck' I mean just that. Heavy as the door was, it rattled like thin slats when I pounded my fist against it.

CHAPTER XIV: I GO IN FOR ACTION

That second knock was a wow, and no mistake.

It brought response from inside. There was a jolt, the slipping of a chair, a whispered voice – another, I thought, which sounded like a man's. Feet crossed to the door, and Michelle Gorgon spoke. His voice was soft again, but there was still a tremor in it.

'There, there, Mr. Williams. A little difficulty – family difficulty, that you would not understand. And please don't pound like that again. I'll be with you in a minute. I—'

Feet moved across the floor. Feet that didn't belong to Michelle Gorgon, by the door. Feet that were too heavy for that delicate, crippled woman in the big chair.

I know I was silly. It wasn't any of my business. If I had any sense I'd have lifted my hat and left the place. Yet, I'm the sort of a guy who does silly things, and likes to do them. Why think it out and reason it? Reason's a damn poor excuse, most times, for not having guts. I didn't reason then – and I didn't think it out. I obeyed the impulse. And the impulse was to – well – here was a chance to talk to Doctor Gorgon. And in a way, at least, I understood – and he would understand in a minute. Damn it, he didn't expect me to keep pounding on that door, like an hysterical woman.

'Open that door – and keep the lady there,' I said. 'No talking like a book now, Doctor. You'll have to talk like a man for once. Open the door now, or, by God! I'll put a bullet through the lock.'

He answered.

'If you do that you will wake the house. Men who might not understand.' Feet were moving quickly inside – heavy feet, that were weighted under a burden, I thought. The woman was being taken from the room by another door.

'No more wind, Doc.' I was giving him the truth now. 'Open the door, or get out of the way while a bullet goes through the lock.'

'Williams, I—'

And that was that. Doctor Gorgon might speak just to hear himself talk, but I didn't. There was a single roar of my gun, the splintering of wood – and a shattered lock. My hand on the knob, my shoulders hunched, with a thrust of my body I had that door open and was in the room. The time for talk was over. When I want an 'in' I generally get an 'in'. And when I take a shot at a lock, that ends that lock. Forty-four is the caliber of my guns. Maybe old fashioned and not much in use today – but a forty-four can certainly do a surprising lot of damage.

This was my field, my game. I didn't more than step through that door when I slammed it behind me and took one quick slant at Doctor Gorgon. His eyes were staring now, but for a different reason than his usual attitude – the 'nothing can excite me' stuff. Well – I won't say staring – rather, bulging. The deep blue pools were hitting high tide, and sort of flooding their banks.

But both his hands were empty, and a curtain on the far side of the library was swinging slightly as I caught a glimpse of the trouser leg of a man.

I brought up my gun, leveled it on that waving curtain and the disappearing leg, and gave the boy who owned the blue trousered limb a chance to live.

'You behind the curtain. Stop – or I'll—'

'Stop!' Doctor Gorgon's voice rang out. 'There has been a grave misunderstanding. You may return Madame to the room at once.'

And Madame was returned. Michelle Gorgon may have known a lot more words than I did, but, believe me, the few words I have serve my purpose at times. This was one of those times.

Two men carried the woman. She shrieked as they brought her back, in a kind of a swing chair, between them. Personally, they were rather stupid looking fellows but they knew what a gun was and the purpose of it, and the havoc it might raise, for they kept their eyes riveted on mine.

And Madame bellowed when they brought her in. She was not a pretty sight now, worse even than before. Her hair streamed over her forehead and her mouth was twisting spasmodically.

She sort of gasped out her words.

'Michelle – please – good God! not like this. That any man could see me like this – my hair—' She was trying to fix her hair with that twisted hand, and making a mess out of it.

Well, I was into it now, and I stepped across the room and stood before her.

Doctor Gorgon crossed quickly to her too, smoothed back her hair and patted her hand. He was leaning down and looking at her. I pulled at his shoulder and straightened him.

'Madame,' I said, 'you called for help. What—'

'She is not well.' Michelle Gorgon horned in quickly – rather too quickly, I thought, though I don't know why I thought it. 'She has had a sudden illusion that she would see some one again – some one very dear to her. And unless she is more careful, that illusion will come true – much more careful.' And as I turned sharply on him, 'I mean her health, of course. As you see, it is not—'

'Can the chatter.' And turning to the woman, 'What's the trouble, lady?' Her eyes were suddenly alive.

'Trouble – trouble. I dreamed it. I do not know. Take me away, Michelle. That a man should see me like this, when I was once so beautiful. A young man too. Take me away. But tell him, Michelle. Let me hear you tell the gentleman how very beautiful I was before. Tell him.' There was almost a child-like anxiety in her voice, a sudden quick flash to her eyes, that died in the making, a simper in her voice, a coquettish tilt to her head that was either disgusting or tragic, I wasn't sure which.

'Yes, she was a very beautiful woman, Mr. Williams. Very beautiful indeed.' Michelle Gorgon leaned close to her again and looked into her eyes. 'Indeed—' he said very slowly, 'she was once – once very beautiful.'

The woman screamed, threw herself back in the chair and lay quite still. I was very close to her – very close to Michelle Gorgon. He had said nothing to her that I hadn't heard. Certainly he had not touched her, or even pulled 'a face on her.'

'Take Madame to Mrs. O'Connor.' Gorgon spoke to the men who held the chair – then to me, 'With your permission, of course.' And there was a bit of a sneer to his voice.

'Sure. It's all right by me,' I said easily. But, damn it, I didn't feel entirely at ease. Not that I was sorry I shot through that lock. Maybe it was a mistake, maybe it wasn't. But we all make lots of mistakes. None, more than I. I'm not a lad who won't admit a thing is wrong, just because he did it. Not me. But – well if it was wrong it was just too damn bad. Nothing could change it now. Nothing I could do then would take a forty-four bullet and shove it back into my gun again. Why cry over it?

'Explain the – the explosion,' Michelle Gorgon said to one of the men. And when the man he spoke to looked at me rather blankly, 'You might say to the servants that Madame has caused a disturbance. That is all.' He watched them carry the woman from the room, even walked to the curtains and pulled the rug that covered her legs slightly closer about her feet, and held the curtains open as they passed from view. Then he turned to me.

'You might have killed me with that shot,' he said. 'Absurd, of course – but I could swear I felt or heard the bullet pass very close to me. The newspapers evidently do not exaggerate your – your idiosyncrasies. You do not know it, Williams, but you took quite an advantage of me. I allow nothing untoward to happen in my house.'

He was talking more, I think to pull himself together. And one thing struck me. I hadn't noticed it before. Maybe it was because he was disturbed, but when he threw a big word into his conversation he seemed to grope for it – feel for it, as if he tried it out first in his own mind before he spoke it. He walked up and down a bit as he talked, finally paused, looked at me a moment, and walking to the wall pressed a button.

The man who came to the door I had rather demolished was old, bent, and every inch the trained servant. Michelle Gorgon looked at him a moment, hesitated, then spoke.

'The No. 1 Sherry, Carleton – Carleton.' He repeated the name 'Carleton' very slowly, as if he liked the sound of it and hoped that I would. Then to the man again, 'Madame has had a spell. We are very fond of her, Carleton – very fond of her indeed. We must put up with a great deal.'

'Very good, sir. The No. 1 Sherry.' And the man left the room.

Michelle Gorgon had exaggerated, to say the least, when he told me the servants had retired.

'There, there, Williams.' Michelle Gorgon paced the room slowly as he talked. 'You have made it a trying evening. I do not believe, though, that the shot was heard outside, or below. It was unfortunate, and I forgive you. I was angry of course, to see – to see Madame so.' He shrugged his shoulders and half extended his arms. 'It is my burden, my cross, and I am afraid there are times when I do not bear it like a man. I hope you will need no further explanation. You are my guest. May I simply say that the lady is my wife and that she met with a very serious accident, which maimed her body and affected her mind. She has never seen her face since the accident. The shock might kill her. We watch her rather closely. As you see, there are no mirrors in this room. But the reflection in the glass of a picture, the highly polished surface of a cigarette case, and such objects, have given her more than a suspicion. But she does not know the whole truth. Only a mirror could tell her that.

'I have been advised to send her away – a private hospital. But she does not wish to go.' He looked dreamily at the ceiling, as if in reminiscent thought. 'It would be better for her, of course, far better. But we cling to sentiment, Williams, almost childishly hang onto the subconscious allurements of the past. Indeed, she was a very beautiful, and a very accomplished woman. Like—' He paused, the door opened, and the servant entered with a tray.

'Like The Flame.' I helped him out. I don't know why that was on my mind, but it was.

'Like The Flame – yes,' he said very slowly. He reached for a glass, lifted the bottle and poured me out a drink, and taking one himself, motioned Carleton to place the tray and bottle on the table.

'You, if you are a judge, will appreciate this wine,' he held the amber glass, with its long stem, before the lamp. 'I have a friend who puts a seal upon it before it leaves France. It comes from the very cellars of the Marguery, in Paris. My own seal is placed upon each bottle before it is even moved from the shelf. It is very rare and—'

Michelle Gorgon paused and looked at a white card which lay upon the tray. He half bowed to me, stayed Carleton with a raised hand and said:

'You'll excuse me, Williams.' And he turned over the card, read it through carefully, moved his eyebrows a bit, but did not permit his eyes to blink.

'I told him, sir—' Carleton started.

'Apologies are unnecessary, Carleton. He would not have come unless— You may tell him to come in.' A moment's hesitation, and just before Carleton passed out the door, 'A bottle of whisky. We must not be inhospitable.' And to me, 'It is my brother, Joe. You do not object, I am sure.'

Maybe I did object. At least unconsciously, for I half came to my feet. Then I shrugged my shoulders but said nothing. Joe Gorgon had pushed himself to the top as a racketeer because of his speed with a gun. Yet, I don't believe there's a lad living today, or dead either for that matter, who can pull on me. But then, a lad with a gun hand like that wouldn't be dead, which gave me the thought that Joe Gorgon was still alive.

'You will excuse me again, Williams.' Doctor Gorgon picked up a bit of paper beside the telephone on the table, studied it a moment, turned it face down and glanced at the clock on the mantel. It was eighteen minutes past two.

'It is almost like a play,' he went on. 'Each scene set to intrigue the audience. Each scene—. But this will be my brother, Joe. An impetuous man, dynamic, invigorating. But let me know what you think of the Sherry.'

I watched him sip his and heard him say, as he tipped the glass.

'Here's to crime – your business, and mine.'

And, damn it, the 'mine' was gotten off in a way that made the wine stick in my throat before going down. Sinister, crafty, evil. There was no expression on his face, but for a moment I thought that I saw the real man.

The man I had seen a part of that minute when Madame – or whatever fancy name you'd hang on her – was discovered in the room. A stern face, an intelligent face. Nothing of the sensual or animal in it. Yet, again, for a fraction of a second I saw, or felt that I saw, the real Michelle Gorgon, and it gave me a certain satisfaction.

CHAPTER XV: DEATH STRIKES AGAIN

Joe Gorgon walked into the room. His eyes flashed and his lips twitched as he saw me. He had known I was there, all right. There were no two ways about that. He hardly noticed the quick steps of Carleton, but he did spot the bottle of whisky the servant placed on the table, poured himself a quick and a generous drink and threw it into him before he spoke a word. Somehow I felt that Joe was the kind of a lad for me, the kind of a lad to do business with. His first words were classic, as I understand the classic. He looked at his brother and jerked a thumb toward me.

'What's he here for?' And then quickly, 'Williams and me had words tonight. I have a message for you, alone. God in—'

He stopped, poured himself another drink, knocked it off, stared at his brother, Michelle Gorgon, a moment, half raised a hand as if to slap it down upon the table, changed his mind and threw himself into a chair, crossing his legs in a position of ease. Just a position, mind you. Joe Gorgon was a worried man.

'What's he here for!' Michelle Gorgon repeated his brother's words. 'I might ask you the same question about yourself, Joe. I invited Mr. Williams up to pay me a visit. That's more than you – but no matter. My home is chaos. My—' And suddenly, 'Why am I indebted to you for this visit?'

'I want to see you alone,' said Joe. And leaning forward, 'I've got to see you alone.'

I liked the byplay between the brothers. The one, Joe, the best known character on Broadway. The other, well, no man could lay a finger to Doctor Michelle Gorgon.

'Got to!' Michelle Gorgon leaned slightly forward. 'Got to – Joseph. Really, I'm afraid you forget—' and a smile, at least a smile with his lips – or anyway, a twist to his lips, 'You forget the duty of a host to his guest.'

'Cripes!' Joe Gorgon came to his feet. 'Williams is here. He knows something. He—. Damn it, Mike – he's not going out of here a—'

I fingered my gun, of course, raised my pocket slightly too. Even thought of pulling the rod out and laying it on my knees, in a sociable way. But I didn't. I took another sip of the wine and understood why Joe drank whisky. Not that the wine wasn't good. It was probably great stuff, great stuff for a garden party. But you'd have to go at it wholesale to get a kick out of it.

'When thieves fall out honest men get their due,' was going strong with me – of course, fully realizing that the honest man must have his hand on a rod and a finger caressing a trigger – or he'd get a 'due' that would be surprising to him.

Joe Gorgon stopped talking. Michelle's eyelids never flickered. The good natured twist to his mouth, that might be better described as tolerance rather than a smile, never changed. But the pupils of his eyes seemed to contract, as if you looked too long at a thing in a bright light, and found it getting smaller and smaller, yet sharper, as it got smaller. His right hand went below the table, and he lifted a book and tossed it across the polished surface so that it spun slightly before it struck Joe's outstretched hand and lay still.

Joe's hand fell upon the book. His mean little eyes grew large as his brother's contracted. He sort of clutched at his side when he spoke.

'For me?' he said. 'Good God! you're not giving that book to me!' And his face cleared slightly as he glanced at me. 'For Williams.'

'Maybe. I hope not.' Michelle Gorgon turned his eyes on me, and I looked down at the expensively bound volume. I saw the title stamped in gold upon the cover.

'*The Tanglewood Tales*,' I read, '*by Nathaniel Hawthorne.*'

I took another sip of the wine, leaned out, and with my free left hand flipped back the pages. It was a de luxe edition, and the volume opened at once to THE GORGON'S HEAD. I grinned up at Michelle.

'For me?' I said, fingering the book.

'I hope not,' said Michelle Gorgon again. 'Indeed, I hope not. But it's not all fancy, Race, that mythical tale of Hawthorne's. History repeats itself.'

'I want to speak to you alone.' Joe Gorgon threw off another drink, and his brother glanced disparagingly at the bottle and sipped his wine.

'Anything you have to say, Joe, can be said in front of Williams, here.'

'No, it can't,' said Joe. And the liquor was doing him some good, for he glared back at his brother now. 'This talking around corners may be good stuff with your crowd, not mine. Williams, here, is one of my kind. He wants straight talk. At least, he gives straight talk. You're—. Yes, damn it, I'll get it in. You're sitting on the edge of a volcano and—. I have a message to deliver to you, alone.'

And that was my cue. I thought I knew why Joe Gorgon had visited his brother. I thought I knew the message he had to deliver. I had seen that message of mine throw Joe higher than a kite. Why not work it for a double header? Why not find what effect it would have on the Third Gorgon, the brains of the three brothers? Why not deliver that message myself? And I decided to try it. I said:

'Why argue the point out? I delivered a little message to Joe, here. He wants to pass it on to you. I'll save you trouble and give it to you myself, Doctor.' And before Joe could horn in I shot it out, with all my flair for the dramatic, and with the memory of Joe's contorted map when he heard it.

'Michelle Gorgon,' I said. 'The Devil is Unchained.'

It worked twice on Joe. He stretched out a hand quickly and grabbed his brother's arm. His face twisted, and his lips parted at the corners. And he watched carefully the features of his brother, Michelle; watched, I thought, for Michelle to give a single shriek, lie down and roll over.

But Michelle Gorgon still smiled with his lips. He said simply:

'How droll. What a droll message!'

'Don't you understand?' Joe Gorgon shook his brother by the arm. 'Have these years so dulled your—'

'Stop!' Michelle Gorgon shot the words through his teeth. There was an animal–like viciousness in the way his head shot forward, as he glared at his brother. 'You're trying to push a peanut wagon across this living room, just as you pushed it on Canal street twenty-three years ago. You had your stand then, Joe. You protected that stand. You enticed rival vendors up an alley and put the fear of Joe Gorgon into their hearts, and went your way and protected your corner, and sold two bags of peanuts where you had sold one before. And now, in your heart you're still running the same peanut racket, still entertaining the same fears, still drinking the same poison. Now—' Michelle Gorgon paused. The phone rang sharply on the table beside him.

'You'll pardon me, gentlemen.' He half bowed to me, very seriously, and to his brother with a touch of sarcasm. 'I think that I am to have a message that will be of much interest to each one of us, more so than Williams' rather em – epigrammatic reference to the devil.'

He picked up the phone and said:

'Doctor Gorgon speaking. Yes, I understand. I have not been at home. Oh, I see. No, I was not asleep. I am interested in all that affects the life, the tranquil life, of our city.' A long pause, and then, 'Thank you very much. I shall read of it at breakfast, in the morning.'

He placed the receiver on the hook. Carefully filled up his wine glass, lit a cigarette and settled back comfortably in the chair. He eyed us now. Those same unblinking globes, his elbows on the arm of his chair, the tips of his fingers on either hand coming slowly together. It was some time before he spoke, and then only in way of forestalling the sudden words that started from Joe Gorgon.

'It's a funny world,' said Michelle Gorgon slowly. 'A very funny world indeed. It will hardly interest either of you. But I just received a message that an Italian gentleman, lately landed in this country, was stabbed to death at Doctor Elrod's Sanitarium. Ah – most distressing. Most distressing.'

CHAPTER XVI: ON THE SPOT

Of course I understood what Michelle Gorgon meant. Giovoni, whom Colonel McBride and I had gone to so much trouble to protect – Colonel McBride very nearly losing his life when we moved the Italian gentleman from the city hospital to Doctor Elrod's Sanitarium – was dead. Murdered within a few hours. I knew it. I believed it. But—.

'No—' I cried out as I jumped to my feet. 'What time – and where were you, Doctor Michelle Gorgon?' I stopped and sat down again. But this time when I stretched out my hand, it reached for Joe Gorgon's bottle of whisky and not the No. 1 Sherry.

'Really,' said Michelle Gorgon, 'your emotions, Williams, do you proud. A poor Italian gentleman. How distressing. But you were saying something about—. Was it – er – that an evil spirit had broken his chains?' And leaning forward slightly, 'Or was it that the devil was chained again, chained this time forever, in death.'

Confused? Yes, I was confused, and mad. Was this the reason that Michelle Gorgon had brought me to his home? So that I would be with him? So that he would know I could not be interfering with this murder he had planned? For that he had planned it I had little doubt. As to Joe, it seemed a cinch that he wasn't in it. His eyes just bulged.

Michelle Gorgon walked slowly around the table and laid a hand upon his brother's shoulder.

'Like our good friend, Williams, here, Joseph, you are a man of action. And I daresay it serves our purpose and is necessary in our every day life. But we must not forget that the physical is only an impulse, directed by the mental. When it is not so, we are told that it is reactionary, impulsive, instinctive, maybe – which is simply the polite way of placing us on the level with animals. When the brain ceases to function and leaves the body, it becomes a useless thing, no matter, Joe, if that brain is not a part of that particular body.' A pause. 'I see I confuse you there. But try and remember that a brain is necessary to the body, to your body, whether it be your brain or my brain, Joe. One brain, then, may control many bodies – but many bodies can not control one brain. It—' Michelle Gorgon stopped and looked at the bewildered face of his brother. 'But no matter,' he said quickly. 'You understand that I am always ready to help and advise you. Ready and anxious, even, but never compelled to. In plain words, your visit here tonight was unnecessary and inopportune. You have seen that.'

'Yes—' said Joe, 'I have seen that. And, the visit of Williams?'

Michelle Gorgon smiled at me.

'A weakness of mine, Joe. A pretty vanity, which all great minds are subject to. For the present you have nothing to worry you. You may sleep and play and—' He looked at the bottle and shrugged his shoulders. 'Mr. Race Williams has been taken care of for tonight.' He put his hand before his mouth, stifled a yawn or an affected yawn. 'The hour is late. You will excuse me, Williams, I know. The interview is over.'

I hadn't had my say; hadn't had half a chance to open up, and now, damn it, he didn't give me the opportunity. Joe Gorgon had moved toward the hall door. Of course I moved with him. Maybe I should have held my ground and believed in the Sanctity of the Home stuff. But I didn't. And it was too late now. Like a woman, Michelle Gorgon had had the last word. He turned, sought the little door that his wife had gone through before, and left us flat.

There was nothing for me to do but leave – leave with Joe Gorgon, presumably New York's biggest and most feared racketeer.

We passed out the front door, across the roof under the covered canopy, and through the thick, steel door which let us into the upper hall of the apartment house.

'He's a great guy, isn't he, Race?' Joe pushed out his chest and looked me over.

The elevator door clanged open, a sleepy eyed operator banged the door closed, and we descended to the street.

Silently Joe and I made our way through the spacious hall with its great pillars and towering plants – out onto Park Avenue.

'Williams,' Joe Gorgon didn't threaten. He spoke his stuff like a man. 'You know me and I know you. Judgeships have been bought and sold before your time and before my time – and will be long after it. Things haven't changed any in the city. It's simply newspaper competition. My world – our world – is a rather small one, after all. I've never laid a sucker on the spot. Men want money – you and me and them. You're a persistent bird and no mistake. You rile a guy – rile him bad. But you can't change life. I daresay there ain't a lad in the city today better informed than you. Yet, you can't do anything to me – nor Mike.' He half looked back up the apartment as he chucked in the 'Mike.' 'Well – Michelle may talk in circles, but when he strikes he strikes straight and hard.'

'Well,' I said, 'come to the point.'

'Yeah.' He bit at a match and spat a piece of it in the gutter. 'It's a bad time for too much excitement. How much do you want to chuck the game and take up golf?'

'I don't play golf,' I told him.

'Oh – I mean—' He paused, scratched the other end of the match on the box and stuck it to a black cigar. 'All right. You and me have made our names stand out a bit. We've both seen plenty of trouble. Now, you're asking for it. That's it, isn't it?'

'I guess so, Joe,' I said.

'Okay!' He looked at me a moment and grinned. 'The look of a Gorgon.' But his smile was pleasant. 'It's a silly racket. But it's paid dividends in the right places. You'd be surprised if you knew the sales increase in Hawthorne's bit of work. But – take care of yourself. S'long.'

Joe Gorgon turned, and was gone. There were no two ways about what he meant. In the language of the underworld, Race Williams was on the spot.

I went home. Any way you look at it, it had been a busy night. On the spot. Well, it wasn't the first time I was put on the spot and wouldn't be the last, I hoped. If I took a little trip for my health every time I was threatened I'd have been around the world a hundred or more times, and still traveling. No, sir, there would be nothing for yours truly, Race Williams, to do for a living unless it was conducting world tours.

That doesn't mean I didn't take the threat of the Gorgons seriously. Besides which, it rather pleased and flattered me. In the first place, they had something to fear from me. A dope fiend might be knocked over on the public street. An unknown Italian might be stabbed to death in a hospital. But the doing in of Race Williams is a different thing, again. Besides, which, some of the best racketeers in the city have been after me, and missed. But they didn't stay after me very long.

I'm not a lad who runs when the bullets fly – at least, if I do run, I run forward and not backward. And if Joe Gorgon wouldn't have any touch of conscience about putting a bullet in me, I wouldn't have any either about putting one in him. An even break, that.

Jerry was waiting up for me.

'There's a lad been calling you on the phone. Sputtered, he did – and seemed to think you spent your time with the receiver clamped to your ear. Trying to make a telephone operator out of me too, and—'

'Did he hang a tag on himself, Jerry?' I asked.

'No. He said you'd know. And for you not to go out again until he got you. He'd ring every fifteen minutes. But, Gawd! He's been buzzing up the bell every five, I think. There you are. Seven minutes, by the clock.' Jerry pushed his hands out as the phone rang.

It was my client, Colonel McBride. His mouth was full of words, his words full of sputters. He sounded like a bunch of Japanese fire-crackers.

But I got enough.

'The man, Giovoni – dead – murdered – stabbed to death in the hospital.'

'I know,' I said. Giovoni, of course, was our little friend that I had carted about.

'How – how do you know?' he demanded breathlessly.

'Does it matter?' I asked him. 'The question is, how did they know where he was? But here's a surprise for you. I spent the evening, or the last hour, with Doctor Michelle Gorgon. Some one was kind enough to ring him up and tell him of the murder. How important was Giovoni? I mean, to you, not himself.'

'Important!' He fairly gasped the words. 'Giovoni was Michelle Gorgon's father-in-law. He was everything. The man who could return Doctor Gorgon to Italy for a brutal murder – clear him out of the country – straighten—'

When he stopped for breath I encouraged.

'His father-in-law?' I didn't get that. The woman called Madame had not looked like a wop.

The fire-crackers went on.

'Yes, at least, I think so. I was told that. Oh – damn it – I have nothing to go on, now. Giovoni never talked much, never gave me much information. He wanted to confront Michelle Gorgon and denounce him. Pay him back for – Michelle Gorgon killed Giovoni's daughter years back, in Italy. It was a brutal murder. Damn it, man, he saw his daughter murdered, watched it, helpless and—'

So he, Giovoni, was not the father of Madame.

'He told you this? He—'

'No, he didn't tell me. He was an old man. He lived his life, spent his days, in an Italian prison. It was vengeance to him. Toney, who you said was killed, told me, the little drug addict. I brought Giovoni from Italy. Now he's dead. How did they know where he was?'

'You must have talked to some one.'

'No one, not a soul. I learned enough from Giovoni and Toney. I have sent an agent to Naples to investigate the story that Michelle Gorgon killed his wife there, over twenty years ago. She was Giovoni's daughter, and her name was Rose Marie. The story is that Michelle Gorgon was convicted of the crime, and escaped. It may be another week before I learn the truth from Italy. In that week of waiting we will leave Michelle Gorgon alone – make him feel that he is safe from the crimes of the past, that he actually committed himself – at least, if the whole thing is not a fabric of lies or the hallucinations of a drug crazed mind. It is possible that Toney may have misled both Giovoni and me.

'Would you be willing, Mr. Williams? I need your services against the Gorgons if this proves true or false, and I will mail you a check in the morning as a retainer. But don't come to see me. Don't ring me up. I want Michelle Gorgon to think that I have dropped you, perhaps even dropped him. I will get in touch with you when I hear from Italy, or from one who knows much, but will not talk yet. It may be only a few days. It may be a week. What do you say? Will you risk it? The pay will be good.'

'Don't forget to mail the check in the morning,' was my answer.

CHAPTER XVII: INFLUENCE VERSUS GUN-PLAY

As a matter of fact it was ten days before I again heard from my client, Colonel Charles Halsey McBride. But the check had come, and where it wasn't a fortune, it was for ten thousand dollars. Which is plenty of jack, as real money goes today.

But I kept to the letter of Colonel McBride's instruction. I didn't frequent any place where I might meet the Gorgons. That was a little tough. It might look to the Gorgons as if I were afraid of that 'on the spot' threat. Also, I still had the envelope containing the currency and jewelry which Michelle Gorgon had asked me to return to his brother, Eddie. Yep, the temptation was strong to look Eddie up and slip it in his hand. For the money and jewelry were given to The Flame by Eddie – as an inducement, I guess, to bring her into the Gorgon outfit. But Doctor Michelle Gorgon had looked at The Flame and seen bigger things for her. So it was that he suggested rather sarcastically that I return the money and jewelry to Eddie Gorgon.

Anyway, since the killing of Toney, the little drug addict, not far from the Golden Dog night club, Eddie had sort of disappeared from his usual haunts in the city. That is, for several days. The last couple of days he was back again. But I understood that the police were not looking for him. Such was the power of Michelle Gorgon – or the so-called cleverness of the police in giving Eddie a free run. Take your choice.

But, as I said, it was ten days before I heard from Colonel McBride. Then, on Thursday evening, at exactly eleven-fifteen, he called me on the phone.

'I should have called you before.' He got down to business. 'Giovoni, Toney, it all seemed so strange. Yet Toney came over on the boat with the Gorgon brothers, over twenty years ago. They were called Gorgonette them. Michelle was twenty-seven then, but looked younger, Joe no more than in his twenties, and Eddie just a small boy. Williams, we may have to start over, try to prove something here in New York. You see, I thought we could pin this crime of years back on Michelle Gorgon. No excitement in the city; no involving others; no influence, no bribery, no jury fixing to fight against. Just the turning of Michelle Gorgon over to the Italian authorities for the murder of his wife years back. Now the Italian investigation seems to have proved a – well – entirely false.'

'There must be something in it. Giovoni was murdered. Toney was murdered. And certainly by the Gorgons. Why kill them if they didn't fear what they could say?'

'Yes. But, Williams, we should have a long talk. My life was attempted yesterday. Some one else has told me that Michelle Gorgon did kill his wife in Italy. But on top of that I have indisputable evidence from my agent in Naples that Michelle Gorgon, or Michelle Gorgonette was never married in Italy. But, enough talk on the phone. I am wondering if I should come to see you or have you come and—'

'I'll come and see you,' I cut in quickly. 'The Gorgons have killed two men, who for all they know may have told you something. There was an attempt on your life, you say. If the Gorgons think you know too much, then you are a menace to them. And get this straight, Colonel. The Gorgons have a direct and efficient way of dealing with menaces. I've been looking up the Gorgon record during the past week. And I guess I can name as many murders that they committed as any dick on the Force, including your friend, Sergeant O'Rourke. But naming them and presenting them as evidence to a jury are two different stories, which the Gorgons know as well as I do.

'It's well known in the underworld that Joe Gorgon shot down Lieutenant Carlsley over four years ago. Yet, they couldn't even get the grand jury to indict Joe. Then there's Eddie Gorgon's brutal murder of the laundry owner who defied the laundry racket and paid for it with his life. At least four people saw that murder. No graft there. The jury was composed of honest citizens. That was straight out and out terror. One witness was drowned; another had disappeared; and two others changed their stories right on the witness stand, giving a description of a murderer that would better fit any man in the city of New York than it would Eddie Gorgon. Friends gave Eddie a dinner and presented him with a loving cup the night he was freed.

'And what's more, you're right about Michelle Gorgon. He's the brains of the whole show. Directs the killing, covers himself, and never has a hand in it. "Murder in the abstract" is what he calls it. He—' I paused, strained my ear against the receiver. Not a sound. 'Are you listening?' I asked, just in a natural voice. No one likes to shoot his trap off just to hear himself talk. At least, I don't.

'Are you listening?' I tried again, his time louder. Perhaps an anxious note came into my voice as I strained my ears to catch the faintest breath. And I thought that I heard something. A distant voice, or a buzzer, or, damn it, maybe just the odd sounds that the telephone wires put on as an added attraction to the subscriber.

I jiggled the receiver hook, spoke quickly – maybe louder – maybe fearfully. Just instinct. Just those nerves I talk about in others and deny having myself. But somehow I felt that tragedy had suddenly stepped into that distant room, that something had happened to—. And then, when I was sure, and about to jerk the receiver back on the hook and dash from the room, his voice came, low, soft – and maybe it was caution in it instead of fear, maybe an anxiety instead of dread, maybe—. But he whispered, for I barely caught the words.

'Come down then. I've got a visitor. I think maybe I'll learn the truth.'
The voice died. The receiver clicked across the wire, and silence. But

had there been a roar – the beginning of a roar, just before that receiver dropped back upon the hook, or had there—? Hell, these Gorgon boys could stir up fancies. Fancies? I thought of the dead snow-bird before the night club, the little Italian with the knife in his chest, the—.

'Jerry,' I grabbed up my hat and stepped to the apartment door, 'I'm going out again. And put your hat on. I'm taking you bye-bye.'

Jerry's eyes shone, his lips parted and his big, uneven teeth jumped into the sudden gap. But he didn't say anything. He didn't have to get ready. Though I seldom took Jerry with me on any such errand he always hoped that I would, and was always ready. Besides which, Jerry knew his underworld by being kicked around it, not from books or the papers. And he was the best shadow since Mary's little lamb fell foul of some mint sauce.

It didn't take Jerry long to turn the corner, dash to the garage and rush my car out. And we were on our way.

'Big thing you're going on, isn't it, Boss?' Jerry just bubbled with enthusiasm.

'Big enough, Jerry,' I told him, as I skipped over to Fifth Avenue. I like action, none better. Maybe I got a thrill now. I daresay I was the only man in the city of New York, or out of it, that the Gorgons had put on the spot, and still lived. And what's more, still intended to remain alive.

Jerry tried again.

'Them Gorgons ain't it?' And when I looked at him, 'When I followed Big Joe I knew who lived in the swell dump he went to. His brother, the Doctor. It's gospel in the right places that Joe never makes a big move but the Doctor advises it. He never pushed no cart on the Avenue, did the Doctor. He never played any gat in Joe's rise. Most of the big timers don't even know the Doctor to speak to. But they know what Joe means when he says, "I'll think it over," or "I'll tell ya tomorrow." I remember once O'Hara, the big bootlegger, the wise money, hearing him say to Joe Gorgon, a year or two before O'Hara got bumped off, and I came with you—'

'All right, Jerry,' I helped him out. This lingering over a story was Jerry's way of finding out if I were interested, 'what did Mr. O'Hara pull on Mr. Joseph Gorgon?'

'It was a liquor deal, I think, a big one, for control of the entire Bronx. When Joe told him what was what, O'Hara says, "Are you speaking through your own mouth, Joe, or through the mouth of the Third Gorgon?" And, Bing! Like that, when Joe gave him the office that he was simply an echo, O'Hara smacked right in on the deal – like nothing at all. I hear as how the Doctor makes judges now, and sells justice at so much a head. They say as how he can pull a murderer right out of the Tombs for the right price. That's how he gets his money, and—. But if it was me, I'd say this Eddie Gorgon is the worst of the lot. Shoot you in the back like THAT.' He snapped his fingers.

'In the back, eh Jerry?'

'Yeah. That's his way, unless it's a snow-bird. Do you think he got little Toney that night?'

'Maybe.' I was listening though. 'But I think, Jerry, if I had to fear any man, I'd pick the influence to fear. It comes natural and sometimes easy to pop at a guy who's standing behind a rod he didn't aim right, or pull the trigger quick enough. But influence, you see, hasn't any body.'

Jerry scratched his head.

'It don't sound right.' He seemed to think aloud. 'But I think I get what you mean. This Third Gorgon don't sport no firearms. That may be hot stuff for the police, or you, with your finicky ideas. But there's a hundred or more guys in the city who'd find it much easier to give a guy the works who's unarmed than—'

'But those guys won't. Maybe there's no reason for them to do it. And maybe a good reason why they shouldn't. You wouldn't want to be the guy who knocked over Joe Gorgon's brother, would you?'

'No,' said Jerry, 'I wouldn't. But Joe Gorgon only kills for business, for necessity, while Eddie—. Well – he's got the killer instinct, Boss. You might duck in and out, and hide from influence – but you can't do nothing with a gun against your back.'

'And that's the point,' I told him. 'It's influence, Jerry, that puts that gun against your back, whether it's Eddie's gun or Joe's gun, or a hundred or more other guns. If you kill a rat, another takes its place. If you kill a dozen rats, a dozen take their place. But if you kill influence, you kill where the rats breed. How the devil can you walk in and shoot down an unarmed man,' and, very slowly, 'and get away with it?'

'Well, they all get it sooner or later,' Jerry said, philosophically. 'But if Eddie Gorgon was after me, like I hear as how he's after you, I'd forget influence and shoot the guts out of Eddie Gorgon.'

Not elegant? Maybe not. But practical just the same. I simply said:

'Eddie Gorgon is only a common murderer, and as such not to be worried about. You see, it's influence again, Jerry. If it wasn't for his brother, he'd have been taken for a ride or roasted at Sing Sing long ago. Now, get this training into your head. A common murderer is only as good as the gun he draws, if you can forget what's behind him. But—. Here's where we lay up. My business is just around the corner.'

446

CHAPTER XVIII: ON THE LONELY STREET

We parked the car and I took Jerry as far as the corner with me. Colonel McBride's hangout was Number 137.

'No. 137,' I told Jerry, as I tried to point out the house down the street. 'It's possible—' and I stepped back from the corner. Of course I couldn't be sure, that is, as to the identity of the man who moved restlessly in the shadows across from 137, but one thing was certain. He was conspicuous enough to be a flat-foot; defiant enough to give the office to any marauder that No. 137 was protected by the law and not a safe place to bother. I often wonder why the police go in so much to prevent crime, that is, temporarily, by a display of law, when a little cagy work might capture the criminal and prevent the crime permanently.

'Stick around,' I told Jerry. 'If you see any one you fancy, follow him and give me a report later.' And as Jerry grinned up at me, I gave him the orders he liked so well. 'On your own, Jerry,' I said, 'Scout around the block behind, if you like.'

'Right'o, Boss.' Jerry half raised a hand in salute. And I turned the corner and walked toward 137. Nearly half a short block, it was, and I'm telling you that, for some reason, no one ever found a block so enmeshed with danger, maybe imaginary danger. But you've got to admit that since I was in this case every trick had been taken by the Gorgons. And now the fear, well, I won't admit the word fear, maybe, but anyway, the apprehension that the Gorgons were about to take another trick – yep, in spite of the fact that a bulky shadow, without an attempt at concealment, was crossing the street before I got halfway down the block. And that bulky shadow had all the earmarks of a headquarters detective.

So things were safe enough from that position. I spun on my heel and turned quickly back, slipping close to the shadows of the old houses. Once I looked over my shoulder. The man was hurrying toward me. I increased my pace, reached the corner again and turned it quickly, paused by the building and stuck my eye back down the street.

The man was on my side of the street now, on the house No. 137's side. He had his hat in his hand and was scratching his head. Twice he stepped toward the corner and twice he drew back again. I couldn't even see his face, yet I thought that I could read his mind. He was told to watch that house, to watch who came to it. It wasn't up to him to think for himself.

Finally he hurried back down the street, paused for a moment before 137, and then quickly crossed the street and hurried up the steps of the house opposite. I smiled at that. It struck me that I was to gather the impression that he was an ordinary householder, going home, while he watched me from the darkness of the doorway.

I shrugged my shoulders. There are front doors as well as back doors. After all, I might be wrong about this watcher. But anyway, I wanted my visit to be private.

My car was still parked in the middle of the block, but Jerry was gone. I knew Jerry's way. He'd walk clean around that block. I skipped down to the next side street. It wouldn't be so hard to measure off the distance, slip down an alley, straddle a fence and drop into the rear yard of 137.

But I didn't do that little thing. Just about where I guessed the house behind 137 should be two figures emerged and crossed quickly to a big sedan parked by the curb. You could clearly make the figures out, though to recognize them was not so easy. There was not enough light. But one was big enough to be Colonel Charles Halsey McBride.

As that black sedan door opened, the smaller one of the two men paused, drew back a bit and quickly shoved off the arm of the other, that clutched at his. I jerked out a gun and ran down the street.

One of those two men, the one I thought my client, the Colonel, had thrown up his hands and cried out. A figure had suddenly jumped from the closed car and clutched him. Two other shadows bounded down the steps from a dark vestibule and were on him from behind. Almost in the time it takes to tell it, that one man was bundled into the car and the other man had escaped and was running down the street, away from me.

There was no chance to overtake that car. It had jumped ahead in second gear and was dashing down the block. I saw it swing into Broadway under a light, sway perilously as it turned left, and disappeared from view. But I thought too that I saw a slim, boyish form come from an areaway and start in pursuit of the man who had fled. And with a little gulp of satisfaction I thought that I recognized that slim pursuing figure as my assistant, Jerry.

Now, I could have gotten the man who ran down the block in the same direction the fleeing car had taken. He wasn't very fast, and slightly bent, and rather uncertain.

But just as I took out after him came more trouble from behind me. I heard the tires skid as a car turned the corner from the same direction I had come. I jumped quickly for the first retreat. A two foot drop into a basement entrance. Turning, I leveled my gun as the car screeched to a stop at the curb. The occupants of that car had seen me all right, for two men hopped to the street.

I put my gun in my pocket and called out to the broad shouldered man who was slipping along with his back close to the building, toward my hiding place. I had gotten a good look at his map.

'Glory be to God, Race Williams,' said Sergeant O'Rourke. 'Surely it's not you that's making all this disturbance! You'll be the bloke that started down the street a few minutes ago, just before the light flashed.'

'What light?' I asked him.

'The – well – the Colonel's. If he needed help he had only to flash his light on and off in the front room, where he sleeps. And he did just that.'

'When?' I asked.

'Less than three minutes ago.'

I counted up quickly. The time to leave his room, go down the stairs, pass through the lower floor into the back yard, climb the high fence that must be there and pass through the alley to the street. And he hadn't left that alley in a hurry. Just a slow walk, and—.

'He couldn't have flashed a light in his front room,' I told O'Rourke, 'less than three minutes ago.'

'But he did.' O'Rourke nodded emphatically as he grinned. 'I had me own eyes on it. I thought maybe the – some one might try and pay him a visit, so I left the way open for an "in", you understand. Not an "out". And it'll be about three minutes, now, since the light flashed. The boys will be playing the front door, while we take the back. Come on, Race. The Colonel will be safe as a fiddle, with his door locked and his gun in his hand and the police busting in. Make it snappy. I've got a few boys across from the front of the house who'll be in by now. I took no chances.'

I grabbed O'Rourke's arm as I followed him into the alley, two other dicks closing in behind us.

And I told him what I had seen, watched his feet hesitate, watched his hands that were gripping the high fence let go their hold, as the full significance of what I said caught him.

'You don't think one of those men was the Colonel?' O'Rourke asked anxiously; then shaking me, 'You do?'

'I do.' I gave him the truth.

'Did the other man have a gun in his ribs and—? But he couldn't. The Colonel's door was heavy. Two windows facing on the street with a man below them and one in the house across the way, watching. No, he wouldn't open that door for any one. That, he promised me. But come on. Maybe it was—'

'Two other fellows,' I started sarcastically, and stopped. What was the good of riding O'Rourke now? If damage was done, it was done. And, another thing. It struck me suddenly. O'Rourke, or no one else, could have prevented the man leaving that house. Certainly, if it was the Colonel, he went of his own free will. Maybe, under some threat, maybe, under some promise, maybe, with some one he trusted. Maybe—. But the light! If he had flashed the light as the pre-prepared signal to O'Rourke, then he had gone in fear. But that light! He wouldn't have had time. And I gave it up. We were over the fence, in the yard, at the foot of the steps leading to the back door.

O'Rourke gave his orders in a low voice. Placing men carefully to watch the cellar windows, and then growling roughly for me to come on, he climbed the steps to the rear kitchen door – found it open and entered the house.

Lights were blazing now. Flatties pounded through the rooms. Some of them I knew, some I didn't. Some were the best detectives on the city Force. A tall, straight figure with iron gray hair spoke to O'Rourke.

'The front room is empty. The bed has not been slept in. Evidently he wasn't expecting to retire at – at the time whatever it was happened. But the Colonel's gone.'

'Yes,' said O'Rourke. 'No sign of any one. Search the house.'

'Men going through it now,' said the gray haired dick. And as a lad holding an axe came into the room, black and disheveled, 'About the cellar, Tim?'

'Even stirred up the coal.' A round Irish face grinned. 'Not a chance for a mouse to hide away.'

'You got the axe, I see. Give it to me.' The old dick addressed Tim.

'Er, what for?' demanded O'Rourke.

'There's a closet door that's locked, and a key missing, in his nib's bedroom.' The dick jerked a thumb upward. 'It may mean nothing, but we'll have a look.'

'Give me that axe.' O'Rourke took the axe, pounded up the stairs, with me at his heels. He nodded to the cop who stood in the outer room, and walked to the closet door in the bedroom. He pulled at the knob and said:

'Hi, Colonel.' Listened a moment, half lifted the axe and put it down again, and turned to the cop. 'Don't want anything disturbed here. Papers and the likes of that. A strong man should jerk that door smack off its hinges.' He grabbed at the door. A quick jerk, and O'Rourke cursed. The door held fast. Then he spotted the lamp cord knotted to the end of the bed, and it took his mind off the door. But it was curled on the floor and no longer hung over the sill, as it did when I first visited that house.

'A lad might have come up by that, slipped through the bedroom, and, damn it, I forgot about this window. But how the devil could he throw it down to himself? Certainly he didn't leave by it and—'

'I don't think that fits this racket.' And I told O'Rourke about Toney, the little snow-bird who had left the house where he had sought protection.

'The lad who was killed last week.' O'Rourke nodded. 'That's what comes of being so secretive. This Colonel has more information coming to him than you'd find in the World Almanac. He tells you this and he tells you that, and shuts up like a clam when you want to know the how of it. Passes his word to stoolies, his word of honor as a gentleman, he tells me. Now, see what comes of it? Two men dead, and me not even knowing where the Italian, Giovoni, was till I looked at his dead body at Elrod's Sanitarium. I'm to take orders, Race.' He looked at me suddenly, 'I think we'll keep quiet on this – this disappearance 'till we hear something. It will be the biggest and worst thing in the world if the Colonel turns up dead. You know who he is, of course.'

'Of course,' I said. 'Colonel Charles Halsey McBride, friend of the deputy police commissioner, and no doubt working secretly for him.'

'Well, it sounds good, in theory. And one can't blame the Commissioner for showing the district attorney's office, and maybe state officials, that he can take care of his own department. If Michelle Gorgon rides, it bursts up the biggest racket the city has ever known. Just now, I'd lay you a hundred to one that I can name twenty-five murders in New York that Michelle Gorgon is responsible for, directly responsible for. Yet, I'd lay you another hundred to one that I couldn't prove a one of them in a court of law. I—' He threw up his head. Some one called him.

'Coming!' said O'Rourke, in answer to a shout from down stairs. 'I'll leave you here, Race to keep an eye on that locked closet door. I wouldn't keep a thing from you. But men are men, and you couldn't expect them to coddle to an outsider. Come on!' he said to the cop by the door, and following that cop out into the hall he closed the door behind him.

What a break for an amateur detective! To go over the room alone, find those hundreds of little clews that the regular police officer misses. You know what I mean. The man is found dead in his palatial library. The police search the place. And then the amateur detective discovers in one corner of the room a cord of wood, or under the bed an Austin car, that the hard boiled Inspector of police had overlooked. Oh, I daresay there are clews, if guys are willing to leave them. But a burnt cigar ash only tells me that some one has smoked a cigar, and nothing more. Real clews, to me, are letters, letters that any guy able to read can understand.

I jerked around from the desk I was pawing over. A key had clicked in a lock, the lock of the closet door.

I stepped a little to one side, drew a bead about the center of that door, saw the knob turn, but heard no click as the latch was slowly slipped back again when the door gave an inch. Then that closet door opened very slowly. Wider – wider – and I saw the figure.

The face was very pale and slightly dirty beneath the long peaked hat. The blue shirt was rather a bad fit, at least, baggy, and little hands were shoved in jacket pockets. A man's clothes and a boy's figure it may have been. But I knew her at once, of course. It was The Flame, alias Florence Drummond. The Girl with the Criminal Mind.

CHAPTER XIX: THE FLAME FIGHTS FOR FREEDOM

Well—' The Flame sort of gasped, as if breathing had suddenly become a luxury, after the closet. 'I'm in a mess, I guess.'

'You guess right,' I said, when I got my own breath back, but I didn't lower my gun.

She smiled a wan little smile as she looked at my gun, and lifted both her hands from her jacket pockets, empty.

'There isn't time for a plea, Race, even an explanation, if I had any. What are you going to do – about me?'

'What do you think?' Maybe I sneered slightly. 'You picked the Gorgons as little playmates. There have been two murders already, and may be another, now. You,' and with a smile of my own, 'you even have put me, or are in with those who have put me on the spot.'

'God in heaven!' she half threw up her hands. 'Don't preach. And there have been as many spots picked out for you, in your day, as for a leopard.'

'You're in bad, Florence.' I came a little closer to her. She looked very tired; there were rings under her eyes. 'There's no reason I should protect you. If you'll sell out the Gorgons, I'll—'

'A stool-pigeon! You want to make a stoolie out of The Flame. You—. I might tell you that letting me go may mean a man's life. I might tell you—. But just one question. Will you let me go? Yes or no.'

'Florence,' I ignored her question, 'if I get you out of this. If—. What will you promise me. What will—'

'Don't play the heavy dick. I'll never squeal, for a price, if I could squeal.' She glanced quickly down at the watch upon her wrist. 'Well, shout out, or stand aside.'

She pushed by me suddenly and made for the door, just as if she didn't know the whole house was thick with police.

I clutched her by the arm and swung her back. She spun, and looked at me. There was hatred, or anger, or defiance, in her eyes. Then she read the truth in mine, I guess, because her eyes went sort of fearful, like a frightened animal, before I spoke.

'The Flame,' I said, as I gripped her arm tighter, 'has swung with her mind and her eyes the honor of many men. You know something, and, by God! you're going to talk. You've made monkeys out of me long enough. Yes, you're right.' I looked straight into her eyes. 'I'm going to turn you in to the cops.'

And she wilted. Was in my arms, her little head upon my shoulder, her arms about my neck. She was sobbing softly. I leaned down and forced up her head. The tears in her eyes were real, the quiver to her lips seemed hardly possible of acting. It was the girl again, but this time without the sparkle of youth in her eyes, the laughter on her lips, and—.

'Race,' she said. 'Race, Race, give me a break. Give me a—. You can't hold me like this and turn me in to the police. You don't know what it may mean. Why, why – let me go. Let me go.'

Maybe I held her the tighter. Maybe I bit my lip. Maybe I even brushed back her hair. I looked straight down at her a moment, and spoke words that my lips formed but my brain never directed. The truth too, perhaps, though who is to tell it.

'Florence,' I said, 'I love you.'

She raised herself on her toes, the sparkle blazed through the mist in her eyes, and – oh, damn it – she kissed me, held me so a moment, then jerking herself free smiled up at me.

'That's what I wanted, Race, that's what I needed to make me—. Goodbye.' She thrust the key of the closet door into my hand, turned again toward the hall door, as my hand shot out and gripped her by the arm.

'You're – you're not going to let me go?' I guess just bewilderment raced over her face at that moment.

'No,' I said very slowly, 'I'm not going to let you go.'

'But you must, now – after – after—'

'I've got to keep you,' I interrupted. 'I've got to turn you in. It isn't you I'm going to live with. It isn't your eyes I'm going to look into the rest of my life. It's myself I've got to live with. It's myself I've got to face in the glass each morning. Maybe I'm hard, cruel. Maybe, as more than one paper has said, I'm a natural killer. Maybe— But, by God! I've never sold out a client, and I won't now. I—'

And I stopped. Feet beat down stairs, along the hall outside the door, seemed to hesitate, then go slowly on, to fall heavily upon other stairs.

'All right,' The Flame said slowly and with an effort, I thought. But she had a way of pulling herself together, and a way of putting something into her eyes that cut like a lash. 'You let me go and I'll give back to you the life of your client.'

I thought that one out.

'Your word, your honor?'

'The honor of The Flame.' She laughed, like a shovel being scraped over a cellar floor. 'I'll give you back the life of your client. That's the whole ticket. Take it or leave it.' And she folded her arms defiantly.

'When?'

'I'll meet you in,' again her eyes went to her watch, 'In thirty minutes, at Maria's Cafe.'

'Maria's been closed by the police, two days ago,' I said.

'Not for you or for me. I told Rudolph Myer to tell you to meet me there anyway. I had something to—. You got the message?'

'No,' I said, 'I didn't.'

'No? Well, perhaps not. What do you say?'

'But how to get you out of here.' I scratched my head. What about O'Rourke? Would I take him into my confidence? Would he let The Flame go, or—? No. I thought I knew how a cop would feel about that. And I thought of the window, the lamp cord. But there would be a cop in the alley. I might call him off. I might—. I turned to The Flame.

She was at the door, had it partly open, was peering into the hall.

'You can't – the police – droves of them,' I whispered hurriedly. 'The window, maybe, if—'

She shook her head and put her finger on her lips. It was in my mind to detain her now. Not because of any duty to a client, though. Because, well, I didn't believe a rabbit could slip through that cordon of police.

I shrugged my shoulders. After all, had I made a right decision? Was it because of my client that I let The Flame go? Or was I just anxious for an excuse not to be the one that turned her in? If the Colonel were dead, they might even hold her for murder.

'At Maria's Cafe, then,' she whispered. And as my hand stretched toward her arm, 'I have an "out",' and she was gone, closing the door silently behind her.

Perhaps it was the best way out. I wouldn't be responsible if she were caught now. And I found myself listening for her feet in the hall, listening vainly. Not a sound. But they wouldn't shoot a woman. They wouldn't—. And I remembered suddenly that The Flame was dressed as a man, also, with a little pang, that The Flame, for all I knew, might be armed and that—. Damn it, which had I let free in that house? The woman of evil or the girl of good?

I threw open the door and listened. Voices from below, just murmurs. Heavy feet on the floor above. Feet that turned and came down the stairs. Loud feet. A dick nodded to me in the dim light, his hand clutching at the banister.

'I don't know what the racket is,' he said, 'but except for them two servants, the man and his wife upstairs, frightened silly, and who never heard a sound, the house is empty.'

'Yeah.' I tried to listen. Would there be a shout as they caught The Flame, or would there be a shot as The Flame was spotted, lurking in some dark corner? Or, and I waited as the cop looked over my shoulder into the room, and then went on his way.

Maybe there were visions of a crumpled little body at the foot of a flight of stairs, a white, childish face, eyes that had no sparkle – and—.

A minutes, two, three, perhaps five passed. Then feet coming up the stairs; Sergeant O'Rourke's gruff voice; his hand upon my shoulder, pushing me into the room. And he spoke.

'Hello!' He stood, looking at the open closet door. Then he turned to me, looked at my hand, and the key I held stupidly in it. 'You found the key, eh?'

'Sure,' I said. 'On the desk, under the blotter, near the phone.' But I still stood by the door, listening.

'Empty, of course.' O'Rourke was in and out of the closet. 'Well, Race, it's a big racket, a big responsibility.' A moment of silence. 'Guess I'll shift the burden, though the orders were to act alone.' He ran fingers through his mottled hair, 'I guess I'll give the Commissioner a buzz.' He reached for the telephone. 'It may turn out a mess if we keep it from the press too long, what with the district attorney's office wondering about it and the entire blame falling on the shoulders of the Commissioner if—. Colonel McBride is quite a lad, you know.'

'Wait.' I held O'Rourke's hand. 'It's just possible I—'

'I – what?' demanded O'Rourke, his hand gripping the phone.

'I may stir up something. Wait.'

'Wait?' gulped O'Rourke. 'Well, I'll pass the "wait" along to the Commissioner. It's his show. I don't want to be an official goat, after all these years.'

We both straightened. The phone rang.

'Now what the hell?' said O'Rourke eagerly, and as he jerked off the receiver, 'Yeah, what do you want?'

A moment's pause, and then from O'Rourke:

'Who wants to know? Who are you? Why, unless I know you, you can't. All right, he's here.' O'Rourke pushed the phone to me, his hand over the mouthpiece.

'Guy wants you. Don't sound like the Colonel. Don't sound like any one. A mouth full of marbles. Better take it.'

'Race,' said a disguised, mechanical voice, that I couldn't recognize.

'Right,' I said. 'Race Williams.'

'Talk a bit, so I can be sure.'

And I did, pressing the receiver close to my ear and pushing O'Rourke off with my shoulder. O'Rourke had a curious turn of mind.

'Now you talk,' I finished.

'It's Rudolph Myer,' came the faint message. 'Tried to get you at your apartment. The Flame must see you at the Cafe Maria. It means a lot, so she says. Suit yourself about going. Some one may be listening. Why she can't put over her own message, I don't know. But she said to come alone, unseen.'

'How did you know I was—'

And I turned to O'Rourke. The click over the wire told me that Myer had cut me off. There's no percentage in talking to yourself.

'Who was that?' asked O'Rourke.

'It was – a lad about another case. I told him to call me here.'

'Mighty liberal with your client's phone.' O'Rourke bit off the end of a cigar, spat it across the room, and added, more sarcastically, 'And forgot you told him you'd be here.'

'Well—' I said. 'Then it's business, this business. I've got to leave you.'

'Sure!' nodded O'Rourke. 'I'll give you an "out" down stairs. The boys wouldn't pass the district attorney through this house tonight without my orders. Remember that.'

'Okay. And sit tight for a bit, O'Rourke. I'll give you a jingle later.'

O'Rourke looked at me before he spoke. Then he said very seriously:

'God! Race – it would be a great thing if your yen for gun-play developed in the right direction, if a certain party, a certain Gorgon got a little round hole in his forehead.'

'Yes,' was the best I could answer. Damn it all, was I getting nerves? Was I still listening for the sharp report that would tell me The Flame was— But I pulled myself together and looked hard at O'Rourke.

'Don't put a tail on me tonight,' I said.

'No.' He seemed to think, and then, 'No, I won't. But remember what I said about the district attorney himself not getting out of here tonight without my Okay.' And raising his voice as he walked with me to the stairs, 'Brophey, see Williams to the corner and let him ride – alone.'

I chewed over O'Rourke's last crack about the district attorney not getting out. I didn't get it then, unless – unless—. But certainly, after the cards O'Rourke and I had dealt each other over the years, he couldn't distrust me. As to holding out on him, he couldn't resent that. It had been our way of playing the game, always. If you don't talk to any one, you can't suspect any one of giving your plans away. When things go wrong, then, you can lay your finger smack on your own chest and nail the guy who's to blame. That much is gospel.

CHAPTER XX: AT MARIA'S CAFE

I had a little time to kill and entered an all night drug store, called up my apartment. Not actually expecting that Jerry would be back, you understand, but just not bent on missing any tricks. Jerry had not returned yet. I hoped he had spotted and, maybe, followed the man who had run when Colonel McBride was grabbed.

Then I drove around the town a bit, just getting the air. And I didn't exactly do any thinking, that is, constructive thinking. But, mostly, I never do. The Flame had certainly pulled a Houdini on the police and Sergeant O'Rourke. Was she still hidden in that house, or had she walked smack through the police net unseen, or had she bought her way out?

There's nothing fantastic about bribery. It's a matter of how much, and the type of man the receiver of the bribe is. You don't have to know him first. It works, from a ten spot to a strange speed cop, to a grand for a police captain, who has found the stock market a sucker's game, but hasn't recognized himself as that sucker yet.

The Flame was clever. There are no two ways about that. She had gotten into the house, maybe, even arranged that bit of kidnaping. Doctor Michelle Gorgon had picked himself some rare talent when he picked The Flame and – my hand went to my breast pocket. Damn it, I was still carrying around that envelope containing that bit of change and the jewelry which I had been requested to turn over to Eddie Gorgon.

Maybe The Flame would answer some questions at the Cafe Maria. The Flame had already intended to meet me there, before she popped out of that closet. And you know—. Well, we're all a bit of a fool, I guess. Somehow I wasn't worried so much about The Flame any more. A guy gets cocky at times. I had held her, told her I loved her. And – she loved me. There were no two ways about that. Any lad who had held The Flame as I did—. But the time was drawing near, so I sped over to Maria's Cafe.

According to my custom I left my car around the corner, walked leisurely down the block, spotted the darkness of the entrance, and went to the little side door down a few steps and knocked.

The door opened almost at once. I nodded as I recognized the bartender.

'Hello, Race.' He opened the door far enough for me to slip into the dimness of the hall, but spotted almost at once the bulge in my right jacket pocket.

'Gawd!' he sort of laughed. 'And me thinking it was just an affair of the heart.'

'There's a lady waiting to see me, Fred?' It was half a question, half a statement.

'Yeah.' He nodded. 'The little room back of the bar.'

'Any one in the bar?'

'No. The Federal officers have closed us up.'

'You're a nice boy, Fred.' I followed him into the bar. 'I wouldn't like to see anything happen to you.' No threat. Just a warning in my words.

'Cripes!' He slowed, and looked at me. 'You ain't got nothing up your sleeve, I don't know about?'

'Nothing up my sleeve. Be sure there's nothing up yours.' I followed him to the door in the rear, down another hall and to another small door.

'You weren't dragged in here.' Fred gave me the words over his shoulder. 'And the door "out" ain't barred and locked now.' He put a hand on the knob. 'What do you say? Got a change of mind? Want to beat it?'

'Do your stuff,' was my say.

'Right!' He spun the knob, shoved open the door and chirped, 'The gent to see you.' He turned quickly, pushed by me and closed the door after him. I heard his feet slipping over the uncarpeted floor of the outer hall.

The room was like any other back room of a speak-easy. A single dome light hung from the ceiling, giving a sharp light. There were eight or ten tables, plain wooden armchairs drawn close to them. Not piled up on top, for they wouldn't be doing any cleaning for a bit. The room still reeked of bum hooch. The open window on the alley didn't help much. There was an old fashioned mantel to one side, above a fireplace that had been bricked up, and a battered but shining silver loving cup supposedly in the center of that mantel.

And, alone in that room, was The Flame. No dirty masculine get-up now. Silk stockings, black skirt, and a tight fitting, worsted sweater coat affair. To crown that off she had a beret cocked on the side of her head, and a cigarette perched jauntily between her lips.

'You did turn up,' she said. 'But then, you would. You always were a fool for courage. Sit down.'

I walked to the window, closed it, and pulled down the heavy shade. I'd rather chance slow death by poison air than a bullet in the back. There was another exit, with a key in the door. I spun the key and turned the knob. It locked all right. An alcove recess, with dirty curtains, proved to be a blind. Just a closet with shelves. Across from that was the door I had entered by. There was no key in the lock. I kicked a chair in front of the door, stuffed a cigarette into my mouth, saw that The Flame was close to the mantel, so dragged up a chair and sat beside her. I could see the window and the door with the chair against it, and had the alcove on the right.

The Flame started. It was the old racket all over again.

'Race, I'll make you a proposition. I'll chuck the Gorgon outfit if you do. I'll chuck the city. We'll cross the pond, hop down to the Riviera, and—'

'Same old hoey,' I cut in. 'Florence, you've given that to any guy you wanted to make – make for the time being – make and then break.'

'Yes.' She nodded very seriously. 'I have. Because I've always thought of it. Thought of it with you, Race.' A hand crept across the table and rested on one of mine. 'We could meet every day, spend long evenings together, understand each other – and bust up the show or stick together for life. There's something big between us, something I never understood. There's been times when I wished you were dead. Times—'

'Florence,' I cut in, 'I'm here for one purpose only. Your promise. I want to know where—'

'Yes, that's so.' She seemed to be listening. 'It's not a good place to talk names here. But, somehow, I wanted you to know.' She leaned forward now, and barely whispered the words. 'I don't know about you, sometimes you simply blunder through things. I've hashed up my life; maybe I wouldn't go if you wished it, maybe I'm hell bent for destruction. But you're looking at a woman now, not a girl. A woman that's going straight to her death, who's got to go through with it.'

I didn't like that talk. Somehow I believed it though. Somehow—. And I stiffened. There, slightly to my left, the knob of a door was turning – the door I had pushed the chair against. I didn't say anything to The Flame. I simply laid both my elbows on the smeared table, my hands up close to my chin, one hand also close to the shoulder holster beneath my left armpit.

The door moved slightly too, very slightly, not enough to even push the chair – that is, the chair by the door. But it moved my chair – or, at least I moved my chair enough to bring me directly facing that turning knob which put my back to the alcove closet, and left me just about on the opposite side of the table from The Flame.

The Flame looked up as I moved. The color seemed to suddenly drain out of her face. Her fingers half reached for her handbag upon the table, hesitated, and she stretched her hand to the mantel and lifted down the loving cup, looking it over. Then she read aloud the inscription on it.

'To Eddie Gorgon,' she read, very slowly. 'On the occasion of his return to the Maria Club – August 27th–1929.' She read it in such a low voice, such a forced, almost ominous voice, that it startled me. But I remembered that dinner too. It was the day Eddie Gorgon was released from the Tombs, when the jury failed to convict him for the murder of an East Side laundry man, who had courageously fought against the then notorious Laundry racketeers.

The door knob quit turning. The door gave a sudden jerk and a voice spoke behind me, by those curtains, from the little alcove closet that I thought had no 'out'. Yep, I had let that door take my attention.

'Don't move,' said the voice of Eddie Gorgon. 'This time, Race, we'll be satisfied with the bullet in your back, where the bullet in any rat should be found. That a girl, Florence. Read him again what's on the cup.'

Trapped? Certainly. Trapped like a child. I could hear Eddie Gorgon cross the floor; knew that he stood a few feet behind me. And there I was, with my right hand under my left armpit, the fingers clasping a gun that I – I could never use. Why hadn't I made sure of that closet? Certainly, those shelves in it hid another door. Was it my stupidity, or my conceit, or my belief in The Flame, or—.

I looked at Florence. I wanted to see how she took it. I wanted to see if at the last minute she would regret my death. I wanted—. And her face was deathly white. She had betrayed me into the hands of the enemy and was paying a price for it. But a hell of a lot of good that would do me now.

'Show him the cup. Read him again what's on the cup.' Eddie mouthed the words. 'Just once more, then I'll let him have it.'

The girl moved the cup. Her eyes sought mine, mine hers, until the cup blocked them both. Yes, the cup blocked them both. And I saw something else. I saw the sinister, rat-like eyes, the twisted lips, and the gun too, the gun held in a steady hand but a thin hand. For Eddie Gorgon seemed long and gaunt – some sixteen or more feet tall, and his arm was as thin as a match stick. And I knew. I was looking at Eddie's reflection in the polished surface of the oval cup.

It was in my mind to draw, swing and fire. All that, of course, while Eddie Gorgon pressed the trigger of his gun. It couldn't save my life. He was too close to miss, too close not to have a chance to fire several times. Just the one chance that I might take him over the hurdles with me.

There was no use to make excuses to myself. Eddie Gorgon had entered that closet while some lad attracted my attention at the moving door. No, I wasn't proud of that moment. There might be one excuse for it, and the worst kind of an excuse. My own vanity. Perhaps subconsciously I had thought that once I had told The Flame I loved her I was safe. That the ambition of her life was realized, that if she could have me she would never think of—. And then just one thought. He travels farthest who travels alone. But The Flame was talking.

'Easy does it, Eddie,' she said. 'Race might talk. You know what he might tell, what your brother wants to know. What—'

'This is my show,' Eddie snarled in on her. 'Look the rat in the eyes, kid. Watch 'em dim. Not a move, Race. Keep them elbows so I can see them. Just a single jerk of your shoulders, and out you go.'

And what was I doing? Just sitting there waiting for death to strike through the mouth of a blazing gun held in the hand of an underworld rat, a common murderer, I had told Jerry.

No. Plainly in that cup I could see the long, gawky form of Eddie Gorgon. My elbows never moved their position on that table. But my hand moved – my fingers moved. Already my right hand had pulled my gun from the shoulder holster, eased it out and shoved it up toward my shoulder. And The Flame still held the cup in her hands – very steady.

Would I try one quick jerk and a shot over my shoulder at Eddie? Maybe I'd have to. The reflection in that cup was clear enough, the features of Eddie, the skinny appearing extended arm, the snub-nosed automatic, the barrel of which appeared long enough, as reflected in that cup, to be a rifle barrel. And—.

'Don't shoot yet, Eddie,' The Flame said. 'I got him here for you, didn't I? I want him to answer a question.'

And my gun crept slowly higher up my left shoulder, my arm never moving, my elbows steady upon the table – just my wrist curling upward and my head moving slightly sideways, slowly sideways. I hoped Eddie was far enough behind me not to see my gun – at least, until it had crept up and over my shoulder.

'Yeah,' snarled Eddie Gorgon. 'But what about me? You made a deal with me. You let me horn you in with us Gorgons, played me for a sucker until Michelle came along, and then what, then what? I got a mind to snuff you, too.'

'It's all the same.' The Flame seemed to half appeal. 'It's the same business, the same racket. I have to listen to Michelle just as you have to listen to him. Whether you brought me in or he brought me in, I'd be working for him just the same. I—'

'That may be Michelle's idea, but not mine,' said Eddie quickly. 'He could have your mind, but not me. I was staking your body, not your mind. Besides which, I still think you've got a yen for this dick. I've played the game, taken orders, done Michelle's dirty work. But no man can take my woman. No, by God! not even Michelle. And Michelle would never know but it was an accident if I knocked you over.'

My gun was higher, right on my shoulder now. Not over enough to show, Just—. The face of Eddie looked so long and lean in that cup, the eyes were so close together.

'Eddie,' and The Flame's voice was soft and low, 'don't talk like that. I saw in Michelle only your interest. I saw only—'

'I seen your face and I seen Michelle's there in your apartment, when you stuck me up. His talk of "in the abstract!" Well, the abstract wasn't in his eyes then. He was just a man who wanted a woman, my woman, and you were just a woman who wanted a man, a bigger man than Eddie Gorgon. You knew what Michelle might mean to you, and you dropped me. Michelle didn't want no mind, he wanted a body. You sold yourself to me, I paid you cash. And, tonight, after the dick, Williams, crashes out I'll—. But he'll take it first.'

And my gun was up. I won't say that I read the will to fire suddenly in Eddie's reflection in the cup. I won't say that I recognized it in his voice, though I think I did. I won't even say that The Flame's sudden shrill cry did the trick.

But she did call out.

'Now, Race!'

Zip! Like that. My finger closed upon the trigger – and I threw myself forward on the table.

CHAPTER XXI: THE MAN IN THE WINDOW

There were two roars, a clang like a bell in a shooting gallery – and I was on my feet. If the cup didn't betray me I had placed a hunk of lead smack between Eddie Gorgon's eyes.

And Eddie Gorgon stood there, his mouth hanging open in surprise. I jerked up my gun to fire again, but I didn't fire. Eddie's gun hung by his side, then his fingers opened and he dropped it to the floor. Not a mark of a bullet on him. No hole in the center of his forehead. And I saw his eyes just before he folded himself up like a jackknife and sank to the floor. Eddie Gorgon had died on his feet, and only a missing tooth or two in the mouth that hung open, and the tiny bubbles forming on his lips – red bubbles – told me where the bullet had gone. Not exactly a perfect shot, maybe, but a serviceable one just the same. I'm no miracle man.

After all, Eddie Gorgon had meant to kill me, and he was dead. I shrugged my shoulders. The thing I had pressed that trigger to do had been accomplished.

The Flame was on her feet too – and clutching the cup to her. She was very white and very shaky, and I noticed that she turned her head from the body. I saw too that the cup had a hole in it – that the first two letters of the word EDDIE were missing. That was the bell-like ring then, as Eddie's bullet hit the cup.

'Did you—? He didn't hit you, Florence?' I was close to her now, supporting her trembling body and placing the cup on the table.

'No, no. It was the cup – saved me. His cup – saved me – and you too.'

'You saved my life, Florence. I—. And after trapping me here.'

'Fool, fool,' she cried out, beating me away as I would have held her. 'I've taken on too much and can't think it out. You, you won't think. It seems impossible and too grotesque to believe, but we must believe it, must. I've never trapped you.' And suddenly pushing me from her and backing away:

'You have nothing to thank me for, Race. He had to go. He had to die. Brains – brains – brains. And it took the animal in Eddie to nearly ruin everything. I can't die yet. I mustn't die yet. I'll die with him, as she died with him, for she died. Damn his soul, what a living death she died!'

Which was all confusing to me, you've got to admit.

The Flame didn't raise a hand this time to stop me as I went toward her. She didn't need to. It was her face, the distorted hatred of it, or was it fear, that I took for hate, or perhaps it was horror. Anyway, I held my ground and simply looked at her, turned, and picking up the cup wiped it clean of finger-prints and placed it back on the mantel.

'We better get out of here, Florence. The shot, the man by the door. The bartender, Fred, and—'

'You can be sure that there is not a soul in this house tonight, right now. If the shot was heard, it was heard outside.' She clutched at her throat and half glanced at the body.

'He's lying there,' she said. 'After all, he was human. Made by the same hand that made you and me and Michelle, and even good people we read about. I must lie like that some day. Soon – very soon – and I know it – and go on toward it. But he's lying there, Race, a human, like you and me. Is he dead?'

I took another look at Eddie, lifted his hand and let it fall back again. I didn't need any medical certificate of death to tell me the truth. It had to be Eddie or me, and – well – if I wasn't exactly glad it was Eddie, I was glad it wasn't me.

'He's dead,' I told The Flame, felt the long envelope in my pocket bend as I knelt so – the envelope which Michelle Gorgon had asked me to deliver to his brother, Eddie. I drew it out. To leave it with Eddie now, there on his chest, would be a gruesome sort of humor, maybe. But it wasn't that which made me stick it back in my pocket. Some one beside the Gorgon crowd might first find Eddie. No need to advertise this bit of killing yet. At least there was no need to implicate The Flame, if others knew about that money and jewelry in the envelope.

No one but Fred, the bartender, had seen me come into the Maria Cafe, and Fred was off for the night. Wise men of the underworld don't speak of the events which precede violent death, at least, to the police, they don't. And certainly it wouldn't take a lot of brain work on the part of either of the Gorgon brothers to guess who sent Eddie bye-bye.

'Come!' The Flame went to the window and threw it open, and let in the cool night air. It felt good. I turned, looked the room over once for any sign of my visit, was satisfied with the inspection and reached the window in time to take the girl by the arm.

'You forget, Florence, what I came here for. I want to know where Colonel McBride is. Is he alive?'

'Yes, he must be. Let us get away from here first. Surely,' she looked at me as I still held her arm, 'we can talk as well in the alley.'

'Yeah, with every ash can concealing a gunman, for all I know? You trapped me twice. You—. Oh, I give you credit for saving my life, Florence. But you change so quickly that I can't chance it. This may be one of your weak, or perhaps, from your point of view, one of your strong moments. Anyway, to love The Flame is to die,' and somewhat bitterly maybe, 'and I put myself on that sucker list tonight, in the house of Colonel McBride when you popped out of the closet. Oh, I'm not blaming you, Florence. I'm beginning to think that label you've won is not just a moniker of the night. The Girl with the Criminal Mind.'

She swung suddenly on me, her hands gripping my arms above the elbows, her eyes looking into mine. Anxious, fearful, haunted eyes. Different than I had ever seen her before. But then, The Flame was always different. Of course women are supposed to faint at violent death, but then, The Flame never ran true to biological or physiological, or what have you, form. Still the death of Eddie had knocked her, it seemed. Yep, The Flame was out of character, or maybe, in character. No one knew the real Flame, I guess, least of all me.

'One question, Race, just one question now. Do you, do you love me?'

'I don't know.' I guess that was the truth.

'Did you mean what you said, there in Colonel McBride's house, when you thought I must be caught or killed? You, you said you loved me, you know. Did you mean it?'

'Yes, I meant it then,' I told her, almost viciously. 'And maybe I mean it now. It's a queer thing though, Florence. No one can lay a finger to it. But love you or not, I don't trust you. I don't think you even trust yourself. I—'

She half glanced at the body again, and shivered slightly. And I let her slip over the sill and drop into the alley. Yes, I let her. But I very nearly stepped on her heels, I dropped so quickly after her.

'You better put out the light,' she told me. 'I imagine that's the way Eddie would have done it, if it were you lying in there. You see, the place is closed. They expect, or Eddie expected, to let the crime ride. Maybe it would be days before they were supposed to find you.'

'Then you did trap me,' I cut in.

'Ah,' she swung on me suddenly, 'then you didn't believe I trapped you. You tried to believe it, but couldn't. That's it, isn't it?' She shook me by the shoulders. 'You couldn't believe it. Try as you might, you could not believe it.'

'Couldn't!' And maybe my laugh was queer. Maybe I didn't want to believe it, but that I didn't was a different thing, again. Inside of me, maybe, I denied it to myself. But I'm a reasoning man, and certainly I believed it.

'You mean to tell me that you didn't know Eddie was there!' I demanded.

'No, I didn't know. I don't expect you to believe me. But I didn't know until I heard him, saw him.'

'But who told Eddie? Fred, the bartender?'

'Fred didn't know whom I was to meet, until you came. He didn't know I was to meet any one until five minutes before you came. That he got in touch with Eddie, or that Eddie just happened to come here, would be impossible.'

'And you didn't have Eddie come to the apartment, your apartment, that night he jumped me from the window?' There certainly was disbelief in my voice.

'No,' she said slowly, 'I didn't.'

'Quite a coincidence, quite a coincidence. And I don't believe in coincidences.'

'Nor do I.' She snapped that back at me as she slipped down the alley and we reached the street. 'But I do believe in using your brains, just once in a while, Race. You can't plug on always like you do.' And with what might have been a smile, 'There won't always be a woman, a woman with a criminal mind, to lift loving cups for you and—'

'Florence,' I said, 'what of Colonel McBride? You promised if I let you go—'

'Oh, I may have lied to you, to get away. It might have been a promise I can never keep. But I'll try, I'll try. Michelle Gorgon knows where he is, and I—. Michelle Gorgon is friendly toward me.'

'Yes,' I said, 'he is.' And with an effort I stuck to my client. 'What about Colonel McBride?'

'Well.' She blazed up. 'Michelle Gorgon wants information from him. He wants to know who is behind McBride, where McBride learns things, and—. Race, go to Michelle, tell him you'll quit the case.'

'Quit for that mountebank!' I sniffed. 'I should say not. A client hired me, and——. But I'll go to Michelle Gorgon all right.'

'If you stay on the case, nothing can save your life now, now that Eddie is dead. Don't you see? Michelle Gorgon loves me. And superstition or not, to love The Flame is to die.' Her lips curled, and her smile was more sad than sinister.

'Death for me too, then.' I half laughed. I could feel her fingers bite into my arm, but she did not speak.

'Florence,' I said. 'You love this man, this Michelle Gorgon. You have been swept off your feet by his influence, his money, his air of superiority, and his admiration for—'

She turned on me viciously. Then, after a moment, she said, almost softly:

'But, yes, he attracts me greatly. To have him love me, want me. It is the ambition of my life.'

She tried to go. I held her arm. But I couldn't say anything. She looked straight at me and spoke again.

'Race, use your head. When the day comes that you believe in me, absolutely trust me, take pencil and paper and go over this, all of this, from the beginning – from the very second that you stepped into the case. Think who is the best informed one you know, of you and me, and—' Then suddenly, 'O'Rourke brought you into this, didn't he?'

'No, he didn't.'

'No – No – But he must have. He must have. It couldn't have been—'

'It was—' And I stopped. I couldn't trust her.

'Rudolph Myer, maybe.' She thought aloud. Then, 'No. That wouldn't be logical. That wouldn't—. But of course it was Rudolph Myer.'

She turned suddenly, flung both arms about my neck, and kissed me. And she left me. Walked smack out of the alley just as a harness bull turned the corner and sauntered leisurely down the street, half a block away.

As for me. I went back down that alley, hopped in the window again and turned out the light. I'd pay a little visit to Michelle Gorgon before Eddie's body was cold.

But I wasn't to pay my little visit to Michelle Gorgon just then. Feet sounded in the alley outside, feet that hit heavily for a moment against stone, then moved cautiously toward that window. It was a cinch that those feet belonged to a heavy body that had dropped from the fence dividing the houses.

It wasn't the harness bull from outside then. My first impulse was to beat it by the front way. My second, to stick it out. It might be one of the Gorgon outfit, come to see if Eddie had disposed of me. There was only one way to find out, that was to wait and see what broke. Nothing dangerous in my position now. There I was, close to one side of the window, my back pushed against the wall, my gun in my hand. No, there was nothing to be alarmed about.

A form blotted out the faint semblance of light from the window. Not light enough there to recognize a man, or anywhere near it. But light enough to barely make out the bulkiness of huge shoulders, and the whiteness of a face. For a moment I got a thrill. To myself I said, 'The Second Gorgon, Joe Gorgon.' My finger squeezed a gun trigger slightly. I was beginning to dislike the Gorgons.

A white hand crept over the sill. A split second later a pencil of light bit into the darkness, crept along the floor, picked out a lifeless foot, ran quickly up the body of Eddie Gorgon and smacked on the side of his face. I rather liked that. The dead gangster lay so that you could not recognize him. My friend at the window would have to come into the room if he wanted to identify the thing that had been Eddie Gorgon, feared racketeer.

He did just that little thing. And what's more, he didn't like it overmuch. Not from any lack of moral courage, I guess, but from the physical effort. For although he started in the window without a moment's hesitation, he didn't like the bodily exertion, for I heard him grunt plainly.

CHAPTER XXII: O'ROURKE HAS A HUNCH

He was in the room now, across to the body, leaning over and turning the dead face into the light of the flash. He whistled softly, muttered something to himself that didn't seem like a curse, and I was smack behind him, my gun in his back.

'Don't move, brother,' I said, 'unless you want to lie down beside your little playmate. Now – that flash. Good.' And the man laughed, and the light struck his face.

Maybe I laughed too, but not with quite as much mirth. The hard, grizzled map I looked into was that of the 'honest cop', Detective Sergeant O'Rourke.

'Well,' I said, 'what are you going to do?'

And I didn't drop my gun. The first thing I thought of then was Rudolph Myer, a habeas corpus writ, and the amount of bail. Not that I didn't trust O'Rourke, but he might be the efficient cop now, not the loyal friend. Through and through O'Rourke was a cop.

'What am I going to do?' He ignored my gun, walked to the window, closed it, pulled down the shade and pressed the electric button. 'It's what are you going to do, and what did you do?'

'I took your advice,' I told him, 'and laid a bullet in one of the Gorgons.

It was self-defense, and more. I was, was trapped here. And you put a tail on me, after you promised you wouldn't.'

'Well,' he said, 'it don't look like you were trapped. Let's talk it out, Race. You and me are in the same racket and under the same boss, but working at odds. And I ain't above telling you now, that I got you into the Gorgon mess. But that's confidential.'

'*You* got me in. I thought—'

'You thought it was Rudolph Myer, and so it was. That was my little plan. I didn't want you to know. But no matter, now. Working the same game or not, here's a lad been croaked. We can't just pretend it never happened, you know. We'll run it through as a matter of form. There's big people behind you. McBride, if he's alive.'

'He's alive,' I told O'Rourke. 'Don't charge me with this shooting. Let me put it in a form of a complaint. I went to the Maria Cafe, was attacked, and shot a man in self-defense – and I call on the authorities to investigate the attack on me. Then it's the district attorney's move against me. I'll be ready with bail, and—'

'Good stuff, and does credit to your honest nature.' O'Rourke grinned. 'But Eddie isn't going to be missed that bad. At least, by the police department. You may not know it exactly, but you're just as much a part of the city's police system, with their rights,' and with a little grimace, 'and without their restrictions, as I am. I've got a lot of authority, and a big lad to take the blame, if things go wrong. We'll let it stand as a gang killing for a little bit, at least, to outsiders.'

'O'Rourke.' I cut in with a sudden idea. 'Could you keep this quiet, just for a few hours, maybe, until—' And I went into the thing. 'I want to see Michelle Gorgon. I want a good talk with him. I—. But if he knows I got his brother, well, it won't give me a chance to work on this thing. Every—'

'I know,' said O'Rourke, rubbing his chin. 'How long do you want?'

'A couple of hours.'

'It's after twelve,' said O'Rourke, snapping out his watch. 'I'll give you until morning, five o'clock, or if you can make it earlier, better still. But you can't go to Michelle Gorgon now – not quite yet.' And very slowly, 'His wife was moved last night to a private hospital down town. Do you know what that means, Race?'

'No,' I said, 'I don't.'

'But I think I do.' O'Rourke nodded vigorously. 'Nothing can happen in Doctor Gorgon's home. He's through with her. She's going to die.'

'But she couldn't. He wouldn't dare murder his own wife. That would be the end. The—'

'He murdered his wife years ago. But who the wife was—?' he scratched his head. 'The best detective in the city has been to Italy, Race, and if that little Giovoni spoke the truth, there's no evidence to show that Michelle Gorgon was ever married before, in Italy or any place else. I tell you, I've been working on Michelle Gorgon for over a year, and it wasn't until this judgeship business came up and Colonel McBride was secretly called in by his buddy, the Deputy Commissioner, that I carried authority in it. The Commissioner himself is behind McBride. I tell you, this judgeship business is nothing to Michelle Gorgon's murder racket. He has many enemies, of course. But when an enemy becomes big enough for him to notice – that enemy dies.

'But if I couldn't find out anything about Michelle Gorgon's former wife, whose, at least claimed to be, father-in-law got rubbed out the other night – I have found out plenty about his present wife. More than any man in the world knows; more than Michelle Gorgon himself knows; more than the wife herself knows. Laugh that off.' There was a ring of pride in his voice.

'And Gorgon's wife––. What do you intend to do?'

'I intend to talk to her. I understand she's slightly loose in the upper story. And I know that she had a terrible accident, airplane accident, in which Michelle Gorgon didn't get hurt, and I understand that she had a gentleman friend, for she was a very beautiful woman. There's a story that Michelle Gorgon maimed her purposely, but like his other activities it can't be proved. Anyway, she didn't jump from the plane, but crashed with it. I want to talk to her before anything happens to her. That's that. If that isn't playing the game with you, Race, nothing is.'

'But you promised not to put a tail on me, and––'

'So that rankles. Well, forget it. I didn't. No more questions about that, now. Let it drop. But the phone in Colonel McBride's house leaked as soon as it rang. Anyway, we'll forget who you came here to meet. But come on. We'll have to chance the discovery of the body. You'd have chanced that anyway.'

'Isn't it a little late for a hospital interview?' I asked.

'Sure,' said O'Rourke. 'But if it were four in the morning I'd go anyway. It isn't something, I think, that can be delayed overlong.

'You know, Race,' O'Rourke told me, when we were safely out of the Maria Cafe and speeding to the private hospital in my car, 'you're a man of your word and I'm a man of mine. Remember that. We've got to work fast on this, before something else happens. I work for the city. I work against time. I use stool-pigeons. Play on crooks who have been, or think they have been, double crossed. Even ignore some small crime if the individual will give information concerning a bigger one. I thought I'd go any length to reach my ends, and I have – I did. I've stirred up thoughts of passion, hatred, and vengeance. Now and here's a terrible thing for a lad who's been an honest cop over twenty years to say. If you were to put a bullet between them cute eyes of Michelle Gorgon, I'd, well, I don't ask you to do it and I don't say I'd thank you for doing it, but I'd sleep easier at night and, and, by God! I might even go on the witness stand and perjure myself that I saw Doctor Gorgon draw a rod and heard him threaten to kill you.'

'You've got a little hatred for this bird yourself, O'Rourke.'

'Yes,' he said, 'I have. But it isn't so much hatred of Michelle Gorgon, but fear, fear of what I've done, fear of the uncontrollable fires I lit. But maybe the day will come, Race, when you'll be wanting to put a little lead bullet between these same two eyes of mine.'

I laughed and said:

'It wouldn't be a hard mark to hit.'

'No,' said O'Rourke, very seriously, 'it wouldn't. But this'll be the place. And it's as respectable as it looks.' I stopped the car before the building, as O'Rourke talked on. 'Ritzy too, and high priced. There's a doctor's name behind this institution that's gospel to the medical profession; a lad to run it who hasn't had ten minutes to himself to hobnob in the underworld since he graduated from medical school. It looks just like the sort of a place to faze the lowly Mick, known as Detective Sergeant O'Rourke. So, under those conditions, we'll go through with it. In we go.'

And in we went.

Somehow O'Rourke seemed different to me. He talked more. Was it nerves? But surely, after his years as the most active detective on the police force, he wouldn't get finicky over a few murders more or less. I guess, maybe, he was just the man hunter on the hunt. The eagerness gets under your skin, you know. Still, he seemed different. But then, every one seemed different. Maybe we were all feeling that sinister air of superiority of the Third Gorgon. And I grinned to myself – of the Second Gorgon now. After all, Eddie was one of them. Eddie was protected by his association and relationship. And you couldn't get away from the fact that all Eddie needed now was a shovel and some loose dirt.

The nurse who let us in was not so much surprised, but the lad in the white coat, who came out of the little room behind her, was more than surprised. He was shocked, and let us know it.

'Mrs. Gorgon – really. You can't see her, of course. And at this hour, under no circumstances.'

'I know it's irregular.' O'Rourke scratched his head.

'Irregular!' Doctor Importance, in the white coat, elevated his nose to avoid the stench of our presence. 'It's impossible.'

'Police business.' O'Rourke produced his shield. 'And damned important police business. We'll see the lady at once.'

The nose came down and had to breathe the same air with us.

'May I—? You have authority, of course.' But there wasn't much confidence in the young doctor's voice. He was simply repeating something he had read some place.

'You see the ticket of admission to the show.' O'Rourke shoved the badge up higher. 'I'll see Mrs. Gorgon now, just us two. Or if you want to stand on ceremony, I'll bring in the boys and make a party of it.'

'I – I may notify Doctor Revel?' he half stammered. 'It's – We couldn't disturb the other patients. Surely you wouldn't – Good God! It's not a raid. Not a raid, here.'

'Never mind Doctor Revel. Come on, shake a leg.' And we were all three leaving the room.

There was no doubt that O'Rourke had bulldozed the young doctor into taking us to Mrs. Gorgon's, or Madame's room.

'She has a weak heart, a very weak heart. You'll—'

'Tut, tut, young feller, me lad.' O'Rourke was patronizing. 'We're here to protect her.' And as we left the elevator and entered the little white room, O'Rourke said, 'Doctor Revel will be glad we came. You can notify him now.' With that he pushed the young doctor into the hall, hesitated a moment, saw the nurse that came down the long corridor toward us, and holding the door open, said:

'We're police officers, Miss. We've got to question Mrs. Gorgon. Better come along with us.' And to me, 'I'm taking a chance, Race, but I think it's justified – but we better have this young lady with us.'

O'Rourke switched on the light, closed the young doctor out in the hall, motioned the nurse toward the bed, and finding no key in the lock, dragged a chair against the door. The nurse was bright but slightly nervous. However, if she resented our presence, or even found it distasteful, she didn't let us know it. She obeyed O'Rourke to the letter.

We stood back while she approached the bed and spoke to the restless form upon it. The brown eyes opened now and blinked in the light – searching – fearful – dead, haunted eyes. Perhaps as the eyes of The Flame had been, for a moment.

'Two gentlemen to see you, Madame. Two gentlemen,' the nurse repeated, softly. 'They want to talk to you. They—'

And Madame saw us. A withered hand went to the scraggy hair; a sheet was jerked quickly up to hide the discoloration on her neck, and almost as quickly the twisted hand went back under the clothes again. She spoke, her teeth getting in the way of her words.

'They mustn't see me, Miss Agnes – not like this. I'm not ready to receive callers. Two gentlemen, Miss Agnes? One a young man, a handsome young man, like—. No – no.' And off she went under the covers.

But I won't go into the tricks of Madame. Both O'Rourke and I were glad we had the nurse, Miss Agnes, with us.

She looked at us once, more questioning than disdainfully. But O'Rourke held his ground.

'I must talk to her,' he told the nurse, and at her suggestion we parked ourselves behind the bed screen while Madame was made what she called 'respectable'.

She talked too. Clearly enough sometimes, incoherently at others.

She sort of wandered on.

'No mirror, Miss Agnes. But then, I never have a mirror. What do you think the gentlemen wish, Miss Agnes? The young man, now – he came to see me once before. My skin does not feel so soft and beautiful – but then, my hand has lost its sense of touch. A little more powder, my dear. I'm sure, a little powder. It's my vanity, Miss Agnes.' She lowered her voice to a hoarse whisper. 'My husband was always so jealous,' and she giggled. It was a girlish giggle. It was eerie. 'Now, why can't I see myself, just once. He was a musician, so young, so handsome. He adored me, played to me, wrote a song just for me. And this accident. No, he mustn't see my twisted body. But my face, it is still beautiful, my eyes, at least. Michelle always said so, until last week. There – put my hand beneath the coverlet, and—'

We stepped out and saw the woman. What a hideous sight she was! Far worse now for the powder and rouge and nightcap on her head. But most of all it was the glint in her eyes – the simper to cracked lips that were now a vivid red. The yellow skin, great patches of it raw flesh, that were more horrible for the thickness of the rouge and the great daubs of powder.

'Madame is ready,' said the nurse, Miss Agnes, looked at us. Partly in warning, maybe, for the woman was indeed terrible to look at.

O'Rourke jerked erect, went to the bed and sat down upon it.

'Mrs. Gorgon,' he said. 'We – I'm a friend. I heard you had some trouble. You wanted to talk about it with me.'

'Trouble, to talk with you? I thought—. But then, maybe it is not true – and it is my face also. It was a very beautiful face. Who are you?'

'I am a police officer. I—'

The door knob turned, the chair slipped, and O'Rourke swung his head and spoke to me.

'Keep him in the hall,' he said.

And I did. I pushed through the door and backed the gray haired man into the hall before me. He was wearing a dark dressing gown, and plenty of dignity.

'I am Doctor Revel,' he said. 'What is the meaning of this intrusion?'

And you had to admire the doctor. He didn't fuss and fume, and I didn't give him any heavy line.

'Police duty.' I let it go at that, but I blocked the doorway.

The doctor looked at his wrist watch.

'Let me see your warrant,' he said.

'Everything's Okay,' I told him. 'You have no cause for alarm. It—'

'If things were strictly as they should be, you would have seen me first.'

'You can take the matter up with Headquarters in the morning, if you're not satisfied with the proceedings.' I pretended an indifference.

'That has already been attended to.' The doctor nodded. 'At least, the police precinct nearest the hospital has been called. To me, the matter is very serious indeed. I can not of course create a disturbance in the hospital; there are some very sick people here. The disturbance, my dear friend, will be created tomorrow, make very sure of that.' The doctor had a mean sort of calm about him.

The woman inside screamed. The nurse spoke quickly. I think O'Rourke cursed, but I'm not sure. But the doctor stiffened, and I stuck my head back in the door and said:

'The head doctor's here and he's not friendly and he's telephoned the precinct.'

And the doctor stepped by me and into the room. Of course I could have stopped him, but I didn't. I wasn't fooling with any medical student now, and I knew it. This guy cut some ice.

He ignored O'Rourke and went straight to the woman on the bed, bent over her a moment, pulled out the twisted hand, pressed his other hand across her forehead, spoke quickly to the nurse, and I saw the bottle from which she measured the drops. It was digitalis. A strong heart stimulant.

O'Rourke and I stood around like a couple of saps. At length the doctor turned on O'Rourke and backed us toward the door.

'Well—' he said, when he had us in the hall, 'have you an explanation?'

O'Rourke stiffened, and the bulldog chin shot out. The cop was ever dominant. He wouldn't take water even then. He was a tough old bird, and no mistake.

'Yes, I have,' he said. 'You read about the murder in Elrod's Sanitarium last week. Do you want to see that poor woman there snuffed out the same way? Don't high hat me, Doctor. I've been on the Force too long. And don't look so hurt. You read your papers. If you don't, some one must have told you. You know who that woman is. You know who brought her here. And you know what the name Gorgon stands for – unless you simply think, like a lot of others, that it stands for money only.'

It was good stuff. The doctor didn't seem so cocky. Oh, his dignity was still there, but it had dents all over it. Finally he won out, and said:

'Are you hinting that my cupidity made me, made me take in this unfortunate woman?'

'I'm hinting at nothing,' said O'Rourke. 'Doctor Gorgon buys what he wants. That woman's life is in grave danger, and not from what's ailing her. I came in, didn't I? And he came in, didn't he?' O'Rourke jerked a thumb at me. 'Now, what's to prevent some one else coming in, who hasn't got the woman's interest at heart, like us? And you can't throw hard looks and pompous words down the muzzle of a murderer's gun. Nor will they wait while you notify the nearest precinct.'

Doctor Revel had a mental picture of the stabbing at Elrod's, I guess. A mental picture that for the first time he permitted himself to think might happen in his tony establishment. His placid map and dignity of bearing were playing him false.

'I never guessed. I didn't know.' He wiped the beads of sweat from his forehead. O'Rourke wasn't a bad talker, a bad cop. 'Why didn't you tell me? Why—'

'Because I thought maybe you'd do just what you did do. Start the phone working. Get the newspapers into it, and—'

'The papers? The newspapers? The woman must go, of course. She's strong enough to move. We can't keep her here. She must go.' The doctor was getting panicky. The word 'murder' had thrown him.

'I thought—' O'Rourke started – clamped his mouth shut again and looked down the hall.

The slow old fashioned elevator had come to a stop. The door opened almost silently and a figure stepped into the light. It was Doctor Michelle Gorgon. Malacca cane, gray suède gloves, black ribbon dangling from his glasses, and all.

CHAPTER XXIII: DOCTOR MICHELLE GORGON

'Really,' Michelle Gorgon said when he reached us. 'Doctor Revel, Mr Williams, and our dear friend, Sergeant O'Rourke. Surely something must have happened. Not, Madame, not a bad turn. Not—'

'You'll have to move your wife, Doctor Gorgon.' Doctor Revel got that off first crack. 'We can't have a scandal here. We—'

'Scandal! You will explain yourself, Doctor.' And Michelle Gorgon's voice was just the right pitch, just the right touch of doubtful indignation.

O'Rourke didn't try to stop Revel. I guess it would have been useless just then.

'Sergeant O'Rourke tells me that your wife – that she may be murdered here, and—'

'Good Lord! an attempt on her life.' Michelle Gorgon clutched at his heart – and, damn it! looked as if he meant it.

'No – no. But there will be – there is to be—. Sergeant O'Rourke—' And O'Rourke horned in.

'It's like this,' he said easily. 'I was tipped off that there would be, or might be, an attempt on her life. I came here to see that everything was right, just right. No objections to that, eh, Doctor Gorgon?'

'Most certainly not. Most commendable.' Michelle Gorgon nodded approval. 'But, really, it seems absurd. Why should any one wish to harm her? Poor thing, she has not long for this world, I'm afraid.'

'Vengeance on you, Doctor,' said O'Rourke. 'That might be it.'

'On me, on me. But surely. Ah! yes, I see. This imaginary hue and cry in the yellow sheets. Connecting me up with my brother's activities. We make enemies in life, of course. We—' He put both hands to his head. Not tragically, not dramatically even – rather, a natural movement – which, if acting, was superb. 'My wife, Madame. I shall see her. I shall comfort her.' This, as Madame called out.

And he did comfort her. At least he quieted her in the few minutes he was alone in the room with his wife, while we stood in the hall, Doctor Revel still insisting that the woman be moved, and O'Rourke just as insistent that she stay at the hospital.

'You can't throw her out tonight. The papers would get hold of you and razz you. To move her would work right into their hands if—' And O'Rourke, seeing that that wasn't a good line, killed it with a sudden snap to his lips. Doctor Revel was interested in human life, of course. But naturally he was interested in the reputation of his establishment. Certainly, any one will admit that a murder in his hospital wouldn't help business any.

'I'll tell you,' said O'Rourke. 'I could put a couple of men in the house for you, or better still, one inside and one outside.'

'Wouldn't that be conspicuous?' But Doctor Revel was coddling to the idea now.

'They'll be in plain clothes. You might even tack a white coat on the inside one. He can stay by the woman's door. That'll protect your hospital, my reputation, and the woman's life. But here's Doctor Gorgon.' And O'Rourke turned and told Michelle Gorgon what was on his mind.

Michelle Gorgon seemed enthusiastic.

'Excellent, Sergeant. Madame won't have to know, and won't have to be unprotected. That is settled then, though I think and hope that Sergeant O'Rourke's information about that unfortunate woman is – is erroneous. But you disturbed her, Sergeant. Oh, unintentionally, I know. What you said to her I could not discover, of course, from her. Her mind does not function coherently on the same thought for five minutes. Does it, Doctor?' He smiled encouragingly at Doctor Revel.

'She is lucid at times,' said Revel. 'She talks often of some imaginary poet or musician whom she loves. She would rather die before he could see her as she is, and – and—. Huh – huh—' The doctor cleared his throat as Michelle Gorgon frowned slightly. 'Nothing odd in that hallucination, sir. To the contrary, rather to be expected.'

'No,' O'Rourke whispered to me. 'Nothing wrong in that, Race, because it happens to be the truth.'

Then the front doorbell rang, and a cop was at the door, and some explanations were in order in the little reception room below.

Michelle Gorgon insisted that Doctor Revel see the patient, Madame, once more before he left.

'It will ease my mind, Doctor,' Gorgon said. 'It is some time since I was interested actively in medicine. I have brought her a few books, rather trashy, Doctor. Love stories, the old ten and fifteen cent variety. But she seems to be able to read them, or get snatches from them, for they ease her mind. Kindly let her have the light on until she becomes calmer. I do not wish to interfere, of course, with the regulations of the hospital, but she has been in the habit of awakening and reading until one-thirty, or playing at reading. She likes, too, to be alone when she reads. Miss Agnes can wait outside her door, or – as you see fit.'

Doctor Revel left us. Five minutes later he returned. Not a word had been spoken between us as we waited.

'Mrs. Gorgon is rather restless and disturbed, but didn't wish to talk to me,' Doctor Revel told Michelle Gorgon.

'There is no danger!' Michelle Gorgon came to his feet. 'Nothing—'

'If you mean that she may take a bad turn in the night. Certainly not. Not more than any other night. But I expect that she will have a restless night, a most unsatisfactory night.'

And he looked around at the three of us, seemingly to place the blame equally between us.

'May I drive you gentlemen home?' There was perhaps the slightest twist to Michelle Gorgon's lips as he spoke.

'I'll stay here for a bit,' said O'Rourke. And when Doctor Revel frowned, 'Just till I get a man over. And I won't disturb your patient further tonight.'

Michelle Gorgon looked at me.

'And you, my dear Williams, will you favor me with your company?'

'I don't know if I'll favor you – but I'll go along with you. I'd like a talk with you.'

'Talk, talk seriously?' He stopped and looked down at me as we descended the steps of the private hospital.

'Seriously.' I nodded, and meant it.

'Then you will come home with me, to my sanctuary, to my library. You're not afraid, of course?'

'Hardly.' I shrugged my shoulders. 'Are you?'

'Really, you joke. Really, Williams, I would fear you more dead than living. For the memory of the dead always so far outshines and even magnifies the petty significance of the living.'

'I don't get that,' I told him. And what's more, I wasn't sure that he got it. Somehow I had the idea that Doctor Gorgon's pretty vanities with words were simply the wish being father to the thought, and in his case, perhaps, farther from the thought. In plain words, I mean he'd like to be considered one of the literati, and was far from it.

'No, perhaps you don't understand it. But tonight I shall not be epigrammatic. You will get in?' We had reached his car.

'No. I've got my own boat, and may need it later. I'll follow you home.'
Michelle Gorgon shook his head.

'Do not follow me.' And when I showed some surprise, 'Precede me. To follow is dangerous. It might be misunderstood. Your life may become very precious to me. I am glad you have not run across my brother, Eddie. You see, he understands that your sudden evaporation from our every day existence would not be entirely displeasing to me. You are very fortunate, Williams. For the time being, I have taken you off what we so vulgarly hear expressed as "the spot".'

'Why?' I stopped as I moved toward my car, behind his.

'Why?' He hesitated a moment, and then, 'Because I have suddenly decided to go out in society. Because I have decided to marry again. I would rather, for a bit, at least until after this marriage, be compared with the living rather than the dead.'

'But you are married.' The thing just blurted out.

'So I am, so I am.' He playfully tapped me on the chest with a long, delicate finger. 'But I have a feeling that it will not be for long. There are times when I really believe I have psychic power. This is one of those times.'

'But who are you to—'

'Tut, tut, Williams. A man does not announce a bride while he has a wife living. But take care of yourself. My car will follow yours closely. Do not fail to visit me. I shall make you a most enticing offer of money, and introduce you to my future wife.'

'But a man does not announce a bride while he has a wife living.' I repeated his crack half sarcastically.

'Quite so, quite so,' he told me. 'And I repeat – I shall introduce you to my future bride.'

With that he was gone, stepping into the huge Rolls Royce, the door of which a man held open for him.

CHAPTER XXIV: HIGH-PRICED INFORMATION

I started toward my car, hesitated and stood in the middle of the sidewalk. Had that last crack of his been a threat against his wife's life? Should I go and tell O'Rourke? Should I—. But the Rolls still stood at the curb and O'Rourke surely expected more than I did that the woman's life might be attempted. Also O'Rourke and another cop were already in that private hospital. One thing was sure. O'Rourke was a thorough police officer. Only the best men would watch over Madame's life, and—

'The night air grows chilly,' Michelle Gorgon was calling from the window of his car. 'If you would rather postpone our little talk, and chat with the genial Sergeant O'Rourke, it is perfectly agreeable to me.'

'Be right with you,' I said confidentially, hopped into my car, stepped on the starter, shoved the old girl in second gear, and was away, shooting down the street before the big Rolls Royce could even get moving.

No, sir, I didn't believe that business of taking me off the spot, or if I did believe it, I wasn't going to test out the accuracy of my instinct in such matters. It might be easy for Michelle Gorgon to pass the word along to certain racketeers, 'Empty your machine gun into the car I'm following.'

I burnt up the city streets, lost track of the Rolls entirely, and had my car parked around the corner and was waiting in the pretentious lobby of the Park Avenue apartment when Michelle Gorgon came in.

'An astounding man, Williams, most astounding.' He shook my shoulders playfully. 'You do everything with such enthusiasm. Now, when I wish speed,' he went on, as we rode up in the elevator, 'I take the airplane. I'm a great believer in the future of air travel, perhaps, even the present. I have more than one plane of my own.'

'Yes,' I said, 'I've heard about your plane. Your wife likes it too, I suppose.' And the sneer would not keep out of my voice.

Michelle Gorgon looked at the elevator operator, but said nothing until we had alighted at the top floor and the elevator door closed behind us. Then he said:

'That was untactful, and if not unkind, at least thoughtless. I am a man, Williams, who is no longer young. It has only been given me in life to love two women.'

'Then you were married twice.' I wasn't trying to be tactful.

'Not yet,' he told me, let himself in the heavy steel door, and we walked across the roof, up the steps of the porch and into the bungalow. Once again I found myself in the library. Once again the old servant brought the No. 1 Sherry and left us alone.

I got up, walked about the room, spotted the door behind the curtain, that Madame had left by on a previous occasion and found it locked. Michelle Gorgon watched me without objection, but with a little twist to his thin lips, and perhaps a narrowness to his eyes, though they never blinked. Just regarded me steadily, like the unblinking orbs of a young baby.

One thing I made certain of. That was – that no one was hiding in that room, or behind those curtained windows. Now, I'd fix my chair, back against read solid plaster and keep it there. I wouldn't be trapped again. Not twice in one night, by a Gorgon, anyway.

'You are perfectly safe here,' Michelle Gorgon told me. 'Besides, Sergeant O'Rourke knows you came with me.' And he added, rather suggestively I thought, 'Sergeant O'Rourke also knows that I came here with you, as does my servant.'

I looked up.

'What do you mean?'

'That Sergeant O'Rourke probably knows why you came here.'

'Do you know why?' My hand was on my gun now; I was leaning slightly forward. 'Do you know why I took a chance like this, coming here alone with you, to your home, again?'

'Yes,' he said, 'I do know. To threaten me with physical violence unless I disclose certain information to you. That would be your way.'

That startled me. In fact, that was almost exactly what was on my mind, but not altogether.

'You're partly right,' I told him. 'But not to threaten you, Michelle Gorgon, to act. You know my ways. You took your chance when you brought me here. Colonel McBride has paid me, trusted me. He has disappeared.'

'Not an affair of the heart, I hope.' Michelle Gorgon looked up at me from his easy chair.

And that was that. Not heroic, nor moving picture stuff. Not the sort of blood that runs through the body of a hero, maybe. But I was alone in that room, with probably the greatest murderer who ever cheated the hot seat. I took two steps forward, and had him by the throat. And I was talking.

'Now, where's McBride? You don't believe in the physical, Doctor Gorgon, except in the abstract. Well, you'll believe in it now. Where—' My fingers started to tighten upon that throat, but stopped. Those eyes held me, still staring, still unblinking, and yet there was nothing of alarm in them. Perhaps, just a touch of the curious. He spoke very slowly as he watched me.

'You are acting rather childishly, Race Williams. Just a moment—' he cut that in quickly, as my fingers started to tighten and I started to talk. 'Let me assure you,' he went on, 'that all arrangements are made for such a contingency as this. I believe, if I wished, I could go through physical violence, even torture, with a silent tongue, but,' and he actually smiled, 'I will not put myself to the test. I am just as determined a man as Colonel McBride. I imagine he has resisted pressure. But the point is – if you so much as close those fingers on my throat, the place will be alive with servants, not gunmen, maybe, but servants. I assure you that my system of protection here is unassailable.'

He didn't speak like a man who was bluffing. He didn't – I let go of his throat and stepped back. I had something else up my sleeve.

'You may be right,' I told him. 'You may have a system that will protect you from physical violence. But what would prevent me placing a bullet smack between those cute eyes of yours?' Somehow, O'Rourke's words crept in then.

'Well,' he smiled with his lips, and actually sipped the sherry, 'you and I would call it, shall I say, ethics. My brothers would call it "lack of guts." And do you know, Williams, I think that my brothers would be right.'

Maybe he was right. Maybe he wasn't. I was fingering my gun speculatively. Oh, it's a weakness. I guess he was right, after all. It's the 'woman' in all of us. I just couldn't bring myself to press that trigger and snuff him out. Couldn't? And I wondered. The men he had murdered, the man, Colonel McBride, whom he now spoke of as being under 'pressure', which probably meant 'torture'. And, I let the trigger of my gun slip back and forth slowly. Who was the woman he was going to marry? Was it The Flame? I half raised my gun.

Did he read what was in my face, or was there anything in my face? I don't know, and so he couldn't. But I have always had an idea that at that moment Doctor Gorgon was nearer to death than he ever was before. And so did he, for he cut in quickly, and his eyes blinked now.

'Also,' he said slowly, 'it would be most disastrous for the Colonel, most disastrous.'

'What you're telling me practically amounts to a confession.' I tried police work.

'Hardly.' And his smile came back as my gun went down on my knees. 'Let us not be children at play. You knew that I knew where Colonel McBride was before you came here. O'Rourke knows that I know. At Albany they know that it is my hand that guides the destiny of our courts. The rookies on the police force know that, when a man dies who has displeased the right people, that it is the hand of a Gorgon who directs that death. But what does it avail them? Nothing. Absolutely nothing! Protection is money. I have that. Protection is influence. I have that. Protection is fear. I have established that. Big men have sought my influence because it gratifies their ambition. They have taken my money because it gratifies their greed. And they've taken my orders because they recognize fear. And I can gratify that emotion to the last degree.'

He was leaning forward now. And suddenly he unclosed his hand and hurled a bit of paper across the table at me. I unfolded it with my left hand as I watched him.

'The soul of Rose Marie cries out for vengeance,' was all that was now written on that paper. But a word, two words or perhaps three, following the word 'vengeance' had been carefully erased.

And the face that I had seen once before in that room was looking at me now. The face I had seen that first night, when Michelle Gorgon found his wife in the library. The contorted, evil features that Michelle Gorgon couldn't control. What a rotten soul the beast must have. The distorted mouth, the eyes now protruding, the lips quivering like an animal's. Yep, Michelle Gorgon was just what Joe was, what Eddie had been. Just an underworld rat. And this time his face stayed coarse and evil when he spoke.

'I'll give you one hundred thousand dollars for the name of the person who wrote that message, who for the past week has been sending those messages. Who—'

'What do you mean?'

'What do I mean!' He fairly cried out the words. 'Who is it that rings the phone at night? Who is it that speaks that same message in the cracked voice of a man who tries to imitate a woman? Yet, it is a woman's trick. But there can be no woman, no man either, no living man, now. Don't you see? Don't you understand? No one in the world but myself knows who that – who Rose Marie is.'

'Your first wife, in Italy.' I tried to throw him.

He only laughed.

'McBride thinks of a first wife, in Italy. The shrewdest Italian detective on the Force has visited my home town in Italy, traced me until I left for America, traced every move I made since leaving the boat in New York, twenty-three years ago. But they know nothing. Giovoni told them nothing. Williams, I offer you one hundred thousand dollars for the name of the person behind McBride, behind O'Rourke. The person who tells them so much, but no more. The person who seeks a personal vengeance against me. The only thing in life I have feared. And I don't know, don't know who it is, nor why it is.'

'Rose Marie, eh?' I was looking at the name.

'Yes, Rose Marie. Let that help you. But, one hundred thousand dollars for the name of the person. It's a lot of money.' He was calmer now. 'I have the cash here, ready to pay. Crisp, new bills.'

'But suppose I don't know who wrote it?' I wouldn't admit I didn't know, yet. Which, from his next words, was an unnecessary precaution on my part.

'Of course you don't know. If you knew what this person—' he spread his arms far apart. 'Colonel McBride don't know, or he would have acted. But Colonel McBride knows who the person is, for that person gave him such information as he has. That person suddenly decided to work it alone. Yes, McBride knows who it is, and McBride won't tell. Won't tell yet.' A drawer in the table came open.

'One hundred thousand dollars. I have it here. It is yours if you will tell me the name of every one, and what's taken place, to the least detail, since you entered this attempt to eliminate the Gorgons, last week.'

I shrugged my shoulders.

'You'd be wasting your money,' I said, but I was trying to think. Was some one onto Michelle Gorgon? Did some one know what that little Italian, Giovoni, had known, and was that some one waiting to get a good price for that information from Colonel McBride? But that couldn't be. If it was simply a question of money they'd blackmail Michelle Gorgon. So I tried that question on him while he seemed ready to talk.

'Has any one tried to shake you down?'

'No, no. There is something deeper than that, far deeper. I can not understand it. But this person who knows, keeps it, keeps the knowledge from all but me. Why? Why?'

'Why do you tell me, why put anything into my hands?'

'Put anything into your hands!' His voice was scornful. 'McBride was told, and O'Rourke was told, that I murdered my wife back in Italy. They—. But no matter. You have been told it too. But like every other accusation against me, it fell through, when—'

'Giovoni died,' I tried.

Michelle Gorgon ignored that. He said:

'I tell you because, because it may be that such – certain information may come to you – and I assure you, Williams, that it will be to your best interests to sell that information to me. But some one told McBride of Giovoni, some one told McBride of – but no matter. The subject is dropped. You will remember it only when you wish money. If I could, could—' He took his head in his hands and pressed the temples at the sides.

Then he changed suddenly.

'And now, Williams, for my little treat. I wish to take you below with me. Just a few floors. It is perfectly safe. Really, you're not alarmed? I promise you that I shall interest you.'

CHAPTER XXV: APARTMENT 12-D

But I was alarmed. Not afraid, you understand. There's a deal of difference between the two, at least, in my way of thinking, there is. And you've got to admit that I've got to live or die on my way of thinking, and not some one else's.

'Maybe I am like you in some things, Williams. If I have made my plans I go through with them no matter what may threaten.' This, as we left the bungalow and entered the upper hall of the apartment. 'Yes, go through with them even if they lead to destruction. For, like Aristotle, I must follow my star.'

'Like Napoleon, you mean.' For once I knew something that he didn't and had to get my oar in like a kid.

'Napoleon. Yes, I said Napoleon.' He fairly snapped the words, and for the first time I saw color in his cheeks. He did have his weak side then, and, damn it! it was brought out by a reflection on his – well – I suppose the word is culture, which is rather a laugh there.

'I meant Napoleon,' he said as we entered the elevator, 'if perhaps I didn't say it. You can see, then, how disturbed I am tonight.' And in a louder voice, directed to the elevator operator, 'Very much disturbed. Madame is very ill, John. I'm quite worried about her. The twelfth floor, please.'

'I'm sorry, sir. I hope it's nothing serious.' The operator didn't appear overinterested, but Michelle went on.

'Not serious from a medical point of view; not serious physically, John. But then, they have not watched over Madame as I have. It's her mental condition. There have been times when I was afraid she'd do herself a harm. She's threatened it. I spoke of it tonight, didn't I, Williams?'

'No, you didn't.' I looked at him strangely. He was a talker, there was no doubt about that. But I had not expected that he'd hold forth with the elevator operator on his domestic affairs, at least the mental afflictions of his wife.

'But I should have mentioned it to you, Williams. It worries me greatly.' This, as we stepped out on the twelfth floor and I followed him down the wide hall to a mahogany door, labeled 12-D.

A moment's wait while a bell buzzed far back behind that door.

'It's all right, Williams. I am going to introduce you to my future bride,' and as a maid opened the door, 'I am expected, of course, Lillian.'

'Of course, sir,' said the colored maid, and held the door open for us to enter.

'A little surprise, Lillian. Don't mention that I've brought a friend. Not a word, now.' And something passed from Michelle Gorgon's hand to the maid's hand as we entered a beautifully furnished living room.

Was I a fool to come? I didn't know. But I'd have come anyway, and bride or no bride my hand still rested on the gun in my jacket pocket. I remembered that I wasn't in the 'sanctuary' of Michelle Gorgon now, and though I remembered also that the elevator man, John, had seen us get off at the twelfth floor and that O'Rourke knew I was in the building – Well, I'm noble minded and all that, but I wasn't a good enough citizen to be willing to play the part of the corpse that finally roasted this inhuman murderer, Michelle Gorgon.

And that was that. There was a sound of laughter and running feet, and a girl was across the room. Two arms were around Michelle's neck.

'It was nice, nice of you to come, and I stayed up. Who—' She dropped to the floor and looked at me. 'What is he doing here?' And the girlish sparkle went out of those eyes; the youthful softness went from her face. It was the woman now. The woman of the night. As I had expected, but never let myself believe, it was The Flame, Florence Drummond. The Girl with the Criminal Mind. And perhaps half a hundred other aliases in her innocent young life.

Bitter? Yes, I was bitter. Only a short while ago she had told me that she loved me. Maybe Michelle Gorgon's presence had some strange power over her. I had half thought that from her previous actions. But, she had not felt his presence when she ran from that room to greet him.

'You see, I'm disturbing the lady.' I half turned toward the door.

'Ah! Yes, yes.' Michelle Gorgon seemed to be enjoying himself. 'We just stopped in, Florence. I have an engagement, and I wanted to tell you that I couldn't visit you tonight.'

'If it's a test—' The girl looked sharply at him.

'If it is, it's not for you, my dear.' Michelle sort of plucked at her arm. 'My confidence in myself, the beautiful things I can shower on you, in the wonderful places I can take you. In—' And turning to me, 'Just a minute, Williams. For the last time, you are looking on The Flame, The Girl with the Criminal Mind. Now, that mind will be occupied with nothing more criminal than making a man happy by, by—'. He went very close to her but still watched me. 'By allowing him to adore her,' he finished.

And The Flame laughed.

'You're somewhat of a dumb bunny, Michelle.' Her voice was that of the young girl again, but her eyes and face weren't. She looked at me defiantly as she stretched both hands upon his shoulders. 'You too listen to the gossip of the street, Michelle.' She put her head close to him and whispered something softly. I didn't get it, but somehow it riled me just the same. I said, purely vindictively, and perhaps without point, but anyway what was on my chest.

'High class house, this. No references needed to get an apartment here, I guess.'

Michelle Gorgon shook his head.

'On the contrary, the clientele is picked most carefully. Miss Drummond's references were of the best. From the owner of the apartment himself.' And with a smile, 'You see, the deeds to this property happen to be in my name.'

While I tried to laugh that one off Michelle Gorgon raised an arm and placed it about The Flame's shoulder. What did it all mean? Was Florence tired of poverty, and taking riches? Was she tired of being ruled, and wanted to rule? Was—? And Michelle drew her close to him, his eyes ever on me, steady, staring things. Watching me, not in alarm or fear; more, a curious glint, as if he had brought me there for this very purpose. To watch how I took it.

Maybe I didn't take it well. My left hand clenched at my side, my right caressed the butt of a heavy caliber six-gun in my jacket pocket.

The temptation was strong to slap him down. Maybe I would have acted upon that temptation. Maybe I wouldn't have. But the thought came then. Was The Flame, after all, the one lured by wealth, by the strange influence of this man? Or was Michelle Gorgon the one lured? Lured, as so many other men had been, by the fascination of this strange girl? Was Michelle Gorgon now the moth attracted by the flame?

Any way you put it, I turned my head, hesitated a moment, then walked toward the exit door. I heard The Flame say:

'And these strange messages, this shadow that bothers you, Michelle. Can't I—'

'Uh-huh.' At least Michelle Gorgon made a funny noise in his throat that sounded like that before he said, 'At a time like this, Florence, why bring that up?' He was annoyed, and showed it.

But Michelle Gorgon reached the apartment door almost the same time I did. We passed out into the wide hall together. He hadn't gotten my goat, and I'd show him he hadn't. I said:

'I thought a man doesn't introduce his future bride with a wife still living.'

'No, not with a wife still living. I have a presentiment that—' He paused and looked at his watch, and smiled with his lips. 'But the offer I made you, Race, the money I will pay for the name of the one behind McBride, behind O'Rourke. Tut, tut, don't answer yet. The shadow that overhangs my – yes, my life – will be wiped out, as all other shadows have been wiped out that threatened a Gorgon, The Gorgon.

'Since you've entered this, shall we call it a case, what has happened? Who has taken every trick? Toney, the little Italian drug addict. He died before he spoke out the whole truth to McBride. Giovoni. He died before he spoke out the whole truth to McBride. Every one who has stood in my way has died.'

'Every one but your wife.' I was thinking of his talk of marrying The Flame.

'I have told you that I am psychic. I have a feeling now, a strong feeling now, that the wife you speak of, God rest her soul – is dead.'

He pressed the two elevator buttons. The one for an up car and the other for a down, and we waited. Almost at once the machinery broke into life. There was the hum of a motor far below. But it was the down car that came first. Just before the elevator reached our floor, Michelle Gorgon said:

'No. A man never introduces his future bride while his wife is living.' And, damn it! he rubbed his hands together, as if he gloated over something, something which I could not believe. 'You have been with me all the evening, Race, no one is to deny that. What a nice alibi for a husband who might be suspected of murder. The abstract, Williams. The abstract is—'

The door of the car clanked open and I stepped within.

'Every trick.' Michelle Gorgon stood by the door a minute. 'And not a single one for you.'

'No. No.' Maybe it was foolish, maybe it wasn't. But I was mad – damn good and mad. Anyway, I did it. I shoved my hand quickly into my pocket and drew out that envelope. The envelope Michelle had asked me so sarcastically to deliver to his brother, Eddie.

'I won't get a chance to deliver this message, Doctor.' I tried to keep the vindictiveness and the gloating out of my own voice, but I guess they crept in. After all I'm only human. 'So, since you'll see Eddie before I do, I'll ask you to deliver this.'

He just eyed me, steadily, unblinkingly, as his hand stretched out for the envelope. But I didn't give it to him then.

'I'll just put Eddie's address on the envelope for you,' I told him, jerked out my pencil and scribbled quickly upon the white surface. Then I shoved it into his hand, pushed him back from the door, slammed it shut and said:

'Down, John. Make it snappy.'

Maybe I'd made a mistake, but I didn't care. I'd have done it again any time, under the same circumstances. I'll bet that grin was wiped off his lips, and the unblinking baby-like stare out of his eyes. For I had written on that envelope:

Eddie Gorgon, Esq.,
Slab One,
The City Morgue.

CHAPTER XXVI: MURDER IN THE ABSTRACT

As I left the building and hurried to my car, yes, hurried, I thought to myself: There, let Michelle Gorgon count up the tricks in the game, and laugh that one off.

There was nothing to do now, of course, but tip O'Rourke off that Eddie Gorgon's body could be picked up and carted away, for Michelle Gorgon to deliver the envelope to.

Michelle Gorgon was some boy. He had a way of getting at you, a convincing way. I thought of Colonel McBride, and more than half wished that I had gone through with the thing and sunk fingers into that white, delicate skin of Michelle Gorgon, until he told me where Colonel McBride was. And then, there was The Flame. I didn't try to think overmuch on that. I didn't want to think about that.

There was also the guy who had something on Michelle Gorgon, knew who his first wife was, if there was a first wife. At least, knew enough to put fear into Michelle Gorgon. It looked as if, for once in his younger days, Michelle Gorgon had gone in for a bit of murder that wasn't in the abstract, after all. But enough of that.

One other dominant thought. Michelle Gorgon's crack about 'a bride and a living wife,' and his crack about having psychic power. I entered a subway station and found a telephone booth, decided to pass up the hospital as a call at that hour, but buzzed O'Rourke at home. His wife answered my jingle. She was not reassuring.

'The Sergeant,' Mrs. O'Rourke always called him that, 'hasn't been home. But he called a little while ago, saying he wouldn't be home tonight at all. And him only a Sergeant, with the worries of an Inspector.' And after a few more natural complaints, she told me, 'He said, if you called him, Mr. Williams, for you to come straight to – to some hospital. I don't mind the name of it, but—.

And I hung up on the good lady, dashed from the station, sprang into my car and made monkeys out of the few traffic lights which were still operating.

O'Rourke was the first lad I saw when the cop by the door of the hospital stood aside for me to enter. O'Rourke didn't wait, or couldn't wait. Anyway, he led me smack into a little room and chirped it out.

'She's dead, Race. Yes, I know, with a cop in the alley and me at the door – in the hall, mind you.'

'Shot?' I said.

'No.' His laugh wasn't pleasant. 'I'm not as bad a cop as that.' He clasped his hands together. 'Poisoned. Murdered by her husband, just the same as if he stuck a knife in her chest and turned the blade. But you won't get a verdict on it, not a chance. There ain't a jury in the country, nor the medical examiner for that matter, but will call it suicide.'

'What sort of poison?'

'There was no label on the bottle, but the smell of burnt almonds was strong. Prussic acid. I guess we all agree on that.'

'And how— Who do you think gave it to her?'

'She gave it to herself, you fool. I tell you I was at the door, Donnelly under the window. Michelle Gorgon left it for her. I can swear to that. But who's to believe it? Not the doctors. Not the medical examiner. And certainly no twelve men in a jury box. There's enough evidence to disprove that Michelle Gorgon brought it here. Listen!' And O'Rourke gave me the whole show.

'Most of the time I heard Madame moving in the bed. Then she sort of cried out. Miss Agnes, who was writing right across from me, on the other side of the door, went in to her. I went as far as the door, and looked in. Madame waved us out. She spoke too, said she was all right. She was holding a book very tightly closed in her hand, but she didn't want anything, wouldn't take anything. And Miss Agnes came out and closed the door. Madame asked that the door be closed, when we left it open a crack.

'She was restless, Race, very restless. And I couldn't swear that she didn't get out of that bed and crawl across the room. But I would swear to that if it would roast Michelle Gorgon.

'The whole thing seemed silly, my sitting there like that, when I ought to be out on the McBride hunt, and I was just about to call it a night and put another lad on the door, when – well – it's almost funny. I didn't hear anything, unless you can hear a sudden quiet. But Madame wasn't restless any more, hadn't been for some time – hadn't—. And I called to Miss Agnes. Not because I was alarmed at the quiet, but because I just wanted to have a last look at Madame before I left.

'And,' O'Rourke's hand went under his collar, 'she was dead, Race, and in one hand was the empty bottle that had held the poison, and in the other withered hand— Well, make a guess.'

'The book of love stories,' I tried.

'Wrong,' said O'Rourke. 'In the other hand she held a tiny mirror. For the first time, she looked at her face in a mirror – and took her life. That'll be the verdict, and don't you forget it.'

I put my oar in.

'But who gave her the mirror? Who left her the mirror and poison? Michelle Gorgon, of course. He had the opportunity when we were out of the room, and—'

'Yes, he did. If that was all there was to it we might pin it on him, at least as manslaughter. But there is more to it. The devilish cunning of the man, or—. But listen to this. Beneath her bed was an open bag, the small, over-night bag she brought with her to the hospital. And that bag had an inside flap, a sort of secret pocket, that was now open. No—' he saw the question on my lips, 'Miss Agnes had put the bag in the small closet. She hadn't noticed the flap when she unpacked the bag – it was well hidden. And she hadn't noticed since early evening if the bag was still in the closet or under the bed. But in the pocket beneath the flap that now hung open was another tiny bottle of the same poison. Pointing out nicely to a jury where Madame hid her poison, maybe for weeks.

'Brophey sums it up like any dick, any lawyer for the defense would, and any jury would believe. Madame had secreted that poison there for the moment she could bear her terrible affliction no longer. And the mirror too – for the day she got the nerve to look at herself. For the mirror was a pocket affair, and could be hidden in a case. The case was on the bed beside her.'

'And you sum it up, O'Rourke?'

'Like you,' he said harshly. 'Michelle Gorgon planned this for a long time. He came here tonight, gave her the mirror and the poison. Maybe he threatened her, maybe he didn't. Maybe she had been pleading for the chance to end her life. But he did it. Defiantly, while I was there. Just laughed at me.'

'Murder in the abstract.' I thought aloud.

'Abstract or no abstract, the woman's dead. God!' O'Rourke threw up both his hands, 'if I only had the guts to lay a hand on him and drag him in for it.'

'No, O'Rourke, you can't do that. With what Michelle Gorgon told me, for he knew his wife was going to die, and what you suspect – well – the jury would just think it a police frame-up. We couldn't hang the crime on him.'

'No, we couldn't,' O'Rourke admitted grudgingly. 'Doctor Revel says it's quite possible that Madame crawled to the closet and got the bag. But he'd like it a straight suicide, with no investigation, of course.'

'Of course.' I agreed. 'Did you – did some one notify Doctor Michelle Gorgon?'

'Yes. He should have been here by this. Word was left with his servant. Gorgon had stepped out of his apartment for the moment.'

'Yes.' I thought aloud. 'He was with me.'

And now what? I suddenly realized that I had entirely forgotten, in the rapid happenings, that I had had no word of my boy, Jerry, whom I had left waiting for me when I went to visit Colonel McBride. Jerry, who had disappeared when I decided to make my appearance at the Colonel's house from the rear instead of the front. Jerry, whom I thought I had seen leave an areaway far down the street and follow the person – the man who had left McBride's house with Colonel McBride. Jerry, who might be able to tell me who––. But no more thought. I had forgotten Jerry. I'd give my home a buzz now and see if he had returned.

But first I told O'Rourke about my message to Michelle Gorgon, but not of the envelope, for I didn't want to bring The Flame into it – at least, yet. Just that I had wised Michelle Gorgon up as to where they could find his brother, Eddie's, body. At the City Morgue.

'Good!' O'Rourke snapped up the phone on the little table. 'I'll have the boys pick up the stiff, just say I was tipped off to a bump in Maria's Cafe. Let the surprise and joy be theirs.' And he grinned at me, but his grin had lost much of its spontaneous good nature.

As for me. I grabbed myself another phone and buzzed my number. And this time I got results. I'm telling you I breathed easier when Jerry's voice came over the wire.

'Never mind me, Jerry,' I cut short his interest. 'Did you recognize the lad who left the block in such a hurry?'

And Jerry did. And Jerry told me so. And the name of the man brought back to me the words of The Flame. 'Use your brains. Go over this thing from the beginning.'

And I did go over it – did think. And the thoughts I got were amazing, astounding, but not unbelievable. When I came to, O'Rourke was standing beside me.

'O'Rourke,' I said, 'now that that bit of shooting is out, I think I'll go down and talk to Rudolph Myer.'

'But I'll cover you. The Commissioner will cover you, if we don't find the Colonel. Hell! Race,' he cut in on himself, 'you said to sit tight on that, you might know something.'

'Might,' I said. 'I will know something soon. But just for safety's sake I'll get over to Rudolph Myer. You can't tell who might step over your head.'

'The Commissioner's head too?'

'Who is Rose Marie?' The question just came to me.

'God!' said O'Rourke. 'If we knew that we'd know everything. Toney said it was Michelle Gorgon's wife. Giovoni spoke of Rose Marie as Michelle Gorgon's wife. And – oh, some one else said it was Michelle Gorgon's wife. But we've gone back over the years and Michelle Gorgon was never married in Italy.'

'Couldn't Michelle have been married under another name?'

'He could have, but he wasn't.'

'But if Giovoni was his father-in-law, then – then who was Giovoni's daughter, and who was her husband?'

'Giovoni's daughter's name was Rose Marie, all right. We've established that as a fact. And she was brutally murdered, too, by her husband. We've established that too, even if it was many years ago. But Michelle Gorgon's name in Italy was Gorgonette, and Rose Marie's husband's name was Nicholas Tremporia and he was a Greek. He escaped after the murder, and was picked up on the railroad tracks on a dock near Naples. Fairly ruined by the train, he was. We only found that out since Giovoni was murdered. So you see, if Giovoni had lived and talked his head off, it wouldn't have hurt Michelle Gorgon any. Giovoni was a little bugs, I guess.'

'Then why have him killed?'

'I don't know,' O'Rourke said despairingly. 'Something else, maybe. But certainly Michelle Gorgon was not Giovoni's son-in-law. That much is established beyond a doubt.'

'Yes?' I chewed that one over, but I didn't like it. There didn't seem any sense, then, in the kicking over of Giovoni. The phone rang and O'Rourke answered it. I had already started for the door.

O'Rourke held up his hand. I waited until the call was over. Then O'Rourke said, and though his voice was calm, it was a false calm:

'You needn't bother about Rudolph Myer. The body of Eddie Gorgon has – disappeared.'

'Disappeared!'

'Well, it isn't there in the Maria Cafe,' snapped O'Rourke. 'Choose your own word for it. But if there's no corpse there's no criminal lawyer necessary. That much is a cinch.'

'Nevertheless,' I told him, as I passed through the hall to the front door,

'I'm a boy scout and believe in preparedness. I'm going to see Rudolph Myer. Wait here. I think something is going to break.'

And smack at the front door I bumped into Doctor Michelle Gorgon.

'Ah! Race Williams,' he said, and though he looked at me unblinkingly I read hatred in his eyes, 'I have another presentiment, quite contrary to former thoughts of you. It is that you are about to die; to be found with—' He broke off as O'Rourke followed me to the door. Then he said, 'I have just heard of Madame's sad end. How distressing. Most distressing, Detective Sergeant O'Rourke.'

CHAPTER XXVII: THE KILLER INSTINCT

But I was gone, hurrying to my car, speeding down the street. Something big was about to break. Any possible doubt that Colonel McBride was held prisoner by the Gorgon outfit was dissipated by my conversation with Michelle Gorgon, and that the man was being tortured for information – information that seemed imperative to the liberty, if not actually the life, of Michelle Gorgon seemed also sure. I shuddered slightly. Michelle Gorgon possessed, in his best moments, not the least touch of human compassion. Now, with his very life in the balance, he'd do anything to get that information from Colonel McBride.

Another thing was certain. McBride would have to be rescued very quickly. There wasn't one chance in a hundred that he would be let free, even if he talked, and I remembered that set jaw of his, the determined eyes. Oh, it may have knocked him to see another killed, shot down before his eyes, as I had shot down the lad the night we were moving Giovoni to the private sanitarium – and it may have unnerved him to think that Toney and Giovoni, whom he wished to protect, met their death, but I didn't think he'd talk, and I knew what that would mean for him.

With this important thing on my mind I was going to consult my lawyer, Rudolph Myer? That's right. That's exactly what I was going to do. As I drove down town and through Greenwich Village to Rudolph Myer's house, I thought upon, and even enlarged upon, if that could be done, the sufferings that Colonel McBride was to be put through, was now going through, or had been put through. Not nice thoughts? No, decidedly not. Nevertheless, I had them, and I held them, for they stirred a hate and a passion, and perhaps even a lust to kill. Bad business? Maybe. But my business tonight was bad business.

There was no guard at Rudolph Myer's house, and I'm not sure if there was a light, though I think one shone beneath the second story window shade, that overlooked the side alley. Side alley? That's right. For I was looking the place over. Rudolph Myer and I were good friends. Had been so for a good many years. He was my lawyer in many instances, and a mighty good one, if a high priced one. But I never begrudged him a cent I paid him.

Now, I guessed that I knew Rudolph well enough to play a practical joke on him. Sort of slip in and surprise him. And surprise him I certainly would. He was alone in that house. The only servant he had left each night. There was nothing for him to fear. He was the friend of the unfortunate, the criminal. The finest fixer in the city of New York.

I went to the back, crossed the stone court, carefully up-ended an ash can, stood upon it and rapped myself a little hole in the window pane. No feeling for electric burglar alarm wires. No need of that. I had been in that room too often not to know. Rudolph Myer knew crooks. He was a firm believer in that saying that any crook who wanted 'in' got 'in' – if he wanted 'in' bad enough.

Well, I'm no crook, but I wanted 'in' bad enough. I just stuck my fingers through the hole, snapped back the window lock, lifted it carefully, slowly, silently, and stepped into the room. My rubber soled shoes made no noise across the linoleum of the kitchen and even less noise as I crossed the thick rug of the dining room, through to the hall and onto the wooden stairs. I picked the front stairs because, well, they were less likely to make noise – had no door bottom and top – and besides which, they would bring me up to the hall and close to that door, the door of the room from which I thought that tiny light had peeped.

All stairs are creaky, of course, no exception to this old outfit. But I had luck, in a way. Some one was moving around up stairs – some one was moving quickly, furtively, quietly back and forth, back and forth across the floor.

I made the upper hall, took a couple of quick steps down it, guided by a light from a partly open door, and stopped dead before that door as the quickly moving feet inside ceased, and some one seemed to listen.

Then it wasn't 'seemed' any more. Some one was listening. For the person in that room had held his breath, and then let it go again in a sort of whistling sound.

Finally the feet crossed to the door, paused, fingers reached to the side of the door and pushed it open wider, and I stepped through the opening and faced Rudolph Myer.

Certainly he was surprised. Maybe even shocked. He rubbed his hands across his eyes as if he wasn't sure, then half straightened his bent shoulders and tried playing at the corners of his mouth with the thumb and index finger of his right hand. He was fully dressed, and a hat and top coat lay over the end of the bed.

'Surprise!' I said, closed the door behind me and spun the key in the lock. Then I looked around the room as he backed away from me. One suitcase already packed stood shut by the bed. It had heavy straps around it. The other was a big affair and needed another shirt or a couple of socks before locking. There was little doubt that Rudolph intended to go bye-bye. Five minutes later and—. But I hadn't been five minutes later. Why dwell on that?

And Rudolph Myer spoke first.

'Race, Race Williams. How did you get in? And why?'

'And the answer is – Who cares? I won't waste time, Myer.' I backed him across the room, my eyes on him. 'You two-timing skunk! After all these years you sell me out. You left the house of Colonel McBride tonight with McBride. You trapped him into the hands of the Gorgons. You two-timed him as you did me.'

'I didn't,' he cried out. 'It's a lie. Before God I swear I didn't.'

And I had him by the throat, forced him to his knees.

'Don't try to lie out of it. My boy, Jerry, was down the block and saw you. They're torturing McBride,' I told him, and my voice shook. 'You know me, Myer. I don't have to threaten you. You've kidded me about my shooting, for I've paid you well. Now, you double-crossed me and I'm going to kill you, kill you.' I squeezed his throat tighter, saw his eyes bulge, watched his tongue protrude, then I thrust him from me. Disgusted? Maybe. Through with him? Not me.

Rudolph Myer stretched a hand, let it slip into his open suitcase and half pulled out an automatic. I liked that. He couldn't possibly believe he had a chance against me with a gun, yet he tried to get one. Why? Because he was afraid. He read the truth in my blazing eyes.

I didn't fire. I simply leaned over and rapped his knuckles with the nose of my forty-four. Then I kicked his gun under the bed and told him what was on my chest.

'Listen, Myer.' And I didn't have to do any acting to get my part over. 'Understand this. I've come here tonight for the purpose of killing you.'

'That would be – murder.' He half lay, half knelt on the floor.

'You can't murder a rat,' I told him. 'Anyway, what difference does the name it goes by matter to you, or to me either? No one saw me come here. No one will see me go. And don't be thinking up wise cracks. Let me tell you what I know.

'You got me into this Gorgon case, because the Gorgons knew I was coming in anyway. You found out that McBride was coming on, to help the Commissioner. You knew that O'Rourke had been after the Gorgons for years. Michelle Gorgon probably told you. He has a way of hearing things, through crooked officials, and crooked, shyster lawyers, like you.

'You knew where McBride planned to take Giovoni, to Elrod's Sanitarium. You told Gorgon and he had him murdered. And it was you who told me The Flame wanted to see me at her rooms, and you, alone, who knew I was going to meet The Flame there. Then you told the

Gorgons, or at least, Eddie Gorgon, and you let Eddie think that The Flame sent the message. I don't know why, I don't care why, but you did it again at Maria's Café, and Eddie Gorgon died. You somehow got McBride out of his house tonight and into the Gorgon trap. I don't know how you did it, why you did it, though I guess you were paid for it.'

'No, no. Not then, Race. It was The Flame. I wanted her. I loved her. I thought—'

'The Flame? You!' I had to laugh.

'Why not?' And Rudolph Myer's beady eyes snapped back to life. 'Many have, others have. Am I any different? I'm not so young, but neither is Michelle Gorgon. I'm not so, not—. Don't you see, Race? What she did to others she did to me. And, Race, she led me on. I swear she did. I've done business for Michelle Gorgon. She got it out of me, all out of me. She sucked me dry of every bit of information, then laughed in my face and—'

He read it in my eyes. He clutched at my coat now, kneeling there at my feet.

'Don't kill me, don't. I know you can get away with it. I know the man-made laws can't touch you. But you've never done that. Never gone in for murder, Race. Never—. You've lived clean. There's other laws beside those of man. There's God's.'

'There's the laws of God and the laws of man, Myer. And there's the law of death, for the rat, for the stoolie, for the two-timer. You sent Giovoni to his death. You sent Colonel McBride to worse than death. You tried to send me to death, and – By God! you've got to pay the price.' I half raised my gun.

Was I going to kill him then? I don't know, so you don't know. But certainly Rudolph Myer thought he knew. He screamed out as he clutched at my knees and begged for life.

'I'll tell you where McBride is if you let me go. Don't you see? It was The Flame, The Girl with the Criminal Mind. Am I made of different stuff than other men? Isn't there blood in my body too? And she laughed at me and told me she loved you, and you only. And, and—. God! Race, I was mad, mad. I wanted you dead. I thought, if you were – if you—. Don't, don't kill me. It'll be death for McBride. Death for The Flame.'

Was it to save McBride that my finger didn't close on that trigger, or was it because of The Flame? What Rudolph Myer said might easily be true, for I guess most any man would fall a victim to The Flame. Most any would, and many had. Or was it simply that I couldn't get up the guts to press that trigger and snap out Myer's life? Or—? But I did say:

'You, you wouldn't know where McBride is.'

'Yes, I do. I do! Promise, give me your word that you won't – won't kill me if I tell you.'

'If I save McBride, you can go free,' I told him. 'But I'll know if you lie about him. I know more than you think. To begin with, I know that you fled down that street, stopped in a telephone booth in a drug store and made two telephone calls. One to me, the other to—'

'To Michelle Gorgon,' he told me, and I believed him. Then he gave me his story.

'Michelle Gorgon found out that Colonel McBride was coming to the city by the request of the Police Commissioner, through the Deputy Commissioner. He had me worm my way into McBride's confidence by telling him things about the Gorgons – things that O'Rourke had already unearthed, but were not evidence. McBride told me about this Giovoni, but no more than his name and that he had arrived in New York, and was taken sick. He didn't tell me where he was, nor where he was going to take him. That was the night before I met you. I watched McBride's house and saw him go to Doctor Elrod's Sanitarium the following morning. So I knew that would be where he'd take Giovoni. I was working, alone, for Michelle Gorgon. Joe or Eddie knew nothing about my connection with Michelle. Michelle Gorgon liked to play without his brothers once in a while. It strengthened his hold over them.'

'Did Michelle have you notify Eddie when The Flame had you date me up for her, both those times?'

'No. I did it myself. I let Eddie think it came from The Flame. I wanted you—. I, I loved The Flame.'

That was a funny one, maybe – but easy to believe.

CHAPTER XXVIII: THE POLICE HORN IN

I looked at my watch. The 'whys' the 'wherefores' of the thing were not as important as knowing where McBride was. I told Myer to talk, and quickly. He did. He said:

'I went to see Colonel McBride. He expected me and left the kitchen door open, as he didn't want the police to know I was there. He was telephoning, up stairs. I whistled up to him from the kitchen door. I was nervous. I thought I heard some one in one of the front rooms, so I kept in the dark. I thought it might be the police. Colonel McBride came down to me. I pretended excitement. I told him I had some one in a car on the street behind, who would tell him all about Rose Marie, and how she was murdered. I told him the person wouldn't come in, for him to come out. He said he was expecting you, Race, but he came with me when I said it would only take a minute. He—' Myer had the good grace to gulp, anyway, 'He trusted me. Joe Gorgon was out in the car, with some others and—. I didn't know they intended to torture him. That's the truth.'

'And they told you where they were going to take him?'

'No,' he said, 'they didn't. But I had a – a colleague around the corner with a car to follow them. I – well – I like to have information of my own if things go wrong, like now.' He looked at my gun and tried to smile.

I nodded at that. It would be like Myer. Slippery – never trusting any one. Always with a card up his sleeve. Yes – I believed him.

Then he gave me the address where Joe Gorgon and his racketeers had taken Colonel McBride. Ricorro's garage. A notorious, all night garage, where the front doors never closed. I had a hunch Myer was speaking the truth. Somehow, at such times you KNOW.

One more question I couldn't help. I had always looked on Myer as a straight shooter to the one who paid him, if crooked every other way, and certainly not in the cesspool of the city's rackets.

'What made you double-cross McBride, Myer?' I asked. 'Did Michelle Gorgon hold something over your head?'

'Not in the sense of blackmail, if you mean that.' Rudolph Myer had recovered quickly and was on his feet now, lighting a cigarette with a shaky hand. 'I don't think any one could ever get anything on me again. No, Michelle Gorgon's methods are much simpler and much more direct. He came to me, Race, and pounded a long finger against my chest. "I need you, Myer," he said. "Come come, we won't quibble. I'll pay you well to act for me. I always do. It's not for you to decide, but for me to decide. You're in with me now, till I'm through with you – or you're dead by morning." That was all he said, Race. That was all he needed to say. I know my city. I know my law, and know too what little protection it could offer me. I'd have felt safer hearing my sentence of death passed by a judge in court. For law or no law, I knew as well, or even better than any man, that Michelle Gorgon is above the law. And – and I wanted very much to live.'

And the worst of it was, it was true.

But I didn't kill any more time. And I didn't listen to Rudolph Myer's protestations when I took those straps from the bag and a couple of bathrobe cords from the closet and trussed him up.

'I daresay you can work yourself free of those straps, but not these,' I said, as I jerked out my irons and fastened them about his ankles. 'I'll come back and release you as soon as Colonel McBride is free. Now, anything else to tell me? For your life depends on my success.'

He could take that any way he liked – but he talked. He said:

'Joe Gorgon'll be there tonight, not Michelle though. How many Joe will have with him I don't know, but he won't trust many in this – this, I don't think.'

And I gagged him. But his eyes bothered me. They were watching that bag, the closed bag. I wondered why, tried to open the bag and found it locked, started to take the gag out of Myer's mouth, saw the excitement in his eyes and tried his vest pocket – and there was the key, attached to the generous watch chain.

I snapped open that bag and got a jar. No wonder Myer was interested in that bag. He was afraid to tell me about it, and was afraid not to. The bag was full of money. Crisp, new bills of large denominations. Rudolph Myer, then, had been leaving the city for an extended visit. I didn't have to count it. But I closed the bag, carried it to the closet and chucked it behind a lot of clothes.

'I don't blame you, worrying,' I told him. 'That's a lot of jack. But it'll be safe there until I return.'

There were many things I wanted to ask him. Each one perhaps more important than the other. But there wasn't time. Not long now before dawn, and the life of Colonel McBride at stake. Who was Rose Marie? Why did she cry out for vengeance? Did Myer know whose voice on the phone so upset Michelle Gorgon? I didn't wait for that information. I only stopped long enough down stairs to put through a call to O'Rourke.

'Hop a subway,' I told him, 'and I'll pick you up at The Bridge. Don't argue. I've got a line on McBride. The time for chin–chin is passed. Snap into it.'

Well, I had used my brains for once, as The Flame had suggested, but I hadn't used them until Jerry told me that Rudolph Myer was the man who escaped down the street after the attack and abduction of Colonel McBride. Then, maybe it wasn't much thinking. I just got a kaleidoscope picture of past events and knew that Rudolph Myer was my meat.

I met O'Rourke and I told him what was on my chest.

'They'll kill McBride if we come in force, yet we can't chance an attack alone. Just one man may be guarding that garage and maybe ten. Here's the ticket. I know Ricorro's. It's an all–night garage. The big front doors are always open. It would look bad if they closed them now. I'm for betting they'll be open.'

'Ricorro's Garage!' O'Rourke stroked his chin. 'Well, it's got a bad enough name, though we've never really pinned a thing on Ricorro. And you don't know if McBride is in the basement below or on the floor above.'

'I don't know even if he's there at all. But dying men are supposed to speak the truth. And I'm telling you, O'Rourke, Rudolph Myer was as near death as any man who ever peeped a final message. But I'm strong for the basement. Here's the lay. There may be a way out that we don't know of. You get a raiding squad and cover the block, but not till I'm inside.'

'You and me inside,' O'Rourke horned in.

'No. Just me. This is my racket. If I'm discovered, they may think I'm alone, and not kill McBride. I work alone. If you're with me – but you have a wife and kid.'

O'Rourke laughed.

'I've been reported killed so many times, and given up by the ambulance surgeon so many times, that the old lady wouldn't even get a bad turn. Besides which, what has the old lady got to do with police business? As for my kid, well, he's going to be a copper, Race – a real copper.' And suddenly bursting out on me, 'Where do you get the stuff that you're the only living man in New York with any guts, any eye – and any gun hand? I'll be a—'

I switched that talk and turned to McBride's interest. Finally O'Rourke saw it enough my way to let me flop into the garage first. Once the surprise was over, he'd follow. That seemed fair enough. What I was mostly afraid of were spies. Watchers on the outside, who'd give the alarm as soon as the cops got anywhere near the garage.

O'Rourke put through a call for the boys to meet us. He had a picked crew waiting and ready, and told me it wouldn't take five minutes to fill that garage with flatties. I didn't like waiting for the coppers there in the dark street some six blocks from Ricorro's Garage. I get restless just before a bit of action, not nervous, you understand, sort of rarin' to go, and the longer I wait the worse I get. So I spent my time telling O'Rourke all that had taken place in my talk with Michelle Gorgon, and his offer of a hundred thousand dollars for the name of the party behind McBride, the party who rang up Michelle Gorgon. Of the note, 'Rose Marie cries out for Vengeance—' with a couple of words erased at the end of it.

'Yeah, Michelle Gorgon would like to know.' O'Rourke chewed an unlighted cigar. 'McBride could tell him, but won't. I could tell him, but won't. I—.

'O'Rourke,' I cut in, 'I've laid my cards on the table. What about yours? Who is the one who knows so much, and why can't you get the information from that party?'

'Because I can't,' snapped O'Rourke. 'And I have passed my—. Well – I can't tell you who it is – that's flat.' And suddenly changing the subject, 'Who'd think it of Rudolph Myer? Imagine it! The police have been trying to get something on Myer for years and always failed, and finally he mixes himself up with a bit of murder, kidnaping, maybe torture, and what have you, all at once. There's no understanding human nature, Race. But it'll just show you what a lad we're dealing with in Michelle Gorgon. Certainly he must have put the stony, Gorgon look on Myer. And you say Myer was ready to jump the city, bags packed and all. But why? He never guessed you were onto him. He couldn't know that Jerry saw and recognized him. Maybe he was just leaving for a day or so, on business, business for the Gorgons, Michelle Gorgon.'

'Not Myer.' I nodded confidently. And I told O'Rourke of the suitcase full of money. 'Did that look like a short trip?' I asked.

'Yeah?' And O'Rourke let his mouth hang open a minute. 'One hundred thousand dollars for the name of the one behind McBride,' he said thoughtfully. 'For the one who strikes fear in Michelle Gorgon's stomach, for he hasn't any heart. One hundred thousand dollars for even a hint of who it might be. One hundred thousand dollars for—' And O'Rourke suddenly clutched me by the arm. 'You don't think – think that bag contained exactly one hundred thousand dollars?'

'It might. Why? You don't think—?'

'But I do think, exactly what you think now. That Rudolph Myer knew, or guessed, and sold the information to Michelle Gorgon. It—. Wait.' And O'Rourke climbed suddenly from the car, went back into that all-night drug store, and following him to the corner I saw him step into the telephone booth.

'Phew—' he rubbed his forehead when he came out. 'At least, no harm has been done yet.'

'O'Rourke—' I started, and stopped. The riot squad was on the job. Two big cars were coming down the street.

Now, I didn't have things my own way. O'Rourke did agree with me that the police cars stay five blocks from Ricorro's. But O'Rourke trailed along with me to within a couple of blocks of the garage – then I let him out of my boat.

'I don't know what you told the cops, O'Rourke,' was my final message to him, 'but I'm certain that a police parade will kill the show.'

'Nothing to worry about,' O'Rourke told me. 'They've got orders to wait, then surround the block. I'll sort of keep an eye on you.'

'Too much interest, and McBride dies.' I took the hand that O'Rourke held out to me. And I grinned as I put the police whistle into my pocket. Why argue over that?

'You've sure got guts, Race,' he said simply, and I drove off.

CHAPTER XXIX: JOE GORGON DOES HIS STUFF

There are times when I feel that I earn my money. This was one of them. I had an idea that one man, working alone, might get to McBride. One man, driving alone into that garage, would probably not send a signal of warning to Joe Gorgon. One man might—. But I swung the corner, dashed down the main street, spotted the wide open doors of Ricorro's Garage and drove smack in. I want to tell you it was a big moment.

Certainly I got service – service one doesn't expect in a garage.

A lad sitting on the running board of a truck jumped to his feet and came quickly toward me. He carried a wrench in his hand. Though he was dolled up like a car washer I recognized him as I stepped from the car, and what's more, he recognized me. He was more or less of a well known gangster. And I had the advantage of him. Where he didn't expect me I expected him, or one of his kind.

We faced each other a split second only, as I stepped from the running board. My car protected us from being seen from the little lighted room that would be an office.

He never spoke, never more than half raised that wrench, when I let him have it. Just a single up-swing of my right hand, and the barrel of my gun crashed home. Yes, I know. If I were real high minded I'd have hit him with my fist. But I'm not high minded, and besides, my knuckles bruise easily and I have yet to see the head that will dent my rod.

His eyes did a 'Charlie Chaplin' as his knees gave. Then he laid down on the floor. So much for that. I don't waste time on these birds, and I didn't waste time now.

Not a soul in that dimly lit garage as I crossed the smeared cement floor to that little office. Boy, what a break! As I pushed open the door, Ricorro's fat little form was coming toward me. He stopped dead in the center of that office and gaped at me. Then he turned quickly to the roll-top desk.

'Don't be a fool, Ricorro,' I told him. 'It's Race Williams. I'm killing tonight.'

Melodramatic? Sure. Who's to deny that? But then, in the new underworld of our great city, melodrama is real life – and death too. Anyway, it was the kind of talk Ricorro understood. He stopped dead, chucked up both his hands and stood so. He knew his stuff, did Ricorro; knew my reputation also. Life in the underworld had taught him that the man with the gun talks, and the man without a gun listens.

A sudden noise behind me and I half swung aside, so as to face both Ricorro and the office door. Then I shrugged my shoulders and let it go at that. O'Rourke was there, slightly out of breath, slightly red of face, but with a gun in his hand. He must have run the two blocks.

'I'm sorry, Race. I had to—. Look out!'

A revolver cracked. A figure, or rather, the shadow of a figure fled down the little hall back of the office, where he had been hiding. With a warning to O'Rourke, I dashed into that little hallway. There wasn't much to fear from a lad who couldn't shoot better than to miss both of us.

'Watch that bird, Ricorro, O'Rourke,' was all I said as I got under way.

I saw the running figure through the glass of the door which led into the garage again. Just another door where Ricorro could go in and out, and miss people he didn't want to see in the front.

Now, had this scurrying rat spoiled the party? If Joe Gorgon was in the basement, did he hear the shot? Somehow, I thought not. The motor of my car was still running. The floor was of thick cement. And as I dashed into the dimness of the garage I called out my warning to the fleeing, ducking figure ahead.

I could have shot him, but I didn't. I thought I knew his kind, his breed. I thought he'd drop his gun and cry out for mercy at the first warning. But he didn't. He ducked quickly behind a car, fired once from the darkness, where I couldn't see him, and I cursed out my big heart, or my assurance that he'd stop when I warned him.

Now the going was not so good. This lad was bent on warning the others or making his escape. But while he was loose in that garage he was a real menace – both to my plans and my life. And I saw him again – far in the rear now, a dim figure between two cars. He was kneeling on the floor, pulling at something. I covered him and again called out. You have to admit I was giving him a break.

And this time he had to have it. He raised his gun and it spouted flame. And that was enough of that. I only fired once, saw him sort of straighten, clutch at his chest and go down. I don't go in to miss. It's not good business.

I was on him before he could fire again, that is, if he was alive, to fire again. And he was alive, but not in condition to cause trouble. Besides which, he had shown me the entrance to the basement. A great slab of heavy timber in the cement floor, with an iron ring in it.

I grabbed his gun, took a grip on that iron ring, lifted the trap door and started down wooden steps. Things were as quiet as the grave below. The grave! I wondered. But faint heart never filled a spade flush, or rescued a McBride, and I believe in going after things with a bit in my teeth.

I didn't find blackness below. As soon as I spotted enough light I jumped those steps two at a time and made the bottom. A quickly moving figure is much harder to hit than a slowly moving one. That makes sense, though a lot of people think you must creep up on an enemy to be effective.

If Joe Gorgon had heard those shots, he wasn't in the open, waiting. The basement was musty and damp. Perhaps half a dozen cars stood out weirdly in the dim yellowish light. There were barrels, that looked as if they might contain oil; a part of a car here and another part there. Loose lumber, old tires, and great hunks of tin, or what looked like great hunks of tin.

There were no little side rooms, no locked doors. No doors at all, except two big ones which, I thought, opened into the car elevator, for I had spotted doors like them directly above.

But you couldn't tell. The doors might be a blind. I stepped over to them, and stepped back from them again. Low, but distinct, just the same, was the hum of an elevator. Was it going up or down? I thought down, then KNEW down. For, as I raised my gun, those doors opened and – Colonel McBride stood smack before me, right in the center of that elevator. Despite the fact that I was looking from the light into the semi-darkness of the unlighted elevator, I recognized him. His face was white, bruised, and cut too. But he was standing on his feet. Standing alone. And I saw the bulky shadow behind him just as that bulky shadow saw me. It was Joe Gorgon.

From behind McBride Joe Gorgon fired. No word of warning. Just a spit of orange blue flame, and a sudden icy coldness across my cheek, as if some one had pulled a red hot iron over it. Yes – I mean that. It was a coldness that burnt.

Joe Gorgon had half turned his great bulk sideways, so that he was completely protected from my fire by Colonel McBride. Joe wasn't like his brother, Eddie. He didn't gloat over his kill. And what's more, he wasn't going to talk himself out of his kill. He was drawing a bead now over McBride's shoulder – his head low, his eye down close to McBride's arm – just a fraction of a sight from under that arm. Joe didn't hurry, but he didn't lag either. Maybe a second. Maybe two. Maybe less, even.

I had to do it. I wasn't fifteen feet from the standing, staring, sort of lifeless McBride, and the hidden crouching bulk of Joe Gorgon. It was my death, McBride's death, or—.

And I did it. I jumped forward and fired, to be closer even when my heavy forty-four found its mark. I fired smack at the right arm of Colonel McBride.

Just the roar and the flash of my gun echoing upon the roar and the flash of Joe Gorgon's single shot. It worked. McBride crumpled to the floor. Joe Gorgon jumped sort of in the air, half spun, fired wildly, and I laid my next bullet smack between his eyes. Just a little round hole, ever growing larger. Joe Gorgon waved his hands once. His right foot came slowly up, like a lad in the slow motion pictures. Then he pitched forward on his face.

Yep, a forty-four is a mighty handy weapon, even if old fashioned. My bullet had gone through the fleshy part of McBride's arm as if it were papier-mâché, and landing in Joe's shoulder had knocked him back, just as if you'd hit him with a battering ram.

But it was McBride I was thinking of. He was so white and silent. The blood was pouring from his arm just above the elbow. An awkward place to tackle, but I did the best I could to make a tourniquet with my handkerchief and pencil as I blew frantically upon the police whistle. Police whistle! Imagine it! I never thought I'd have use for one of those things. But now, I was glad O'Rourke had forced it on me. The thing was over! McBride was safe, and Joe Gorgon—. Already his body was cold enough for little devils to be skating on his chest.

They came. Half a dozen plainclothesmen, a police surgeon, and O'Rourke leading them.

'I had a doctor in the car,' O'Rourke said, 'though I should have brought an undertaker. Joe's dead of course. And he got McBride first!'

'He did not!' I told O'Rourke emphatically.

Then I explained the necessity of plugging McBride, felt O'Rourke dabbing at my neck with a handkerchief, and for the first time realized that the warm stream running under my collar was not perspiration, but blood, and that the bullet had been closer to doing me in than I thought, for the wound was along the side of my neck and not my cheek. Queer, that? Maybe. But queer or not, it was the truth just the same. I guess it's much easier to see where you plug another guy than to know where you're hit yourself. But why bother? After the police surgeon had fixed up McBride I let him play around my neck. And he did. With a gallon or two of iodine, and a lot of conversation as to what might have happened if the bullet had been a fraction of an inch to the right.

CHAPTER XXX: A LETTER FROM THE DEAD

McBride came around in that little office up stairs and talked a bit. I listened but didn't get it at all.

'I never told him,' Colonel McBride said over and over, until he seemed to get his bearings better. 'Joe Gorgon threatened me and struck me with his gun while my hands and feet were bound. And then he decided to go after me in earnest. A hot iron that he heated in the little stove up stairs. It was the shot that saved me, for he stopped and listened. Then untied my feet, and with a gun pressed against my back led me to the elevator.'

'Yes, we know all that,' I cut in. That wasn't very important now. 'How did they get you here – Rudolph Myer, wasn't it?'

'Yes, though he may be an innocent party to it. He came to me and said that the girl had decided to talk. That she would tell me everything. That she was waiting in the car on the street behind. That seemed right. She had promised to come to my house. Promised to, at least—'

'What girl?' I asked quickly.

'The Flame, of course. She—'

But O'Rourke was at him – shutting him up – speaking hurriedly.

I turned on O'Rourke.

'The Flame? She knows! The voice on the wire that so worried Michelle Gorgon; the cracked voice of a man trying to imitate a woman. The Flame? Why, she's going to marry Michelle Gorgon. She's—. Come, O'Rourke, out with it.'

'Now, now, Race.' And as two white coated lads came in with a stretcher for Colonel McBride, O'Rourke finished, 'I guess it's time you knew everything, but it's not for me to tell you. I passed my word to The Flame. Come, we'll go up to her apartment and see her. Tut, tut, don't look at me like that, Race. She'll be expecting us.'

And up to her apartment we did go. And maybe I did look at him 'like that'. Like what? Oh, like anything O'Rourke thought I looked like.

Think! The Flame had said, 'Think.' And the one thing I couldn't do as we made that trip up Park Avenue was – think.

This time we drove straight to the door of the flashy apartment. The dawn was breaking in the sky. Brophey, the detective who had been at McBride's house after his disappearance, stepped from the shadows and saluted O'Rourke. O'Rourke explained the dick's presence before the apartment to me.

'When I left you in the car by the drug store,' he said, 'I made a couple of calls. One, was to cover this apartment and drag in Michelle Gorgon.'

'On what charge?'

'The murder of his wife,' said O'Rourke. 'I couldn't think of any better charge, and even if I couldn't hold him it wouldn't look so bad. Prussic acid is hard to buy – especially by a crippled, half witted woman who has never been on the street alone since her – her accident.'

'I think that was a mistake,' I told O'Rourke, and meant it.

'I had another reason. I had to do it to protect The Flame. Any luck, Brophey?' he asked the dick.

'Doctor Michelle Gorgon has not come in,' Brophey said, 'And The Fla— Miss Drummond has not gone out – at least, since I've been here.'

'Good!' said O'Rourke as we passed into the apartment house. 'We'll see The Flame.' And as I started to question him again, 'Just a jaunt to the twelfth floor, Race, then it's up to her.'

The night man didn't like the hour we sought The Flame. O'Rourke didn't argue. He showed his badge, pushed the elevator man, John, back and said, 'Twelfth floor, and no lip.'

Another plainclothesman, who was sitting on the cold stairs beside the elevator, came to his feet when we reached the twelfth floor. O'Rourke was thorough, anyway. But certainly Michelle Gorgon would get wind of the police display and not return. I said as much to O'Rourke.

'I didn't want him to return,' said O'Rourke. 'I didn't want to make the pinch unless he came here for The Flame. I'd of had to pinch him to save her. Anything stirring, Cohen?'

'Not a thing,' said Cohen. 'No one in or out of 12-D since I've been here.'

It took time to get into that apartment. At last the colored maid, Lillian, opened the door.

'Miss Drummond?' said O'Rourke. 'Miss—' And the girl didn't have to tell us. We both read it in her face. But when she came out with it, it startled me just the same. Florence, The Flame, had received a telephone call and left the house, perhaps a half hour earlier.

'Just before the boys got here,' said O'Rourke, the mental figuring showing on his face.

'Miss Florence left a letter for a Mr. Williams—' the maid started, but O'Rourke had shoved by her and was into the living room, snatching an envelope quickly from the table. He held it a moment in his hand, then tore it open. When I followed him and grabbed at his arm, he said:

'All right, it's for you.' He chucked the envelope in the basket and handed me several sheets of paper. Then he turned to the maid. She was frightened. She was talking.

'You're the police, ain't you, Mister?' she said to O'Rourke. 'Well, Miss Florence acted funny. There were two telephone calls. The first woke me up. I didn't hear what she said.'

'That would be my call.' O'Rourke thought aloud.

'The second call came right after it,' the maid went on. 'I didn't try to listen but I couldn't help it.' Which meant she had her ear to the keyhole, I thought, but said nothing. 'Of course I didn't hear what came over that wire, but I heard Miss Florence say, "All right – the airport."'

'What airport – My God! What airport?' And O'Rourke was shaking her by the shoulders and saying over and over, 'Good God! he's going to do it again.' And suddenly, to me, when there was nothing more to get from the now thoroughly frightened maid:

'Read that, Race. Read all The Flame wrote.'

He picked up the phone, and I heard him say, 'Roosevelt Field airstation. Damn the number! This is police headquarters.'

But I was reading the closely and hastily written letter The Flame had left for me. It started bluntly enough – but here it is.

'I love you, Race.

'What a beginning for the last will and testament of The Flame. At least, the last if you should read this.

'I am going back a great many years. I never knew my real father or mother. I was brought up in an orphanage outside of Harrisburg, Pennsylvania. But in that orphanage I had a mother's love. It was my sister who stood between me and the heartaches, and even the brutality of the institutions of those days. She gave up opportunities of adoption, suffered undeserved punishments, to give herself a bad name so that she would not be taken from me. For she was not the incorrigible girl the orphanage authorities painted her. She was good and kind and beautiful, and the criminal instinct in my mind was not in hers.

'She was older than I – much older. Then one day a lady took me away. That was Mrs. Drummond. A kind, wealthy, and somewhat foolish widow. She believed those stories about my sister – that she was bad, and never let me see her or speak of her.

'Then Mrs. Drummond married Lu Roper, and later she died – an unhappy woman. I called him my stepfather. If Lu Roper did not actually plant the seed of crime in my childish mind, at least he developed it to its present perfection. But he is dead now. Criminal! Murderer! Gang leader! You remember him.

'I learned later that my sister escaped from the orphanage – ran away when she was held illegally after coming of age. She never knew what became of me. I never knew what became of her – except, that it was charged that she took money with her from that orphanage, which charge I never did believe. I never tried to find her. I never wished to find her. It would have broken her heart to know that I wear – and deservedly wear – the name: The Girl with the Criminal Mind.

'Things were done rather shabbily back when I was adopted. And that's why I did not inherit the money from Mrs. Drummond that I should have received. But other things were brought up in that fight for Mrs. Drummond's wealth.

'One man, Race – a fair and honest man – in his pursuit of Doctor Michelle Gorgon, came as far as that court when Mrs. Drummond's money was being kept from me. He was a clever, determined man. I joined forces, to a certain extent, with this man – but why hide his name? He will tell you now. He was Detective Sergeant O'Rourke. And this is what he discovered:

'The wife of Michelle Gorgon was my sister. And Michelle Gorgon had taken her in an airplane, and––. But you know that terrible story. Michelle Gorgon didn't expect my sister would live. But she did live, maimed and twisted in body; wracked and dead of mind. He did this because she was going to leave him – for another man – some one she loved only in her heart and soul, and would love only so – until she was free of her husband, Michelle Gorgon.

'So I went in with O'Rourke and Colonel McBride. Such is my mind. I wanted – not justice, Race – but vengeance, I guess.

'And I learned who Michelle Gorgon really was. I learned who Giovoni was. He was an Italian criminal, known as "The Devil" years ago. I gave Giovoni into the hands of Colonel McBride, but I didn't tell him all I knew. I couldn't. I wouldn't. Until I was sure that the so-called Michelle Gorgon had purposely planned my sister's terrible "accident". Rudolph Myer helped me, but until tonight I didn't suspect how much he really understood.

'Toney, the little drug addict, came over on the boat from Italy with the Gorgon brothers twenty-three years ago. He knew the truth. There was no Michelle Gorgon. Michelle Gorgon met his death in Naples, beneath a train, twenty-three years before. And it was the escaped murderer of Giovoni's daughter, Rose Marie – Nicholas Tremporia – who took his place. He came to America as Michelle Gorgon – or Gorgonette – as the Gorgon brothers were then called.

'The immigration laws were not so strict in those days. Michelle Gorgon's body was mangled beyond recognition by the train, and it was wearing Nicholas Tremporia's clothes and carrying Nicholas Tremporia's papers and little possessions – which gives the idea that, perhaps, after all, the death of Michelle Gorgon was not an accident – but that he was laid, drugged, upon the tracks by Joe Gorgon and Nicholas Tremporia, as Eddie was but a child then. For Michelle Gorgon had money; had a good reputation in his home town. And, again, what points to his murder is the fact that Joe Gorgon was as much upset by the coming of Giovoni as was his supposed brother, Michelle. Let us still, for clearness, call him Michelle.

'So much for that. I did not tell what I knew to Colonel McBride. Toney did not tell what he knew to Colonel McBride. We left it in the hands of Giovoni to identify the murderer of his daughter.

'After Giovoni died and Michelle Gorgon thought himself safe, I began to hound him – with telephone calls – little notes, which, if another found them, would mean his end. Each night I'd send him a note, that read:
'THE SOUL OF ROSE MARIE CRIES OUT FOR VENGEANCE – MR. NICHOLAS TREMPORIA.

I paused a moment in reading the letter. I recalled the note Michelle Gorgon had shown me – the words that were erased at the end of it, and knew they were the three words he feared so much. MR. NICHOLAS TREMPORIA.

O'Rourke was still telephoning. I heard him calling the airport at Newark. I went on reading.

'I know now that my sister is dead. I know now that Rudolph Myer sold me out. I know that – because Sergeant O'Rourke telephoned me that Michelle knew it was I who held his secret. But I am not certain that it can be proven, now, that Michelle Gorgon is really Nicholas Tremporia.

'I know too, Race, that if ever you read this it is Goodbye. For I have just received word from Michelle Gorgon to meet him at the airport. He knows, now, that I was the voice on the wire – that I sent him those notes – and no doubt knows, too, that his wife was my sister. But he doesn't know that I know he knows. Yes – I am going with him. If he plans my death, he will perhaps tell me the truth first – that he purposely maimed his wife – my sister. He may gloat over his vengeance on me. But it will be worth death to—.

'I love you, Race. Since you are reading this note; since you have kept your word with me. Since your honor would forbid you opening this letter after reading what was on the envelope – until now.

Goodbye. Look for my body in Northern Westchester. But let me hope it will not lie there alone.

'To the End,

'The Girl with the Criminal Mind,

'FLORENCE.'

CHAPTER XXXI: DEATH FROM THE SKY

I laid down the letter and looked at O'Rourke. He was still telephoning, madly.

'Newark airport, yeah. Michelle Gorgon – no. Not at all. I—' And down went the receiver.

It wasn't the time yet to have things out with O'Rourke. The Flame was dead. She had more than hinted as much. But she couldn't be if she had only left the apartment a short while before. Another thing in that letter struck me. 'Since your honor would forbid you opening this letter after reading what was on the envelope.'

O'Rourke was buzzing the phone again. I said to him in a cracked voice: 'Is there an airport in Westchester – northern Westchester?'

And he didn't answer me. The receiver clicked up and down. O'Rourke was an almanac of information. I heard him calling an airport some eight or ten miles above White Plains.

As for me. I'm not a dumb ox altogether. I was fishing into that waste basket for the envelope that O'Rourke had tossed there. And I found it, spread it out, and read what was written on it.

'Race – I trust to your honor not to read this note until twelve o'clock, noon.' I looked at my watch. It was now exactly twenty minutes to five. I guess my eyes got a little harder as they looked at O'Rourke. He had made sure I wouldn't see what was on that envelope. But I didn't say anything. He was talking on the phone.

'Never heard of Michelle Gorgon! Well, it's damn near time you bought a New York newspaper. No order for a plane to go up – none gone up – and wait – just a minute. Any plane there owned by a Miss Drummond? A—. That's it. That's it. Her pilot dropped in with it early in the week? Listen. Get in touch with the police and see that – that that plane—. Listen – Damn it!' He pounded the hook up and down. 'The fool's cut off. Central— Damn it, give me that number I—' O'Rourke dropped the receiver. 'Some one cut the wires, I'll bet. Come on, Race. There's a chance yet.'

'Yes, a chance yet.' I faced him as he stood up. 'So you're the light haired boy who got The Flame into his—. Who let her take this trip tonight. Who—. And you once suggested a bullet between your own eyes, O'Rourke, once—' Maybe my hand touched my gun. 'Why didn't you warn her?'

'But I did,' said O'Rourke. 'As soon as you told me about that pile of jack in Rudolph Myer's bag I rang her up and warned her not to open the door to any one, that my men would be there shortly. For her not to see Michelle Gorgon, and—'

'Maybe you did.' I thought of the letter. 'She knew and she went anyway. God! O'Rourke. How could you do it? How—'

'If we've got to differ, Race, let it be later. Maybe, in a different way, I think as much of The Flame as you do. I'll talk now. She's talked in that letter. But let's be friends now, Race, at least allies. It looks like The Flame went, purposely, to her death. Come on. To the airport in Westchester. There's a chance.'

'There's no chance,' I told him, as we hurried from the apartment. 'He's taking her as he took his wife. The Flame crossed him. She was out to ruin him, and he knows it.'

The sky was brightening as we dashed through the city streets. I wasn't quite my own man. I let Brophey drive the police car, and I sat in the back with O'Rourke. That car carried the police insignia. There would be less delays.

'Look here.' O'Rourke leaned close to me and spoke. 'I saw a chance to get the Gorgons through The Flame. And I was right. She found out more in a month than I had found out in a year. But she wouldn't tell me, wouldn't tell McBride. At least, not until she was sure, beyond any doubt, that Michelle Gorgon had maimed her sister. She was afraid I told her that simply to get her in with me.'

'Then she was working for you all along.'

'Yes and no,' said O'Rourke. 'In a way she was working with me, but really working for herself. But I thought, once she was convinced of the truth, she would turn Michelle Gorgon in. It was she who found out that Toney came over on the ship with the Gorgons, though what that information was worth I never did know. It was she who discovered, through Toney, about Giovoni. But Giovoni wouldn't talk out until he could confront Michelle Gorgon. Besides, he was taken desperately ill, aboard ship. But we got enough from him to know that he was called "The Devil" years back. And you never suspected The Flame?'

'No.' And suddenly, 'You knew she was at McBride's house that night, in the locked closet?'

'Sure,' said O'Rourke. 'I thought as much as soon as I found that closet door locked, and remembered that I had told The Flame about McBride signalling me with the light, for help – when she warned me that he should never be unprotected. She had come in the back way, through the door that was left open for Rudolph Myer. She knew, or felt, that McBride was in great danger and came to warn him. She hid in one of the front rooms when McBride came down stairs to meet Rudolph Myer. She thought it was the police though, and never suspected McBride was leaving by the back door with some one. So she didn't see with whom he left. But the moment she knew he was gone she suspected some trap of the Gorgons, ran up those stairs and flashed the danger signal with the light.

'Yes, I suspected she was there in the closet, but I didn't know for sure until I met her in the hall and gave her safe passage from the house. That's what I meant when I said to you that the district attorney himself couldn't leave that house without my Okay. You must have thought me an awful hick cop. But she didn't want you to know too much, Race. She was afraid you would give the show away trying to protect her, but in her heart I think she wanted you out of the case, because she thought you'd – well – get yourself a hole in the ground.'

'I never thought of her working in with the police.'

'And she wasn't,' snapped O'Rourke. 'It was vengeance, or retribution, or a great love – or a great hate. But each day I thought she would get the proof from Michelle Gorgon himself that he had maimed his wife, her sister. And then, I thought, she'd blow it all to me. Now, she's gone with him, knowing that he's onto her. Why?'

'Do you think – maybe she don't – didn't understand you?'

'Hell! I told her flat, that Rudolph Myer had sold her out to Michelle Gorgon. Then I gave her the office to sit tight. The Flame's no child, you know.'

'No.' Death – destruction. All that The Flame had told me came up before me now. 'O'Rourke,' I said slowly, 'I don't know. But if The Flame's dead, get away from me – get—. Good God! I—. We've been almost pals. I—. Why didn't you tell me The Flame was in it – with – with us?'

'I couldn't. I passed my word. She wouldn't help me unless I did. And I also passed my word not to ask you into the case. In a way, I broke that promise. I had McBride bring you in – through Myer.'

'And the note, with what was written on the envelope. She trusted to my honor, and—'

'That's it,' said O'Rourke. 'There's too much honor, been too damned much honor. If you hadn't read that note we wouldn't be on our way to save her now. I'm a stickler about my own honor, Race, yet not a guardian of yours. It's best you read it, and—'

'Yes,' I said, 'it's best that I read it.'

'Good!' He stuck out his hand, but I didn't see it. Finally he put it back in his pocket. 'We must all go our way according to our light,' he said.

'Yeah. I thought you were a friend, a real friend. And you're just, just a cop,' was the best I could give him.

'But an honest cop,' said O'Rourke. 'An honest cop.'

Brophey could drive. And the police siren screeched but little in the city streets. No talk, now, between us. Up Broadway to Van Cortland Park, through the park to Central Avenue. Sometimes sixty, sometimes sixty-five. It was then that I wished I had my own car. Out on that long stretch of concrete road I could have pushed it to eighty, and perhaps ninety on that down grade just before you reach that slight upswing to the Tuckahoe Road. But, be fair about it. That down grade is quite some curve and maybe, maybe—. But this is not an automobile tour I'm writing about – nor a real estate ad for 'Buy in Westchester' – nor even a treatise on the merits of certain automobile motors. It was a race against death. At least, I hoped it was. But maybe, after all, it was just a race with death, to find death.

It was perhaps five miles out of White Plains that I saw O'Rourke stick his head out of the window, then lean forward and tap the driver, Brophey, on the shoulder. The brakes ground; the car came to a stop just at a cross road. And that was the first time I came to life, and heard plainly the roar of a motor – an airplane motor.

Looking up I saw the plane. A biplane, pretty high. But even at that distance one could see that the motor was sputtering, and that the plane was circling. Then it suddenly dived, hesitated a moment, seemed to gain altitude and shoot toward the west and on a beeline with the road to our right.

And we were after it. A pitiful, hopeless little trio, in that modern invention known as the automobile, as helpless and as prehistoric as if we ran on foot, armed with huge clubs cut from the trees. Still, we sped down that road in the wake of the slowly diminishing plane.

Sixty! Sixty-five! A curve in the road, our wheels in the roadbed, a sudden jerk and we were straightened out again, with great empty fields behind the trees to our left. And again O'Rourke had tapped our driver, Brophey, on the shoulder. Again the brakes. This time we stopped beneath the shadows of a cluster of huge trees.

'Drive her off, in the grass there, out of the way,' said O'Rourke.

'Good God!' I said to O'Rourke, as we climbed from the car, 'I know it's no use and all that, but it seems like doing something to keep going. At least trying to save her life.'

O'Rourke spoke.

'Here, keep in the protection of those trees. I haven't trailed Michelle Gorgon all these weeks without knowing his car when I see it. And that Rolls of his was parked in the field back there. Look!'

And I looked through the foliage. Yep, there was the outline of a car all right. But it wasn't the car I looked at. It was the figure that stood so still beside a tree. A figure that seemed like part of the landscape, or a scarecrow. Then it moved, and I knew that it was human. The figure watched that plane, the plane which had turned now and was coming back over the field. And then I saw the flash. Not for certain, not for sure.

But O'Rourke cried out.

'The plane's on fire, and some one is jumping.'

A far distant figure, with a great hump on its back, balanced, swayed, seemed to clutch at a wing – then pitched out, swung slowly and came hurtling toward the earth. I waited, breathless, for a sudden jerk of that body and the great silk of a parachute to check the flight, and send the form drifting gently to earth. But no parachute opened. The body began to turn rapidly now; hands gripped frantically at the air; even legs seemed to be attempting to entwine space.

'Good God!' said O'Rourke, 'he's thrown her from the plane, and—'

The falling body struck in some trees, went crashing through them, and I sunk my head in my arms. So, destruction and death! That was the end of The Flame – that was—.

'And he ain't having such an easy time of it.' O'Rourke gripped me by the shoulder. 'The plane's on fire. Something's gone wrong. Look! It's out of control, entirely.'

And it was. Fascinated, I watched that plane. Twisting, turning, diving, ever falling – ever nearer to the ground – ever—. And it swerved suddenly, about a hundred feet from the ground – seemed to straighten, then shoot upward, dip again, and dash straight toward a clump of trees not a hundred yards away from us.

'You can't do anything for – for her.' And the words choked in O'Rourke's throat. 'But him, the dirty, lousy murderer! We've got him red handed this time. In death The Flame gave him to us.'

And we were running across that field. I'm not sure just what happened. But I think the plane paused in its drop, turned its nose up so suddenly that you could hear struts hum – snap, even – and with a crash it dove smack into a tree, twisted slightly, seemed to fall, and hung there.

You could see it blazing now.

'Quick!' shouted O'Rourke, dashing by me. 'The damn thing may blow up in a minute. We—'

'Let him burn to death,' I cried out, and the next instant thought better of it. I hurled O'Rourke from me as we reached the now blazing wreck, jumped and caught a branch, and swung myself into the tree beside the plane.

I saw it all, and didn't care. I saw the jury filing from the room. I knew my story in that second's flash. I'd say I thought that Michelle Gorgon had a gun in his hand – and I shot him in self-defense. For I was going to kill him – put a bullet right through his head before ever O'Rourke could stop me. Catch Michelle Gorgon for the murder of The Flame? Hang murder on such a notorious racketeer – who could influence judges, keep witnesses silent, intimidate jurors? No – he was going before a jury now that he couldn't buy, couldn't intimidate, a Judge he couldn't fix.

And I saw him crouched there in the cock-pit. He'd know too. The flames flashed back suddenly, whipped by a touch of wind.

'All right, Doctor Michelle Gorgon,' I cried out, almost mad with rage and hate, and something else, something that made me half sob out the words before I killed him. But I wanted him to know. He must know. And he would know. For his body stirred, his head low on his chest beneath the helmet, tried to rise.

My right hand gripped my gun. My left hand stretched in, clutched at the face that was turned from me. I jerked that head around, and – and looked straight into the wide, questioning, frightened eyes of The Flame – Florence Drummond.

CHAPTER XXXII: THE END OF THE RACKET

I don't know how I got The Flame out of that cock-pit. Maybe O'Rourke and Brophey did most of it. Maybe they didn't. But, anyway, she was on the grass beside us.

O'Rourke was hollering something about water. Brophey was yapping about a flask in the car, and I held The Flame close in my arms.

'It wasn't murder, Race,' she said over and over. 'It wasn't that. I ripped the parachute pack on his back with my knife when we got into the plane. But I told him, I did tell him before he jumped. I couldn't help it. I – but he was gone – on the edge – and he left me there to burn with it – crash with it – for my parachute was useless. He had seen to that.'

'Ssh.' I warned her. 'O'Rourke will hear.' Maybe he did hear, and maybe he didn't. But, anyway, he was running across the fields, running to where the body of Michelle Gorgon had dropped through the trees. I could barely make out the unshapely mass on the ground.

And The Flame talked.

'I had to know about my sister. I had to know if he really planned it so that she was crippled like that. That's why I went to meet him when he telephoned me. You see, the plane was in my name. Michelle brought it to the airport only a few days ago. He registered it at the field under my name because he was afraid, then, that the truth could come out about Rose Marie. He was afraid – deadly afraid – of that voice on the wire, and was ready for a get-away. He told me everything, once we were in the air. Gloated over the way he had broken my sister. Told me, too, that he had killed her – made her kill herself.

'It was a horrible crime, that murder of my sister. He played upon both her mental and physical weakness. Told her that in the secret flap of her bag was a bottle of poison, and a mirror. And told her that if she were alive in two hours' time he would bring to see her the man she loved – the man who had loved her.'

She stopped a minute and rubbed at her dry eyes. The Flame didn't know how to cry, I guess. Then she went on.

'I couldn't protect myself, Race. I had not expected him to act so quickly. Before we were off the ground he had taken my gun – and the mechanic who turned our propeller struck me a blow on the head. I was stunned, didn't fully recover until we were up in the air, high up.

'He was clever, Race. The mechanic was one of his men. That mechanic would swear that I had gone up alone. Michelle was to set fire to the plane, leap with a parachute, be picked up by a man waiting with his car and driven back to the city.

'"This was to be our bridal chariot," he said. "Now – it's your coffin, Florence. Like your sister, you crossed me. I loved you; I could have made you very happy. But you proved yourself a rat and a stool–pigeon. I give you death. I fight my own battles, I do not need the police."'

'"And I too can fight my own battles,' I cried out, as he tossed something on the hot engine and did something to the controls. "Don't jump, Michelle Gorgon! You've planned for me to be burnt to death in this blazing plane. I—" as I saw him on the edge of the cock-pit, his gun covering me, his index finger cocked through the loop of his parachute chord, "I ripped the pack on your back with a knife as soon as you climbed into the plane. I cut your parachute. You'll – you'll have to burn with me."

'He seemed to hesitate for a moment – then he smiled and stretched his hand back over his shoulder. The plane lurched. He cried out once, slipped, tottered – and fell. It seemed like hours that I heard his terrible screech of horror. Then the earth coming up, the trees and the crash – and you. But I swear I warned him that I cut—'

I put my hand across her mouth. O'Rourke was coming back.

'I'll telephone at the first town and have them pick up that Rolls and that mechanic at the field – and then have a look at Rudolph Myer,' O'Rourke said, as we climbed into the police car. 'And to ease your mind, Race. That lad was as dead as old King Tut, and it was our mutual friend, Michelle Gorgon.'

'Yes, and anything The Flame had to do with it was self-defense, and—'

'You talk too much.' O'Rourke looked at me as he lit a big black cigar, and I gathered The Flame close to me in the back of the machine. 'You know, the body of Gorgon still hung in the trees when I reached it.' And when I looked at him, surprised – for I had seen plainly that the body was on the ground, 'I say it still hung in the trees. Get that! I know it, for I had to cut that parachute pack to ribbons with my knife to get him loose. Cut it to ribbons, understand!' And after a pause, while he glared at me, 'It's funny it didn't open right, but then, they very often don't, and there's no explaining – no explaining it.'

After all, O'Rourke wasn't a bad scout. But Michelle Gorgon was dead, and Michelle Gorgon had held The Flame in his arms. And – oh, I wasn't superstitious or anything like that. That thought had nothing to do with my moving over in a corner of the back seat and sticking a cigarette in my mouth. I – I just needed a smoke, I guess.

Any more to it? Well – hardly. The body of Eddie Gorgon turned up in the river three days later. We could only guess that Michelle Gorgon had some of his crowd put it there. Why? Well – maybe because he didn't want it discovered in the underworld, just then, that some one – particularly a lad known as Race Williams – had the guts to shoot his brother, Eddie – or the lad every one thought was his brother, Eddie.